PENGUIN BOOKS

TRILOGY OF DEATH

P. D. James was born in Oxford in 1920 and educated at Cambridge High School. From 1949 to 1968 she worked in the National Health Service as an administrator, and the experience she gained from her job helped her with the background for *Shroud for a Nightingale*, *The Black Tower* and *A Mind to Murder*. In 1968 she entered the Home Office as Principal, working with the Police Department concerned with the forensic science service and later in the Criminal Policy Department. She retired in 1979 and is currently a Fellow of the Royal Society of Literature, a governor of the BBC and a member of the boards of the Arts Council and the British Council. P. D. James has twice been the winner of the Silver Dagger Award of the Crime Writers Association and in 1987 was awarded the Diamond Dagger Award for services to crime writing. In 1983 she received the OBE and was created a life peer in 1991. She has been a widow for over twenty-five years and has two children and five grandchildren.

Her other novels include *Cover Her Face*, *Unnatural Causes*, *Death of an Expert Witness*, *A Taste for Death* and *Devices and Desires* which was shortlisted for the *Sunday Express* Book of the Year Award in 1989. She is co-author, with T. A. Critchley, of *The Maul and the Pear Tree*. Penguin also publish *A Dalgliesh Trilogy*, which contains the novels *Shroud for a Nightingale*, *The Black Tower* and *Death of an Expert Witness*.

P. D. JAMES

TRILOGY OF DEATH

AN UNSUITABLE JOB FOR A WOMAN
INNOCENT BLOOD
THE SKULL BENEATH THE SKIN

PENGUIN BOOKS
IN ASSOCIATION WITH FABER & FABER

PENGUIN BOOKS

Published by the Penguin Group
Penguin Books Ltd, 27 Wrights Lane, London W8 5TZ, England
Penguin Books USA Inc., 375 Hudson Street, New York, New York 10014, USA
Penguin Books Australia Ltd, Ringwood, Victoria, Australia
Penguin Books Canada Ltd, 10 Alcorn Avenue, Toronto, Ontario, Canada M4V 3B2
Penguin Books (NZ) Ltd, 182–190 Wairau Road, Auckland 10, New Zealand

Penguin Books Ltd, Registered Offices: Harmondsworth, Middlesex, England

An Unsuitable Job for a Woman first published by Faber & Faber 1972
Published in Penguin Books in association with Faber & Faber 1989

Innocent Blood first published by Faber & Faber 1980
Published in Penguin Books in association with Faber & Faber 1989

The Skull beneath the Skin first published in Great Britain by Faber & Faber 1982
Published in Canada by Lester & Orpen Dennys Ltd 1983
Published in Penguin Books in association with Faber & Faber 1989

This omnibus edition published in Penguin Books 1992
5 7 9 10 8

Printed in England by Clays Ltd, St Ives plc
Set in 10/12 pt Monophoto Baskerville

CONTENTS

AN UNSUITABLE JOB FOR A WOMAN

For Jane and Peter who kindly allowed two of my characters to live at 57 Norwich Street

AUTHOR'S NOTE

A crime novelist, by virtue of his unpleasant craft, has the duty to create at least one highly reprehensible character in each book and it is perhaps inevitable that from time to time their sanguinary misdeeds should impinge upon the dwellings of the just. A writer whose characters have chosen to act out their tragicomedy in an ancient university city is in particular difficulty. He can, of course, call it Oxbridge, invent colleges named after improbable saints and send his characters boating on the Camsis, but this timid compromise merely confuses characters, readers and the author alike, with the result that no one knows precisely where he is and two communities are offered opportunities for offence instead of one.

The greater part of this story is unrepentantly set in Cambridge, a city in which, undeniably, there live and work policemen, coroners, doctors, students, college servants, flower sellers, Dons, scientists, and even, no doubt, retired Majors. None of them, to my knowledge, bears the slightest resemblance to his counterpart in this book. All the characters, even the most unpleasant, are imaginary; the city, happily for us all, is not.

P. D. J.

CHAPTER ONE

On the morning of Bernie Pryde's death – or it may have been the morning after, since Bernie died at his own convenience, nor did he think the estimated time of his departure worth recording – Cordelia was caught in a breakdown of the Bakerloo Line outside Lambeth North and was half an hour late at the office. She came up from Oxford Circus underground into the bright June sunshine, sped past the early morning shoppers scanning the windows of Dickins and Jones and plunged into the cacophony of Kingly Street, threading her way between the blocked pavement and the shining mass of cars and vans which packed the narrow street. The hurry she knew was irrational, a symptom of her obsession with order and punctuality. There were no appointments booked; no clients to be interviewed; no case outstanding; not even a final report to be written. She and Miss Sparshott, the temporary typist, at Cordelia's suggestion were circulating information about the Agency to all the London solicitors in the hope of attracting custom; Miss Sparshott would probably be busy with it now, eyes straying to her watch, tapping out her staccato irritation at every minute of Cordelia's lateness. She was an unprepossessing woman with lips permanently taut as if to prevent the protruding teeth from springing from her mouth, a receding chin with one coarse hair which grew as quickly as it was plucked, and fair hair set in stiff corrugated waves. That chin and mouth seemed to Cordelia the living refutation that all men are born equal and she tried from time to time to like and sympathize with Miss Sparshott, with a life lived in bed-sitting-rooms, measured in the five-penny pieces fed to the gas stove and circumscribed by fell seams and hand hemming. For Miss Sparshott was a skilled dressmaker, an assiduous attender at the GLC evening classes. Her clothes were beautifully made but so dateless that they were never actually in fashion; straight skirts in grey or black which were exercises in how to sew a pleat or insert a zip fastener;

blouses with mannish collars and cuffs in insipid pastel shades on which she distributed without discretion her collection of costume jewellery; intricately cut dresses with hems at the precise length to emphasize her shapeless legs and thick ankles.

Cordelia had no premonition of tragedy as she pushed open the street door which was kept perpetually on the latch for the convenience of the secretive and mysterious tenants and their equally mysterious visitors. The new bronze plaque to the left of the door gleamed brightly in the sun in incongruous contrast to the faded and dirt-encrusted paint. Cordelia gave it a short glance of approval.

Pryde's Detective Agency
(*Props:* Bernard G. Pryde   Cordelia Gray)

It had taken Cordelia some weeks of patient and tactful persuasion to convince Bernie that it would be inappropriate to append the words 'ex-CID Metropolitan Police' to his name or prefix 'Miss' to hers. There had been no other problem over the plaque since Cordelia had brought no qualifications or relevant past experience to the partnership and indeed no capital, except her slight but tough twenty-two-year-old body, a considerable intelligence which Bernie, she suspected, had occasionally found more disconcerting than admirable, and a half exasperated, half pitying affection for Bernie himself. It was obvious very early to Cordelia that in some undramatic but positive way life had turned against him. She recognized the signs. Bernie never got the enviable front left hand seat in the bus; he couldn't admire the view from the train window without another train promptly obscuring it; the bread he dropped invariably fell buttered side downwards; the Mini, reliable enough when she drove it, stalled for Bernie at the busiest and most inconvenient intersections. She sometimes wondered whether, in accepting his offer of a partnership in a fit of depression or of perverse masochism, she was voluntarily embracing his ill-luck. She certainly never saw herself as powerful enough to change it.

The staircase smelt as always of stale sweat, furniture polish and disinfectant. The walls were dark green and were invariably damp whatever the season as if they secreted a miasma of desperate respectability and defeat. The stairs, with their ornate wrought-iron balustrade, were covered with split and stained linoleum patched by the landlord in various and contrasting colours only when a tenant complained. The Agency was on the third floor. There was no clatter of typewriter keys as Cordelia entered and she saw that Miss Sparshott was engaged in cleaning her machine, an ancient Imperial which was a constant cause of justified complaint. She looked up, her face blotched with resentment, her back as rigid as the space bar.

'I've been wondering when you would turn up, Miss Gray. I'm concerned about Mr Pryde. I think he must be in the inner office but he's quiet, very quiet, and the door's locked.'

Cordelia, chill at heart, wrenched at the door handle:

'Why didn't you do something?'

'Do what, Miss Gray? I knocked at the door and called out to him. It wasn't my place to do that, I'm only the temporary typist, I've no authority here. I should have been placed in a very embarrassing position if he had answered. After all, he's entitled to use his own office I suppose. Besides, I'm not even sure if he's there.'

'He must be. The door's locked and his hat is here.'

Bernie's trilby, the stained brim turned up all round, a comedian's hat, was hanging on the convoluted hatstand, a symbol of forlorn decrepitude. Cordelia was fumbling in her shoulder-bag for her own key. As usual, the object most required had fallen to the bottom of the bag. Miss Sparshott began to clatter on the keys as if to disassociate herself from impending trauma. Above the noise she said defensively:

'There's a note on your desk.'

Cordelia tore it open. It was short and explicit. Bernie had always been able to express himself succinctly when he had something to say:

'I'm sorry, partner, they've told me it's cancer and I'm taking the easy way out. I've seen what the treatment does to people and I'm not having any. I've made my will and it's with my solicitor. You'll find his name in the desk. I've left the business to you. Everything, including *all* the equipment. Good luck and thank you.' Underneath with the inconsiderateness of the doomed he had scribbled a final unfair plea:

'If you find me alive, for God's sake wait before calling help. I rely on you for this, partner. Bernie.'

She unlocked the door of the inner office and went inside, closing the door carefully behind her.

It was a relief to see that there was no need to wait. Bernie was dead. He lay slumped over the desk as if in an extremity of exhaustion. His right hand was half clenched and an open cut-throat razor had slithered over the desk top leaving a thin trail of blood like a snail's track and had come to rest precariously poised on the extreme edge of the desk. His left wrist, scored with two parallel cuts, lay palm upwards in the enamel bowl which Cordelia used for the washing-up. Bernie had filled it with water but it was now brimful with a pale pinky liquid smelling sickly sweet, through which the fingers, curved as if in supplication and looking as white and delicate as those of a child, gleamed as smooth as wax. The blood and water had overflowed on to the desk and floor soaking the oblong of garish rug which Bernie had recently bought in the hope of impressing visitors with his status but which Cordelia privately thought had only drawn attention to the shabbiness of the rest of the office. One of the cuts was tentative and superficial but the other had gone deep as the bone and the severed edges of the wound, drained of blood, gaped cleanly like an illustration in an anatomy textbook. Cordelia remembered how Bernie had once described the finding of a prospective suicide when he was first on the beat as a young constable. It was an old man huddled into a warehouse doorway who had slashed his wrist with a broken bottle – but who had later been dragged back to reluctant half-life because an immense clot of blood had blocked the severed veins. Bernie, remembering, had taken precautions to ensure that his blood would not clot. He had, she noticed, taken another precaution; there was an empty teacup, the one in which she served his afternoon tea, on the right of the desk with a grain or two of powder, aspirin perhaps or a barbiturate, staining the rim and side. A dried trickle of mucus, similarly stained, hung from the corner of his mouth. His lips were pursed and half open like those of a sleeping child, petulant and vulnerable. She put her head round the office door and said quietly:

'Mr Pryde is dead; don't come in. I'll ring the police from here.'

The telephone message was taken calmly, someone would come round. Sitting beside the body to wait and feeling that she needed to make some gesture of pity and comfort Cordelia laid her hand gently on Bernie's hair. Death had as yet no power to diminish these cold and nerveless cells and the hair felt roughly and unpleasantly alive like that of an animal. Quickly she took her hand away and tentatively touched the side of his forehead. The skin was clammy and very cold. This was death; this was how Daddy had felt. As with him, the gesture of pity was meaningless and irrelevant. There was no more communication in death than there had been in life.

She wondered when exactly Bernie had died. No one now would ever know. Perhaps Bernie himself had not known. There must, she supposed, have been one measurable second in time in which he had ceased to be Bernie and had become this unimportant but embarrassingly unwieldy weight of flesh and bone. How odd that a moment of time so important to him should pass without his knowledge. Her second foster mother, Mrs Wilkes, would have said that Bernie did know, that there was a moment of indescribable glory, shining towers, limitless singing, skies of triumph. Poor Mrs Wilkes! Widowed, her only son dead in the war, her small house perpetually noisy with the foster children who were her livelihood, she had needed her dreams. She had lived her life by comfortable maxims stored like nuggets of coal against the winter. Cordelia thought of her now for the first time in years and heard again the tired, determinedly cheerful voice 'If the Lord doesn't call on his way out, He'll call on his way back.' Well, going or coming, He hadn't called on Bernie.

It was odd but somehow typical of Bernie that he should have retained a dogged and invincible optimism about the business even when they had nothing in the cash box but a few coins for the gas meter and yet had given up hope of life without even a struggle. Was it perhaps that he had subconsciously recognized that neither he nor the Agency had any real future and had decided that this way he could yield up both life and livelihood with some honour? He had done it effectively but messily, surprisingly so for an ex-policeman versed in the ways of death. And then she realized why he had chosen the razor and the drugs. The gun. He hadn't really taken the easy way out. He could have used the gun, but he had wanted her to have it; he had bequeathed it to her together with the rickety filing cabinets, the antique typewriter, the scene-of-crime kit, the Mini, his shock-proof and waterproof wrist watch, the blood-soaked rug, the embarrassingly large stock of writing paper with the ornate heading *Pryde's Detective Agency – We take a Pride in our Work. All* the equipment; he had underlined all. He must have meant to remind her about the gun.

She unlocked the small drawer at the base of Bernie's desk to which only she and he had a key and drew it out. It was still in the suede draw-string bag which she had made for it, with three rounds of ammunition packed separately. It was a pistol, a .38 semi-automatic; she had never known how Bernie had come by it but she was certain that he had no licence. She had never seen it as a lethal weapon, perhaps because Bernie's boyishly naïve obsession with it had reduced it to the impotence of a child's toy. He had taught her to become – at any rate in theory – a creditable shot. They had driven for practice into the depths of Epping Forest and her memories of the gun were linked with dappled shade and the rich smell of decaying leaves. He had fixed a target to a convenient tree; the gun was loaded with blanks. She could still hear the excited staccato orders. 'Bend your knees slightly. Feet apart. Arm full length. Now place the left hand against the barrel, cradling it. Keep your eyes on the target. Arm straight, partner, arm straight! Good! Not bad; not bad; not bad at all.' 'But, Bernie,' she had said, 'we can never fire it! We haven't a licence.' He had smiled, the sly self-satisfied smile of superior knowledge. 'If we ever fire in anger it will be to save our lives. In such an eventuality the question of a licence is irrelevant.' He had been pleased with this rotund sentence and had repeated it, lifting his heavy face to the sun like a dog. What, she wondered, had he seen in imagination? The two of them crouching behind a boulder on some desolate moor, bullets pinging against the granite, the gun passed smoking from hand to hand?

He had said: 'We'll have to go carefully with the ammunition.

Not that I can't get it of course . . .' The smile had become grim, as if at the memory of those mysterious contacts, those ubiquitous and obliging acquaintances whom he had only to summon from their shadow world.

So he had left her the gun. It had been his most prized possession. She slipped it, still shrouded, into the depths of her shoulder-bag. It was surely unlikely that the police would examine the drawers of the desk in a case of obvious suicide but it was as well to take no risk. Bernie had meant her to have the gun and she wasn't going to give it up easily. With her bag at her feet she sat down again by the body. She said a brief, convent-taught prayer to the God she wasn't sure existed for the soul which Bernie had never believed he possessed and waited quietly for the police.

The first policeman to arrive was efficient but young, not yet experienced enough to hide his shock and distaste at the sight of violent death nor his disapproval that Cordelia should be so calm. He didn't spend long in the inner office. When he came out he meditated upon Bernie's note as if a careful scrutiny could extract some inner meaning from the bald sentence of death. Then he folded it away.

'I'll have to keep this note for the present, Miss. What did he get up to here?'

'He didn't get up to anything. This was his office. He was a private detective.'

'And you worked for this Mr Pryde? You were his secretary?'

'I was his partner. It says so in the note. I'm twenty-two. Bernie was the senior partner; he started the business. He used to work for the Metropolitan Police in the CID with Superintendent Dalgliesh.'

As soon as the words were spoken, she regretted them. They were too propitiatory, too naïve a defence of poor Bernie. And the name Dalgliesh, she saw, meant nothing to him. Why should it? He was just one of the local uniformed branch. He couldn't be expected to know how often she had listened with politely concealed impatience to Bernie's nostalgic reminiscences of his time in the CID before he was invalided out, or to his eulogies on the virtues and wisdom of Adam Dalgliesh. 'The Super – well, he was just an Inspector then – always taught us . . . The Super once described a case . . . If there was one thing the Super couldn't stand . . .'

Sometimes she had wondered whether this paragon had actually existed or whether he had sprung impeccable and omnipotent from Bernie's brain, a necessary hero and mentor. It was with a shock of surprise that she had later seen a newspaper picture of Chief Superintendent Dalgliesh, a dark, sardonic face which, on her closer scrutiny, disintegrated into an ambiguity of patterned micro dots, giving nothing away. Not all the wisdom Bernie so glibly recalled was the received gospel. Much, she suspected, was his own philosophy. She in turn had devised a private litany of disdain: supercilious, superior, sarcastic Super; what wisdom, she wondered, would he have to comfort Bernie now.

The policeman had made discreet telephone calls. He now prowled around the outer office, hardly bothering to hide his puzzled contempt at the shabby second-hand furniture, the battered filing cabinet with one drawer half open to reveal teapot and mugs, the worn linoleum. Miss Sparshott, rigid at an ancient typewriter, gazed at him with fascinated distaste. At last he said:

'Well, suppose you make yourselves a nice cup of tea while I wait for the police surgeon. There is somewhere to make tea?'

'There's a small pantry down the corridor which we share with the other tenants on this floor. But surely you don't need a surgeon? Bernie's dead!'

'He's not officially dead until a qualified medical practitioner says so.' He paused: 'It's just a precaution.'

Against what, Cordelia wondered – judgement, damnation, decay? The policeman went back into the inner office. She followed him and asked softly:

'Couldn't you let Miss Sparshott go? She's from a secretarial agency and we have to pay for her by the hour. She hasn't done any work since I arrived and I doubt whether she will now.'

He was, she saw, a little shocked by the apparent callousness of concerning herself with so mercenary a detail while standing within touching distance of Bernie's body, but he said willingly enough:

'I'll just have a word with her, then she can go. It isn't a nice place for a woman.'

His tone implied that it never had been.

Afterwards, waiting in the outer office, Cordelia answered the inevitable questions.

'No, I don't know whether he was married. I've a feeling that he was divorced; he never talked about a wife. He lived at 15, Cremona Road, SE1. He let me have a bed-sitting-room there but we didn't see much of each other.'

'I know Cremona Road; my aunt used to live there when I was a kid – one of those streets near the Imperial War Museum.'

The fact that he knew the road seemed to reassure and humanize him. He ruminated happily for a moment.

'When did you last see Mr Pryde alive?'

'Yesterday at about five o'clock when I left work early to do some shopping.'

'Didn't he come home last night?'

'I heard him moving around but I didn't see him. I have a gas ring in my room and I usually cook there unless I know he's out. I didn't hear him this morning which is unusual, but I thought he might be lying in. He does that occasionally when it's his hospital morning.'

'Was it his hospital morning today?'

'No, he had an appointment last Wednesday but I thought that they might have asked him to come back. He must have left the house very late last night or before I woke early this morning. I didn't hear him.'

It was impossible to describe the almost obsessional delicacy with which they avoided each other, trying not to intrude, preserving the other's privacy, listening for the sound of flushing cisterns, tiptoeing to ascertain whether the kitchen or bathroom was empty. They had taken infinite trouble not to be a nuisance to each other. Living in the same small terraced house they had hardly seen each other outside the office. She wondered whether Bernie had decided to kill himself in his office so that the little house would be uncontaminated and undisturbed.

At last the office was empty and she was alone. The police surgeon had closed his bag and departed; Bernie's body had been manoeuvred down the narrow staircase watched by eyes from the half-opened doors of other offices; the last policeman had left. Miss Sparshott had gone for good, violent death being a worse insult than a typewriter which a trained typist ought not to be expected to use or lavatory accommodation which was not at all what she had been accustomed to. Alone in the emptiness and silence Cordelia felt the need of physical action. She began vigorously to clean the inner office, scrubbing the blood stains from desk and chair, mopping the soaked rug.

At one o'clock she walked briskly to their usual pub. It occurred to her that there was no longer any reason to patronize the Golden Pheasant but she walked on unable to bring herself to so early a disloyalty. She had never liked the pub or the landlady and had often wished that Bernie would find a nearer house, preferably one with a large bosomy barmaid with a heart of gold. It was, she suspected, a type commoner in fiction than in real life. The familiar lunch-time crowd was clustered around the bar and, as usual, Mavis presided behind it wearing her slightly minatory smile, her air of extreme respectability. Mavis changed her dress three times a day, her hair style once every year, her smile never. The two women had never liked each other although Bernie had galumphed between them like an affectionate old dog, finding it convenient to believe that they were great mates and unaware of or ignoring the almost physical crackle of antagonism. Mavis reminded Cordelia of a librarian known to her in childhood who had secreted the new books under the counter in case they should be taken out and soiled. Perhaps Mavis's barely suppressed chagrin was because she was forced to display her wares so prominently, compelled to measure out her bounty before watchful eyes. Pushing a half pint of shandy and a Scotch egg across the counter in response to Cordelia's order, she said:

'I hear you've had the police round.'

Watching their avid faces, Cordelia thought, they know about it, of course; they want to hear the details; they may as well hear them. She said:

'Bernie cut his wrists twice. The first time he didn't get to the vein; the second time he did. He put his arm in water to help the bleeding. He had been told that he had cancer and couldn't face the treatment.'

That, she saw, was different. The little group around Mavis glanced at each other, then quickly averted their eyes. Glasses were momentarily checked upon their upward way. Cutting one's wrist was something which other people did but the sinister little crab had his claws of fear into all their minds. Even Mavis looked as if she saw his bright claws lurking among her bottles. She said:

'You'll be looking for a new job, I suppose? After all, you can hardly keep the Agency going on your own. It isn't a suitable job for a woman.'

'No different from working behind a bar; you meet all kinds of people.'

The two women looked at each other and a snatch of unspoken dialogue passed between them clearly heard and understood by both.

'And don't think, now he's dead, that people can go on leaving messages for the Agency here.'

'I wasn't going to ask.'

Mavis began vigorously polishing a glass, her eyes still on Cordelia's face.

'I shouldn't think your mother would approve of you staying on alone.'

'I only had a mother for the first hour of my life, so I don't have to worry about that.'

Cordelia saw at once that the remark had deeply shocked them and wondered again at the capacity of older people to be outraged by simple facts when they seemed capable of accepting any amount of perverse or shocking opinion. But their silence, heavy with censure, at least left her in peace. She carried her shandy and Scotch egg to a seat against the wall and thought without sentimentality about her mother. Gradually out of a childhood of deprivation she had evolved a philosophy of compensation. In her imagination she had enjoyed a lifetime of love in one hour with no disappointments and no regrets. Her father had never talked about her mother's death and Cordelia had avoided questioning him, fearful of learning that her mother had never held her in her arms, never regained consciousness, never perhaps even known that she had a daughter. This belief in her mother's love was the one fantasy which she could still not entirely risk losing although its indulgence had become less necessary and less real with each passing year. Now, in imagination, she consulted her mother. It was just as she expected: her mother thought it an entirely suitable job for a woman.

The little group at the bar had turned back to their drinks. Between their shoulders she could see her own reflection in the mirror above the bar. Today's face looked no different from yesterday's face; thick, light brown hair framing features which looked as if a giant had placed a hand on her head and the other under her chin and gently squeezed the face together; large eyes, browny-green under a deep fringe of hair; wide cheek bones; a gentle, childish mouth. A cat's face she thought, but calmly decorative among the reflection of coloured bottles and all the bright glitter of Mavis's bar. Despite its look of deceptive youth it could be a secret, uncommunicative face. Cordelia had early learnt stoicism. All her foster parents, kindly and well-meaning in their different ways, had demanded one thing of her – that she should be happy. She had quickly learned that to show unhappiness was to risk the loss of love. Compared with this early discipline of concealment, all subsequent deceits had been easy.

The Snout was edging his way towards her. He settled himself down on the bench, his thick rump in its appalling tweed pressed close to hers. She disliked the Snout although he had been Bernie's only friend. Bernie had explained that the Snout was a police informer and did rather well. And there were other sources of income. Sometimes his friends stole famous pictures or valuable jewellery. Then the Snout, suitably instructed, would hint to the police where the loot could be found. There was a reward for the Snout to be subsequently shared, of course, among the thieves, and a pay-off, too, for the detective, who after all had done most of the work. As Bernie had pointed out, the insurance company got off lightly, the owners got their property back intact, the thieves were in no danger from the police and the Snout and the detective got their pay-off. It was the system. Cordelia, shocked, had not liked to protest too much. She suspected that Bernie too had done some snouting in his time, although never with such expertise or with such lucrative results.

The Snout's eyes were rheumy, his hand around the glass of whisky was shaking.

'Poor old Bernie, I could see he had it coming to him. He'd been losing weight for the last year and he had that grey look to him, the cancer complexion, my dad used to call it.'

At least the Snout had noticed; she hadn't. Bernie had always seemed to her grey and sick-looking. A thick, hot thigh edged closer.

'Never had any luck, poor sod. They chucked him out of the CID. Did he tell you? That was Superintendent Dalgliesh, Inspector at the time. Christ, he could be a proper bastard; no second chance from him, I can tell you.'

'Yes, Bernie told me,' Cordelia lied. She added: 'He didn't seem particularly bitter about it.'

'No use, is there, in being bitter? Take what comes, that's my motto. I suppose you'll be looking for another job?'

He said it wistfully as if her defection would leave the Agency open for his exploitation.

'Not just yet,' said Cordelia. 'I shan't look for a new job just yet.'

She had made two resolutions: she would keep on Bernie's business until there was nothing left with which to pay the rent, and she would never come into the Golden Pheasant again as long as she lived.

This resolution to keep the business going survived the next four days – survived discovery of the rent book and agreement which revealed that Bernie hadn't, after all, owned the little house in Cremona Road and that her tenancy of the bed-sitting-room was illegal and certainly limited; survived learning from the Bank Manager that Bernie's credit balance would barely pay for his funeral and from the garage that the Mini was shortly due for an overhaul; survived the clearing up of the Cremona Road house. Everywhere was the sad detritus of a solitary and mismanaged life.

The tins of Irish stew and baked beans – had he never eaten anything else? – stacked in a carefully arranged pyramid as if in a grocer's window; large tins of metal and floor polish, half-used, with their contents dried or congealed; a drawer of old rags used as dusters but stiff with an amalgam of polish and dirt; a laundry basket unemptied; thick woollen combinations felted with machine washing and stained brown about the crotch – how could he have borne to leave those for discovery?

She went daily to the office, cleaning, tidying, rearranging the filing. There were no calls and no clients and yet she seemed always busy. There was the inquest to attend, depressing in its detached almost boring formality, in its inevitable verdict. There was a visit to Bernie's solicitor. He was a dispirited, elderly man with an office inconveniently situated near Mile End Station who took the news of his client's death with lugubrious resignation as if it were a personal affront, and after a brief search found Bernie's will and pored over it with puzzled suspicion, as if it were not the document he himself had recently drawn up. He succeeded in giving Cordelia the impression that he realized that she had been Bernie's mistress – why else should he have left her the business? – but that he was a man of the world and didn't hold the knowledge against her. He took no part in arranging the funeral except to supply Cordelia with the name of a firm of undertakers; she suspected that they probably gave him a commission. She was relieved after a week of depressing solemnity to find that the funeral director was both cheerful and competent. Once he discovered that Cordelia wasn't going to break down in tears or indulge in the more histrionic antics of the bereaved, he was happy to discuss the relative price and the merits of burial and cremation with conspiratorial candour.

'Cremation every time. There's no private insurance, you tell me? Then get it all over as quickly, easily and cheaply as possible. Take my word, that's what the deceased would want nine times out of ten. A grave's an expensive luxury these days – no use to him – no use to you. Dust to dust, ashes to ashes; but what about the process in between? Not nice to think about, is it? So why not get it over as quickly as possible by the most reliable modern methods? Mind you, Miss, I'm advising you against my own best interests.'

Cordelia said:

'It's very kind of you. Do you think we ought to have a wreath?'

'Why not, it'll give it a bit of tone. Leave it to me.'

So there had been a cremation and one wreath. The wreath had been a vulgarly inappropriate cushion of lilies and carnations, the flowers already dying and smelling of decay. The cremation service had been spoken by the priest with carefully controlled speed and with a suggestion of apology in his tone as if to assure his hearers that, although he enjoyed a special dispensation, he didn't expect them to believe the unbelievable. Bernie had passed to his burning to the sound of synthetic music and only just on time, to judge by the impatient rustlings of the cortège already waiting to enter the chapel.

Afterwards Cordelia was left standing in the bright sunlight, feeling the heat of the gravel through the soles of her shoes. The air was rich and heavy with the scent of flowers. Swept suddenly with desolation and a defensive anger on Bernie's behalf, she sought a scapegoat and found it in a certain Superintendent of the Yard. He had kicked Bernie out of the only job he had ever wanted to do; hadn't troubled to find out what happened to him later; and, most irrational indictment of all, he hadn't even bothered to come to the funeral. Bernie had needed to be a detective as other men needed to paint, write, drink or fornicate. Surely the CID was large enough to accommodate one man's enthusiasm and inefficiency? For the first time Cordelia wept for Bernie; hot tears blurred and multiplied the long line of waiting hearses with their bright coronets so that they seemed to stretch in an infinity of gleaming chrome and trembling flowers. Untying the black chiffon scarf from her head, her only concession to mourning, Cordelia set off to walk to the tube station.

She was thirsty when she got to Oxford Circus and decided to have tea in the restaurant at Dickins and Jones. This was unusual and an extravagance but it had been an unusual and extravagant day. She lingered long enough to get full value for her bill and it was after a quarter past four when she returned to the office.

She had a visitor. There was a woman waiting, shoulders against the door – a woman who looked cool and incongruous against the dirty paintwork and the greasy walls. Cordelia caught her breath in surprise, her upward rush checked. Her light shoes had made no sound on the stairway and for a few seconds she saw her visitor unobserved. She gained an impression, immediate and vivid, of competence and authority and an intimidating rightness of dress. The woman was wearing a grey suit with a small stand-away collar which showed a narrow band of white cotton at the throat. Her black patent shoes were obviously expensive; a large black bag with patch pockets was slung from her left shoulder. She was tall and her hair, prematurely white, was cut short and moulded to her head like a cap. Her face was pale and long. She was reading *The Times*, the paper folded so that she could hold it in her right hand. After a couple of seconds, she became aware of Cordelia and their eyes met. The woman looked at her wrist watch.

'If you are Cordelia Gray, then you're eighteen minutes late. This notice says that you would return at four o'clock.'

'I know, I'm sorry.' Cordelia hurried up the last few steps and fitted the Yale key into the lock. She opened the door.

'Won't you come in?'

The woman preceded her into the outer office and turned to face her without giving the room even a glance.

'I was hoping to see Mr Pryde. Will he be long?'

'I'm sorry; I've just come back from his cremation. I mean . . . Bernie's dead.'

'Obviously. Our information was that he was alive ten days ago. He must have died with remarkable speed and discretion.'

'Not with discretion. Bernie killed himself.'

'How extraordinary!' The visitor seemed to be struck by its extraordinariness. She pressed her hands together and for a few seconds walked restlessly about the room in a curious pantomime of distress.

'How extraordinary!' she said again. She gave a little snort of laughter. Cordelia didn't speak, but the two women regarded each other gravely. Then the visitor said:

'Well, I seem to have had a wasted journey.'

Cordelia breathed an almost inaudible 'Oh no!' and resisted an absurd impulse to fling her body against the door.

'Please don't go before talking to me. I was Mr Pryde's partner and I own the business now. I'm sure I could help. Won't you please sit down?'

The visitor took no notice of the offered chair.

'No one can help, no one in the world. However that is beside the point. There is something which my employer particularly wants to know – some information he requires – and he had decided that Mr Pryde was the person to get it for him. I don't know if he would consider you an effective substitute. Is there a private telephone here?'

'In here, please.'

The woman walked into the inner office, again with no sign that its shabbiness had made any impression on her. She turned to Cordelia.

'I'm sorry, I should have introduced myself. My name is Elizabeth Leaming and my employer is Sir Ronald Callender.'

'The conservationist?'

'I shouldn't let him hear you call him that. He prefers to be called a microbiologist, which is what he is. Please excuse me.'

She shut the door firmly. Cordelia, feeling suddenly weak, sat down at the typewriter. The keys, oddly familiar symbols encircled in black medallions, shifted their pattern before her tired eyes, then at a blink clicked back to normality. She grasped the sides of the machine, cold and clammy to the touch, and talked herself back to calmness. Her heart was thudding.

'I must be calm, must show her that I am tough. This silliness is only the strain of Bernie's funeral and too much standing in the hot sun.'

But hope was traumatic; she was angry with herself for caring so much.

The telephone call took only a couple of minutes. The door of the inner office opened; Miss Leaming was drawing on her gloves.

'Sir Ronald has asked to see you. Can you come now?'

Come where, thought Cordelia, but she didn't ask.

'Yes, shall I need my gear?'

The gear was Bernie's carefully designed and fitted-out scene-of-crime case with its tweezers, scissors, fingerprinting equipment, jars to collect specimens; Cordelia had never yet had occasion to use it.

'It depends upon what you mean by your gear, but I shouldn't think so. Sir Ronald wants to see you before deciding whether to offer you the job. It means a train journey to Cambridge but you should get back tonight. Is there anyone you ought to tell?'

'No, there's only me.'

'Perhaps I ought to identify myself.' She opened her handbag. 'Here is an addressed envelope. I'm not a white slaver in case they exist and in case you're frightened.'

'I'm frightened of quite a number of things but not of white slavers and if I were, an addressed envelope would hardly reassure me. I'd insist on telephoning Sir Ronald Callender to check.'

'Perhaps you would like to do so?' suggested Miss Leaming without rancour.

'No.'

'Then shall we go?' Miss Leaming led the way to the door. As they went out to the landing and Cordelia turned to lock the office behind her, her visitor indicated the notepad and pencil hanging together from a nail on the wall.

'Hadn't you better change the notice?'

Cordelia tore off her previous message and after a moment's thought wrote:

I am called away to an urgent case. Any messages pushed through the door will receive my immediate and personal attention on return.

'That,' pronounced Miss Leaming, 'should reassure your clients.' Cordelia wondered if the remark was sarcastic; it was impossible to tell from the detached tone. But she didn't feel that Miss Leaming was laughing at her and was surprised at her own lack of resentment at the way in which her visitor had taken charge of events. Meekly, she followed Miss Leaming down the stairs and into Kingly Street.

They travelled by the Central Line to Liverpool Street and caught the 17.36 train to Cambridge with plenty of time. Miss Leaming bought Cordelia's ticket, collected a portable typewriter and a briefcase of papers from the left luggage department and led the way to a first-class carriage. She said:

'I shall have to work in the train; have you anything to read?'

'That's all right. I don't like talking when I'm travelling either. I've got Hardy's *Trumpet Major* – I always have a paperback in my bag.'

After Bishops Stortford they had the compartment to themselves but only once did Miss Leaming look up from her work to question Cordelia.

'How did you come to be working for Mr Pryde?'

'After I left school I went to live with my father on the continent. We travelled around a good deal. He died in Rome last May after a heart attack and I came home. I had taught myself some shorthand and typing so I took a job with a secretarial agency. They sent me to Bernie and after a few weeks he let me help him with one or two of the cases. He decided to train me and I agreed to stay on permanently. Two months ago he made me his partner.'

All that had meant was that Cordelia gave up a regular wage in return for the uncertain rewards of success in the form of an equal share of the profits together with a rent-free bed-sitting-room in Bernie's house. He hadn't meant to cheat. The offer of the partnership had been made in the genuine belief that she would recognize it for what it was; not a good conduct prize but an accolade of trust.

'What was your father?'

'He was an itinerant Marxist poet and an amateur revolutionary.'

'You must have had an interesting childhood.'

Remembering the succession of foster mothers, the unexplained incomprehensible moves from house to house, the changes of schools, the concerned faces of Local Authority Welfare Officers and school teachers desperately wondering what to do with her in the holidays, Cordelia replied as she always did to this assertion, gravely and without irony.

'Yes, it was very interesting.'

'And what was this training you received from Mr Pryde?'

'Bernie taught me some of the things he learnt in the CID: how to search the scene of a crime properly, how to collect exhibits, some elementary self-defence, how to detect and lift fingerprints – that kind of thing.'

'Those are skills which I hardly feel you will find appropriate to this case.'

Miss Leaming bent her head over her papers and did not speak again until the train reached Cambridge.

*

Outside the station Miss Leaming briefly surveyed the car-park and led the way towards a small black van. Standing beside it rigidly as a uniformed chauffeur, was a stockily built young man dressed in an open-necked white shirt, dark breeches and tall boots who Miss Leaming introduced casually and without explanation as 'Lunn'. He nodded briefly in acknowledgement of the introduction but did not smile. Cordelia held out her hand. His grip was momentary but remarkably strong, crushing her fingers; suppressing a grimace of pain she saw a flicker in the large mud-brown eyes and wondered if he had hurt her deliberately. The eyes were certainly memorable and beautiful, moist calves' eyes heavily lashed and with the same look of troubled pain at the unpredictability of the world's terrors. But their beauty emphasized rather than redeemed the unattractiveness of the rest of him. He was, she thought, a sinister study in black and white with his thick, short neck and powerful shoulders straining the seams of his shirt. He had a helmet of strong black hair, a pudgy slightly pock-marked face and a moist petulant mouth; the face of a ribald cherub. He was a man who sweated profusely; the underarms of his shirt were stained and the cotton stuck to the flesh emphasizing the strong curve of the back and the obtrusive biceps.

Cordelia saw that the three of them were to sit squashed together in the front of the van. Lunn held open the door without apology except to state:

'The Rover's still in dock.'

Miss Leaming hung back so that Cordelia was compelled to get in first and sit beside him. She thought: 'They don't like each other and he resents me.'

She wondered about his position in Sir Ronald Callender's household. Miss Leaming's place she had already guessed; no ordinary secretary however long in service, however indispensable, had quite that air of authority or talked of 'my employer' in that tone of possessive irony. But she wondered about Lunn. He didn't behave like a subordinate but nor did he strike her as a scientist. True, scientists were alien creatures to her. Sister Mary Magdalen was the only one she had known. Sister had taught what the syllabus dignified as general science, a hotch-potch of elementary physics, chemistry and biology unceremoniously lumped together. Science subjects were in general little regarded at the Convent of the Immaculate Conception, although the arts were well taught. Sister Mary Magdalen had been an elderly and timid nun, eyes puzzled behind steel-rimmed spectacles, her clumsy fingers permanently stained with chemicals, who had apparently been as surprised as her pupils at the extraordinary explosions and fumes which her activities with test tube and flask had occasionally produced. She had been more concerned to demonstrate the incomprehensibility of the universe and the inscrutability of God's laws than to reveal scientific principles and in this she had certainly succeeded. Cordelia felt that Sister Mary Magdalen would be no help to her in dealing with Sir Ronald Callender; Sir Ronald who had campaigned in the cause of conservation long before his interest became a popular obsession, who had represented his country at international conferences on ecology and been knighted for his services to conservation. All this Cordelia, like the rest of the country, knew from his television appearances and the Sunday colour supplements. He was the establishment scientist, carefully uncommitted politically, who personified to everyone's reassurance the poor boy who had made good and stayed good. How, Cordelia wondered, had he come to think of employing Bernie Pryde?

Uncertain how far Lunn was in his employer's or Miss Leaming's confidence, she asked carefully:

'How did Sir Ronald hear about Bernie?'

'John Bellinger told him.'

So the Bellinger bonus had arrived at last! Bernie had always expected it. The Bellinger case had been his most lucrative, perhaps his only, success. John Bellinger was the director of a small family firm which manufactured specialized scientific instruments. The previous year his office had been plagued by an outbreak of obscene letters and, unwilling to call in the police, he had telephoned Bernie. Bernie, taken on the staff at his own suggestion as a messenger, had quickly solved a not very difficult problem. The writer had been Bellinger's middle-aged and highly regarded personal secretary. Bellinger had been grateful. Bernie, after anxious thought and consultation with Cordelia, had sent in a bill the size of which had astounded them both and the bill had been promptly paid. It had kept the Agency going for a month. Bernie had said: 'We'll get a bonus from the Bellinger case, see if we don't. Anything can happen in this job. He only chose us by picking our name from the telephone directory but now he'll recommend us to his friends. This case could be the beginning of something big.'

And now, thought Cordelia, on the day of Bernie's funeral, the Bellinger bonus had arrived.

She asked no more questions and the drive, which took less than thirty minutes, passed in silence. The three of them sat thigh to thigh, but distanced. She saw nothing of the city. At the end of Station Road by the War Memorial the car turned to the left and soon they were in the country. There were wide fields of young corn, the occasional stretch of tree-lined dappled shade, straggling villages of thatched cottages and squat red villas strung along the road, low uplands from which Cordelia could see the towers and spires of the city, shining with deceptive nearness in the evening sun. Finally, there was another village, a thin belt of elms fringing the road, a long curving wall of red brick and the van turned in through open wrought-iron gates. They had arrived.

The house was obviously Georgian, not perhaps the best Georgian, but solidly built, agreeably proportioned and with the look of all good domestic architecture of having grown naturally out of its site. The mellow brick, festooned with wisteria, gleamed richly in the evening sun so that the green of the creeper glowed and the whole house looked suddenly as artificial and unsubstantial as a film set. It was essentially a family house, a welcoming house. But now a heavy silence lay over it and the rows of elegantly proportioned windows were empty eyes.

Lunn, who had driven fast but skilfully, braked in front of the porch. He stayed in his seat while the two women got out then drove the van round the side of the house. As she slid down from the high seat Cordelia could glimpse a range of low buildings, topped with small ornamental turrets, which she took to be stables or garages. Through the wide-arched gateway she could see that the grounds dropped slowly away to give a far vista of the flat Cambridgeshire countryside, patterned with the gentle greens and fawns of early summer. Miss Leaming said:

'The stable-block has been converted into laboratories. Most of the east side is now glass. It was a skilful job by a Swedish architect, functional but attractive.'

For the first time since they had met her voice sounded interested, almost enthusiastic.

The front door was open. Cordelia came into a wide, panelled hall with a staircase curving to the left, a carved stone fireplace to the right. She was aware of a smell of roses and lavender, of carpets gleaming richly against polished wood, of the subdued ticking of a clock.

Miss Leaming led the way to a door immediately across the hall. It led to a study, a room book-lined and elegant, one with a view of wide lawns and a shield of trees. In front of the french windows was a Georgian desk and behind the desk sat a man.

Cordelia had seen his photographs in the press and knew what to expect. But he was at once smaller and more impressive than she had imagined. She knew that she was facing a man of authority and high intelligence; his strength came over like a physical force. But as he rose from his seat and waved her to a chair, she saw that he was slighter than his photographs suggested, the heavy shoulders and impressive head making the body look top-heavy. He had a lined, sensitive face with a high-bridged nose, deep-set eyes on which the lids weighed heavily and a mobile, sculptured mouth. His black hair, as yet unflecked with grey, lay heavily across his brow. His face was shadowed with weariness and, as Cordelia came closer, she could detect the twitch of a nerve in his left temple and the almost imperceptible staining of the veins in the irises of the deep-set eyes. But his compact body, taut with energy and latent vigour, made no concession to tiredness. The arrogant head was held high, the eyes were keen and wary under the heavy lids. Above all he looked successful. Cordelia had seen that look before, had recognized it from the back of crowds as, inscrutable, they had watched the famous and notorious pass on their way – that almost physical glow, akin to sexuality and undimmed by weariness or ill-health, of men who knew and enjoyed the realities of power.

Miss Leaming said:

'This is all that remains of Pryde's Detective Agency – Miss Cordelia Gray.'

The keen eyes looked into Cordelia's.

'We take a Pride in our Work. Do you?'

Cordelia, tired after her journey at the end of a momentous day, was in no mood for jokes about poor Bernie's pathetic pun. She said:

'Sir Ronald, I have come here because your secretary said that you might want to employ me. If she's wrong, I would be glad to know so that I can get back to London.'

'She isn't my secretary and she isn't wrong. You must forgive my discourtesy; it's a little disconcerting to expect a burly ex-policeman and to get you. I'm not complaining, Miss Gray; you might do very well. What are your fees?'

The question might have sounded offensive but it wasn't; he was completely matter-of-fact. Cordelia told him, a little too quickly, a little too eagerly.

'Five pounds a day and expenses, but we try to keep those as low as possible. For that, of course, you get my sole services. I mean I don't work for any other client until your case is finished.'

'And is there another client?'

'Well, not just at present but there very well could be.' She went on quickly:

'We have a fair-play clause. If I decide at any stage of the investigation that I'd rather not go on with it, you are entitled to any information I have gained up to that point. If I decide to withhold it from you, then I make no charge for the work already done.'

That had been one of Bernie's principles. He had been a great man for principles. Even when there hadn't been a case for a week, he could happily discuss the extent to which they would be justified in telling a client less than the full truth, the point at which the police ought to be brought into an inquiry, the ethics of deception or lying in the service of truth. 'But no bugging,' Bernie would say, 'I set my face firmly against bugging. And we don't touch industrial sabotage.'

The temptation to either wasn't great. They had no bugging

equipment and wouldn't have known how to use it if they had, and at no time had Bernie been invited to touch industrial sabotage.

Sir Ronald said:

'That sounds reasonable but I don't think this case will present you with any crisis of conscience. It is comparatively simple. Eighteen days ago my son hanged himself. I want you to find out why. Can you do that?'

'I should like to try, Sir Ronald.'

'I realize that you need certain basic information about Mark. Miss Leaming will type it out for you, then you can read it through and let us know what else you require.'

Cordelia said:

'I should like you to tell me yourself, please.'

'Is that necessary?'

'It would be helpful to me.'

He settled again into his chair and picked up a stub of pencil, twisting it in his hands. After a minute he slipped it absent-mindedly into his pocket. Without looking at her, he began to speak.

'My son Mark was twenty-one on the 25th April this year. He was at Cambridge reading history at my old college and was in his final year. Five weeks ago and without warning, he left the university and took a job as gardener with a Major Markland, who lives in a house called Summertrees outside Duxford. Mark gave me no explanation of this action either then or later. He lived alone in a cottage in Major Markland's grounds. Eighteen days later he was found by his employer's sister hanging by the neck from a strap knotted to a hook in the sitting-room ceiling. The verdict at the inquest was that he took his life while the balance of his mind was disturbed. I know little of my son's mind but I reject that comfortable euphemism. He was a rational person. He had a reason for his action. I want to know what it was.'

Miss Leaming, who had been looking out of the french windows to the garden, turned and said with sudden vehemence:

'This lust always to know! It's only prying. If he'd wanted us to know, he'd have told us.'

Sir Ronald said:

'I'm not prepared to go on in this uncertainty. My son is dead. *My* son. If I am in some way responsible, I prefer to know. If anyone else is responsible I want to know that too.'

Cordelia looked from one to the other. She asked:

'Did he leave a note?'

'He left a note but not an explanation. It was found in his typewriter.'

Quietly Miss Leaming began to speak:

'Down the winding cavern we groped our tedious way, till a void boundless as the nether sky appeared beneath us, and we held by the roots of trees and hung over this immensity; but I said: if you please we will commit ourselves to this void and see whether providence is here also.'

The husky, curiously deep voice came to an end. They were silent. Then Sir Ronald said:

'You claim to be a detective, Miss Gray. What do you deduce from that?'

'That your son read William Blake. Isn't it a passage from *The Marriage of Heaven and Hell*?'

Sir Ronald and Miss Leaming glanced at each other. Sir Ronald said:

'So I am told.'

Cordelia thought that Blake's gently unemphatic exhortation, devoid of violence or despair, was more appropriate to suicide by drowning or by poison – a ceremonious floating or sinking into oblivion – than to the trauma of hanging. And yet there was the analogy of falling, of launching oneself into the void. But this speculation was indulgent fantasy. He had chosen Blake: he had chosen hanging. Perhaps other and more gentle means were not to hand; perhaps he had acted upon impulse. What was it that the Super always said? 'Never theorize in advance of your facts.' She would have to look at the cottage.

Sir Ronald said, with a touch of impatience.

'Well, don't you want the job?'

Cordelia looked at Miss Leaming but the woman did not meet her eyes.

'I want it very much. I was wondering whether you really wanted me to take it.'

'I'm offering it to you. Worry about your own responsibilities, Miss Gray, and I'll look after mine.'

Cordelia said:

'Is there anything else that you can tell me? The ordinary things. Was your son in good health? Did he seem worried about his work or his love affairs? About money?'

'Mark would have inherited a considerable fortune from his maternal grandfather had he reached the age of twenty-five. In the meantime, he received an adequate allowance from me, but from the date of leaving college he transferred the balance back to my own account and instructed his Bank Manager to deal similarly with any future payments. Presumably he lived on his earnings for the last two weeks of his life. The post-mortem revealed no illnesses and his tutor testified that his academic work was satisfactory. I, of course, know nothing of his subject. He didn't confide in me about his love affairs – what young man does to his father? If he had any, I would expect them to be heterosexual.'

Miss Leaming turned from her contemplation of the garden. She held out her hands in a gesture which could have been resignation or despair:

'We knew nothing about him, nothing! So why wait until he's dead and then start finding out?'

'And his friends?' asked Cordelia quietly.

'They rarely visited here but there were two I recognized at the inquest and the funeral: Hugo Tilling from his own college and his sister who is a post-graduate student at New Hall, studying philology. Do you remember her name, Eliza?'

'Sophie. Sophia Tilling. Mark brought her here to dinner once or twice.'

'Could you tell me something about your son's early life? Where was he educated?'

'He went to a pre-prep school when he was five and to a prep school subsequently. I couldn't have a child here running unsupervised in and out of the laboratory. Later, at his mother's wish – she died when Mark was nine months old – he went to a Woodard

Foundation. My wife was what I believe is called a High Anglican and wanted the boy educated in that tradition. As far as I know, it had no deleterious effect on him.'

'Was he happy at prep school?'

'I expect he was as happy as most eight-year-olds are, which means that he was miserable most of the time, interposed with periods of animal spirits. Is all this relevant?'

'Anything could be. I have to try to get to know him, you see.'

What was it that the supercilious, sapient, superhuman Super had taught? 'Get to know the dead person. Nothing about him is too trivial, too unimportant. Dead men can talk. They can lead directly to their murderer.' Only this time, of course, there wasn't a murderer. She said:

'It would be helpful if Miss Leaming could type out the information you have given to me and add the name of his college and his tutor. And please may I have a note signed by you to authorize me to make inquiries.'

He reached down to a left-hand drawer in the desk, took out a sheet of writing-paper and wrote on it; then he passed it to Cordelia. The printed heading read: *From Sir Ronald Callender, F.R.C., Garforth House, Cambridgeshire.* Underneath he had written: *The bearer, Miss Cordelia Gray, is authorized to make inquiries on my behalf into the death on 26th May of my son Mark Callender.* He had signed and dated it. He asked:

'Is there anything else?'

Cordelia said:

'You talked about the possibility of someone else being responsible for your son's death. Do you quarrel with the verdict?'

'The verdict was in accordance with the evidence which is all one can expect of a verdict. A court of law is not constituted to establish the truth. I'm employing you to make an attempt at that. Have you everything you need? I don't think we can help you with any more information.'

'I should like a photograph.' They looked at each other nonplussed. He said to Miss Leaming:

'A photograph. Have we a photograph, Eliza?'

'There is his passport somewhere but I'm not sure where. I have that photograph I took of him in the garden last summer. It shows him fairly clearly, I think. I'll get it.' She went out of the room. Cordelia said:

'And I should like to see his room, if I may. I assume that he stayed here during his vacations?'

'Only occasionally, but of course he had a room here. I'll show it to you.'

The room was on the second floor and at the back. Once inside, Sir Ronald ignored Cordelia. He walked over to the window and gazed out over the lawns as if neither she nor the room held any interest for him. It told Cordelia nothing about the adult Mark. It was simply furnished, a schoolboy's sanctum, and looked as if little had been changed in the last ten years. There was a low white cupboard against one wall with the usual row of discarded childhood toys; a teddy bear, his fur scuffed with much cuddling and one beady eye hanging loose; painted wooden trains and trucks; a Noah's Ark, its deck a-tumble with stiff-legged animals topped by a round-faced Noah and his wife; a boat with limp dejected sail; a miniature dartboard. Above the toys were two rows of books. Cordelia went over to examine them. Here was the orthodox library of the middle-class child, the approved classics handed down from generation to generation, the traditional lore of Nanny and mother. Cordelia had come to them late as an adult; they had found no place in her Saturday comic and television-dominated childhood. She said:

'What about his present books?'

'They're in boxes in the cellar. He sent them here for storage when he left college and we haven't had time to unpack them yet. There hardly seems any point in it.'

There was a small round table beside the bed and on it a lamp and a bright round stone intricately holed by the sea, a treasure picked up, perhaps, from some holiday beach. Sir Ronald touched it gently with long tentative fingers then began rolling it under his palm over the surface of the table. Then, apparently without thinking, he dropped it into his pocket.

'Well,' he said. 'Shall we go down now?'

They were met at the foot of the stairs by Miss Leaming. She looked up at them as slowly they came down side by side. There was such controlled intensity in her regard that Cordelia waited almost with apprehension for her to speak. But she turned away, her shoulders drooping as if with sudden fatigue, and all she said was:

'I've found the photograph. I should like it back when you've finished with it please. I've put it in the envelope with the note. There isn't a fast train back to London until nine thirty-seven, so perhaps you would care to stay for dinner?'

The dinner party which followed was an interesting but rather odd experience, the meal itself a blend of the formal and casual which Cordelia felt was the result of conscious effort rather than chance. Some effect, she felt, had been aimed at but whether of a dedicated band of co-workers meeting together at the end of a day for a corporate meal, or the ritual imposition of order and ceremony on a diverse company, she wasn't sure. The party numbered ten: Sir Ronald Callender, Miss Leaming, Chris Lunn, a visiting American Professor, whose unpronounceable name she forgot as soon as Sir Ronald introduced her, and five of the young scientists. All the men, including Lunn, were in dinner-jackets, and Miss Leaming wore a long skirt of patchwork satin below a plain sleeveless top. The rich blues, greens and reds gleamed and changed in the candle-light as she moved, and emphasized the pale silver of her hair and the almost colourless skin. Cordelia had been rather nonplussed when her hostess left her in the drawing room and went upstairs to change. She wished that she had something more competitive than the fawn skirt and green top, being at an age to value elegance more highly than youth.

She had been shown to Miss Leaming's bedroom to wash and had been intrigued by the elegance and simplicity of the furniture and the contrasting opulence of the adjacent bathroom. Studying her tired face in the mirror and wielding her lipstick, she had wished she had some eye shadow with her. On impulse, and with a sense of guilt, she had pulled open a dressing-table drawer. It was filled with a variety of make-up; old lipsticks in colours long out of date; half-used bottles of foundation cream; eye pencils; moisturizing creams; half-used bottles of scent. She had rummaged, and eventually found a stick of eye shadow which, in view of the wasteful muddle of discarded items in the drawer, she had had little compunction in using. The effect had been bizarre but striking. She could not compete with Miss Leaming but at least she looked five years older. The disorder in the drawer had surprised her and she had had to resist the temptation to see if the wardrobe and the other drawers were in a similar state of disarray. How inconsistent and how interesting human beings were! She thought it astonishing that such a fastidious and competent woman should be content to live with such a mess.

The dining room was at the front of the house. Miss Leaming placed Cordelia between herself and Lunn, a seating which held little prospect of pleasurable conversation. The rest of the party sat where they wished. The contrast between simplicity and elegance showed in the table arrangements. There was no artificial light and three silver branched candlesticks were placed at regular intervals down the table. Between them were set four wine carafes made of thick green glass with curved lips, such as Cordelia had often seen in cheap Italian restaurants. The place-mats were of plain cork, but the forks and spoons were antique silver. The flowers were set in low bowls, not skilfully arranged but looking as if they were casualties of a garden storm, blooms which had snapped off in the wind and which someone had thought it kind to place in water.

The young men looked incongruous in their dinner-jackets, not ill at ease since they enjoyed the essential self-esteem of the clever and successful, but as if they had picked up the suits second-hand or at a fancy dress costumier and were participating in a charade. Cordelia was surprised at their youth; she guessed that only one was over thirty. Three were untidy, fast talking, restless young men with loud emphatic voices who took no notice of Cordelia after the first introduction. The other two were quieter and one, a tall black-haired boy with strong irregular features, smiled at her across the table and looked as if he would like to have sat within speaking distance.

The meal was brought in by an Italian manservant and his wife who left the cooked dishes on hot plates on a side table. The food was plentiful and the smell almost intolerably appetizing to

Cordelia, who hadn't realized until then just how hungry she was. There was a dish heaped high with glistening rice, a large casserole of veal in a rich, mushroom sauce, a bowl of spinach. Beside it on the cold table was a large ham, a sirloin of beef and an interesting assortment of salads and fruit. The company served themselves, carrying their plates back to the table with whatever combination of food, hot or cold, they fancied. The young scientists piled their plates high and Cordelia followed their example.

She took little interest in the conversation except to notice that it was predominantly about science and that Lunn, although he spoke less than the others, spoke as their equal. He should, she thought, have looked ridiculous in his rather tight dinner-jacket but, surprisingly, he looked the most at ease, the second most powerful personality in the room. Cordelia tried to analyse why this was so, but was defeated. He ate slowly, with finicky attention to the arrangement of the food on his plate, and from time to time, smiled secretly into his wine.

At the other end of the table Sir Ronald was peeling an apple and talking to his guest, his head inclined. The green rind slid thinly over his long fingers and curved down towards his plate. Cordelia glanced at Miss Leaming. She was staring at Sir Ronald with such unwavering and speculative concern, that Cordelia uncomfortably felt that every eye present must be irresistibly drawn to that pale disdainful mask. Then, Miss Leaming seemed to become aware of her glance. She relaxed and turned to Cordelia:

'When we were travelling here together you were reading Hardy. Do you enjoy him?'

'Very much. But I enjoy Jane Austen more.'

'Then you must try to find an opportunity of visiting the Fitzwilliam Museum in Cambridge. They have a letter written by Jane Austen. I think you'll find it interesting.'

She spoke with the controlled artificial brightness of a hostess trying to find a subject to interest a difficult guest. Cordelia, her mouth full of veal and mushrooms, wondered how she would manage to get through the rest of the meal. Luckily, however, the American professor had caught the word 'Fitzwilliam' and now called down the table to inquire about the Museum's collection of majolica in which, apparently, he was interested. The conversation became general.

It was Miss Leaming who drove Cordelia to the station, Audley End this time instead of Cambridge; a change for which no reason was given. They didn't speak about the case during the drive. Cordelia was exhausted with tiredness, food and wine and allowed herself to be firmly taken in hand and placed in the train without attempting to gain any further information. She didn't really think she would have got it. As the train drew out, her tired fingers fumbled with the flap of the strong white envelope which Miss Leaming had handed to her and she drew out and read the enclosed note. It was expertly typed and set out, but told her little more than she had already learnt. With it was the photograph. She saw the picture of a laughing boy, his head half-turned towards the camera, one hand shielding his eyes from the sun. He was wearing jeans and a vest and was half lying on the lawn, a pile of books on the grass beside him. Perhaps he had been working there under the trees when she had come out of the french windows with her camera and called imperiously to him to smile. The photograph told Cordelia nothing except that for one recorded second at least, he had known how to be happy. She placed it back in the envelope; her hands closed protectively over it. Cordelia slept.

CHAPTER TWO

Next morning Cordelia left Cremona Road before seven o'clock. Despite her tiredness the night before, she had made her major preparations before she went to bed. They hadn't taken long. As Bernie had taught her, she checked systematically the scene-of-crime kit, an unnecessary routine since nothing had been touched since, in celebration of their partnership, he had first set it up for her. She put ready the polaroid camera; sorted into order the road maps from the jumble pushed into the back of his desk; shook out the sleeping bag and rolled it ready; filled a carrier bag with iron rations from Bernie's store of tinned soup and baked beans; considered, and finally decided to take, their copy of Professor Simpson's book on forensic medicine and her own Hacker portable radio; checked the first-aid kit. Finally, she found herself a fresh notebook, headed it *Case of Mark Callender* and ruled up the last few pages ready for her expense account. These preliminaries had always been the most satisfying part of a case, before boredom or distaste set in, before anticipation crumbled into disenchantment and failure. Bernie's planning had always been meticulous and successful; it was reality which had let him down.

Finally, she considered her clothes. If this hot weather continued, her Jaeger suit, bought from her savings after much careful thought to see her through almost any interview, would be uncomfortably hot, but she might have to interview the head of a college and the dignified professionalism best exemplified by a suit would be the effect to aim at. She decided to travel in her fawn suede skirt with a short-sleeved jumper and pack jeans and warmer jumpers for any field work. Cordelia enjoyed clothes, enjoyed planning and buying them, a pleasure circumscribed less by poverty than by her obsessive need to be able to pack the whole of her wardrobe into one medium sized suitcase like a refugee perpetually ready for flight.

Once she had shaken free from the tentacles of north London,

Cordelia enjoyed the drive. The Mini purred along and Cordelia thought that it had never run so sweetly. She liked the flat East Anglian countryside, the broad streets of the market towns, the way in which the fields grew unhedged to the edge of the road, the openness and freedom of the far horizons and wide skies. The country matched her mood. She had grieved for Bernie and would grieve for him again, missing his comradeship and his undemanding affection, but this, in a sense, was her first case and she was glad to be tackling it alone. It was one that she thought she could solve. It neither appalled nor disgusted her. Driving in happy anticipation through the sunbathed countryside, the boot of the car carefully packed with her gear, she was filled with the euphoria of hope.

When she finally reached Duxford village she had difficulty at first in finding Summertrees. Major Markland was apparently a man who thought that his importance warranted omitting the name of the road from his address. But the second person she stopped to ask was a villager who was able to point the way, taking infinite trouble over the simple directions as if fearing that a perfunctory answer would have seemed discourteous. Cordelia had to find a suitable place to turn and then drive back a couple of miles, for she had already passed Summertrees.

And this, at last, must be the house. It was a large Victorian edifice of red brick, set well back, with a wide turfed verge between the open wooden gate leading to the drive and the road. Cordelia wondered why anyone should have wanted to build such an intimidatingly ugly house or, having decided to do so, should have set down a suburban monstrosity in the middle of the countryside. Perhaps it had replaced an earlier, more agreeable house. She drove the Mini on to the grass but at some distance from the gate and made her way up the drive. The garden suited the house; it was formal to the point of artificiality and too well kept. Even the rock plants burgeoned like morbid excrescences at carefully planned intervals between the terrace paving-stones. There were two rectangular beds in the lawn, each planted with red-rose trees and edged with alternate bands of lobelia and alyssum. They looked like a patriotic display in a public park. Cordelia felt the lack of a flag-pole.

The front door was open, giving a view of a dark, brown-painted hall. Before Cordelia could ring, an elderly woman came round the corner of the house trundling a wheelbarrow full of plants. Despite the heat, she was wearing wellington boots, a jumper and long tweed skirt and had a scarf tied round her head. When she saw Cordelia she dropped the handle of the wheelbarrow and said:

'Oh, good morning. You've come from the church about the jumble, I expect?'

Cordelia said:

'No, not the jumble. I'm from Sir Ronald Callender. It's about his son.'

'Then I expect you've called for his things? We wondered when Sir Ronald was going to send for them. They're all still at the cottage. We haven't been down there since Mark died. We called him Mark, you know. Well, he never told us who he was which was rather naughty of him.'

'It isn't about Mark's things. I want to talk about Mark himself. Sir Ronald has engaged me to try to find out why his son killed himself. My name is Cordelia Gray.'

This news seemed to puzzle rather than disconcert Mrs Markland. She blinked at Cordelia rapidly through troubled, rather stupid, eyes and clutched at the wheelbarrow handle as if for support.

'Cordelia Gray? Then we haven't met before, have we? I don't think I know a Cordelia Gray. Perhaps it would be better if you came into the drawing room and talked to my husband and sister-in-law.'

She abandoned the barrow where it stood in the middle of the path and led the way into the house, pulling off her head scarf and making ineffective pats at her hair. Cordelia followed her through the sparsely furnished hall, smelling of floor polish, with its clutter of walking sticks, umbrellas and mackintoshes draping the heavy oak hatstand, and into a room at the back of the house.

It was a horrible room, ill-proportioned, bookless, furnished not in poor taste but in no taste at all. A huge sofa of repellent design and two armchairs surrounded the fireplace and a heavy mahogany table, ornately carved and lurching on its pedestal, occupied the centre of the room. There was little other furniture. The only pictures were framed groups, pale oblong faces too small to identify posed in straight innominate lines in front of the camera. One was a regimental photograph; the other had a pair of crossed oars above two rows of burly adolescents, all of whom were wearing low peaked caps and striped blazers. Cordelia supposed it to be a school boating club.

Despite the warmth of the day, the room was sunless and cold. The doors of the french windows were open. On the lawn outside were grouped a large swinging sofa with a fringed canopy, three cane chairs sumptuously cushioned in a garish blue cretonne, each with its footrest, and a wooden slatted table. They looked part of a setting for a play in which the designer had somehow failed to catch the mood. All the garden furniture looked new and unused. Cordelia wondered why the family should bother to sit indoors on a summer morning while the lawn was so much more comfortably furnished.

Mrs Markland introduced Cordelia by sweeping her arm in a wide gesture of abandonment and saying feebly to the company in general:

'Miss Cordelia Gray. It isn't about the church jumble.'

Cordelia was struck by the resemblance that husband and wife and Miss Markland bore to each other. All three reminded her of horses. They had long, bony faces, narrow mouths above strong, square chins, eyes set unattractively close, and grey, coarse-looking hair which the two women wore in thick fringes almost to their eyes. Major Markland was drinking coffee from an immense white cup, much stained about the rim and sides, which had been set on a round tin tray. He held *The Times* in his hands. Miss Markland was knitting, an occupation which Cordelia vaguely felt was inappropriate to a hot summer morning.

The two faces, unwelcoming, only partly curious, regarded her with faint distaste. Miss Markland could knit without looking at the needles, an accomplishment which enabled her to fix Cordelia with sharp, inquisitive eyes. Invited by Major Markland to sit, Cordelia perched on the edge of the sofa, half expecting the smooth cushion to let out a rude noise as it subsided beneath her. She found it, however, unexpectedly hard. She composed her face into the appropriate expression – seriousness combined with efficiency and a touch of propitiatory humility seemed about right, but she wasn't sure that she managed to bring it off. As she sat there, knees demurely together, her shoulder-bag at her feet, she was unhappily aware that she probably looked more like an eager seventeen-year-old facing her first interview than a mature business woman, sole proprietor of Pryde's Detective Agency.

She handed over Sir Ronald's note of authority and said:

'Sir Ronald was very distressed on your account, I mean it was awful for you that it should happen on your property when you'd been so kind in finding Mark a job he liked. His father hopes you won't mind talking about it; it's just that he wants to know what made his son kill himself.'

'And he sent you?' Miss Markland's voice was a compound of disbelief, amusement and contempt. Cordelia didn't resent rudeness. She felt Miss Markland had a point. She gave what she hoped was a credible explanation. It was probably true.

'Sir Ronald thinks that it must have been something to do with Mark's life at university. He left college suddenly, as you may know, and his father was never told why. Sir Ronald thought that I might be more successful in talking to Mark's friends than the more usual type of private detective. He didn't feel that he could trouble the police; after all, this sort of inquiry isn't really their kind of job.'

Miss Markland said grimly:

'I should have thought it was precisely their job; that is, if Sir Ronald thinks there's something odd about his son's death . . .'

Cordelia broke in:

'Oh no, I don't think there's any suggestion of that! He's quite satisfied with the verdict. It's just that he badly wants to know what made him do it.'

Miss Markland said with sudden fierceness:

'He was a drop-out. He dropped out of university, apparently he dropped out of his family obligations, finally he dropped out of life. Literally.'

Her sister-in-law gave a little bleat of protest.

'Oh, Eleanor, is that quite fair? He worked really well here. I liked the boy. I don't think –'

'I don't deny that he earned his money. That doesn't alter the fact that he was neither bred nor educated to be a jobbing gardener. He was, therefore, a drop-out. I don't know the reason and I have no interest in discovering it.'

'How did you come to employ him?' asked Cordelia.

It was Major Markland who answered.

'He saw my advertisement in the *Cambridge Evening News* for a gardener and turned up here one evening on his bicycle. I suppose he cycled all the way from Cambridge. It must have been about five weeks ago, a Tuesday I think.'

Again Miss Markland broke in:

'It was Tuesday, May 9th.'

The Major frowned at her as if irritated that he couldn't fault the information.

'Yes, well, Tuesday the 9th. He said that he had decided to leave university and take a job and that he'd seen my advertisement. He admitted that he didn't know much about gardening but said that he was strong and was willing to learn. His inexperience didn't worry me; we wanted him mostly for the lawns and for the vegetables. He never touched the flower garden; my wife and I see to that ourselves. Anyway, I quite liked the look of the boy and I thought I'd give him a chance.'

Miss Markland said:

'You took him because he was the only applicant who was prepared to work for the miserable pittance you were offering.' The Major, so far from showing offence at this frankness, smiled complacently.

'I paid him what he was worth. If more employers were prepared to do that, the country wouldn't be plagued with this inflation.' He spoke as one to whom economics were an open book.

'Didn't you think it was odd, his turning up like that?' asked Cordelia.

'Of course I did, damned odd! I thought he had probably been sent down; drink, drugs, revolution, you know the sort of thing they get up to at Cambridge now. But I asked him for the name of his tutor as a referee and rang him, a fellow called Horsfall. He wasn't particularly forthcoming but he did assure me that the boy had left voluntarily and to use his own words, his conduct while in college had been almost boringly irreproachable. I need not fear that the shades of Summertrees would be polluted.'

Miss Markland turned her knitting and broke into her sister-in-law's little cry of 'What can he have meant by that?' with the dry comment:

'A little more boredom of that kind would be welcome from the city of the plains.'

'Did Mr Horsfall tell you why Mark had left college?' asked Cordelia.

'I didn't inquire. That wasn't my business. I asked a plain question and I got a more or less plain answer, as plain as you can expect from those academic types. We certainly had no complaint about the lad while he was here. I speak as I find.'

'When did he move into the cottage?' asked Cordelia.

'Immediately. That wasn't our idea, of course. We never advertised the job as residential. However, he'd obviously seen the cottage and taken a fancy to the place and he asked if we'd mind if he camped out there. It wasn't practicable for him to cycle in from Cambridge each day, we could quite see that, and as far as we knew there was no one in the village who could put him up. I can't say I was keen on the idea; the cottage needs a lot doing to it. Actually we have it in mind to apply for a conversion grant and then get rid of the place. It wouldn't do for a family in its present state but the lad seemed keen on roughing it there, so we agreed.'

Cordelia said:

'So he must have inspected the cottage before he came for the job?'

'Inspected? Oh, I don't know. He probably snooped around to see what the property was like before he actually came to the door. I don't know that I blame him, I'd have done the same myself.'

Mrs Markland broke in:

'He was very keen on the cottage, very keen. I pointed out that there was no gas or electricity but he said that that wouldn't worry him; he'd buy a primus stove and manage with lamps. There's water laid on, of course, and the main part of the roof is really quite sound. At least I think it is. We don't go there you know. He seemed to settle in very happily. We never actually visited him, there was no need, but as far as I could see he was looking after himself perfectly well. Of course as my husband said, he was very inexperienced; there were one or two things we had to teach him, like coming up to the kitchen early every morning for the orders. But I liked the boy; he was always working hard when I was in the garden.'

Cordelia said:

'I wonder if I might have a look at the cottage?'

The request disconcerted them. Major Markland looked at his wife. There was an embarrassed silence and for a moment Cordelia feared that the answer would be no. Then Miss Markland stabbed her needles into the ball of wool and got to her feet:

'I'll come with you now,' she said.

The grounds of Summertrees were spacious. First there was the formal rose garden, the bushes closely planted and grouped according to variety and colour like a market garden, the name tags fixed at precisely the same height from the earth. Next was the kitchen garden cut in two by a gravel path with evidence of Mark Callender's work in the weeded rows of lettuce and cabbages, the patches of dug earth. Finally they passed through a gate into a small orchard of old and unpruned apple trees. The scythed grass, smelling richly of hay, lay in thick swathes round the gnarled trunks.

At the furthest end of the orchard was a thick hedge, so overgrown that the wicket gate into the rear garden of the cottage was at first difficult to see. But the grass around it had been trimmed and the gate opened easily to Miss Markland's hand. On the other side was a thick bramble hedge, dark and impenetrable and obviously allowed to grow wild for a generation. Someone had hacked a way through, but Miss Markland and Cordelia had to bend low to avoid catching their hair on its tangled tentacles of thorn.

Once free of this barrier, Cordelia lifted her head and blinked in the bright sunshine. She gave a little exclamation of pleasure. In the short time in which he had lived here Mark Callender had created a little oasis of order and beauty out of chaos and neglect. Old flower beds had been discovered and the surviving plants tended; the stone path had been scraped free of grass and moss; a minute square of lawn to the right of the cottage door had been cut and weeded. On the other side of the path a patch about twelve feet square had been partly dug. The fork was still in the earth, driven deep about two feet from the end of the row.

The cottage was a low, brick building under a slate roof. Bathed in the afternoon sunshine, and despite its bare, rain-scoured door, its rotted window-frames and the glimpse of exposed beams in the roof, it had the gentle melancholy charm of age which hadn't yet degenerated into decay. Just outside the cottage door, dropped casually side by side, was a pair of heavy gardening shoes encrusted with earth.

'His?' asked Cordelia.

'Who else's?'

They stood together for a moment contemplating the dug earth. Neither spoke. Then they moved to the back door. Miss Markland fitted the key into the lock. It turned easily as if the lock had been recently oiled. Cordelia followed her into the sitting-room of the cottage.

The air was cool after the heat of the garden but unfresh, with a taint of contagion. Cordelia saw that the plan of the cottage was simple. There were three doors, one straight ahead obviously led to the front garden but was locked and barred, the joints hung with cobwebs as if it hadn't been opened for generations. One to the right led, as Cordelia guessed, to the kitchen. The third door was ajar and she could glimpse through it an un-carpeted wooden stairway leading to the first floor. In the middle of the room was a wooden-topped table, the surface scarred with much scrubbing, and with two kitchen chairs, one at each end. In the middle of the table a blue ribbed mug held a posy of dead flowers, black brittle stems bearing sad tatters of unidentifiable plants, their pollen staining the surface of the table like golden dust. Shafts of sunlight cut across the still air; in their beams a myriad of motes, specks of dust and infinitesimal life danced grotesquely.

To the right was a fireplace, an old-fashioned iron range with ovens each side of the open fire. Mark had been burning wood and papers; there was a mound of white ash in the grate and a pile of kindling wood and small logs placed ready for the next evening. On one side of the fire was a low wooden slatted chair with a faded cushion and on the other a wheel-backed chair with the legs sawn off, perhaps to make it low enough for nursing a child. Cordelia thought that it must have been a beautiful chair before its mutilation.

Two immense beams, blackened with age, ran across the ceiling. In the middle of one was fixed a steel hook, probably once used for hanging bacon. Cordelia and Miss Markland looked at it without speaking; there was no need for question and answer. After a moment they moved, as if by common consent, to the two fireside chairs and sat down. Miss Markland said:

'I was the one who found him. He didn't come up to the kitchen for the day's orders so after breakfast I walked down here to see if he had overslept. It was nine twenty-three exactly. The door was unlocked. I knocked, but there was no reply so I pushed it open. He was hanging from that hook with a leather belt round his neck. He was wearing his blue cotton trousers, the ones he usually worked in, and his feet were bare. That chair was lying on its side on the floor. I touched his chest. He was quite cold.'

'Did you cut him down?'

'No. He was obviously dead and I thought it better to leave the body until the police arrived. But I did pick up the chair and place it so that it supported his feet. That was an irrational action, I know, but I couldn't bear to see him hanging there without releasing the pressure on his throat. It was, as I've said, irrational.'

'I think it was very natural. Did you notice anything else about him, about the room?'

'There was a half-empty mug of what looked like coffee on the table and a great deal of ash in the grate. It looked as if he had been burning papers. His portable typewriter was where you see it now, on that side table; the suicide note was still in the machine. I read it, then I went back to the house, told my brother and sister-in-law what had happened and rang the police. After the police arrived I brought them to this cottage, and confirmed what I had seen. I never came in here again until this moment.'

'Did you, or Major and Mrs Markland, see Mark on the night he died?'

'None of us saw him after he stopped work at about six-thirty. He was a little later that evening because he wanted to finish mowing the front lawn. We all saw him putting the mower away, then walking across the garden towards the orchard. We never saw him alive again. No one was at home at Summertrees that night. We had a dinner party at Trumpington – an old army colleague of my brother. We didn't get home until after midnight. By then, according to the medical evidence, Mark must have been dead about four hours.'

Cordelia said:

'Please tell me about him.'

'What is there to tell? His official hours were eight-thirty to six o'clock, with an hour for lunch and half an hour for tea. In the evenings he would work in the garden here or round the cottage. Sometimes in his lunch hour he would cycle to the village store. I used to meet him there from time to time. He didn't buy much – a loaf of wholemeal bread, butter, the cheapest cut of bacon, tea, coffee – the usual things. I heard him ask about free-range eggs and Mrs Morgan told him that Wilcox at Grange Farm would always sell him half a dozen. We didn't speak when we met, but he would smile. In the evenings once the light had faded, he used to read or type at that table. I could see his head against the lamplight.'

'I thought Major Markland said that you didn't visit the cottage?'

'They don't; it holds certain embarrassing memories for them. I do.' She paused and looked into the dead fire.

'My fiancé and I used to spend a great deal of time here before the war when he was at Cambridge. He was killed in 1937, fighting in Spain for the Republican cause.'

'I'm sorry,' said Cordelia. She felt the inadequacy, the insincerity of her response and yet, what else was there to say? It had all happened nearly forty years ago. She hadn't heard of him before. The spasm of grief, so brief that it was hardly felt, was no more than a transitory inconvenience, a sentimental regret for all lovers who died young, for the inevitability of human loss.

Miss Markland spoke with sudden passion as if the words were being forced out of her:

'I don't like your generation, Miss Gray. I don't like your arrogance, your selfishness, your violence, the curious selectivity of your compassion. You pay for nothing with your own coin, not even for your ideals. You denigrate and destroy and never build. You invite punishment like rebellious children, then scream when you are punished. The men I knew, the men I was brought up with, were not like that.'

Cordelia said gently:

'I don't think Mark Callender was like that either.'

'Perhaps not. At least the violence he practised was on himself.' She looked up at Cordelia searchingly.

'No doubt you'll say I'm jealous of youth. It's a common enough syndrome of my generation.'

'It ought not to be. I can never see why people should be jealous. After all, youth isn't a matter of privilege, we all get the same share of it. Some people may be born at an easier time or be richer or more privileged than others, but that hasn't anything to do with being young. And being young is terrible sometimes. Don't you remember how terrible it could be?'

'Yes, I remember. But I remember other things, too.'

Cordelia sat in silence, thinking that the conversation was strange but somehow inevitable and that, for some reason, she didn't resent it. Miss Markland looked up.

'His girl-friend visited him once. At least, I suppose she was his girl-friend or why should she have come? It was about three days after he started work.'

'What was she like?'

'Beautiful. Very fair, with a face like a Botticelli angel – smooth, oval, unintelligent. She was foreign, French, I think. She was also rich.'

'How could you tell that, Miss Markland?' Cordelia was intrigued.

'Because she spoke with a foreign accent; because she arrived driving a white Renault which I took to be her own car; because her clothes, although odd and unsuitable for the country, weren't cheap; because she walked up to the front door and announced that she wanted to see him with the confident arrogance that one associates with the rich.'

'And did he see her?'

'He was working in the orchard at the time, scything the grass. I took her down to him. He greeted her calmly and without embarrassment and took her to sit in the cottage until it was time for him to stop work. He seemed pleased enough to see her but not, I thought, either delighted or surprised. He didn't introduce her. I left them together and returned to the house before he had the chance to. I didn't see her again.'

Before Cordelia could speak she said suddenly:

'You're thinking of living here for a time, aren't you?'

'Will they mind? I didn't like to ask in case they said no.'

'They won't know, and if they did, they wouldn't care.'

'But do you mind?'

'No. I shan't worry you and I don't mind.' They were talking in whispers as if in church. Then Miss Markland got up and moved to the door. She turned.

'You've taken on this job for the money, of course. Why not? But if I were you I'd keep it that way. It's unwise to become too personally involved with another human being. When that human being is dead, it can be dangerous as well as unwise.'

Miss Markland stumped off down the garden path and disappeared through the wicket gate. Cordelia was glad to see her go. She was fidgeting with impatience to examine the cottage. This was where it had happened; this was where her job really began.

What was it that the Super had said? 'When you're examining a building look at it as you would a country church. Walk round it first. Look at the whole scene inside and out; then make your deductions. Ask yourself what you saw, not what you expected to see or what you hoped to see, but what you saw.'

He must be a man then who liked country churches and that at least was a point in his favour; for this, surely, was genuine Dalgliesh dogma. Bernie's reaction to churches, whether country or town, had been one of half-superstitious wariness. Cordelia decided to follow the advice.

She made her way first to the east side of the cottage. Here, discreetly set back and almost smothered by the hedge, was a wooden privy with its latched stable-like door. Cordelia peeped inside. The privy was very clean and looked as if it had been recently repainted. When she pulled the chain, to her relief, the bowl flushed. There was a roll of lavatory paper hanging by a string from the door and nailed beside it a small plastic bag contained a crumpled collection of orange papers and other soft wrappings. He had been an economical young man. Next to the privy was a large dilapidated shed containing a man's bicycle, old but well cared for, a large tin of white emulsion paint with the lid rammed down hard and a clean brush up-ended in a jam jar beside it, a tin bath, a few clean sacks, and a collection of gardening tools. All were shining clean and were neatly disposed against the wall or supported on nails.

She moved to the front of the cottage. This was in marked contrast to the southern aspect. Here Mark Callender had made no attempt to tackle the waist-high wilderness of nettles and grass which stifled the small front garden and almost obliterated the path. A thick climbing shrub sprinkled with small white flowers had thrust its black and thorned boughs to bar the two ground floor windows. The gate leading to the lane had stuck and would open only wide enough for a visitor to squeeze through. On each side a holly tree stood sentinel, its leaves grey with dust. The front hedge of privet was head-high. Cordelia could see that on either side of the path there had once been twin flower beds edged with large round stones which had been painted white. Now most of the stones had sunk out of sight among the encroaching weeds and nothing remained of the beds but a tangle of wild and straggling roses.

As she took a last look at the front garden, her eye caught a flash of colour half trodden among the weeds at the side of the path. It was a crumpled page of an illustrated magazine. She smoothed it open and saw that it was a colour photograph of a female nude. The woman had her back to the camera and was bending forward, gross buttocks splayed above booted thighs. She was smiling saucily over her shoulder in a blatant invitation made more grotesque by the long androgynous face which even tactful lighting couldn't make other than repellent. Cordelia noted the date at the top of the page; it was the May edition. So the magazine, or at least the picture, could have been brought to the cottage while he was there.

She stood with it in her hand trying to analyse the nature of her disgust which seemed to her excessive. The picture was vulgar and salacious but no more offensive or indecent than dozens on view in the side-streets of London. But as she folded it away in her bag – for it was evidence of a kind – she felt contaminated and depressed. Had Miss Markland been more percipient than she knew? Was she, Cordelia, in danger of becoming sentimentally obsessed with the dead boy? The picture probably had nothing to do with Mark; it could easily have been dropped by some visitor to the cottage. But she wished that she hadn't seen it.

She passed round to the west of the cottage and made one more discovery. Hidden behind a clump of elder bushes was a small well about four feet in diameter. It had no superstructure but was closely fitted with a domed lid made of strong slatted wood and fitted at the top with an iron hoop. Cordelia saw that the cover was padlocked to the wooden rim of the well and the lock, although rusty with age, held firm at her tug. Someone had taken the trouble to see that there was no danger here to exploring children or visiting tramps.

And now it was time to explore the interior of the cottage. First the kitchen. It was a small room with a window over the sink looking east. It had obviously been recently painted and the large table which took up most of the room had been covered with a red plastic cloth. There was a poky larder containing half a dozen tins of beer, a jar of marmalade, a crock of butter and the mouldy heel of a loaf. It was here in the kitchen that Cordelia found the explanation to the disagreeable smell which had struck her on entering the cottage. On the table was an open bottle of milk about half full, the silver top crumpled beside it. The milk was solid and furred with putrefaction; a bloated fly was sucking at the rim of the bottle and still stuck to its feast as, instinctively, she tried to flick it away. On the other side of the table was a twin-burner paraffin stove with a heavy pot on one burner. Cordelia tugged at the close-fitting lid and it came off suddenly, letting out a rich repulsive smell. She opened the table drawer and stirred the mess with a spoon. It looked like beef stew. Chunks of greenish meat, soapy looking potatoes and unidentifiable vegetables floated up through the scum like drowned and putrefying flesh. Beside the sink was an orange box placed on one side and used as a vegetable store. The potatoes were green, the onions had shrunk and sprouted, the carrots were wrinkled and limp. So nothing had been cleaned up, nothing had been removed. The police had taken away the body and any evidence they required but no one, neither the Marklands nor the boy's family or friends, had bothered to come back to clean up the pathetic leavings of his young life.

Cordelia went upstairs. A cramped landing led to two bedrooms, one obviously unused for years. Here the window frame had rotted, the ceiling plaster had crumbled and a faded paper patterned with roses was peeling away with the damp. The second and larger room was the one in which he had slept. There was a single iron bed with a hair mattress and on it a sleeping-bag and a bolster folded in two to make a high pillow. Beside the bed was an old table with two candles, stuck with their own wax to a cracked plate, and a box of matches. His clothes were hung in the single cupboard, a pair of bright green corduroy trousers, one or two shirts, pullovers and one formal suit. A few underclothes, clean but not ironed, were folded on the ledge above. Cordelia fingered the pullovers. They were hand knitted in thick wool and intricate patterns and there were four of them. Someone, then, had cared enough about him to take some trouble on his behalf. She wondered who.

She ran her hands over his meagre wardrobe, feeling for pockets. She found nothing except a slim, brown leather wallet in the bottom left-hand pocket of his suit. Excitedly she carried it over to the window hoping that it might contain a clue – a letter, perhaps, a list of names and addresses, a personal note. But the wallet was empty except for a couple of pound notes, his driving licence and a blood donor's card issued by the Cambridge blood transfusion service, which showed his group to be B rhesus negative.

The uncurtained window gave a view of the garden. His books were arranged on the window shelf. There were only a few of them: several volumes of the *Cambridge Modern History*; some

Trollope and Hardy; a complete William Blake; school textbook volumes of Wordsworth, Browning and Donne; two paperbacks on gardening. At the end of the row was a white leather-bound book which Cordelia saw was the Book of Common Prayer. It was fitted with a finely wrought, brass clasp and looked much used. She was disappointed in the books; they told her little beyond his superficial tastes. If he had come to this solitary life to study, to write or to philosophize he had come singularly ill-equipped.

The most interesting thing in the room was above the bed. It was a small oil painting about nine inches square. Cordelia studied it. It was certainly Italian and probably, she thought, late fifteenth century. It showed a very young tonsured monk reading at a table, his sensitive fingers enleafed between the pages of his book. The long, controlled face was taut with concentration, the heavy-lidded eyes were fixed on the page. Behind him, a view from the open window was a miniature of delight. Cordelia thought that one would never tire of looking at it. It was a Tuscan scene showing a walled city with towers enclosed by cypresses, a river winding like a silver stream, a gaudily clad procession preceded by banners, yoked oxen working in the fields. She saw the picture as a contrast between the worlds of intellect and action and tried to remember where she had seen similar paintings. The comrades – as Cordelia always thought of that ubiquitous band of fellow-revolutionaries who attached themselves to her father – had been very fond of exchanging messages in art galleries and Cordelia had spent hours walking slowly from picture to picture, waiting for the casual visitor to pause beside her and whisper his few words of warning or information. The device had always struck her as a childish and unnecessarily histrionic way of communicating, but at least the galleries were warm and she had enjoyed looking at the pictures. She enjoyed this picture; he had obviously liked it too. Had he also liked that vulgar illustration which she had found in the front garden? Were they both an essential part of his nature?

The tour of inspection over, she made herself coffee using a packet from his store cupboard and boiling the water on the stove. She took a chair from the sitting-room and sat outside the back door with the mug of coffee in her lap, her head stretched back to feel the sun. She was filled with a gentle happiness as she sat there, contented and relaxed, listening to the silence, her half-closed lids impressed with the visage of the sun. But now it was time to think. She had examined the cottage in accordance with the Super's instructions. What did she now know about the dead boy? What had she seen? What could she deduce?

He had been almost obsessively neat and tidy. His garden tools were wiped after use and carefully put away, his kitchen had been painted and was clean and ordered. Yet he had abandoned his digging less than two feet from the end of a row; had left the uncleaned fork in the earth; had dropped his gardening shoes casually at the back door. He had apparently burnt all his papers before killing himself, yet had left his coffee mug unwashed. He had made himself a stew for his supper which he hadn't touched. The preparation of the vegetables must have been done earlier in the same day, or perhaps the day before, but the stew was clearly intended for supper that night. The pot was still on the stove and was full to the brim. This wasn't a heated-up meal, one left from the evening before. This surely meant that he had only made the decision to kill himself after the stew had been prepared and had been put on the stove to cook. Why should he trouble to prepare a meal that he knew he wouldn't be alive to eat?

But was it likely, she wondered, that a healthy young man coming in from an hour or two of hard digging and with a hot meal waiting should be in that mood of boredom, *accidie*, anguish or despair which could lead to suicide? Cordelia could remember times of intense unhappiness, but she couldn't recall that they had followed purposeful outdoor exercise in the sun with a meal in prospect. And why the mug of coffee, the one which the police had taken away to analyse? There were tins of beer in the larder; if he had come in thirsty from his digging, why not open one of those? Beer would have been the quickest, the obvious way of quenching thirst. Surely no one, however thirsty, would brew and drink coffee just before a meal. Coffee came after food.

But suppose someone had visited him that evening. It wasn't likely to have been someone calling with a casual message as he passed by; it was important enough for Mark to break off his digging even within two feet of the end of a row and invite the visitor into the cottage. It was probably a visitor who didn't like or drink beer – could that mean a woman? It was a visitor who wasn't expected to stay for supper but yet was at the cottage long enough to be offered some refreshment. Perhaps it was someone on the way to his own evening meal. Obviously, the visitor hadn't been invited to supper earlier or why would the two of them have begun the meal by drinking coffee and why would Mark have worked so late in the garden instead of coming in to change? So it was an unexpected visitor. But why was there only one mug of coffee? Surely Mark would have shared it with his guest or, if he preferred not to drink coffee, would have opened a tin of beer for himself. But there was no empty beer can in the kitchen and no second mug. Had it perhaps been washed and put away? But why should Mark wash one mug and not the other? Was it to conceal the fact that he'd had a visitor that evening?

The jug of coffee on the kitchen table was almost empty and the bottle of milk only half full. Surely more than one person had taken milk and coffee. But perhaps that was a dangerous and unwarranted deduction; the visitor might well have had his mug refilled.

But suppose it wasn't Mark who had wished to conceal the fact that a visitor had called that night; suppose it wasn't Mark who had washed and put away the second mug; suppose it was the visitor who had wished to conceal the fact of his presence. But why should he bother to do that since he couldn't know that Mark was going to kill himself? Cordelia shook herself impatiently. This, of course, was nonsense. Obviously the visitor wouldn't have washed up the mug if Mark were still there and alive. He would only have obliterated the evidence of his visit if Mark were already dead. And if Mark had been dead, had been strung up on that hook before his visitor had left the cottage, then could this really be suicide? A word dancing at the back of Cordelia's mind, an amorphous half-formed jangle of letters, came suddenly into focus and, for the first time, spelt out clearly the blood-stained word. Murder.

Cordelia sat on in the sun for another five minutes finishing her coffee, then she washed up the mug and hung it back on a hook in the larder. She walked down the lane to the road, where the Mini was still parked on the grass verge outside Summertrees, glad of the instinct that had led her to leave it out of sight of the house. Letting in the clutch gently, she drove it slowly down the lane looking carefully from side to side for a possible parking place; to leave it outside the cottage would only advertise her presence. It was a pity that Cambridge wasn't closer; she could then have used Mark's bicycle. The Mini wasn't necessary to her task but would be inconveniently conspicuous wherever she left it.

But she was lucky. About fifty yards down the lane was the entrance to a field, a wide grass verge with a small copse at one side. The copse looked damp and sinister. It was impossible to believe that flowers could spring from this tainted earth or bloom among these scarred and misshapen trees. The ground was scattered with old pots and pans, the up-ended skeleton of a pram, a battered and rusty gas stove. Beside a stunted oak a matted heap of blankets was disintegrating into the earth. But there was space for her to drive the Mini off the road and under cover of a kind. If she locked it carefully it would be better here than outside the cottage and at night, she thought, it would be unobserved.

But now, she drove it back to the cottage and began to unpack. She moved Mark's few underclothes to one side of the shelf and set her own beside them. She laid her sleeping-bag on the bed over his, thinking that she would be glad of the extra comfort. There was a red tooth-brush and half-used tube of toothpaste in a jamjar on the kitchen window ledge; she placed her yellow brush and her own tube beside them. She hung her towel next to his across the cord which he had fixed between two nails under the kitchen sink. Then she made an inventory of the contents of the larder and a list of the things she would need. It would be better to buy them in Cambridge; she would only draw attention to her presence if she shopped locally. The saucepan of stew and the half bottle of milk were a worry. She couldn't leave them in the kitchen to sour the cottage with the stench of decay but she was reluctant to throw the contents away. She considered whether to photograph them but decided against it, tangible objects were better evidence. In the end she carried them out to the shed and shrouded them thickly with a piece of old sacking.

Last of all, she thought about the gun. It was a heavy object to carry with her all the time but she felt unhappy about parting with it, even temporarily. Although the back door of the cottage could be locked and Miss Markland had left her the key, an intruder would have no difficulty in breaking in through a window. She decided that the best plan would be to secrete the ammunition among her underclothes in the bedroom cupboard but to hide the pistol separately in or near the cottage. The exact place cost her a little thought, but then she remembered the thick and twisting limbs of the elder bush by the well; by reaching high, she was able to feel for a convenient hollow near the fork of a branch and could slip the gun, still shrouded in its draw-string bag, among the concealing leaves.

At last she was ready to leave for Cambridge. She looked at her watch; it was half-past ten; she could be in Cambridge by eleven and there would still be two hours of the morning to go. She decided that her best plan would be to visit the newspaper office first and read the account of the inquest, then to see the police; after that she would go in search of Hugo and Sophia Tilling.

She drove away from the cottage with a feeling very like regret, as if she were leaving home. It was, she thought, a curious place, heavy with atmosphere and showing two distinct faces to the world like facets of a human personality; the north, with its dead thorn-barred windows, its encroaching weeds, and its forbidding hedge of privet, was a numinous stage for horror and tragedy. Yet the rear, where he had lived and worked, had cleared and dug the garden and tied up the few flowers, had weeded the path, and opened the windows to the sun, was as peaceful as a sanctuary. Sitting there at the door she had felt that nothing horrible could ever touch her; she was able to contemplate the night alone there without fear. Was it this atmosphere of healing tranquillity, she wondered, that had attracted Mark Callender? Had he sensed it before he took the job, or was it in some mysterious way the result of his transitory and doomed sojourn there? Major Markland had been right; obviously Mark had looked at the cottage before he went up to the house. Had it been the cottage he wanted or the job? Why were the Marklands so reluctant to come to the place, so reluctant that they obviously hadn't visited it even to clean up after his death? And why had Miss Markland spied on him, for surely such close observation was very close to spying? Had she only confided that story about her dead lover to justify her interest in the cottage, her obsessional preoccupation with what the new gardener was doing? And was the story even true? That ageing body heavy with latent strength, that equine expression of perpetual discontent, could she really once have been young, have lain perhaps with her lover on Mark's bed through the long, warm evenings of long-dead summers? How remote, how impossible and grotesque it all seemed.

Cordelia drove down Hills Road, past the vigorous memorial statue of a young 1914 soldier striding to death, past the Roman Catholic church and into the centre of the city. Again she wished that she could have abandoned the car in favour of Mark's bicycle. Everyone else seemed to be riding and the air tinkled with bells like a festival. In these narrow and crowded streets even the compact Mini was a liability. She decided to park it as soon as she could find a place and set out on foot in search of a telephone. She had decided to vary her programme and see the police first.

But it didn't surprise her when at last she rang the police station to hear that Sergeant Maskell, who had dealt with the Callender case, was tied up all the morning. It was only in fiction that the people one wanted to interview were sitting ready at home or in their office, with time, energy and interest to spare. In real life, they were about their own business and one waited on their convenience, even if, untypically, they welcomed the attention of Pryde's Detective Agency. Usually they didn't. She mentioned Sir Ronald's note of authority to impress her hearer with the authenticity of her business. The name was not without influence. He went away to inquire. After less than a minute he came back to say that Sergeant Maskell could see Miss Gray at two-thirty that afternoon.

So the newspaper office came first after all. Old files were at least accessible and could not object to being consulted. She quickly found what she wanted. The account of the inquest was brief, couched in the usual formal language of a court report. It told her little that was new, but she made a careful note of the main evidence. Sir Ronald Callender testified that he hadn't spoken to his son for over a fortnight before his death, when Mark had telephoned to tell his father of his decision to leave college and to take a job at Summertrees. He hadn't consulted Sir Ronald before making the decision nor had he explained his reasons. Sir Ronald had subsequently spoken to the Master, and the college authorities were prepared to take his son back for the next academic year if he changed his mind. His son had never spoken to him of suicide and had no health or money worries as far as he was aware. Sir Ronald's testimony was followed by a brief reference to other evidence. Miss Markland described how she had found the body; a forensic pathologist testified that the cause of death was asphyxia due to strangulation; Sergeant Maskell recounted the measures he had thought it proper to take and a report from the forensic science laboratory was submitted which stated that a mug of coffee found on the table had been analysed and found harmless. The verdict was that the deceased died by his own hand while the balance of his mind was disturbed. Closing the heavy file, Cordelia felt depressed. It looked as if the police work had been thorough. Was it really possible that these experienced professionals had overlooked the significance of the unfinished digging, the gardening shoes dropped casually at the back door, the untouched supper?

And now, at midday, she was free until half-past two. She could explore Cambridge. She bought the cheapest guide book she could find from Bowes and Bowes, resisting the temptation to browse among the books, since time was short and pleasure must be rationed. She stuffed her shoulder-bag with a pork pie and fruit bought from a market stall and entered St Mary's church to sit quietly and work out her itinerary. Then for an hour and a half she walked about the city and its colleges in a trance of happiness.

She was seeing Cambridge at its loveliest. The sky was an infinity of blue from whose pellucid depths the sun shone in unclouded but gentle radiance. The trees in the college gardens and the avenues leading to the Backs, as yet untouched by the heaviness of high summer, lifted their green tracery against stone and river and sky. Punts shot and curtsied under the bridges, scattering the gaudy water fowl, and by the rise of the new

Garret Hostel bridge the willows trailed their pale, laden boughs in the darker green of the Cam.

She included all the special sights in her itinerary. She walked gravely down the length of Trinity Library, visited the Old Schools, sat quietly at the back of King's College Chapel marvelling at the upward surge of John Wastell's great vault spreading into curved fans of delicate white stone. The sunlight pouring through the great windows staining the still air, blue, crimson and green. The finely carved Tudor roses, the heraldic beasts supporting the crown, stood out in arrogant pride from the panels. Despite what Milton and Wordsworth had written, surely this chapel had been built to the glory of an earthly sovereign, not to the service of God? But that didn't invalidate its purpose nor blemish its beauty. It was still a supremely religious building. Could a non-believer have planned and executed this superb interior? Was there an essential unity between motive and creation? This was the question which Carl alone among the comrades would have been interested to explore and she thought of him in his Greek prison, trying to shut her mind to what they might be doing to him and wishing his stocky figure at her side.

During her tour she indulged in small particular pleasures. She bought a linen tea cloth printed with a picture of the chapel from the stall near the west door; she lay on her face on the shorn grass above the river by Kings Bridge and let the cold green water eddy round her arms; she wandered among the book stalls in the market place and after careful reckoning bought a small edition of Keats printed on India paper and a cotton kaftan patterned in greens, blues and browns. If this hot weather continued it would be cooler than a shirt or jeans for wear in the evenings.

Finally, she returned to King's College. There was a seat set against the great stone wall which ran from the chapel down to the river bank and she sat there in the sun to eat her lunch. A privileged sparrow hopped across the immaculate lawn and cocked a bright insouciant eye. She threw him scraps from the crust of her pork pie and smiled at his agitated peckings. From the river floated the sound of voices calling across the water, the occasional scrunch of wood on wood, the harsh call of a duckling.

Everything about her – the pebbles bright as jewels in the gravel path, the little shafts of grass at the verge of the lawn, the sparrow's brittle legs – was seen with an extraordinary intensity as if happiness had cleared her eyes.

Then memory recalled the voices. First her father's:

'Our little fascist was educated by the papists. It accounts for a lot. How on earth did it happen, Delia?'

'You remember, Daddy. They muddled me up with another C. Gray who was a Roman Catholic. We both passed the eleven plus exam the same year. When they discovered the mistake they wrote to you to ask if you minded my staying on at the Convent because I'd settled there.'

He hadn't in fact replied. Reverend Mother had tried tactfully to conceal that he hadn't bothered to answer and Cordelia had stayed on at the Convent for the six most settled and happy years of her life, insulated by order and ceremony from the mess and muddle of life outside, incorrigibly Protestant, uncoerced, gently pitied as one in invincible ignorance. For the first time she learned that she needn't conceal her intelligence, that cleverness which a succession of foster mothers had somehow seen as a threat. Sister Perpetua had said:

'There shouldn't be any difficulty over your 'A' Levels if you can go on as you are at present. That means that we plan for university entrance in two years' time from this October. Cambridge, I think. We might as well try for Cambridge, and I really don't see why you shouldn't stand a chance of a scholarship.'

Sister Perpetua had herself been at Cambridge before she entered the Convent and she still spoke of the academic life, not with longing or regret, but as if it had been a sacrifice worthy of her vocation. Even the fifteen-year-old Cordelia had recognized that Sister Perpetua was a real scholar and had thought it rather unfair of God to bestow a vocation on one who was so happy and useful as she was. But for Cordelia herself, the future had, for the first time, seemed settled and full of promise. She would go to Cambridge and Sister would visit her there. She had a romantic vision of wide lawns under the sun and the two of them walking in Donne's paradise. 'Rivers of knowledge are there, arts and sciences flow from thence; gardens that are walled in; bottomless depths of unsearchable councils are there.' By the aid of her own brain and Sister's prayers she would win her scholarship. The prayers occasionally worried her. She had absolutely no doubt of their efficacy since God must necessarily listen to one who at such personal cost had listened to Him. And if Sister's influence gave her an unfair advantage over the other candidates – well, that couldn't be helped. In a matter of such importance neither Cordelia nor Sister Perpetua had been disposed to fret over theological niceties.

But this time Daddy had replied to the letter. He had discovered a need for his daughter. There were no 'A' Levels and no scholarship and at sixteen Cordelia finished her formal education and began her wandering life as cook, nurse, messenger and general camp-follower to Daddy and the comrades.

But now by what devious routes and for what a strange purpose she had come at last to Cambridge. The city didn't disappoint her. In her wanderings she had seen lovelier places, but none in which she had been happier or more at peace. How indeed, she thought, could the heart be indifferent to such a city where stone and stained glass, water and green lawns, trees and flowers were arranged in such ordered beauty for the service of learning. But as regretfully she rose at last to go, brushing the few crumbs from her skirt, a quotation, untraced and unsought, came into her mind. She heard it with such clarity that the words might have been spoken by a human voice – a young masculine voice, unrecognized and yet mysteriously familiar: 'Then saw I that there was a way to hell even from the gates of heaven.'

The police headquarters building was modern and functional. It represented authority tempered with discretion; the public were to be impressed but not intimidated. Sergeant Maskell's office and the Sergeant himself conformed to this philosophy. He was surprisingly young and elegantly dressed, with a square, tough face wary with experience and a long but skilfully cut hair style which, Cordelia thought, could only just have satisfied the Force requirements, even for a plain-clothes detective. He was punctiliously polite without being gallant and this reassured her.

It wasn't going to be an easy interview, but she had no wish to be treated with the indulgence shown to a pretty but importunate child. Sometimes it helped to play the part of a vulnerable and naïve young girl eager for information – this was a role in which Bernie had frequently sought to cast her – but she sensed that Sergeant Maskell would respond better to an unflirtatious competence. She wanted to appear efficient, but not too efficient. And her secrets must remain her own; she was here to get information, not to give it.

She stated her business concisely and showed him her note of authority from Sir Ronald. He handed it back to her, remarking without rancour:

'Sir Ronald said nothing to me to suggest that he was not satisfied with the verdict.'

'I don't think that's in question. He doesn't suspect foul play. If he did, he would have come to you. I think he has a scientist's curiosity to know what made his son kill himself and he couldn't very well indulge that at public expense. I mean, Mark's private miseries aren't really your problem, are they?'

'They could be if the reasons for his death disclosed a criminal offence – blackmail, intimidation – but there was never any suggestion of that.'

'Are you personally satisfied that he killed himself?'

The Sergeant looked at her with the sudden keen intelligence of a hunting dog on the scent.

'Why should you ask that, Miss Gray?'

'I suppose because of the trouble you took. I've interviewed Miss Markland and read the newspaper report of the inquest. You called in a forensic pathologist; you had the body photographed before it was cut down; you analysed the coffee left in his drinking mug.'

'I treated the case as a suspicious death. That's my usual practice. This time the precautions proved unnecessary, but they might not have been.'

Cordelia said:

'But something worried you, something didn't seem right?'

He said, as if reminiscing:

'Oh, it was straightforward enough to all appearances. Almost the usual story. We get more than our share of suicides. Here is a young man who gave up his university course for no apparent reason and went to live on his own in some discomfort. You get the picture of an introspective, rather solitary student, one who doesn't confide in his family or friends. Within three weeks after leaving college he's found dead. There's no sign of a struggle; no disturbance in the cottage: he leaves a suicide note conveniently in the typewriter, much the kind of suicide note you would expect. Admittedly, he took the trouble to destroy all the papers in the cottage and yet left the garden fork uncleaned and his work half-completed, and bothered to cook himself a supper which he didn't eat. But all that proves nothing. People do behave irrationally, particularly suicides. No, it wasn't any of those things which gave me a bit of worry; it was the knot.'

Suddenly he bent down and rummaged in the left-hand drawer of his desk.

'Here,' he said. 'How would you use this to hang yourself, Miss Gray?'

The strap was about five feet long. It was a little over an inch wide and was made of strong but supple brown leather, darkened in places with age. An end was tapered and pierced with a row of metal-bound eye holes, the other was fitted with a strong brass buckle. Cordelia took it in her hands; Sergeant Maskell said:

'That was what he used. Obviously it's meant as a strap, but Miss Leaming testified that he used to wear it wound two or three times round his waist as a belt. Well, Miss Gray, how would you hang yourself?'

Cordelia ran the strap through her hands.

'First of all, of course, I'd slip the tapered end through the buckle to make a noose. Then, with the noose round my neck, I'd stand on a chair underneath the hook in the ceiling and draw the other end of the strap over the hook. I'd pull it up fairly tight and then make two half hitches to hold it firm. I'd pull hard on the strap to make sure that the knot didn't slip and that the hook would hold. Then I'd kick away the chair.'

The Sergeant opened the file in front of him and pushed it across the desk.

'Look at that,' he said. 'That's a picture of the knot.'

The police photograph, stark in black and white, showed the knot with admirable clarity. It was a bowline on the end of a low loop and it hung about a foot from the hook.

Sergeant Maskell said:

'I doubt whether he would be able to tie that knot with his hands above his head, no one could. So he must have made the noose first just as you did and then tied the bowline. But that can't be right either. There were only a few inches of strap between the buckle and the knot. If he'd done it that way, he wouldn't have had sufficient play on the strap to get his neck through the noose. There's only one way he could have done it. He made the noose first, pulled it until the strap fitted his neck like a collar and then tied the bowline. Then he got on the chair, placed the loop over the nail and kicked the chair away. Look, this will show you what I mean.'

He turned over a new page of the file and suddenly thrust it towards her.

The photograph, uncompromising, unambiguous, a brutal surrealism in black and white, would have looked as artificial as a sick joke if the body were not so obviously dead. Cordelia felt her heart hammering against her chest. Beside this horror Bernie's death had been gentle. She bent her head low over the file so that her hair swung forward to shield her face and made herself study the pitiable thing in front of her.

The neck was elongated so that the bare feet, their toes pointed like a dancer's, hung less than a foot from the floor. The stomach muscles were taut. Above them the high rib cage looked as brittle as a bird's. The head lolled grotesquely on the right shoulder like a horrible caricature of a disjointed puppet. The eyes had rolled upwards under half-open lids. The swollen tongue had forced itself between the lips.

Cordelia said calmly:

'I see what you mean. There are barely four inches of strap between the neck and the knot. Where is the buckle?'

'At the back of the neck under the left ear. There's a photograph of the indentation it made in the flesh later in the file.'

Cordelia did not look. Why, she wondered, had he shown her this photograph? It wasn't necessary to prove his argument. Had he hoped to shock her into a realization of what she was meddling in; to punish her for trespassing on his patch; to contrast the brutal reality of his professionalism with her amateurish meddling; to warn her perhaps? But against what? The police had no real suspicion of foul play; the case was closed. Had it, perhaps, been the casual malice, the incipient sadism of a man who couldn't resist the impulse to hurt or shock? Was he even aware of his own motives?

She said:

'I agree he could only have done it in the way you described, if he did it. But suppose someone else pulled the noose more tight about his neck, then strung him up. He'd be heavy, a dead weight. Wouldn't it have been easier to make the knot first and then hoist him on to the chair?'

'Having first asked him to hand over his belt?'

'Why use a belt? The murderer could have strangled him with a cord or a tie. Or would that have left a deeper and identifiable mark under the impression of the strap?'

'The pathologist looked for just such a mark. It wasn't there.'

'There are other ways, though; a plastic bag, the thin kind they pack clothes in, dropped over his head and held tight against his face; a thin scarf; a woman's stocking.'

'I can see you would be a resourceful murderess, Miss Gray. It's possible, but it would need a strong man and there would have to be an element of surprise. We found no sign of a struggle.'

'But it could have been done that way?'

'Of course, but there was absolutely no evidence that it was.'

'But if he were first drugged?'

'That possibility did occur to me; that's why I had the coffee analysed. But he wasn't drugged, the PM confirmed it.'

'How much coffee had he drunk?'

'Only about half a mug, according to the PM report, and he died immediately afterwards. Sometime between seven and nine p.m. was as close as the pathologist could estimate.'

'Wasn't it odd that he drank coffee before his meal?'

'There's no law against it. We don't know when he intended to eat his supper. Anyway, you can't build a murder case on the order in which a man chooses to take his food and drink.'

'What about the note he left? I suppose it isn't possible to raise prints from typewriter keys?'

'Not easily on that type of key. We tried but there was nothing identifiable.'

'So in the end you accepted that it was suicide?'

'In the end I accepted that there was no possibility of proving otherwise.'

'But you had a hunch? My partner's old colleague – he's a Superintendent of the CID – always backed his hunches.'

'Ah, well, that's the Met, they can afford to indulge themselves. If I backed all my hunches I'd get no work done; it isn't what you suspect, it's what you can prove that counts.'

'May I take the suicide note and the strap?'

'Why not, if you sign for them? No one else seems to want them.'

'Could I see the note now, please?'

He extracted it from the file and handed it to her. Cordelia began to read to herself the first half-remembered words:

A void boundless as the nether sky appeared beneath us . . .

She was struck, not for the first time, by the importance of the written word, the magic of ordered symbols. Would poetry hold its theurgy if the lines were printed as prose, or prose be so compelling without the pattern and stress of punctuation? Miss Leaming had spoken Blake's passage as if she recognized its beauty yet here, spaced on the page, it exerted an even stronger power.

It was then that two things about the quotation caught at her breath. The first was not something which she intended to share with Sergeant Maskell but there was no reason why she should not comment on the second.

She said:

'Mark Callender must have been an experienced typist. This was done by an expert.'

'I didn't think so. If you look carefully you'll see that one or two of the letters are fainter than the rest. That's always the sign of an amateur.'

'But the faint letters aren't always the same ones. It's usually the keys on the edges of the keyboard which the inexperienced typist hits more lightly. And the spacing here is good until nearly the end of the passage. It looks as if the typist suddenly realized that he ought to disguise his competence but hadn't time to retype the whole passage. And it's strange that the punctuation is so accurate.'

'It was probably copied direct from the printed page. There was a copy of Blake in the boy's bedroom. The quotation is from Blake, you know, the Tyger tyger burning bright poet.'

'I know. But if he typed it from the book, why bother to return the Blake to his bedroom?'

'He was a tidy lad.'

'But not tidy enough to wash up his coffee mug or clean his garden fork.'

'That proves nothing. As I said, people do behave oddly when they're planning to kill themselves. We know that the typewriter was his and that he'd had it for a year. But we couldn't compare the typing with his work. All his papers had been burnt.'

He glanced at his watch and got to his feet. Cordelia saw that the interview was over. She signed a chit for the suicide note and the leather belt, then shook hands and thanked him formally for his help. As he opened the door for her he said, as if on impulse:

'There's one intriguing detail you may care to know. It looks as if he was with a woman some time during the day on which he died. The pathologist found the merest trace – a thin line only – of purple-red lipstick on his upper lip.'

CHAPTER THREE

New Hall, with its Byzantine air, its sunken court and its shining domed hall like a peeled orange, reminded Cordelia of a harem; admittedly one owned by a sultan with liberal views and an odd predilection for clever girls, but a harem none the less. The college was surely too distractingly pretty to be conducive to serious study. She wasn't sure, either, whether she approved of the obtrusive femininity of its white brick, the mannered prettiness of the shallow pools where the goldfish slipped like blood-red shadows between the water-lilies, its artfully planted saplings. She concentrated on her criticism of the building; it helped to prevent her being intimidated.

She hadn't called at the Lodge to ask for Miss Tilling, afraid that she might be asked her business or refused admission; it seemed prudent just to walk in and chance to luck. Luck was with her. After two fruitless inquiries for Sophia Tilling's room, a hurrying student called back at her:

'She doesn't live in college but she's sitting on the grass over there with her brother.'

Cordelia walked out of the shadow of the court into bright sunlight and over turf as soft as moss towards the little group. There were four of them, stretched out on the warm-smelling grass. The two Tillings were unmistakably brother and sister. Cordelia's first thought was that they reminded her of a couple of pre-Raphaelite portraits with their strong dark heads held high on unusually short necks, and their straight noses above curved, foreshortened upper lips. Beside their bony distinction, the second girl was all softness. If this were the girl who had visited Mark at the cottage, Miss Markland was right to call her beautiful. She had an oval face with a neat slender nose, a small but beautifully formed mouth, and slanted eyes of a strikingly deep blue which gave her whole face an oriental appearance at variance with the fairness of her skin and her long blonde hair. She was wearing an ankle-length dress of fine mauve patterned cotton, buttoned high at the waist but with no other fastening. The gathered bodice cupped her full breasts and the skirt fell open to reveal a pair of tight fitting shorts in the same material. As far as Cordelia could see, she wore nothing else. Her feet were bare and her long, shapely legs were untanned by the sun. Cordelia reflected that those white voluptuous thighs must be more erotic than a whole city of sunburnt limbs and that the girl knew it. Sophia Tilling's dark good looks were only a foil to this gentler, more entrancing beauty.

At first sight the fourth member of the party was more ordinary. He was a stocky, bearded young man with russet curly hair and a spade-shaped face, and was lying on the grass by the side of Sophie Tilling.

All of them, except the blonde girl, were wearing old jeans and open-necked cotton shirts.

Cordelia had come up to the group and had stood over them for a few seconds before they took any notice of her. She said:

'I'm looking for Hugo and Sophia Tilling. My name is Cordelia Gray.' Hugo Tilling looked up:

'What shall Cordelia do, love and be silent.'

Cordelia said:

'People who feel the need to joke about my name usually inquire after my sisters. It gets very boring.'

'It must do. I'm sorry. I'm Hugo Tilling, this is my sister, this is Isabelle de Lasterie and this is Davie Stevens.'

Davie Stevens sat up like a jack-in-the-box and said an amiable 'Hi.'

He looked at Cordelia with a quizzical intentness. She wondered about Davie. Her first impression of the little group, influenced perhaps by the college architecture, had been of a young sultan taking his ease with two of his favourites and attended by the captain of the guard. But, meeting Davie Stevens's steady intelligent gaze, that impression faded. She suspected that, in this seraglio, it was the captain of the guard who was the dominant personality.

Sophia Tilling nodded and said 'Hullo.'

Isabelle did not speak but a smile beautiful and meaningless spread over her face. Hugo said:

'Won't you sit down, Cordelia Gray, and explain the nature of your necessities?'

Cordelia knelt gingerly, wary of grass stains on the soft suede of her skirt. It was an odd way to interview suspects – only, of course, these people weren't suspects – kneeling like a suppliant in front of them. She said:

'I'm a private detective. Sir Ronald Callender has employed me to find out why his son died.'

The effect of her words was astonishing. The little group, which had been lolling at ease like exhausted warriors, stiffened with instantaneous shock into a rigid tableau as if struck to marble. Then, almost imperceptibly, they relaxed. Cordelia could hear the slow release of held breath. She watched their faces. Davie Stevens was the least concerned. He wore a half-rueful smile, interested but unworried, and gave a quick look at Sophie as if in complicity. The look was not returned; she and Hugo were staring rigidly ahead. Cordelia felt that the two Tillings were carefully avoiding each other's eyes. But it was Isabelle who was the most shaken. She gave a gasp and her hand flew to her face like a second-rate actress simulating shock. Her eyes widened into fathomless depths of violet blue and she turned them on Hugo in desperate appeal. She looked so pale that Cordelia half expected her to faint. She thought:

'If I'm in the middle of a conspiracy, then I know who is its weakest member.'

Hugo Tilling said:

'You're telling us that Ronald Callender has employed you to find out why Mark died?'

'Is that so extraordinary?'

'I find it incredible. He took no particular interest in his son when he was alive, why begin now he's dead?'

'How do you know he took no particular interest?'

'It's just an idea I had.'

Cordelia said:

'Well, he's interested now even if it's only the scientist's urge to discover truth.'

'Then he'd better stick to his microbiology, discovering how to make plastic soluble in salt water, or whatever. Human beings aren't susceptible to his kind of treatment.'

Davie Stevens said with casual unconcern:

'I wonder that you can stomach that arrogant fascist.'

The gibe plucked at too many chords of memory. Wilfully obtuse, Cordelia said:

'I didn't inquire what political party Sir Ronald favours.'

Hugo laughed.

'Davie doesn't mean that. By fascist Davie means that Ronald Callender holds certain untenable opinions. For example, that all men may not be created equal, that universal suffrage may not necessarily add to the general happiness of mankind, that the tyrannies of the left aren't noticeably more liberal or supportable than the tyrannies of the right, that black men killing black men is small improvement on white men killing black men in so far as the victims are concerned and that capitalism may not be responsible for all the ills that flesh is heir to from drug addiction to poor syntax. I don't suggest that Ronald Callender holds all or indeed any of these reprehensible opinions. But Davie thinks that he does.'

Davie threw a book at Hugo and said without rancour:

'Shut up! You talk like the *Daily Telegraph*. And you're boring our visitor.'

Sophie Tilling asked suddenly:

'Was it Sir Ronald who suggested that you should question us?'

'He said that you were Mark's friends; he saw you at the inquest and funeral.'

Hugo laughed:

'For God's sake, is that his idea of friendship?'

Cordelia said:

'But you were there?'

'We went to the inquest – all of us except Isabelle, who, we thought, would have been decorative but unreliable. It was rather dull. There was a great deal of irrelevant medical evidence about the excellent state of Mark's heart, lungs and digestive system. As far as I can see, he would have gone on living for ever if he hadn't put a belt round his neck.'

'And the funeral – were you there too?'

'We were, at the Cambridge Crematorium. A very subdued

affair. There were only six of us present in addition to the undertaker's men; we three, Ronald Callender, that secretary/housekeeper of his and an old nanny-type dressed in black. She cast rather a gloom over the proceedings, I thought. Actually she looked so exactly like an old family retainer that I suspect she was a policewoman in disguise.'

'Why should she be? Did she look like one?'

'No, but then you don't look like a private eye.'

'You've no idea who she was?'

'No, we weren't introduced; it wasn't a chummy kind of funeral. Now I recall it, not one of us spoke a single word to any of the others. Sir Ronald wore a mask of public grief, the King mourning the Crown Prince.'

'And Miss Leaming?'

'The Queen's Consort; she should have had a black veil over her face.'

'I thought that her suffering was real enough,' said Sophie.

'You can't tell. No one can. Define suffering. Define real.'

Suddenly Davie Stevens spoke, rolling over on to his stomach like a playful dog.

'Miss Leaming looked pretty sick to me. Incidentally, the old lady was called Pilbeam; anyway, that was the name on the wreath.'

Sophie laughed:

'That awful cross of roses with the black-edged card? I might have guessed it came from her; but how do you know?'

'I looked, honey. The undertaker's men took the wreath off the coffin and propped it against the wall so I took a quick butcher's. The card read "With sincere sympathy from Nanny Pilbeam".'

Sophie said:

'So you did, I remember now. How beautifully feudal! Poor old nanny, it must have cost her a packet.'

'Did Mark ever talk about a Nanny Pilbeam?' Cordelia asked.

They glanced at each other quickly. Isabelle shook her head. Sophie said 'Not to me.'

Hugo Tilling replied:

'He never talked about her, but I think I did see her once before the funeral. She called at college about six weeks ago – on Mark's twenty-first birthday actually, and asked to see him. I was in the Porter's Lodge at the time and Robbins asked me if Mark was in college. She went up to his room and they were there together for about an hour. I saw her leaving, but he never mentioned her to me either then or later.'

And soon afterwards, thought Cordelia, he gave up university. Could there be a connection? It was only a tenuous lead, but she would have to follow it.

She asked out of a curiosity that seemed both perverse and irrelevant.

'Were there any other flowers?'

It was Sophie who replied:

'A simple bunch of unwired garden flowers on the coffin. No card. Miss Leaming, I suppose. It was hardly Sir Ronald's style.'

Cordelia said:

'You were his friends. Please tell me about him.'

They looked at each other as if deciding who should speak. Their embarrassment was almost palpable. Sophie Tilling was picking at small blades of grass and rolling them in her hands. Without looking up, she said:

'Mark was a very private person. I'm not sure how far any of us knew him. He was quiet, gentle, self-contained, unambitious. He was intelligent without being clever. He was very kind; he cared about people, but without inflicting them with his concern. He had little self-esteem but it never seemed to worry him. I don't think there is anything else we can say about him.'

Suddenly Isabelle spoke in a voice so low that Cordelia could hardly catch it. She said:

'He was sweet.'

Hugo said with a sudden angry impatience:

'He was sweet and he is dead. There you have it. We can't tell you any more about Mark Callender than that. We none of us saw him after he chucked college. He didn't consult us before he left, and he didn't consult us before he killed himself. He was, as my sister has told you, a very private person. I suggest that you leave him his privacy.'

'Look,' said Cordelia, 'you went to the inquest, you went to the funeral. If you had stopped seeing him, if you were so unconcerned about him, why did you bother?'

'Sophie went out of affection. Davie went because Sophie did. I went out of curiosity and respect; you mustn't be seduced by my air of casual flippancy into thinking that I haven't a heart.'

Cordelia said obstinately:

'Someone visited him at the cottage on the evening he died. Someone had coffee with him. I intend to find out who that person was.'

Was it her fancy that this news surprised them? Sophie Tilling looked as if she were about to ask a question when her brother quickly broke in:

'It wasn't any of us. On the night Mark died we were all in the second row of the dress circle of the Arts Theatre watching Pinter. I don't know that I can prove it. I doubt whether the booking clerk has kept the chart for that particular night, but I booked the seats and she may remember me. If you insist on being tediously meticulous, I can probably introduce you to a friend who knew of my intention to take a party to the play; to another who saw at least some of us in the bar in the interval; and to another with whom I subsequently discussed the performance. None of this will prove anything; my friends are an accommodating bunch. It would be simpler for you to accept that I am telling the truth. Why should I lie? We were all four at the Arts Theatre on the night of 26th May.'

Davie Stevens said gently:

'Why not tell that arrogant bastard Pa Callender to go to hell and leave his son in peace, then find yourself a nice simple case of larceny?'

'Or murder,' said Hugo Tilling.

'Find yourself a nice simple case of murder.'

As if in obedience to some secret code, they began getting up, piling their books together, brushing the grass cuttings from their clothes. Cordelia followed them through the courts and out of college. Still in a silent group they made their way to a white Renault parked in the forecourt.

Cordelia came up to them and spoke directly to Isabelle.

'Did you enjoy the Pinter? Weren't you frightened by that dreadful last scene when Wyatt Gillman is gunned down by the natives?'

It was so easy that Cordelia almost despised herself. The immense violet eyes grew puzzled.

'Oh, no! I did not care about it, I was not frightened. I was with Hugo and the others, you see.'

Cordelia turned to Hugo Tilling.

'Your friend doesn't seem to know the difference between Pinter and Osborne.'

Hugo was settling himself into the driving seat of the car. He twisted round to open the back door for Sophie and Davie. He said calmly:

'My friend, as you choose to call her, is living in Cambridge, inadequately chaperoned I'm happy to say, for the purpose of learning English. So far her progress has been erratic and in some respects disappointing. One can never be certain how much my friend has understood.'

The engine purred into life. The car began to move. It was then that Sophie Tilling thrust her head out of the window and said impulsively:

'I don't mind talking about Mark if you think it will help. It won't, but you can come round to my house this afternoon if you like – 57 Norwich Street. Don't be late; Davie and I are going on the river. You can come too if you feel like it.'

The car accelerated. Cordelia watched it out of sight. Hugo raised his hand in ironic farewell but not one of them turned a head.

Cordelia muttered the address to herself until it was safely written down: 57 Norwich Street. Was that the address where Sophie lodged, a hostel perhaps, or did her family live in Cambridge? Well, she would find out soon enough. When ought she to arrive? Too early would look over eager; too late and they might have set out for the river. Whatever motive prompted Sophie Tilling to issue that belated invitation, she mustn't lose touch with them now.

They had some guilty knowledge; that had been obvious. Why else had they reacted so strongly to her arrival? They wanted the facts of Mark Callender's death to be left undisturbed. They would try to persuade, cajole, even to shame her into abandoning the case. Would they, she wondered, also threaten? But why? The most likely theory was that they were shielding someone. But again, why? Murder wasn't a matter of climbing late into college, a venial infringement of rules which a friend would automatically condone and conceal. Mark Callender had been their friend. Someone whom he knew and trusted had pulled a strap tight round his neck, had watched and listened to his agonized choking, had strung his body on a hook like the carcase of an animal. How could one reconcile that appalling knowledge with Davie Stevens's slightly amused and rueful glance at Sophie, with Hugo's cynical calm, with Sophie's friendly and interested eyes? If they were conspirators, then they were monsters. And Isabelle? If they were shielding anyone, it was most likely to be her. But Isabelle de Lasterie couldn't have murdered Mark. Cordelia remembered those frail sloping shoulders, those ineffective hands almost transparent in the sun, the long nails painted like elegant pink talons. If Isabelle were guilty, she hadn't acted alone. Only a tall and very strong woman could have heaved that inert body on to the chair and up to the hook.

Norwich Street was a one-way thoroughfare and, initially, Cordelia approached it from the wrong direction. It took her some time to find her way back to Hills Road, past the Roman Catholic church and down the fourth turning to the right. The street was terraced with small brick houses, obviously early Victorian. Equally obviously, the road was on its way up. Most of the houses looked well cared for; the paint on the identical front doors was fresh and bright; lined curtains had replaced the draped lace at the single ground-floor windows and the bases of the walls were scarred where a damp course had been installed. Number fifty-seven had a black front door with the house number painted in white behind the glass panel above. Cordelia was relieved to see that there was space to park the Mini. There was no sign of the Renault among the almost continuous row of old cars and battered bicycles which lined the edge of the pavement.

The front door was wide open. Cordelia pressed the bell and stepped tentatively into a narrow white hall. The exterior of the house was immediately familiar to her. From her sixth birthday she had lived for two years in just such a Victorian terraced cottage with Mrs Gibson on the outskirts of Romford. She recognized the steep and narrow staircase immediately ahead, the door on the right leading to the front parlour, the second door set aslant which led to the back parlour and through it to the kitchen and yard. She knew that there would be cupboards and a curved alcove on each side of the fireplace: she knew where to find the door under the stairs. Memory was so sharp that it imposed on this clean, sun-scented interior the strong odour of unwashed napkins, cabbage and grease which had permeated the Romford house. She could almost hear the children's voices calling her outlandish name across the rookery of the primary school playground across the road, stamping the asphalt with the ubiquitous Wellington boots which they wore in all seasons, flailing their thin jerseyed arms: 'Cor, Cor, Cor!'

The furthest door was ajar and she could glimpse a room painted bright yellow and spilling over with sunlight. Sophie's head appeared.

'Oh, it's you! Come in. Davie has gone to collect some books from college and to buy food for the picnic. Would you like tea now or shall we wait? I'm just finishing the ironing.'

'I'd rather wait, thank you.'

Cordelia sat down and watched while Sophie wound the flex around the iron and folded the cloth. She glanced around the room. It was welcoming and attractive, furnished in no particular style or period, a cosy hotchpotch of the cheap and the valuable, unpretentious and pleasing. There was a sturdy oak table against the wall; four rather ugly dining chairs; a Windsor chair with a plump yellow cushion; an elegant Victorian sofa covered with brown velvet and set under the window; three good Staffordshire figures on the mantelshelf above the hooded wrought-iron grate. One of the walls was almost covered with a notice-board in dark cork which displayed posters, cards, *aides-mémoire*, and pictures cut from magazines. Two, Cordelia saw, were beautifully photographed and attractive nudes.

Outside the yellow-curtained window the small walled garden was a riot of greenery. An immense and multi-flowered hollyhock burgeoned against a tatty looking trellis; there were roses planted in Ali Baba jars and a row of pots of bright-red geraniums lined the top of the wall.

Cordelia said:

'I like this house. Is it yours?'

'Yes, I own it. Our grandmother died two years ago and left Hugo and me a small legacy. I used mine for the down payment on this house and got a local authority grant towards the cost of conversion. Hugo spent all of his laying down wine. He was ensuring a happy middle age; I was ensuring a happy present. I suppose that's the difference between us.'

She folded the ironing cloth on the end of the table and stowed it away in one of the cupboards. Sitting opposite to Cordelia, she asked abruptly:

'Do you like my brother?'

'Not very much. I thought he was rather rude to me.'

'He didn't mean to be.'

'I think that's rather worse. Rudeness should always be intentional, otherwise it's insensitivity.'

'Hugo isn't at his most agreeable when he's with Isabelle. She has that effect on him.'

'Was she in love with Mark Callender?'

'You'll have to ask her, Cordelia, but I shouldn't think so. They hardly knew each other. Mark was my lover, not hers. I thought I'd better get you here to tell you myself since someone's bound to sooner or later if you go around Cambridge ferreting out facts about him. He didn't live here with me, of course. He had rooms in college. But we were lovers for almost the whole of last year. It ended just after Christmas when I met Davie.'

'Were you in love?'

'I'm not sure. All sex is a kind of exploitation, isn't it? If you mean, did we explore our own identities through the personality of the other, then I suppose we were in love or thought that we were. Mark needed to believe himself in love. I'm not sure I know what the word means.'

Cordelia felt a surge of sympathy. She wasn't sure either. She thought of her own two lovers; Georges whom she had slept with because he was gentle and unhappy and called her Cordelia, a real name, her name, not Delia, Daddy's little fascist; and Carl who was young and angry and whom she had liked so much that it seemed churlish not to show it in the only way which seemed to him important. She had never thought of virginity as other than a temporary and inconvenient state, part of the general insecurity and vulnerability of being young. Before Georges and Carl she had been lonely and inexperienced. Afterwards she had been lonely and a little less inexperienced. Neither affair had given her the longed-for assurance in dealing with Daddy or the landladies, neither had inconveniently touched her heart. But for Carl she had felt tenderness. It was just as well that he had left Rome before his love-making had become too pleasurable and he too important to her. It was intolerable to think that those strange gymnastics might one day become necessary. Love-making, she had decided, was overrated, not painful but surprising. The alienation between thought and action was so complete. She said:

'I suppose I only meant were you fond of each other, and did you like going to bed together?'

'Both of those things.'

'Why did it end? Did you quarrel?'

'Nothing so natural or uncivilized. One didn't quarrel with Mark. That was one of the troubles about him. I told him that I didn't want to go on with the affair and he accepted my decision as calmly as if I were just breaking a date for a play at the Arts. He didn't try to argue or dissuade me. And if you're wondering whether the break had anything to do with his death, well you're wrong. I wouldn't rank that high with anyone, particularly not Mark. I was probably fonder of him than he was of me.'

'So why did it end?'

'I felt that I was under moral scrutiny. It wasn't true; Mark wasn't a prig. But that's how I felt, or pretended to myself that I felt. I couldn't live up to him and I didn't even want to. There was Gary Webber, for example. I'd better tell you about him; it explains a lot about Mark. He's an autistic child, one of the uncontrollable, violent ones. Mark met him with his parents and their other two children on Jesus Green about a year ago; the children were playing on the swings there. Mark spoke to Gary and the boy responded to him. Children always did. He took to visiting the family and looking after Gary one evening a week so that the Webbers could get out to the pictures. During his last two vacs he stayed in the house and looked after Gary completely while the whole family went off for a holiday. The Webbers couldn't bear the boy to go to hospital; they'd tried it once and he didn't settle. But they were perfectly happy to leave him with Mark. I used to call in some evenings and see them together. Mark would hold the boy on his lap and rock him backwards and forwards for hours at a time. It was the one way to quieten him. We disagreed about Gary. I thought he would be better dead and I said so. I still think it would be better if he died, better for his parents, better for the rest of the family, better for him. Mark didn't agree. I remember saying:

'"Oh well, if you think it reasonable that children should suffer so that you can enjoy the emotional kick of relieving them –" After that the conversation became boringly metaphysical. Mark said:

'"Neither you nor I would be willing to kill Gary. He exists. His family exists. They need help which we can give. It doesn't matter what we feel. Actions are important, feelings aren't."'

Cordelia said:

'But actions arise out of feelings.'

'Oh, Cordelia, don't you start! I've had this particular conversation too many times before. Of course they do!'

They were silent for a moment. Then Cordelia, reluctant to shatter the tenuous confidence and friendship which she sensed was growing between them, made herself ask:

'Why did he kill himself – if he did kill himself?' Sophie's reply was as emphatic as a slammed door.

'He left a note.'

'A note perhaps. But, as his father pointed out, not an explanation. It's a lovely passage of prose – at least I think so – but as a justification for suicide it just isn't convincing.'

'It convinced the jury.'

'It doesn't convince me. Think, Sophie! Surely there are only two reasons for killing oneself. One is either escaping from something or to something. The first is rational. If one is in intolerable pain, despair or mental anguish and there is no reasonable chance of a cure, then it's probably sensible to prefer oblivion. But it isn't sensible to kill oneself in the hope of gaining some better existence or to extend one's sensibilities to include the experience of death. It isn't possible to experience death. I'm not even sure it's possible to experience dying. One can only experience the preparations for death, and even that seems pointless since one can't make use of the experience afterwards. If there's any sort of existence after death we shall all know soon enough. If there isn't, we shan't exist to complain that we've been cheated. People who believe in an afterlife are perfectly reasonable. They're the only ones who are safe from ultimate disillusionment.'

'You've thought it all out, haven't you? I'm not sure that suicides do. The act is probably both impulsive and irrational.'

'Was Mark impulsive and irrational?'

'I didn't know Mark.'

'But you were lovers! You slept with him!'

Sophie looked at her and cried out in angry pain.

'I didn't know him! I thought I did, but I didn't know the first thing about him!'

They sat without speaking for almost two minutes. Then Cordelia asked:

'You went to dinner at Garforth House didn't you? What was it like?'

'The food and the wine were surprisingly good, but I don't suppose that's what you had in mind. The dinner party wasn't otherwise memorable. Sir Ronald was amiable enough when he noticed I was there. Miss Leaming, when she could tear her obsessive attention from the presiding genius, looked me over like a prospective mother-in-law. Mark was rather silent. I think he'd taken me there to prove something to me, or perhaps to himself; I'm not sure what. He never talked about the evening or asked me what I thought. A month later Hugo and I both went to dinner. It was then I met Davie. He was the guest of one of the research biologists and Ronald Callender was angling to get him. Davie did a vac job there in his final year. If you want the inside dope on Garforth House, you should ask him.'

Five minutes later Hugo, Isabelle and Davie arrived. Cordelia had gone upstairs to the bathroom and heard the car stop and the jabber of voices in the hall. Footsteps passed beneath her towards the back parlour. She turned on the hot water. The gas boiler in the kitchen immediately gave forth a roar as if the little house were powered by a dynamo. Cordelia let the tap run, then stepped out of the bathroom, closing the door gently behind her. She stole to the top of the stairs. It was hard luck on Sophie to waste her hot water, she thought guiltily; but worse was the sense of treachery and shabby opportunism as she crept down the first three stairs and listened. The front door had been closed but the door to the back parlour was open. She heard Isabelle's high unemphatic voice:

'But if this man Sir Ronald is paying her to find out about Mark, why cannot I pay her to stop finding out?'

Then Hugo's voice, amused, a little contemptuous:

'Darling Isabelle, when will you learn that not everyone can be bought?'

'She can't, anyway. I like her.'

It was Sophie speaking. Her brother replied:

'We all like her. The question is, how do we get rid of her?'

Then for a few minutes there was a murmur of voices, words undistinguishable, broken by Isabelle.

'It is not, I think, a suitable job for a woman.'

There was the sound of a chair scraping against the floor, a shuffle of feet. Cordelia darted guiltily back into the bathroom and turned off the tap. She recalled Bernie's complacent admonition when she had asked whether they needed accept a divorce case.

'You can't do our job, partner, and be a gentleman.' She stood watching at the half-open door. Hugo and Isabelle were leaving. She waited until she heard the front door close and the car drive away. Then she went down to the parlour. Sophie and Davie were together, unpacking a large carrier bag of groceries. Sophie smiled and said:

'Isabelle has a party tonight. She has a house quite close to here in Panton Street. Mark's tutor, Edward Horsfall, will probably be there and we thought it might be useful for you to talk to him about Mark. The party's at eight o'clock but you can call for us here. Just now we're packing a picnic; we thought we'd take a punt on the river for an hour or so. Do come if you'd like to. It's really much the pleasantest way of seeing Cambridge.'

*

Afterwards, Cordelia remembered the river picnic as a series of brief but intensely clear pictures, moments in which sight and sense fused and time seemed momentarily arrested while the sunlit image was impressed on her mind. Sunlight sparkling on the river and gilding the hairs of Davie's chest and forearms; the flesh of his strong upper arms speckled like an egg; Sophie lifting her arm to wipe the sweat from her brow as she rested between thrusts of the punt pole; green-black weeds dragged by the pole from mysterious depths to writhe sinuously below the surface; a bright duck cocking its white tail before disappearing in a flurry of green water. When they had rocked under Silver Street Bridge a friend of Sophie's swam alongside, sleek and snout-nosed like an otter, his black hair lying like blades across his cheeks. He rested his hands on the punt and opened his mouth to be fed chunks of sandwiches by a protesting Sophie. The punts and canoes scraped and jostled each other in the turbulence of white water racing under the bridge. The air rang with laughing voices and the green banks were peopled with half-naked bodies lying supine with their faces to the sun.

Davie punted until they reached the higher level of the river and Cordelia and Sophie stretched out on the cushions at opposite ends of the punt. Thus distanced it was impossible to carry on a private conversation; Cordelia guessed that this was precisely what Sophie had planned. From time to time, she would call out snatches of information as if to emphasize that the outing was strictly educational.

'That wedding cake is John's – we're just passing under Clare bridge, one of the prettiest, I think. Thomas Grumbald built it in 1639. They say he was only paid three shillings for the design. You know that view, of course; it's a good view of Queen's, though.'

Cordelia's courage failed her at the thought of interrupting this desultory tourist's chat with the brutal demand:

'Did you and your brother kill your lover?'

Here, rocking gently on the sunlit river, the question seemed both indecent and absurd. She was in danger of being lulled into a gentle acceptance of defeat; viewing all her suspicions as a neurotic hankering after drama and notoriety, a need to justify her fee to Sir Ronald. She believed that Mark Callender had been murdered because she wanted to believe it. She had identified with him, with his solitariness, his self-sufficiency, his alienation from his father, his lonely childhood. She had even – most dangerous presumption of all – come to see herself as his avenger. When Sophie took over the pole, just past the Garden House Hotel, and Davie edged his way along the gently rocking punt and stretched himself out beside her, she knew that she wouldn't be able to mention Mark's name. It was out of no more than a vague, unintrusive curiosity that she found herself asking:

'Is Sir Ronald Callender a good scientist?' Davie took up a short paddle and began lazily to stir the shining water.

'His science is perfectly respectable, as my dear colleagues would say. Rather more than respectable, in fact. At present the lab is working on ways of expanding the use of biological monitors to assess pollution of the sea and estuaries; that means routine surveys of plants and animals which might serve as indicators. And they did some very useful preliminary work last year on the degradation of plastics. R.C. isn't so hot himself, but then you can't expect much original science from the over fifties. But he's a great spotter of talent and he certainly knows how to run a team if you fancy that dedicated, one for all, band of brothers approach. I don't. They even publish their papers as the Callender Research Laboratory, not under individual names. That wouldn't do for me. When I publish, it's strictly for the glory of David Forbes Stevens and, incidentally, for the gratification of Sophie. The Tillings like success.'

'Was that why you didn't want to stay on when he offered you a job?'

'That among other reasons. He pays too generously and he asks too much. I don't like being bought and I've a strong objection to dressing up every night in a dinner-jacket like a performing monkey in a zoo. I'm a molecular biologist. I'm not looking for the holy grail. Dad and mum brought me up as a Methodist and I don't see why I should chuck a perfectly good religion which served me very well for twelve years just to put the great scientific principle of Ronald Callender in its place. I distrust these sacerdotal scientists. It's a bloody wonder that little lot at Garforth House aren't genuflecting three times a day in the direction of the Cavendish.'

'And what about Lunn? How does he fit in?'

'Oh, that's boy's a bloody wonder! Ronald Callender found him in a children's home when he was fifteen – don't ask me how – and trained him to be a lab assistant. You couldn't find a better. There isn't an instrument made which Chris Lunn can't learn to understand and care for. He's developed one or two himself and Callender has had them patented. If anyone in that lab is indispensable it's probably Lunn. Certainly Ronald Callender cares a damn sight more for him than he did for his son. And Lunn, as you might guess, regards R.C. as God Almighty, which is very gratifying for them both. It's extraordinary really, all that violence which used to be expressed in street fights and coshing old ladies, harnessed to the service of science. You've got to hand it to Callender. He certainly knows how to pick his slaves.'

'And is Miss Leaming a slave?'

'Well, I wouldn't know just what Eliza Leaming is. She's responsible for the business management and, like Lunn, she's probably indispensable. Lunn and she seem to have a love-hate relationship, or, perhaps, a hate-hate relationship. I'm not very clever at detecting these psychological nuances.'

'But how on earth does Sir Ronald pay for it all?'

'Well that's the thousand dollar question, isn't it? It's rumoured that most of the money came from his wife and that he and Elizabeth Leaming between them invested it rather cleverly. They certainly needed to. And then he gets a certain amount from contract work. Even so, it's an expensive hobby. While I was there they were saying that the Wolvington Trust were getting interested. If they come up with something big – and I gather it's below their dignity to come up with something small – then most of Ronald Callender's troubles should be over. Mark's death must have hit him. Mark was due to come into a pretty substantial fortune in four years' time and he told Sophie that he intended to hand most of it over to Dad.'

'Why on earth should he do that?'

'God knows. Conscience money, perhaps. Anyway, he obviously thought it was something that Sophie ought to know.'

Conscience money for what, Cordelia wondered sleepily. For not loving his father enough? For rejecting his enthusiasms? For being less than the son he had hoped for? And what would happen to Mark's fortune now? Who stood to gain by Mark's death? She supposed that she ought to consult his grandfather's will and find out. But that would mean a trip to London. Was it really worth it?

She stretched back her face to the sun and trailed one hand in the river. A splash of water from the punt pole stung her eyes. She opened them and saw that the punt was gliding close to the bank and under the shade of overhanging trees. Immediately in front of her a torn branch, cleft at the end and thick as a man's body, hung by a thread of bark and turned gently as the punt passed beneath it. She was aware of Davie's voice; he must have been talking for a long time. How odd that she couldn't remember what he'd been saying!

'You don't need reasons for killing yourself; you need reasons for not killing yourself. It was suicide, Cordelia. I should let it go at that.'

Cordelia thought that she must have briefly slept, since he seemed to be answering a question she couldn't remember having asked. But now there were other voices, louder and more insistent. Sir Ronald Callender's: 'My son is dead. *My* son. If I am in some way responsible, I'd prefer to know. If anyone else is responsible, I want to know that too.' Sergeant Maskell's: 'How would you use this to hang yourself, Miss Gray?' The feel of the belt, smooth and sinuous, slipping like a live thing through her fingers.

She sat bolt upright, hands clasped around her knees, with such suddenness that the punt rocked violently and Sophie had to clutch at an overhanging branch to keep her balance. Her dark face, intriguingly foreshortened and patterned with the shadow of leaves, looked down at Cordelia from what seemed an immense height. Their eyes met. In that moment Cordelia knew how close she had come to giving up the case. She had been suborned by the beauty of the day, by sunshine, indolence, the promise of comradeship, even friendship, into forgetting why she was here. The realization horrified her. Davie had said that Sir Ronald was a good picker. Well, he had picked her. This was her first case and nothing and no one was going to hinder her from solving it.

She said formally:

'It was good of you to let me join you, but I don't want to miss the party tonight. I ought to talk to Mark's tutor and there may be other people there who could tell me something. Isn't it time that we thought about turning back?'

Sophie turned her glance on Davie. He gave an almost imperceptible shrug. Without speaking, Sophie drove the pole hard against the bank. The punt began slowly to turn.

Isabelle's party was due to begin at eight o'clock but it was nearly nine when Sophie, Davie and Cordelia arrived. They walked to the house which was only five minutes from Norwich Street; Cordelia never discovered the exact address. She liked the look of the house and wondered how much it was costing Isabelle's father in rent. It was a long, white, two-storey villa with tall curved windows and green shutters, set well back from the street, with a semi-basement and a flight of steps to the front door. A similar flight led down from the sitting-room to the long garden.

The sitting-room was already fairly full. Looking at her fellow guests, Cordelia was glad that she had bought the kaftan. Most people seemed to have changed although not necessarily, she thought, into something more attractive. What was aimed at was originality; it was preferable to look spectacular, even bizzare, than to appear nondescript.

The sitting-room was elegantly but insubstantially furnished and Isabelle had impressed on it her own untidy, impractical and iconoclastic femininity. Cordelia doubted whether the owners had provided the ornate crystal chandelier, far too heavy and large for the room, which hung like a sunburst from the middle of the ceiling, or the many silken cushions and curtains which gave the room's austere proportions something of the ostentatious opulence of a courtesan's boudoir. The pictures, too, must surely be Isabelle's. No house owner letting his property would leave pictures of this quality on the walls. One, hanging above the fireplace, was of a young girl hugging a puppy. Cordelia gazed at it in excited pleasure. Surely she couldn't mistake that individual blue of the girl's dress, that marvellous painting of the cheeks and plump young arms, which simultaneously absorbed and reflected light – lovely, tangible flesh. She cried out involuntarily so that people turned to look at her:

'But that's a Renoir!'

Hugo was at her elbow. He laughed.

'Yes; but don't sound so shocked, Cordelia. It's only a small Renoir. Isabelle asked Papa for a picture for her sitting-room. You didn't expect him to provide a print of the Haywain or one of those cheap reproductions of Van Gogh's boring old chair.'

'Would Isabelle have known the difference?'

'Oh, yes. Isabelle knows an expensive object when she sees one.'

Cordelia wondered whether the bitterness, the hard edge of contempt in his voice, was for Isabelle or for himself. They looked across the room to where she stood, smiling at them. Hugo moved towards her like a man in a dream and took her hand. Cordelia watched. Isabelle had dressed her hair in a high cluster of curls, Grecian style. She was wearing an ankle-length dress of cream matt silk, with a very low square neckline and small intricately tucked sleeves. It was obviously a model and should, Cordelia felt, have looked out of place at an informal party. But it didn't. It merely made every other woman's dress look like an improvisation and reduced her own, whose colours had seemed muted and subtle when she bought it, to the status of a gaudy rag.

Cordelia was determined to get Isabelle alone some time during the evening but could see that it wasn't going to be easy. Hugo stuck tenaciously to her side, steering her among her guests with one proprietorial hand on her waist. He seemed to be drinking steadily and Isabelle's glass was always filled. Perhaps as the evening wore on they would get careless and there would be a chance to separate them. In the meantime, Cordelia decided to explore the house, and a more practical matter, to find out before she needed it where the lavatory was. It was the kind of party where guests were left to find out these things for themselves.

She went up to the first floor and making her way down the passage pushed gently open the door of the far room. The smell of whisky met her immediately; it was overpowering and Cordelia instinctively slipped into the room and closed the door behind her, afraid that it might permeate the house. The room, which was in an indescribable state of disarray, wasn't empty. On the bed and half covered by the counterpane a woman was lying; a woman with bright ginger hair splayed over the pillow and wearing a pink silk dressing-gown. Cordelia walked up to the bed and looked down at her. She was insensible with drink. She lay there emitting puffs of foul, whisky-laden breath which rose like invisible balls of smoke from the half-open mouth. Her lower lip and jaw were tense and creased, giving the face a look of stern censoriousness as if she disapproved strongly of her own condition. Her thin lips were thickly painted, the strong purple stain had seeped into the cracks around the mouth so that the body looked parched in an extremity of cold. Her hands, the gnarled fingers brown with nicotine and laden with rings, lay quietly on the counterpane. Two of the talon-like nails were broken and the brick-red varnish on the others was cracked or peeled away.

The window was obstructed by a heavy dressing-table. Averting her eyes from the mess of crumpled tissues, open bottles of face-cream, spilt powder and half-drunk cups of what looked like black coffee, Cordelia squeezed behind it and pushed open the window. She gulped in lungfuls of fresh, cleansing air. Below her in the garden, pale shapes moved silently over the grass and between the trees like the ghosts of long dead revellers. She left the window open and went back to the bed. There was nothing here that she could do but she placed the cold hands under the counterpane and, taking a second and warmer gown from the hook on the door, tucked it around the woman's body. That, at least, would compensate for the fresh air blowing across the bed.

That done, Cordelia slipped back into the passage, just in time to see Isabelle coming out of the room next door. She shot out an arm and half dragged the girl back into the bedroom. Isabelle gave a little cry, but Cordelia planted her back firmly against the door and said in a low, urgent whisper:

'Tell me what you know about Mark Callender.'

The violet eyes slewed from door to window as if desperate for escape.

'I wasn't there when he did it.'

'When who did what?'

Isabelle retreated towards the bed as if the inert figure, who was now groaning stertorously, could offer support. Suddenly the woman turned on her side and gave a long snort like an animal in pain. Both girls glanced at her in startled alarm. Cordelia reiterated:

'When who did what?'

'When Mark killed himself; I wasn't there.'

The woman on the bed gave a little sigh. Cordelia lowered her voice:

'But you were there some days earlier, weren't you? You called at the house and inquired for him. Miss Markland saw you. Afterwards you sat in the garden and waited until he'd finished work.'

Was it Cordelia's imagination that the girl suddenly seemed more relaxed, that she was relieved at the innocuousness of the question?

'I just called to see Mark. They gave me his address at the college Lodge. I went to visit him.'

'Why?' The harsh question seemed to puzzle her. She replied simply:

'I wanted to be with him. He was my friend.'

'Was he your lover too?' asked Cordelia. This brutal frankness was surely better than asking whether they had slept together, or gone to bed together – stupid euphemisms which Isabelle might not even understand: it was hard to tell from those beautiful but frightened eyes just how much she did understand.

'No, Mark was never my lover. He was working in the garden and I had to wait for him at the cottage. He gave me a chair in the sun and a book until he was free.'

'What book?'

'I don't remember, it was very dull. I was dull too until Mark came. Then we had tea with funny mugs that had a blue band, and after tea we went for a walk and then we had supper. Mark made a salad.'

'And then?'

'I drove home.'

She was perfectly calm now. Cordelia pressed on, aware of the sound of footsteps passing up and down the stairs, of the ring of voices.

'And the time before that? When did you see him before that tea party?'

'It was a few days before Mark left college. We went for a picnic in my car to the seaside. But first we stopped at a town – St Edmunds town, is it? – and Mark saw a doctor.'

'Why? Was he ill?'

'Oh no, he was not ill, and he did not stay long enough for what you call it – an examination. He was in the house a few minutes only. It was a very poor house. I waited for him in the car, but not just outside the house you understand.'

'Did he say why he went there?'

'No, but I do not think he got what he wanted. Afterwards he was sad for a little time, but then we went to the sea and he was happy again.'

She, too, seemed happy now. She smiled at Cordelia, her sweet, unmeaning smile. Cordelia thought: it's just the cottage that terrifies her. She doesn't mind talking about the living Mark, it's his death she can't bear to think about. And yet, this repugnance wasn't born of personal grief. He had been her friend; he was sweet; she liked him. But she was getting on very well without him.

There was a knock at the door. Cordelia stood aside and Hugo came in. He lifted an eyebrow at Isabelle and, ignoring Cordelia, said:

'It's your party, ducky; coming down?'

'Cordelia wanted to talk to me about Mark.'

'No doubt. You told her, I hope, that you spent one day with him motoring to the sea and one afternoon and evening at Summertrees and that you haven't seen him since.'

'She told me,' said Cordelia. 'She was practically word perfect. I think she's safe to be let out on her own now.'

He said easily:

'You shouldn't be sarcastic, Cordelia, it doesn't suit you. Sarcasm is all right for some women, but not for women who are beautiful in the way that you are beautiful.'

They were passing down the stairs together to meet the hubbub in the hall. The compliment irritated Cordelia. She said:

'I suppose that woman on the bed is Isabelle's chaperone. Is she often drunk?'

'Mademoiselle de Congé? Not often as drunk as that, but I admit that she is seldom absolutely sober.'

'Then oughtn't you to do something about it?'

'What should I do? Hand her over to the twentieth-century Inquisition – a psychiatrist like my father? What has she done to us to deserve that? Besides, she is tediously conscientious on the few occasions when she's sober. It happens that her compulsions and my interest coincide.'

Cordelia said severely:

'That may be expedient but I don't think it very responsible and it isn't kind.'

He stopped in his tracks and turned towards her, smiling directly into her eyes.

'Oh, Cordelia, you talk like the child of progressive parents who has been reared by a nonconformist nanny and educated at a convent school. I do like you!'

He was still smiling as Cordelia slipped away from them and infiltrated into the party. She reflected that his diagnosis hadn't been so very far wrong.

She helped herself to a glass of wine, then moved slowly round the room listening unashamedly to scraps of conversation, hoping to hear Mark's name mentioned. She heard it only once. Two girls and a very fair, rather insipid young man were standing behind her. One of the girls said:

'Sophie Tilling seems to have recovered remarkably quickly from Mark Callender's suicide. She and Davie went to the cremation, did you know? Typical of Sophie to take her current lover to see the previous one incinerated. I suppose it gave her some kind of a kick.'

Her companion laughed.

'And little brother takes over Mark's girl. If you can't get beauty, money and brains, settle for the first two. Poor Hugo! He suffers from a sense of inferiority. Not quite handsome enough; not quite clever enough – Sophie's First must have shaken him – not quite rich enough. No wonder he has to rely on sex to give him confidence.'

'And, even there, not quite . . .'

'Darling, you should know.'

They laughed and moved away. Cordelia felt her face burning. Her hand shook almost spilling her wine. She was surprised to find how much she cared, how much she had come to like Sophie. But that, of course, was part of the plan, that was Tilling strategy. If you can't shame her into giving up the case, suborn her; take her on the river; be nice to her; get her on our side. And it was true, she was on their side, at least against malicious detractors. She comforted herself with the censorious reflection that they were as bitchy as guests at a suburban cocktail party. She had never in her life attended one of those innocuous if boring gatherings for the routine consumption of gossip, gin and canapés but, like her father who had never attended one either, she found no difficulty in believing that they were hot beds of snobbery, spite and sexual innuendo.

A warm body was pressing against her. She turned and saw Davie. He was carrying three bottles of wine. He had obviously heard at least part of the conversation, as the girls had no doubt intended, but he grinned amiably.

'Funny how Hugo's discarded women always hate him so much. It's quite different with Sophie. Her ex-lovers clutter up Norwich Street with their beastly bicycles and broken-down cars. I'm always finding them in the sitting-room drinking my beer and confiding to her the awful trouble they're having with their present girls.'

'Do you mind?'

'Not if they don't get any further than the sitting-room. Are you enjoying yourself?'

'Not very much.'

'Come and meet a friend of mine. He's been asking who you are.'

'No thank you, Davie. I must keep myself free for Mr Horsfall. I don't want to miss him.'

He smiled at her, rather pityingly she thought, and seemed about to speak. But he changed his mind and moved away, clutching the bottles to his chest and shouting a cheerful warning as he edged himself through the throng.

Cordelia worked her way around the room, watching and listening. She was intrigued by the overt sexuality; she had thought that intellectuals breathed too rarefied air to be much interested in the flesh. Obviously this was a misapprehension. Come to think of it, the comrades, who might have been supposed to live in randy promiscuity, had been remarkably staid. She had sometimes felt that their sexual activities were prompted more by duty than instinct, more a weapon of revolution or a gesture against the bourgeois mores they despised than a response to human need. Their basic energies were all devoted to politics. It was not difficult to see where most of the energies of those present were directed.

She needn't have worried about the success of the kaftan. A number of men showed themselves willing or even eager to detach themselves from their partners for the pleasure of talking to her. With one particularly, a decorative and ironically amusing young historian, Cordelia felt that she could have spent an entertaining evening. To enjoy the sole attention of one agreeable man and no attention at all from anyone else was all she ever hoped from a party. She wasn't naturally gregarious and, alienated by the last six years from her own generation, found herself intimidated by the noise, the underlying ruthlessness and the half-understood conventions of these tribal matings. And she told herself firmly that she wasn't here to enjoy herself at Sir Ronald's expense. None of her prospective partners knew Mark Callender or showed any interest in him, dead or alive. She mustn't get herself tied for the evening to people who had no information to give. When this seemed a danger and the talk became too beguiling, she would murmur her excuses and slip away to the bathroom or into the shadows of the garden where little groups were sitting on the grass smoking pot. Cordelia couldn't be mistaken in that evocative smell. They showed no disposition to chat and here, at least, she could stroll in privacy gaining courage for the next foray, for the next artfully casual question, the next inevitable response.

'Mark Callender? Sorry – we never met. Didn't he go off to sample the simple life and end by hanging himself or something?'

Once she took refuge in Mademoiselle de Congé's room, but she saw that the inert figure had been unceremoniously dumped on a cushion of pillows on the carpet and that the bed was being occupied for quite another purpose.

She wondered when Edward Horsfall would arrive or whether he would arrive at all. And if he did, would Hugo remember or bother to introduce her? She couldn't see either of the Tillings in the hot crush of gesticulating bodies which by now had crammed the sitting-room and spilled into the hall and half-way up the stairs. She was beginning to feel that this would be a wasted evening when Hugo's hand fell on her arm. He said:

'Come and meet Edward Horsfall. Edward, this is Cordelia Gray; she wants to talk about Mark Callender.'

Edward Horsfall was another surprise. Cordelia had subconsciously conjured up the picture of an elderly don, a little distrait with the weight of his learning, a benevolent if detached mentor of the young. Horsfall could not have been much over thirty. He was very tall, his hair falling long over one eye, his lean body curved as a melon rind, a comparison reinforced by the pleated yellow shirt-front under a jutting bow-tie.

Any half-acknowledged, half-shameful hope which Cordelia may have nourished that he would immediately take to her and be happily ungrudging of his time so long as they were together was quickly dispersed. His eyes were restless, flicking obsessively back to the door. She suspected that he was alone by choice, deliberately keeping himself free from encumbrances until the hoped-for companion arrived. He was so fidgety that it was difficult not to be fretted by his anxiety. She said:

'You don't have to stay with me all the evening you know, I only want some information.'

Her voice recalled him to an awareness of her and to some attempt at civility.

'That wouldn't exactly be a penance. I'm sorry. What do you want to know?'

'Anything you can tell me about Mark. You taught him history didn't you? Was he good at it?'

It wasn't a particularly relevant question but one which she felt all teachers might respond to as a start.

'He was more rewarding to teach than some students I'm afflicted with. I don't know why he chose history. He could very well have read one of the sciences. He had a lively curiosity about physical phenomenon. But he decided to read history.'

'Do you think that was to disoblige his father?'

'To disoblige Sir Ronald?' He turned and stretched out an arm for a bottle. 'What are you drinking? There's one thing about Isabelle de Lasterie's parties, the drink is excellent, presumably because Hugo orders it. There's an admirable absence of beer.'

'Doesn't Hugo drink beer then?' asked Cordelia.

'He claims not to. What were we talking about? Oh, yes, disobliging Sir Ronald. Mark said that he chose history because we have no chance of understanding the present without understanding the past. That's the sort of irritating cliché people come out with at interviews, but he may have believed it. Actually, of course, the reverse is true, we interpret the past through our knowledge of the present.'

'Was he any good?' asked Cordelia. 'I mean, would he have got a First?'

A First, she naïvely believed, was the ultimate in scholastic achievement, the certificate of pronounced intelligence that the recipient carried unchallenged through life. She wanted to hear that Mark was safe for a First.

'Those are two separate and distinct questions. You seem to be confusing merit with achievement. Impossible to predict his class, hardly a First. Mark was capable of extraordinarily good and original work but he limited his material to the number of his original ideas. The result tended to be rather thin. Examiners like originality but you've got to spew up the accepted facts and orthodox opinions first if only to show that you've learnt them. An exceptional memory and fast legible handwriting; that's the secret of a First. Where are you, incidentally?' He noticed Cordelia's brief look of incomprehension.

'At what college?'

'None; I work. I'm a private detective.'

He took this information in his stride.

'My uncle employed one of those once to find out if my aunt was being screwed by their dentist. She was, but he could have found out more easily by the simple expedient of asking them. His way, he lost the services of a wife and of a dentist simultaneously and paid through the nose for information he could have got for nothing. It made quite a stir in the family at the time. I should have thought that the job was –'

Cordelia finished the sentence for him.

'An unsuitable job for a woman?'

'Not at all. Entirely suitable I should have thought, requiring, I imagine, infinite curiosity, infinite pains and a penchant for interfering with other people.' His attention was wandering again. A group near to them were talking and snatches of the conversation came to them.

'– typical of the worst kind of academic writing. Contempt for logic; a generous sprinkling of vogue names; spurious profundity and bloody awful grammar.'

The tutor gave the speakers a second's attention, dismissed their academic chat as beneath his notice and condescended to transfer his attention but not his regard back to Cordelia.

'Why are you so interested in Mark Callender?'

'His father has employed me to find out why he died. I was hoping that you might be able to help. I mean, did he ever give you a hint that he might be unhappy, unhappy enough to kill himself? Did he explain why he gave up college?'

'Not to me. I never felt that I got near him. He made a formal goodbye, thanked me for what he chose to describe as my help, and left. I made the usual noises of regret. We shook hands. I was embarrassed, but not Mark. He wasn't, I think, a young man susceptible to embarrassment.'

There was a small commotion at the door and a group of new arrivals pushed themselves noisily into the throng. Among them was a tall, dark girl in a flame-coloured frock, open almost to the waist. Cordelia felt the tutor stiffen, saw his eyes fixed on the new arrival with an intense, half-anxious, half-supplicating look, which she had seen before. Her heart sank. She would be lucky now to get any more information. Desperately trying to recapture his attention, she said:

'I'm not sure that Mark did kill himself. I think it could have been murder.'

He spoke inattentively, his eyes on the newcomers.

'Unlikely, surely. By whom? For what reason? He was a

negligible personality. He didn't even provoke a vague dislike except possibly from his father. But Ronald Callender couldn't have done it if that's what you're hoping. He was dining in Hall at High Table on the night Mark died. It was a college feast night. I sat next to him. His son telephoned him.'

Cordelia said eagerly, almost tugging at his sleeve,

'At what time?'

'Soon after the meal started, I suppose. Benskin, he's one of the college servants, came in and gave him the message. It must have been between eight and eight-fifteen. Callender disappeared for about ten minutes then returned and got on with his soup. The rest of us still hadn't reached the second course.'

'Did he say what Mark wanted? Did he seem disturbed?'

'Neither. We hardly spoke through the meal. Sir Ronald doesn't waste his conversational gifts on non-scientists. Excuse me, will you?'

He was gone, threading his way through the throng towards his prey. Cordelia put down her glass and went in search of Hugo.

'Look,' she said, 'I want to talk to Benskin, a servant at your college. Would he be there tonight?'

Hugo put down the bottle he was holding.

'He may be. He's one of the few who live in college. But I doubt whether you would winkle him out of his lair on your own. If it's all that urgent, I'd better come with you.'

The college porter ascertained with curiosity that Benskin was in the college and Benskin was summoned. He arrived after a wait of five minutes during which Hugo chatted to the porter and Cordelia walked outside the Lodge to amuse herself reading the college notices. Benskin arrived, unhurrying, imperturbable. He was a silver-haired, formally dressed old man, his face creased and thick skinned as an anaemic blood orange, and would, Cordelia thought, have looked like an advertisement for the ideal butler, were it not for an expression of lugubrious and sly disdain.

Cordelia gave him sight of Sir Ronald's note of authority and plunged straight into her questions. There was nothing to be gained by subtlety and since she had enlisted Hugo's help, she had little hope of shaking him off. She said:

'Sir Ronald has asked me to inquire into the circumstances of his son's death.'

'So I see, Miss.'

'I am told that Mr Mark Callender telephoned his father while Sir Ronald was dining at High Table on the night his son died and that you passed the message to Sir Ronald shortly after dinner began?'

'I was under the impression at the time that it was Mr Callender who was ringing, Miss, but I was mistaken.'

'How can you be sure of that, Mr Benskin?'

'Sir Ronald himself told me, Miss, when I saw him in college some few days after his son's death. I've known Sir Ronald since he was an undergraduate and I made bold to express my condolences. During our brief conversation I made reference to the telephone call of 26th May and Sir Ronald told me that I was mistaken, that it was not Mr Callender who had called.'

'Did he say who it was?'

'Sir Ronald informed me that it was his laboratory assistant, Mr Chris Lunn.'

'Did that surprise you – that you were wrong, I mean?'

'I confess that I was somewhat surprised, Miss, but the mistake was perhaps excusable. My subsequent reference to the incident was fortuitous and in the circumstances regrettable.'

'Do you really believe that you misheard the name?'

The obstinate old face did not relax.

'Sir Ronald could have been in no doubt about the person who telephoned him.'

'Was it usual for Mr Callender to ring his father while he was dining in college?'

'I had never previously taken a call from him, but then answering the telephone is not part of my normal duties. It is possible that some of the other college servants may be able to help but I hardly think that an inquiry would be productive or that the news that college servants had been questioned would be gratifying to Sir Ronald.'

'Any inquiry which can help ascertain the truth is likely to be gratifying to Sir Ronald,' said Cordelia. Really, she thought, Benskin's prose style is becoming infectious. She added more naturally:

'Sir Ronald is very anxious to find out everything possible about his son's death. Is there anything that you can tell me, any help that you can give me, Mr Benskin?'

This was perilously close to an appeal but it met with no response.

'Nothing, Miss. Mr Callender was a quiet and pleasant young gentleman who seemed, as far as I was able to observe him, to be in good health and spirits up to the time he left us. His death has been very much felt in the college. Is there anything else, Miss?'

He stood patiently waiting to be dismissed and Cordelia let him go. As she and Hugo left college together and walked back into Trumpington Street she said bitterly:

'He doesn't care, does he?'

'Why should he? Benskin's an old phoney but he's been at college for seventy years and he's seen it all before. A thousand ages in his sight are but an evening gone. I've only known Benskin distressed once over the suicide of an undergraduate and that was a Duke's son. Benskin thought that there were some things that college shouldn't permit to happen.'

'But he wasn't mistaken about Mark's call. You could tell that from his whole manner, at least I could. He knows what he heard. He isn't going to admit it, of course, but he knows in his heart he wasn't mistaken.'

Hugo said lightly:

'He was being the old college servant, very correct, very proper; that's Benskin all over. "The young gentlemen aren't what they were when I first came to college." I should bloody well hope not! They wore side whiskers then and noblemen sported fancy gowns to distinguish them from the plebs. Benskin would bring all that back if he could. He's an anachronism, pottering through the court hand in hand with a statelier past.'

'But he isn't deaf. I deliberately spoke in a soft voice and he heard me perfectly. Do you really believe that he was mistaken?'

'Chris Lunn and his son are very similar sounds.'

'But Lunn doesn't announce himself that way. All the time I

was with Sir Ronald and Miss Leaming they just called him Lunn.'

'Look, Cordelia, you can't possibly suspect Ronald Callender of having a hand in his son's death! Be logical. You accept, I suppose, that a rational murderer hopes not to be found out. You admit, no doubt, that Ronald Callender, although a disagreeable bastard, is a rational being. Mark is dead and his body cremated. No one except you has mentioned murder. Then Sir Ronald employs you to stir things up. Why should he if he's got something to hide? He doesn't even need to divert suspicion, there is no suspicion.'

'Of course I don't suspect him of killing his son. He doesn't know how Mark died and he desperately needs to know. That's why he's taken me on. I could tell that at our interview; I couldn't be wrong about that. But I don't understand why he should have lied about the telephone call.'

'If he is lying there could be half a dozen innocent explanations. If Mark did ring the college it must have been something pretty urgent, perhaps something which his father didn't want to make public, something which gives a clue to his son's suicide.'

'Then why employ me to find out why he killed himself?'

'True, wise Cordelia; I'll try again. Mark asked for help, perhaps an urgent visit which Dad refused. You can imagine his reaction. "Don't be ridiculous, Mark, I'm dining at High Table with the Master. Obviously I can't leave the cutlets and claret just because you telephone me in this hysterical way and demand to see me. Pull yourself together." That sort of thing wouldn't sound so good in open court; coroners are notoriously censorious.' Hugo's voice took on a deep magisterial tone. '"It is not for me to add to Sir Ronald's distress, but it is, perhaps, unfortunate that he chose to ignore what was obviously a cry for help. Had he left his meal immediately and gone to his son's side this brilliant young student might have been saved." Cambridge suicides, so I've noticed, are always brilliant; I'm still waiting to read the report of an inquest where the college authorities testify that the student only just killed himself in time before they kicked him out.'

'But Mark died between seven and nine p.m. That telephone call is Sir Ronald's alibi!'

'He wouldn't see it like that. He doesn't need an alibi. If you know you're not involved and the question of foul play never arises, you don't think in terms of alibis. It's only the guilty who do that.'

'But how did Mark know where to find his father? In his evidence Sir Ronald said that he hadn't spoken to his son for over two weeks.'

'I can see you have a point there. Ask Miss Leaming. Better still, ask Lunn if it was, in fact, he who rang the college. If you're looking for a villain Lunn should suit admirably. I find him absolutely sinister.'

'I didn't know that you knew him.'

'Oh, he's pretty well known in Cambridge. He drives that horrid little closed van around with ferocious dedication as if he were transporting recalcitrant students to the gas chambers. Everyone knows Lunn. Seldom he smiles and smiles in such a way as if he mocked himself and scorned his spirit that could be moved to smile at anything. I should concentrate on Lunn.'

They walked on in silence through the warm scented night while the waters sang in the runnels of Trumpington Street. Lights were shining now in college doorways and in porters' lodges and the far gardens and inter-connecting courts, glimpsed as they passed, looked remote and ethereal as in a dream. Cordelia was suddenly oppressed with loneliness and melancholy. If Bernie were alive they would be discussing the case, cosily ensconced in the furthest corner of some Cambridge pub, insulated by noise and smoke and anonymity from the curiosity of their neighbours; talking low-voiced in their own particular jargon. They would be speculating on the personality of a young man who slept under that gentle and intellectual painting, yet who had bought a vulgar magazine of salacious nudes. Or had he? And if not, how had it come to be in the cottage garden? They would be discussing a father who lied about his son's last telephone call; speculating in happy complicity about an uncleaned spade, a row of earth half dug, an unwashed coffee mug, a quotation from Blake meticulously typed. They would be talking about Isabelle who was terrified and Sophie who was surely honest and Hugo who certainly knew something about Mark's death and who was clever but not as clever as he needed to be. For the first time since the case began Cordelia doubted her ability to solve it alone. If only there were someone reliable in whom she could confide, someone who would reinforce her confidence. She thought again of Sophie, but Sophie had been Mark's mistress and was Hugo's sister. They were both involved. She was on her own and that, when she came to think about it, was no different from how essentially it had always been. Ironically, the realization brought her comfort and a return of hope.

At the corner of Panton Street they paused and he said:

'You're coming back to the party?'

'No, thank you, Hugo; I've got work to do.'

'Are you staying in Cambridge?'

Cordelia wondered whether the question was prompted by more than polite interest. Suddenly cautious, she said:

'Only for the next day or two. I've found a very dull but cheap bed and breakfast place near the station.'

He accepted the lie without comment and they said goodnight. She made her way back to Norwich Street. The little car was still outside number fifty-seven, but the house was dark and quiet as if to emphasize her exclusion and the three windows were as blank as dead rejecting eyes.

She was tired by the time she got back to the cottage and had parked the Mini on the edge of the copse. The garden gate creaked at her hand. The night was dark and she felt in her bag for her torch and followed its bright pool round the side of the cottage and to the back door. By its light she fitted the key into the lock. She turned it and, dazed with tiredness, stepped into the sitting-room. The torch, still switched on, hung loosely from her hand, making erratic patterns of light on the tiled floor. Then in one involuntary movement it jerked upwards and shone full on the thing that hung from the centre hook of the ceiling. Cordelia gave a cry and clutched at the table. It was the bolster from her bed, the bolster with a cord drawn tight about one end making a grotesque and bulbous head, and the other end stuffed into a pair of Mark's trousers. The legs hung pathetically flat and empty, one lower than the other. As she stared at it in fascinated horror, her heart hammering, a slight breeze wafted in from the open door and it swung slowly round as if twisted by a living hand.

She must have stood there rooted with fear and staring wild-eyed at the bolster for seconds only, yet it seemed minutes before she found the strength to pull out a chair from the table and take the thing down. Even in the moment of repulsion and terror she remembered to look closely at the knot. The cord was attached to the hook by a simple loop and two half hitches. So, either her secret visitor had chosen not to repeat his former tactics, or he hadn't known how the first knot had been tied. She laid the bolster on the chair and went outside for the gun. In her tiredness she had forgotten it, but now she longed for the reassurance of the hard cold metal in her hand. She stood at the back door and listened. The garden seemed suddenly full of noises, mysterious rustlings, leaves moving in the slight breeze like human sighs, furtive scurryings in the undergrowth, the bat-like squeak of an animal disconcertingly close at hand. The night seemed to be holding its breath as she crept out towards the elder bush. She waited, listening to her own heart, before she found courage to turn her back and stretch up her hand to feel for the gun. It was still there. She sighed audibly with relief and immediately felt better. The gun wasn't loaded but that hardly seemed to matter. She hurried back to the cottage, her terror assuaged.

It was nearly an hour before she finally went to bed. She lit the lamp and, gun in hand, made a search of the whole cottage. Next she examined the window. It was obvious enough how he had got in. The window had no catch and was easy to push open from outside. Cordelia fetched a roll of Scotch tape from her scene-of-crime kit and, as Bernie had shown her, cut two very narrow strips and pasted them across the base of the pane and the wooden frame. She doubted whether the front windows could be opened but she took no chances and sealed them in the same way. It wouldn't stop an intruder but at least she would know next morning that he had gained access. Finally, having washed in the kitchen, she went upstairs to bed. There was no lock on her door but she wedged it slightly open and balanced a saucepan lid on the top of the frame. If anyone did succeed in getting in, he wouldn't take her by surprise. She loaded the gun and placed it on her bedside table, remembering that she was dealing with a killer. She examined the cord. It was a four-foot length of ordinary strong string, obviously not new and frayed at one end. Her heart sank at the hopelessness of trying to identify it. But she labelled it carefully, as Bernie had taught her, and packed it in her scene-of-crime kit. She did the same with the curled strap and the typed passage of Blake, transferring them from the bottom of her shoulder-bag to plastic exhibit envelopes. She was so weary that even this routine chore cost her an effort of will. Then she placed the bolster back on the bed, resisting an impulse to sling it on the floor and sleep without it. But, by then, nothing – neither fear nor discomfort – could have kept her awake. She lay for only a few minutes listening to the ticking of her watch before tiredness overcame her and bore her unresisting down the dark tide of sleep.

CHAPTER FOUR

Cordelia was awakened early next morning by the discordant chattering of the birds and the strong clear light of another fine day. She lay for several minutes stretching herself within her sleeping-bag, savouring the smell of a country morning, that subtle and evocative fusion of earth, sweet wet grass and stronger farmyard smell. She washed in the kitchen as Mark had obviously done, standing in the tin bath from the shed and gasping as she poured saucepans of cold tap water over her naked body. There was something about the simple life which disposed one to these austerities. Cordelia thought it unlikely that, in any circumstances, she would willingly have bathed in cold water in London or so much relished the smell of the paraffin stove superimposed on the appetizing sizzle of frying bacon, or the flavour of her first strong mug of tea.

The cottage was filled with sunlight, a warm friendly sanctum from which she could safely venture out to whatever the day held. In the calm peace of a summer morning the little sitting-room seemed untouched by the tragedy of Mark Callender's death. The hook in the ceiling looked as innocuous as if it had never served its dreadful purpose. The horror of that moment when her torch had first picked out the dark swollen shadow of the bolster moving in the night breeze now had the unreality of a dream. Even the memory of the precautions of the night before were embarrassing viewed in the unambiguous light of day. She felt rather foolish as she unloaded the gun, secreted the ammunition among her underclothes, and hid the pistol in the elder bush, watching carefully to see that she wasn't observed. When the washing-up was done and the one tea cloth washed through and hung out to dry, she picked a small posy of pansies, cowslips and meadowsweet from the far end of the garden and set them on the table in one of the ribbed mugs.

She had decided that her first task must be to try to trace

Nanny Pilbeam. Even if the woman had nothing to tell her about Mark's death or his reason for leaving college, she would be able to speak about his childhood and boyhood; she, probably better than anyone, would know what his essential nature had been. She had cared enough about him to attend the funeral and to send an expensive wreath. She had called on him in college on his twenty-first birthday. He had probably kept in touch with her, might even have confided in her. He had no mother and Nanny Pilbeam could have been, in some sense, a substitute.

As she drove into Cambridge Cordelia considered tactics. The probability was that Miss Pilbeam lived somewhere in the district. It was unlikely that she actually lived in the city since Hugo Tilling had only seen her once. From his brief account of her, it sounded as if she were old and probably poor. It was unlikely, therefore, that she would travel far to attend the funeral. It was apparent that she hadn't been one of the official mourners from Garforth House, hadn't been invited by Sir Ronald. According to Hugo, none of the party had even spoken to each other. This hardly suggested that Miss Pilbeam was the elderly and valued retainer of tradition, almost one of the family. Sir Ronald's neglect of her on such an occasion intrigued Cordelia. She wondered just what Miss Pilbeam's position in the family had been.

If the old lady lived near Cambridge, she had probably ordered the wreath at one of the city florists. Villages were very unlikely to provide this kind of service. It had been an ostentatious wreath, which suggested that Miss Pilbeam had been prepared to spend lavishly and had probably gone to one of the larger florists. The likelihood was that she had ordered it personally. Elderly ladies, apart from the fact that they were seldom on the telephone, like to attend to these matters direct, having, Cordelia suspected, a well-founded suspicion that only face-to-face confrontation and the meticulous recital of one's precise requirements extracted the best service. If Miss Pilbeam had come in from her village by train or by bus, she had probably selected a shop somewhere near the centre of the city. Cordelia decided to begin her search by inquiring of passers-by if they could recommend the name of a good florist.

She had already learned that Cambridge was not a city for the cruising motorist. She drew up and consulted the folding map at the back of her guide book and decided to leave the Mini on the car park next to Parker's Piece. Her search might take some time and would be best done on foot. She daren't risk a parking fine nor the impounding of the car. She checked her watch. It was still only a few minutes after nine o'clock. She had made a good start to the day.

The first hour was disappointing. The people of whom she inquired were anxious to be helpful but their ideas of what constituted a reliable florist somewhere near the centre of the city were peculiar. Cordelia was directed to small greengrocers selling a few bunches of cut flowers as a side line, to the supplier of gardening equipment who dealt in plants but not in wreaths, and once to a funeral director. The two florists' shops which at first sight seemed possible had never heard of Miss Pilbeam and had provided no wreaths for the Mark Callender funeral. A little weary with much walking and beginning to feel despondent, Cordelia decided that the whole quest had been unreasonably sanguine. Probably Miss Pilbeam had come in from Bury St Edmunds or Newmarket and had bought the wreath in her own town.

But the visit to the undertakers was not wasted. In reply to her inquiry, they recommended the name of a firm which 'provided a very nice class of wreath, Miss, really very nice indeed.' The shop was further from the centre of the city than Cordelia had expected. Even from the pavement it smelt of weddings or funerals, as one's mood dictated, and as she pushed open the door Cordelia was welcomed by a gush of warm air which caught at the throat. There were flowers everywhere. Large green buckets lined the walls holding clumps of lilies, irises and lupins; smaller containers were packed tight with wallflowers and marigolds and stocks; there were frigid bundles of tight-budded roses on thornless stems, each flower identical in size and colour and looking as if it had been cultivated in a test tube. Pots of indoor plants, decorated with variegated ribbon, lined the path to the counter like a floral guard of honour.

There was a room at the back of the shop where two assistants were working. Through the open door Cordelia watched them. The younger, a languid blonde with a spotted skin, was assistant executioner, laying open roses and freesias, predestined victims, graded according to type and colour. Her senior whose status was denoted by a better fitting overall and an air of authority, was twisting off the flower heads, piercing each mutilated bloom with wire and threading them closely on to a huge bed of moss in the shape of a heart. Cordelia averted her eyes from this horror.

A buxom lady in a pink smock appeared behind the counter apparently from nowhere. She was as pungently scented as the shop, but had obviously decided that no ordinary floral perfume could compete and that she had better rely on the exotic. She smelt of curry powder and pine so strongly that the effect was practically anaesthetizing.

Cordelia said her prepared speech:

'I'm from Sir Robert Callender of Garforth House. I wonder whether you can help us? His son was cremated on 3rd June and their old nurse very kindly sent a wreath, a cross of red roses. Sir Ronald has lost her address and very much wants to write to her. The name is Pilbeam.'

'Oh, I don't think we executed any orders of that type for 3rd June.'

'If you would be kind enough to just look in the book –'

Suddenly the young blonde looked up from her work and called out:

'It's Goddard.'

'I beg your pardon, Shirley?' said the buxom lady repressively.

'The name's Goddard. The card on the wreath said Nanny Pilbeam, but the customer was a Mrs Goddard. Another lady came to inquire from Sir Ronald Callender and that was the name she gave. I looked it up for her. Mrs Goddard, Lavender Cottage, Ickleton. One cross, four foot long in red roses. Six pounds. It's there in the book.'

'Thank you very much,' said Cordelia fervently. She smiled her thanks impartially at the three of them and left quickly in case she got embroiled in an argument about the other inquirer from Garforth House. It must have looked odd, she knew, but the three of them would no doubt enjoy themselves discussing it after she had left. Lavender Cottage, Ickleton. She kept repeating the address to herself until she was at a safe distance from the shop and could pause to write it down.

Her tiredness seemed miraculously to have left her as she sped back to the car park. She consulted her map. Ickleton was a village near the Essex border about ten miles from Cambridge. It wasn't far from Duxford so that she would be retracing her steps. She could be there in less than half an hour.

But it took longer than she had expected to thread her way through the Cambridge traffic and it wasn't until thirty-five minutes later, that she came to Ickleton's fine flint and pebble church with its broach spire, and drove the Mini close to the church gate. It was a temptation to take a brief look inside, but she resisted it. Mrs Goddard might even now be preparing to catch the Cambridge bus. She went in search of Lavender Cottage.

It wasn't, in fact, a cottage at all but a small semi-detached house of hideous red brick at the end of the High Street. There was only a narrow strip of grass between the front door and the road and neither smell nor sight of lavender. The iron knocker, in the form of a lion's head, fell heavily, shaking the door. The response came, not from Lavender Cottage, but from the next house. An elderly woman appeared, thin, almost toothless and swathed in an immense apron patterned with roses. She had carpet slippers on her feet, a woollen cap decorated with a bobble on her head and an air of lively interest in the world in general.

'You'll be wanting Mrs Goddard, I daresay?'

'Yes. Could you tell me where I could find her?'

'She'll be over at the graveyard, I don't doubt. She usually is this time of a fine morning.'

'I've just come from the church. I didn't see anyone.'

'Bless you, Miss, she's not at the church! They haven't been burying us there for many a year now. Her old man is where they'll be putting her in time, in the cemetery on Hinxton Road. You can't miss it. Just keep straight on.'

'I'll have to go back to the church for my car,' said Cordelia. It was obvious that she was going to be watched out of sight and it seemed necessary to explain why she was departing in the opposite direction to the one indicated. The old woman smiled and nodded and came out to lean on her gate for a better view of Cordelia's progress down the High Street, nodding her head like a marionette so that the bright bobble danced in the sun.

The cemetery was easily found. Cordelia parked the Mini on a convenient patch of grass where a signpost pointed the footpath to Duxford and walked the few yards back to the iron gates. There was a small flint chapel of rest with an apse at the east end and beside it an ancient wooden seat green with lichen and spattered with bird lime which gave a view of the whole burial ground. A wide swathe of turf ran straight down the middle and on each side were the graves, variously marked with white marble crosses, grey headstones, small rusted circles of iron heeling over towards the smooth turf and bright splashes of flowers patch-worked over the newly dug earth. It was very peaceful. The burial ground was surrounded by trees, their leaves scarcely stirring in the calm, hot air. There was little sound except the chirruping of crickets in the grass and from time to time the nearby ringing of a railway level-crossing bell and the swooping horn of a diesel train.

There was only one other person in the graveyard, an elderly woman bending over one of the far graves. Cordelia sat quietly on the seat, arms folded in her lap, before making her way silently down the grass path towards her. She knew with certainty that this interview was going to be crucial yet paradoxically she was in no hurry to begin. She came up to the woman and stood, still unnoticed, at the foot of the grave.

She was a small woman dressed in black, whose old-fashioned straw hat, its brim wreathed with faded net, was screwed to her hair with an immense black-bobbed hatpin. She knelt with her back to Cordelia showing the soles of a pair of misshapen shoes from which her thin legs stuck out like sticks. She was weeding the grave; her fingers, darting like a reptile's tongue over the grass, plucked at small, almost undetectable weeds. At her side was a punnet holding a folded newspaper and a gardening trowel.

From time to time, she dropped into the punnet her little mush of weeds.

After a couple of minutes, during which Cordelia watched her in silence, she paused satisfied and began smoothing the surface of the grass as if comforting the bones underneath. Cordelia read the inscription carved deep on the headstone. 'Sacred to the memory of Charles Albert Goddard beloved husband of Annie who departed this life 27th August 1962, aged 70 years. At rest.' At rest; the commonest epitaph of a generation to whom rest must have seemed the ultimate luxury, the supreme benediction.

The woman rested back for a second on her heels and contemplated the grave with satisfaction. It was then that she became aware of Cordelia. She turned a bright much wrinkled face towards her and said without curiosity or resentment at her presence:

'It's a nice stone, isn't it?'

'Yes, it is. I was admiring the lettering.'

'Cut deep that is. It cost a mint of money but it was worth it. That'll last, you see. Half the lettering here won't it's that shallow. It takes the pleasure out of a cemetery. I like to read the gravestones, like to know who people were and when they died and how long the women lived after they buried their men. It sets you wondering how they managed and whether they were lonely. There's no use in a stone if you can't read the lettering. Of course, this stone looks a bit top-heavy at present. That's because I asked them to leave space for me: "Also to Annie his wife, departed this life, . . ." and then the date: that'll even it up nicely. I've left the money to pay for it.'

'What text were you thinking of having?' inquired Cordelia.

'Oh, no text! At rest will be good enough for the both of us. We shan't be asking more of the good Lord than that.'

Cordelia said:

'That cross of roses you sent to Mark Callender's funeral was beautiful.'

'Oh, did you see it? You weren't at the funeral were you? Yes, I was pleased with it. They made a nice job of it, I thought. Poor boy, he hadn't much else, had he?'

She looked at Cordelia with benign interest:

'So you knew Mr Mark? Would you be his young lady perhaps?'

'No, not that, but I care about him. It's odd that he never talked about you, his old nurse.'

'But I wasn't his nurse, my dear, or at least, only for a month or two. He was a baby then, it meant nothing to him. No, I was nurse to his dear mother.'

'But you visited Mark on his twenty-first birthday?'

'So he told you that, did he? I was glad to see him again after all those years, but I wouldn't have pushed myself on him. It wouldn't have been right, his father feeling as he did. No, I went to give him something from his mother, to do something she had asked me to do when she was dying. Do you know, I hadn't seen Mr Mark for over twenty years – odd, really, considering that we didn't live that far apart – but I knew him at once. He had a great look of his mother about him, poor boy.'

'Could you tell me about it? It's not just curiosity; it's important for me to know.'

Leaning for support on the handle of her basket, Mrs Goddard got laboriously to her feet. She picked at a few short blades of grass adhering to her skirt, felt in her pocket for a pair of grey cotton gloves and put them on. Together they made their way slowly down the path.

'Important, is it? I don't know why it should be. It's all in the past now. She's dead, poor lady, and so is he. All that hope and promise come to nothing. I haven't spoken to anyone else about it, but then who would care to know?'

'Perhaps we could sit on this bench and talk together for a time?'

'I don't see why we shouldn't. There's nothing to hurry home for now. Do you know, my dear, I didn't marry my husband until I was fifty-three and yet I miss him as if we had been childhood sweethearts. People said I was a fool to take on a man at that age but you see I had known his wife for thirty years, we were at school together, and I knew him. If a man's good to one woman, he'll be good to another. That's what I reckoned and I was right.'

They sat side by side on the bench gazing over the green swathe towards the grave. Cordelia said:

'Tell me about Mark's mother.'

'She was a Miss Bottley, Evelyn Bottley. I went to her mother as under-nursemaid before she was born. There was only little Harry then. He was killed in the war on his first raid over Germany. His Dad took it very hard; there was never anyone to match Harry, the sun shone out of his eyes. The master never really cared for Miss Evie, it was all the boy with him. Mrs Bottley died when Evie was born and that may have made a difference. People say that it does, but I've never believed it. I've known fathers who loved a baby even more – poor innocent things, how can they be blamed? If you ask me, it was just an excuse for not taking to the child, that she killed her mother.'

'Yes, I know a father who made it an excuse too. But it isn't their fault. We can't make ourselves love someone just because we want to.'

'More's the pity, my dear, or the world would be an easier place. But his own child, that's not natural!'

'Did she love him?'

'How could she? You won't get love from a child if you don't give love. But she never had the trick of pleasing him, of humouring him – he was a big man, fierce, loud talking, frightening to a child. He would have done better with a pretty, pert little thing, who wouldn't have been afraid of him.'

'What happened to her? How did she meet Sir Ronald Callender?'

'He wasn't Sir Ronald then, my dear. Oh, dear no! He was Ronny Callender the gardener's son. They lived at Harrogate you see. Oh, such a lovely house they had! When I first went into service there they had three gardeners. That was before the war, of course. Mr Bottley worked in Bradford; he was in the wool trade. Well, you were asking about Ronny Callender. I remember him well, a pugnacious, good-looking lad but one who kept his thoughts to himself. He was clever that one, oh he was clever! He got a scholarship to the grammar school and did very well.'

'And Evelyn Bottley fell in love?'

'She may have done, my dear. What there was between them when they were young, who can tell. But then the war came and he went away. She was wild to do something useful and they took her on as a VAD, though how she passed the medical I'll never know. And then they met again in London as people did in the war and the next thing we knew they were married.'

'And came to live here outside Cambridge?'

'Not until after the war. At first she kept on with her nursing and he was sent overseas. He had what the men call a good war; we'd call it a bad war I daresay, a lot of killing and fighting, imprisonment and escaping. It ought to have made Mr Bottley proud of him and reconciled to the marriage but it didn't. I think he thought that Ronny had his eye on the money, because there was money to come, no doubt about that. He may have been right, but who's to blame the boy? My mother used to say, "Don't marry for money, but marry where money is!" There's no harm in looking for money as long as there's kindness as well.'

'And do you think there was kindness?'

'There was never unkindness that I could see, and she was mad about him. After the war he went up to Cambridge. He'd always wanted to be a scientist and he got a grant because he was ex-service. She had some money from her father and they bought the house he lives in now so that he could live at home when he was studying. It didn't look the same then, of course. He's done a lot to it since. They were quite poor then and Miss Evie managed with practically no one to help, only me. Mr Bottley used to come and stay from time to time. She used to dread his visits, poor darling. He was looking for a grandchild, you see, and one didn't come. And then Mr Callender finished at the university and got a job teaching. He wanted to stay on at college to be a don or something like that, but they wouldn't have him. He used to say it was because he hadn't influence, but I think he may not have been quite clever enough. In Harrogate we thought he was the cleverest boy in the grammar school. But then, Cambridge is full of clever men.'

'And then Mark was born?'

'Yes, on the 25th April 1951, nine years after they were married. He was born in Italy. Mr Bottley was that pleased when she became pregnant that he increased the allowance and they used to spend a lot of holidays in Tuscany. My lady loved Italy, always had, and I think she wanted the child to be born there. Otherwise she wouldn't have gone on holiday in the last month of her pregnancy. I went to visit her about a month after she came home with the baby and I've never seen a woman so happy. Oh, he was a lovely little boy!'

'But why did you visit her; weren't you living and working there?'

'No, my dear. Not for some months. She wasn't well in the early days of her pregnancy. I could see that she was strained and unhappy and then one day Mr Callender sent for me and told me that she had taken against me and that I'd have to leave. I wouldn't have believed it, but when I went to her she just put out her hand and said: "I'm sorry, Nanny, I think it would be better if you went."

'Pregnant women have strange fancies, I know, and the baby was so important to them both. I thought she might have asked me to come back afterwards and so she did, but not living in. I took a bed-sitting-room in the village with the postmistress and used to give four mornings a week to my lady and the rest to other ladies in the village. It worked very well, really, but I missed the baby when I wasn't with him. I hadn't seen her often during her pregnancy but once we met in Cambridge. She must have been near the end of her time. She was very heavy, poor dear, dragging herself along. At first she pretended that she hadn't noticed me and then she thought better of it and came across the road. "We're off to Italy next week, Nanny," she said. "Isn't it lovely?" I said: "If you're not careful, my dear, that baby will be a little Italian," and she laughed. It seemed as though she couldn't wait to get back to the sun.'

'And what happened after she came home?'

'She died after nine months, my dear. She was never strong, as I said, and she caught influenza. I helped look after her and I'd have done more but Mr Callender took over the nursing himself. He couldn't bear anyone else to be near her. We only had a few minutes together just before she died and it was then that she asked me to give her prayer-book to Mark on his twenty-first birthday. I can hear her now: "Give it to Mark when he's twenty-one, Nanny. Wrap it up carefully and take it to him when he comes of age. You won't forget will you?" I said: "I'll not forget, my darling, you know that." Then she said a strange thing. "If you do, or if you die before then, or if he doesn't understand, it won't really matter. It will mean that God wants it that way."'

'What do you think she meant?'

'Who's to say, my dear? She was very religious was Miss Evie, too religious for her own good, I sometimes thought. I believe we should accept our own responsibilities, solve our own problems, not leave it all to God as if He hadn't enough to be thinking about with the world in the state it is. But that's what she said not three hours before she died and that's what I promised. So when Mr Mark was twenty-one, I found out what college he was at and went to see him.'

'What happened?'

'Oh, we had a very happy time together. Do you know, his father had never spoken about his mother. That sometimes happens when a wife dies but I think a son ought to know about his mother. He was full of questions, things that I thought his father would have told him.

'He was glad to get the prayer-book. It was a few days later that he came to see me. He asked the name of the doctor who had treated his mother. I told him that it was old Dr Gladwin. Mr Callender and she had never had any other doctor. I used to think it a pity sometimes, Miss Evie being so frail. Dr Gladwin must have been seventy then, and although there were people who wouldn't say a word against him, I never thought much of him myself. Drink, you know, my dear; he was never really reliable. But I expect he's gone to his rest long since, poor man. Anyway, I told Mr Mark the name and he wrote it down. Then we had tea and a little chat and he left. I never saw him again.'

'And no one else knows about the prayer-book?'

'No one in the world, my dear. Miss Leaming saw the florist's name on my card and asked them for my address. She came here the day after the funeral to thank me for attending but I could see it was only curiosity. If she and Sir Ronald were so pleased to see me, what was to stop them from coming over and shaking hands? She as good as suggested that I was there without an invitation. An invitation to a funeral! Who ever heard of such a thing?'

'So you told her nothing?' asked Cordelia.

'I've told no one but you, my dear, and I'm not sure why I've told you. But no, I didn't tell her. I never liked her, to tell you the truth. I'm not saying there was anything between her and Sir Ronald, not while Miss Evie was alive anyway. There was never any gossip and she lived in a flat in Cambridge and kept herself to herself, I'll give her that. Mr Callender met her when he was teaching science at one of the village schools. She was the English mistress. It wasn't until after Miss Evie died that he set up his own laboratory.'

'Do you mean that Miss Leaming has a degree in English?'

'Oh, yes, my dear! She wasn't trained as a secretary. Of course she gave up the teaching when she started working for Mr Callender.'

'So you left Garforth House after Mrs Callender died? You didn't stay on to care for the baby?'

'I wasn't wanted. Mr Callender employed one of those new college-trained girls and then, when Mark was still only a baby, he was sent away to school. His father made it plain that he didn't like me to see the child and after all, a father has his rights. I wouldn't have gone on seeing Mr Mark knowing that his father didn't approve. It would have only put the boy in a false position. But now he's dead and we've all lost him. The coroner said that he killed himself, and he may have been right.'

Cordelia said:

'I don't think he killed himself.'

'Don't you, my dear? That's kind of you. But he's dead, isn't he, so what does it matter now? I think it's time for me to go home. If you don't mind, I won't ask you to tea, my dear, I'm a little tired today. But you know where to find me, and if ever you want to see me again, you'll always be welcome.'

They made their way out of the burial ground together. At the gates, they parted. Mrs Goddard patted Cordelia on the shoulder with the clumsy affection she might have shown to an animal, then walked off slowly towards the village.

As Cordelia drove round the curve of the road, the level crossing came into sight. A train had just passed and the barriers were being raised. Three vehicles had been caught at the crossing and the last in line was quickest away, accelerating past the first two cars as they bumped slowly over the rails. Cordelia saw that it was a small black van.

Later Cordelia remembered little of the journey back to the cottage. She drove fast, concentrating on the road ahead, trying to control her rising excitement by meticulous attention to gears and brakes. She drove the Mini hard against the front hedge, careless of whether it were seen. The cottage looked and smelt just as she had left it. She had almost expected to find it ransacked and the prayer-book gone. Sighing with relief, she saw that the white spine was still there among the taller and darker covers. Cordelia opened it. She hardly knew what she expected to find; an inscription perhaps, or a message, cryptic or plain, a letter folded between the leaves. But the only inscription could have no possible relevance to the case. It was written in a shaky, old-fashioned hand; the steel nib had crawled spider-like over the page. 'To Evelyn Mary on the occasion of her confirmation, with love from her Godmother, 5th August 1934.'

Cordelia shook the book. No slip of paper fluttered out. She skimmed through the pages. Nothing.

She sat on the bed drooping with disappointment. Had it been unreasonable to imagine that there was something significant in the bequest of the prayer-book; had she fabricated a promising edifice of conjecture and mystery on an old woman's confused recollections of a perfectly ordinary and understandable action – a devout and dying mother leaving a prayer-book to her son? And even if she hadn't been wrong, why should the message still be there? If Mark had found a note from his mother, placed between the leaves, he might well have destroyed it after reading.

And if he hadn't destroyed it, someone else might have done so. The note, if it ever existed, was now probably part of the shifting heap of white ash and charred debris in the cottage grate.

She shook herself out of her despondency. There was still a line of inquiry to pursue; she would try to trace Dr Gladwin. After a second's thought she put the prayer-book in her bag. Looking at her watch, she saw that it was nearly one o'clock. She decided to have a picnic lunch of cheese and fruit in the garden and then set off again for Cambridge to visit the central library and consult a medical directory.

Less than an hour later she found the information she wanted. There was only one Dr Gladwin still on the register who could have attended Mrs Callender as an old man of over seventy, twenty years ago. He was Emlyn Thomas Gladwin who had qualified at St Thomas's Hospital in 1904. She wrote down the address in her note book: 4 Pratts Way, Ixworth Road, Bury St Edmunds. Edmunds town! The town which Isabelle had said that she and Mark had visited on their way to the sea.

So the day hadn't been wasted after all – she was following in Mark Callender's footsteps. Impatient to consult a map she went over to the atlas section of the library. It was now two-fifteen. If she took the A45 road direct through Newmarket she could be in Bury St Edmunds in about an hour. Allow an hour for the visit to the doctor and another for the return journey. She could be home at the cottage before half-past five.

She was driving through the gentle unemphatic countryside just outside Newmarket when she noticed the black van following her. It was too far away to see who was driving but she thought it was Lunn and that he was alone. She accelerated, trying to keep the distance between them, but the van drew a little nearer. There was no reason, of course, why Lunn shouldn't be driving to Newmarket on Sir Ronald Callender's business, but the sight of the squat little van perpetually in her driving mirror was disconcerting. Cordelia decided to throw him off. There were few side turns on the road she was travelling and the country was unfamiliar to her. She decided to wait until she reached Newmarket and seize what opportunity offered.

The main through-street of the town was a tangle of traffic and every turn seemed to be blocked. It was only at the second set of traffic lights that Cordelia saw her chance. The black van was caught at the intersection about fifty yards behind. As the light turned green, she accelerated quickly and swung round to the left. There was another turn to the left and she took it, then one to the right. She drove on through unfamiliar streets, then after about five minutes, stopped at an intersection and waited. The black van did not appear. It looked as if she had succeeded in shaking him off. She waited for another five minutes, then made her way slowly back to the main road and joined in the flow of eastward traffic. Half an hour later she had passed through Bury St Edmunds and was driving very slowly down the Ixworth Road, watching for Pratts Way. Fifty yards farther on she came to it, a row of six small stucco houses standing back from a lay-by. She stopped the car outside number four remembering Isabelle, biddable and docile, who had obviously been told to drive further on and wait in the car. Was that because Mark thought the white Renault too conspicuous? Even the arrival of the Mini had provoked interest. There were faces at upper windows and a small group of children had mysteriously appeared, clustered around a neighbouring gate and watching her with wide and expressionless eyes.

Number four was a depressing house; the front garden was unweeded and the fence had gaps where the planks had rotted or been wrenched apart. The external paint had flaked away to the bare wood and the brown front door had peeled and blistered in the sun. But Cordelia saw that the bottom windows were shining and that the white net curtains were clean. Mrs Gladwin was probably a careful housewife, struggling to keep up her standards but too old for the heavy work and too poor to afford help. Cordelia felt benevolent towards her. But the woman, who, after some minutes, finally opened to her knock – the bell was out of order – was a disconcerting antidote to her sentimental pity. Compassion died before those hard distrustful eyes, that mouth tight as a trap, the thin arms clasped in a bony barrier across her chest as if to repel human contact. It was difficult to guess her age. Her hair, screwed back into a small tight bun, was still black but her face was deeply lined and the sinews and veins stood out in the thin neck like cords. She was wearing carpet slippers and a gaudy cotton overall. Cordelia said:

'My name is Cordelia Gray. I wondered if I could talk to Dr Gladwin, if he's in. It's about an old patient.'

'He's in, where else would he be? He's in the garden. You'd better go through.'

The house smelt horrible, an amalgam of extreme old age, the sour taint of excreta and stale food, with an overlay of strong disinfectant. Cordelia went through to the garden, carefully avoiding looking at the hall or kitchen since curiosity might seem impertinent.

Dr Gladwin was sitting in a high Windsor chair placed in the sun. Cordelia had never seen a man so old. He seemed to be wearing a woollen track suit, his swollen legs were encased in immense felt slippers and there was a knitted patchwork shawl across his knees. His two hands hung over the arms of the chair as if too heavy for the frail wrists, hands stained and brittle as autumn leaves which trembled with a gentle insistence. The high-domed skull, spiked with a few grey bristles, looked as small and vulnerable as a child's. The eyes were pale yolks swimming in their glutinous blue-veined whites.

Cordelia went to him and called him gently by his name. There was no response. She knelt on the grass at his feet and looked up into his face.

'Dr Gladwin, I wanted to talk to you about a patient. It was a long time ago. Mrs Callender. Do you remember Mrs Callender of Garforth House?'

There was no reply. Cordelia knew that there wouldn't be. Even to ask again seemed an outrage. Mrs Gladwin was standing beside him as if displaying him to a wondering world.

'Go on, ask him! It's all in his head you know. That's what he used to tell me. "I'm not one for records and notes. It's all in my head."'

Cordelia said:

'What happened to his medical records when he gave up practice? Did anyone take them over?'

'That's what I've just told you. There never were any records.

And it's no use asking me. I told the boy that too. The doctor was glad enough to marry me when he wanted a nurse, but he didn't discuss his patients. Oh, dear no! He was drinking all the practice profits away, but he could still talk about medical ethics.'

The bitterness in her voice was horrible. Cordelia could not meet her eyes. Just then she thought she saw the old man's lips move. She bent down her head and caught the one word. 'Cold.'

'I think he's trying to say that he's cold. Is there another shawl perhaps that he could have round his shoulders?'

'Cold! In this sun! He's always cold.'

'But perhaps another blanket would help. Shall I fetch it for you?'

'You let him be, Miss. If you want to look after him, then look after him. See how you enjoy keeping him clean like a baby, washing his nappies, changing the bed every morning. I'll get him another shawl, but in two minutes he'll be pushing it off. He doesn't know what he wants.'

'I'm sorry,' said Cordelia helplessly. She wondered whether Mrs Gladwin was getting all the help available, whether the District Nurse called, whether she had asked her doctor to try to find a hospital bed. But these were useless questions. Even she could recognize the hopeless rejection of help, the despair which no longer had energy even to look for relief. She said:

'I'm sorry; I won't trouble either of you any further.'

They walked back together through the house. But there was one question Cordelia had to ask. When they reached the front gate she said:

'You talked about a boy who visited. Was his name Mark?'

'Mark Callender. He was asking about his mother. And then about ten days later we get the other one calling.'

'What other one?'

'He was a gentleman all right. Walked in as if he owned the place. He wouldn't give a name but I've seen his face somewhere. He asked to see Dr Gladwin and I showed him in. We were sitting in the back parlour that day as there was a breeze. He went up to the doctor and said "Good afternoon, Gladwin" loudly as if talking to a servant. Then he bent down and looked at him.

Eye to eye they were. Then he straightened up, wished me good day and left. Oh, we're getting popular, we are! Any more of you and I'll have to charge for the show.'

They stood together at the gate. Cordelia wondered whether to hold out her hand but sensed that Mrs Gladwin was willing her not to go. Suddenly the woman spoke in a loud and gruff voice, looking straight ahead.

'That friend of yours, the boy who came here. He left his address. He said he wouldn't mind sitting with the doctor on a Sunday if I wanted a break; he said he could get them both a bit of dinner. I have a fancy to see my sister at Haverhill this Sunday. Tell him he can come over if he wants to.'

The capitulation was ungracious, the invitation grudging. Cordelia could guess what it had cost her to give it. She said impulsively:

'I could come on Sunday instead. I've got a car, I could get here sooner.'

It would be a day lost to Sir Ronald Callender, but she wouldn't charge him. And even a private eye was surely entitled to a day off on Sundays.

'He won't want a slip of a girl. There's things to do for him that need a man. He took to that boy. I could see that. Tell him he can come.'

Cordelia turned to her.

'He would have come, I know he would. But he can't. He's dead.'

Mrs Gladwin did not speak. Cordelia put out a tentative hand and touched her sleeve. There was no response. She whispered:

'I'm sorry. I'll go now.' She nearly added 'If there's nothing I can do for you,' but stopped herself in time. There was nothing she or anyone could do.

She looked back once as the road bent towards Bury and saw the rigid figure still at the gate.

Cordelia wasn't sure what made her decide to stop at Bury and walk for ten minutes in the Abbey gardens. But she felt she couldn't face the drive back to Cambridge without calming her spirits and the glimpse of grass and flowers through the great Norman doorway was irresistible. She parked the Mini on Angel Hill, then walked through the gardens to the river bank. There she sat for five minutes in the sun. She remembered that there was money spent on petrol to be recorded in her notebook and felt for it in her bag. Her hand brought out the white prayer-book. She sat quietly thinking. Suppose she had been Mrs Callender and had wanted to leave a message, a message which Mark would find and other searchers might miss. Where would she place it? The answer now seemed childishly simple. Surely somewhere on the page with the collect, gospel and epistle for St Mark's Day. He had been born on April 25th. He had been named after the Saint. Quickly she found the place. In the bright sunlight reflected from the water she saw what a quick rustle through the pages had missed. There against Cranmer's gentle petition for grace to withstand the blasts of false doctrine was a small pattern of hieroglyphics so faint that the mark on the paper was little more than a smudge. She saw that it was a group of letters and figures.

E M C
A A
14.1.52

The first three letters, of course, were his mother's initials. The date must be that on which she wrote the message. Hadn't Mrs Goddard said that Mrs Callender had died when her son was about nine months old? But the double A? Cordelia's mind chased after motoring associations before she remembered the card in Mark's wallet. Surely these two letters under an initial could only show one thing, the blood group. Mark had been B. His mother was AA. There was only one reason why she should have wanted him to have that information. The next step was to discover Sir Ronald Callender's group.

She almost cried out with triumph as she ran through the gardens and turned the Mini again towards Cambridge. She hadn't thought out the implications of this discovery, or even whether her arguments were valid. But at least she had something to do, at least she had a lead. She drove fast, desperate to get to the city before the post office closed. There, she seemed to remember, it was possible to get a copy of the Executive Council's list of local doctors. It was handed over. And now for a telephone. She knew only one house in Cambridge where there was a chance of being left in peace to telephone for up to an hour. She drove to 57, Norwich Street.

Sophie and Davie were at home playing chess in the sitting-room, fair head and dark almost touching over the board. They showed no surprise at Cordelia's plea to use the telephone for a series of calls.

'I'll pay, of course. I'll make a note of how many.'

'You'll want the room to yourself, I expect?' said Sophie. 'We'll finish the game in the garden, Davie.'

Blessedly incurious they carried the chess board with care through the kitchen and set it up on the garden table. Cordelia drew a chair to the table and settled down with her list. It was formidably long. There was no clue where to begin but perhaps those doctors with group practices and addresses near the centre of the city would be the best bet. She would start with them, ticking off their names after each call. She remembered another reported pearl of the Superintendent's wisdom: 'Detection requires a patient persistence which amounts to obstinacy.' She thought of him as she dialled the first number. What an intolerably demanding and irritating boss he must have been! But he was almost certainly old now – forty-five at least. He had probably eased up a bit by now.

But an hour's obstinacy was unfruitful. Her calls were invariably answered; one advantage of ringing a doctor's surgery was that the telephone was at least manned. But the replies, given politely, curtly or in tones of harassed haste by a variety of respondents from the doctors themselves to obliging daily women prepared to convey a message, were the same. Sir Ronald Callender was not a patient of this practice. Cordelia repeated her formula. 'I'm so sorry to have troubled you. I must have misheard the name.'

But after nearly seventy minutes of patient dialling she struck lucky. The doctor's wife answered.

'I'm afraid you've got the wrong practice. Dr Venables looks after Sir Ronald Callender's household.'

This was luck indeed! Dr Venables wasn't on her preliminary list and she wouldn't have reached the V's for at least another hour. She ran her finger down the names and dialled for the last time.

It was Dr Venables' nurse who answered. Cordelia spoke her prepared piece:

'I'm ringing for Miss Leaming from Garforth House. I'm sorry to trouble you but could you please remind us of Sir Ronald Callender's blood group? He wants to know it before the Helsinki Conference next month.'

'Just a minute, please.' There was a brief wait; the sound of footsteps returning.

'Sir Ronald is Group A. I should make a careful note of it if I were you. His son had to ring a month or so ago with the same inquiry.'

'Thank you! Thank you! I'll be careful to make a note.' Cordelia decided to take a risk.

'I'm new here, assisting Miss Leaming, and she did tell me to note it down last time but stupidly I forgot. If she should happen to call, please don't tell her that I had to trouble you again.'

The voice laughed, indulgent to the inefficiency of the young. After all, it wasn't likely to inconvenience her much.

'Don't worry, I shan't tell her. I'm glad she's got herself some help at last. Everyone's well, I hope?'

'Oh, yes! Everyone's fine.'

Cordelia put down the receiver. She looked out of the window and saw that Sophie and Davie were just finishing their game and were putting the pieces back in the box. She had just finished in time. She knew the answer to her query but she still had to verify it. The information was too important to leave to her own vague recollection of the Mendelian rules of inheritance gleaned from the chapter on blood and identity in Bernie's book on forensic medicine. Davie would know, of course. The quickest way would be to ask him now. But she couldn't ask Davie. It would mean going back to the public library, and she would have to hurry if she were to be there before it closed.

But she got there just in time. The librarian, who by now had got used to seeing her, was as helpful as ever. The necessary reference book was quickly produced. Cordelia verified what she had already known. A man and wife both of whose bloods were A could not produce a B group child.

Cordelia was very tired by the time she got back to the cottage. So much had happened during one day; so much had been discovered. It seemed impossible that less than twelve hours previously she had started out on her search for Nanny Pilbeam with only a vague hope that the woman, if she could be found, might provide a clue to Mark Callender's personality, might tell her something about his formative years. She was exhilarated by the success of the day, restless with excitement, but too mentally exhausted to tease out the tangle of conjecture which lay knotted at the back of her mind. At present the facts were disordered; there was no clear pattern, no theory which would at once explain the mystery of Mark's birth, Isabelle's terror, Hugo and Sophie's secret knowledge, Miss Markland's obsessive interest in the cottage, Sergeant Maskell's almost reluctant suspicions, the oddities and unexplained inconsistencies which surrounded Mark's death.

She busied herself about the cottage with the energy of mental overtiredness. She washed the kitchen floor, laid a fire on top of the heap of ash in case the next evening should be chilly, weeded the back flower patch, then made herself a mushroom omelette and ate it sitting, as he must have done, at the simple table. Last of all, she fetched the gun from its hiding pace and set it on the table beside the bed. She locked the back door carefully and drew the curtains across the window, checking once more that the seals were intact. But she didn't balance a saucepan on the top of her door. Tonight that particular precaution seemed childish and unnecessary. She lit her bedside candle then went to the window to choose a book. The night was balmy and windless; the flame of the candle burned steadily in the still air. Outside, darkness had not yet fallen but the garden was very quiet, the peace broken only by the distant crescendo of a car on the main road or the cry of a night bird. And then, seen dimly through the gloaming, she glimpsed a figure at the gate. It was Miss Markland. The woman hesitated, hand on the latch, as if wondering whether to enter the garden. Cordelia slipped to one side, back pressed against the wall. The shadowy figure was so still that it seemed as if she sensed a watching presence and had frozen like an animal surprised. Then, after two minutes, she moved away and was lost among the trees of the orchard. Cordelia relaxed, took a copy of *The Warden* from Mark's row of books, and wriggled into her sleeping-bag. Half an hour later, she blew out the candle and stretched her body comfortably for the slow acquiescent descent into sleep.

She stirred in the early hours and was instantly awake, eyes wide open in the half darkness. Time lay suspended; the still air was expectant as if the day had been taken by surprise. She could hear the ticking of her wrist watch on the bedside table and could see beside it the crooked, comforting outline of the pistol, the black cylinder of her torch. She lay and listened to the night. One lived so seldom in these still hours, the time most often slept or dreamt away, that one came to them tentative and unpractised like a creature newly born. She wasn't aware of fear, only of an all-embracing peace, a gentle lassitude. Her breathing filled the room, and the still, uncontaminated air seemed to be breathing in unity with her.

Suddenly, she realized what had woken her. Visitors were coming to the cottage. She must subconsciously in some brief phase of uneasy sleep have recognized the sound of a car. Now there was the whine of the gate, the rustle of feet, furtive as an animal in undergrowth, a faint, broken murmur of voices. She wriggled out of her sleeping-bag and stole to the window. Mark hadn't attempted to clean the glass of the front windows; perhaps he hadn't had time, perhaps he welcomed their occluding dirt. Cordelia rubbed her fingers with desperate haste against the gritty accretion of years. But, at last, she felt the cold smooth glass. It squeaked with the friction of her fingers, high and thin like an animal's squeal so that she thought the noise must betray her. She peered through the narrow strip of clear pane into the garden below.

The Renault was almost hidden by the high hedge but she could see the front of the bonnet gleaming by the gate and the two pools of light from the side lamps shining like twin moons on the lane. Isabelle was wearing something long and clinging; her pale figure trembled like a wave against the dark of the hedge. Hugo was only a black shadow at her side. But then he turned and Cordelia saw the flash of a white shirt-front. They were both in evening dress. They came together quietly up the path and conferred briefly at the front door, then moved towards the corner of the cottage.

Snatching up her torch, Cordelia rushed on silent, naked feet down the stairs and threw herself across the sitting-room to unlock the back door. The key turned easily and silently. Hardly daring to breathe she retreated back into the shadows at the foot of the stairs. She was just in time. The door opened, letting in a shaft of paler light. She heard Hugo's voice:

'Just a minute, I'll strike a match.'

The match flared, illuminating in a gentle, momentary light the two grave anticipatory faces, Isabelle's immense and terrified eyes. Then it went out. She heard Hugo's muttered curse followed by the scratch of the second match striking against the box. This time he held it high. It shone on the table, on the mute accusing hook; on the silent watcher at the foot of the stairs. Hugo gasped; his hand jerked and the match went out. Immediately, Isabelle began to scream.

Hugo's voice was sharp.

'What the hell –'

Cordelia switched on her torch and came forward.

'It's only me; Cordelia.'

But Isabelle was beyond hearing. The screams rang out with such piercing intensity that Cordelia half feared that the Marklands must hear. The sound was inhuman, the shriek of animal terror. It was cut short by the swing of Hugo's arm; the sound of a slap; a gasp. It was succeeded by a second of absolute silence, then Isabelle collapsed against Hugo sobbing quietly.

He turned harshly on Cordelia:

'What the hell did you do that for?'

'Do what?'

'You terrified her, lurking there. What are you doing here anyway?'

'I could ask you that.'

'We came to collect the Antonello which Isabelle lent to Mark when she came to supper with him, and to cure her of a certain morbid obsession with this place. We've been to the Pitt Club Ball. It seemed a good idea to call here on our way home. Obviously, it was a bloody stupid idea. Is there any drink in the cottage?'

'Only beer.'

'Oh God, Cordelia, there would be! She needs something stronger.'

'There isn't anything stronger, but I'll make coffee. You set a light to the fire. It's laid.'

She stood the torch upright on the table and lit the table lamp, turning the wick low, then helped Isabelle into one of the fireside chairs.

The girl was trembling. Cordelia fetched one of Mark's heavy sweaters and placed it round her shoulders. The kindling began to flame under Hugo's careful hands. Cordelia went into the kitchen to make coffee, laying her torch on its side at the edge of the window-sill so that it shone on the oil stove. She lit the stronger of the two burners and took from the shelf a brown earthenware jug, the two blue-rimmed mugs and a cup for herself. A second and chipped cup held the sugar. It took only a couple of minutes to boil half a kettle of water and to pour it over the coffee grains. She could hear Hugo's voice from the sitting-room, low, urgent, consolatory, interposed with Isabelle's monosyllabic replies. Without waiting for the coffee to brew she placed it on the only tray, a bent tin one patterned with a chipped picture of Edinburgh castle, and carried it into the sitting-room, setting it down in the hearth. The faggots spluttered and blazed, shooting out a falling shower of bright sparks which patterned Isabelle's dress with stars. Then a stouter brand caught flame and the fire glowed with a stronger, more mellow, heart.

As she bent forward to stir the coffee Cordelia saw a small beetle scurrying in desperate haste along the ridges of one of the small logs. She picked up a twig from the kindling still in the hearth and held it out as a way of escape. But it confused the beetle still more. It turned in panic and raced back towards the flame, then doubled in its tracks and fell finally into a split in the wood. Cordelia wondered whether it briefly comprehended its dreadful end. Putting a match to a fire was such a trivial act to cause such agony, such terror.

She handed Isabelle and Hugo their mugs and took her own. The comforting smell of fresh coffee mingled with the resinous tang of the burning wood. The fire threw long shadows over the tiled floor and the oil lamp cast its gentle glow over their faces. Surely, thought Cordelia, no murder suspects could have been interrogated in a cosier setting. Even Isabelle had lost her fears. Whether it was the reassurance of Hugo's arm across her shoulders, the stimulus of the coffee or the homely warmth and crackle of the fire, she seemed almost at ease.

Cordelia said to Hugo:

'You said that Isabelle was morbidly obsessed by this place. Why should she be?'

'Isabelle's very sensitive; she isn't tough like you.'

Cordelia privately thought that all beautiful women were tough – how else could they survive? – and that Isabelle's fibres could compare well for resilience with her own. But nothing would be gained by challenging Hugo's illusions. Beauty was fragile, transitory, vulnerable. Isabelle's sensitivities must be protected. The toughies could look after themselves. She said:

'According to you, she's only been here once before. I know that Mark Callender died in this room, but you hardly expect me to believe that she's grieving over Mark. There's something that both of you know and it would be better if you told me now. If you don't I shall have to report to Sir Ronald Callender that Isabelle, your sister and you are somehow concerned in his son's death and it will be up to him to decide whether to call in the police. I can't see Isabelle standing up to even the mildest police questioning, can you?'

Even to Cordelia it sounded a stilted, sententious little speech, an unsubstantiated accusation backed up by an empty threat. She half expected Hugo to counter it with amused contempt. But he looked at her for a minute as if assessing more than the reality of the danger. Then he said quietly:

'Can't you accept my word that Mark died by his own hand and that if you do call in the police it will cause unhappiness and distress to his father, to his friends and be absolutely no help to anyone?'

'No, Hugo, I can't.'

'Then if we do tell you what we know, will you promise that it won't go any further?'

'How can I, any more than I can promise to believe you?'

Suddenly Isabelle cried:

'Oh, tell her, Hugo! What does it matter?'

Cordelia said:

'I think that you must. I don't think you've any choice.'

'So it seems. All right.' He put his coffee mug down in the hearth and looked into the fire.

'I told you that we went – Sophie, Isabelle, Davie and I – to the Arts Theatre on the night Mark died but that, as you've probably guessed, was only three-quarters true. They had only three seats left when I booked so we allocated them to the three people mostly likely to enjoy the play. Isabelle goes to the theatre to be seen rather than to see and is bored by any show with a cast of less than fifty, so she was the one left out. Thus neglected by her current lover, she very reasonably decided to seek consolation with the next.'

Isabelle said with a secret, anticipatory smile:

'Mark was not my lover, Hugo.'

She spoke without rancour or resentment. It was a matter of putting the record straight.

'I know. Mark was a romantic. He never took a girl to bed – or anywhere else that I could see – until he judged that there was an adequate depth of inter-personal communication, or whatever jargon he used, between them. Actually, that's unfair. It's my father who uses bloody awful meaningless phrases like that. But Mark agreed with the general idea. I doubt whether he could enjoy sex until he'd convinced himself that he and the girl were in love. It was a necessary preliminary – like undressing. I gather that with Isabelle the relationship hadn't reached the necessary depths, hadn't achieved the essential emotional rapport. It was only a matter of time, of course. Where Isabelle was concerned, Mark was as capable of self-deception as the rest of us.'

The high, slightly hesitant voice was edged with jealousy.

Isabelle said, slowly and patiently, like a mother explaining to a wilfully obtuse child:

'Mark never made love to me, Hugo.'

'That's what I'm saying. Poor Mark! He exchanged the substance for the shadow and now he has neither.'

'But what happened that night?'

Cordelia spoke to Isabelle, but it was Hugo who replied.

'Isabelle drove here and arrived shortly after half-past seven. The curtains were drawn across the back window, the front one is impenetrable anyway, but the door was open. She came in. Mark was already dead. His body was hanging by the strap from that hook. But he didn't look as he did when Miss Markland found him next morning.'

He turned to Isabelle:

'You tell her.' She hesitated. Hugo bent forward and kissed her lightly on the lips.

'Go on, tell. There are some unpleasantnesses which all Papa's money can't entirely shield from you and this, darling, is one.'

Isabelle turned her head and looked intently into the four corners of the room as if satisfying herself that the three of them were really alone. The irises of her remarkable eyes were purple in the firelight. She leaned towards Cordelia with something of the confiding relish of a village gossip about to relate the latest scandal. Cordelia saw that her panic had left her. Isabelle's agonies were elemental, violent but short lived, easily comforted. She would have kept her secret while Hugo instructed her to keep it, but she was glad of his order of release. Probably her instinct told her that the story, once told, would lose the sting of terror. She said:

'I thought I would call to see Mark and, perhaps, that we would have supper together. Mademoiselle de Congé was not well and Hugo and Sophie were at the theatre and I was bored. I came to the back door because Mark had told me that the front door would not open. I thought that I might see him in the garden, but he was not there, only the garden fork in the ground and his shoes at the door. So I pushed open the door. I did not knock because I thought that I would be a surprise for Mark.'

She hesitated and looked down into the mug of coffee, twisting it between her hands.

'And then?' prompted Cordelia.

'And then I saw him. He was hanging there by the belt from that hook in the ceiling and I knew he was dead. Cordelia, it was horrible! He was dressed like a woman in a black bra and black lace panties. Nothing else. And his face! He had painted his lips, all over his lips, Cordelia, like a clown! It was terrible but it was funny too. I wanted to laugh and scream at the same time. He didn't look like Mark. He didn't look like a human being at all. And on the table there were three pictures. Not nice pictures, Cordelia. Pictures of naked women.'

Her wide eyes stared into Cordelia's, dismayed, uncomprehending. Hugo said:

'Don't look like that, Cordelia. It was horrible for Isabelle at the time and disagreeable to think about now. But it isn't so very uncommon. It does happen. It's probably one of the more innocuous of sexual deviations. He wasn't involving anyone but himself. And he didn't mean to kill himself; that was just bad luck. I imagine that the buckle of the belt slipped and he never had a chance.' Cordelia said:

'I don't believe it.'

'I thought you might not. But it's true, Cordelia. Why not come with us now and ring Sophie? She'll confirm it.'

'I don't need confirmation of Isabelle's story. I already have that. I mean I still don't believe that Mark killed himself.'

As soon as she spoke she knew that it had been a mistake. She shouldn't have revealed her suspicions. But it was too late now and there were questions she had to ask. She saw Hugo's face, his quick impatient frown at her obtuseness, her obstinacy. And then she detected a subtle change of mood; was it irritation, fear, disappointment? She spoke directly to Isabelle.

'You said that the door was open. Did you notice the key?'

'It was in this side of the door. I saw it when I went out.'

'What about the curtains?'

'They were like now, across the window.'

'And where was the lipstick?'

'What lipstick, Cordelia?'

'The one used to paint Mark's lips. It wasn't in the pockets of his jeans or the police would have found it, so where was it? Did you see it on the table?'

'There was nothing on the table except the pictures.'

'What colour was the lipstick?'

'Purple. An old lady's colour. No one would choose such a colour I think.'

'And the underclothes, could you describe them?'

'Oh, yes! They were from M & S. I recognized them.'

'You mean that you recognized those particular ones, that they were yours?'

'Oh, no Cordelia! They were not mine. I never wear black underclothes. I only like white next to my skin. But they were the kind I usually buy. I always get my underclothes from M & S.'

Cordelia reflected that Isabelle was hardly one of the store's best customers, but that no other witness would have been as reliable when it came to details, particularly of clothes. Even in that moment of absolute terror and revulsion, Isabelle had noticed the type of underclothes. And if she said that she hadn't seen the lipstick, then it was because the lipstick hadn't been there to see.

Cordelia went on inexorably:

'Did you touch anything, Mark's body perhaps, to see if he was dead?'

Isabelle was shocked. The facts of life she could take in her stride, but not the facts of death.

'I couldn't touch Mark! I touched nothing. And I knew that he was dead.'

Hugo said: 'A respectable, sensible law-abiding citizen would have found the nearest telephone and rung the police. Luckily Isabelle is none of these things. Her instinct was to come to me.

She waited until the play ended, and then met us outside the theatre. When we came out she was pacing up and down the pavement on the other side of the road. Davie, Sophie and I came back here with her in the Renault. We only stopped briefly at Norwich Street to collect Davie's camera and flash.'

'Why?'

'That was my idea. Obviously, we had no intention of letting the fuzz and Ronald Callender know how Mark had died. Our idea was to fake a suicide. We planned to dress him in his own clothes, clean his face and then leave him for someone else to find. We hadn't it in mind to fake a suicide note; that was a refinement somewhat outside our powers. We collected the camera so that we could photograph him as he was. We didn't know what particular law we were breaking in faking a suicide, but there must have been one. You can't do the simplest service for your friends these days without it being liable to misconstruction by the fuzz. If there were trouble we wanted some evidence of the truth. We were all fond of Mark in our different ways, but not fond enough to risk a murder charge. However, our good intentions were frustrated. Someone else had got here first.'

'Tell me about it.'

'There's nothing to tell. We told the two girls to wait in the car, Isabelle because she had already seen enough and Sophie because Isabelle was too frightened to be left alone. Besides, it seemed only fair to Mark to keep Sophie out of it, to prevent her from seeing him. Don't you find it odd, Cordelia, this concern one has for the susceptibilities of the dead?'

Thinking of her father and Bernie, Cordelia said:

'Perhaps it's only when people are dead that we can safely show how much we cared about them. We know that it's too late for them to do anything about it.'

'Cynical but true. Anyway, there was nothing for us to do here. We found Mark's body and this room as Miss Markland described them at the inquest. The door was open, the curtains drawn across. Mark was naked except for his blue jeans. There were no magazine pictures on the table and no lipstick on his face. But there was a suicide note in the typewriter and a mound of ash in the grate. It looked as if the visitor had made a thorough job of it. We didn't linger. Someone else – perhaps someone from the house – might have turned up at any minute. Admittedly, it was very late by then but it seemed an evening for people to pop in. Mark must have had more visitors that night than during his whole time at the cottage; first Isabelle; then the unknown samaritan; then us.'

Cordelia thought that there had been someone before Isabelle. Mark's murderer had been there first. She asked suddenly:

'Someone played a stupid trick on me last night. When I got back here from the party there was a bolster slung from that hook. Did you do that?'

If his surprise were not genuine, then Hugo was a better actor than Cordelia thought possible.

'Of course I didn't! I thought you were living in Cambridge not here. And why on earth should I?'

'To warn me off.'

'But that would be crazy! It wouldn't warn you off, would it? It might scare some women, but not you. We wanted to convince you that there was nothing to investigate about Mark's death. That sort of trick would only convince you that there was. Someone else was trying to scare you. The most likely person is the one who came here after us.'

'I know. Someone took a risk for Mark. He – or she – won't want me ferreting around. But he would have got rid of me more sensibly by telling me the truth.'

'How could he know whether to trust you? What will you do now, Cordelia? Go back to town?'

He was trying to keep his voice casual but she thought she detected the underlying anxiety. She replied.

'I expect so. I'll have to see Sir Ronald first.'

'What will you tell him?'

'I'll think of something. Don't worry.'

Dawn was staining the eastern sky and the first chorus of birds was noisily contradicting the new day before Hugo and Isabelle left. They took the Antonello with them. Cordelia saw it taken down with a pang of regret as if something of Mark was leaving the cottage. Isabelle examined the picture closely with a grave professional eye before tucking it under her arm. Cordelia thought that she was probably generous enough with her possessions, both people and pictures, provided they were on loan only, to be returned promptly on demand and in the same condition as when she parted with them. Cordelia watched from the front gate as the Renault, with Hugo driving, moved out of the shadow of the hedge. She lifted her hand in a formal gesture of farewell like a weary hostess speeding her final guests, then turned back to the cottage.

The sitting-room seemed empty and cold without them. The fire was dying and she hastily pushed in the few remaining sticks from the hearth and blew on them to kindle the flame. She moved restlessly about the little room. She was too lively to go back to bed, but her short and disturbed night had left her edgy with tiredness. But her mind was tormented by something more fundamental than lack of sleep. For the first time she knew that she was afraid. Evil existed – it hadn't needed a convent education to convince her of that reality – and it had been present in this room. Something here had been stronger than wickedness, ruthlessness, cruelty or expedience. Evil. She had no doubt that Mark had been murdered, but with what diabolical cleverness it had been done! If Isabelle told her story, who now would ever believe that he hadn't died accidentally, but by his own hand? Cordelia had no need to refer to her book on forensic medicine to know how it would appear to the police. As Hugo had said, these cases weren't so very uncommon. He, as a psychiatrist's son, would have heard or read of them. Who else would know? Probably any reasonably sophisticated person. But it couldn't have been Hugo. Hugo had an alibi. Her mind revolted at the thought that Davie or Sophie could have participated in such a horror. But how typical that they should have collected the camera. Even their compassion had been overlaid with self-concern. Would Hugo and Davie have stood here, under Mark's grotesque body, calmly discussing distance and exposure before taking the photograph which would, if necessary, exonerate them at his expense?

She went into the kitchen to make tea, glad to be free of the malignant fascination of that hook in the ceiling. Previously it had hardly worried her, now it was as obtrusive as a fetish. It seemed to have grown since the previous night, to be growing still as it drew her eyes compulsively upwards. And the sitting-room itself had surely shrunk; no longer a sanctum but a claustrophobic cell, tawdry and shameful as an execution shed. Even the bright morning air was redolent with evil.

Waiting for the kettle to boil she made herself contemplate the day's activities. It was still too early to theorize; her mind was too preoccupied with horror to deal rationally with its new knowledge. Isabelle's story had complicated, not illumined the case. But there were still relevant facts to be discovered. She would go on with the programme she had already planned. Today she would go to London to examine Mark's grandfather's will.

But there were still two hours to get through before it was time to start out. She had decided to travel to London by train and to leave the car at Cambridge station since this would be both quicker and easier. It was irritating to have to spend a day in town when the heart of the mystery so obviously lay in Cambridgeshire, but for once she wasn't sorry at the prospect of leaving the cottage. Shocked and restless, she wandered aimlessly from room to room and prowled around the garden, fretting to be away. Finally in desperation she took hold of the garden fork and completed the digging of Mark's unfinished row. She wasn't sure that this was wise; Mark's interrupted work was part of the evidence for his murder. But other people, including Sergeant Maskell, had seen it and could testify if necessary, and the sight of the partly completed job, of the fork still askew in the soil, was unbearably irritating. When the row was completed she felt calmer and she dug on without pausing for another hour before carefully cleaning the fork and placing it with the other tools in the garden shed.

At last it was time to go. The seven o'clock weather forecast had prophesied thundery storms in the south-east so she put on her suit, the heaviest protection she had brought with her. She hadn't worn it since Bernie's death and she discovered that the waist band was uncomfortably loose. She had lost some weight. After a moment's thought, she took Mark's belt from the scene-of-crime kit and wound it twice round her waist. She felt no repugnance as the leather tightened against her. It was impossible to believe that anything he had ever touched or owned could frighten or distress her. The strength and heaviness of the leather so close to her skin was even obscurely comforting and reassuring as if the belt were a talisman.

CHAPTER FIVE

The storm broke just as Cordelia alighted from the number 11 bus outside Somerset House. There was a jagged flash of lightning and, almost instantaneously, the thunder crashed like a barrage round her ears and she raced across the inner courtyard between the ranks of parked cars through a wall of water while the rain spouted around her ankles as if the paving stones were being raked with bullets. She pushed open the door and stood draining pools of water on the mat and laughing aloud with relief. One or two of the people present glanced up from their perusal of wills and smiled at her, while a motherly looking woman behind the counter tut-tutted her concern. Cordelia shook her jacket over the mat then hung it on the back of one of the chairs and tried ineffectually to dry her hair with her handkerchief before approaching the counter.

The motherly woman was helpful. Consulted by Cordelia on the correct procedure, she indicated the shelves of heavy, bound volumes in the middle of the hall and explained that the wills were indexed under the surname of the testator and the year in which the document was lodged with Somerset House. It was for Cordelia to trace the catalogue number and bring the volume to the desk. The original will would then be sent for and she could consult it for a fee of 20 pence.

Not knowing when George Bottley had died, Cordelia was in some perplexity where to begin her search. But she deduced that the will must have been made after the birth, or at least the conception, of Mark, since he had been left a fortune by his grandfather. But Mr Bottley had also left money to his daughter and this part of his fortune had come on her death to her husband. The strong probability was that he had died before her, since otherwise he would surely have made a new will. Cordelia decided to begin her search with the year of Mark's birth, 1951.

Her deductions proved correct. George Albert Bottley of

Stonegate Lodge, Harrogate, had died on 26th July 1951, exactly three months and one day after the birth of his grandson and only three weeks after making his will. Cordelia wondered whether his death had been sudden and unexpected or whether this was the will of a dying man. She saw that he had left an estate of nearly three quarters of a million pounds. How had he made this, she wondered? Surely not all from wool. She heaved the heavy book across to the counter, the clerk wrote the details on a white form and pointed out the way to the cashier's office. Within a surprisingly few minutes of paying what seemed to her a modest fee, Cordelia was seated under the light at one of the desks near the window with the will in her hands.

She hadn't liked what she had heard about George Bottley from Nanny Pilbeam and she didn't like him any better after reading his will. She had feared that the document might be long, complicated and difficult to understand; it was surprisingly short, simple and intelligible. Mr Bottley directed that all his possessions should be sold, 'since I wish to prevent the usual unseemly wrangling over bric-à-brac'. He left modest sums to servants in his employ at the time of his death but there was no mention, Cordelia noticed, of his gardener. He bequeathed half of the residue of his fortune to his daughter, absolutely, 'now that she has demonstrated that she has at least one of the normal attributes of a woman.' The remaining half he left to his beloved grandson Mark Callender on attaining his twenty-fifth birthday, 'by which date, if he hasn't learned the value of money, he will at least be of an age to avoid exploitation.' The income from the capital was left to six Bottley relations, some of them, apparently, only distant kinsmen. The will recreated a residual trust; as each beneficiary died his share would be distributed among the survivors. The testator was confident that this arrangement would promote in the beneficiaries a lively interest in each others' health and survival while encouraging them to achieve the distinction of longevity, no other distinction being within their reach. If Mark died before his twenty-fifth birthday the family trust would continue until all the beneficiaries were dead and the capital would then be distributed among a formidable list of charities chosen, as far as Cordelia could see, because they were well known and successful rather than because they represented any personal concern or sympathy on the part of the testator. It was as if he had asked his lawyers for a list of the more reliable charities, having no real interest in what happened to his fortune if his own issue were not alive to inherit it.

It was a strange will. Mr Bottley had left nothing to his son-in-law yet had apparently been unworried by the possibility that his daughter, whom he knew not to be strong, might die and leave her fortune to her husband. In some respects it was a gambler's will and Cordelia wondered again how George Bottley had made his fortune. But, despite the cynical unkindness of its comments, the will was neither unfair nor ungenerous. Unlike some very rich men he hadn't attempted to control his great fortune from beyond the grave, obsessively determined that not one penny should ever get into unfavoured hands. His daughter and his grandson had both been left their fortunes absolutely. It was impossible to like Mr Bottley but difficult not to respect him. And the implications of his will were very clear. No one stood to gain by Mark's death except a long list of highly respectable charities.

Cordelia made a note of the main clauses of the will, more because of Bernie's insistence on meticulous documentation than from any fear of forgetting them; slipped the receipt for 20p into the expenses page of her notebook; added the cost of her cheap day return ticket from Cambridge and her bus fare, and returned the will to the counter. The storm had been as short as it was violent. The hot sun was already drying the windows and the puddles lay bright on the rain-washed courtyard. Cordelia decided that she ought to charge Sir Ronald for half a day only and spend the rest of her time in London at the office. There might be post to collect. There might even be another case awaiting her.

But the decision was a mistake. The office seemed even more sordid than when she had left it and the air smelt sour in contrast to the rain-washed streets outside. There was a thick film of dust over the furniture and the bloodstain on the rug had deepened into a brick-brown which looked even more sinister than the original bright red. There was nothing in the letter-box but a final demand from the electricity board and a bill from the stationer. Bernie had paid dearly – or rather, had not paid – for the despised writing paper.

Cordelia wrote a cheque for the electricity bill, dusted the furniture, made one last and unsuccessful attempt to clean the rug. Then she locked the office and set off to walk to Trafalgar Square. She would seek consolation in the National Gallery.

She caught the 18.16 train from Liverpool Street and it was nearly eight o'clock before she arrived back at the cottage. She parked the Mini in its usual place in the shelter of the copse and made her way round the side of the cottage. She hesitated for a moment wondering whether to collect the gun from its hiding place but decided that this could wait until later. She was hungry and the first priority was to get a meal. She had carefully locked the back door and had stuck a thin strip of Scotch tape across the window-sill before leaving that morning. If there were any more secret visitors she wanted to be warned. But the tape was still intact. She felt in her shoulder-bag for the key and, bending down, fitted it into the lock. She wasn't expecting trouble outside the cottage and the attack took her completely by surprise. There was the half-second of pre-knowledge before the blanket fell but that was too late. There was a cord around her neck pulling the mask of hot stifling wool taut against her mouth and nostrils. She gasped for breath and tasted the dry strong-smelling fibres on her tongue. Then a sharp pain exploded in her chest and she remembered nothing.

The movement of liberation was a miracle and a horror. The blanket was whipped off. She never saw her assailant. There was a second of sweet reviving air, a glimpse, so brief that it was barely comprehended, of blinding sky seen through greenness, and then she felt herself falling, falling in helpless astonishment into cold darkness. The fall was a confusion of old nightmares, unbelievable seconds of childhood terrors recalled. Then her body hit the water. Ice-cold hands dragged her into a vortex of horror. Instinctively, she had closed her mouth at the moment of impact and she struggled to the surface through what seemed an eternity of cold encompassing blackness. She shook her head and, through her stinging eyes, she looked up. The black tunnel that stretched above her ended in a moon of blue light. Even as she looked, the well lid was dragged slowly back like the shutter of a camera. The moon became a half moon; then a crescent. At last there was nothing but eight thin slits of light.

Desperately she trod water, reaching tentatively for the bottom. There was no bottom. Frantically moving hands and feet, willing herself not to panic, she felt around the walls of the well for a possible foothold. There was none. The funnel of bricks, smooth, sweating with moisture, stretched around and above her like a circular tomb. As she gazed upwards they writhed, expanded, swayed and reeled like the belly of a monstrous snake.

And then she felt a saving anger. She wouldn't let herself drown, wouldn't die in this horrible place, alone and terrified. The well was deep but small, the diameter barely three feet. If she kept her head and took time, she could brace her legs and shoulders against the bricks and work her way upwards.

She hadn't bruised or stunned herself against the walls as she fell. Miraculously she was uninjured. The fall had been clean. She was alive and capable of thought. She had always been a survivor. She would survive.

She floated on her back, bracing her shoulders against the cold walls, spreading her arms and digging her elbows into the interstices of the bricks to get a better grip. Shuffling off her shoes, she planted both feet against the opposite wall. Just beneath the surface of the water, she could feel that one of the bricks was slightly unaligned. She curved her toes around it. It gave her a precarious but welcome foothold for the start of the climb. By means of it, she could lift her body out of the water and could relieve for a moment the strain on the muscles of her back and thighs.

Then slowly she began to climb, first shifting her feet one after the other in tiny sliding steps, then humping up her body inch by painful inch. She kept her eyes fixed on the opposite curve of the wall, willing herself not to look down, nor up, counting progress by the width of each brick. Time passed. She couldn't see Bernie's watch, although its ticking seemed unnaturally loud, a regular obtrusive metronome to the thumping of her heart and the fierce gasping of her breath. The pain in her legs was intense and her shirt was sticking to her back with a warm, almost comforting effusion, which she knew must be blood. She willed herself not to think of the water beneath her or of the thin, but widening clefts of light above. If she were to survive, all her energy must be harnessed for the next painful inch.

Once, her legs slipped and she slithered back several yards before her feet, scrabbling ineffectually against the slimy walls, at last found a purchase. The fall had grazed her injured back and left her whimpering with self-pity and disappointment. She scourged her mind into courage and began climbing again. Once she was gripped by cramp and lay stretched as if on a rack until the agony passed and her fixed muscles could move. From time to time her feet found another small foothold and she was able to stretch her legs and rest. The temptation to stay in comparative safety and ease was almost irresistible and she had to will herself to start again on the slow tortuous climb.

It seemed that she had been climbing for hours, moving in a parody of a difficult labour towards some desperate birth. Darkness was falling. The light from the well top was wider now but less strong. She told herself that the climb wasn't really difficult. It was only the darkness and loneliness which made it seem so. If this were a fabricated obstacle race, an exercise in the school gymnasium, surely she could have done it easily enough. She filled her mind with the comforting images of rib stools and vaulting horses, of the fifth form shouting their encouragement. Sister Perpetua was there. But why wasn't she looking at Cordelia? Why had she turned away? Cordelia called her and the figure turned slowly and smiled at her. But it wasn't Sister after all. It was Miss Leaming, the lean pale face sardonic under the white veil.

And now when she knew that, unaided, she could get no further, Cordelia saw salvation. A few feet above her was the bottom rung of a short wooden ladder fixed to the last few feet of the well. At first she thought that it was an illusion, a phantasm born of exhaustion and despair. She shut her eyes for a few minutes; her lips moved. Then she opened her eyes again. The ladder was still there, seen dimly but comfortingly solid in the fading light. She lifted impotent hands towards it knowing, even as she did so, that it was out of reach. It could save her life and she knew that she hadn't the strength to reach it.

It was then, without conscious thought or scheming, that she remembered the belt. Her hand dropped to her waist feeling for the heavy brass buckle. She undid it and drew the long snake of leather from her body. Carefully she threw the buckled end towards the bottom rung of the ladder. The first three times the metal struck the wood with a sharp crack but didn't fall over the rung; the fourth time it did. She pushed the other end of the belt gently upwards and the buckle dropped towards her until she could reach out her hand and grasp it. She fastened it to the other end to form a strong loop. Then she pulled, at first very gently and then harder until most of her weight was on the strap. The relief was indescribable. She braced herself against the brickwork, gathering strength for the final triumphant effort. Then it happened. The rung, rotted at its joints, broke loose with a harsh tearing sound and spun past her into darkness, just missing her head. It seemed minutes rather than seconds before the distant splash reverberated round the wall.

She unbuckled the belt and tried again. The next rung was a foot higher and the throw more difficult. Even this small effort was exhausting in her present state and she made herself take time. Every unsuccessful throw made the next more difficult. She didn't count the number of attempts, but at last the buckle fell over the rung and dropped towards her. When it snaked within reach she found that she could only just buckle the strap. The next rung would be too high. If this one broke, it would be the end.

But the rung held. She had no clear memory of the last half hour of the climb but at last she reached the ladder and strapped herself firmly to the uprights. For the first time she was physically safe. As long as the ladder held she needn't fear falling. She let herself relax into brief unconsciousness. But then the wheels of the mind which had been spinning blissfully free, took hold again and she began to think. She knew that she had no hope of moving the heavy wooden cover unaided. She stretched out both hands and pushed against it but it didn't shift, and the high concave dome made it impossible for her to brace her shoulders against the wood. She would have to rely on outside help and that wouldn't come till daylight. It might not come even then, but she pushed the thought away. Sooner or later someone would come. She could hope to hold on, thus strapped, for several days. Even if she lost consciousness there was a chance that she would be rescued alive. Miss Markland knew that she was at the cottage; her things were still there. Miss Markland would come.

She gave thought to how she could attract attention. There was room to push something between the boards of wood if only she had something sufficiently stiff to push. The edge of the buckle was possible provided she strapped herself more tightly. But she must wait until the morning. There was nothing she could do now. She would relax and sleep and await rescue.

And then the final horror burst upon her. There would be no rescue. Someone would be coming to the well, coming on quiet and stealthy feet under the cover of darkness. But it would be her murderer. He had to return; it was part of his plan. The attack, which at the time had seemed so astonishingly, so brutally stupid, hadn't been stupid at all. It was intended to look like an accident. He would come back that night and remove the well cover again. Then, some time next day or within the next few days, Miss Markland would blunder through the garden and discover what had happened. No one would ever be able to prove that Cordelia's death wasn't an accident. She recalled the words of Sergeant Maskell: 'It isn't what you suspect; it's what you can prove.' But this time would there even be suspicion? Here was a young, impulsive, over-curious young woman living at the cottage without the owner's authority. She had obviously decided to explore the well. She had smashed the padlock, drawn back the lid with the coil of rope which the killer would leave ready to be found, and tempted by the ladder, had let herself down those few steps until the final rung broke beneath her. Her prints and no one else's would be found on the ladder, if they took the trouble to look. The cottage was utterly deserted; the chance that her murderer would be seen returning was remote. There was nothing she could do but wait until she heard his footsteps, his heavy breathing, and the lid was drawn slowly back to reveal his face.

After the first intensity of terror, Cordelia waited for death without hope and without further struggle. There was even a kind of peace in resignation. Strapped like a victim to the uprights of the ladder she drifted mercifully into brief oblivion and prayed that it might be so when her killer returned, that she might not be conscious at the moment of the final blow. She had no longer any interest in seeing her murderer's face. She wouldn't humiliate herself by pleading for her life, wouldn't beg for mercy from a man who had strung up Mark. She knew that there would be no mercy.

But she was conscious when the well lid began slowly to move. The light came in above her bowed head. The gap widened. And then she heard a voice, a woman's voice, low, urgent and sharp with terror.

'Cordelia!'

She looked up.

Kneeling at the rim of the well, her pale face immense and seeming to float disembodied in space like the phantasm of a nightmare, was Miss Markland. And the eyes which stared into Cordelia's face were as wild with terror as her own.

Ten minutes later Cordelia was lying slumped in the fireside chair. Her whole body ached and she was powerless to control her violent shivering. Her thin shirt was stuck to her wounded back and every shift of movement was pain. Miss Markland had put a light to the kindling and was now making coffee. Cordelia could hear her moving to and fro in the little kitchen and could smell the stove as it was turned high and, soon, the evocative aroma of coffee. These familiar sights and sounds would normally have been reassuring and comforting, but now she was desperate to be alone. The killer would still return. He had to return, and when he did, she wanted to be there to meet him. Miss Markland brought in the two mugs and pressed one into Cordelia's shivering hands. She stumped upstairs and came down with one of Mark's jumpers which she wound round the girl's neck. Her terror had left her, but she was as agitated as a young girl sharing her first half-shameful adventure. Her eyes were wild, her whole body trembled with excitement. She sat down directly in front of Cordelia and fixed her with her sharp inquisitive eyes.

'How did it happen? You must tell me.'

Cordelia had not forgotten how to think.

'I don't know. I can't remember anything that happened before

I hit the water. I must have decided to explore the well and lost my balance.'

'But the well lid! The lid was in place!'

'I know. Someone must have replaced it.'

'But why? Who would have come this way?'

'I don't know. But someone must have seen it. Someone must have dragged it back.'

She said more gently:

'You saved my life. How did you notice what had happened?'

'I came to the cottage to see if you were still here. I came earlier today but there was no sign of you. There was a coil of rope – the one that you used, I expect – left in the path and I stumbled over it. Then I noticed that the lid wasn't quite in place and that the padlock had been smashed.'

'You saved my life,' said Cordelia again, 'but please go now. Please go. I'm all right, really I am.'

'But you aren't fit to be left alone! And that man – the one who replaced the lid – he might return. I don't like to think of strangers snooping around the cottage and you here alone.'

'I'm perfectly safe. Besides, I have a gun. I only want to be left in peace to rest. Please don't worry about me!'

Cordelia could detect the note of desperation, almost of hysteria, in her own voice.

But Miss Markland seemed not to hear. Suddenly she was on her knees in front of Cordelia and pouring out a spate of high, excited chatter. Without thought and without compassion, she was confiding to the girl her terrible story, a story of her son, the four-year-old child of herself and her lover, who had broken his way through the cottage hedge and fallen into the well to his death. Cordelia tried to shake herself free from the wild eyes. It was surely all a fantasy. The woman must be mad. And if it were true, it was horrible and unthinkable and she could not bear to hear it. Sometime later she would remember it, remember every word, and think of the child, of his last terror, his desperate cry for his mother, the cold suffocating water dragging him to his death. She would live his agony in nightmares as she would relive her own. But not now. Through the spate of words, the self-accusations, the terror recalled, Cordelia recognized the note of liberation. What to her had been horror, to Miss Markland had been release. A life for a life. Suddenly Cordelia could bear it no longer. She said violently:

'I'm sorry! I'm sorry! You've saved my life and I'm grateful. But I can't bear to listen. I don't want you here. For God's sake go!'

All her life she would remember the woman's hurt face, her silent withdrawal. Cordelia didn't hear her go, didn't remember the soft closing of the door. All she knew was that she was alone. The shaking was over now although she still felt very cold. She went upstairs and pulled on her slacks and then unwound Mark's jumper from her neck and put it on. It would cover the blood stains on her shirt and the warmth was immediately comforting. She was moving very quickly. She felt for the ammunition, took her torch and let herself out of the back door of the cottage. The gun was where she had left it, in the fold of the tree. She loaded it and felt its familiar shape and heaviness in her hand. Then she stood back among the bushes and waited.

It was too dark to see the dial of her wrist-watch but Cordelia reckoned that she must have waited there immobile in the shadows for nearly half an hour before her ears caught the sound for which she was waiting. A car was approaching down the lane. Cordelia held her breath. The sound of the engine reached a brief crescendo and then faded away. The car had driven on without stopping. It was unusual for a car to pass down the lane after dark and she wondered who it could be. Again she waited, moving deeper into the shelter of the elder bush so that she could rest her back against the bark. She had been clutching the gun so tightly that her right wrist ached and she moved the pistol to her other hand and rotated the wrist slowly, stretching the cramped fingers.

Again she waited. The slow minutes passed. The silence was broken only by the furtive scuffling of some small night prowler in the grass and the sudden wild hoot of an owl. And then once more she heard the sound of an engine. This time the noise was faint and it came no closer. Someone had stopped a car further up the road.

She took the gun in her right hand, cradling the muzzle with her left. Her heart was pounding so loudly that she felt its wild hammering must betray her. She imagined rather than heard the thin whine of the front gate but the sound of feet moving round the cottage was unmistakable and clear. And now he was in sight, a stocky, broad-shouldered figure, black against the light. He moved towards her and she could see her shoulder-bag hanging from his left shoulder. The discovery disconcerted her. She had completely forgotten the bag. But now she had realized why he had seized it. He had wanted to search it for evidence, but it was important that, finally, it should be discovered with her body in the well.

He came forward gently on tip-toe, his long simian arms held stiffly away from his body like a caricature of a film cowboy ready for the draw. When he got to the rim of the well he waited and the moon struck the white of his eyes as he gazed slowly round. Then he bent down and felt in the grass for the coil of rope. Cordelia had laid it where Miss Markland had found it, but something about it, some slight difference perhaps in the way it was coiled, seemed to strike him. He rose uncertainly and stood for a moment with the rope dangling from his hand. Cordelia tried to control her breathing. It seemed impossible that he should not hear, smell or see her, that he should be so like a predator yet without the beast's instinct for the enemy in the dark. He moved forward. Now he was at the well. He bent and threaded one end of the rope through the iron hoop.

Cordelia moved with one step out of the darkness. She held the gun firmly and straight as Bernie had shown her. This time the target was very close. She knew that she wouldn't fire but, in that moment, she knew too what it was that could make a man kill. She said loudly:

'Good evening, Mr Lunn.'

She never knew whether he saw the gun. But for one unforgettable second, as the clouded moon sailed into the open sky, she saw his face clearly; saw the hate, the despair, the agony and the rictus of terror. He gave one hoarse cry, threw down the shoulder-bag and the rope and rushed through the garden in a blind panic. She gave chase, hardly knowing why, or what she hoped to achieve, determined only that he shouldn't get back to Garforth House before her. And still she didn't fire the gun.

But he had an advantage. As she threw herself through the gate she saw that he had parked the van some fifty yards up the road and left the engine running. She chased after him but could see that it was hopeless. Her only hope of catching up with him was to get the Mini. She tore down the lane feeling in her shoulder-bag as she ran. The prayer book and her note book were both gone but her fingers found the car keys. She unlocked the Mini, threw herself in and reversed it violently on to the road. The rear lights of the van were about a hundred yards ahead of her. She didn't know what speed it could do, but doubted whether it could out-pace the Mini. She trod on the accelerator and gave pursuit. She turned left out of the lane on to the subsidiary road and now she could see the van still ahead. He was driving fast and was holding the distance. Now the road turned and for a few seconds he was out of sight. He must be getting very close now to the junction with the Cambridge road.

She heard the crash just before she herself reached the junction, an instantaneous explosion of sound which shook the hedges and made the little car tremble. Cordelia's hands tightened momentarily on the wheel and the Mini jerked to a stop. She ran forward round the corner and saw before her the gleaming, headlamp-lit surface of the main Cambridge road. It was peopled with running shapes. The transporter, still upright, was an immense oblong mass blocking the skyline, a barricade slewed across the road. The van had crumpled under its front wheels like a child's toy. There was a smell of petrol, a woman's harsh scream, the squeal of braking tyres. Cordelia walked slowly up to the transporter. The driver was still in his seat, gazing rigidly ahead, his face a mask of dedicated concentration. People were shouting at him, stretching out their arms. He didn't move. Someone – a man in a heavy leather coat and goggles – said:

'It's shock. We'd better drag him clear.'

Three figures moved between Cordelia and the driver. Shoulders heaved in unison. There was a grunt of effort. The driver was lifted out, rigid as a manikin, his knees bent, his clenched hands held out as if still grasping the immense wheel. The shoulders bent over him in secret conclave.

There were other figures standing round the crushed van. Cordelia joined the ring of anonymous faces. Cigarette-ends glowed and faded like signals, casting a momentary glow on the shaking hands, the wide, horrified eyes. She asked:

'Is he dead?' The man in goggles replied laconically:

'What do you think?'

There was a girl's voice, tentative, breathless.

'Has anyone called the ambulance?'

'Yeah. Yeah. That chap in the Cortina's gone off to 'phone.'

The group stood irresolute. The girl and the young man to whom she was clinging began to back away. Another car stopped. A tall figure was pushing his way through the crowd. Cordelia heard a high, authoritative voice.

'I'm a doctor. Has anyone called the ambulance?'

'Yes, sir.'

The reply was deferential. They stood aside to let the expert through. He turned to Cordelia, perhaps because she was nearest.

'If you didn't witness the accident, young woman, you'd better get on your way. And stand back, the rest of you. There's nothing that you can do. And put out those cigarettes!'

Cordelia walked slowly back to the Mini, placing each foot carefully before the other like a convalescent trying her first painful steps. She drove carefully round the accident, bumping the Mini on the grass verge. There was the wail of approaching sirens. As she turned off the main road, her driving mirror glowed suddenly red and she heard a whoosh of sound followed by a low, concerted groan which was broken by a woman's high, single scream. There was a wall of flame across the road. The doctor's warning had been too late. The van was on fire. There was no hope now for Lunn; but then, there never had been.

Cordelia knew that she was driving erratically. Passing cars hooted at her and flashed their lights and one motorist slowed down and shouted angrily. She saw a gate and drew in off the road and switched off the engine. The silence was absolute. Her hands were moist and shaking. She wiped them on her handkerchief and laid them in her lap feeling that they were separate from the rest of her body. She was hardly aware of a car passing and then slowing to a halt. A face appeared at the window. The voice was slurred and nervous but horribly ingratiating. She could smell the drink on his breath.

'Anything wrong, Miss?'

'Nothing. I've just stopped for a rest.'

'No point in resting alone – a pretty girl like you.'

His hand was on the door handle. Cordelia felt in her shoulder-bag and drew out the gun. She pushed it into his face.

'It's loaded. Go away at once or I'll shoot.'

The menace in her voice struck cold even to her own ears. The pale, moist face disintegrated with surprise, the jaw fell. He backed away.

'Sorry, Miss, I'm sure. My mistake. No offence.'

Cordelia waited until his car was out of sight. Then she turned on the engine. But she knew that she couldn't go on. She turned off the engine again. Waves of tiredness flowed over her, an irresistible tide, gentle as a blessing, which neither her exhausted mind nor body had the will to resist. Her head fell forward and Cordelia slept.

CHAPTER SIX

Cordelia slept soundly but briefly. She didn't know what woke her, whether the blinding light of a passing car sweeping across her closed eyes or her own subconscious knowledge that rest must be rationed to a brief half hour, the minimum necessary to enable her to do what had to be done before she could give herself over to sleep. She eased her body upright, feeling the stab of pain in her strained muscles and the half-pleasurable itch of dried blood on her back. The night air was heavy and odorous with the heat and scents of the day; even the road winding ahead looked tacky in the glare of her headlights. But Cordelia's chilled and aching body was still grateful for the warmth of Mark's jersey. For the first time since she had pulled it over her head she saw that it was dark green. How odd that she hadn't noticed its colour before!

She drove the rest of the journey like a novice, sitting bolt upright, eyes rigidly ahead, hands and feet tense on the controls. And here at last were the gates of Garforth House. They loomed in her headlights far taller and more ornamental than she remembered them, and they were closed. She ran from the Mini praying that they wouldn't be locked. But the iron latch, although heavy, rose to her desperate hands. The gates swung soundlessly back.

There were no other cars in the drive and she parked the Mini some little way from the house. The windows were dark and the only light, gentle and inviting, shone through the open front door. Cordelia took the pistol in her hand and, without ringing stepped into the hall. She was more exhausted in body than when she had first come to Garforth House, but tonight she saw it with a new intensity, her nerves sensitive to every detail. The hall was empty, the air expectant. It seemed as if the house had waited for her. The same smell met her of roses and lavender, but tonight she saw that the lavender came from a huge Chinese bowl set on a side table. She recalled the insistent ticking of a clock, but now she noticed for the first time the delicate carving on the clock case, the intricate scrolls and whirls on the face. She stood in the middle of the hall, swaying slightly, the pistol held lightly in her drooping right hand, and looked down. The carpet was a formal geometrical design in rich olive greens, pale blues and crimson, each pattern shaped like the shadow of a kneeling man. It seemed to draw her to her knees. Was it perhaps an eastern prayer mat?

She was aware of Miss Leaming coming quietly down the stairs towards her, her long red dressing-gown sweeping round her ankles. The pistol was taken suddenly but firmly from Cordelia's unresisting hand. She knew that it had gone because her hand felt suddenly lighter. It made no difference. She could never defend herself with it, never kill a man. She had learnt that about herself when Lunn had run from her in terror. Miss Leaming said:

'There is no one here you need defend yourself against, Miss Gray.'

Cordelia said:

'I've come to report to Sir Ronald. Where is he?'

'Where he was the last time you came here, in his study.'

As before, he was sitting at his desk. He had been dictating and the machine was at his right hand. When he saw Cordelia, he switched it off, then walked to the wall and pulled the plug from the socket. He walked back to the desk and they sat down opposite each other. He folded his hands in the pool of light from the desk lamp and looked at Cordelia. She almost cried out with shock. His face reminded her of faces seen grotesquely reflected in grubby train windows at night – cavernous, the bones stripped of flesh, eyes set in fathomless sockets – faces resurrected from the dead.

When he spoke his voice was low, reminiscent.

'Half an hour ago I learned that Chris Lunn was dead. He was the best lab assistant I ever had. I took him out of an orphanage fifteen years ago. He never knew his parents. He was an ugly, difficult boy, already on probation. School had done nothing for him. But Lunn was one of the best natural scientists I've ever known. If he'd had the education, he'd have been as good as I am.'

'Then why didn't you give him his chance, why didn't you educate him?'

'Because he was more useful to me as a lab assistant. I said that he could have been as good as I am. That isn't quite good enough. I can find plenty of scientists as good. I couldn't have found another lab assistant to equal Lunn. He had a marvellous hand with instruments.'

He looked up at Cordelia, but without curiosity, apparently without interest.

'You've come to report, of course. It's very late, Miss Gray, and, as you see, I'm tired. Can't it wait until tomorrow?'

Cordelia thought that this was as close to an appeal as he could ever bring himself. She said:

'No, I'm tired too. But I want to finish the case tonight, now.' He picked up an ebony paper-knife from the desk and, without looking at Cordelia, balanced it on his forefinger.

'Then tell me, why did my son kill himself? I take it that you do have news for me? You would hardly have burst in here at this hour without something to report.'

'Your son didn't kill himself. He was murdered. He was murdered by someone he knew very well, someone he didn't hesitate to let into the cottage, someone who came prepared. He was strangled or suffocated, then slung up on that hook by his own belt. Last of all, his murderer painted his lips, dressed him in a woman's underclothes and spread out pictures of nudes on the table in front of him. It was meant to look like accidental death during sexual experiment; such cases aren't so very uncommon.'

There was half a minute of silence. Then he said with perfect calmness:

'And who was responsible, Miss Gray?'

'You were. You killed your son.'

'For what reason?' He might have been an examiner, putting his inexorable questions.

'Because he discovered that your wife wasn't his mother, that the money left to her and to him by his grandfather had come by fraud. Because he had no intention of benefiting by it a moment longer, nor of accepting his legacy in four years' time. You were afraid that he might make this knowledge public. And what about the Wolvington Trust? If the truth came out, that would be the end of their promised grant. The future of your laboratory was at stake. You couldn't take the risk.'

'And who undressed him again, typed out that suicide note, washed the lipstick from his face?'

'I think I know, but I shan't tell you. That's really what you employed me to discover, isn't it? That's what you couldn't bear not to know. But you killed Mark. You even prepared an alibi just in case it was needed. You got Lunn to ring you at college and announce himself as your son. He was the one person you could rely on absolutely. I don't suppose you told him the truth. He was only your lab assistant. He didn't require explanations, he did what you told him. And even if he did guess the truth, he was safe, wasn't he? You prepared an alibi which you dared not use, because you didn't know when Mark's body was first discovered. If someone had found him and faked that suicide before you had claimed to have spoken to him on the telephone, your alibi would have been broken, and a broken alibi is damning. So you made a chance to talk to Benskin and put matters right. You told him the truth; that it was Lunn who had rung you. You could rely on Lunn to back up your story. But it wouldn't really matter, would it, even if he did talk? No one would believe him.'

'No, any more than they will believe you. You've been determined to earn your fee, Miss Gray. Your explanation is ingenious; there is even a certain plausibility about some of the details. But you know, and I know, that no police officer in the world would take it seriously. It's unfortunate for you that you couldn't question Lunn. But Lunn, as I said, is dead. He burnt to death in a road accident.'

'I know, I saw. He tried to kill me tonight. Did you know that? And earlier, he tried to scare me into dropping the case. Was that because he had begun to suspect the truth?'

'If he did try to kill you, he exceeded his instructions. I merely asked him to keep an eye on you. I had contracted for your sole and whole-time services, if you remember; I wanted to be sure I was getting value. I am getting value of a kind. But you mustn't indulge your imagination outside this room. Neither the police nor the courts are sympathetic to slander nor to hysterical nonsense. And what proof have you? None. My wife was cremated. There is nothing alive or dead on this earth to prove that Mark was not her son.'

Cordelia said:

'You visited Dr Gladwin to satisfy yourself that he was too senile to give evidence against you. You needn't have worried. He never did suspect, did he? You chose him as your wife's doctor because he was old and incompetent. But I have one small piece of evidence. Lunn was bringing it to you.'

'Then you should have looked after it better. Nothing of Lunn except his bones has survived that crash.'

'There are still the female clothes, the black pants and the bra. Someone might remember who bought them, particularly if that person was a man.'

'Men do buy underclothes for their women. But if I were planning such a murder, I don't think buying the accessories would worry me. Would any harassed shop girl at the cash desk of a popular multiple store remember a particular purchase, a purchase paid for with cash, one of a number of innocuous items, all presented together at the busiest time of the day? The man might even have worn a simple disguise. I doubt whether she would even notice his face. Would you really expect her to remember, weeks afterwards, to identify one of thousands of customers and identify him with sufficient certainty to satisfy a jury? And if she did, what would it prove unless you have the clothes in question? Be sure of one thing, Miss Gray, if I needed to kill I should do it efficiently. I should not be found out. If the police ever learn how my son was found, as they well may do since, apparently, someone other than yourself knows it, they will only believe with greater certainty that he killed himself. Mark's death was necessary and, unlike most deaths, it served a purpose. Human beings have an irresistible urge towards self-sacrifice. They die for any reason or none at all, for meaningless abstractions like patriotism, justice, peace; for other men's ideals, for other men's power, for a few feet of earth. You, no doubt, would give your life to save a child or if you were convinced that the sacrifice would find a cure for cancer.'

'I might. I like to think that I would. But I should want the decision to be mine, not yours.'

'Of course. That would provide you with the necessary emotional satisfaction. But it wouldn't alter the fact of your dying nor the result of your death. And don't say that what I'm doing here isn't worth one single human life. Spare me that hypocrisy. You don't know and you're incapable of understanding the value of what I'm doing here. What difference will Mark's death make to you? You'd never heard of him until you came to Garforth House.'

Cordelia said:

'It will make a difference to Gary Webber.'

'Am I expected to lose everything I've worked for here because Gary Webber wants someone to play squash or discuss history with?'

Suddenly he looked Cordelia full in the face. He said sharply:

'What is the matter? Are you ill?'

'No I'm not ill. I knew that I must be right. I knew that what I had reasoned was true. But I can't believe it. I can't believe that a human being could be so evil.'

'If you are capable of imagining it, then I'm capable of doing it. Haven't you yet discovered that about human beings, Miss Gray? It's the key to what you would call the wickedness of man.'

Suddenly Cordelia could no longer bear this cynical antiphony. She cried out in passionate protest.

'But what is the use of making the world more beautiful if the people who live in it can't love one another?'

She had stung him at last into anger.

'Love! The most overused word in the language. Has it any meaning except the particular connotation which you choose to give it? What do you mean by love? That human beings must learn to live together with a decent concern for each other's welfare? The law enforces that. The greatest good of the greatest number. Beside that fundamental declaration of common sense all other philosophies are metaphysical abstractions. Or do you define love in the Christian sense, caritas? Read history, Miss Gray. See to what horrors, to what violence, hatred and repression the religion of love has led mankind. But perhaps you prefer a more feminine, more individual definition; love as a passionate commitment to another's personality. Intense personal commitment always ends in jealousy and enslavement. Love is more destructive than hate. If you must dedicate your life to something, dedicate it to an idea.'

'I mean love, as a parent loves a child.'

'The worse for them both, perhaps. But if he doesn't love, there is no power on earth which can stimulate or compel him to. And where there is no love, there can be none of the obligations of love.'

'You could have let him live! The money wasn't important to him. He would have understood your needs and kept silent.'

'Would he? How could he – or I – have explained his rejection of a great fortune in four years' time? People at the mercy of what they call their conscience are never safe. My son was a self-righteous prig. How could I put myself and my work in his hands?'

'You are in mine, Sir Ronald.'

'You are mistaken. I am in no one's hand. Unfortunately for you that tape recorder is not working. We have no witnesses. You will repeat nothing that has been said in this room to anyone outside. If you do I shall have to ruin you. I shall make you unemployable, Miss Gray. And first of all I shall bankrupt that pathetic business of yours. From what Miss Leaming told me it shouldn't be difficult. Slander can be a highly expensive indulgence. Remember that if you are ever tempted to talk. Remember this too. You will harm yourself; you will harm Mark's memory; you will not harm me.'

Cordelia never knew how long the tall figure in the red dressing-gown had been watching and listening in the shadow of the door. She never knew how much Miss Leaming had heard or at what moment she had stolen quietly away. But now she was aware of the red shadow moving soundlessly over the carpet, eyes on the figure behind the desk, the gun held closely against her breast. Cordelia watched in fascinated horror, not breathing. She knew exactly what was going to happen. It must have taken less than three seconds but they passed as slowly as minutes. Surely there had been time to cry out, time to warn, time to leap forward and wrench the gun from that steady hand? Surely there had been time for him to cry out? But he made no sound. He half rose, incredulous, and gazed at the muzzle in blind disbelief. Then he turned his head towards Cordelia as if in supplication. She would never forget that last look. It was beyond terror, beyond hope. It held nothing but the blank acceptance of defeat.

It was an execution, neat, unhurried, ritually precise. The bullet went in behind the right ear. The body leapt into the air, shoulders humped, softened before Cordelia's eyes as if the bones were melting into wax, and lay discarded at last over the desk. A thing; like Bernie; like her father.

Miss Leaming said:

'He killed my son.'

'Your son?'

'Of course. Mark was my son. His son and mine. I thought you might have guessed.'

She stood with the gun in her hand gazing with expressionless eyes through the open window to the lawn. There was no sound. Nothing moved. Miss Leaming said:

'He was right when he said that no one could touch him. There was no proof.'

Cordelia cried out appalled:

'Then how could you kill him? How could you be so sure?'

Without releasing her hold on the pistol, Miss Leaming put her hand into the pocket of her dressing-gown. The hand moved over the desk top. A small gilt cylinder rolled over the polished wood towards Cordelia, then rocked into stillness. Miss Leaming said:

'The lipstick was mine. I found it a minute ago in the pocket of his dress suit. He hadn't worn that suit since he last dined in Hall on Feast night. He was always a magpie. He put small objects instinctively into his pockets.'

Cordelia had never doubted Sir Ronald's guilt but now every nerve was desperate for reassurance.

'But it could have been planted there! Lunn could have put it there to incriminate him.'

'Lunn didn't kill Mark. He was in bed with me at the time Mark died. He only left my side for five minutes and that was to make a telephone call shortly after eight o'clock.'

'You were in love with Lunn!'

'Don't look at me like that! I only loved one man in my life and he's the one I've just killed. Talk about things you understand. Love had nothing to do with what Lunn and I needed from each other.'

There was a moment's silence. Then Cordelia said:

'Is there anyone in the house?'

'No. The servants are in London. No one is working late at the lab tonight.'

And Lunn was dead. Miss Leaming said with weary resignation:

'Hadn't you better phone the police?'

'Do you want me to?'

'What does it matter?'

'Prison matters. Losing your freedom matters. And do you really want the truth to come out in open court? Do you want everyone to know how your son died and who killed him? Is that what Mark himself would want?'

'No. Mark never believed in punishment. Tell me what I have to do.'

'We've got to work quickly and plan carefully. We have to trust each other and we have to be intelligent.'

'We are intelligent. What must we do?'

Cordelia took out her handkerchief and dropping it over the gun, took the weapon from Miss Leaming and placed it on the desk. She grasped the woman's thin wrist and pushed her protesting hand against Sir Ronald's palm, pulling against the instinctive recoil, forcing the stiff but living fingers against the soft unresisting hand of the dead.

'There may be firing residue. I don't really know much about that, but the police may test for it. Now wash your hands and get me a pair of thin gloves. Quickly.'

She went without a word. Left alone, Cordelia looked down at the dead scientist. He had fallen with his chin against the desk top and his arms swinging loosely at his sides, an awkward, uncomfortable-looking pose which gave him the appearance of peering malevolently over his desk. Cordelia could not look at his eyes, but she was conscious of feeling nothing, not hatred, or anger, or pity. Between her eyes and the sprawled figure swung an elongated shape, head hideously crooked, toes pathetically pointed. She walked over to the open window and looked out over the garden with the casual curiosity of a guest kept waiting in a strange room. The air was warm and very still. The scent of roses came in waves through the open window, alternately sickening sweet and then as elusive as a half-caught memory.

This curious hiatus of peace and timelessness must have lasted less than half a minute. Then Cordelia began to plan. She thought about the Clandon case. Memory pictured herself and Bernie, sitting astride a fallen log in Epping Forest and eating their picnic lunch. It brought back the yeasty smell of fresh rolls, butter and tangy cheese, the heavy fungoid smell of summer woods. He had rested the pistol on the bark between them and had mumbled at her through the bread and cheese. 'How would you shoot yourself behind the right ear? Go on, Cordelia – show.'

Cordelia had taken the pistol in her right hand, index finger lightly resting on the trigger, and with some difficulty had strained back her arm to place the muzzle of the gun against the base of the skull. 'Like that?' 'You wouldn't, you know. Not if you were used to a gun. That's the little mistake Mrs Clandon made and it nearly hanged her. She shot her husband behind the right ear with his service revolver and then tried to fake a suicide. But she pressed the wrong finger on the trigger. If he'd really shot himself behind the right ear he'd have pressed the trigger with his thumb and held the revolver with his palm round the back of the butt. I remember that case well. It was the first murder I worked on with the Super – Inspector Dalgliesh, as he was then. Mrs Clandon confessed in the end.' 'What happened to her, Bernie?' 'Life. She'd probably have got away with manslaughter if she hadn't tried to fake a suicide. The jury didn't much like what they heard about Major Clandon's little habits.'

But Miss Leaming couldn't get away with manslaughter; not unless she told the whole story of Mark's death.

She was back in the room now. She handed Cordelia a pair of thin cotton gloves. Cordelia said:

'I think you'd better wait outside. What you don't see you won't have the trouble of forgetting. What were you doing when you met me in the hall?'

'I was getting myself a nightcap, a whisky.'

'Then you would have met me again coming out of the study

as you took it up to your room. Get it now and leave the glass on the side table in the hall. That's the kind of detail the police are trained to notice.'

Alone again, Cordelia took up the gun. It was astonishing how repulsive she found this inert weight of metal now. How odd that she should ever have seen it as a harmless toy! She rubbed it thoroughly with the handkerchief erasing Miss Leaming's prints. Then she handled it. It was her gun. They would expect to find some of her prints on the butt together with those of the dead man. She placed it again on the desk top and drew on the gloves. This was the more difficult part. She handled the pistol gingerly and took it over to the inert right hand. She pressed his thumb firmly against the trigger, then wound the cold, unresisting hand round the back of the butt. Then she released his fingers and let the gun fall. It struck the carpet with a dull thud. She peeled off the gloves and went out to Miss Leaming in the hall, closing the study door quietly behind her.

'Here, you'd better put these back where you found them. We mustn't leave them lying around for the police to find.'

She was gone only a few seconds. When she returned, Cordelia said:

'Now we must act the rest just as it would have happened. You meet me as I come out of the room. I have been with Sir Ronald about two minutes. You put down your glass of whisky on the hall table and walk with me to the front door. You say – what would you say?'

'Has he paid you?'

'No, I'm to come in the morning for my money. I'm sorry it wasn't a success. I've told Sir Ronald that I don't want to go on with the case.'

'That's your concern, Miss Gray. It was a foolish business in the first place.'

They were walking out of the front door now. Suddenly Miss Leaming turned to Cordelia and said urgently and in her normal voice:

'There's one thing you had better know. It was I who found Mark first and faked the suicide. He'd rung me earlier in the day and asked me to call. I couldn't get away until after nine because of Lunn. I didn't want him to be suspicious.'

'But didn't it occur to you when you found Mark that there might be something odd about the death? The door was unlocked although the curtains were drawn. The lipstick was missing.'

'I suspected nothing until tonight when I stood in the shadows and heard you talking. We're all sexually sophisticated these days. I believed what I saw. It was all horror but I knew what I had to do. I worked quickly, terrified that someone would come. I cleaned his face with my handkerchief dampened with water from the kitchen sink. It seemed that the lipstick would never come off. I undressed him and pulled on his jeans which had been thrown over the back of a chair. I didn't wait to put on his shoes, that didn't seem important. Typing the note was the worst part. I knew that he would have his Blake with him somewhere in the cottage and that the passage I chose might be more convincing than an ordinary suicide note. The clattering of the typewriter keys sounded unnaturally loud in the quietness; I was terrified that someone would hear. He had been keeping a kind of journal. There wasn't time to read it but I burnt the typescript in the sitting-room grate. Last of all, I bundled up the clothes and the pictures and brought them back here to be burnt in the lab incinerator.'

'You dropped one of the pictures in the garden. And you didn't quite succeed in cleaning the lipstick from his face.'

'So that's how you guessed?'

Cordelia didn't reply immediately. Whatever happened she must keep Isabelle de Lasterie out of the case.

'I wasn't sure if it was you who had been there first but I thought it must have been. There were four things. You didn't want me to investigate Mark's death; you read English at Cambridge and could have known where to find that Blake quotation; you are an experienced typist and I didn't think that the note had been typed by an amateur despite the late attempt to make it look like Mark's work; when I was first at Garforth House and asked about the suicide note you spoke the whole of the Blake quotation; the typed version was ten words short. I first noticed that when I visited the police station and was shown the note. It pointed direct to you. That was the strongest evidence I had.'

They had reached the car now and paused together. Cordelia said:

'We mustn't waste any more time before ringing the police. Someone may have heard the shot.'

'It's not likely. We're some distance from the village. Do we hear it now?'

'Yes. We hear it now.' There was a second's pause then Cordelia said:

'What was that? It sounded like a shot.'

'It couldn't have been. It was probably a car backfiring.'

Miss Leaming spoke like a bad actress, the words were stilted, unconvincing. But she spoke them; she would remember them.

'But there isn't a car passing. And it came from the house.'

They glanced at each other, then ran back together through the open door into the hall. Miss Leaming paused for a moment and looked Cordelia in the face before she opened the study door. Cordelia came in behind her. Miss Leaming said:

'He's been shot! I'd better phone the police.'

Cordelia said:

'You wouldn't say that! Don't ever think like that! You'd go up to the body first and then you'd say:

'"He's shot himself. I'd better phone the police."'

Miss Leaming looked unemotionally at her lover's body, then glanced round the room. Forgetting her role, she asked:

'What have you done in here? What about fingerprints?'

'Never mind. I've looked after that. All you have to remember is that you didn't know I had a gun when I first came to Garforth House; you didn't know Sir Ronald took it from me. You haven't seen that gun until this moment. When I arrived tonight you showed me into the study and met me again when I came out two minutes later. We walked together to the car and spoke as we have just spoken. We heard the shot. We did what we have just done. Forget everything else that has happened. When they question you, don't embroider, don't invent, don't be afraid to say you can't remember. And now – ring the Cambridge police.'

Three minutes later they were standing together at the open door waiting for the police to arrive. Miss Leaming said:

'We mustn't talk together once they're here. And, afterwards, we mustn't meet or show any particular interest in each other. They'll know that this can't be murder unless we two are in it together. And why should we conspire together when we've only met once before, when we don't even like each other?'

She was right, thought Cordelia. They didn't even like each other. She didn't really care if Elizabeth Leaming went to prison; she did care if Mark's mother went to prison. She cared, too, that the truth of his death should never be known. The strength of that determination struck her as irrational. It could make no difference to him now and he wasn't a boy who had cared over much what people thought of him. But Ronald Callender had desecrated his body after death; had planned to make him an object, at worse of contempt, at best of pity. She had set her face against Ronald Callender. She hadn't wanted him to die; wouldn't have been capable herself of pressing the trigger. But he was dead and she couldn't feel regret, nor could she be an instrument of retribution for his murderer. It was expedient, no more than that, that Miss Leaming shouldn't be punished. Gazing out into the summer night and waiting for the sound of the police cars, Cordelia accepted once and for all the enormity and the justification of what she had done and was still planning to do. She was never afterwards to feel the least tinge of regret or of remorse.

Miss Leaming said:

'There are things you probably want to ask me, things I suppose you've a right to know. We can meet in King's College Chapel after Evensong on the first Sunday after the inquest. I'll go through the screen into the chancel, you stay in the nave. It will seem natural enough for us to meet by chance there, that is if we are both still free.'

Cordelia was interested to see that Miss Leaming was taking charge again. She said:

'We shall be. If we keep our heads this can't go wrong.'

There was a moment's silence. Miss Leaming said:

'They're taking their time. Surely they should be here by now?'

'They won't be much longer.'

Miss Leaming suddenly laughed and said with revealing bitterness:

'What is there to be frightened of? We shall be dealing only with men.'

So they waited quietly together. They heard the approaching cars before the headlamps swept over the drive, illuminating every pebble, picking out the small plants at the edge of the beds, bathing the blue haze of the wisteria with light, dazzling the watchers' eyes. Then the lights were dimmed as the cars rocked gently to a stop in front of the house. Dark shapes emerged and came unhurriedly but resolutely forward. The hall was suddenly filled with large, calm men, some in plain clothes. Cordelia effaced herself against the wall and it was Miss Leaming who stepped forward, spoke to them in a low voice and led them into the study.

Two uniformed men were left in the hall. They stood talking together, taking no notice of Cordelia. Their colleagues were taking their time. They must have used the telephone in the study because more cars and men began to arrive. First the police surgeon, identified by his bag even if he hadn't been greeted with:

'Good evening Doc. In here please.'

How often he must have heard that phrase! He glanced with brief curiosity at Cordelia as he trotted through the hall, a fat, dishevelled little man, his face crumpled and petulant as a child when forcibly woken from sleep. Next came a civilian photographer carrying his camera, tripod and box of equipment; a fingerprint expert; two other civilians who Cordelia, instructed in procedure by Bernie, guessed were scene-of-crime officers. So they were treating this as a suspicious death. And why not? It was suspicious.

The head of the household lay dead, but the house itself seemed to have come alive. The police talked, not in whispers, but in confident normal voices unsubdued by death. They were professionals doing their job, working easily to the prescribed routine. They had been initiated into the mysteries of violent death; its victims held no awe for them. They had seen too many bodies: bodies scraped off motorways; loaded piecemeal into ambulances; dragged by hook and net from the depths of rivers; dug putrefying from the clogging earth. Like doctors, they were kind and condescendingly gentle to the uninstructed, keeping inviolate their awful knowledge. This body, while it breathed, had been more important than others. It wasn't important now, but it could still make trouble for them. They would be that much more meticulous, that much more tactful. But it was still only a case.

Cordelia sat alone and waited. She was suddenly overcome with tiredness. She longed for nothing but to put down her head on the hall table and sleep. She was hardly aware of Miss Leaming passing through the hall on her way to the drawing-room, of the tall officer talking to her as they passed. Neither took any notice of the small figure in its immense woollen jersey, sitting against the wall. Cordelia willed herself to stay awake. She knew what she had to say; it was all clear enough in her mind. If only they would come to question her and let her sleep.

It wasn't until the photographer and the print man had finished their work that one of the senior officers came out to her. She was never afterwards able to recall his face but she remembered his voice, a careful, unemphatic voice from which every tinge of emotion had been excluded. He held out the gun towards her. It was resting on his open palm, protected by a handkerchief from the contamination of his hand.

'Do you recognize this weapon, Miss Gray?'

Cordelia thought it odd that he should use the word weapon. Why not just say gun?

'I think so. I think it must be mine.'

'You aren't sure?'

'It must be mine, unless Sir Ronald owned one of the same make. He took it from me when I first came here four or five days ago. He promised to let me have it back when I called tomorrow morning for my pay.'

'So this is only the second time you've been in this house?'

'Yes.'

'Have you ever met Sir Ronald Callender or Miss Leaming before?'

'No. Not until Sir Ronald sent for me to undertake this case.'

He went away. Cordelia rested her head back against the wall and took short snatches of sleep. Another officer came. This time he had a uniformed man with him, taking notes. There were more questions. Cordelia told her prepared story. They wrote it down without comment and went away.

She must have dozed. She awoke to find a tall, uniformed officer standing over her. He said:

'Miss Leaming is making tea in the kitchen, Miss. Perhaps you would like to give her a hand. It's something to do, isn't it?'

Cordelia thought; they're going to take away the body. She said:

'I don't know where the kitchen is.'

She saw his eyes flicker.

'Oh, don't you, Miss? You're a stranger here, are you? Well, it's this way.'

The kitchen was at the back of the house. It smelt of spice, oil and tomato sauce, bringing back memories of meals in Italy with her father. Miss Leaming was taking down cups from a vast dresser. An electric kettle was already hissing steam. The police officer stayed. So they weren't to be left alone. Cordelia said:

'Can I help?' Miss Leaming did not look at her.

'There are some biscuits in that tin. You can put them out on a tray. The milk is in the fridge.'

Cordelia moved like an automaton. The milk bottle was an icy column in her hands, the biscuit tin lid resisted her tired fingers and she broke a nail prising it off. She noticed the details of the kitchen – a wall calendar of St Theresa of Avila, the saint's face unnaturally elongated and pale so that she looked like a hallowed Miss Leaming; a china donkey with two panniers of artificial flowers, its melancholy head crowned with a miniature straw hat; an immense blue bowl of brown eggs.

There were two trays. The police constable took the larger from Miss Leaming and led the way into the hall. Cordelia followed with the second tray, holding it high against her chest like a child, permitted as a privilege to help mother. Police officers gathered round. She took a cup herself and returned to her usual chair.

And now there was the sound of yet another car. A middle-aged woman came in with a uniformed chauffeur at her shoulder. Through the fog of her tiredness, Cordelia heard a high, didactic voice.

'My dear Eliza, this is appalling! You must come back to the Lodge tonight. No, I insist. Is the Chief Constable here?'

'No, Marjorie, but these officers have been very kind.'

'Leave them the key. They'll lock up the house when they've finished. You can't possibly stay here alone tonight.'

There were introductions, hurried consultations with the detectives in which the newcomer's voice was dominant. Miss Leaming went upstairs with her visitor and reappeared five minutes later with a small case, her coat over her arm. They went off together, escorted to the car by the chauffeur and one of the detectives. None of the little party glanced at Cordelia.

Five minutes later the Inspector came up to Cordelia, key in hand.

'We shall lock up the house tonight, Miss Gray. It's time you were getting home. Are you thinking of staying at the cottage?'

'Just for the next few days, if Major Markland will let me.'

'You look very tired. One of my men will drive you in your own car. I should like a written statement from you tomorrow. Can you come to the station as soon as possible after breakfast? You know where it is?'

'Yes, I know.'

One of the police panda cars drove off first and the Mini followed. The police driver drove fast, lurching the little car around the corners. Cordelia's head lolled against the back of the seat and, from time to time, was thrown against the driver's arm. He was wearing shirt sleeves and she was vaguely conscious of the comfort of the warm flesh through the cotton. The car window was open and she was aware of hot night air rushing against her face, of the scudding clouds, of the first unbelievable colours of the day staining the eastern sky. The route seemed strange to her and time itself disjointed; she wondered why the car had suddenly stopped and it took a minute for her to recognize the tall hedge bending over the lane like a menacing shadow, the ramshackle gate. She was home. The driver said:

'Is this the place, Miss?'

'Yes, this is it. But I usually leave the Mini further down the lane on the right. There's a copse there where you can drive it off the road.'

'Right, Miss.'

He got out of the car to consult the other driver. They moved on slowly for the last few yards of the journey. And now, at last, the police car had driven away and she was alone at the gate. It was an effort to push it open against the weight of the weeds and she lurched round the cottage to the back door like a drunken creature. It took some little time to fit the key into the lock, but that was the last problem. There was no longer a gun to hide; there was no longer need to check the tape sealing the windows. Lunn was dead and she was alive. Every night that she had slept at the cottage Cordelia had come home tired, but never before had she been as tired as this. She made her way upstairs as if sleepwalking and, too exhausted even to zip herself into her sleeping-bag, crept underneath it and knew nothing more.

And at last – it seemed to Cordelia after months, not days, of waiting – there was another inquest. It was as unhurried, as unostentatiously formal, as Bernie's had been, but there was a difference. Here, instead of a handful of pathetic casuals who had sneaked into the warmth of the back benches to hear Bernie's obsequies, were grave-faced colleagues and friends, muted voices, the whispered preliminaries of lawyers and police, an indefinable sense of occasion. Cordelia guessed that the grey-haired man escorting Miss Leaming must be her lawyer. She watched him at work, affable but not deferential to the senior police, quietly solicitous for his client, exuding a confidence that they were all engaged in a necessary if tedious formality, a ritual as unworrying as Sunday Matins.

Miss Leaming looked very pale. She was wearing the grey suit she had worn when Cordelia first met her but with a small black hat, black gloves and a black chiffon scarf knotted at her throat. The two women did not look at each other. Cordelia found a seat at the end of a bench and sat there, unrepresented and alone. One or two of the younger policemen smiled at her with a reassuring but pitying kindness.

Miss Leaming gave her evidence first in a low, composed voice. She affirmed instead of taking the oath, a decision which caused a brief spasm of distress to pass over her lawyer's face. But she gave him no further cause for concern. She testified that Sir Ronald had been depressed at his son's death and, she thought, had blamed himself for not knowing that something was worrying Mark. He had told her that he intended to call in a private detective, and it had been she who had originally interviewed Miss Gray and had brought her back to Garforth House. Miss Leaming said that she had opposed the suggestion; she had seen no useful purpose in it, and thought that this futile and fruitless inquiry would only remind Sir Ronald of the tragedy. She had not known that Miss Gray possessed a gun nor that Sir Ronald had taken it from her. She had not been present during the whole of their preliminary interview. Sir Ronald had escorted Miss Gray to view his son's room while she, Miss Leaming, had gone in search of a photograph of Mr Callender for which Miss Gray had asked.

The coroner asked her gently about the night of Sir Ronald's death.

Miss Leaming said that Miss Gray had arrived to give her first report shortly after half-past ten. She herself had been passing through the front hall when the girl appeared. Miss Leaming had pointed out that it was late, but Miss Gray had said that she wanted to abandon the case and get back to town. She had showed Miss Gray into the study where Sir Ronald was working. They had been together, she thought, for less than two minutes. Miss Gray had then come out of the study and she had walked with her to her car; they had only talked briefly. Miss Gray said that Sir Ronald had asked her to call back in the morning for her pay. She had made no mention of a gun.

Sir Ronald had, only half an hour before that, received a telephone call from the police to say that his laboratory assistant, Christopher Lunn, had been killed in a road accident. She had not told Miss Gray the news about Lunn before her interview with Sir Ronald; it hadn't occurred to her to do so. The girl had gone almost immediately into the study to see Sir Ronald. Miss Leaming said that they were standing together at the car talking when they heard the shot. At first she had thought it was a car backfiring but then she had realized that it had come from the house. They had both rushed into the study and found Sir Ronald lying slumped over his desk. The gun had dropped from his hand to the floor.

No, Sir Ronald had never given her any idea that he contemplated suicide. She thought that he was very distressed about the death of Mr Lunn but it was difficult to tell. Sir Ronald was not a man to show emotion. He had been working very hard recently and had not seemed himself since the death of his son. But Miss Leaming had never for a moment thought that Sir Ronald was a man who might put an end to his life.

She was followed by the police witnesses, deferential, professional, but managing to give an impression that none of this was new to them; they had seen it all before and would see it again.

They were followed by the doctors, including the pathologist, who testified in what the court obviously thought was unnecessary detail to the effect of firing a jacketed hollow-cavity bullet of ninety grains into the human brain. The coroner asked:

'You have heard the police evidence that there was the print of Sir Ronald Callender's thumb on the trigger of the gun and a palm marked smudged around the butt. What would you deduce from that?'

The pathologist looked slightly surprised at being asked to deduce anything but said that it was apparent that Sir Ronald had held the gun with his thumb on the trigger when pointing it against his head. The pathologist thought that it was probably the most comfortable way, having regard to the position of the wound of entry.

Lastly, Cordelia was called to the witness box and took the oath. She had given some thought to the propriety of this and had wondered whether to follow Miss Leaming's example. There were moments, usually on a sunny Easter morning, when she wished that she could with sincerity call herself a Christian; but for the rest of the year she knew herself to be what she was – incurably agnostic but prone to unpredictable relapses into faith. This seemed to her, however, a moment when religious scrupulosity was an indulgence which she couldn't afford. The lies she was about to tell would not be the more heinous because they were tinged with blasphemy.

The coroner let her tell her story without interruption. She sensed that the court was puzzled by her but not unsympathetic. For once, the carefully modulated middle-class accent, which in her six years at the convent she had unconsciously acquired, and which in other people often irritated her as much as her own voice had irritated her father, was proving an advantage. She wore her suit and had bought a black chiffon scarf to cover her head. She remembered that she must call the coroner 'sir'.

After she had briefly confirmed Miss Leaming's story of how she had been called to the case, the coroner said:

'And now, Miss Gray, will you explain to the court what happened on the night Sir Ronald Callender died?'

'I had decided, sir, that I didn't want to go on with the case. I hadn't discovered anything useful and I didn't think there was anything to discover. I had been living in the cottage where Mark Callender had spent the last weeks of his life and I had come to think that what I was doing was wrong, that I was taking money for prying into his private life. I decided on impulse to tell Sir Ronald that I wanted to finish the case. I drove to Garforth House. I got there about ten-thirty. I knew it was late but I was anxious to get back to London the next morning. I saw Miss Leaming as she was crossing the hall and she showed me straight into the study.'

'Will you please describe to the court how you found Sir Ronald?'

'He seemed to be tired and distracted. I tried to explain why I wanted to give up the case but I'm not sure that he heard me. He said I was to come back next morning for my money and I said that I had only proposed to charge expenses, but that I would like to have my gun. He just waved a hand in dismissal and said, "Tomorrow morning, Miss Gray. Tomorrow morning."'

'And then you left him?'

'Yes, sir. Miss Leaming accompanied me back to the car and I was just about to drive away when we heard the shot.'

'You didn't see the gun in Sir Ronald's possession while you were in the study with him?'

'No, sir.'

'He didn't talk to you about Mr Lunn's death or give you any idea that he was contemplating suicide?'

'No, sir.'

The coroner doodled on the pad before him. Without looking at Cordelia, he said:

'And now, Miss Gray, will you please explain to the court how Sir Ronald came to have your gun.'

This was the difficult part, but Cordelia had rehearsed it. The Cambridge police had been very thorough. They had asked the same questions over and over again. She knew exactly how Sir Ronald had come to have the gun. She remembered a piece of Dalgliesh dogma, reported by Bernie, which had seemed to her at the time more appropriate advice for a criminal than a detective. 'Never tell an unnecessary lie; the truth has great authority. The cleverest murderers have been caught, not because they told the one essential lie, but because they continued to lie about unimportant detail when the truth could have done them no harm.'

She said:

'My partner, Mr Pryde, owned the gun and was very proud of it. When he killed himself I knew that he meant me to have it. That was why he cut his wrists instead of shooting himself, which would have been quicker and easier.'

The coroner looked up sharply.

'And were you there when he killed himself?'

'No, sir. But I found the body.'

There was a murmur of sympathy from the court; she could feel their concern.

'Did you know that the gun wasn't licensed?'

'No, sir, but I think I suspected that it might not have been. I brought it with me on this case because I didn't want to leave it in the office and because I found it a comfort. I meant to check up on the licence as soon as I got back. I didn't expect ever to use the gun. I didn't really think of it as a lethal weapon. It's just that this was my first case and Bernie had left it to me and I felt happier having it with me.'

'I see,' said the coroner.

Cordelia thought that he probably did see and so did the court. They were having no difficulty in believing her because she was telling the somewhat improbable truth. Now that she was about to lie, they would go on believing her.

'And now will you please tell the court how Sir Ronald came to take the gun from you?'

'It was on my first visit to Garforth House when Sir Ronald was showing me his son's bedroom. He knew that I was the sole owner of the Agency, and he asked me if it wasn't a difficult and rather frightening job for a woman. I said that I wasn't frightened but that I had Bernie's gun. When he found that I had it with me in my bag he made me hand it over to him. He said that he didn't propose to engage someone who might be a danger to other people or herself. He said that he wouldn't take the responsibility. He took the gun and the ammunition.'

'And what did he do with the gun?'

Cordelia had thought this one out carefully. Obviously he hadn't carried it downstairs in his hand or Miss Leaming would have seen it. She would have liked to have said that he put it into a drawer in Mark's room but she couldn't remember whether the bedside table had had any drawers. She said:

'He took it out of the room with him; he didn't tell me where. He was only away for a moment and then we went downstairs together.'

'And you didn't set eyes on the gun again until you saw it on the floor close to Sir Ronald's hand when you and Miss Leaming found his body?'

'No, sir.'

Cordelia was the last witness. The verdict was quickly given, one that the court obviously felt would have been agreeable to Sir Ronald's scrupulously exact and scientific brain. It was that the deceased had taken his own life but that there was no evidence as to the state of his mind. The coroner delivered at length the obligatory warning about the danger of guns. Guns, the court were informed, could kill people. He managed to convey that unlicensed guns were particularly prone to this danger. He pronounced no strictures on Cordelia personally although it was apparent that this restraint cost him an effort. He rose and the court rose with him.

After the coroner had left the bench the court broke up into little whispering groups. Miss Leaming was quickly surrounded. Cordelia saw her shaking hands, receiving condolences, listening with grave assenting face to the first tentative proposals for a memorial service. Cordelia wondered how she could ever have feared that Miss Leaming would be suspected. She herself stood a little apart, delinquent. She knew that the police would charge her with illegal possession of the gun. They could do no less. True, she would be lightly punished, if punished at all. But for the rest of her life she would be the girl whose carelessness and naïveté had lost England one of her foremost scientists.

As Hugo had said, all Cambridge suicides were brilliant. But about this one there could be little doubt. Sir Ronald's death would probably raise him to the status of genius.

Almost unnoticed, she came alone out of the courtroom on to Market Hill. Hugo must have been waiting; now he fell into step with her.

'How did it go? I must say death seems to follow you around, doesn't it?'

'It went all right. I seem to follow death.'

'I suppose he did shoot himself?'

'Yes. He shot himself.'

'And with your gun?'

'As you will know if you were in court. I didn't see you.'

'I wasn't there, I had a tutorial, but the news did get around. I shouldn't let it worry you. Ronald Callender wasn't as important as some people in Cambridge may choose to believe.'

'You know nothing about him. He was a human being and he's dead. The fact is always important.'

'It isn't, you know, Cordelia. Death is the least important thing about us. Comfort yourself with Joseph Hall. "Death borders upon our birth and our cradle stands in the grave." And he did choose his own weapon, his own time. He'd had enough of himself. Plenty of people had had enough of him.'

They walked together down St Edward's Passage towards King's Parade. Cordelia wasn't sure where they were making for. Her need at present was just to walk, but she didn't find her companion disagreeable.

She asked:

'Where's Isabelle?'

'Isabelle is home in Lyons. Papa turned up unexpectedly yesterday and found that mademoiselle wasn't exactly earning her wages. Papa decided that dear Isabelle was getting less – or it may have been more – out of her Cambridge education than he had expected. I don't think you need worry about her. Isabelle is safe enough now. Even if the police do decide that it's worthwhile going to France to question her – and why on earth should they? – it won't help them. Papa will surround her with a barrage of lawyers. He's not in a mood to stand any nonsense from Englishmen at present.'

'And what about you? If anyone asks you how Mark died, you'll never tell them the truth?'

'What do you think? Sophie, Davie and I are safe enough. I'm reliable when it comes to essentials.'

For a moment Cordelia wished that he were reliable in less essential matters. She asked:

'Are you sorry about Isabelle leaving?'

'I am rather. Beauty is intellectually confusing; it sabotages common sense. I could never quite accept that Isabelle was what she is: a generous, indolent, over-affectionate and stupid young woman. I thought that any woman as beautiful as she must have an instinct about life, access to some secret wisdom which is beyond cleverness. Every time she opened that delicious mouth I was expecting her to illumine life. I think I could have spent all my life just looking at her and waiting for the oracle. And all she could talk about was clothes.'

'Poor Hugo.'

'Never poor Hugo. I'm not unhappy. The secret of contentment is never to allow yourself to want anything which reason tells you you haven't a chance of getting.'

Cordelia thought that he was young, well off, clever, even if not clever enough, handsome; there wasn't much that he would have to forgo on that or any other criteria.

She heard him speaking:

'Why not stay in Cambridge for a week or so and let me show you the city? Sophie would let you have her spare room.'

'No thank you, Hugo. I have to get back to town.'

There was nothing in town for her, but with Hugo there would be nothing in Cambridge for her either. There was only one reason for staying in this city. She would remain at the cottage until Sunday and her meeting with Miss Leaming. After that, as far as she was concerned, the case of Mark Callender would be finished for good.

Sunday afternoon Evensong was over and the congregation, who had listened in respectful silence to the singing of responses, psalms and anthem by one of the finest choirs in the world, rose and joined with joyous abandon in the final hymn. Cordelia rose and sang with them. She had seated herself at the end of the row close to the richly carved screen. From here she could see into the chancel. The robes of the choristers gleamed scarlet and white; the candles flickered in patterned rows and high circles of golden light; two tall and slender candles stood each side of the softly illuminated Reubens above the high altar, seen dimly as a distant smudge of crimson, blue and gold. The blessing was pronounced, the final amen impeccably sung and the choir began to file decorously out of the chancel. The south door was opened and sunlight flooded into the chapel. The members of the college who had attended divine service strolled out after the Provost and Fellows in casual disarray, their regulation surplices dingy and limp over a cheerful incongruity of corduroy and tweed. The great organ snuffled and groaned like an animal gathering breath, before giving forth its magnificent voice in a Bach fugue. Cordelia sat quietly in her chair, listening and waiting. Now the congregation was moving down the main aisle – small groups in bright summer cottons whispering discreetly, serious young men in sober Sunday black, tourists clutching their illustrated guides and half embarrassed by their obtrusive cameras, a group of nuns with calm and cheerful faces.

Miss Leaming was one of the last, a tall figure in a grey linen dress and white gloves, her head bare, a white cardigan slung carelessly around her shoulders against the chill of the chapel. She was obviously alone and unwatched and her careful pretence of surprise at recognizing Cordelia was probably an unnecessary precaution. They passed out of the chapel together.

The gravel path outside the doorway was thronged with people. A little party of Japanese, festooned with cameras and accessories, added their high staccato jabber to the muted Sunday afternoon chat. From here the silver stream of the Cam was invisible but the truncated bodies of punters glided against the far bank like puppets in a show, raising their arms above the pole and turning to thrust it backwards as if participating in some ritual dance. The great lawn lay unshadowed in the sun, a quintessence of greenness staining the scented air. A frail and elderly Don in gown and mortarboard was limping across the grass; the sleeves of his gown caught a stray breeze and billowed out so that he looked like a winged and monstrous crow struggling to rise. Miss Leaming said, as if Cordelia had asked for an explanation:

'He's a Fellow. The sacred turf is, therefore, uncontaminated by his feet.'

They walked in silence by Gibbs Building. Cordelia wondered when Miss Leaming would speak. When she did, her first question was unexpected.

'Do you think you'll make a success of it?'

Sensing Cordelia's surprise, she added impatiently:

'The Detective Agency. Do you think you'll be able to cope?'

'I shall have to try. It's the only job I know.'

She had no intention of justifying to Miss Leaming her affection and loyalty to Bernie; she would have had some difficulty in explaining it to herself.

'Your overheads are too high.'

It was a pronouncement made with all the authority of a verdict.

'Do you mean the office and the Mini?' asked Cordelia.

'Yes. In your job I don't see how one person in the field can bring in sufficient income to cover expenses. You can't be sitting in the office taking orders and typing letters and be out solving cases at the same time. On the other hand, I don't suppose you can afford help.'

'Not yet. I've been thinking that I might rent a telephone answering service. That will take care of the orders although, of course, clients much prefer to come to the office and discuss their case. If I can only make enough in expenses just to live, then any fees can cover the overheads.'

'If there are any fees.'

There seemed nothing to say to this and they walked on in silence for a few seconds. Then Miss Leaming said:

'There'll be the expenses from this case anyway. That at least should help towards your fine for illegal possession of the gun. I've put the matter in the hands of my solicitors. You should be getting a cheque fairly soon.'

'I don't want to take any money for this case.'

'I can understand that. As you pointed out to Ronald, it falls under your fair deal clause. Strictly speaking you aren't entitled to any. All the same, I think it would look less suspicious if you took your expenses. Would thirty pounds strike you as reasonable?'

'Perfectly, thank you.'

They had reached the corner of the lawn and had turned to walk towards King's Bridge. Miss Leaming said:

'I shall have to be grateful to you for the rest of my life. That for me is an unaccustomed humility and I'm not sure that I like it.'

'Then don't feel it. I was thinking of Mark, not of you.'

'I thought you might have acted in the service of justice or some such abstraction.'

'I wasn't thinking about any abstraction. I was thinking about a person.'

They had reached the bridge now and leaned over it side by side to look down into the bright water. The paths leading up to the bridge were, for a few minutes, empty of people. Miss Leaming said:

'Pregnancy isn't difficult to fake, you know. It only needs a loose corset and judicious stuffing. It's humiliating for the woman of course, almost indecent if she happens to be barren. But it isn't difficult, particularly if she isn't closely watched. Evelyn wasn't. She had always been a shy, self-contained woman. People expected her to be excessively modest about her pregnancy. Garforth House wasn't filled with friends and relations swapping horror stories about the antenatal clinic and patting her stomach. We had to get rid of that tedious fool Nanny Pilbeam, of course. Ronald regarded her departure as one of the subsidiary benefits of the pseudo pregnancy. He was tired of being spoken to as if he were still Ronnie Callender, the bright grammar school boy from Harrogate.'

Cordelia said:

'Mrs Goddard told me that Mark had a great look of his mother.'

'She would. She was sentimental as well as stupid.'

Cordelia did not speak. After a few moments' silence Miss Leaming went on:

'I discovered that I was carrying Ronald's child at about the same time as a London specialist confirmed what the three of us already guessed, that Evelyn was most unlikely to conceive. I wanted to have the baby; Ronald desperately wanted a son; Evelyn's father was obsessional about his need for a grandson and was willing to part with half a million to prove it. It was all so easy. I resigned from my teaching job and went off to the safe anonymity of London and Evelyn told her father she was pregnant at last. Neither Ronald nor I had any conscience about defrauding George Bottley. He was an arrogant, brutal, self-satisfied fool who couldn't imagine how the world would continue without his issue to supervise it. He even subsidized his own deceit. The cheques for Evelyn began to arrive, each with a note imploring her to look after her health, to consult the best London doctors, to rest, to take a holiday in the sun. She had always loved Italy, and Italy became part of the plan. The three of us would meet in London every two months and fly together to Pisa. Ronald would rent a small villa outside Florence and, once there, I became Mrs Callender and Evelyn became me. We had only daily servants and there was no need for them to look at our passports. They got used to our visits and so did the local doctor who was called in to supervise my health. The locals thought it flattering that the English lady should be so fond of Italy that she came back month after month, so close to her confinement.'

Cordelia asked:

'But how could she do it, how could she bear to be there with you in the house, watching you with her husband, knowing that you were going to have his child?'

'She did it because she loved Ronald and couldn't bear to lose him. She hadn't been much success as a woman. If she lost her husband, what else was there for her? She couldn't have gone back to her father. Besides, we had a bribe for her. She was to have the child. If she refused, then Ronald would leave her and seek a divorce to marry me.'

'I would rather have left him and gone off to scrub doorsteps.'

'Not everyone has a talent for scrubbing doorsteps and not everyone has your capacity for moral indignation. Evelyn was religious. She was, therefore, practised in self-deception. She convinced herself that what we were doing was best for the child.'

'And her father? Didn't he ever suspect?'

'He despised her for her piety. He always had. Psychologically he could hardly indulge that dislike and at the same time think her capable of deceit. Besides, he desperately needed that grandchild. It wouldn't have entered his mind that the child might not be hers. And he had a doctor's report. After our third visit to Italy we told Dr Sartori that Mrs Callender's father was concerned about her care. At our request he wrote a reassuring medical report on the progress of the pregnancy. We went to Florence together a fortnight before the baby was due and stayed there until Mark arrived. Luckily he was a day or two before time. We'd had the foresight to put back the expected date of delivery so that it genuinely looked as if Evelyn had been caught unexpectedly by a premature birth. Dr Sartori did what was necessary with perfect competence and the three of us came home with the baby and a birth certificate in the right name.'

Cordelia said:

'And nine months later Mrs Callender was dead.'

'He didn't kill her, if that's what you're thinking. He wasn't really the monster that you imagine, at least, not then. But in a sense we did both destroy her. She should have had a specialist, certainly a better doctor than that incompetent fool Gladwin. But the three of us were desperately afraid that an efficient doctor would know that she hadn't borne a child. She was as worried as we were. She insisted that no other doctor be consulted. She had grown to love the baby, you see. So she died and was cremated and we thought we were safe for ever.'

'She left Mark a note before she died, nothing but a scribbled hieroglyphic in her prayer book. She left him her blood group.'

'We knew that the blood groups were a danger. Ronald took blood from the three of us and made the necessary tests. But after she was dead even that worry ended.'

There was a long silence. Cordelia could see a little group of tourists moving down the path towards the bridge. Miss Leaming said:

'The irony of it is that Ronald never really loved him. Mark's grandfather adored him; there was no difficulty there. He left half his fortune to Evelyn and it came automatically to her husband. Mark was to get the other half on his twenty-fifth birthday. But Ronald never cared for his son. He found that he couldn't love him, and I wasn't allowed to. I watched him grow up and go to school. But I wasn't allowed to love him. I used to knit him endless jerseys. It was almost an obsession. The patterns got more intricate and the wool thicker as he grew older. Poor Mark, he must have thought that I was mad, this strange discontented woman whom his father couldn't do without but wouldn't marry.'

'There are one or two of the jerseys at the cottage. What would you like me to do with his things?'

'Take them away and give them to anyone who needs them. Unless you think I ought to unpick the wool and knit it up into something new? Would that be a suitable gesture, do you think, symbolic of wasted effort, pathos, futility?'

'I'll find a use for them. And his books?'

'Get rid of them too. I can't go again to the cottage. Get rid of everything if you will.'

The little group of tourists was very close now but they seemed engrossed in their own chatter. Miss Leaming took an envelope out of her pocket and handed it to Cordelia.

'I've written out a brief confession. There's nothing in it about Mark, nothing about how he died or what you discovered. It's just a brief statement that I shot Ronald Callender immediately after you had left Garforth House and coerced you into supporting my story. You'd better put it somewhere safe. One day you may need it.'

Cordelia saw that the envelope was addressed to herself. She didn't open it. She said:

'It's too late now. If you regret what we did, you should have spoken earlier. The case is closed now.'

'I've no regrets. I'm glad that we acted as we did. But the case may not be over yet.'

'But it is over! The inquest has given its verdict.'

'Ronald had a number of very powerful friends. They have influence and, periodically, they like to exercise it if only to prove that they still have it.'

'But they can't get this case reopened! It practically takes an act of parliament to change a coroner's verdict.'

'I don't say that they'll try to do that. But they may ask questions. They may have what they describe as a quiet word in the right ear. And the right ears are usually available. That's how they work. That's the sort of people they are.'

Cordelia said suddenly:

'Have you a light?'

Without question or protest Miss Leaming opened her handbag and handed over an elegant silver tube. Cordelia didn't smoke and was unused to lighters. It took three clicks before the wick burst into flame. Then she leaned over the parapet of the bridge and set fire to the corner of the envelope.

The incandescent flame was invisible in the stronger light of the sun. All Cordelia could see was a narrow band of wavering purple light as the flame bit into the paper and the charred edges widened and grew. The pungent smell of burning was wafted away on the breeze. As soon as the flame tinged her fingers, Cordelia dropped the envelope, still burning, and watched it twist and turn as it floated down small and frail as a snowflake to be lost at last in the Cam. She said:

'Your lover shot himself. That is all that either of us need to remember now or ever.'

They didn't speak again about Ronald Callender's death, but walked silently along the elm-lined path towards the Backs. At one point Miss Leaming glanced at Cordelia and said in a tone of angry petulance:

'You look surprisingly well!'

Cordelia supposed that this brief outburst was the resentment of the middle-aged at the resilience of the young which could so quickly recover from physical disaster. It had only taken one night of long and deep sleep to return her to the state which Bernie, with irritating coyness, used to describe as bright eyed and bushy tailed. Even without the benison of a hot bath the broken skin on her shoulders and back had healed cleanly. Physically, the events of the last fortnight had left her unscathed. She wasn't so sure about Miss Leaming. The sleek platinum hair was still swathed and shaped immaculately to the bones of the head; she still carried her clothes with cool distinction as if it were important to appear the competent and unharassed helpmate of a famous man. But the pale skin was now tinged with grey; her eyes were deeply shadowed, and the incipient lines at the side of the mouth and across the forehead had deepened so that the face, for the first time, looked old and strained.

They passed through King's Gate and turned to the right. Cordelia had found a place and had parked the Mini within a few yards of the gate; Miss Leaming's Rover was further down Queen's Road. She shook hands firmly but briefly with Cordelia and said goodbye as unemotionally as if they were Cambridge acquaintances, parting with unusual formality after an unexpected meeting at Evensong. She didn't smile. Cordelia watched the tall, angular figure striding down the path under the trees towards John's Gate. She didn't look back. Cordelia wondered when, if ever, they would see each other again. It was difficult to believe that they had met only on four occasions. They had nothing in common except their sex, although Cordelia had realized during the days following Ronald Callender's murder the strength of that female allegiance. As Miss Leaming herself had said, they didn't even like each other. Yet each held the other's safety in her hands. There were moments when their secret almost horrified Cordelia by its immensity. But these were few and would get fewer. Time would inevitably diminish its importance. Life would go on. Neither of them would ever forget completely while the brain cells still lived, but she could believe that a day might come when they would glimpse each other across a theatre or restaurant or be borne unprotestingly past on an underground escalator and would wonder whether what they both recalled in the shock of recognition had really once happened. Already, only four days after the inquest, Ronald Callender's murder was beginning to take its place in the landscape of the past.

There was no longer anything to keep her at the cottage. She spent an hour obsessionally cleaning and tidying rooms which no one would enter, probably for weeks. She watered the mug of cowslips on the sitting-room table. In another three days they would be dead and no one would notice, but she couldn't bear to throw out the still living flowers. She went out to the shed and contemplated the bottle of sour milk and the beef stew. Her first impulse was to take both and empty them down the lavatory. But they were part of the evidence. She wouldn't need that evidence again, but ought it to be completely destroyed? She recalled Bernie's reiterated admonition: 'Never destroy the evidence.' The Super had been full of cautionary tales to emphasize the importance of that maxim. In the end she decided to photograph the exhibits, setting them up on the kitchen table and paying great attention to exposure and light. It seemed a fruitless, somewhat ridiculous, exercise and she was glad when the job was done and the unsavoury contents of bottle and pan could be disposed of. Afterwards she carefully washed them both and left them in the kitchen.

Last of all she packed her bag and stowed her gear in the Mini together with Mark's jerseys and books. Folding the thick wool, she thought of Dr Gladwin sitting in his back garden, his shrunken veins indifferent to the sun. He would find the jerseys useful, but she couldn't take them to him. That kind of gesture might have been accepted from Mark, but not from her.

She locked the door and left the key under a stone. She couldn't face Miss Markland again and had no wish to hand it back to any other member of the family. She would wait until she got to London, then send a brief note to Miss Markland thanking her for her kindness and explaining where the key could be found. She walked for the last time round the garden. She wasn't sure what impulse led her to the well but she came up to it with a shock of surprise. The soil around the rim had been cleared and dug and had been planted with a circle of pansies, daisies and small clumps of alyssum and lobelia, each plant looking well established in its hollow ring of watered earth. It was a bright oasis of colour among the encroaching weeds. The effect was pretty but ridiculous and disquietingly odd. Thus strangely celebrated, the well itself looked obscene, a wooden breast topped by a monstrous nipple. How could she have seen the well cover as a harmless and slightly elegant folly?

Cordelia was torn between pity and revulsion. This must be the work of Miss Markland. The well, which for years had been to her an object of horror, remorse and reluctant fascination, was now to be tended as a shrine. It was ludicrous and pitiable and Cordelia wished that she hadn't seen it. She was suddenly terrified of meeting Miss Markland, of seeing the incipient madness in her eyes. She almost ran out of the garden, pulled the gate shut against the weight of the weeds and drove finally away from the cottage without a backward glance. The case of Mark Callender was finished.

CHAPTER SEVEN

Next morning she went to the Kingly Street office promptly at nine o'clock. The unnaturally hot weather had broken at last and when she opened the window, a keen breeze shifted the layers of dust on desk and filing cabinet. There was only one letter. This was in a long stiff envelope and was headed with the name and address of Ronald Callender's solicitors. It was very brief.

'Dear Madam, I enclose a cheque for £30.00 being expenses due to you in respect of the investigation which you carried out at the request of the late Sir Ronald Callender into the death of his son Mark Callender. If you agree this sum, I would be grateful if you would sign and return the attached receipt.'

Well, as Miss Leaming had said, it would at least pay part of the fine. She had sufficient money to keep the Agency going for another month. If there were no further cases by that time, there was always Miss Feakins and another temporary job. Cordelia thought of the Feakins Secretarial Agency without enthusiasm. Miss Feakins operated, and that was the appropriate word, from a small office as squalid as Cordelia's own, but which had a desperate gaiety imposed upon it in the form of multi-coloured walls, paper flowers in a variety of urn-like containers, china ornaments and a poster. The poster had always fascinated Cordelia. A curvaceous blonde, clad in brief hot pants and laughing hysterically, was leap-frogging over her typewriter, a feat she managed to perform with a maximum of exposure while clutching a fistful of five pound notes in each hand. The caption read:
'Be a Girl Friday and join the fun people. All the best Crusoes are on our books.'

Beneath this poster Miss Feakins, emaciated, indefatigably cheerful and tinsled like a Christmas tree, interviewed a dispirited trail of the old, the ugly and the virtually unemployable. Her milch cows seldom escaped into permanent employment. Miss Feakins would warn against the unspecified dangers of accepting a permanent job much as Victorian mothers warned against sex. But Cordelia liked her. Miss Feakins would welcome her back, her defection to Bernie forgiven, and there would be another of those furtive telephone conversations with the fortunate Crusoe, made with one bright eye on Cordelia, a brothel madam recommending her latest recruit to one of her fussier customers. 'Most superior girl – well educated – you'll like her – and a worker!' The emphasis of amazed wonder on the last word was justified. Few of Miss Feakins' temporaries, beguiled by advertisements, seriously expected to have to work. There were other and more efficient agencies but only one Miss Feakins. Bound by pity and an eccentric loyalty, Cordelia had little hope of escaping that glittering eye. A series of temporary jobs with Miss Feakins' Crusoes might, indeed, be all that was left to her. Didn't a conviction for illegal possession of a weapon under Section 1 of the Firearms Act 1968 count as a criminal record, barring one for life from socially responsible and safe jobs in the civil service and local government?

She settled down at the typewriter, with the yellow telephone directory to hand, to finish sending out the circular letter to the last twenty solicitors on the list. The letter itself embarrassed and depressed her. It had been concocted by Bernie after a dozen preliminary drafts and, at the time, it hadn't seemed too unreasonable. But his death and the Callender case had altered everything. The pompous phrases about a comprehensive professional service, immediate attendance in any part of the country, discreet and experienced operators and moderate fees, struck her as ridiculously, even dangerously, pretentious. Wasn't there something about false representation in the Trades Description Act? But the promise of moderate fees and absolute discretion was valid enough. It was a pity, she thought drily, that she couldn't get a reference from Miss Leaming. Alibis arranged; inquests attended; murders efficiently concealed; perjury at our own special rates.

The raucous burr of the telephone startled her. The office was so quiet and still that she had taken it for granted that no one would call. She stared at the instrument for several seconds, wide-eyed and suddenly afraid, before stretching out her hand.

The voice was calm and assured, polite but in no way deferential. It uttered no threat, yet to Cordelia, every word was explicit with menace.

'Miss Cordelia Gray? This is New Scotland Yard. We wondered whether you would be back at your office yet. Could you please make it convenient to call here sometime later today? Chief Superintendent Dalgliesh would like to see you.'

It was ten days later that Cordelia was called for the third time to New Scotland Yard. The bastion of concrete and glass off Victoria Street was, by now, fairly familiar to her although she still entered it with a sense of temporarily discarding part of her identity, like leaving shoes outside a mosque.

Superintendent Dalgliesh had imposed little of his own personality on his room. The books in the regulation bookcase were obviously textbooks on law, copies of regulations and Acts of Parliament, dictionaries and books of reference. The only picture was a large water-colour of the old Norman Shaw building on the Embankment painted from the river, an agreeable study in greys and soft ochres lit by the bright golden wings of the RAF Memorial. On this visit, as on previous occasions, there was a bowl of roses on his desk, garden roses with sturdy stems and thorns curved like strong beaks, not the etiolated scentless blooms of a West End florist.

Bernie had never described him; had only fathered on him his own obsessive, unheroic, rough-hewn philosophy. Cordelia, bored by his very name, had asked no questions. But the Superintendent she had pictured was very different from the tall, austere figure who had risen to shake her hand when she first came into this room and the dichotomy between her private imaginings and the reality had been disconcerting. Irrationally, she had felt a twinge of irritation against Bernie for so putting her at a disadvantage. He was old of course, over forty at least, but not as old as she had expected. He was dark, very tall and loose-limbed where she had expected him to be fair, thickset and stocky. He was serious and spoke to her as if she were a responsible adult, not avuncular and condescending. His face was sensitive without being weak and she liked his hands and his voice and the way she could see the structure of his bones under the skin. He sounded gentle and kind, which was cunning since she knew that he was dangerous and cruel, and she had to keep reminding herself of how he had treated Bernie. At some moments during the interrogation she had actually wondered whether he could be Adam Dalgliesh the poet.

They had never been alone together. On each of her visits a policewoman, introduced as Sergeant Mannering, had been present, seated at the side of the desk with her notebook. Cordelia felt that she knew Sergeant Mannering well, having met her at school in the person of the head girl, Teresa Campion-Hook. The two girls could have been sisters. No acne had ever marked their shiningly clean skins; their fair hair curled at precisely the regulation length above their uniformed collars: their voices were calm, authoritarian, determinedly cheerful but never strident; they exuded an ineffable confidence in the justice and logic of the universe and the rightness of their own place in it. Sergeant Mannering had smiled briefly at Cordelia as she came in. The look was open, not overtly friendly since too generous a smile might prejudice the case, but not censorious either. It was a look which disposed Cordelia to imprudence; she disliked looking a fool before that competent gaze.

She had at least had time before her first visit to decide on tactics. There was little advantage and much danger in concealing facts which an intelligent man could easily discover for himself. She would disclose, if asked, that she had discussed Mark Callender with the Tillings and his tutor; that she had traced and interviewed Mrs Goddard; that she had visited Dr Gladwin. She decided to say nothing about the attempt on her life or about her visit to Somerset House. She knew which facts it would be vital to conceal: Ronald Callender's murder; the clue in the prayer-book; the actual way in which Mark had died. She told herself firmly that she mustn't be drawn into discussing the case, mustn't talk about herself, her life, her present job, her ambitions. She remembered what Bernie had told her. 'In this country, if people won't talk, there's nothing you can do to make them, more's the pity. Luckily for the police most people just can't keep their mouths shut. The intelligent ones are the worst. They just have to show

how clever they are, and once you've got them discussing the case, even discussing it generally, then you've got them.' Cordelia reminded herself of the advice she had given to Elizabeth Leaming: 'Don't embroider, don't invent, don't be afraid to say you can't remember.'

Dalgliesh was speaking:

'Have you thought of consulting a solicitor, Miss Gray?'

'I haven't got a solicitor.'

'The Law Society can give you the names of some very reliable and helpful ones. I should think about it seriously if I were you.'

'But I should have to pay him, shouldn't I? Why should I need a solicitor when I'm telling the truth?'

'It's when people start telling the truth that they most often feel the need of a solicitor.'

'But I've always told the truth. Why should I lie?' The rhetorical question was a mistake. He answered it seriously as if she had really wanted to know.

'Well, it could be to protect yourself – which I don't think likely – or to protect someone else. The motive for that could be love, fear or a sense of justice. I don't think you've known any of the people in this case long enough to care for them deeply so that rules out love, and I don't think you would be very easy to frighten. So we're left with justice. A very dangerous concept, Miss Gray.'

She had been closely questioned before. The Cambridge police had been very thorough. But this was the first time she had been questioned by someone who knew; knew that she was lying; knew that Mark Callender hadn't killed himself; knew, she felt desperately, all there was to know. She had to force herself to an acceptance of reality. He couldn't possibly be sure. He hadn't any legal proof and he never would have. There was no one alive to tell him the truth except Elizabeth Leaming and herself. And she wasn't going to tell. Dalgliesh could beat against her will with his implacable logic, his curious kindness, his courtesy, his patience. But she wouldn't talk, and in England there was no way in which he could make her.

When she didn't reply, he said cheerfully:

'Well, let's see how far we've got. As a result of your inquiries you suspected that Mark Callender might have been murdered.

You haven't admitted that to me but you made your suspicions plain when you visited Sergeant Maskell of the Cambridge police. You subsequently traced his mother's old nurse and learned from her something of his early life, of the Callender marriage, of Mrs Callender's death. Following that visit you went to see Dr Gladwin, the general practitioner who had looked after Mrs Callender before she died. By a simple ruse you ascertained the blood group of Ronald Callender. There would only be point in that if you suspected that Mark wasn't the child of his parents' marriage. You then did what I would have done in your place, visited Somerset House to examine Mr George Bottley's will. That was sensible. If you suspect murder, always consider who stands to gain by it.'

So he had found out about Somerset House and the call to Dr Venables. Well, it was to be expected. He had credited her with his own brand of intelligence. She had behaved as he would have behaved.

She still didn't speak. He said:

'You didn't tell me about your fall down the well. Miss Markland did.'

'That was an accident. I don't remember anything about it, but I must have decided to explore the well and over-balanced. I was always rather intrigued by it.'

'I don't think it was an accident, Miss Gray. You couldn't have pulled the lid free without a rope. Miss Markland tripped over a rope, but it was coiled neatly and half-hidden in the undergrowth. Would you have even troubled to detach it from the hook if you'd only been exploring?'

'I don't know. I can't remember anything that happened before I fell. My first memory is hitting the water. And I don't see what this has to do with Sir Ronald Callender's death.'

'It might have a great deal to do with it. If someone tried to kill you, and I think that they did, that person could have come from Garforth House.'

'Why?'

'Because the attempt on your life was probably connected with your investigation into Mark Callender's death. You had become a danger to someone. Killing is a serious business. The professionals don't like it unless it's absolutely essential and even the amateurs are less happy-go-lucky about murder than you might expect. You must have become a very dangerous woman to someone. Someone replaced that well lid, Miss Gray; you didn't fall through solid wood.'

Cordelia still said nothing. There was a silence, then he spoke again:

'Miss Markland told me that after your rescue from the well she was reluctant to leave you alone. But you insisted that she should go. You told her that you weren't afraid to be alone in the cottage because you had a gun.'

Cordelia was surprised how much this small betrayal hurt. Yet, how could she blame Miss Markland? The Superintendent would have known just how to handle her, probably persuaded her that frankness was in Cordelia's own interest. Well, she could at least betray in her turn. And this explanation, at least, would have the authority of truth.

'I wanted to get rid of her. She told me some dreadful story about her illegitimate child falling down the well to his death. I'd only just been rescued myself. I didn't want to hear it, I couldn't bear it just then. I told her a lie about the gun just to make her go. I didn't ask her to confide in me, it wasn't fair. It was only a way of asking for help and I hadn't any to give.'

'And didn't you want to get rid of her for another reason? Didn't you know that your assailant would have to return that night; that the well cover would have to be dragged clear again if your death were to look like an accident?'

'If I'd really thought that I was in any danger I should have begged her to take me with her to Summertrees House. I wouldn't have waited alone in the cottage without my gun.'

'No, Miss Gray, I believe that. You wouldn't have waited there alone in the cottage that night without your gun.'

For the first time Cordelia was desperately afraid. This wasn't a game. It never had been, although at Cambridge the police interrogation had held some of the unreality of a formal contest in which the result was both foreseeable and unworrying since one of the opponents didn't even know he was playing. It was real enough now. If she were tricked, persuaded, coerced into telling him the truth, she would go to prison. She was an accessory after the fact. How many years did one get for helping to conceal murder? She had read somewhere that Holloway smelt. They would take away her clothes. She would be shut up in a claustrophobic cell. There was remission for good conduct but how could one be good in prison? Perhaps they would send her to an open prison. Open. It was a contradiction in terms. And how would she live afterwards? How would she get a job? What real personal freedom could there ever be for those whom society labelled delinquent?

She was terrified for Miss Leaming. Where was she now? She had never dared ask Dalgliesh, and Miss Leaming's name had hardly been mentioned. Was she even now in some other room of New Scotland Yard being similarly questioned? How reliable would she be under pressure? Were they planning to confront the two conspirators with each other? Would the door suddenly open and Miss Leaming be brought in, apologetic, remorseful, truculent? Wasn't that the usual ploy, to interview conspirators separately until the weaker broke down? And who would prove the weaker?

She heard the Superintendent's voice. She thought he sounded rather sorry for her.

'We have some confirmation that the pistol was in your possession that night. A motorist tells us that he saw a parked car on the road about three miles from Garforth House and when he stopped to inquire if he could help he was threatened by a young woman with a gun.'

Cordelia remembered that moment, the sweetness and silence of the summer night suddenly overlaid by his hot, alcoholic breath.

'He must have been drinking. I suppose the police stopped him for a breath test later that night and now he's decided to come up with this story. I don't know what he expects to gain by it but it isn't true. I wasn't carrying a gun. Sir Ronald took the pistol from me on my first night at Garforth House.'

'The Metropolitan Police stopped him just over the force border. I think he may persist in his story. He was very definite. Of course, he hasn't identified you yet but he was able to describe the car. His story is that he thought you were having trouble with it and stopped to help. You misunderstood his motives and threatened him with a gun.'

'I understood his motives perfectly. But I didn't threaten him with a gun.'

'What did you say, Miss Gray?'

'Leave me alone or I'll kill you.'

'Without the gun, surely that was an empty threat?'

'It would always have been an empty threat. But it made him go.'

'What exactly did happen?'

'I had a spanner in the front pocket of the car and when he shoved his face in at the window I grasped that and threatened him with it. But no one in his right senses could have mistaken a spanner for a gun!'

But he hadn't been in his right senses. The only person who had seen the gun in her possession that night was a motorist who hadn't been sober. This, she knew, was a small victory. She had resisted the momentary temptation to change her story. Bernie had been right. She recalled his advice; the Superintendent's advice; this time she could almost hear it spoken in his deep slightly husky voice: 'If you're tempted to crime, stick to your original statement. There's nothing that impresses the jury more than consistency. I've seen the most unlikely defence succeed simply because the accused stuck to his story. After all, it's only someone else's word against yours; with a competent counsel that's half-way to a reasonable doubt.'

The Superintendent was speaking again. Cordelia wished that she could concentrate more clearly on what he was saying. She hadn't been sleeping very soundly for the past ten days – perhaps that had something to do with this perpetual tiredness.

'I think that Chris Lunn paid you a visit on the night he died. There's no other reason that I could discover why he should have been on the road. One of the witnesses to the accident said that he came out in the little van from that side road as if all the devils in hell were following him. Someone was following him – you, Miss Gray.'

'We've had this conversation before. I was on my way to see Sir Ronald.'

'At that hour? And in such a hurry?'

'I wanted to see him urgently to tell him that I'd decided to drop the case. I couldn't wait.'

'But you did wait, didn't you? You went to sleep in the car on the side of the road. That's why it was nearly an hour after you'd been seen at the accident before you arrived at Garforth House.'

'I had to stop. I was tired and I knew it wasn't safe to drive on.'

'But you knew too, that it was safe to sleep. You knew that the person you had most to fear from was dead.'

Cordelia didn't reply. A silence fell on the room but it seemed to her a companionable not an accusing silence. She wished that she wasn't so tired. Most of all, she wished that she had someone to talk to about Ronald Callender's murder. Bernie wouldn't have been any help here. To him the moral dilemma at the heart of the crime would have held no interest, no validity, would have seemed a wilful confusion of straightforward facts. She could imagine his coarse and facile comment on Eliza Leaming's relations with Lunn. But the Superintendent might have understood. She could imagine herself talking to him. She recalled Ronald Callender's words that love was as destructive as hate. Would Dalgliesh assent to that bleak philosophy? She wished that she could ask him. This, she recognized, was her real danger – not the temptation to confess but the longing to confide. Did he know how she felt? Was this, too, part of his technique?

There was a knock at the door. A uniformed constable came in and handed a note to Dalgliesh. The room was very quiet while he read it. Cordelia made herself look at his face. It was grave and expressionless and he continued looking at the paper long after he must have assimilated its brief message.

She thought that he was making up his mind to something. After a minute he said:

'This concerns someone you know, Miss Gray. Elizabeth Leaming is dead. She was killed two days ago when the car she was driving went off the coast road south of Amalfi. This note is confirmation of identity.'

Cordelia was swept with relief so immense that she felt physically sick. She clenched her fist and felt the sweat start on her brow. She began to shiver with cold. It never occurred to her that he might be lying. She knew him to be ruthless and clever but she had always taken it for granted that he wouldn't lie to her. She said in a whisper:

'May I go home now?'

'Yes. I don't think there's much point in your staying, do you?'

'She didn't kill Sir Ronald. He took the gun from me. He took the gun –'

Something seemed to have happened to her throat. The words wouldn't come out.

'That's what you've been telling me. I don't think you need trouble to say it again.'

'When do I have to come back?'

'I don't think you need come back unless you decide that there's something you want to tell me. In that well-known phrase, you were asked to help the police. You have helped the police. Thank you.'

She had won. She was free. She was safe, and with Miss Leaming dead, that safety depended only on herself. She needn't come back again to this horrible place. The relief, so unexpected and so unbelievable, was too great to be borne. Cordelia burst into dramatic and uncontrollable crying. She was aware of Sergeant Mannering's low exclamation of concern and a folded white handkerchief handed to her by the Superintendent. She buried her face in the clean, laundry-smelling linen and blurted out her pent-up misery and anger. Strangely enough – and the oddness of it struck her even in the middle of her anguish – her misery was centred on Bernie. Lifting a face disfigured with tears and no longer caring what he thought of her, she blurted out a final, irrational protest:

'And after you'd sacked him, you never inquired how he got on. You didn't even come to the funeral!'

He had brought a chair over and had seated himself beside her. He handed her a glass of water. The glass was very cold but comforting and she was surprised to find how thirsty she was. She sipped the cold water and sat there hiccuping gently. The hiccups made her want to laugh hysterically but she controlled herself. After a few minutes he said gently:

'I'm sorry about your friend. I didn't realize that your partner was the Bernie Pryde who once worked with me. It's rather worse than that, actually. I'd forgotten all about him. If it's any consolation to you, this case might have ended rather differently if I hadn't.'

'You sacked him. All he ever wanted was to be a detective and you wouldn't give him a chance.'

'The Metropolitan Police hiring and firing regulations aren't quite as simple as that. But it's true that he might still have been a policeman if it hadn't been for me. But he wouldn't have been a detective.'

'He wasn't that bad.'

'Well, he was, you know. But I'm beginning to wonder if I didn't underrate him.'

Cordelia turned to hand him back the glass and met his eyes. They smiled at each other. She wished that Bernie could have heard him.

Half an hour later Dalgliesh was seated opposite the Assistant Commissioner in the latter's office. The two men disliked each other but only one of them knew this and he was the one to whom it didn't matter. Dalgliesh made his report, concisely, logically, without referring to his notes. This was his invariable habit. The AC had always thought it unorthodox and conceited and he did so now. Dalgliesh ended:

'As you can imagine, sir, I'm not proposing to commit all that to paper. There's no real evidence and as Bernie Pryde used to tell us, hunch is a good servant but a poor master. God, how that man could churn out his horrible platitudes! He wasn't unintelligent, not totally without judgement, but everything, including ideas, came apart in his hands. He had a mind like a police notebook. Do you remember the Clandon case, homicide by shooting? It was in 1954 I think.'

'Ought I to?'

'No. But it would have been helpful if I had.'

'I don't really know what you're talking about, Adam. But if I understand you aright, you suspect that Ronald Callender killed his son. Ronald Callender is dead. You suspect that Chris Lunn tried to murder Cordelia Gray. Lunn is dead. You suggest that Elizabeth Leaming killed Ronald Callender. Elizabeth Leaming is dead.'

'Yes, it's all conveniently tidy.'

'I suggest we leave it that way. The Commissioner incidentally has had a telephone call from Dr Hugh Tilling, the psychiatrist. He's outraged because his son and daughter have been questioned about Mark Callender's death. I'm prepared to explain his civil duties to Dr Tilling, he's already well aware of his rights, if you really feel it necessary. But will anything be gained by seeing the two Tillings again?'

'I don't think so.'

'Or by bothering the Sureté about that French girl who Miss Markland claims visited him at the cottage?'

'I think we can spare ourselves that embarrassment. There's only one person now alive who knows the truth of these crimes and she's proof against any interrogation we can use. I can comfort myself with the reason. With most suspects we have an invaluable ally lurking at the back of their minds to betray them. But whatever lies she's been telling, she's absolutely without guilt.'

'Do you think that she's deluded herself that it's all true?'

'I don't think that young woman deludes herself about anything. I took to her, but I'm glad I shan't be encountering her again. I dislike being made to feel during a perfectly ordinary interrogation that I'm corrupting the young.'

'So we can tell the Minister that his chum died by his own hand?'

'You can tell him that we are satisfied that no living finger pressed that trigger. But perhaps not. Even he might be capable of reasoning that one out. Tell him that he can safely accept the verdict of the inquest.'

'It would have saved a great deal of public time if he'd accepted it in the first place.'

The two men were silent for a moment. Then Dalgliesh said:

'Cordelia Gray was right. I ought to have inquired what happened to Bernie Pryde.'

'You couldn't be expected to. That wasn't part of your duties.'

'Of course not. But then one's more serious neglects seldom are part of one's duty. And I find it ironic and oddly satisfying that Pryde took his revenge. Whatever mischief that child was up to in Cambridge, she was working under his direction.'

'You're becoming more philosophical, Adam.'

'Only less obsessive, or perhaps merely older. It's good to be able to feel occasionally that there are some cases which are better left unsolved.'

The Kingly Street building looked the same, smelt the same. It always would. But there was one difference. Outside the office a man was waiting, a middle-aged man in a tight blue suit, pig eyes sharp as flint among the fleshy folds of the face.

'Miss Gray? I'd nearly given you up. My name's Fielding. I saw your plate and just came up by chance, don't you know.'

His eyes were avaricious, prurient.

'Well now, you're not quite what I expected, not the usual kind of Private Eye.'

'Is there anything I can do for you, Mr Fielding?'

He gazed furtively round the landing, seeming to find its sordidness reassuring.

'It's my lady friend. I've reason to suspect that she's getting a bit on the side. Well – a man likes to know where he stands. You get me?'

Cordelia fitted the key into the lock.

'I understand, Mr Fielding. Won't you come in?'

INNOCENT BLOOD

CONTENTS

BOOK ONE

Proof of Identity

ONE

The social worker was older than she had expected; perhaps the nameless official who arranged these matters thought that greying hair and menopausal plumpness might induce confidence in the adopted adults who came for their compulsory counselling. After all, they must be in need of reassurance of some kind, these displaced persons whose umbilical cord was a court order, or why had they troubled to travel this bureaucratic road to identity? The social worker smiled her encouraging professional smile. She said, holding out her hand:

'My name is Naomi Henderson and you're Miss Philippa Rose Palfrey. I'm afraid I have to begin by asking you for some proof of identity.'

Philippa nearly replied: 'Philippa Rose Palfrey is what I'm called. I'm here to find out who I am,' but checked herself in time, sensing that such an affectation would be an unpropitious beginning to the interview. They both knew why she was here. And she wanted the session to be a success; wanted it to go her way without being precisely clear what way that was. She unclipped the fastening of her leather shoulder-bag and handed over in silence her passport and the newly acquired driving licence.

The attempt at reassuring informality extended to the furnishing of the room. There was an official-looking desk, but Miss Henderson had moved from behind it as soon as Philippa was announced, and had motioned her to one of the two vinyl-covered armchairs on each side of a low table. There were even flowers on the table, a small blue bowl lettered 'a present from Polperro'. It held a mixed bunch of roses. These weren't the scentless, thornless buds of the florist's window. These were garden roses, recognized from the garden at Caldecote Terrace: Peace, Superstar, Albertine, the blossoms overblown, already peeling with only one or two tightly furled buds, darkening at the lips and destined never to open. Philippa wondered if the social worker had brought them in from her own garden. Perhaps she was retired, living in the country, and had been recruited part-time for this particular job. She could picture her clumping round her rose bed in the brogues and serviceable tweeds she was wearing now, snipping away at roses which were due for culling, might just last out the London day. Someone had watered the flowers over-enthusiastically. A milky bead lay like a pearl between two yellow petals and there was a splash on the table top. But the imitation mahogany wouldn't be stained; it wasn't really wood. The roses gave forth a damp sweetness; but they weren't really fresh. In these easy chairs no visitor had ever sat at ease. The smile which invited her confidence and trust across the table was bestowed by courtesy of section twenty-six of the Children Act 1975. She had taken trouble with her appearance, but then she always did, presenting herself to the world with self-conscious art, daily re-making herself in her own image. The aim this morning had been to suggest that no trouble had in fact been taken, that this interview had induced no special anxiety, warranted no exceptional care. Her strong corn-coloured hair, bleached by the summer so that no two strands were exactly the same gold, was drawn back from a high forehead and knotted in a single heavy plait. The wide mouth with its strong, curved upper lip and sensuous droop at each corner was devoid of lipstick, but she had applied her eyeshadow with care, emphasizing her most remarkable feature, the luminous, slightly protuberant green eyes. Her honey-coloured skin glistened with sweat. She had lingered too long in the Embankment Gardens, unwilling to arrive early, and in the end had had to hurry. She wore sandals and a pale green open-necked cotton shirt above her corduroy trousers. In contrast to this casual informality, the careful ambiguity about money or social class, were the possessions which she wore like talismen: the slim gold watch, the three heavy Victorian rings, topaz, cornelian, peridot, the leather Italian bag slung from her left shoulder. The contrast was deliberate. The advantage of remembering virtually nothing before her eighth birthday, the knowledge that she was illegitimate, meant that there was no phalanx of the living dead, no pious ancestor worship, no conditioned reflexes of thought to inhibit the creativity with which she presented herself to the world. What she aimed to achieve was singularity, an impression of intelligence, a look that could be spectacular, even eccentric, but never ordinary.

Her file, clean and new, lay open before Miss Henderson.

Across the table Philippa could recognize some of the contents: the orange and brown Government information sheet, a copy of which she had obtained from the Citizens' Advice Bureau in north London where there had been no risk that she would be known or recognized; her letter to the Registrar General written five weeks ago, the day after her eighteenth birthday, in which she had requested the application form which was the first document to identity; a copy of the form itself. The letter was tagged on top of the file, stark white against the buff of bureaucracy. Miss Henderson fingered it. Something about it, the address, the quality of the heavy linen-based paper apparent even in a copy, evoked, Philippa thought, a transitory unease. Perhaps it was a recognition that her adoptive father was Maurice Palfrey. Given Maurice's indefatigable self-advertisement, the stream of sociological publications which flowed from his department, it would be odd if a senior social worker hadn't heard of him. She wondered whether Miss Henderson had read his *Theory and Technique in Counselling: A Guide for Practitioners*, and if so, how much she had been helped in bolstering her clients' self-esteem – and what a significant word 'client' was in social-work jargon – by Maurice's lucid exploration of the difference between developmental counselling and Gestalt therapy.

Miss Henderson said:

'Perhaps I ought to begin by telling you how far I'm able to help you. Some of this you probably already know, but I find it useful to get it straight. The Children Act 1975 made important changes in the law relating to access to birth records. It provides that adopted adults, that is people who are at least eighteen years old, may if they wish apply to the Registrar General for information which will lead them to the original record of their birth. When you were adopted you were given a new birth certificate, and the information which links your present name, Philippa Rose Palfrey, with your original birth certificate is kept by the Registrar General in confidential records. It is this linking information which the law now requires the Registrar General to give you if you want it. The 1975 Act also provides that anyone adopted before 12th November 1975, that is before the Act was passed, must attend an interview with a counsellor before they can be given the information. The reason for this is that Parliament was concerned about making the new arrangements retrospective since over the years many natural parents gave up their children for adoption and adopters took on the children on the understanding that their natural parentage would remain unknown. So you have come here today so that we can consider together the possible effect of any inquiries you may make about your natural parents, both on yourself and on other people, and so that the information you are now seeking, and to which you have, of course, a legal right, is provided in a helpful and appropriate manner. At the end of our talk, and if you still want it, I shall be able to give you your original name, the name of your natural mother, possibly, but not certainly, the name of your natural father and the name of the court where your adoption order was made. I shall also be able to give you an application form which you can use to apply to the Registrar General for a copy of your original birth certificate.'

She had said it all before. It came out a little too pat. Philippa said:

'And there's a standard charge of two pounds fifty pence for the birth certificate. It seems cheap at the price. I know all that. It's in the orange and brown pamphlet.'

'As long as it's quite clear. I wonder if you'd like to tell me when you first decided to ask for your birth record. I see that you applied as soon as you were eighteen. Was this a sudden decision or had you been thinking about it for some time?'

'I decided when the 1975 Act was passed. I was fifteen then and taking my O-levels. I don't think I gave it a great deal of thought at the time. I just made up my mind that I'd apply as soon as I was legally able to.'

'Have you spoken to your adoptive parents about it?'

'No. We're not exactly a communicative family.'

Miss Henderson let that pass for the moment.

'And what exactly did you have in mind? Do you want just to know who your natural parents are, or are you hoping to trace them?'

'I'm hoping to find out who I am. I don't see the point of stopping at two names on a birth certificate. There may not even be two names. I know I'm illegitimate. The search may all come to nothing. I know that my mother is dead so I can't trace her, and I may never find my father. But at least if I can find out who my mother was I may get a lead to him. He may be dead too, but I don't think so. Somehow I'm certain that my father is alive.'

Normally she liked her fantasies at least tenuously rooted in reality. Only this one was different, out of time, wildly improbable and yet impossible to relinquish, like an ancient religion whose archaic ceremonies, comfortingly familiar and absurd, somehow witness to an essential truth. She couldn't remember why she had originally set her scene in the nineteenth century, or why, learning so soon that this was a nonsense since she had been born in 1960, she had never updated the persistent self-indulgent imaginings. Her mother, a slim figure dressed as a Victorian parlour-maid, an upswept glory of golden hair under the goffered cap with its two broderie Anglaise streamers, ghost-like against the tall hedge which surrounded the rose garden. Her father in full evening dress striding like a god across the terrace, down the broad walk, under the spray of the fountains. The sloping lawn, drenched by the mellow light of the last sun, glittering with peacocks. The two shadows merging into one shadow, the dark head bending to the gold.

'My darling, my darling. I can't let you go. Marry me.'

'I can't. You know I can't.'

It had become a habit to conjure up her favourite scenes in the minutes before she fell asleep. Sleep came in a drift of rose leaves. In the earliest dreams her father had been in uniform, scarlet and gold, his chest beribboned, sword clanking at his side. As she grew older she had edited out these embarrassing embellishments. The soldier, the fearless rider to hounds had become the aristocrat scholar. But the essential picture remained.

There was a globule of water creeping down the petal of the yellow rose. She watched it, fascinated, willing it not to fall. She had distanced her thoughts from what Miss Henderson had been saying. Now she made an effort to attend. The social worker was asking about her adoptive parents:

'And your mother, what does she do?'

'My adoptive mother cooks.'

'You mean she works as a cook?' The social worker modified this as if conscious that it could imply some derogation, and added: 'She cooks professionally?'

'She cooks for her husband and her guests and me. And she's a juvenile court magistrate but I think she only took that on to please my adoptive father. He believes that a woman should have a job outside the home, provided, of course, that it doesn't interfere with his comfort. But cooking is her enthusiasm. She's good enough at it to cook professionally, although I don't think she was ever properly taught except at evening classes. She was my father's secretary before they married. I mean that cooking is her hobby, her interest.'

'Well, that's nice for your father and you.'

Presumably that hint of encouraging patronage was by now too unconsciously acquired to be easily disciplined. Philippa gazed at the woman stonily, noted it, took strength from it.

'Yes, we're both greedy, my adoptive father and I. We can both eat voraciously without putting on weight.'

That, she supposed, implied something of an appetite for life, not indiscriminate since they were both appreciative of good food; perhaps a reinforcement of their belief that one could indulge without having to pay for indulgence. Greed, unlike sex, involved no commitment except to one's self, no violence except to one's own body. She had always taken comfort from her discernment about food and drink. That, at least, could hardly have been caught from his example. Even Maurice, convinced environmentalist that he was, would hardly claim that a nose for claret could be so easily acquired. Learning to enjoy wine, discovering that she had a palate, had been one more reassuring affirmation of inherited taste. She recalled her seventeenth birthday; the three bottles on the table before them, the labels shrouded. She couldn't recall that Hilda had been with them. Surely she must have been present for a family birthday dinner, but in memory she and Maurice celebrated alone. He had said:

'Now tell me which you prefer. Forget the purple prose of the colour supplements, I want to know what you think in your own words.'

She had tasted them again, holding the wine in her mouth, sipping water between each sampling since she supposed that this was the proper thing to do, watching his bright challenging eyes.

'This one.'

'Why?'

'I don't know. I just like it best.'

But he would expect a more considered judgement than that. She added:

'Perhaps because with this one I can't distinguish taste from smell and from the feel of it in the mouth. They aren't separate sensations, it's a trinity of pleasure.'

She had chosen the right one. There always was a right answer and a wrong answer. This had been one more test successfully passed, one more notch on the scale of approval. He couldn't entirely reject her, couldn't send her back; she knew that. An adoption order couldn't be revoked. That made it the more important that she should justify his choice of her, that she should give value for money. Hilda, who worked for hours in the kitchen preparing their meals, ate and drank little. She would sit, anxious eyes fixed on them as they shovelled in their food. She gave and they took. It was almost too psychologically neat. Miss Henderson asked:

'Do you resent them for adopting you?'

'No, I'm grateful. I was lucky. I don't think I'd have done well with a poor family.'

'Not even if they loved you?'

'I don't see why they should. I'm not particularly lovable.'

She hadn't done well with a poor family, of that at least she could be certain.. She hadn't done well with any of her foster parents. Some smells: her own excreta, the rotting waste outside a restaurant, a young child bundled into soiled clothes on its mother's lap pressed against her by the lurch of a bus, these could evoke a momentary panic that had nothing to do with disgust. Memory was like a searchlight sweeping over the lost hinterland of self, illuminating scenes with total clarity, the colours gaudy as a child's comic, edges of objects hard as blocks, scenes which could lie for months unremembered in that black wasteland, not rooted, as were other childish memories, in time and place, not rooted in love.

'Do you love them, your adoptive parents?'

She considered. Love. One of the most used words in the language, the most debased. Héloïse and Abelard. Rochester and Jane Eyre. Emma and Mr Knightly. Anna and Count Vronsky. Even in the narrow connotation of heterosexual love it meant exactly what you wanted it to mean.

'No. And I don't think they love me. But we suit each other on the whole. That's more convenient, I imagine, than living with people that you love but don't suit.'

'I can see that it could be. How much were you told about the circumstances of your adoption? About your natural parents?'

'As much, I think, as my adoptive mother could tell me. Maurice never talks about it. My adoptive father's a university lecturer, a sociologist. Maurice Palfrey, the sociologist who can write English. His first wife and their son died in a car crash when the boy was three. She was driving. He married my adoptive mother nine months afterwards. They discovered that she couldn't have children so they found me. I was being fostered at the time so they took over the care of me and after six months applied to the county court and got an adoption order. It was a private arrangement, the kind of thing your new Act would make illegal. I can't think why. It seems to me a perfectly sensible way of going about it. I've certainly nothing to complain of.'

'It worked very well for thousands of children and their adopters, but it had its dangers. We wouldn't want to go back to the days when unwanted babies lay in rows of cots in nurseries so that adoptive parents could just go and pick out the one they fancied.'

'I don't see why not. That seems to me the only sensible way, as long as the children are too young to know what's happening. That's how you'd pick a puppy or a kitten. I imagine that you need to take to a baby, to feel that this is a child that you want to rear, could grow to love. If I needed to adopt, and I never would, the last thing I'd want would be a child selected for me by a social worker. If we didn't take to each other I wouldn't be able to hand it back without the social services department striking me off the books as being one of those neurotic self-indulgent women who want a child for their own satisfaction. And what other possible reason could there be for wanting an adopted child?'

'Perhaps to give that child a better chance.'

'Don't you mean, to have the personal satisfaction of giving that child a better chance? It amounts to the same thing.'

She wouldn't bother to refute that heresy, of course. Social-work theory didn't err. After all, its practitioners were the new priesthood, the ministry of unbelievers. She merely smiled and persevered:

'Did they tell you anything about your background?'

'Only that I'm illegitimate. My adoptive father's first wife came from the aristocracy, an earl's daughter, and was brought up in a Palladian mansion in Wiltshire. I believe that my mother was one of the maids there, who got herself pregnant. She died soon after I was born and no one knew who my father was. Obviously he wasn't a fellow servant; she couldn't have kept that particular secret from the servants' hall. I think he must have been a visitor to the house. There are only two things I can remember clearly about my life before I was eight; one is the rose garden at Pennington, the other is the library. I think that my father, my real father, was there with me. It's possible that one of the upper servants at Pennington put my adoptive father in touch with me after his first wife died. He never speaks about it. I only learned as much as that from my adoptive mother. I suppose Maurice thought that I'd do because I was a girl. He wouldn't want a boy to bear his name unless he were really his son. It would be terribly important to him to know that a son was really his own.'

'That's understandable, isn't it?'

'Of course. That's why I'm here. It's important for me to know that my parents really were my own.'

'Well, let's say that you think it important.'

Her eyes dropped to the file. There was a rustle of papers. 'So you were adopted on 7th January 1969. You must have been eight. That's quite old.'

'I suppose they thought it was better than taking a very young baby and having broken nights. And my adoptive father could see that I was all right, physically all right, that I wasn't stupid.

There wasn't the same risk as with a young baby. I know that there are stringent medical examinations, but one can never be quite sure, not about intelligence anyway. He couldn't have borne to find himself saddled with a stupid child.'

'Is that what he told you?'

'No, it's what I've thought out for myself.'

One fact she could be sure of, that she came from Pennington. There was a childhood memory more clear even than that of the rose garden: the Wren library. She knew that she had once stood there under that exuberant seventeenth-century stuccoed ceiling with its garlands and cherubs, had stared down that vast room at the Grinling Gibbons carvings richly spilling from the shelves, at the Roubiliac busts set above the bookcases, Homer, Dante, Shakespeare, Milton. In memory she saw herself standing at the great chart table reading from a book. The book had been almost too heavy to hold. She could still recall the ache in her wrists and the fear that she might drop it. And she was certain that her real father had been with her; that she had been reading aloud to him. She was so sure that she belonged at Pennington that sometimes she was tempted to believe that the Earl had been her father. But the fantasy was unacceptable and she rejected it, faithful to the original version of the visiting aristocrat. The Earl must have known if he had fathered a child on one of his servants, and surely, surely he wouldn't have rejected her totally, left her unsought and unrecognized for eighteen years. She had never been back to the house, and now that the Arabs had bought it and it had become a Moslem fortress she never would. But when she was twelve she had searched in Westminster reference library for a book on Pennington and had read a description of the library. There had been a picture too. The confirmation had jolted her heart. It was all there, the plaster ceiling, the Grinling Gibbons carvings, the busts. But her memory had come first. The child standing beside the chart table holding the book in her aching hands must have existed.

She scarcely heard the rest of the counselling. If it had to be done, she supposed that Miss Henderson was making a good enough job of it. But it was no more than a statutory nuisance, the way in which uneasy legislators had salved their consciences.

None of the arguments so conscientiously put forward could shake her resolve to track down her father. And how could their meeting, however delayed, be unwelcome to him? She wouldn't be coming empty-handed. She had her Cambridge scholarship to lay at his feet.

She said, wrenching her mind back to the present:

'I can't see the point of this compulsory counselling. Are you supposed to dissuade me from tracing my father? Either our legislators think I have a right to know, or they don't. To give me the right and at the same time officially try to discourage me from exercising it seems muddled thinking even for Parliament. Or do they just have a bad conscience about retrospective legislation?'

'Parliament wants adopted people to think carefully about the implications of what they're doing, what it could mean for themselves, for their adoptive parents, for their natural parents.'

'I have thought. My mother is dead, so it can't hurt her. I don't propose to embarrass my father. I want to know who he is, or was, if he's dead. That's all. If he's still alive, I should like to meet him, but I'm not thinking of bursting in on a family party and announcing that I'm his bastard. And I don't see how any of this concerns my adoptive parents.'

'Wouldn't it be wise, and kinder, to discuss it first with your adoptive parents?'

'What is there to discuss? The law gives me a right. I'm exercising it.'

Thinking back on the counselling session that evening at home, Philippa couldn't remember the precise moment when the information she sought had been handed to her. She supposed that the social worker must have said something: 'Here, then, are the facts you are seeking' was surely too pretentious and theatrical for Miss Henderson's detached professionalism. But some words must have been said, or had she merely taken the General Register Office paper from the file and passed it over in silence?

But here it was at last in her hands. She stared at it in disbelief, her first thought that there had been some bureaucratic muddle. There were two names, not one, on the form. Her natural parents were shown as Mary Ducton and Martin John Ducton. She muttered the words to herself. The names meant nothing to her, stirred no memory, evoked no sense of completeness, of forgotten knowledge resurrected at a word to be recognized and acknowledged. And then she saw what must have happened. She said, hardly realizing that she spoke aloud:

'I suppose they married my mother off when they found out that she was pregnant. Probably to a fellow servant. They must have been making that kind of tactful arrangement for generations at Pennington. But I hadn't realized that I was placed for adoption before my mother died. She must have known that she hadn't long to live and wanted to be sure that I would be all right. And, of course, if she were married before I was born the husband would be registered as my father. Nominally I suppose I'm legitimate. It's helpful that she did have a husband. Martin Ducton must have been told that she was pregnant before he agreed to the marriage. She may even have told him before she died who my real father was. Obviously the next step is to trace Martin Ducton.'

She picked up her shoulder-bag and held out her hand to say goodbye. She only half heard Miss Henderson's closing words, the offer of any future help she could give, reiterated advice that Philippa discuss her plans with her adoptive parents, the gently urged suggestion that if she were able to trace her father it should be done through an intermediary. But some words did penetrate her consciousness:

'We all need our fantasies in order to live. Sometimes relinquishing them can be extraordinarily painful, not a rebirth into something exciting and new, but a kind of death.'

They shook hands, and Philippa, looking into her face for the first time with any real interest, seeing her for the first time as a woman, detected there a fleeting look which, had she not known better, she might have mistaken for pity.

TWO

She posted her application and cheque to the Registrar General that evening, 4th July 1978, enclosing, as she had done previously, a stamped addressed envelope. Neither Maurice nor Hilda was curious about her private correspondence but she didn't want to risk an officially labelled reply falling through the letter-box. She spent the next few days in a state of controlled excitement which, for most of the time, drove her out of the house, afraid that Hilda might wonder at her restlessness. Pacing round the lake in St James's Park, hands deep in her jacket pockets, she calculated when the birth certificate might arrive. Government departments were notoriously slow, but surely this was a simple enough matter. They had only to check their records. And they wouldn't be coping with a rush of applications. The Act had been passed in 1975.

In exactly one week, on Tuesday 11th July, she saw the familiar envelope on the mat. She took it at once to her own room, calling out to Maurice from the stairs that there was no post for him. She carried it over to the window as if her eyes were growing weaker and she needed more light. The birth certificate, new, crisp, so much more imposing than the shortened form which had served her, as an adopted person, for so long, seemed at first reading to have nothing to do with her. It recorded the birth of a female, Rose Ducton, on 22nd May 1960 at 41 Bancroft Gardens, Seven Kings, Essex. The father was shown as Martin John Ducton, clerk; the mother as Mary Ducton, housewife.

So they had left Pennington before she was born. That, perhaps, wasn't surprising. What was unexpected was that they should have moved so far from Wiltshire. Perhaps they had wanted to cut themselves off entirely from the old life, from the gossip, from memories. Perhaps someone had found him a job in Essex, or he might have been returning to his home county. She wondered what he was like, this spurious accommodating father, whether he had been kind to her mother. She hoped that she could like or at least respect him. He might still live at 41 Bancroft Gardens, perhaps with a second wife and a child of his own. Ten years wasn't such a long time. She used the telephone extension in her room to ring Liverpool Street Station. Seven Kings was on the eastern suburban line and in the rush hour there were trains every ten minutes. She left without waiting for breakfast. If there were time, she would get coffee at the station.

The 9.25 train from Liverpool Street was almost empty. It was still early enough for Philippa to be travelling against the commuter tide. She sat in her corner seat, her eyes moving from side to side as the train racketed through the urban sprawl of the eastern suburbs; rows of drab houses with blackened bricks and patched roofs from which sprang a tangle of television aerials, frail crooked fetishes against the evil eye; layered high-rise flats smudged in a distant drizzle of rain; a yard piled high with the glitter of smashed cars in symbolic proximity to the regimented crosses of a suburban graveyard; a paint factory, a cluster of gasometers; pyramids of grit and coal piled beside the track; wastelands rank with weeds; a sloping green bank rising to suburban gardens with their washing lines and tool sheds and children's swings among the roses and hollyhocks. The eastern suburbs, so euphoniously and inappropriately named, Maryland, Forest Gate, Manor Park, were alien territory to her, as unvisited and remote from the preoccupations of the last ten years as were the outer suburbs of Glasgow and New York. None of her school friends lived east of Bethnal Green, although a number, unvisited, were reputed to have houses in the few unspoilt Georgian squares off the Whitechapel Road, self-conscious enclaves of culture and radical chic among the tower blocks and the industrial wasteland. Yet the grimy, unplanned urban clutter through which the train rocked and clattered struck some dormant memory, was familiar even in its strangeness, unique despite its bleak uniformity. Surely it wasn't because she had been this way before. Perhaps it was just that the scenery flashing by was so predictably dreary, so typical of the grey purlieus of any large city, that forgotten descriptions, old pictures and newsprint, snatches of film jumbled in her imagination to produce this sense of recognition. Perhaps everyone had been here before. This drab no man's land was part of everyone's mental topography.

There were no taxis at Seven Kings Station. She asked the ticket collector the way to Bancroft Gardens. He directed her down the High Street, left down Church Lane, then first on the right. The High Street ran between the railway and the shopping arcade of small businesses with flats above, a launderette, a newsagent, a greengrocer and a supermarket with shoppers already queuing at the checkpoints.

There was one scene so vividly recalled, validated by smell and sound and remembered pain which it was impossible to believe she had imagined. A woman wheeling a baby in a pram down just such a street. Herself, little more than a toddler, half stumbling beside the pram, clutching at the handle. The square paving stones speckled with light, unrolling beneath the whirling pram wheels, faster and faster. Her grip slipping on the moist warm metal and the desperate fear that she would lose hold, would be left behind, trampled and kicked under the wheels of the bright red buses. Then a shouted curse. The slap stinging her cheek. A jerk which nearly tore her arm from its socket, and the woman's hand fastening her grip once more on the pram handle. She had called the woman auntie. Auntie May. How extraordinary that she should remember the name now. And the child in the pram had worn a red woolly cap. Its face had been smeared with mucus and chocolate. She remembered that she had hated the child. It must have been winter. The street had been a glare of light and there had been a necklace of coloured bulbs swinging above the greengrocer's stall. The woman had stopped to buy fish. She remembered the slab, bright with red-eyed herrings shedding their glistening scales, the strong oleaginous smell of kippers. It could have been this street, only there was no fishmonger here now. She looked down at the paving stones, mottled with rain. Were these the ones over which she had stumbled so desperately? Or was this street, like the terrain each side of the railway, only one more scene from an imagined past?

Turning from the High Street into Church Lane was stepping from drab commercial suburbia into leafy privacy and cosy domesticity. The narrow street, its verge planted with plane trees, curved gently. Perhaps before the First War it had indeed been a lane leading to an ancient village church, a building long since demolished or destroyed by bombing in the Second War. All she could see now was a distant stunted spire which looked as if it had been fabricated from slabs of synthetic stone, and topped by a weather-vane instead of a cross because of some understandable confusion about the building's function.

And here at last was Bancroft Gardens. Stretching out of sight on either side of the road were identical semi-detached houses, each with a path running down the side. They might, she thought, be architecturally undistinguished, but at least they were on a human scale. The gates and railings had been removed and the front gardens were bounded with low brick walls. The front bay windows were square and turreted, a long vista of ramparted respectability. But the uniformity of the architecture was broken by the individuality of the residents. Every front garden was different, a riot of massed summer flowers, squares of lawn meticulously cut and shaped, stone slabs set about with urns bearing geraniums and ivy.

When Philippa reached number 41 she stopped, amazed. The house stood out from its neighbours by a garish celebration of eccentric taste. The yellow London bricks had been painted a shiny red outlined with white pointing. It looked like a house built with immense toy bricks. The crenellations of the bay were alternately red and blue. The window was curtained with net looped across and caught up with satin bows. The original front door had been replaced by one with an opaque glass panel and was painted bright yellow. In the front patch of garden an artificial pond of glass was surrounded by synthetic rocks, on which three gnomes with expressions of grinning imbecility were perched with fishing-rods.

As soon as she had pressed the doorbell – it let out a musical jingle – Philippa sensed that the house was empty. The owners were probably at work. She tried once more, but there was no reply. Resisting the temptation to peer through the letter-box, she decided to try next door. At least they would know whether Ducton still lived at 41 or where he had gone. The house had no bell and the thud of the knocker sounded unnaturally loud and peremptory. There was no reply. She waited a full minute and was lifting her hand again when she heard the shuffle of feet. The door was opened on a chain, and she glimpsed an elderly woman in apron and hairnet who gave her the unwelcoming suspicious stare of someone to whom no morning visitor at the front door bodes other than ill. Philippa said:

'I'm sorry to disturb you, but I wonder if you can help me. I'm looking for a Mr Martin Ducton who lived next door ten years ago. There isn't anyone at home there and I thought you might be able to help.'

The woman said nothing, but stood transfixed, one brown claw-like hand still on the door-chain, the only visible eye staring blankly at Philippa's face. Then there were more steps, firmer and heavier but still muffled. A male voice said:

'Who is it, Ma? What's up?'

'It's a girl, she's asking for Martin Ducton.'

The woman's voice was a whisper, sibilant with wonder and a kind of outrage. A chubby male hand released the chain, and the woman stood there, dwarfed by her son. He was wearing slacks topped with a singlet. On his feet were red carpet slippers. Perhaps, thought Philippa, he was a bus driver or conductor relaxing on his rest day. It hadn't been a good time to call. She said apologetically:

'I'm sorry to trouble you, but I'm trying to trace a Mr Martin Ducton. He used to live next door. I wondered whether you might know what happened to him.'

'Ducton? He's dead, isn't he? Been dead best part of nine years. Died in Wandsworth Prison.'

'In prison?'

'Where else would he be, fucking murderer? He raped that kid, and then he and his missus strangled her. What's he to do with you then? You a reporter or something?'

'Nothing. Nothing. It must be the wrong Ducton. Perhaps I've mistaken the name.'

'Someone been having you on more likely. Ducton he was. Martin Ducton. And she was Mary Ducton. Still is.'

'She's alive then?'

'As far as I know. Coming out soon, I shouldn't wonder. Must've done near ten years by now. Not that she'll be coming back next door. Four families have had that place since the Ductons. It always goes cheap, that house. Young couple bought it six months ago. It's not everyone fancies a place where a kid's been done in. Upstairs in the front room it was.'

He nodded his head towards number 41, but his eyes never met Philippa's face. The woman said suddenly:

'They should've been hung.'

Philippa, astonished, heard herself reply:

'Hanged. The word is hanged. They should have been hanged.'

'That's right,' said the man.

He turned to his mother.

'Buried the kid in Epping Forest didn't they? Isn't that what they did with her, Ma? Buried her in Epping Forest. Twelve years old she was. You remember, Ma?'

Perhaps the woman was deaf. His last words were an impatient shout. She didn't answer. Still staring at Philippa, she said:

'Her name was Julie Scase. I remember now. They killed Julie Scase. But they never got as far as the forest. Caught with the kid's body in the car boot they was. Julie Scase.'

Philippa made herself ask through lips so stiff that she could hardly form the words:

'Did they have any children? Did you know them?'

'No. We weren't here then. We moved here from Romford after they were inside. There was talk of a kid, a girl, weren't it, who was adopted. Best thing for the poor little bugger.'

Philippa said:

'Then it's not the same Ducton. This Ducton had no children. I've been given the wrong address. I'm sorry to have troubled you.'

She walked away from them down the road. Her legs felt swollen and heavy, weighted bolsters which had no connection with the rest of her body, yet which carried her forward. She looked down at the paving stones, using them as a guide like a drunkard under test. She guessed that the woman and her son were still watching her, and when she had gone about twenty yards she made herself turn round and gaze back at them stolidly. Immediately they disappeared. Alone now in the empty road, no longer under surveillance, she found that she couldn't go on. She stretched her hands towards the brick wall bordering the nearest garden, found it and sat. She felt faint and a little sick, her heart constricted like a hot pulsating ball. But she mustn't faint here, not in this street. Somehow she must get back to the station. She let her head drop between her knees and felt the blood pound back into her forehead. The faintness passed but the nausea was worse. She sat up again, shutting her eyes against the reeling houses, taking deep gulps of the flower-scented air. Then she opened her eyes and made herself concentrate on the things she could touch and feel. She ran her fingers over the roughness of the wall. Once it had been topped with iron railings. She could feel the coarse grain of the cement-filled holes where they had pierced the brickwork. Perhaps the railings had been taken away in the war to be melted down for armaments. She gazed fixedly at the paving stone under her feet. It was pricked with light, set with infinitesimal specks, bright as diamonds. Pollen from the gardens had blown over it and there was a single flattened rose petal like a drop of blood. How extraordinary that a paving stone should be so varied, should reveal under the intensity of her gaze such gleaming wonders. These things at least were real, and she was real – more vulnerable, less durable than bricks and stones but still present, visible, an identity. If people passed, surely they would be able to see her. A youngish woman came out of the house two doors down and walked towards her, pushing a pram with an older child trotting beside it and holding on to the handle. The woman glanced at Philippa, but the child dragged his steps then turned and gazed back at her with a wide, incurious gaze. He had let go of the pram handle and she found herself struggling to her feet, holding out her arms towards him in warning or entreaty. Then the mother stopped and called to him and the child ran up to her and grasped the pram again.

She watched them until they turned the corner into the High Street. It was time to go. She couldn't sit here all day fastened to the wall as if it were a refuge, the one solid reality in a shifting world. Some words of Bunyan came into her mind and she found herself speaking them aloud:

'"Some also have wished that the next way to their father's house were here, and that they might be troubled no more with either hills or mountains to go over, but the way is the way and there is an end."'

She didn't know why the words comforted her. She wasn't particularly fond of Bunyan and she couldn't see why the passage should speak to her confused mind in which disappointment, anguish and fear struggled for mastery. But as she walked back to the station she spoke the passage over and over again as if the words were in their own way as immutable and solid as the pavement on which she trod. 'The way is the way, and there is an end.'

THREE

When he was working, and that was most of the year, Maurice Palfrey used his room at college. The sociology department had swelled since his appointment as senior lecturer, borne on the sixties' tide of optimism and secular faith, and had overflown into an agreeable late eighteenth-century house owned by the college in a Bloomsbury square. He shared the house with the Department of Oriental Studies, colleagues notable for their unobtrusiveness and for the number of their visitors. A succession of small, dark, spectacled men and saried women slid daily through the front door and disappeared into an uncanny silence. He seemed always to be encountering them on the narrow stairs; there were steppings back, bowings, slant-eyed smiles; but only an occasional footfall creaked the upper floor. He felt the house to be infected with secret, mice-like busyness.

His room had once been part of the elegant first-floor drawing-room, its three tall windows and wrought-iron balcony overlooking the square gardens, but it had been divided to provide a room for his secretary. The grace of the proportions had been destroyed and the delicately carved overmantel, the George Morland oil which had always hung in the business room at Pennington and which he had placed above it, the two Regency chairs looked pretentious and spurious. He felt the need to explain to visitors that he hadn't furnished his room with reproductions. And the conversion hadn't been a success. His secretary had to pass through his room to get to hers and the clatter of the typewriter through the thin partition was so irritating a metallic *obbligato* to his meetings that he had to tell Molly to stop working when he had visitors. It was difficult to concentrate during meetings when he was aware that she was sitting next door glowering across her machine in sullen, ostentatious idleness. Elegance and beauty had been sacrificed for a utility which wasn't even efficient. Helena, on her first visit to the room, had merely said: 'I don't like conversions' and hadn't visited again. Hilda, who hadn't appeared to notice or care about the room's proportions, had left the department after their marriage and had never come back.

The habit of working away from home had begun after his marriage to Helena when she had bought 68 Caldecote Terrace. Walking hand in hand through the empty echoing rooms like exploring children, folding back the shutters so that the sun came through in great shafts and lay in pools on the unpolished boards, the pattern of their future together had been laid down. She had made it plain that there would be no intrusion of his work into their domestic life. When he had suggested that he would need a study she had pointed out that the house was too small, the whole of the top floor was needed for the nursery and the nanny. She was prepared, apparently, to wash and cook with the aid of daily help, but not to look after her child. She had enumerated their necessities, the drawing-room, dining-room, their two bedrooms and the spare bedroom. There had been no study at Pennington; the suggestion seemed to her eccentric. And there could hardly be a library. She had been brought up with the Wren library at Pennington, and to her any other private library was merely a room in which people kept books.

Now, when he had long ago worked through his grief – and how accurately some of his colleagues had described that interestingly painful psychological process – when he could distance himself even from humiliation and pain, he was intrigued by the moral eccentricity which could, apparently without compunction, father on him another man's child, yet which was outraged by the thought of abortion. He recalled their words when she had told him about the child. He had asked:

'What do you want to do about it, have an abortion?'

'Of course not. Don't be so bourgeois, darling.'

'Abortion can be thought of as distasteful, undesirable, dangerous or even morally wrong if you think in those terms. I don't see what's bourgeois about it.'

'It's all those things. Why on earth should you suppose I want an abortion?'

'You might feel that the baby would be a nuisance.'

'My old nanny is a nuisance, so is my father. I don't kill them off.'

'Then what do you want to do?'

'Marry you, of course. You are free, aren't you? You haven't a wife secreted away somewhere?'

'No, I haven't a wife. But my darling love, you can't want to marry me.'

'I never know what I want. I'm only really sure of what I don't want. But I think we'd better marry.'

It had been the commonest, the most obvious of cheats, and he the most gullible of victims. But he had been in love for the first and only time, a state which he now realized didn't conduce to clear thinking. Poets were right to call love a madness. His love had certainly been a kind of insanity in the sense that his thought processes, his perception of external reality, even his physical life, appetite, digestion, sleep, all had been disturbed. Small wonder that he hadn't calculated with what flattering speed she had singled him out during that short holiday at Perugia, how short the time between that first appraising look across the dining-room table to getting him into her bed.

It was true that she only knew what she didn't want. Her needs had seemed to him reassuringly modest, her unwants had all the force of strong desire. He was surprised that they had found the house in Caldecote Terrace so quickly. All districts of London were apparently impossible for her. Hampstead was too trendy, Mayfair too expensive, Bayswater vulgar, Belgravia too smart. And they had been restricted in choice by her refusal to contemplate a mortgage. It was useless for him to point out the advantages of tax relief. A nineteenth-century earl had once mortgaged Pennington, to the embarrassment of his encumbered heirs. A mortgage was bourgeois. In the end they had found Caldecote Terrace in Pimlico and here she had given him, however casual the gift, the four happiest years of his life. Her death, Orlando's death, had taught him all he knew about suffering. He was glad now that no premature knowledge had despoiled those first few months of grief. It hadn't been until two years after his marriage to Hilda, seeking medical advice on their childlessness, that he had learnt the truth; that he could never father a child. That period of mourning for a woman who hadn't existed, for a son who wasn't his son, now seemed to him a debt discharged, not without honour, a secular grace.

He had grieved more for Orlando than for Helena. Helena's death had been the loss of a joy to which he had never felt entitled, which had never seemed quite real, which he had hoped, rather than expected, would last. Some part of his mind had accepted her loss as inevitable; death could not part them more completely than could life. But for Orlando he had mourned with an elemental violence of grief, a wordless scream of anguish. The death of a beautiful, intelligent and happy child had always seemed to him an outrage, and this child had been his son. His grief had seemed to embrace a cosmic fellowship of suffering. He had indulged no inordinate hopes for Orlando, fostered on his child no high ambition, had asked only that he should continue to exist in his beauty, his loving kindness, his peculiarly uncoordinated grace.

And it was because Orlando had died that he had married Hilda. He knew that their friends found the marriage an enigma. It was easily explained. Hilda was the only one among his friends, his colleagues, who had wept for Orlando. The day after his return from the funeral at Pennington – the depositing of Helena and Orlando in the family vault had symbolized for him the final separation, they lay now with their own kind – she had come into his office with the morning post. He could remember how she had looked, the white schoolgirl's blouse, the skirt which she had pressed that morning, he could see the impress of the iron across the front pleat. She stood there at the door looking at him. All she said was: 'That little boy. That little boy.' He had watched while her face stiffened and then disintegrated with grief. Two tears oozed from her eyes and ran unchecked over her cheeks.

She had only known Orlando briefly on the few occasions when his nurse had brought him into the office. But she had wept for him. His colleagues had written and spoken their condolences, averting their eyes from a grief they could not assuage. Death was in poor taste. They had treated him with sympathetic wariness, as if he were suffering from a slightly embarrassing disease. She only had paid Orlando the tribute of a spontaneous tear.

And that had been the beginning. It had led to the first invitation to dinner, to their theatre dates, to the curious courtship which had merely reinforced their misconceptions about each other. He had persuaded himself that she was teachable, that she had a goodness and simplicity which could meet his complicated needs, that behind the bland gentle face was a mind which only needed the stimulus of his loving concern to break into some kind of flowering, what he was never precisely sure. And she had been so different from Helena. It had been flattering to give instead of to take, to be the one who was loved instead of the one who loved. And so, with what to some of his colleagues had seemed indecent haste, they had come to that Registry Office wedding. Poor girl, she had hoped for a white wedding in church. That quiet exchange of contracts could hardly have seemed to her or her parents like a proper marriage. She had got through it in an agony of embarrassment, afraid perhaps that the registrar had thought that she was pregnant.

He was suddenly aware of his restlessness. He walked across to the tall window and looked out over the dishevelled square. Although the slight rain had now stopped, the plane trees were bedraggled and scraps of sodden litter lay unmoving on the spongy grass. This slow dripping away of the summer matched his mood. He had always disliked the hiatus between academic years when the detritus of the last term had scarcely been cleared away, yet the next was already casting its shadow. He couldn't remember when the conscientious performance of duty had replaced enthusiasm, or when conscientiousness had finally given way to boredom. What worried him now was that he approached each academic term with an emotion more disturbing than boredom, something between irritation and apprehension. He knew that he no longer saw his students as individuals, no longer had any wish to know or communicate except on the level of tutor to student, and even here there was no trust between them. There seemed to have been a reversal of roles, he the student, they the instructors. They sat in the ubiquitous uniform of the young, jeans and sweaters, huge clumpy plimsolls, open-necked shirts topped with denim jackets, and gazed at him with the fixity of inquisitors waiting for any deviation from orthodoxy. He told himself that they were no different from his former students, graceless, not very intelligent, uneducated if education implied the ability to write their own language with elegance and precision, to think clearly, to discriminate or enjoy. They were filled with the barely suppressed anger of those who have grabbed for themselves sufficient privilege to know just how little privilege they would ever achieve. They didn't want to be taught, having already decided what they preferred to believe.

He had become increasingly petty, irritated by details, by the diminishing, for example, of their forenames, Bill, Bert, Mike, Geoff, Steve. He wanted to inquire peevishly if a commitment to Marxism was incompatible with a disyllabic forename. And their vocabulary provoked him. In his last series of seminars on the juvenile law they had talked always of 'kids'. The mixture of condescension and sycophancy in the word repelled him. He himself had used the words 'children' and 'young people' punctiliously and had sensed that it had annoyed them. He had found himself talking to them like a pedantic schoolmaster to the lower third:

'I've corrected some of the grammar and spelling. This may seem bourgeois pedantry, but if you plan to organize revolution you'll have to convince the intelligent and educated as well as the gullible and ignorant. It might be worthwhile trying to develop a prose style which isn't a mixture of sociological jargon and the standard expected from the C stream of a comprehensive school. And "obscene" means "lewd", "indecent", "filthy", it can't properly be used to describe Government policy in not implementing the recommendations of the Finer Report on one-parent families, reprehensible as that decision may be.'

Mike Beale, chief instigator of student power, had received back his last essay muttering under his breath. It had sounded like 'fucking bastard' and might indeed have been 'fucking bastard' except that Beale was incapable of an invective which didn't include the word 'fascist'. Beale had just completed his second year. With luck he would graduate next autumn, departing to take a social-work qualification and find himself a job with a local authority, no doubt to teach juvenile delinquents that the occasional minor act of robbery with violence was a natural response of the underprivileged to capitalist tyranny and to promote political awareness among those council-house tenants looking for an excuse not to pay their rents. But he would be replaced by others. The academic machine would grind on, and what was so extraordinary was that essentially he and Beale were on the same side. He had been too publicly committed and for too long to renege now. Socialism and sociology. He felt like an old campaigner who no longer believes in his cause but finds it enough that there is a battle and he knows his own side.

He stuffed into his briefcase the few letters he had found waiting for him in his cubby-hole that morning. One was from a Socialist Member of Parliament enlisting his help with the General Election which he took for granted would come in early October. Would Maurice talk on one of the television party political broadcasts? He supposed he would accept. The box sanctified, conferred identity. The more familiar the face, the more to be trusted. The other was yet another appeal to him to apply for the Chair in social work at a northern university. He could understand the concern among social workers about the Chair. There had been a number of recent appointments outside the field of social work. But what the protesters couldn't see was that what mattered was the quality of the academic work and of the research, not the discipline of the applicant. With the present competition for Chairs sociology needed to demonstrate its academic respectability, not pursue a spurious professionalism. He was becoming increasingly irritated by the sensitivity of colleagues, unsure of themselves, feeling morbidly undervalued, complaining that they were expected to remedy all the ills of society. He only wished that he could cure his own.

He put away the last few papers and locked his desk drawer. He remembered that tonight the Cleghorns were coming to dinner. Cleghorn was one of the trustees of a fund set up to investigate the causes and treatment of juvenile delinquency, and Maurice had a post-graduate student who was looking for a research job for the next couple of years. The advantage of giving regular dinner parties was that when one was angling for a favour an invitation to dine didn't look too blatant a ploy. Closing the door, he wondered without much curiosity where Philippa had been going that morning so early, and whether she would remember the Cleghorns and get home in time to do the dining-room flowers.

FOUR

When she finally got back to Liverpool Street, Philippa spent the rest of the day walking in the city. It was just after six when she returned to Caldecote Terrace. The rain had nearly stopped and was now so fine that it fell against her warm face as a drifting mist needled with cold. But the pavement stones were as tacky as if it had fallen heavily all day, and a few shallow puddles had collected in the gutter into which occasional dollops dropped with heavy portentousness from a sky as thick and grey as curdled milk. Number 68 looked just as it did when she returned from school on any dull summer evening. This homecoming was outwardly no different from any other. As always the basement kitchen was brightly lit and the rest of the house was in darkness except for a light shining from the hall through the elegant fanlight of the front door.

The kitchen was on the lower ground floor at the front of the house. The dining-room, which was at the back, had french doors to the garden. The whole of the raised ground floor was taken up by the drawing-room; this, too, had access to the garden by a flight of delicately carved and moulded wrought-iron steps. On summer evenings they would carry their coffee down to the patio to the chairs under the fig tree. The walled garden, only thirty feet long, enclosed the scent of roses and white stocks. The patio was set about with white-painted wooden tubs of geraniums glowing blood red in the peculiarly intense light before the setting sun, then bleached as the patio lamps were turned on.

The light was always on in the north-facing kitchen, yet Hilda never drew the curtains. Perhaps she had never realized that, to the upper world, she moved on a lighted stage. She was there now, already starting on the dinner. Philippa crouched down, clutching the railings, and peered through at her. Hilda cooked with a peculiar intensity, moving like a high priestess among the impedimenta of her craft, consulting her recipe book with the keen unblinking scrutiny of an artist examining his model, then briefly laying her hand on each ingredient like a preparatory blessing. She cleaned and tidied the rest of the house obsessively, but as if nothing it contained had anything to do with her, only here in the organized muddle of her kitchen was she at home. This was her habitat. Here she lived doubly caged behind the protecting iron bars on the windows and the spiked railings above, seeing the world pass as a succession of desultory or hurrying feet. Her pale lank hair which normally fell forward over her face was strained back from her eyes with two plastic combs. In the white apron which she invariably wore she looked very young and defenceless, like a schoolgirl, preoccupied with a practical examination, or a newly engaged maid coping with her first dinner party. And it wasn't because she worked in the kitchen that she looked like a servant. All but the wealthiest of the mothers of the girls at school did most of their own cooking. Cookery had become a fashionable craft, almost a cult. Perhaps it was the white apron, the worried eyes which seemed always to expect, almost to invite a rebuke, which made her look like a woman precariously earning her keep.

Philippa had forgotten that the Cleghorns and Gabriel Lomas were coming to dinner. She saw that the meal was to begin with artichokes. Six of them, solidly ornamental, were ranged on the central table ready for the pot. The kitchen, under the glare of the twin fluorescent lights, was as familiar as a picture on a nursery wall. The one wicker chair with its shabby patchwork cushion. It had never been necessary to buy a second since neither Maurice nor Philippa made it a habit to sit in the kitchen chatting with Hilda while she cooked. The shelf of paperback recipe books with their greasy crumpled covers, the calendar hanging beside the wall-mounted telephone with its garish blue picture of Brixham Harbour, the portable television set, black and white since the one colour set was in the drawing-room. Philippa couldn't remember ever seeing Hilda sitting alone in the drawing-room. Why should she? It wasn't her drawing-room. Everything in it had been chosen by Maurice or by his first wife.

Philippa had never heard Maurice speak of Helena, but it never occurred to her that this was because he continued to grieve for her or because he was sensitive to Hilda's feelings. She had long ago decided that he was a man who kept his emotions in compartments. That way there could be no messy spillage from one life to another. From time to time she had felt a vague curiosity about Helena Palfrey, glamorized and dignified as she was for ever by an early and dramatic death. Only once had she seen a picture of Maurice's first wife. It had been at a bring and buy sale held at school in aid of Oxfam. One of the parents had donated a bundle of glossy society magazines. They had sold well, she remembered. People were happy to give a penny or two for the brief pleasures of nostalgia and recollection. They had flicked through them giggling.

'Look, here's Molly and John at Henley. My dear, did we really wear skirts that length?'

Browsing through a bundle displayed for sale, she had seen with a shock of surprise and recognition, Maurice's face. It was a younger Maurice, strange yet utterly familiar, wearing the startled half-fatuous smile of a man suddenly caught by the camera who hasn't had time to decide what expression to assume. It had been taken at a wedding. The caption said: 'Mr Maurice Palfrey and Lady Helena Palfrey chatting to Sir George and Lady Scott-Harries'. And there they were, not chatting to anyone, but staring into the lens, champagne glasses in their hands, as if toasting this second of their joint lives ephemerally recorded in microdots. Lady Helena Palfrey, smiling, stood taller than her husband in her wide-brimmed hat and ridiculously short skirt. Dark hair framed a face which looked no longer young, bony, almost ravaged, heavy-browed. Philippa had torn out the cutting and had kept it, secreted in one of her books, for almost a year. From time to time she had taken it over to the light of her bedroom window to peer at it obsessively, willing it to disclose some clue to the woman's character, to their love, if love there had been, to their joint life together. Eventually, frustrated, she had torn it up and flushed it down the lavatory.

And now, with an equal intensity, she peered through the railings at Maurice's living wife. She was bent over the central table, carefully rolling out fillets of veal. It looked as if the dinner guests were to have veal in wine and mushroom sauce. They would praise the meal, of course; the guests invariably did. Philippa remembered having read that it was the last war which had finally killed the English reticence about the quality of a meal. Now most of the women, and sometimes the men, praised, inquired, exchanged recipes. But with Hilda the praise became effusive, strained, almost embarrassingly insincere. It was as if they needed to reassure or propitiate her, to give her worth in her own eyes. For the whole of her marriage her husband's guests had treated her as if cooking were her only interest, the only topic she could talk about. And now perhaps it was.

There were footsteps coming down the street. Philippa scrambled to her feet, wincing at the pain in her cramped legs. She felt suddenly faint and had to grasp at the spikes of the railings for support. She remembered for the first time that she had walked for nearly seven hours through the streets of London, round the parks, in and out of the City churches, along the Embankment, without stopping to eat. Painfully, she made her way up the steps to the front door.

She turned her key in the lock and passed through the inner porch with its twin panels of Burne-Jones stained glass, an allegory of spring and summer, into the pearl-grey quietness of the hall. She smelled the usual faint smell of lavender and fresh paint, so faint that it was almost illusory, a conditioned response to the familiar objects of home. The delicate banister rail in polished pale mahogany supported by elegant balustrades, unwound from its scroll and curved upwards drawing the eye to the stained glass of the landing window. The two panes were a continuation of the ones in the porch, a garlanded woman with a cornucopia spilling the fruits of autumn, bearded winter with his faggots and stave. By an earlier taste their self-conscious aestheticism and period charm would have been despised; now Maurice, who didn't particularly like them, wouldn't have dreamed of having them removed, probably knowing to a pound the value they added to his property. But the rest of the hall was his taste, his or that of his first wife; the low shelf with his collection of Staffordshire historical groups, bold against the shiny white wood; a pale elongated Nelson dying black-booted in Hardy's arms; Wellington, Field-Marshal's baton on his hip, mounted on his charger Copenhagen; Victoria and Albert with their blond idealized children grouped before the Grand Exhibition; a lighthouse rising from a turbulent sea of unchipped waves, with Grace Darling straining on her oars. Above them, in incongruous proximity but looking somehow right since both combined strength with delicacy, were Maurice's three nineteenth-century Japanese prints in their curved rosewood frames; Nobukazu, Kikugawa, Tokohumi. Like the Staffordshire, which as a child she had been allowed to dust, they were part of her childhood, ferocious warriors with their curved swords, pale moons behind delicate blossomed boughs, the soft pinks and greens of the slant-eyed women in their kimonos. Had she really only known them for ten years? Where then had been those other hallways, forgotten except in nightmares, with their dark dados, the lank greasy mackintoshes hanging inside the door, the smell of cabbage and fish, the claustrophobic horror of the black cupboard under the stairs?

Without taking off her coat she went down to the kitchen. Hilda came out of the pantry, a box of eggs in her hand. Without looking at Philippa she said:

'I'm glad you're back. We've got the Cleghorns for dinner. Can you do the table and the flowers, darling?'

Philippa didn't answer. She felt very calm, light-headed with tiredness, her anger spent. She was glad that she had no need to discipline her voice, that she was in complete control. She closed the kitchen door and leaned her back against it as if barring Hilda's escape. She waited until Hilda, getting no answer, looked up at her. Then she said:

'Why didn't you tell me that my mother was a murderess?'

But she needed to discipline herself after all. Hilda looked so ridiculous, stuck there speechless, mouth gaping, eyes wide with fright, the personification of stage horror, that she had to make a conscious effort to stop herself breaking into nervous laughter. She watched while the box of eggs dropped from Hilda's parting hands as if she had willed them to fall. One bounced free and cracked open, spilling an unbroken dome of yellow, shivering in its glutinous pad of white. Instinctively Philippa stepped towards it. Hilda cried out sharply:

'Don't step in it! Don't step in it!'

Moaning she seized a cloth and dabbed at the yolk. There was a splurge of yellow over the black and white tiles. Still kneeling, she muttered:

'The Cleghorns, they're coming to dinner. I haven't done the table yet. I knew you'd find out! I told him. I always said so. Who told you? Where have you been all day?'

'I applied for a copy of my birth certificate under the Children Act. Then I went to 41 Bancroft Gardens. There was no one in, but a neighbour told me. Then I spent the day walking in the City. After that I came home, I mean I came back here.'

Hilda was still scrubbing at the tiles, smearing the yellow mucus. She said wildly:

'I don't want to talk about it, not now! I've got to get on with dinner. The Cleghorns are coming. It's important to your father.'

'The Cleghorns? How can it be? If they want something from him they'll hardly complain if the food isn't up to expectations. And if he wants something from them, then he's wasting his time if their decision can be swayed by whether the veal is the best they've eaten since they found that intriguing little inn in the Dordogne.'

She explained patiently:

'Look, they don't matter. I matter. Why didn't you tell me?'

'How could we? A thing like that. They killed that girl. Raped and murdered her. She was only twelve! What good would it have done, your knowing? It wasn't your fault. It was nothing to do with you. I don't want to think about it. It was horrible, horrible! There are things you can't tell a child, ever. It would have been too cruel.'

'More cruel than letting me find out?'

Hilda turned on her with a sudden flash of defensive spirit.

'Yes, cruel and wrong! You don't mind so much now. At least you're grown up. You have your own life, your own personality. It can't destroy you now. You wouldn't be talking like this if you really cared. You're excited and angry, and I suppose you're shocked, but you aren't really hurt. It isn't real to you. You stand outside life and look at it as if you aren't really part of it. You watch people as if they're acting on some kind of stage. That's how you were looking down at me just now. You thought I didn't know you were there, but I did. You don't really care what your mother did to that child. It doesn't touch you. Nothing does.'

Philippa stared at Hilda, disconcerted by this unexpected percipience. She cried:

'But I want it to touch me! I want to feel it!'

She thought:

'It's because I don't really believe it yet. All my past is fabrication. This is just a new story, a different angle, to be explored and experienced. Then I shall return to the reality I fabricated for myself, to that unknown father striding across the lawn at Pennington. It is these newcomers, not he, who are the usurpers.'

Hilda was rinsing out the floor-cloth under the tap, muttering above the splash of the water.

'When you came in just now – you knew what you were going to say. I expect you practised it in the train. But you aren't really unhappy. You're not as unhappy as you would have been if you hadn't got your Cambridge scholarship. You're like your father, neither of you can bear to fail.'

'You mean I'm like Maurice. I don't know whether I'm like my father. That's one of the things I mean to find out.'

'It was Parliament, that Act they passed. They had no right. It was breaking faith with adopters. When we took you on we thought that you'd never be able to find out who your parents were.'

'Took you on.' Was that how Hilda had always seen her, as an obligation, a responsibility, a burden? Probably Hilda had never really wanted her. Why should she? A baby adopted from birth, pitiful, dependent, responsive, might have done something for Hilda's frustrated maternal feelings. But what satisfaction could she have expected from a difficult and resentful eight-year-old whose parents had suddenly been taken from her, had disappeared without explanation? No, it had been Maurice's doing. Maurice had demanded his experimental material. But the idea of adoption must have been Hilda's. She must have been the one who had originally agitated for a child. Maurice wouldn't have cared one way or the other. But if there had to be an adopted child to satisfy Hilda's thwarted maternal instinct, then he would at least ensure that they chose one with intelligence but from the worst possible background. If he couldn't have a child of his own, at least he could rear one for the glory of sociological theory. It was surprising that he hadn't selected a second female, carefully matched for age and intelligence, to monitor their joint progress.

After all, every experiment needed a control. How he and Hilda must have enjoyed their secret! Was this what had kept their odd marriage intact, the titillating confederacy of deceit?

She said:

'I could have applied to a court for permission to see my birth certificate once I came of age. That's always been the law, even if people didn't realize it.'

'But you wouldn't have done that, and if you had, at least we'd have been warned. Then we could have told the court and the judge wouldn't have given you permission. But even if he had, it would still have been better than learning it when you were a child.'

'And all those stories? My mother being a servant at Pennington and dying soon after I was born. Did you concoct them together?'

'No, that was me. He just wanted to tell you that we didn't know who your parents were. But I had to tell you something when you asked. The story just grew.'

'And that bit about the letter my mother wrote, the letter to be handed to me when I'm twenty-one?'

Hilda gazed up at her, puzzled.

'I never told you that. What letter? I didn't say anything about a letter.'

So that part must have been her own fabrication. Together she and Hilda, in unconscious collaboration, had created and embellished their joint fantasy, a small detail there, a touch of local colour, snatches of imagined conversation, small descriptions. Sometimes Hilda had been forced by Philippa's obsessional questions into embarrassed evasions, but Philippa had always put these down to Hilda's embarrassment at any mention of Pennington and Maurice's first wife. But she had done it very cleverly, you had to give her that. The story had hung together without obvious inconsistencies. Philippa's mother had been a parlourmaid at Pennington. She had given birth to an illegitimate child and had died shortly afterwards. The baby had been fostered by people in the village, now dead, and then by foster parents in London. Maurice had heard about her on one of his return visits to Pennington after his first wife's death, and had suggested to

Hilda that they should foster the child. The fostering had been successful and had led six months later to adoption. There was no one now to disprove any of it. The present Earl had sold Pennington nine years previously and had taken refuge from taxation and the exigencies of his ex-wives in the south of France. Very few of the original servants lived in Pennington village and none still worked in the house. It had subsequently been sold to an Arab and was now closed to the public. It would have been difficult to disprove the story and Philippa had never had any inclination to try. It had, she realized now, conformed too neatly with her own private imaginings. She had believed it because she had wanted it to be true. And even now, one small part of her mind obstinately refused to relinquish it.

She said bitterly:

'You'd be a good liar in the witness box. I wouldn't have credited you with that much imagination. I knew that it embarrassed you to talk about my mother but I thought that was because she came from Pennington. It must have amused you, fooling me all these years. I hope it was some compensation for having me foisted on you.'

Hilda cried:

'It wasn't like that! I wanted you! We both wanted you! When I found out I couldn't give Maurice a child . . .'

'You make a baby sound like an orgasm. And if that's all he married you for – and I can't think why else – it's a pity he didn't send you to a gynaecologist for a certificate of fertility before you went off together to the Registry Office.'

They heard the quiet thud of the front door closing. Hilda said:

'It's your father! Maurice is home!'

She spoke wildly, terrified, like a woman awaiting a drunken husband. Then she dashed to the bottom of the stairs and called:

'Maurice! Maurice! Come here!'

The footsteps hesitated, then came deliberately down the stairs. He stood in the kitchen doorway watching them. Hilda cried:

'She knows! She found out about that clause in the Children Act. I told you she would. She's got her birth certificate. She's been to Bancroft Gardens.'

He said to Philippa:

'How much do you know?'

'How much is there? That I'm the child of a rapist and a murderess.'

She was glad that he didn't love her, that neither of them loved her, that there was no risk that he would come across to her in spontaneous pity and smother all the shock and misery in his arms. He said calmly:

'I'm sorry, Philippa. I suppose this moment was inevitable, but I wish it didn't have to happen.'

'You should have told me.'

He placed his briefcase on the table, calmly moving the artichokes to make room.

'Even if I agree, and I don't, there hasn't been a moment since the adoption when it seemed the right time to tell. What time precisely would you have chosen? When you were adjusting to living here, when you were eleven and taking the examination into the South London Collegiate, when you were coping with adolescence, working for O-levels, A-levels, the Cambridge scholarship? Ten years pass very quickly, particularly when punctuated with the crises of childhood. With some news, the later the better.'

'Where is she now?'

'Your mother? At Melcombe Grange in the pre-release unit. It's an open prison near York. She's due out I believe in about a month's time.'

'You knew that!'

'I've had an interest in her release date, naturally. But that's all. She's not my responsibility. There's nothing I can do about it.'

'But I can. I can write to her and ask her to come to me. I've saved the money for my European trip. I can take a flat in London and look after her, at least for the two months before I go up to Cambridge.'

The idea, spontaneous, surprising even to her own ears, seemed to have come from outside herself, an impulse not subject to her will. And yet she knew even as she spoke the words that this was what she must do, what she had intended to do from that first moment of learning that her mother was alive. She didn't think about her motives; this wasn't the moment for that egotistical indulgence. But her heart told her that they were corrupt, that this histrionic gesture was born, not out of compassion for that unknown mother, but out of her anger against Maurice, her misery, her own complicated half-acknowledged needs.

He had turned away from her and she couldn't see his face. But his voice was suddenly hard. He said:

'The idea is stupid and dangerous, dangerous for both of you. You owe her nothing, not even the conventional obligations of a child to a parent. All that was expunged with the adoption order. And there's nothing that she has that you need, nothing that she can give you.'

'I wasn't thinking of obligations. And there is something I need that she can give me. Information. Knowledge. A past. She can help me to find out who I am. Don't you understand? She's my mother! I can't wipe that out any more than I can wipe out what she did. I can't suddenly learn that she's alive and not want to meet her, get to know her. What do you expect me to do? Go on as if today had never happened? Concoct a new fantasy to live by? Everything you and Hilda have given me is pretence. This is real.'

Hilda gave a small ridiculous sound between a snort and a sob. Maurice turned and slowly lifted his briefcase from the table. Suddenly he looked and sounded very tired. He said:

'We'll talk about it after dinner. It's a nuisance that the Cleghorns are coming, but we can't put them off at less than an hour's notice. As I said, there's never a convenient moment for this kind of news.'

FIVE

She dressed with care. The guests were only to be the Cleghorns and Gabriel Lomas to even up the numbers, but it wasn't for them that she put on her favourite evening skirt of fine pleated wool and the high-necked green-blue tunic; she was dressing for herself. The skirt and top fulfilled what she most demanded of clothes, that they should be dramatic but easy to put on and sensuously agreeable to wear. She took care with her hair, brushing it until her scalp smarted then winding it in a high top-knot, curling two thin strands with a wetted finger to lie against each cheek. Afterwards she stood and surveyed herself in the full-length glass. This is how I see myself. How do I look to others?

It surprised her that she was so calm; that the long, bony, honey-coloured face, with its high cheekbones, was so clear in its outlines, the eyes so unclouded. She had half expected the image to fudge and quiver like a reflection seen in a distorting mirror. She stretched out her hands, and fingers splayed to meet fingers encountering the cold glass.

She began to pace slowly round the room, looking at it with the appraising eyes of an inquisitive stranger. It stretched the whole length of the house on the top storey where two attics had been converted into one large, low-ceilinged room. Maurice had furnished it for her to her taste when she was twelve. Unlike the rest of the house it was modern, functional, sparsely furnished, giving an impression of airiness, of being suspended in space. It was very light with windows at each end. The southern window gave a view of the small walled garden and York stone patio, of plane trees, of the multitudinous and varied roofs of Pimlico. The furniture was modern, the bed and fitted wall units in pale wood. At this desk she had worked for O- and A-levels and for her Cambridge entrance. On this bed she and Gabriel had groped and twined in that first unsuccessful attempt at making love. The phrase struck her as ridiculous. Whatever they had been making together, it hadn't been love. He had said, gently at first, and then with controlled irritation:

'Stop thinking about yourself. Stop worrying about what you're feeling. Let yourself go.'

But that she had never been able to do. How could you let go of something which you had never felt was yours to relinquish? To let go implied the utter confidence of undisputed possession, the assurance that nothing of oneself could be violated by that transitory, terrifying loss of control.

It surprised her that this initial sexual fiasco hadn't resulted in an estrangement. Like her, he couldn't tolerate failure. And afterwards, unsatisfied and frustrated, she hadn't even managed the expedience of pretence or the grace of generosity. It had been a bad time to recall the warning of his sister; Sarah's voice, cool, amused, a little spiteful:

'My brother seems to look on the upper sixth as his private harem. He's AC/DC by the way. Not that it matters. But it's as well to know these little details before you try to plug in your kettle.'

Pulling on her dressing-gown, she had said:

'Why did you bother? Was it to prove that you can make it with a woman?'

And he had replied:

'What were you trying to prove? That you can make it at all?'

But he had, if anything, been more attentive, more apparently devoted since that disastrous evening, and she suspected that he knew perfectly well why she played her part in their charade. He was high on her list of objects of use and beauty which she planned to take with her to Cambridge. Having the rich and amusing Honourable Gabriel Lomas in tow would do her absolutely no harm with her contemporaries at King's.

Settling down at this desk to write a history essay on the first Saturday morning after the room had been completed, she had learned an early lesson, that undeserved good fortune was resented. Mrs Cooper, Hilda's cleaning woman, had been brought up by Hilda to admire the room. Hilda involved her in any new domestic arrangements, apparently in a desperate attempt to pretend that they liked each other. But Mrs Cooper, unpropitiated, persisted in calling her 'madam' and held aloof as if to demonstrate that ten shillings an hour and a free lunch could buy obsequiousness, but it couldn't buy affection. She had stared round the room before giving her customary unenthusiastic verdict. 'It's very nice, madam, I'm sure.' But she had lingered a few seconds when Hilda left, then coming quickly up to Philippa had pushed her face close to her cheek. The words had come in a hiss of sour breath.

'Bastard. I hope you're grateful. It isn't right. All this for a bastard when decent kids have to make do four in a room. You ought to be in a Home.'

Then her voice had again become respectful:

'Coming, madam.'

Philippa could recall still the shock and anger. But she had learned control. There were no tantrums now. Words, she had discovered, were more effective than screams, more hurtful than kicks and blows. She had said coolly:

'You shouldn't breed four children if you can't afford them. And I expect they'll go on living four to a room if they're as ugly and stupid as you.'

After that Mrs Cooper had handed in her notice, but without giving a reason, and Hilda, as Philippa knew, had been left with an added weight of inadequacy and failure.

She walked across to the bookshelves and ran her hand along the spines of the books. Here was the orthodox library of an upper-middle-class student. With these volumes you could pass an A-level in English literature whatever the year or the syllabus; with luck and a good memory you could even achieve a Cambridge entrance. It wasn't easy to deduce the girl's personal taste, except perhaps that she preferred Turgenev to Tolstoy, Proust to Flaubert, Henry James to Dickens. But here were no battered childhood favourites passed from generation to generation. True the accepted upper-middle-class children's classics were present, the *Just So Stories*, *The Wind in the Willows*; Carroll, and Ransome and Nesbit. They looked read, but they looked, also, as if they had been bought new for this privileged child.

Here on these packed shelves was enough knowledge, wisdom, imagination to sustain her for life. For what life? There wasn't a word which she herself had written, yet it was in this accumulation of other men's thoughts and experiences that she had looked for an affirmation of identity. She thought:

'Even putting on the clothes of my choice was only putting on myself. Naked in the bathroom just now, who was I? I can be described, measured, weighed, my physical processes recorded, given a name, real or unreal, for the convenient documentation of a life. But who am I? But whoever I am, nothing of me comes from Maurice and Hilda. How could it? They've done nothing but provide the props for this charade, the clothes, the artefacts. Even this soliloquy is contrived. Some part of me, that part of me which one day will make me a writer, is watching another me choosing the words to think, deciding what emotions are appropriate to feel.'

She opened the immense fitted wardrobe and rattled the hangers along the rail. The swaying skirts and dresses emitted a faint scent which she recognized as familiar. It must be her own. This girl liked expensive clothes. She bought little but she bought with care. She wore only wool and cotton; obviously she disliked synthetics. She smiled at the facile irony.

She moved over to the noticeboard of charcoal-coloured cork fitted to the wall above the desk unit. It was patterned with postcards, obviously bought on holidays or at art galleries, a school timetable, notices cut from newspapers of forthcoming art exhibitions, *aides-mémoire*, two invitations to parties. She examined the postcards. Hans Holbein's delicate portrait of Cecily Heron; Augustus John's etching of W. B. Yeats; a Renoir nude from the Musée du Jeu de Paume; a Farington aquatint of London Bridge in 1799; a George Brecht. How could one deduce this unknown girl's taste in art from such capricious pickings? They told one nothing except which galleries she had visited.

In this room, she had concocted for herself over ten years a whole mythology of identity. It was slipping away from her now, that dead discredited world. She told herself, nothing has changed; I am the same person as I was yesterday. But who was I yesterday? The room reminded her of a designer's room in a furniture store, its carefully chosen objects disposed around to give the illusion of an absent owner, but one who had no reality except in the designer's mind.

She recalled Hilda's face bending over her to tuck her in at night.

'Where am I when I'm asleep?'

'You're still here, in bed.'

'But how do you know?'

'Because I can see you, silly. I can touch you.'

Only, of course, she very seldom did touch. The three of them lived distanced. That hadn't been Hilda's fault. When Philippa was tucked in at night she had lain rigid, rejecting the final, and in the end merely dutiful, kiss, hating that moist encounter of the flesh more than the rough tickle of the blanket which Hilda always drew from under the sheet and tucked against her face.

'But you know you are here because you can see and touch me. When I'm asleep I can't see or touch anyone.'

'No one can when they're asleep. But you're still here in your bed.'

'If I went into hospital and had an anaesthetic, where would I be then. Not my body, where would *I* be?'

'Best ask Daddy.'

'When I am dead where will I be?'

'With Jesus in Heaven.'

But Hilda had spoken that heresy against Maurice's atheism without conviction.

She was drawn again to the bookcase. Here, surely, if anywhere an answer was to be found. And here, ranked together, were the first editions of Maurice's books, all inscribed in his hand with the name he had bestowed on her. It was surprising in view of this industry that no university had offered him a Chair. Perhaps others prominent in his discipline detected in him a dilettantism, a less than whole-hearted commitment to his subject. Or was it simpler than that? Perhaps the rebarbative arrogance of some of his public criticisms irritated or repelled them, as she suspected it might do his pupils. But here they were, the most recent fruits of his intellectual preoccupations, elegantly written for a sociologist, impeccable in scholarship and style, or so the critics said, the books which partly explained Maurice. Now, of course, she saw that they explained her too. *Nature and Nurture: Genetic and Environmental Interactions in Language Development. Tackling Disadvantage: Social Class, Language and Intelligence. Genes and Environment: Environmental Influences on the Concept of Object Permanence. Schooled to Fail: Class Poverty and Education in Great Britain.* Had he planned one day to add another? *Adoption: A Case Study in the Interaction of Heredity and Environment.*

Last of all she comforted herself with a long look at her most prized possession, the Henry Walton oil painting of the Reverend Joseph Skinner and family which she had chosen as Maurice's gift for her eighteenth birthday. It was an extraordinarily attractive and competent painting with none of the slightly sentimental charm of some of his later works. Here was all the elegance, the order, the confidence and the formal good manners of her favourite period in English history. The Reverend Skinner and his three sons were mounted, his wife and two daughters were seated in a barouche. Behind them was their solid decent house, before them their carriage drive, their shadowed lawn set with oaks. They could have had no crises of identity. The long Skinner faces, the high-arched Skinner noses proclaimed their lineage. And yet they spoke to her, telling her only that they had lived and suffered, endured and died. And so in her time would she.

SIX

Harry Cleghorn who, at forty-five and already balding, still managed to retain his reputation as an up-and-coming politician, looked to Philippa so like a successful Tory back-bencher that she supposed his political career to have been inevitable. He was strongly muscled with a smooth, high-coloured skin, hair so black that it looked dyed, and a moist, rather petulant, mouth whose lips, red at the outlines as if lipsticked, revealed when he spoke an under-bleb of soft pale pink. As far as Philippa could see, he and Maurice had nothing in common except their appearance together as members of the same television chat show and their status as television personalities. But what else did they need to have in common? Differences of background, temperament, interests or political philosophy all faded in the unifying glare which the television studio lights shed on the company of the elect.

Nora Cleghorn faced her across the table, her over-made-up face softened by the candlelight. She must have been attractive when she was twenty to those who liked fair doll-like prettiness, but hers was a beauty which faded early, depending as it did on a pert perfection of skin and colouring, and not on bone structure. She was a silly woman, excessively proud of her husband, but few people disliked her, perhaps because there was something endearingly naïve about a belief that membership of the House of Commons represented the summit of human aspiration. She was, as usual, overdressed for an informal dinner party, gleamingly metallic in a sequined, sleeveless top over a velvet skirt. As their shoulders brushed in the doorway she smelled to Philippa of hot moist coins which had been steeped in scent.

If Nora Cleghorn were over-dressed, so was Gabriel Lomas,

since he was the only man wearing a dinner-jacket. But with Gabriel one knew that sartorial eccentricity was deliberate. Maurice apparently liked him despite – or could it be because of – his affectation of an extreme right-wing Toryism. Perhaps it made a change from the majority of his students. For his part, Gabriel sometimes seemed to Philippa to be excessively interested in Maurice. It was from Gabriel that she had learnt most of what she knew about Helena Palfrey. Since she had almost total recall of any conversation which really interested her, she could perfectly remember one snatch of conversation.

'Your father is like all rich Socialists, there's a Tory inside which he's struggling to keep down.'

She had replied:

'I don't think Maurice qualifies as a rich Socialist. You shouldn't be misled by our life-style. He inherited this house and most of the furniture and pictures from his first wife. Maurice's background is perfectly respectable from the Comrades' point of view. Dad was a Post Office supervisor, leading light in the union. Maurice hasn't rebelled, merely conformed.'

'He married an earl's daughter. I don't call that conforming. Admittedly an eccentric earl who is somewhat of an embarrassment to his class, but there's nothing suspect about his lineage, no Victorian creation there. Admittedly, too, knowing Lady Helena, people wondered why marriage, until she produced a baby seven months later, the only seven-month prem to weigh in at eight and a half pounds.'

'Gabriel, how on earth do you get to know these things?'

'An addiction to petty gossip acquired during childhood, long summer afternoons in Kensington Gardens listening to Nanny and her cronies. Sarah, grossly over-dressed, sitting up in the huge, shabby family pram, me trotting by the side. God, the suffocating boredom of those perambulations round the Round Pond! Be grateful, privileged little bastard that you are, that you were spared them.'

Now as they started on their artichokes, Gabriel was indulging in a minor Maurice tease, pretending to believe that a recent Labour Party political broadcast by a group of Young Socialists had been put out by the Tory Party.

'Naughty of them, although I don't think it will make them any converts. And if they wanted to scare us I think they rather overdid it. Surely even the young Comrades don't actually mouth such a risible combination of spurious philosophy, class hatred and discredited economic theory. And where on earth did they find those singularly unattractive actors? Positively scrofulous most of them. I don't think there's been any research to examine the correlation between acne and left-wing opinions. It might be rather an interesting project for one of your post-graduate students, sir?'

Nora Cleghorn said wonderingly:

'But I thought it was supposed to be a Labour broadcast.'

Her husband laughed:

'You'd certainly be well-advised, Maurice, to keep the young Comrades under wraps until after the election.'

The political discussion was under way as was inevitable. Conversation between Maurice and Harry Cleghorn, thought Philippa, was seldom memorable being usually either a reiteration of their previous television encounter, or a rehearsal for their next. She detached her mind from arguments which she had heard so often before and glanced across the table at Hilda.

Ever since early adolescence, Philippa's reaction to her adoptive mother had been an urge to alter her, to upgrade her, to make her over as she might a dull but still serviceable winter coat. In imagination she applied make-up as if by the judicious application of colour the face could be given definition, rescued from its pallid inconsequence. She had a half-shameful vision of confronting Maurice with a wife transformed, presented with her compliments for his approval, a procuress of his pleasure. Even now she hardly ever looked at her adoptive mother without mentally changing her hairstyle, her clothes. About a year ago, when Hilda had needed a new evening dress, she had tentatively suggested to Philippa that they should shop for it together. Perhaps the invitation had conjured up for her an idealized relationship of mother and daughter, a feminine excursion, half frivolous, conspiratorial. It hadn't been a success. Hilda hated all shops other than those which sold food, was embarrassed by the presence of smarter customers, confused by too abundant a choice, over-deferential to the assistants, shy about undressing. The last store to which Philippa in desperation had taken her had had a large communal dressing-room. What inhibitions of the flesh, she wondered, had caused Hilda to shrink desperately into one corner, trying with ridiculous prudery to undress under cover of her coat while all around her girls and women stripped unselfconsciously to their bras and pants. Philippa had foraged out, desperately hunting among the rails. Nothing looked right on Hilda. Nothing could, since she wore it without confidence, without pleasure, a mute uncomplaining victim offering herself to be adorned for some sacrificial dinner party. In the end they had bought the black woollen skirt she was wearing now, topped by an over-fussy and ill-cut Crimplene blouse. It was the last time they had gone out together, the only time that she had tried to be a daughter. She told herself that she was glad that she need never try again.

Harry Cleghorn's slightly hectoring voice – all his utterances had the resonant boom of the hustings – broke into her comforting disparagement of Hilda, Hilda whose only skills were cooking and deceit.

'Your party claims to understand the so-called working class, but most of you haven't a clue about what they're feeling. Take an old woman living south of the river and holed up on the top of one of your tower blocks. If she can't go out to shop or collect her pension because she's afraid of being mugged, she isn't free in any real sense of that word. Freedom to move about safely in your own capital city is a damned sight more fundamental than the abstractions that the civil liberties lobby prates about.'

'If you could explain how longer prison sentences and tougher detention centre regimes would make it safer.'

Nora Cleghorn licked sauce vinaigrette from her fingers.

'I do think that they ought to hang murderers.'

She spoke in a brightly conversational voice as though, thought Philippa, she were referring to a neighbour's unaccountable omission to hang curtains. There was a moment of complete silence as if she had dropped something precious. In her mind Philippa heard the tinkle of smashing glass. Then Maurice said evenly:

'They? You mean we ought. As it's not a duty I personally

would care to perform, I can hardly expect someone else to do it on my behalf.'

'Oh, Harry would do it, wouldn't you darling?'

'There are one or two I can think of I wouldn't exactly flinch at launching into eternity.'

And this led them, as Philippa knew it would, to a discussion of the century's most notorious child murderess, the name which came up whenever people discussed capital punishment, the touchstone by which liberals tested their response to the death penalty. Philippa wondered if her own mother had served for a longer than normal time because her early release might have stimulated agitation on behalf of that other, more notorious child killer. She glanced across at Hilda, but Hilda's face, half hidden by the two swathes of hair, was bent low over her plate. Artichokes were a convenient starter to an embarrassing meal. They required careful attention. Cleghorn said:

'Having decided that it is wrong to hang murderers, we are now waking up to the fact that they don't conveniently die in prison or just fade away. We're also waking up to the fact that someone has to look after them and that if we don't pay society's custodians properly for a disagreeable job we won't find anyone willing to do it. But obviously, sooner or later, the woman will have to be paroled. I suggest that it might be later.'

Nora Cleghorn said:

'But isn't she supposed to have got terribly religious? I think I read somewhere that she wants to go into a convent or nurse lepers or something.'

Gabriel laughed.

'Poor lepers! They seem always to be selected as the sacrificial victims of someone's contrition. You'd think they had enough troubles already.'

Cleghorn's moist lips fastened on the succulent heart of his artichoke, like a child's on a dummy. A trickle of sauce ran down the side of his mouth. His voice was half muffled in his linen napkin.

'I don't mind who she nurses as long as she keeps away from their children.'

His wife said:

'But if she has really reformed, she wouldn't be agitating to get out of prison, would she?'

Cleghorn spoke impatiently. Philippa had noticed before that he was indulgent to his wife's inanities, but became irritated when she spoke sense.

'Of course she wouldn't. That's the last thing she'd be worried about. After all, if she's hankering to do good, a prison is as suitable a place as any. All this talk about contrition is nonsense. She and her lover tortured a child to death. If she ever comes to an understanding of what she's done, I don't see how she could bear to go on living, let alone start planning for a life outside.'

Gabriel said:

'So we must hope for her own sake that she is unrepentant. But why all this public interest in the state of her soul? I suppose that society has a right to punish her to deter others, and to demand what assurances are possible that she's no longer dangerous before letting her out. What we haven't the right to demand is repentance. That's a matter between her and her god.'

Philippa said:

'Of course. It's as arrogant as me, a Gentile, proclaiming that I've forgiven the Nazis for the holocaust. The statement has no meaning.'

Maurice said drily:

'As little meaning as the statement that repentance is between her and her god.'

Cleghorn laughed:

'Now Maurice, leave the theological argument for your encounter with the Bishop. What are they paying you for the new series, by the way?'

The conversation turned to contracts and the foibles of television producers. There was no more talk of murder. The meal dragged on through the veal, the lemon soufflé, and finally to the leisurely coffee and brandy in the garden. It seemed to Philippa that she had never lived through a longer day. She had woken that morning as a bastard; how short but how endless the hours which had legitimized her into horror and disgrace. It was like experiencing birth and death simultaneously, each separately painful yet both part of the same inexorable process. Now she sat, drained, under the patio lamps and willed the Cleghorns to go.

She was beyond tiredness. Her mind was preternaturally clear yet it fastened on unimportant details which it invested with an egregious significance; Nora Cleghorn's bra strap slipping down a sequined shoulder, her husband's heavy signet ring biting into his little finger, the peach tree gleaming silver under the patio lamp; surely if she stretched out her arm and shook the trunk its leaves would tinkle down in a shower of glistening pellets.

By half-past eleven the talk had become disjointed, perfunctory. Maurice and Cleghorn had completed their academic business and Gabriel, with his half-ironic formality, had taken his leave. But still the Cleghorns lingered in what seemed an obstinate endurance, long after a damp chill had crept across the garden and the purple sky was stained with the arteries of the dying day. It was nearly midnight before they reminded each other that they had a home, said their protracted goodbyes, and made their way through the garden gate to the mews garage and their Jaguar. Philippa was free at last to go to her room.

SEVEN

The letter was more difficult to write than even the most challenging of her weekly school essays. It was astonishing that a short passage of English prose should take so long to compose, that even the most ordinary words should carry such a charge of innuendo, condescension or crass insensitivity. The problems began with the superscription. 'Dear Mother' seemed a startling, almost presumptuous beginning; 'Dear Mrs Ducton' was offensively, almost aggressively formal; 'Dear Mary Ducton' was too obviously a trendy compromise, a confession of defeat. In the end she decided on 'Dear Mother'. That, after all, was the relationship between them, the primal, unalterable, biological tie. To admit the fact needn't imply that it was any more than that.

The first sentence was comparatively easy. She wrote: 'I hope that it won't distress you to receive this letter, but I exercised my right under the Children Act 1975 to apply to the Registrar General for a copy of my birth certificate. Afterwards I went to Bancroft Gardens and learned from a neighbour who you were.'

There was no need to say any more. In that last sentence infamy was plucked from the past, briefly held, then dropped. The words were bloodstained. She went on:

'I should very much like to meet you unless you would much rather not; I could come to Melcombe Grange on any visitors' day if you would let me know when it would be convenient.'

She deleted the second 'much' and hesitated over the last five words, but decided on reflection to leave them in. The sentence didn't satisfy her, but at least it was short and the meaning clear. The next part was more difficult. The words 'released', 'paroled', 'licensed' or 'set free' were pejorative but it was extraordinarily difficult to avoid them. Quickly she scribbled an alternative draft:

'I don't want to force myself on you, but if you haven't anywhere to go . . . anywhere to stay . . . if you haven't finally decided on your plans after you leave Melcombe Grange, would you care to come to me?'

But the last seven words sounded as grudging and patronizing as an invitation to an unwelcome guest. She tried again:

'I shall be taking up my Cambridge scholarship in October and hope to find a flat in London for the next couple of months. If you haven't finally decided on your plans after you leave Melcombe Grange and would care to share the flat, that would be agreeable for me, but please don't feel that you have to say yes.'

It occurred to her that her mother might worry about her share of the rent. Presumably she wouldn't leave prison with very much money. She ought to make it plain that no payment was involved. She began to write that the offer was without obligation, but that bleak commercial note was too reminiscent of a sales catalogue. And there would, after all, be obligations. The demands she would be making of her mother couldn't be satisfied with money. In the end she decided the details could await their meeting. She ended the draft:

'It will only be a small flat – a room for each of us and a kitchen and bathroom – but I hope to find one which will be reasonably central and convenient.'

Convenient for what, she wondered. Covent Garden Opera House, the West End shops, the theatres and restaurants? What sort of life was she implying? What was she visualizing for this stranger who would walk into freedom, if licence from a life sentence was ever freedom, carrying the weight of a dead child? She copied out the draft neatly and signed the letter Philippa Palfrey. She read it through carefully. It was, she thought, disingenuous. She wondered whether her mother would see through the careful words to the truth. There was no real choice for her. She was, in effect, being once again hunted down. The meeting between them was inevitable; if not now, it would come later. There was nothing her mother could do to prevent it.

Perhaps it would have been more honest and, since style depended on honesty, more satisfying to have written the brutal truth.

'If you have nowhere satisfactory to go when you're released from prison, would you care to share a flat with me in London until I go up to Cambridge in October? It can't be longer than that; I'm not intending to alter my life for you. I need to know who I am. If you need a room for two months it would seem a fair exchange. Let me know if you'd like me to come up to Melcombe Grange to talk about it.'

She heard two sets of footsteps mounting the stairs. Then there was a knock. That must be Hilda. Maurice – taught perhaps by Helena – would never have knocked. They stood there, side by side, like a deputation, dressing-gowned, Hilda in her flowered padded nylon, Maurice in his fine scarlet wool, looking diminished and vulnerable, bringing with them a childhood bathtime smell of soap and powder. He said:

'We have to talk, Philippa.'

'I'm too tired. It's after midnight. And what is there to say?'

'At least do nothing until you've seen her, spoken to her.'

'I've already written. I'll post it tomorrow, today I mean. The offer means nothing if it isn't made before we meet. I can't look her over first as if she were goods on approval.'

'You propose then to commit yourself, for weeks, for months, perhaps even for life, to a woman you don't know, who has done nothing for you, who will be nothing but an embarrassment to you, who you probably won't even like. The fact that she happens to be a murderess is irrelevant. It's quixotic, Philippa. Worse, it's self-indulgent stupidity.'

'I didn't say anything about commitment.'

'Of course it's a commitment. You're not engaging a junior

clerk. If she doesn't give satisfaction you can hardly throw her out. What else is it but a commitment?'

'A sensible arrangement to help her over these first two months outside. All I propose to do is to make the offer. She may not even want to see me. If she does it won't necessarily mean that she'll want to share a flat. She's probably made other arrangements. But if she hasn't found anywhere to go, then I'm free for the next few months. At least she'll have a choice.'

'It's not a question of her finding somewhere to go. If she hasn't a family willing to take her back, then the probation service will have found somewhere for her. She won't be homeless. They don't parole lifers unless the aftercare arrangements are approved by the Home Office as satisfactory.'

Hilda said nervously:

'Aren't there hostels, places like that? I've heard they're quite nice. She'll probably go to a hostel just until she's sorted herself out, found herself a job.'

She spoke, thought Philippa, as if her mother were a convalescent being discharged prematurely from hospital. Maurice said:

'Or she'll join up with some woman she's met inside. I don't suppose she's spent all those years entirely alone.'

'You mean a lover? A lesbian?'

He said irritably:

'It's not unknown. You know nothing about her. She let you go out of her life, no doubt because she thought it for the best. Now do the same for her. Hasn't it occurred to you that you may be the last person on earth that she wants to see again?'

'Then all she has to do is say so. I shall write first. I'm not proposing to arrive at the prison unannounced. And if she gave me up it's because she had no choice.'

Hilda's voice was a thin wail of protest.

'But you can't just leave! What are people going to think? What can we say to your friends, to Gabriel Lomas?'

'It's nothing to do with Gabriel. Tell them I'm abroad until October. That's what I was going to do anyway.'

'But they're bound to see you in London. They'll see you with her!'

'What if they do? She won't be branded on her forehead with the divine stigma. I'll think of something to tell your friends if that's all you're worried about. And it's only for a couple of months. People do leave home occasionally.'

Maurice came into the room and walked over to the Henry Walton. Studying the picture, his back to her, he said:

'How much have you read about the murder?'

'I haven't read anything. I know that she killed a child called Julie Scase after my father raped her.'

'You haven't consulted the newspaper reports of the crime?'

'No, I haven't the time to grub about in the archives, and I don't want to.'

'Then I suggest that, before you do anything foolish, make any decision, you get hold of the newspaper cuttings and the trial report and learn the facts.'

'I know the facts. They were told to me this morning with brutal explicitness. I'm not going to spy on my mother before I meet her. If I want any more facts, she can give them to me. And now, please, I'm very tired. I'd like to go to bed.'

EIGHT

Two days later, on Friday 14th July, Norman Scase celebrated simultaneously his fifty-seventh birthday and the last day of his career as a local government accounts clerk. He had told his colleagues that he had been left a modest legacy by an uncle, sufficient to enable him to freeze his pension for three years and to take a premature retirement. The lie worried him; he was unpractised in lying. But something had to be said to explain how a middle-grade unqualified clerk who, to their knowledge, had worn the same suit to work for the last five years could afford the indulgence of an early retirement. He could hardly tell them the truth, that the murderess of his child was due to be released from prison in August and that there were arrangements which he had to make, matters to which he must now devote the whole of his time.

Celebration was not a word he would have used either for the birthday or for his last day at the office. He would have been grateful to have been allowed to slip quietly away as he had at the end of every working day for the last eight years; but there were rituals in the treasurer's department from which not even the least sociable and most private member of the staff was exempt. It was the custom of members of staff who were leaving, getting married, being promoted or retiring to mark the occasion with an invitation either to tea or to sherry, depending on their status and habits and the degree of importance which they attached to the impending change. The invitation was typed by courtesy of the typing pool for those too lowly to have a personal secretary, and circulated by the junior clerical assistant with the miscellaneous departmental notes, circulars and periodicals which went the rounds. On its first appearance Miss Millicent Yelland, the senior personal secretary, would start collecting for a present, tripping conspiratorially from room to room with an envelope to receive donations and a greeting card on which contributors would sign their names under variously worded messages of farewell or good wishes. The choice of card was invariably left to Miss Yelland. At fifty-four she had sublimated her maternal instincts by taking upon herself the role of mother of the division, and had for the past fifteen years promoted, without noticeable success, the fiction that they were all one happy family.

She always took a great deal of trouble, browsing along the racks in the Army and Navy Stores and in the Westminster Abbey Bookshop, and even venturing occasionally as far as Oxford Circus. For more senior staff she usually chose a dog. Dogs were always acceptable, evoking in her mind a mixture of vaguely-felt emotions and aspirations, loyalty and devotion, rough tweeded masculinity, mysterious upper-class activities on grouse moors and among the heather, a restrained good taste. Since a country cottage, with its suggestion of shared connubial bliss, was unsuitable for a widower, and it was impossible to associate Mr Scase with anything as frivolous as bambis or black cats, she decided on a moorland scene featuring a shaggy dog of indeterminate breed with a pheasant in its mouth.

When she examined the card again in her office she had a qualm of doubt. The pheasant, at least she supposed it was a pheasant, looked so very dead, pathetic really, with its drooping neck and glazed eye. It was hardly what you would call a cheerful card. She hoped that Mr Scase didn't disapprove of blood sports.

And when one came to examine it, the expression on the dog's face was really most unpleasant, almost gloating. Well, it would have to do now. She had spent thirty-three pence from the collection of ten pounds – a disappointing sum, but then poor Mr Scase had never particularly put himself out to be popular – and it would be an idiotic waste to buy another card. It was a pity that he was so difficult to choose for. On the death of his wife, eight months ago, about which he had been as reticent as he was about any of his private concerns, she had sent a mourning card on behalf of the division, a silver cross wreathed with violets and forget-me-nots. Afterwards she had wondered whether her choice then had been suitable. He had worked in the division for nearly nine years yet they knew virtually nothing about him except that, like herself, he commuted to Liverpool Street from one of the eastern suburbs. They seldom met on the station and sometimes she wondered if he deliberately avoided her.

Some years previously, emboldened by two glasses of cheap sherry at the office Christmas party, she had asked him whether he had children, and he had replied 'No.' After a few seconds he had added, 'We did have a daughter, but she died young.' Then he had flushed and turned aside as if regretting that brief confidence. She had been made to feel tactless and inquisitive. She had murmured something about being sorry and had moved away, replenishing the outstretched glasses and responding to the office banter. But afterwards she had told herself that to no one else had he spoken about his child, that the confidence, even if involuntary, had been to her alone. She never mentioned it either to him or in the office, but cherished it as a small secret which somehow affirmed her worth in his eyes. And the knowledge of his private tragedy lent him an interest, almost a distinction, which intrigued her. After the death of his wife she found herself indulging a private fantasy. They were both lonely. And he was thoughtful, conscientious. The junior staff didn't appreciate him, just because he insisted on punctuality and a proper standard of work. It took an older woman, a mature woman, to appreciate his qualities. Perhaps here was someone who would be a friend and later, who knew, more than a friend. It wasn't too late for her to make a man happy. She would have someone other than Mother to cook for and care for. But she knew she would have to make the first move.

Inspiration came to her from the advice column of her woman's magazine, where one of the readers wrote that she was interested in a boy in her office, but he had never been more than polite and friendly. There had been no invitation, no date. The answer had been explicit. 'Buy two theatre tickets for something you think he'll like. Then tell him that you've been given the tickets unexpectedly and ask whether he'd care to see the show with you.' It hadn't been an easy ploy for Miss Yelland to put into effect. There had been the difficulty of persuading a neighbour to sit with her mother, the problem of deciding what tickets to buy. In the end, feeling that music was the safest bet, she had queued for two expensive seats for a Brahms concert at the Royal Festival Hall for a Friday night. On the Monday she spoke to him. The few stiff words had been over-rehearsed and her invitation sounded ungracious as well as insincere. He hadn't answered her at first, keeping his eyes on his ledger, and she began to wonder whether he had heard. Then he had got clumsily to his feet, looked briefly into her eyes and murmured:

'It's very kind of you, Miss Yelland, but I never go out in the evenings.'

She had read in his eyes not merely embarrassment, but a kind of panic. Afterwards, scarlet with humiliation since the rejection had been so absolute, she had sought solitude in the ladies' cloakroom. Tearing up the two tickets she flushed them down the lavatory. It was, she knew, a stupidly extravagant gesture. The concert was a popular one; the bookings office could almost certainly have disposed of the tickets. But the gesture was some small comfort to her pride. She had never approached him again, and it seemed to her imagination that he became even more reserved, withdrew more completely beneath his carapace of quiet efficiency. And now he was leaving. For nearly nine years he had circumvented her loving kindness. Now he was escaping for good.

The formal goodbye was arranged for twelve-thirty, and by one o'clock Mr Willcox, the chief accountant in the division, who undertook these ceremonies for staff whose status didn't warrant the personal appearance of the treasurer, was in full flood:

'And if any of you were to ask me, as his senior officer, what I regard as the salient feature of Norman Scase's work in this division, I shouldn't need to hesitate for a single second before giving you my judgement.'

He then hesitated for a nicely-judged half-minute, giving the assembled division time to assume expressions of brightly anticipatory interest as if this fascinating question had indeed been on their lips, while the deputy senior accountant cast lugubrious eyes at the ceiling, the junior personal secretary giggled and Miss Yelland smiled encouragingly at Scase across the throng. The smile wasn't returned. He stood there, holding the canteen glass in his hand, half filled with sweet South African wine, and stared slightly over their heads. He had taken the usual trouble with his appearance, neither more nor less. The formal blue suit was a little shabby now, the sleeves polished by the friction of desk top and ledger. The shirt collar was crumpled but very clean, and the nondescript tie precisely knotted. Standing there, a little apart, like a man under judgement, he reminded Miss Yelland of someone; a picture, a photograph, a newsreel, not someone known to her. Then she remembered. It was one of the accused in the dock at Nuremberg. The mental image, impious, offensive, shocked her; she flushed and gazed fixedly into her sherry as if detected in a solecism. But the memory remained. She fixed her eyes again resolutely on Mr Willcox.

'It would be expressed in a single word,' he pronounced, and proceeded to use a thesaurus. 'Conscientiousness, attention to detail, methodicalness' – he slipped a little over this and Miss Yelland wondered whether there was such a word – 'complete reliability. Whatever he has put his hand to, that task has been carried through to the end with accuracy, neatness and with complete reliability.'

His deputy, lowering his eyes, swallowed his sherry in one gulp, since it was not a taste voluntarily to let linger on the tongue, and thought that if there were a more bloody boring, damning valediction, then he had yet to hear it. He was intrigued by Scase's early retirement. The legacy, of which he had heard rumours, must have been quite a sum if he could afford to go three years early, unless, of course, he had found himself another job and was keeping quiet about it. But that seemed unlikely. Who, these days, would want to take a 57-year-old chap without qualifications?

And so the self-satisfied rhetoric boomed on. Sly innuendoes about what Scase would do with his retirement; congratulations only half jocular, he couldn't prevent the note of envy from creeping in that he could afford to freeze his pension and retire three years before he was due to go; the final conventional wish that he would enjoy a long, prosperous and happy retirement and that the division's little gift would be used to provide some small luxury which would remind him of their affection and respect. The cheque was handed over, there was a brief outbreak of self-conscious clapping in which Mr Willcox joined with a curiously soundless and rhythmic clasping and releasing of his palms like a half-hearted cheer-leader at a revivalist meeting, and all their eyes swivelled and rested on Scase. He blinked at the envelope which had been pressed into his hand, but he didn't open it. One might suppose that he didn't know the convention, that he was supposed to pretend he couldn't find the flap, raise a gratified eyebrow at the size of the cheque, exclaim over the design on the card, and study the inscribed names. But he clutched it in his delicate hands as a child might do, uncertain if it were really his. He said:

'Thank you very much. I shall miss the division in many ways after nearly nine years.'

'Nine years hard,' someone called out, and laughed.

He didn't smile.

'After nearly nine years,' he repeated. 'I shall buy a pair of binoculars with your kind gift, and they will remind me of old friends and colleagues in local government. Thank you.'

Then he smiled. He had a singularly sweet smile, but it was so transitory that those who saw it were left wondering whether there had indeed been that extraordinary transformation. He put down his unfinished drink, shook hands with one or two closest to him, and left them.

Back in the small room which he shared with two other clerks, he had already packed his few belongings in a plastic carrier bag; his cup and saucer carefully wrapped in yesterday's *Daily Telegraph*; a ready reckoner and dictionary; his toilet bag. He gave a last look round. Nothing remained to be done. Making his way to the lift he wondered what they would have said, how they would have looked, if he had spoken quite simply what was in his mind.

'I have to retire early because there is something I must do in the next few months, a task which will take a great deal of time and planning. I have to find and kill the murderess of my child.'

Would the ring of nervously smiling faces have frozen into stark disbelief, the mouths set in their conventional smirks have broken into embarrassed laughter? Or would they have stood in a surrealist charade, still smiling, still nodding, toasting him in their cheap sherry, as if the dreadful words were as meaningless as Mr Willcox's pompous platitudes? The thought that he might actually hear himself speaking the truth had come to him during the last seconds of Mr Willcox's peroration. He hadn't, of course, been seriously tempted to such folly; but it surprised and slightly offended him that so iconoclastic and so melodramatic a conceit should have entered his mind. He was not given to the grand gesture, either in thought or action. Killing Mary Ducton was a duty which he neither wanted to escape, nor could escape even had he wanted to. Certainly he planned to commit a successful murder, in the sense that he intended to avoid detection. It was justice, not martyrdom, that he sought. But never until this afternoon had it occurred to him to wonder what his colleagues would think of him as a prospective killer, and he felt obscurely denigrated, his serious purpose cheapened into melodrama, that the thought should have occurred to him now.

NINE

He took his usual way home over Westminster Bridge, across Parliament Square, down Great George Street and into St James's Park. The quicker way to Liverpool Street Station and the eastern suburban line was by Waterloo and the city line, but he preferred to walk each evening over the river and take the underground from St James's Park. Since Mavis's death he had been in no hurry to get home. There was no hurry now.

St James's Park was crowded, but he managed to find room on a bench beside the lake. Carefully he lowered the holdall with his few belongings and placed it on the path beneath his feet. Staring at the lake through the boughs of a willow, he realized that he had sat in this identical spot eight months previously, in his lunch hour on the day after his wife's death. It had been an unusually cold Friday in November. He could remember a smudged sun high above the lake like a great white moon, and the willow fronds slowly shedding their pale lances on to the water. In these burgeoning rose beds there had been a few tight red buds, blighted by the cold, their stems choked with dead leaves. The lake had been bronzed and wrinkled with, at its centre, a great salver of beaten silver. An old man, surely too old to be employed by the city council, had shuffled along the path past him, spearing the sparse litter. The park then had held an air of sad decrepitude, the handrail of the blue bridge worn by tourists' hands, the fountain silent, the tea house closed for the winter. Now the air was loud with the staccato chatter of tourists, the shrieks and laughter of children. Then, he remembered, there had been one solitary child with his mother. The gulls had risen squawking before his harsh, cracked laughter, and he had stretched out his arms, willing their plump bodies to fall into his palms. Under the far trees patches of early snow had lain between the clumps of grass like the discarded litter of the dead summer.

Remembering that day he could almost feel again the November cold. He shut his eyes against the sunlit greenness of the park, the sheen on the lake; blotted out the calling voices of the children and the distant beat of the band, and willed his mind back to the hospital ward in which Mavis had died.

It had been an inconvenient day and time to die, the Thursday of the major operation list, and at four in the afternoon when the trolleys were coming back from the theatre. These things, he had sensed, were better managed at night when the patients were settled or asleep, when there was time for the nursing staff to turn aside from the battle and minister to those who had already lost it. The staff nurse in charge, harassed, had explained that normally they would have moved his wife into a side ward, but the four side wards were occupied. Perhaps tomorrow. There was the unspoken commitment that if she could die more conveniently then she could die with more comfort. He had sat by her bed behind the drawn curtains. Their pattern was forever fixed in his mind, small pink rosebuds on a pink background, cosy, domestic, a prettification of death. They were not completely drawn, and he could glimpse through the gap the business of the ward, trolleys being wheeled beside the waiting beds with impersonal efficiency, the long-gowned nurses steadying the swinging drip-bottles, voices and passing feet; from time to time a ward orderly put her head round the curtains and asked brightly:

'Tea?'

He took the cup and saucer, thick white china with two lumps of sugar already dissolving in the spill of brown liquid.

Both her arms lay outside the coverlet. He held her left hand, wondering what dreams, if any, peopled the uplands of her valley of the shadow. Surely they couldn't be as tormenting as the nightmares which, in the weeks following Julie's death, had made dreadful her nights so that he would wake to her shrill screams, to the hot sweet smell of sweat and fear. The world she was inhabiting now was surely gentler, or why would she lie so still? The passing expressions of her face, which he watched with detached interest, were the transitory hints of emotions which she could no longer feel, a peevish frown, a sly unconvincing smile which reminded him disconcertingly of Julie as a baby when she had wind, a petulant frown, the illusion of thought. From time to time her eyes flickered and her lips moved. He bent his head to listen.

'Better use a knife. It's more certain. You won't forget?'

'No, I won't forget.'

'You've got the letter?'

'Yes, I've got the letter.'

'Show me.'

He took it from his wallet. Her eyes focused on it with difficulty. She stretched her right hand trembling towards it and touched it as a believer might touch a relic. She tried to fix her eyes on it. Her jaw dropped and began to quiver as if the effort of concentrating on that oblong of creased white paper had released the final disintegration of muscle and flesh. He took her dry hand in his, and pressed it against the envelope. He said:

'I won't forget.'

He remembered when she had written the letter. It had been just one year before, when the cancer had been first diagnosed.

They had been sitting together, distanced, on the sofa watching a television programme about the birds of Antarctica. After he switched off she had said:

'If I don't get better you'll have to do it alone. That might not be easy. You'll need an excuse for finding out where she is. And after she's dead, if they suspect you, you'll have to explain why you traced her. I'll write a letter, a letter of forgiveness. Then you can say that you promised me on my deathbed to deliver it into her hand.'

She must have been planning that, thinking it out all the time they were watching the programme together. He could still remember the sudden jolt of disappointment and fear. Somehow he had believed that her death might release him, that he wouldn't be expected to carry the burden alone. But there was to be no escape. She had written the letter at once, sitting at the kitchen table, and had placed it in an unsealed envelope remembering that he might need to show it to someone, someone in authority, someone who might let him know where the murderess was. He hadn't read it at the time, and he hadn't read it since. He had carried it with him in his wallet. Until this moment, so short a time before her death, she had never mentioned it again.

She sank into unconsciousness. He sat on stiffly beside her, letting the dry hand rest beneath his. A lizard hand, inert, repellent, the loose skin sliding beneath his touch. He told himself that it had cooked for him, worked for him, cleaned his house, washed his clothes. He tried to picture these things, tried to stimulate pity. It meant nothing. He felt pity but it was a diffuse impersonal hopelessness at the inevitability of loss. The ward seemed loud with ineffective activity, meaningless suffering. He knew that if he wept it would be for all of them there, sick and healthy alike, but most of all for himself. He had to make an effort of will not to draw his hand away. He was helped by the thought that the staff nurse might draw back the curtains and would expect to find him sitting thus linked, dispensing the final consolations of the flesh. Love had died. The woman had throttled it to death when she throttled the life out of their child. Perhaps it hadn't been very strong to die so easily and thus vicariously, but it had seemed strong. They had loved, as surely every human being did, each to the limit of his capacity. But they had failed each other at the end. Perhaps she had been the most culpable because the stronger. But somehow he should have been able to help her back to a kind of living. Now there was one way left in which he wouldn't fail her. Their joint purpose must now be his alone. Perhaps the death of the woman would be both an expiation and, for him, a release into some kind of life, a justification of the long, lost years.

She had nourished grief and revenge like a monstrous foetus, ever growing but never delivered. Even her general practitioner, wearily drawing his prescription pad towards him and writing yet another letter for a psychiatric out-patient appointment, made it plain that he thought she had grieved long enough. Grief, after all, was an indulgence, having no merit, no social value, rationed out like coins to the deserving poor, a commodity the strong and self-reliant were too proud to need. Perhaps, he thought, the Victorian habit of formal mourning had its uses. At least it defined the accepted limits of public indulgence. A year in black for a widow, he remembered his grandmother had told him, then six months in grey, then in mauve. Those expensive conventions were not, of course, for her but she had observed them with approval in the large town houses in which she had served as a parlour-maid. How long in black, he wondered, for a raped and murdered child. Not long perhaps. In his grandmother's time there would have been a replacement within a year.

How easily humanity subscribed to the universal commercial imperative: business as usual. You have your life to live, they had told Mavis, and she had gazed at them with huge uncomprehending eyes since, so obviously, she no longer had her life to live. You must think of your husband, her doctor had commanded, and indeed she had thought of him. Lying stiffly, speechlessly, side by side in the double bed of that back suburban bedroom, he had stared into the darkness and seen her thoughts, self-reproachful, like a darker cloud against the blackness of the ceiling, or a contagion spreading from her brain to his. Never once had she turned to him. She had occasionally stretched out a hand, but when he had taken it had withdrawn it as if the flesh which had impregnated her had become repulsive. Once, shy and with a sense of betrayal, he had made himself speak to their doctor. The answer, glib and professional, had done nothing to help. 'She associates physical love with grief, with loss. You must be patient.' Well, he had been patient, patient unto death.

She was trying to speak again. He bent down and caught her breath, sour-sweet with intimations of decay, and had to resist the temptation to put his handkerchief to his mouth to shield him from contamination. He held his breath and tried not to swallow. But in the end he had to take her death into himself. It took her several minutes to get out the words, but when they came between the gibbering lips her voice was surprisingly clear, gruff and deep as it had never been in life.

'Strong,' she said. 'Strong.'

He didn't know what she meant by that word. Was it a final exhortation to him to stay strong in resolution? Or did she mean that the murderess was strong, too strong for him to overcome her if he came unweaponed to the kill. Standing there in the dock of the Old Bailey she hadn't struck him as particularly tall or robust; but perhaps that court, so unexpectedly small, so anonymous, patterned in pale wood, diminished all human beings, guilty and innocent alike. Even the judge, scarlet-sashed under the royal coat of arms, had shrunk to a bewigged marionette. But the years in prison wouldn't have made her less strong. They looked after you in prison. You weren't over-worked or underfed. When you were sick they gave you the best medical care. They saw that you got your exercise. When he and Mavis had talked together about the killing, they had planned to throttle the woman since that was how Julie had died. But Mavis was right. He was on his own now. He had better use a weapon.

He hadn't wanted her to die like this, in bitterness and hate. This too the murderess had taken from them with so much else. Love; the solace of responsive flesh. Companionship, laughter, ambition, hope. And of course Julie. Sometimes to his surprise he almost forgot Julie. And Mavis had lost her God. Like all other believers she had made Him in her own image, a Methodist God, benign, suburban in his tastes, appreciative of cheerful singing and mildly academic sermons, not demanding more than she could give. The Sunday morning chapel had been more a comfortable routine than an imperative to worship. Mavis had been brought up a Methodist and she was not a woman to reject early orthodoxies. But she had never forgiven God for letting Julie die. Sometimes Scase thought that she had never forgiven him. Love had died chiefly because of guilt; their joint guilt; her blame of him, his blame of himself. She would return to it again and again.

'We shouldn't have let her join the Guides. She only agreed because she knew you were keen, that it would please you.'

'I didn't want her to be lonely. I remember what it was like when I was a child.'

'You should have called for her every Thursday. It wouldn't have happened if you'd called for her.'

'But you know she wouldn't let me. She told us that Sally Meakin always walked home with her across the recreation ground.'

But Sally Meakin hadn't. No one had, and Julie had been too ashamed to ask for him to call for her. She had been like him as a child, unattractive, solitary, introspective, coping as best she could with the irrational terrors and uncertainties of childhood. He had guessed why she hadn't taken the short-cut home across the recreation ground. It must have seemed limitless in its dark emptiness, the swings tied up for the night but creaking in the wind, the great upward sweep of the slide gaunt against the sky, the dark recesses of the shelter, smelling of urine, where in the daytime the mothers sat with their prams. So she had walked alone the long way round, down unfamiliar streets, made less frightening because they were so like her own, bordered with cosy, comfortable semi-detached houses with their lighted windows, comforting symbols of security and home. And it was there in one of those dull streets that she had met her murderer. It must have been because the rapist and his house were both so ordinary that he had been able to entice her in. They had warned her punctiliously against speaking to strange men, accepting sweets, going away with them, and they had always thought that her timidity would protect her. But nothing protected her, neither their warnings nor their love. His guilt was less now. Time didn't heal, but it anaesthetized. The human mind could only feel so much. He had read somewhere that even the tortured reached a point beyond which there was no more pain, only the thud of unregarded blows, a limbo beyond suffering that was almost pleasurable. He remembered the first cup of tea he had drunk after Julie's death. He couldn't have forced himself to swallow food, but suddenly he had been intensely thirsty, and the taste of the strong, sweet tea had been marvellously good. No tea before or since had tasted like that. She had only been dead a matter of hours and already the voracious, the treacherous body was able to experience pleasure.

Now, sitting in the sun with his few belongings on the ground between his feet, he accepted again the burden she had laid on him. He would seek out his child's murderess and kill her. He would try to do it without danger to himself since the prospect of prison terrified him, but he would still do it whatever the cost. The strength of this conviction puzzled him. The will for the deed was absolute, yet the justification eluded his questing mind. Surely it wasn't just the need for revenge. That had long ago ceased to motivate him. His grief for Julie, at first almost as lacerating as Mavis's, had long ago faded into a dull acceptance of loss. He could hardly now recall her face. Mavis had destroyed all their photographs of her after the murder. But there were pictures which he kept in his mind, recalling them almost as a duty, an *aide-mémoire* of grief. Taking his daughter into his arms for the first time, the infinitely small cocooned body, the gummed eyelids, the secretive meaningless smile. Julie toddling towards the sea at Southend, clinging tightly to his finger. Julie in her Guide uniform setting the table for dinner with anxious care, qualifying for her hostess badge. Nothing he did to Mary Ducton at whatever cost could bring her back.

Was it the need to keep faith with Mavis? But how could you keep faith with the dead, who by the very act of dying had put themselves for ever beyond the reach of treachery or betrayal? Whatever he did it couldn't touch Mavis, couldn't harm or disappoint her. She wouldn't return a querulous ghost to reproach him with his weakness. No, he wasn't doing it for Mavis. He was doing it for himself. Was it, perhaps, that after nearly fifty-seven years of living he needed to prove himself, nonentity that he was, capable of courage and action, of an act so terrible and irrevocable that, whatever happened to him afterwards, he could never again doubt his identity as a man? He supposed that it might be so, although none of it seemed relevant to him. But surely it was ridiculous, this sense that the act was inescapable, preordained. And yet he knew that it was so.

The sun had gone in. A chill wind moved across the lake, shaking the willows. He felt under the bench for his holdall and made his way slowly to St James's Station and home.

TEN

On Thursday, 20th July, three days after she had received her mother's reply, Philippa took a day return ticket to York and travelled up on the nine o'clock train from King's Cross. The brief information sheet which had been enclosed with her prison visiting order stated that the bus to Melcombe Grange left the York bus station at two o'clock promptly. She was in a state of restless excitement which drove her to action and movement. It would be easier to pass the waiting hours exploring York than to linger in London for a later train.

At the station bookstall at York she bought a guide book, then checked the time of the return train. Then she walked indefatigably down the narrow paved streets of the walled city, Fossgate, Shambles, Petergate, between the timber-framed houses and the elegant Georgian façades, down secret alleyways and in and out of spice-smelling shops, through the eighteenth-century Assembly Rooms, the medieval Merchant Adventurers Hall, hung with the splendid banners of the Guilds, the portraits of their benefactors, through the remains of the Roman baths and into ancient churches. She walked in a medieval dream in which the varied delights of the city, colour and light, form and sound, imposed themselves on a consciousness which was simultaneously heightened yet detached. And so at last she passed under the statue of St Peter, through the west door and into the cool immensity of the Minster. Here she sat and rested, looking up where the great east window stained the quiet air. She had bought a cheese and tomato roll for her lunch, and found herself suddenly hungry, but was reluctant to offend the susceptibilities of other visitors by eating it there. Instead she fixed her gaze where God the Father sat in majesty among His creation, glorified in the splendour of medieval stained glass. Before him was an open book. *Ego sum alpha et omega.* How simple life must be for those who could both lose and find identity in that magnificent assurance. But for herself that way was closed. Hers was a bleaker and more presumptuous creed, but it was not without its comfort and she had no other. Now with myself I will begin and end.

She arrived early at the bus station and was glad that she hadn't lingered over her lunch since the bus, a double decker, rapidly filled. She wondered how many of the passengers were visitors to the prison, how often the same people travelled month after month the same route. The destination board made no mention of the prison but stated simply that the bus went to Moxton via Melcombe. Some passengers seemed to know each other and called out a greeting or edged their way down the aisle to sit together. Most of them carried baskets or humped bulging tote bags on to the rack. About half the passengers were men and they too were laden. But it wasn't a gloomy company nor, she thought, oppressed by any sense of stigma. Each might be carrying a private load of anxiety, but this afternoon, travelling through the bright air, each bore it more lightly. The sun burned through the windows, scorching plastic seats. The bus smelled of hot leather, bodies, newly baked cakes and the strong grass-scented summer breeze. Almost merrily it bore its chattering load through sparse villages, down green shadowed lanes where the laden boughs of the horse chestnuts scraped against the roof, then with a grind of gears, upwards to a high narrow road which ran between dry stone walls. On either side stretched the close-cropped fields, white with sheep.

Only three passengers on the lower deck seemed immune to the general air of cheerful well-being, a middle-aged grey-haired man, dressed with careful formality, who had taken his seat beside Philippa just before the bus moved off and who spent the journey gazing out of the opposite window and restlessly turning a plain gold ring on his third finger, and two middle-aged women who had settled themselves behind her and who talked for most of the journey, one of them in a querulous whine.

'It's want, want, want with her, every bloody month. It's all very well, I said, but I can't do it. I'm keeping your bloody kids on the welfare, bread 20p a loaf and I can't do it. It's wool this month, if you please. Twenty balls! She's knitting herself one of those jerkin things. George won't visit any more. He won't put up with it, not George.'

Her companion said:

'They got wool in Paggett's sale.'

'That's no bloody good. It has to be that new French wool. Eighty pence an ounce, if you please. And what about the kids? If she wants to knit, Darren could do with a pullover. I've got no bloody time for knitting, I told her, stuck in the house, three kids under eight. Pity they don't let her out to look after them herself. I'm the one who's in prison. I told her. I'm the one who's been bloody well sentenced.'

And through it all the grey-haired man sat staring through the window, pulling on his ring.

From time to time she slipped her hand through the flap of her shoulder-bag and touched the envelope containing her mother's letter. It had arrived on Monday 17th July and had been posted two days previously. It was as short and businesslike as Philippa's own and she knew it by heart.

'Thank you for your letter. Your offer is kind, but I think you ought to see me before you decide. I shall understand if you want to change your mind. I think you would be wise to change it. I have applied for a monthly visiting order for you and if you care to come I am of course always here.' It was signed simply Mary Ducton.

The note of sardonic humour in the last line intrigued her. But then, perhaps it had been meant to intrigue. She wondered it if was a self-protective device, a way of lowering in advance the emotional temperature of this first meeting.

Twenty minutes later the bus slowed to turn left down a narrower road into a valley. The signpost said 'Melcombe – 2 miles'. They drove through a village of stone houses, past the Melcombe Arms and a general store and post office, over a humped bridge spanning a shallow fast-running stream, then alongside an eight-foot stone wall. The wall was old but in an excellent state of repair, and it seemed to stretch for miles. Then suddenly it ended and the bus shook to a stop outside two immense wrought-iron gates. They stood wide open. On the wall the notice painted black and white was stark. 'HM Prison, Melcombe Grange.'

It was, she thought, a not entirely unsuitable house for use as a prison for all its stolid domestic origins. It was a sixteenth-century brick-built mansion with wide projecting wings at whose junction with the centre block two heavy castellated towers rose like watch-towers. The rows of tall mullioned windows, coruscated by the sun, were secretive, transomed with stone bars. The doorway was formidable, its heavy ornate porch symbolic of strength and security rather than of the grace of hospitality. It was easy to see that the estate had been institutionalized. The sweep to the main door had been widened to provide a marked parking space for half a dozen cars, and to the right of the house she could see a row of prefabricated huts, craft rooms perhaps or extra dormitories. On the lawn to the left of the main path three women wearing bibbed overalls were tinkering, not very energetically, with a recalcitrant lawnmower. They turned to stare at the stream of approaching visitors without apparent enthusiasm.

The openness, the absence of custodians, the beauty of the house stretching before her in its ageless calm disconcerted and confused her. The bus had gone on its way bearing the last few remaining passengers to the next village. She had forgotten to ask the time of the return journey, and she experienced a moment of irrational panic that, without this information, there could be no return journey, that she was condemned to be stranded here in this prison which was so alarmingly un-prisonlike. The visitors, sure of themselves, knowing what awaited them for good or ill, were streaming down the wide gravel path towards the house. Their shoulders dragged with the weight of their bags. Even the grey-haired man was carrying a bundle of books bound with a strap. Only she was coming empty-handed. She walked slowly after them, heart thumping. One of them, a coloured girl of about her own age, her hair minutely plaited and decorated with green and yellow beads, glanced back then waited for her. She said:

'You're new, aren't you? Saw you on the bus. Who d'you want?'

'I'm visiting Mrs Ducton. Mrs Mary Ducton.'

'Mary? She's in the stable block with my mate. I'm going there. I'll show you.'

'Oughtn't I to report to someone?'

'You report to the warden's office over at the stables. Got your VO have you?'

Seeing Philippa's look of momentary incomprehension, she said:

'Your VO. Visiting Order.'

'Yes, I've got that.'

Her companion led the way round the side of the house to a set of converted stables, across a cobbled yard and through an open door to a small office. There was a woman prison officer there in uniform. The coloured girl handed over her visiting order and dumped her bag on the small table. The woman officer rummaged through the contents with brief expertise. She said in a pleasant Scottish accent:

'My word but you're smart today, Ettie. It beats me how you have the patience to thread in all those beads.'

Ettie grinned and shook her neatly decorative head. The beads danced and jangled, red, yellow and blue. The prison officer turned to Philippa. Philippa held out her pass.

'Oh yes, you're Miss Palfrey. This is your first time, isn't it? The Governor thought you'd like some extra privacy so I've put a notice on the sitting-room door. You'll be all right there for an hour at least. You show Miss Palfrey the sitting-room, will you Ettie, there's a good lass, I can't leave the desk just for a moment.'

The room was a little way down the corridor on the right. A cardboard notice with the word 'engaged' was hung on the door. Ettie didn't open it, but gave the door a gentle kick and said:

'Here you are. See you on the bus maybe.' Then she was gone.

Philippa opened the door slowly. The room was empty. She shut the door and leaned against it for a moment, glad of the comforting strength of wood against her back. Like Miss Henderson's office, this room had a spurious comfort. It was a transit lounge but without the ostentatious vulgarity of an airport waiting-room, unpretentious, stuffy, over-crowded with furniture which looked as if it had been rejected from a dozen different homes. Nothing it contained was memorable. It was designed to be used and then mercifully forgotten. No transient would look back on this room with regret or be tempted to leave a humming chord of her misery or hope on the bleak air. There were too many chairs, assorted in size or shape, disposed around half a dozen small highly polished tables. The walls were plain and smudged in places, as if someone had cleansed them of graffiti. Over the fireplace was a print of Constable's *Hay Wain* and below it on the mantelshelf a glass vase of artificial flowers. In the middle of the room was set a small octagonal table with two facing chairs. In contrast to the informality of the room they looked as if they had been specially arranged. Perhaps a helpful inmate, instructed to see that the room was tidy, had placed them there, seeing every visit as a formal confrontation across an invisible but impregnable grille.

The waiting minutes seemed to stretch for hours. Occasionally footsteps passed the door. It was as cheerfully noisy as school at mid-morning break. Philippa's mind was a turmoil of emotions: excitement, apprehension, resentment, and finally anger. What was she doing abandoned here in this dreary room where the furniture was too clean, the walls too grubby, the flowers artificial? They had a large enough garden, surely they could at least provide fresh flowers. A cell would have been less disquieting to wait in. At least it didn't pretend to be anything but what it was. And why wasn't her mother here, waiting for her? She knew that she was coming, she must have known the time of the bus. What was she finding to do that was more important than being here? Her mind spun with grotesque images. Hair that had once been golden but was now dry as straw, dancing with threaded beads, her mother's face sagging under the weight of make-up, a cigarette hanging from a slack mouth, hands with painted talons stretched out to her throat. She thought: 'Suppose I don't like her. Suppose she can't stand me. We've got to spend two months together. I can't get out of it now. I can't go back to Caldecote Terrace and tell Maurice I made a mistake.' She walked over to the window and looked out across the cobbled courtyard at the second set of stables. She would make herself think about the architecture. Maurice had taught her how to look at buildings. This stable block was later than the house; it might even be neo-Georgian. But the clock turret with its swinging golden cock looked older. Perhaps they had re-erected it when the original stables were demolished. They had made a good job of the conversion. But where was her mother? Why didn't she come?

The door opened. She turned round. Her first impression, but so fleeting that the thought and its rejection were almost simultaneous, was that her mother had sent a friend to break the news that she had changed her mind, that she didn't want to meet her after all. It was stupid to have expected so much older a woman. And, at first, she looked so ordinary, a slight, attractive figure in a grey pleated skirt with a paler cotton shirt blouse and a green scarf knotted at the neck. All her grotesque imaginings fled like shrieking demons before a relic. It was like recognizing oneself. It was the beginning of identity. Surely if she had met this woman anywhere in the world she would have known herself to be flesh of her flesh. Instinctively they each slowly took a chair and regarded each other across the table. Her mother said:

'I'm sorry I've kept you waiting. The bus was early. I didn't want to watch out for it in case you didn't come.'

Philippa knew now from which parent she had inherited her corn-gold hair. But her mother's hair, shaped to her head like a cap and cut in a fringe above her eyes, looked finer and lighter, perhaps because it was streaked with silver. The mouth, wider than her own, had the same curved upper lip, but it was more resolute, the delicate droop at each corner less sensuous. But here was the pattern of her high cheekbones, her slightly arched nose. Only the eyes were different, a luminous grey faintly streaked with green. They held a look of half-startled wariness, of endurance, like those of a patient facing once more the inescapable and painful probing. Her skin might once have been honey-coloured, but now looked clear, almost bloodless. The impression was of a face still attractive, still young, but from which colour had been drained by a perpetual weariness, of watchful eyes which had seen too much for too long.

They didn't touch each other. Neither stretched a hand across the table. Philippa said:

'What shall I call you?'

'Mother. Isn't that why you're here?'

Philippa didn't reply. She wanted to say that she was sorry to have come empty-handed, but was frightened that her mother might reply, 'but you've brought yourself.' It would be intolerable if their first meeting began with such banality. Her mother said:

'You do understand what I did, why you were adopted?'

'I don't understand, but I do know about it. My father raped a child and you killed her.'

It seemed to Philippa that the air between them had solidified, had become the oscillating medium through which their words flickered and spun. Now it trembled, and her mother's face was for a moment blank as if some tenuous link of perception had been broken. She said:

'Did feloniously and with malice aforethought kill one Julie Mavis Scase. It's true, except that they don't use those words any more and it wasn't with malice aforethought. It wasn't meant. But she's just as dead as if it had been. And all murderers tell you that anyway. You don't have to believe it. I don't know why I said it. You must excuse me if I seem socially inept. You are my first visitor for nine years.'

'If you tell me, why shouldn't I believe you?'

'But it's irrelevant. You aren't a romantic, are you? You don't look as if you are. You haven't come here with the idea of proving me innocent? You haven't been reading too many crime novels?'

'I don't read crime novels except Dostoevsky and Dickens.'

The noise from outside was louder now, the voices had become strident, feet were pounding down the corridor. Philippa said:

'They're a noisy lot, aren't they? It's rather like a boarding school.'

'Yes, a boarding school with strict discipline where they take difficult girls off their parents' hands. This part is the old stable block converted into a pre-release hostel. Lifers have to live here for nine months before they let us out. We go out to work. There are a few liberal minded employers in York with an interest in rehabilitating prisoners. After the prison authorities have deducted a contribution towards our keep and paid out pocket money they bank the surplus. I shall have two hundred and thirty pounds forty-eight pence when I leave. I thought – if you still want me – that the money could go towards the rent of the flat.'

'I can pay the rent of the flat. You'll need your two hundred pounds. What do you do? I mean, what kind of job?'

She hoped she didn't sound like a prospective employer. Her mother said:

'I'm a chamber-maid at a hotel. There wasn't much choice of work. Murderers are easier to place than thieves or confidence tricksters, but with unemployment as high as it is the prison has to take what's on offer. But it does mean that I've had my insurance card stamped.'

'Hotel work must be boring.'

'Tiring, but not boring. I'm not afraid of hard work.'

The statement seemed to Philippa out of character, pathetic, almost demeaning. It embarrassed her by its naïvety. It was too close to an appeal, the Victorian kitchen-maid desperate to be taken on. Suddenly she thought of Hilda, bending over the kitchen table. The memory of Hilda at that moment was intrusive and disconcerting. She said:

'Do we have to stay in here? It's lovely in the sun. Can't we go outside?'

'If you'd rather. The warden suggested that we might like to walk round the lawn. Visitors normally have to stay in the house, but she's made an exception for you, for us.'

A gravel path, bordered with lime trees, circled the immense lawn. It was here that they walked. The gravel glinted in the sun and was as hot as cinders to the soles of Philippa's feet. In the distance the bleached skeletons of denuded elms, stricken by Dutch elm disease, stood like pale distorted gibbets against the varying green of oak, beech, horse chestnut and silver birch. Occasionally their black shadows were broken by a path of green sward and she could see tantalizing vistas leading to a circular rose garden, a bulbous stone cherub. The skeleton of a dried beech leaf trembled momentarily on the path before being ground to dust under her feet. Even at the height of summer there were always some dead leaves. Someone somewhere was burning them: there was a sweet, pungent smell redolent of autumn. Surely it was early to be burning leaves. No one burnt leaves in the London parks. This was a country smell, raking memory back to forgotten autumns at Pennington, except that she had never lived at Pennington. The hard boughs of horse chestnut and oak, weighted with summer, the dead leaf, the smoky bonfire tang, the transitory spring sweetness of the lime flowers, all produced in her a momentary confusion, a sense of all seasons coming together in a moment out of time. Perhaps these two months, before she went up to Cambridge, would be similarly lived in a new dimension, not counted against her allotted years. Perhaps she would look back at this visit, uncertain whether it had been spring or autumn, remembering only the discordant scent and sounds, the single dead leaf.

They walked in silence. Philippa tried to analyse her emotions. What was she feeling? Embarrassment? Not that. Comradeship? That was too sturdily complaisant a word for the tenuous link between them. Fulfilment? Peace? No, not peace. Here was a balance between excitement and apprehension, a euphoria which had nothing to do with the mind's quietude. Contentment, perhaps. Now at least I know who I am. I know the worst, I shall know the best. Above all, a sense that it was right to be here, that this deliberate pacing, carefully distanced so that the first touch should not be casual, was a ritual of immense significance, an end and a beginning.

She thought for the first time since she had heard it: 'I like her voice.' It was low, unpractised, tentative, as if English were a language her mother had learned. Words were symbols formed in the mind and seldom spoken. It was strange, thought Philippa, that she would have found it more difficult to live with a whining or grating voice than with the knowledge that this woman had killed a child. Her mother asked:

'What are you going to do? I mean, what job?' She paused. 'I'm sorry. That's the kind of question a ten-year-old gets asked and hates answering.'

'I've known since I was ten. I'm going to be a writer.'

'Are you gathering material? Is that why you're offering to help me? I don't mind. At least I shall have given you something. There's nothing else I've given you.'

It was matter of fact, with no hint of self-pity or of remorse. 'Except my life. Except my life. Except my life.'

'*Hamlet*. It seems strange now, but I hardly knew Shakespeare before I went to prison. I promised myself that I'd read every play and in chronological order. There are twenty-one. I rationed myself to one every six months. That way I could be sure that they would last out the sentence. You can annihilate thought with words.'

The paradox of poetry.

'Yes,' she said. 'I know.'

The gravel path grated Philippa's feet. She said:

'Can't we walk into the garden?'

'We have to keep to this path. Rules. They haven't the staff to hunt people down all over the grounds.'

'But the gate wasn't locked. You could all walk out.'

'Only into another kind of prison.'

Two women, obviously staff, were hurrying across the grass, running gawkily, lurching together. They weren't in uniform, but it was impossible to mistake them for inmates. One had thrown an arm round her companion's shoulder. Their laughter was happy, conspiratorial. Remembering that they mustn't be called warders, Philippa asked:

'The prison officers, how have they treated you?'

'Some like animals, some like recalcitrant children, some like mental patients. I like best those who treat us as prisoners.'

'And those two, running across the grass, who are they?'

'Two friends. They always ask to get posted together. They live together.'

'You mean they're lovers, lesbians? Is there a lot of that in prison?' She remembered Maurice's snide innuendo.

Her mother smiled.

'You make it sound like an infectious disease. Of course it happens. It happens often. People need to be loved. They need to feel that they matter to someone. If you're wondering about me, the answer is no. I wouldn't have had the chance, anyway. In prison or out, people need someone they can despise more than they do themselves. A child killer is at the bottom of the heap, even here. Learn to be alone. Don't draw attention to yourself. That way my sort survive. Your father didn't.'

'What was he like, father?'

'He was a schoolmaster. He hadn't a university degree. His father, your grandfather, was a clerk with an insurance company. I don't suppose any member of the family has ever been to a university. Your father went to a teacher training college. That was regarded as a great achievement. He taught the senior boys at an inner London comprehensive school until he couldn't stand it any more. Then he took a job as a clerk with the Gas Board.'

'But what was he like? What were his interests?'

Her mother's voice was a harsh grate:

'His interest was little girls.'

Perhaps the bleak reply was meant to shock, to jolt her into a fresh awareness of why they were here, pacing the gravel together. Philippa waited until she could be sure that her voice was calm. She said:

'That isn't an interest. That's an obsession.'

'I'm sorry, I shouldn't have said that. I'm not even sure that it's true. It's just that I don't seem able to give you what you want.'

'I don't want anything. I'm not here because of wanting.'

But it seemed to Philippa that her question had been only the first catalogue of wants. I want to know who I am, I want to be approved of, I want to be successful, I want to be loved. The question, 'Then why *are* you here?' hung between them, unasked, unanswerable.

They walked on together in silence. Her mother seemed to be thinking, then she said:

'He liked second-hand books, exploring old churches, roaming city streets, taking a train to Southend for the day and walking to the end of the pier. He liked reading history and biography, never fiction. He lived in his own imagination, not other men's. He disliked his job but hadn't the courage to change it again. He hadn't the courage to change anything. He was one of the meek who are supposed to inherit the earth. He liked you.'

'How did he manage to entice her into the house?'

She disciplined her voice, politely interested, as if the inquiry were about some social trivia. Did he take sugar in his tea? Did he enjoy sports? How did he rape a child?

'He had his right hand bandaged. It was quite genuine. He'd grazed it when he fell over a garden rake and it had become septic. He had just come home from work when he saw her, walking home after her Girl Guide meeting. He told her that he wanted a cup of tea but couldn't manage to fill the kettle.'

Ah, but that had been clever. He had seen a child coming down that suburban street, walking in the dangerous innocence of childhood. A Girl Guide in uniform. Her good deed for the day. He had used the one ploy that might succeed even with a suspicious or timid child. She hadn't sensed danger where there was a need she could meet, something within her power. She could picture the child carefully filling the kettle at the cold tap, lighting the gas for him, offering to stay and make the tea, setting out his cup and saucer with anxious care. He had made use of what was good and kind in her to destroy her. If evil existed, if those four letters placed in that order had any reality, then surely here was evil.

She was aware of her mother's voice.

'He didn't mean to harm her.'

'Didn't he? Then what did he mean?'

'To talk, perhaps. To kiss her. To fondle her. I don't know. Whatever he had in mind, it wasn't rape. He was gentle, timid, weak. I suppose that's why he was attracted to children. I thought I could help him because I was strong. But he didn't want strength. He couldn't cope with it. What he wanted was childishness, vulnerability. He didn't hurt her, you know, not physically. It was a technical rape, but he wasn't violent. I suppose if I hadn't killed her she and her parents would have claimed later that he'd ruined her life, that she could never make a happy marriage. Perhaps they would have been right. The psychologists say that children never get over an early sexual assault. I didn't leave her any life to be spoiled. I'm not excusing him, only you mustn't picture it as worse than it was.'

How could it have been worse than it was, Philippa wondered. A child had been raped and murdered. The physical details she could imagine, had imagined. But the horror, the loneliness, the last terrifying moment; it was no more possible to enter into these by an effort of will than it was physically to feel another's pain.

Pain and fear. To experience either was to be aware for ever of the loneliness of the self.

Maurice, after all, had warned her, in one of their short bouts of disconnected talk during those four days when she had been waiting for her mother's reply:

'None of us can bear too much reality. No one. We all create for ourselves a world in which it's tolerable for us to live. You've probably created yours with more imagination than most. Having gone to that trouble, why demolish it?'

And she in her arrogant confidence had replied:

'Perhaps I shall find out that it would have been better for me if I'd been contented with it. But it's too late now. That world has gone for good. I have to find another. At least this one will be founded on reality.'

'Will it? How do you know that it won't turn out to be just as illusory and far less comfortable?'

'But it must be better to know the facts. You're a scientist – a pseudo-scientist anyway. I thought you held truth to be sacred.'

And he had replied:

'"What is truth", said jesting Pilate, and would not stay for an answer. Facts are sacred, if you can discover them, and as long as you don't confuse them with values.'

They had circled the lawn once and were back at the Grange. Rejecting it, they turned slowly and began retracing their steps. She said:

'Have I any relations on my father's side of the family?'

'Your father was an only child. He had a cousin, but she and her husband emigrated to Canada about the time of the trial. They didn't want anyone to know about the connection. I suppose they're still alive. They hadn't any children and they were both middle-aged then. About forty, I think.'

'And your side?'

'I did have a brother, Stephen, eight years younger than I, but he was killed in Ireland the first year of the troubles, before he was twenty. He was in the army.'

'So my only uncle is dead, and there's no one else?'

'No,' she said gravely, unsmiling. 'Only me. I'm your only blood relation.'

They continued their slow pacing. The sun was hot on Philippa's shoulders. Her mother said:

'They provide tea for visitors, if you'd like a cup.'

'I would, but not here. I'll get it in York. How much longer have we?'

'Before the bus? Another thirty minutes.'

'What do I have to do? I mean, can you just come to me when you leave, or are there formalities?'

She was careful to keep her eyes on the path, unwilling to face what she might see in her mother's eyes. It was the moment of final offer and acceptance. When her mother spoke her voice was controlled.

'The present plan is for me to go to a probation hostel for women in Kensington. I hated the thought of another hostel, but there wasn't any choice, at least for the first month. But I don't think there'll be any difficulty about coming to you instead. They'll send someone to check that you've actually got a flat and the arrangements have to be approved by the Home Office. The first stage is for you to write formally to the Chief Welfare Officer here, but hadn't you better take a week or two to think about it?'

'I have thought about it.'

'What would you normally be doing in these next two months?'

'Probably the same, taking a flat in London. I've left school. I got my Cambridge scholarship last year when I was seventeen. This year I've been taking philosophy and adding to my A-levels just to fill in time. I'm hardly the VSO type – Voluntary Service Overseas. I'm not altering my plans for you, if that's what's worrying you.'

Her mother accepted the lie. She said:

'I shall be an embarrassing flat mate. How will you explain me to your friends?'

'We shan't be seeing my friends. If we do run into them, I shall explain that you're my mother. What else do they need to know?'

Her mother said formally:

'Then, thank you Philippa. Just for the first two months I'd be very glad to join you.'

After that they spoke no more of the future, but walked

together, each with her thoughts, until it was time for Philippa to join the desultory stream of visitors making their way up the wide sun-scorched path towards the gates and the waiting bus.

ELEVEN

Neither Maurice nor Hilda asked any questions when she got home shortly after half-past eight. Not to ask questions was part of Maurice's policy of non-interference; usually he managed to convey the impression of not being particularly interested in knowing. Hilda, who looked flushed and rather sulky, kept a resolute and sullen silence, inquiring only if Philippa had had a good journey. She glanced fearfully at Maurice as she asked this seemingly innocuous question, and appeared not to hear Philippa's answer. The tone was forced; she might have been speaking to a newly arrived and not particularly welcome guest. During a late dinner they sat like strangers; but strangers, after all, were what they were. It was a night when company would have been welcomed, but they drank their vichyssoise and ate their chicken marengo almost in silence. As she finally pushed her chair from the table, Philippa said:

'My mother seems quite glad to share a flat for the next month or so. I'll start looking tomorrow.'

The words came out unnaturally loudly, belligerent as a challenge. She was angry with herself that they should sound so forced, that despite her silent rehearsal throughout dinner speaking them aloud had been so difficult. She had never been frightened of Maurice. Why should she start being frightened of him now? She was eighteen, officially an adult, responsible to no one but herself. She was probably as free now as she was ever likely to be. She had no need to justify her actions. Maurice said:

'You won't find it easy to rent a flat at a price you can afford, not in central London anyway. If you need to borrow money, let me know. Don't go to the bank. There's no point in paying interest at the present rate.'

'I can manage on my own. I've got the money I saved for my European trip.'

'In that case, good luck. You'd better keep your key in case you need to come back. And if you are intending to move out permanently, it would be helpful if we could have as much notice as possible. I could probably find a use for your room.'

He made it sound, thought Philippa, as if he were dismissing an unwelcome paying guest. But that was how he had intended it to sound.

TWELVE

On Monday 17th July, shortly after nine o'clock in the morning, Scase rang a number in the city which he had rung every three months for the last six years. But this time the information he requested wasn't given to him. Nor, as usually happened, was it promised for a few days' time. Instead Eli Watkin asked him to call in at the office as soon as was convenient to him. Within half an hour he was on his way to Hallelujah Passage off Ludgate Hill to see a man whom he had last seen six years ago. Then Mavis had been with him; this time he made his way past St Paul's churchyard and into the dark, narrow little alley on his own.

They had waited for three years after the end of the trial before getting in touch with Eli Watkin Investigations Limited. They found the firm's name in the yellow pages of the London telephone directory among a list of some dozen private detective agencies, sandwiched between Designers and Diamond Merchants. They spent a day in London visiting each office in turn, trying to assess from the address and outward appearance whether it was efficient and reputable. Mavis had wanted to exclude any agency which accepted divorce cases, but Scase had persuaded her that this was an unnecessary limitation of choice. The task wasn't easy. Mutually supportive and determined as they were, they nevertheless felt themselves on alien and frightening territory. They were intimidated by the smart, impersonal-looking offices of the largest concerns, and repelled by the seediness of some of the smallest. In the end they ventured into Eli Watkin Investigations because they liked the name of Hallelujah Passage, the office exuded a Dickensian atmosphere of cheerful amateurism, and Mavis was reassured and cheered by the window box outside the ground-floor window in which the spears of early daffodils were already beginning to show. They were greeted by an elderly typist, then shown upstairs to Mr Eli Watkin himself.

On their entry into his small, claustrophobic office, they had found him squatting before a hissing gas fire, spooning cat food into three saucers while five squalling cats of varied sizes and hues butted against his thin ankles. A matriarchal tabby sat, paws folded, on top of a bookcase, regarding the mêlée with slit-eyed disdain. When the last of the food had been distributed, she jumped lightly down with a switch of her tail and arranged herself at the third bowl. Only then did Eli Watkin stand up to greet them. They had seen a squat, crumpled-faced man with a comb of white hair and heavy-lidded eyes. He had a disconcerting habit of appearing to keep them half closed when speaking, then of suddenly raising them, as if by a conscious effort, to display small but intensely blue eyes. He welcomed them with none of the smarmy condescension which Scase had feared. Nor did he seem at all surprised by their commission. Scase had practised what he intended to say.

'Three years ago a woman, Mary Ducton, was sentenced for life for the murder of our daughter, Julie Mavis Scase. We want to be kept in touch with her. We want to know when she's moved and where, what she's doing, and when she's due to be released. Is that the kind of information you deal in?'

'Well now, it could be. There's no information in the world that you can't get hold of if you're prepared to pay.'

'Would it be expensive?'

'Not that expensive. Where is the lady now? In Holloway? I thought so. Ring me at this number in ten days' time and we'll see what we can do.'

'How do you obtain your information?'

'The way one always gets information, Mr Scase. By paying for it.'

'This is confidential, of course. There's nothing illegal about it, but we don't want other people to know our business.'

'Of course. That is why you pay a little more.'

After that they had telephoned Eli Watkin four times a year. On each occasion he would ring back three days later and tell them what he knew. Within a week a bill would come, 'to professional services rendered'. The amount varied. Sometimes it was as high as twenty pounds, sometimes as low as five. In this way they learned when Mary Ducton came out of her self-imposed isolation and began working in the prison library, when she was moved from Holloway to Durham and from Durham to Melcombe Grange, when she was admitted to the prison hospital for treatment after an assault by three of the other prisoners, when her case was first considered by the parole board. Six months ago he had learned from Eli Watkin that she had been given a conditional release date for August 1978.

It was nearly eleven o'clock when he reached Hallelujah Passage. There was still a window box outside Eli Watkin's office, but now it held nothing but caked earth. The door into the passage was open and the ground-floor office, which was empty, was filled with packing cases. The dingy walls had been stripped; there were oblong shapes where once pictures must have hung. The windows were so filthy that the daylight was almost entirely excluded and he had to feel his way across the tattered linoleum to the uncarpeted stairway.

In the upstairs office Eli Watkin awaited him as he had six years ago. The same gas fire hissed away and he recognized the large roll-topped desk and the two battered filing cabinets. There were no cats now, but it seemed to Scase that there hung on the air the sharp, sour reek of their food. But then he wondered whether what he was smelling was mortal sickness. He could recognize Eli Watkin because the bright blue eyes were the same; nothing else was. The hand held out to grasp his was a cluster of loose bones held together by dry flesh. The face was a yellow death's head from which the eyes blazed with the brilliance of jewels.

Scase said:

'I've called about Mary Ducton. I rang to ask if you'd yet got the actual day of release. You asked me to call.'

'So I did, so I did, Mr Scase. There are some things which are best said face to face. Come in now, will you?'

He went over to the first of the filing cabinets and took from the top drawer a buff folder. The drawer seemed otherwise to be empty. The folder was faded but clean, almost untouched. But then, thought Scase, it had only been handled four times a year. Eli Watkin carried it back to the desk and opened it. Scase saw that it contained copies of his bills and small scraps of paper, notes, perhaps, of telephone conversations. There was nothing else. Watkin said:

'The subject is due to be released from Melcombe Grange prison on Tuesday 15th of August 1978.'

'To what address?'

'Now that I can't be telling you, Mr Scase; it was to have been to a probation hostel in North Kensington, but there's talk at the prison that the arrangement may be changed.'

'When would you be able to let me know? Could I telephone you next week?'

'I shan't be here next week, Mr Scase. By next month the builders will be in converting this place to a coffee and sandwich bar. A little tucked away, I should have thought, to suit the customers, but that's not my worry. I've been paid well enough for the lease. And if you should telephone in six months' time they'll tell you, if there's anyone still here and if they care, that I'm dead. By August fifteenth I shall be in Mexico. I've waited all my life, Mr Scase, to see the floating gardens of Xochimilco, and I'm off in three days' time. This is the last information I'll be giving you. And you, Mr Scase, are my last client.'

Scase said:

'I'm sorry.'

There was nothing else that he could think to say. After a moment he asked:

'And you've no idea what town she'll be travelling to?'

'I imagine she'll come to London. They usually do. She lived in Seven Kings in Essex at the time of the murder, didn't she? Likely as not she'll come to London.'

'Do you know what time they'll release her?'

'It's usually in the morning. I should plan for the morning if I were you. The morning of Tuesday, 15th August.'

Had there been a subtle emphasis on the word 'plan'? Scase said:

'It would be helpful to know. I have to see her personally, to hand her a letter from my wife. I promised Mavis to put it into her hand.'

'I've promised myself all my life that I'd see the floating gardens. Do you believe in reincarnation, Mr Scase?'

'I haven't thought about it. I suppose it could be a comfort to people who need to believe in their own importance.'

'But you can believe in your own importance without myths?'

The swollen lids were suddenly raised and the blue eyes stared at him, unfaded, ironic. He said:

'Killing someone isn't easy, Mr Scase. Even the State has had to give it up. And the State had all the conveniences, you might say, a scaffold, a skilled and experienced operator, the condemned person safely to hand. Are you a skilled operator, Mr Scase?'

He wondered why the words, the implied threat, didn't worry him. And then a glance at that skull, marked out like an anatomist's model with its tributaries of blue veins, at the paper-thin membrane stretched over the jutting bones, told him why. Even the mark of death was enough to make a man virtually harmless. He was already moving away from the petty concerns of the living towards his floating gardens. And what difference did suspicion make? When the murderess was dead he must expect to be the chief, perhaps the only suspect. What mattered was that he should give the police no real evidence, no legal proof. Part of him half believed that they might not look for that proof too assiduously. He said calmly:

'If that's what you believe, aren't you going to warn the police?'

'But that would be unethical, Mr Scase. In my profession I don't often speak to the police, although sometimes they like to speak to me. And you and I have had a long and I think, fruitful professional relationship. You've paid me well over the years for certain information. What you do with it isn't my responsibility. And I have to catch that plane in three days' time.'

Scase said calmly:

'You are mistaken. I have to see the woman, have to hand over a letter, that's all. My wife wanted her to know that we have forgiven her. One can't go on hating for nearly ten years.'

'Very true. Do you read Thomas Mann, Mr Scase? A fine writer. "For the sake of humanity, for the sake of love, let no man's thoughts be ruled by death." I think I have quoted it correctly, but you get the meaning I'm sure. That will be fifty pounds.'

'It's more than I expected. I've only brought forty pounds in cash with me. I've never paid more than thirty before.'

'But this is the final payment, and I think you can say that the information is worth it. But we'll say forty. We don't want any cheques, do we?'

He paid over the eight five-pound notes. Eli Watkin folded them into his wallet. He said:

'I don't think we need trouble this time with a receipt. And now we can add your file to the rest of this rubbish. There are quite a number of secrets and a lot of misery torn up in this sack. Perhaps you'll deal with it. The file cover is rather too stiff for my hands.'

Scase tore up each scrap of paper, then ripped the file cover into small pieces and shook them into the sack in which the debris of Mr Watkin's small business slid in a restless tide of paper. Last of all they shook hands. Watkin's hand was dry and very cold, but his handshake was surprisingly firm; strong enough, surely, to have torn up the file had he chosen. Scase's last sight of him was of him still sitting at his desk, and looking after him with an amused, benignant pity. But his last words were cheerful enough:

'Don't fall over the dustbins, Mr Scase. Wouldn't it be an inconvenient thing now if you were disabled just at this interesting period of your life?'

That afternoon he telephoned the best known of the local house agents and instructed them to put his house on the market. The firm said that they would try to send round their Mr Wheatley early next morning. By ten o'clock Mr Wheatley had arrived. He was younger than Scase had expected – not more than twenty, surely, – with a sharp, unhealthy-looking face, and was dressed with a desperate respectability, presumably to inspire confidence in the efficiency and probity of the firm. The padded shoulders of his cheap, dark blue suit hung loosely on him as if he had chosen it to allow for growth. But he entered with brisk assurance and was hardly through the door before he began surveying the house with a keen appraising eye. He carried a clip-board and measured each room expertly with a spring measuring tape which he used with a flourish. Walking behind him from room to room, Scase saw that he had a small pustule on his neck. It had broken, staining the top of his shirt collar with blood and pus. He found it difficult to take his eyes off it.

'Well, it's a nice little property, sir. Nicely maintained. We shouldn't have much trouble in getting rid of it for you. Mind you, the market isn't quite what it was six months ago. What price were you thinking of?'

'What price do you suggest?'

He wouldn't, Scase knew, put it higher than he needed to. The commission went up with the price, but what really paid was a quick sale and no trouble. And he wouldn't be valuing it himself for all his pursed lips and air of calculation. His firm would have told him exactly what a reasonably well-maintained semi in Alma Road would fetch.

After a couple of minutes spent slowly pacing from hall to sitting-room, from sitting-room to kitchen, he said:

'You might get nineteen and a half if you're lucky. The garden's a bit neglected and these houses haven't got garages. That always brings the price down. People like a garage. We could start at twenty and be prepared to drop.'

'I want a quick sale. I don't mind starting at nineteen and a half.'

'It's up to you, sir. Now, what about viewing? Will you be in this afternoon?'

'No. I'll give you a spare set of keys. I'd like you to show people round. I don't want to see them.'

'That may hold things up a bit, sir. It's a question of staff, you see. We'd have to try and fit a number of viewers in together. Now, if you could arrange to be home early evenings for, say, a couple of weeks . . .'

Scase thought, let them earn their commission.

'I don't want to see anyone. You can hand over the keys if they sign for them and undertake to lock up carefully. There's nothing here for them to steal.'

'Oh, we wouldn't want to do that, sir. Look, if I could tell prospective purchasers that you might take eighteen and a half, or even eighteen at a pinch, I don't think you'll have to wait long.'

'All right. Ask eighteen and a half.'

'There's a young couple on the books who might be interested at eighteen thousand. They've got two kids and you're handy for the school. I'll see if I can get them over this evening.'

'I want a quick sale. Won't they need a mortgage? That takes time.'

'There'll be no difficulty there, sir. They've been saving with a building society. I think you'll find that it will all go very easily if they like the house.'

Taking one last disparaging look at the meanly proportioned front sitting-room, he added:

'Whoever takes it will probably knock that middle wall down and make one large room. Open it up, like. And the kitchen will need remodelling.'

Scase didn't care what they did to it as long as it was quickly sold. He needed the money to finance his enterprise. He and Mavis had always agreed that selling the house might be necessary. He didn't think Mavis had thought beyond the actual deed; at present he wasn't thinking beyond it himself. But the prospect of virtual homelessness, of moving from this snug suburban respectability into an unknown, intimidating world filled him with a mixture of excitement and apprehension. It would be so easy to hang on, to see the house as a familiar refuge to which he could retreat if the hunt got hard or disappointing. As he followed behind Mr Wheatley, watching the silver measure leap out to record the meagre dimensions of kitchen and hall, the house seemed to him like the lair of some small predator, earth-bound, secret, holding within its brown walls the beast's very smell. In the kitchen he imagined that he could see its spoor on the linoleum, could see under the table a litter of fur and bones.

THIRTEEN

Philippa knew that in her search for a furnished, two-roomed flat in central London at a reasonable rent, she was privileged; appearance, age, voice and colour – although no one was so unwise as to hint at race – all were in her favour. She read the truth of her advantage in the appraising eyes and deference of the receptionists and interviewers in the dozen or so flat agencies at which she called. It was an added attraction to them that the lease required was so short – 'only the three months before I go up to Cambridge' – and that she didn't want a joint let. The words, 'just for the two of us, my mother and me, we want to spend some months together in London before I go up to college and she goes abroad', spoken in her confident, educated voice were, as she well knew, a reassuring guarantee of filial duty and respectability. Any of the agents would gladly have let to her if they had had anything suitable to offer. But short-term furnished leases in inner London were exorbitantly priced for the foreign market, and her tentative suggestion of forty to fifty pounds a week was met with incredulous smiles, shakes of the head, and murmurs of the evil effect of the rent restriction acts. She was made to feel guilty of some deception; she had no right to walk in looking so prosperous and admit to such poverty. Losing interest, the agencies took her name and address and promised nothing.

She followed the same daily routine during the first week of her search. She left 68 Caldecote Terrace after breakfast and spent the morning trudging round the agencies. As soon as the lunchtime editions of the evening paper were available, she bought them and marked the possibilities. The next half-hour was spent in a telephone kiosk where, provided with a supply of coins, she began the frustrating task of trying to contact the advertisers on numbers most of which were either perpetually engaged or unobtainable. Then came the viewing; flats whose grimy windows overlooked deep wells which no sunlight could ever penetrate; shared lavatories and bathrooms remote from the flat itself and in a state to encourage permanent constipation; furnished flats where the furniture consisted of the landlord's broken rejects, wardrobes whose doors swung perpetually open, cookers with chipped enamel and food-encrusted ovens, tables with scorched tops and uneven legs, and filthy lumpy beds; landlords whose advertisement for a female tenant had less to do with the probable greater cleanliness of the kitchen than with other more elemental needs.

She was soon forced to widen the area of her search. She came to know a different London and she saw it through different eyes. The city was all things to all men. It reflected and deepened mood; it did not create it. Here the miserable were more miserable, the lonely more bereft, while the prosperous and happy saw reflected in its river and glittering life the confirmation of their deserved success. In its week of seeking, unsuccessfully, for a flat in which she could bear, even temporarily, to live, Philippa felt increasingly depressed and rejected. Once, from the security of Caldecote Terrace she would have seen the meaner streets of north Paddington, Kilburn and Earls Court as fascinating outposts of an alien culture, part of the variety and colour of any capital city. Now with disenchanted and prejudiced eyes she saw only filth and deformity; the bursting bags of uncollected rubbish, the litter which choked the gutters and blew down the passages of the Underground, the walls defaced by the scribbled hate of extremists of the left and right, the crude obscenities with which the platform posters were embellished, the stink of urine overlaid with disinfectant which rose from the stained concrete of the underground walkways, the ugliness of people. Man, fouling his own habitat, couldn't even behave like a good animal.

The alien shrouded bodies crouching on the kerb-side, watching from the open doors, threatened her with their strangeness; the prevailing smells of curry, of herded bodies, of scented women's hair, emphasized the sense of exclusion, of being unwanted in her own city.

And then on the morning of Friday 28th July, walking down Edgware Road after finding that yet another advertised flat had been taken, she saw down a side road an agency which she hadn't before discovered. The most remarkable thing about the Raterite Accommodation Bureau was that it existed at all, or that, existing, it did any business. If larger, cleaner and more imposing agencies were short of properties to rent or manage, it was strange that this seedy unprepossessing establishment attracted prospective landlords. The window was patterned with hand-written cards sellotaped to the smeared glass. Most were brown with age; on some the ink had faded to the colour of thin dried blood. The variety of handwriting and eccentricity of spelling suggested a frequent change of staff and no great discrimination in their choosing. The few clean white cards were intrusive patches of hope which was quickly vitiated by the word 'taken' scrawled across those few which, judging from the reasonable rent demanded, had probably never genuinely been on offer.

Philippa pushed open the door and stepped into a small office containing two desks and a row of four chairs against the wall. On one of these an Indian was sitting in patient resignation. Behind the larger of the two desks a flamboyantly dressed woman with red hair and a multitude of clinking bangles sat smoking a cigarette and doing the crossword in the morning paper. She had the look of a woman who has found life recalcitrant since childhood but has finally succeeded, at some cost to herself, in pounding it into shape. At the second desk a younger, blonde woman was listening with careful uninterest to the volubility of a red-faced, bandy-legged man whose suit of checked tweed and natty, feather-trimmed trilby were more appropriate to the Brighton racecourse than to this seedy office.

The blonde shifted her eyes to Philippa, apparently to indicate that she was now prepared to do business. The bandy-legged man, taking the hint, made for the door.

'Well, see you.'

'See you,' the two women chorused together with a marked lack of enthusiasm.

Philippa said her piece. She was looking for a small, partly furnished, two-roomed flat for herself and her mother in central London for about two months.

'Until I go up to university. There's just the two of us. I don't mind doing something to it if it's basically in good order and fairly central.'

'What sort of rent were you thinking of?'

'What sort of rents are there?'

'Depends. Fifty, sixty, eighty, a hundred and more. We don't usually get anything under fifty a week. It's the Rent Act you see. Doesn't pay a landlord to rent when he can't get the tenants out.'

'Yes, I know all about the Rent Act. I could pay cash in advance.'

The woman at the other desk looked up but didn't speak. The blonde went on:

'Two months, you say? Most landlords look for a bit longer.'

'I thought they liked short lets. Isn't that why they let to foreigners because they know they can get them out? I can promise we'll be out by the autumn.'

The red-headed woman spoke.

'We don't take promises. There'd be an agreement. Mr Wade, the solicitor round the corner, draws it up for us. You did say cash?'

Philippa made herself look hard into the calculating eyes.

'For ten per cent discount.'

The blonde laughed.

'Are you kidding? Anything we get to rent furnished we can let without a discount.'

The woman at the other desk said:

'What about that two-roomed place with kitchen and shared bathroom in Delaney Street?'

'It's taken, Mrs Bealing. That young couple with the kid and the baby on the way. They viewed yesterday. I told you.'

'Let's have a look at the card.'

The blonde opened the top left-hand drawer of her desk and flicked through a card index. The card was passed across. The red-headed woman looked at Philippa.

'Three months' cash in advance. He won't let it go for less than three months. He's asking one hundred and ninety a month. Say five hundred and fifty for the three months, cash down, no cheques. And it's what's called a holiday letting. That means that the Rent Act doesn't apply.'

She had just short of one thousand pounds in her bank account saved from birthday presents and holiday jobs. But money, although she never spent it without thought, had never been important to her. She had always believed that she could earn money. Of all her needs, it seemed to her the most easily acquired. She said with only a moment's hesitation:

'All right. But if it's taken?'

'Please yourself. It's up to you.'

The blonde glanced at Philippa with the amused, slightly contemptuous look of a woman who has long given up expecting people to behave well, but can still gain some satisfaction from watching them behave badly. Philippa nodded. The older woman picked up the telephone and dialled.

'Mr Baker? The Raterite Agency here about the flat. Yes. Yes. Yes. Well, the fact of the matter is that Mr Coates isn't happy. Yes, I know he's in New York. He rang. He doesn't like the idea of your wife managing those narrow stairs, not in her condition. And he doesn't want a let with children. Yes, I know, but I'm the one who makes the decisions and I wasn't here when you came in. And then there would be the pram in the hall. No, it wouldn't be any good writing to him. I don't know where he'll be for the next month or two. Sorry. Yes, we'll let you know. Up to forty pounds a week. Yes. I know, Mr Baker. Yes. We've got all the details. Yes. Yes. I don't think it's very helpful to take that attitude. After all, nothing has been signed.'

She took up her cigarette again, and returned to her paper. Without looking at Philippa she said:

'You can view it now if you like. Number 12, Delaney Street. It's at the bottom of Mell Street off the Edgware Road just this side of Praed Street. Two rooms, one kitchen. Use of bathroom. The bathroom's shared with the lock-up greengrocery on the ground floor. You won't find anything cheaper, not in central London. It's a snip. It'd be twice the price, but Mr Coates went to New York in a hurry and he wants a short let.'

'Is it furnished?'

The blonde said:

'Not so as you'd notice. Well, most people like to bring in their own bits and pieces. But it's a furnished letting.'

'I'd like to view it now, please.'

She signed for the keys, but didn't at once make her way to Delaney Street. It seemed to her that once there the decision would have been made. If she were going to reject the flat she must do so now. She felt the need to stride out vigorously, to co-ordinate thought with action. But the pavement was too crowded; the pressure of bodies, the tangle of pushchairs and trolleys forced her restless feet from the kerb into the stream of traffic. Almost without thinking she turned into the café about a hundred yards down Edgware Road and found a seat at a grubby formica-topped table near the window. A lank-haired waiter in a stained jacket slouched over from the counter and she ordered a coffee. The coffee when it arrived in a plastic cup, pale, lukewarm and tasteless was literally undrinkable. Glancing round at her fellow customers who were not only managing to drink it – although with no apparent signs of pleasure – but had actually bought food, over-cooked hamburgers, flabby chips, fried eggs curling brown at the edges and swimming in grease, she reflected that one at least of Maurice's axioms was true: The poor always got worse value pound for pound than the rich.

The window was festooned with wicker baskets of dusty artificial flowers and trailing vineleaves. Against the glittering panorama of the traffic the pavement was heaving with life. From time to time, faces, grey, brown or black, moved momentarily to the glass to study the price list. They seemed to be staring in at her; face succeeded face like a peripatetic jury, mute witnesses of her moral dilemma.

Nothing she could recognize from her past had equipped her to deal with it. She slipped the key ring on her thumb so that the two keys, the Yale which must be for the shared front door, the Chubb for the door to the flat itself, lay cold and heavy against her palm, reinforcing symbolism. Her moral training – indoctrination Maurice would have called it, smiling a self-satisfied acceptance of his own honesty – had been a matter of semantics, of the intellectualization of a comfortable, ethical conformity. You behaved reasonably well to other people in the interest of certain abstractions: good public order, a pleasant life, natural justice – whatever that meant – the greatest good of the greatest number. Most of all, you behaved well to others to ensure that they behaved well to you. The implication was that the clever, the witty, the beautiful or the rich had less need of these expedients; it was the more seemly in them to set an example.

She could find no answer in her schooling. The South London Collegiate was nominally a Christian foundation but the fifteen minutes' corporate worship with which the school started the day had always seemed to her no more than a convenient celebration of tradition, a way of ensuring that the whole school was present when the headmistress read out the day's notices. Some of the girls practised a religion. Anglicanism, particularly High Anglicanism, was accepted as a satisfying compromise between reason and myth, justified by the beauty of its liturgy, a celebration of Englishness; but essentially it was the universal religion of liberal humanism laced with ritual to suit each individual taste. She had never supposed that for Gabriel, professed High Anglican, it had ever been more. The small number of Roman Catholics, Christian Scientists and Nonconformists were regarded as eccentrics governed by family tradition. Nothing that any of them professed to believe interfered with the central dogma of the whole school, the supremacy of human intelligence. The girls, like their brothers at Winchester, Westminster and St Paul's, were conditioned from childhood to a fierce intellectual competitiveness. She herself had been so conditioned from the time of her entry to the lower school. They were marked for success as if with invisible stigmata; the blessed company of the redeemed, redeemed from monotony, from poverty, from inconsequence, from failure. The universities they would go to, the professions they would choose, the men they would marry, were ranked in a hierarchy, unstated but subtly understood. She didn't feel that this was the only world in which she could find a place. She was a writer; all worlds were open to her. But it was the world into which Maurice had raised himself, into which she had been adopted, and she had no quarrel with it. After her foragings among the philistines this civilized city would always open its doors to her, not as an alien but as a freeman.

She supposed that Dame Beatrice, who visited the school once a week to teach moral philosophy, would have had an answer to her dilemma, if asking more questions and discussing their relevance, whether they had, in fact, any meaning, was an answer. She recalled the last weekly essay, which was in itself a diploma of superiority since only the upper sixth attended Dame Beatrice's lectures.

'Act only on that maxim through which you can at the same time will that it should become a universal law. Discuss with reference to Hegel's Criticism of Kant's System of Moral Philosophy.'

And what relevance had that to the opposing claims to a cheap flat of an ex-convict who was a murderess and a pregnant wife?

Except that the pregnant wife had got there first. There was a notice on the board in the school hall. The Chaplain is available to girls in his study by appointment or on Friday from twelve-thirty to two p.m. and on Wednesday from four to five-thirty. A spiritual stud. He was a humourless man and the girls had giggled at the infelicitous wording. But he would, she supposed, have had his answer:

'Behold, I give you a new commandment, that you love one another.'

But that wasn't possible by an act of will. Surely the faithful were justified in replying 'But Lord, show us how'? And He, that itinerant man/God, whom no one would have heard of if he had died sane and in his bed would have had his answer too: 'I have.'

The café was not the most suitable place for the resolution of a moral dilemma. The noise was appalling and there was a shortage of seats. Harassed women with folded push-chairs and children clutching at their coats were looking for a place. She had sat there long enough. She left a fivepenny tip under the saucer of unfinished coffee, dropped the keys in her shoulder-bag and set off resolutely down the Edgware Road towards Mell Street.

FOURTEEN

Delaney Street was at the Lisson Grove end of Mell Street, a narrow street with, on the left, a terrace of small shops with living accommodation above. There was a pub at the end, the Grenadier, with a swinging sign of some splendour, then a betting shop, secretive behind painted glass, giving out a low murmur like a hive of angry bees. Then came a hairdresser, the front of his window strewn with advertisements for hair tonics and lotions, and the back occupied by four dummy heads. The blank dolls' eyes turned upwards in the gaping sockets, and the wigs, dry as straw, gave the heads the look of guillotine victims of some ancient holocaust, needing only a jagged red line around each severed neck to complete the illusion. The door was open, and Philippa could see two customers awaiting their turn, and a wizened old man, comb poised, busying himself with the back of a customer's neck.

A green door with '12' painted in black and a Victorian iron knocker and letter-box was between a junk shop and a greengrocer whose open-fronted shop had once been the ground floor of the house. On the fascia was painted 'Monty's Fruit and Veg'. Both shops had spilled out on to the pavement. The greengrocer's stall, covered with a mat of lurid artificial grass, was piled with fruit and vegetables, displayed with an eye to artistic effect. An intricate pyramid of oranges gleamed against the dimness of the inner shop; bunches of bananas and grapes hung from a rail above the back of the stall and the boxes of burnished apples, the carrots and tomatoes were arranged in a balanced pattern as if for a church harvest festival. A stocky young man with greasy fair hair straggling to his shoulders, a podgy, amiable face and huge hands, was pouring potatoes from the pan of his scales into the overstretched shopping bag held by the mittened hands of an elderly customer, so well-wrapped against the unkind summer that little of his face was visible between the flat cloth cap and the swathed woollen scarves.

Now that she was here she found herself torn between anxiety to see the flat and a curious reluctance to put the key in the door. It was almost as an exercise in self-control as well as a wish to postpone disappointment that she made herself take stock of her surroundings.

The junk shop looked exciting. Outside there was an assortment of old furniture: four bentwood chairs, two more with broken cane seats, a sturdy kitchen table bearing boxes of paperback novels and old magazines, an ancient treadle sewing-machine, an enamel wash-tub filled with assorted crockery, most of it chipped, and a wooden mangle. Victorian prints and amateur water-colours in a variety of frames rested against the table legs. On the pavement was a square cardboard box of linen in which a couple of young women were rummaging happily. In the shop window every inch of space was occupied. Philippa gained an impression of articles jumbled together, irrespective of merit and, presumably, of price. She could see chipped Staffordshire, delicately painted cups and saucers, dishes and bowls, candlesticks and horse brasses, while an antique doll with a delicate china face and straw-filled bulging legs was perched in the pride of place.

She inserted the Yale key in the lock, aware as she did so of the interested glance of the greengrocer, and found herself in a narrow hall. The hall smelled of apples and loam, a strong rich tang which, she guessed, overlaid less-agreeable smells. It was very narrow – too narrow for a pram, she told herself – and obstructed by two sacks of potatoes and a meshed bag of onions. To the right an open door led into the shop; a second, with a glass panel, gave sight of a back yard. She decided to explore this later, although the glimpse of it immediately filled her mind with visions of climbing plants and geranium-filled tubs. A flight of steep, drugget-covered stairs led to a back room on a half landing. She opened the door gingerly and saw that this was the bathroom. The large old-fashioned bath was heavily stained round the waste-pipe, but otherwise surprisingly clean. There was a small wash-basin encrusted with grime and with a slimy face-flannel jammed into the soap dish. The lavatory had a heavy mahogany seat, a high cistern and a chain, lengthened by string. Another length of string was stretched across the bath. It sagged with the weight of a pair of jeans and two grubby towels.

She went up a further short flight of stairs to the flat door. The key turned in the Chubb lock without difficulty and she passed into a short hall. After the dimness of the stairway the flat seemed full of light, perhaps because the doors to the three rooms were all open. She moved first into the one at the front which she guessed would be the principal room running the whole width of the house. The curtains were drawn back and a single beam of sunlight shone through the dirty window panes so that the air was iridescent with dancing motes of dust. It wasn't large, she judged about fifteen feet by ten, but was pleasantly proportioned with a carved cornice and with two windows facing over the street. On the left-hand wall was a Victorian grate, its hood was patterned with a border of scallop shells and decorated with a design of beribboned grape vines; above it was a plain wooden overmantel. The grate was stuffed with brown and brittle old newspapers, and the tiled surround was littered with cigarette butts, but the air held no taint of cigarette smoke, only the faint autumnal smell of vegetables and apples. The room was shabby. The paint on the window-frames had chipped and flaked to the bare wood. The carpet was a dull green, splodged and ringed in front of the fire as if the occupier had placed his hot cooking pans on the floor. But the wallpaper, patterned in small posies of rosebuds, had faded to a pleasant pinkish brown, and was surprisingly intact, and although the ceiling obviously hadn't been painted for years, there were no ominous cracks, no hanging swathes of lining paper. A long cord with a single unshaded light bulb on the end had been drawn from the middle of the ceiling and stretched over a hood so that the light was suspended over the single divan bed.

The divan was covered with a woollen blanket made of hand-knitted squares in different colours. Philippa drew it back and saw with relief that the mattress was clean, so clean that it looked new. There were two pillows, also new, but no other bedclothes. Between the windows was a small but sturdy oak wardrobe with carved doors. It stood firm when she pulled open the door. Inside were two empty hangers and, folded on the floor, three grey army blankets exuding a smell of mothballs. The only other items of furniture were a wicker chair with a limp fawn cushion, an oblong table with a centre drawer, and a bentwood rocking chair with a wicker seat.

The windows were curtained in a coarse unlined linen, slung from wooden hooks on an old-fashioned bamboo curtain rail. They had the creased, grubby look of curtains which had been laid aside, unused, but the material was good. Standing behind them she looked out over the narrow street. Opposite but about thirty yards to the left was another pub, the Blind Beggar. It was a high Dutch-fronted building with the date 1896 painted in heavy curved numerals on an oval plaque under the central gable. The swinging sign, which was competently painted and highly sentimental, was almost certainly the original. It showed a bent white-haired man with sightless eyes being led by a golden-haired child. A narrow passage ran down the side of the building, separating it from a wasteland bordered with a fence of high corrugated iron. It looked like a bomb site which had been neglected since the war but, she thought, more probably it had been cleared for some development which had been thwarted for lack of money. It had been concreted, but the surface had cracked and grass and weeds waist-high had burgeoned in the crevices. Three vehicles had been parked there, a van and two saloons. They had the isolated battered look of ramshackle rejects abandoned in a small oasis of decrepitude. Next to the car park was a second-hand bookshop. The window was half shuttered but two trestle tables outside the shop were bright with the green and orange of old paperbacks. Next came a small general store, the window plastered with notices of special offers. On the corner of Delaney Street and Mell Street was a launderette. As she watched, a coloured woman came out lugging two plastic bags, presumably of washed clothes, which she humped on to an empty push-chair. But otherwise the road was empty, lapped in a mid-morning lull.

She turned away from the window and looked round the room again with mounting excitement. Something could be made of it. In her mind's eye she saw it transformed, the grate cleaned and polished, the woodwork painted a gleaming white, the curtains washed. Nothing need be done about the walls, she liked the delicate washed-out pink and brown. The floor would be a problem, of course. She turned back a corner of the carpet. Underneath the solid oak boards were dirty but looked undamaged. The most exciting thing to do would be to sand the floor and then polish it so that the natural oak shone with the simplicity and beauty of wood against the darker walls, but she doubted whether that would be possible. Without the use of a car it would be difficult to hire a sanding machine, and there wasn't very much time. She had never realized before just how important a car could be. But the carpet would have to go. She would rip it out, roll it and get rid of it somehow, and replace it with rugs. The room might in the end be bare, but it would have some grace, some individuality. It wouldn't have what her mind's eye pictured as the dreadful compromise between bleakness and claustrophobic cosiness of a prison cell.

She continued her exploration. At the rear were two rooms, a narrow bedroom and the kitchen. Both overlooked the walled yard and, beyond it, the narrow back gardens of the next street. One or two of them had been carefully tended but most were an untidy conglomeration of ramshackle sheds, dismembered motor bikes, broken and discarded children's toys, washing lines and concrete fuel bunkers. But there was a plane tree at the bottom of the garden opposite the bedroom, providing a green light-filled shield for the worst of the clutter, and at least the view had some human interest.

She decided that the small room would have to be hers. It was too like a cell in its proportions to be suitable for her mother. She sat on the single divan bed and assessed the room's possibilities. There was a fitted cupboard on each side of the iron Victorian grate and the walls had been stripped of paper ready for redecoration. She wouldn't need to buy a wardrobe and it would be a simple matter to apply a coat of emulsion. She liked, too, the pine overmantel. Someone had painted it green but the paint was already peeling. It wouldn't be too difficult to strip and polish it. The window-sill was wide enough to hold a plant. She could picture the sill gleaming with white paint, reflecting the green and red of a geranium.

Lastly she went into the kitchen. Here she was agreeably surprised. It was a good-sized room with the sink and teak draining-board in front of the double window. The owner had started here with his redecoration and the walls had been painted white. There was a wooden-topped table, two wheel-backed chairs, a small refrigerator and what looked like a new gas stove. She turned on the gas tap and found to her relief that the supply hadn't been disconnected. He must have left for America in a hurry.

After her inspection she relocked the front door and went finally to explore the back yard whose worst horrors had been obscured from the upstairs windows by an overhanging bough of the plane tree. The outside lavatory with its wooden seat and stone floor obviously hadn't worked for years. But at least it didn't smell. The yard was a mess. There was a bicycle against one wall and the other two were piled with rubbish; empty paint cans, a rotting roll of old carpet, and what looked like the dismembered parts of an ancient gas stove. Here, too, were two battered and malodorous dustbins. She supposed that they would have to be dragged into the street for the weekly collection. Something, she decided, would have to be done about the yard, but it would have to wait its turn.

She looked at her watch. It was time that she went back to the agency and confirmed that she would definitely take the flat. She had thirty pounds with her in cash. Perhaps they would take that as a deposit until she could get to her bank and draw out the rest of the cash. Whatever happened, she mustn't lose it now. As soon as the agreement had been signed she would move in and start work. But first it might be prudent to make the acquaintance of her neighbour.

He had just finished serving a customer and was carefully repairing his pyramid of oranges. She watched him for a moment, knowing that he was aware of her but was waiting for her to make the first move. She said:

'Good morning. Are you Monty?'

'Naw. Monty was me granddad. Dead twenty years.' He hesitated, then added: 'I'm George.'

'I'm Philippa. Philippa Palfrey. My mother and I have just taken the upstairs flat.'

She held out her hand. After another hesitation he wiped his palm against his side and gripped her knuckles hard. She winced as the bones ground together. He said:

'Marty gone to New York then?'

'He's gone somewhere. I suppose he'll be back. It's only a short-term let for two or three months. I was wondering about the bathroom. They said at the agency that we share it. I thought we'd better settle about the cleaning.'

He looked, she thought, a little nonplussed.

'Marty's birds always did the cleaning.'

'Well, I'm no one's bird. But as there are two of us and only you, I don't mind taking responsibility for the bathroom, if that's all right by you.'

'Suits me.'

'We'll do the passage and the stairs, too. Do you mind if I clear up the yard, I mean, just get rid of some of the mess? I thought we might have some pots – geraniums perhaps. I don't suppose it gets much sun with that high wall, but something might grow.'

'I keep me bike in the yard.'

'Oh, I didn't mean I'd move your bike. Of course not. I'd just get rid of those old paint cans and the bits of iron.'

'That's OK by me. That outside WC doesn't work.'

'So I found. It hardly seems worth mending it; after all my mother and I won't be monopolizing the bathroom. We can bath out of shop hours. We'll try to keep it clear for you if you can let us know when you want to use it.'

'Look love, I pee in the bloody place. It's me bog. I can't tell you when I'm going to be took short, not with the amount of beer I drink.'

'I'm sorry. I saw your bath towel there and I thought you might want to bath after you close the shop.'

'That's Marty's towel. I bath at home. There's only two things I want to do up there and I can't tell you when I'll want to do them. OK?'

'Well, that's all right then.'

They looked at each other. He said:

'Marty OK? Doing all right is he?'

'I haven't the least idea. Considering the rent he's asking, he should be doing fine.'

He smiled. Then with the élan of a conjuror his chubby hands picked out four oranges, tossed them into a bag and held it out to her.

'Sample the produce. Monty's best. It's on the house. House-warming present.'

'That's very kind of you. Thank you. I've never had a house-warming present before.'

The action in its generosity and grace disconcerted and touched her. She smiled at him and turned quickly away, afraid that she might cry. She never cried, but it had been a long exhausting week and she was at the end of her search at last. Perhaps it was only tiredness and the relief of finding somewhere when she had almost given up hope that made her so ridiculously sensitive to a simple act of kindness. The bag was too fragile for the weight of the oranges and she had to support them on her hands. She looked down at their gleaming pock-marked skin and felt their solidarity resting on her palms. She bore them upstairs slowly and carefully as if they might crack, then rested the bag against the wall while she unlocked the flat door. She had found during her inspection a shallow Wedgwood patterned bowl in the kitchen cupboard among a miscellany of crockery and half-used tins of coffee and cocoa. She set the oranges in it. Then she placed the bowl precisely in the middle of the kitchen table. It seemed to her that with this action she took possession of the flat.

FIFTEEN

On the following day, Saturday 29th July, Scase took a cheap day return ticket from Victoria to Brighton. He was on his way to buy thc knife. He had been born in Brighton, in a small pub near the station, but his return for the first time since his youth had nothing to do with nostalgia. The purchase of a knife seemed to him of immense significance; he had to make the right choice and to make it without risk that his purchase would afterwards be remembered. That meant that he needed to buy it in a large town, preferably some distance from London, and on the busiest shopping day of the week. He would feel at home in Brighton. There were advantages in not having to cope with so important a purchase and at the same time find his way around a strange town.

His first thought was to buy a hunting or sheath knife from a shop which dealt in camping equipment, but when, after anxiously scrutinizing the window, he ventured inside such a shop, there were no knives on display and the thought of having actually to ask for one, and perhaps of being asked by an assistant, anxious to be helpful, for what precise purpose he wanted it, reinforced his feeling that this wasn't the right place. Wandering among the anoraks, the bed-rolls and the camping gear, he did eventually find a selection of jack-knives hanging from a display board, but he thought that the blades might be too short. He was worried, too, that if he had to act in a hurry his fingers might be too weak to get the blade prised open in time. What he wanted was a simpler weapon. But he did find, and buy, at the camping shop another necessary piece of equipment; a strong canvas rucksack in khaki, about fourteen inches by ten with two metal buckles and a shoulder strap.

In the end he found the knife in the kitchen department of a fashionable household store, new since his time. The goods were displayed in racks; stacks of pretty cups and saucers, earthenware casserole dishes, plain well-designed cutlery and every possible item of equipment for cooking. The store was very busy and he moved with his blood-stained preoccupation among young couples conferring happily over purchases for their homes, families with boisterous children, chattering foreign tourists and the occasional solitary shopper surveying with a discriminating eye the bottles of spices and coffee beans and the jars of preserves. The store seemed to be staffed by pretty girls in summer dresses, much occupied with their own conversations. No one approached him. Customers selected their own items and carried them in the store's baskets to the check-out desk. He would be one of an endless, moving line of people, anonymous, quickly dealt with, not even required to speak.

He took his time at the knife rack, trying them in his hands for weight and balance and for a comfortable feel of the handle in his grasping palm. In the end he chose a strong carving knife with a triangular, eight-inch blade, very sharp at the point and riveted into a plain wooden handle. The blade, razor sharp, was protected with a tough cardboard sheath. The sharp point seemed to him important. It was that first deep thrust into her flesh which he imagined might take all his strength and purpose. That done, the final twist and withdrawal would be little more than a reflex action. He had the right money ready, and after standing in a short queue, was through the check-out within seconds.

He had brought with him to Brighton the binoculars which he had bought as his retiring present. He already had at home a street map of London, but there were two other necessities, and both he bought at Brighton. In a chainstore chemist he purchased the small size of the finest protective gloves which they had on display, and, in another large store, a white transparent mackintosh. Here, but without bothering to try it on, he selected the largest size. If he were to be adequately protected against what might be a gushing fountain of blood, he needed a protective coat which would reach almost to the ground. He put the gloves in the pocket of the mackintosh, then rolled it round the binoculars and the sheathed knife. The bundle fitted easily into the bottom of the rucksack and its wide strap fitted comfortably on his shoulder.

He couldn't be sure why, in the end, he decided after all to visit the Goat and Compasses. Perhaps the reasons were a mixture of the simple and complex; he was, after all, in Brighton and was unlikely to visit here again in the near future, the pub was on his way to the station, he was moving into a new sphere of existence which would distance still further those early traumatic years, it would be interesting to see whether the place had changed. Nothing about it had. It still seemed to crouch under the shadow of the railway arches, a low, dark, claustrophobic pub, liked by its regulars but hardly inviting to the casual passer-by. The wooden-walled public bar was still furnished with the same long oak tables and benches, the walls were still hung with the same maple-framed old photographs of Brighton pier, and groups of sou'wester-clad fishermen before their boats. Opposite and seen through the windows the railway arches still gaped like black menacing mouths. In his childhood the arches had been a place of terror, the lair of the spitting monsters with no necks, whose spittle was death. Always he passed on the other side of the road, not running, in case his padding feet drew their attention, but walking in steady haste, his eyes averted. But then, when he was eleven, he made a pact with them. He used to secrete scraps of his meals, a crust from breakfast, the end of a sausage or a piece of potato from supper, and lay them, a propitiatory offering, at the entrance to the first arch. Returning at night, he would look to see if the offering had been accepted. With part of his mind he knew that the seagulls scavenged there, but when he found that the scraps had gone he went home comforted. But the trains never frightened him. He would lie at night mentally timing their visitation, hands clutching the blanket edge, his eyes fixed on the window, waiting for the preparatory whistle, the approaching rumble, which, almost as soon as he heard it, exploded into a climax of clashing metal and flashing lights while his bed shook under the momentary dazzle of the patterned ceiling.

Sitting there, alone, in the dim corner of the saloon bar with his hands clasped round his glass of lager, he recalled the day when he had first learned that he was ugly. He had been ten years and three months old. His Auntie Gladys and Uncle George were setting out the public bar for the first evening customers. His mother was out with Uncle Ted, the latest of the so-called uncles who came and went in his life, and he was playing alone in the dark little passage between the bar and the sitting-room, sprawled on the floor and taxiing his model of a biplane carefully on to one of the grey squares of the chequered lino. The door to the bar was swinging open and he could hear footsteps, the clink of bottles, chairs being dragged across the floor, and then his uncle's voice:

'Where's Norm? Marge said he wasn't to go out.'

'In his room, I suppose. That kid gives me the willies, George. He's right ugly. He's a proper little Crippen.'

'Oh come off it! He's not that bad, poor little sod. His dad was no oil painting. The kid's no trouble.'

'I grant you that. More healthy if he was. I like a boy with a bit of spirit to him. He creeps around the place like some sodding animal. You got the key to this till, George?'

The voices sank to a murmur. He slid across the floor soundlessly and stole out of the door and up the twisting stairs to his bedroom. There was a rickety oak chest of drawers in front of the window and on top of it an old-fashioned swivel looking-glass, the mirror spotted with age. He hardly ever used it and had to drag the bedside chair across to the chest and stand on it before he saw the thin grubby fingers pressed white against the oak, the toy biplane between them, his face rising to confront him, framed in split mahogany. He gazed at himself stolidly, the protuberant eyes behind the cheap crooked spectacles with their steel rims, the straight fringe of dry brown hair, too thin to obscure the rash of spots across his forehead, the unhealthy pallor of his skin. Ugliness. So this was why his mother didn't love him. The realization didn't surprise him. He didn't love himself. The knowledge that he was ugly and therefore beyond the possibilities of love was only the confirmation of something always known but never, until now, acknowledged, taken in with his milk when she thrust the bottle teat between his gums, mirrored in the anxious disappointed face which bent over his, perpetually present in adults' eyes, heard in the whining nag of her voice. It was too inescapably a part of him to be resented or grieved over. It would have been better for him to have been born with one leg or one eye. People might have been impressed by how well he managed, might have been sorry for him. But this deformity of the spirit was beyond pity as it was beyond healing.

When his mother came home, he followed her up to her room.

'Mummy, who was Crippen?'

'Crippen? What a question. Why d'you want to know?'

'I heard someone talking about him at school.'

'Pity they couldn't find something better to talk about then. He was a murderer. He killed his wife and cut her up and buried her in the cellar. That was a long time ago. In your granddad's time. Hilldrop Crescent. That's where it happened!' Her voice brightened at the wonder of memory's capricious cleverness, then resumed its normal hectoring tone. 'Crippen indeed!'

'What happened to him?'

'He was hanged, of course, what do you think happened to him? Give over talking about him, will you.'

So he was wicked as well as ugly, and in some mysterious way the ugliness and the wickedness belonged together. When he thought about his boyhood he marvelled at the child's stoical acceptance of this yoked burden of physical and moral repulsion, hardly made more bearable by the knowledge of its arbitrariness, or his powerlessness to shift the load from his shoulders.

Two things saved him, delinquency and chess. The first had begun in a small way. He had wandered unobserved into the saloon bar early one Saturday morning before opening time. He liked the bar when it was silent and empty, the round tables with their ornate cast-iron legs and stained tops; the wall clock with its swinging pendulum and flower-painted face measuring the silence with ticks which were too soft to be heard except out of opening hours; the smeared plastic cloth covering the tray holding two of yesterday's sausage rolls, even the smell of beer which permeated the whole house, but which in this smoky brown-clad cabin was strong and potent as a gas; the mysterious dimness behind the counter with its rows of darkly gleaming bottles awaiting the magic moment when the bar lights would be switched on and the liquids would take fire. Venturing behind the bar into this heartland of the forbidden territory, he saw that the till drawer was unlocked and slightly open. Gently he pulled it towards him. And there it was, money; not money in the possession of grown-ups, a symbol of adult power, not a few crumpled notes being stuffed, almost surreptitiously, into his mother's purse in a supermarket, not coins carefully doled out weekly to him to pay for school dinners or his fares. Here was money under his hands, two bundles of notes held together in rubber bands, silver coins, unnaturally bright, looking as heavy as doubloons, coffee-coloured pennies. Afterwards he couldn't recall taking the one-pound note. All he could remember was being back in his own room, terrified, his heart thudding, his back pressed against the door, turning the note over in his hands.

It was never missed, or if it was, he was not suspected. He spent it that morning on a model of a Lotus racing car, and on Monday, brought it out ostentatiously between lessons, and ran it over his desk top. The boy in the next desk looked at it trying to conceal his envy.

'That's the new Lotus, isn't it? Where d'you get it?'

'Bought it.'

'Let's have a look.'

He passed it across, feeling a momentary pang at the loss of its smooth brightness. He said:

'You can keep it if you like.'

'You mean you don't want it?'

He shrugged his shoulders.

'I mean you can have it.'

Thirty pairs of eyes slewed round to witness this marvel. The form bully said:

'Got any more at home?'

'I may have. Why, d'you want one?'

'I don't mind.'

But he did mind. Looking into the face he feared, into the greedy little eyes, Norman rejoiced in the knowledge of just how much he minded.

'I'll bring you one next week. Monday maybe.'

And that was the end of the persecution and the beginning of a year during which he lived at a pitch of inner excitement, of exhilaration and terror, which he had never experienced since. He didn't again steal from the pub takings. Twice more he stole into the saloon bar in hope, but on neither occasion was the till drawer unlocked. Part of him was relieved to be spared the temptation. To risk a second theft would have been too dangerous. But with the beginning of summer and the influx of visitors came other and safer opportunities. In his solitary wanderings after school along the promenade or on the beach his restlessly blinking eyes, so deceptively mild behind steel-rimmed spectacles, grew adept at spotting his chances; a purse casually laid on top of a beach bag, a wallet stuck into a blazer pocket, loose change from paying the deck-chair attendant dropped into the pocket of a coat slung across the back of the canvas. He grew skilful at picking pockets, the tiny marsupial hands insinuating their way under the jacket, into the back trouser pocket. Afterwards, his tactic was always the same. He would wait to examine the spoils until he could be sure that he was unobserved. Usually he would seek the rank-smelling metallic saltiness of the gloom under the great iron girders of the pier, take out the money, then scuffle the purse or wallet under the sand. Apart from coins, he took away only pound notes. To proffer anything larger at a local shop would be to invite suspicion. But, perhaps because he worked alone, was so unremarkable, looked so neat and respectable, there never was suspicion. Only once, during the whole of the year, was he in danger of discovery. He had bought a model of a breakdown van and had been unable to resist playing with it in the hall before school. His mother's eye had been caught by the unexpected brightness.

'That's new isn't it? Where d'you get it?'

'A man gave it to me.'

'What man?' Her voice was sharp, worried.

'Just a man coming out of the bar. A customer.'

'What did you do for it?'

'Nothing. I didn't do anything.'

'Well, what did he ask you to do?'

'Nothing, Mum. He just gave it to me, honest. I didn't do anything.'

'Well don't, that's all! And don't take toys from strangers.'

But in the following autumn, the beginning of the second year at senior school, came Mr Micklewright, a new and enthusiastic young member of staff, with his passion for chess. The school chess club was formed and Norman joined. The game fascinated him. He played every day, needing no opponent since there were published games to work out, strategies which could be developed in secret, books from the public and school library to teach him the subtleties of the various openings. Encouraged by Mr Micklewright's enthusiasm and praise he rapidly became the best player in the school. Then there were the local school competitions, the Southern Championships, and eventually even a photograph in the Brighton Evening Argus, a photograph cut out by his aunt and passed from hand to hand round the saloon bar. That established his fame. From then on he lived the rest of his school life without fear. He stopped stealing because it was no longer necessary for him to steal. Even the spitting monsters deserted the railway arches, leaving nothing but their debris of beer cans, screwed-up cigarette cartons and a brown, mildewed pillow leaking damp feathers against the furthest wall.

On his walk back to the station and his homeward train, he wondered what would have happened to him if he had gone on with the stealing. He couldn't have hoped to have evaded detection for ever. And then what? He would have been officially labelled delinquent; processed through the juvenile justice system; become the unprepossessing object of the machinery of bureaucratic caring. There would have been no respectable career in local government, no meeting with Mavis, no Julie. So much in his life seemed to have depended on that moment when Mr Micklewright set out before his fascinated gaze those mythical warriors whose lives, like his, were governed by such unalterable and arbitrary rules.

When at last he reached home he went to his bedroom and tried on his equipment for murder. He looked at himself in the long wardrobe glass. With the unsheathed knife in his hand, the raincoat hanging in glistening folds from his thin shoulders, he looked like a surgeon gowned for some desperate operation or, perhaps, like the member of a more ancient and sinister priesthood garbed for a ritual slaughter. And yet the image was not wholly terrifying. There was something wrong about it, something almost pathetic. The clothes were right, the naked knife showed the keen edge of fear; but the eyes which met his with their look of mild, almost painful resolution, were the eyes, not of an executioner, but of the victim.

SIXTEEN

On 4th August a probation officer came by appointment to look at the flat. Philippa prepared for the visit with excessive care, cleaning and rearranging the sparse furniture and buying a geranium in a pot to sit on the kitchen window. There was still a lot to do to the flat before it was ready to receive her mother, and only another ten days in which to do it, but she was pleased with her efforts so far. She couldn't remember when she had physically worked harder than during the last week, or with more satisfaction. She had concentrated on her mother's room and it was now nearly ready. The worst job had been taking up the carpet and getting rid of it, but George, hearing her coughing with the dust and struggling on the stairs with the discarded roll, had helped her carry it down and had bribed or persuaded the dustmen to take it away. Then she had spent two days scrubbing and staining the floor. She had brought nothing with her from Caldecote Terrace except one suitcase of clothes and the Henry Walton oil. She had hung it above the fireplace in her mother's room where, although it was not in period, she thought it looked particularly good above the newly gleaming fire hood and the plain but elegant overmantel.

She was glad that she still had some money in reserve. She was surprised how expensive cleaning materials were; how many small items were essential to domestic comfort and how costly they were to buy. The previous owner had left in a box under the sink his set of tools, and after trial and error and much consulting of a book on elementary carpentry borrowed from the Marylebone Road branch of the Westminster library, she managed to make a reasonable job of putting up extra shelves in the kitchen and a coat rack in the hall. She found in the market a cheap batch of old

Victorian tiles and fixed them behind the sink. Some of the jobs she particularly enjoyed; painting the woodwork white, with the sun from the open window warming her arms, searching in the local junk shops and in Church Street market for the extra pieces of furniture they needed. One particularly successful buy was two small cane chairs. They were in perfect condition but painted a particularly repulsive green. After a coat of paint and new patchwork cushions they added a touch of gaiety to the two rooms. George, if he saw her struggling with items of furniture, would temporarily leave his shop and give her a hand. She liked him. They seldom spoke, except when she bought from him the fruit which she ate each day for lunch, but she was aware that there flowed from him a general good will. Once he asked when Mrs Palfrey was expected to arrive. She told him on August the fifteenth, but didn't correct the name.

At night she lay on the narrow bed in the back room in an almost sensuous languor of exhaustion, with the window wide open, listening to the rumble and murmur of London, watching the stain of its night life on the scudding clouds, letting herself be gently shaken into sleep by the shudder of the Underground trains running between Marylebone and Edgware Road.

The probation officer was ten minutes late. When the downstairs bell at last rang Philippa opened the door to a tall, dark-haired woman who looked little older than herself. She was lugging a bulging plastic bag from the Edgware Road supermarket and seemed harassed. She said:

'Philippa Palfrey? I'm Joyce Bungeld. Sorry I'm late. The gasket went. I only got back from holiday this morning and it's been one hell of a day. All the eight O'Briens in court together. They're apparently terrified that I may be made redundant so they go out on a family shop-lifting bash every time I'm away just to prove to the authorities that I'm indispensable. Very pleased with themselves they were, grinning in the box like a row of monkeys, but I could have done without it. You weren't thinking of making tea, were you? I've got a throat like a gravel pit.'

Philippa made the tea, taking down her two new pottery mugs. Her first visitor. She told herself that she mustn't let resentment at the inspection prejudice her enterprise, and was resolved to counter officialdom with at least a show of docility. The probation officer rummaged in her bag and produced a packet of chocolate wholemeal biscuits. She tore open the package and offered it to Philippa. They munched companionably, sipping hot tea, both perched on the kitchen table.

'Your mother has her own room, has she? I see, in here. I like your picture.'

What was she afraid of, thought Philippa, that she and her mother were about to embark on a sophisticated variety of incest? And how could having separate rooms prevent that? She said:

'Don't you want to look at the bathroom? It's on the half landing.'

'No thanks. I'm not a sanitary inspector, thank God. You're here; the flat's here; your mother has someone and some place to come to. That's all I'm interested in. I'll write to the prison CWO tomorrow. You should hear in a day or two. I think they're trying to keep to the original release date, the fifteenth of August.'

'Will it be all right?' Philippa tried to keep the note of anxiety out of her voice.

'I should think so; why not? But it's finally up to the Home Office. Will you be here much? I mean, I suppose you've got a job?'

'Not yet. I thought we'd get one together; hotel work, waitressing, something like that.' She added, with an echo that was only half ironic: 'We're not afraid of hard work.'

'Then you're the only two people in London who aren't. Sorry. I'm feeling a little sour this afternoon. This would be a lovely job if it weren't for the clients. You go up to Cambridge in October, don't you? What had you in mind then?'

'For my mother? Nothing. I imagine she'll look for a cheaper flat if she can't afford to stay on here, or she could take a living-in job, if she can find one. And there's always one of your post-release hostels.'

She thought that the probation officer looked at her a little strangely. Then she said:

'Then she's probably only postponing most of her problems. Still, the first two months are the most difficult for a lifer. That's when they need support. And she did ask to come here. Thanks for the tea.'

The visit had lasted for less than twenty minutes, but Philippa thought that Miss Bungeld had seen all she wanted to see, had asked all the questions which it was necessary to ask. Shutting the street door after her and climbing the stairs she could imagine her report.

'The prisoner's daughter is of full age. She is an intelligent and sensible girl and the accommodation for which three months' rent has been paid in advance appears adequate. The licensee will have her own room and the flat, although small and unpretentious, was clean and tidy when I called. Miss Palfrey intends to find a job working with her mother. I recommend that the arrangements be approved.'

BOOK TWO

An Order of Release

ONE

On Tuesday 15th August, Scase was at York Station beginning his watch by half-past eight in the morning. He had travelled to York the previous evening and had taken a room in a dull commercial hotel close to the station. He could have been lodged in any provincial city. It never occurred to him to visit the Minster or to stroll through the cobbled streets within the city walls. Nothing the city promised could seduce his mind for an instant from the task in hand. He travelled light, carrying only his rucksack, adding nothing but his pyjamas and toilet bag to the sheathed knife, the rolled plastic mackintosh, the binoculars and the thin gloves. He was never now parted from the knife and the other impedimenta of murder. It was not that he expected to be able to kill her during the journey to London, a crowded train was hardly likely to afford opportunity, but it had become necessary to him to carry the knife. It was no longer an object of fascination or horror, but a familiar and potent extension of himself, the part which, when he closed his hand round it, completed him and made him whole. Now, even at night, he felt bereft without the drag of the rucksack on his shoulder, without being able to slip his hand under the flap and run his fingers along the cardboard sheath.

It was a convenient station in which to keep watch. From the outside hall an arched passage led through to the small concourse. To the right was the women's waiting-room. He could glimpse through the door a heavy mahogany table with carved legs, a lumpy couch and a row of carved chairs against the wall. Above the unlit gas fire was a nondescript modern print; it looked like a row of fishing nets strung out to dry. The waiting-room was empty except for one very old woman huddled in sleep among an assortment of bulging packages. There was only one entrance to the station concourse and the indicator showed him that the London trains went from platform 8. Beyond it the cavernous arched roof rose from the pale grey pillars with their ornate capitals. There lay over the station the freshness of the early morning overlaid with the smell of coffee. It waited in what seemed an eerie and portentous calm for the flood of commuter traffic and the chattering throng of the day's first tourists. Scase knew that, waiting alone so early, he would be conspicuous, but he told himself that it didn't matter. No place was more impersonal and anonymous than a railway station, no one would challenge him, and if they did he would say that he was waiting for a friend from London.

The bookstall was open and he bought a *Daily Telegraph*. A paper would be a quick way of hiding his face when she arrived. Then he settled himself on a bench to wait. He never doubted that Eli Watkin had kept faith with him, that this morning was the day of release. But he began to agitate himself with fears that he might not recognize her, that nearly ten years in prison might have changed her fundamentally or so subtly that she would slip past unnoticed. He took from his wallet the one picture that he had of her, cut from the local paper at the time of the trial. She and her husband had been snapped by a commercial photographer on what looked like a promenade at Southend. It was a photograph of two young people laughing, holding hands in the sun. He wondered how the reporter had managed to get hold of it. It told him nothing, and when he held it close to his eyes the image disintegrated into an anonymous pattern of microdots. It was impossible to connect this face with the woman whom he had last seen in the dock at the Old Bailey.

He had sat alone through every day of the three-week trial of his child's murderess, and by the last day nothing had any longer seemed real to him. It was like living in a dream world confined within the clean claustrophobic court-room in which the ordinary conventions of life had been replaced by a different logic, an alien set of values. In that surrealist limbo no one except the professionals had any reality. All present were actors, but only those gowned or bewigged moved and spoke with assurance or knew their parts. The two accused sat side by side in the dock, yet distanced, not looking at each other, hardly moving their eyes. Perhaps if each had stretched out an arm their fingers might have touched, but their arms did not move. Touching was not in the script. The searing hatred which had infected him like a fever during the first days after Julie's death, which had driven him out into the suburban streets, walking endlessly, pointlessly, unseeing, desperately striding on to prevent himself from beating his head against those neat suburban walls and howling for vengeance like a dog; all that passed when he looked at their dead faces, since how could you hate someone who wasn't there, who was merely a bit-player, selected to sit in the dock so that the play could go on? They were the most important characters, yet they had the least to do, were the least regarded. They had a look of ordinariness which, in some dreadful way, wasn't ordinary at all; they were shells of flesh from which not only the spirit was missing. If they were pricked, they wouldn't bleed. The members of the jury seemed afraid to meet their eyes. The judge ignored them. He felt that the drama, so muted, so desultory, could have gone on even without their presence.

The court was very full, yet the air had no taste to it, no smell. Time stretched out to accommodate the leisurely charade. Counsel for the prosecution spoke with calm deliberation, accommodating his speed to the movement of the judge's pen. From time to time there was a hiatus when no one spoke, when the bewigged lawyers would suddenly perk up and watch the judge, and the judge would appear sunk in a private reverie. And then the moment would pass. The judge's pen would move again. Counsel would begin again his slow peroration. The court, almost imperceptibly, would relax.

There was one woman member of the jury from whom he had found it difficult to avert his eyes. Afterwards, whenever he thought about the trial, it was she who dominated his mind. The images of the accused and the judge faded, hers became clearer with the years. She was a stockily built grey-haired woman, wearing upswept diamanté-trimmed spectacles, dressed in a plaid cloak of red, green and yellow, the rolls of tightly curled hair topped with a matching cap. The brim was set straight across her intimidating brow, the crown was bulbous, as if stuffed with paper, the whole topped with a pom-pom in red wool. Like the other jurors, she sat very still throughout the trial, grim-faced under the ridiculous hat, only turning her head like an automaton to look at whoever was speaking, betraying no emotion.

Both the accused had been represented by the same counsel who had attempted in a voice of quiet reasonableness to persuade the jury that rape had been sexual assault, and murder manslaughter. The verdicts, when they came, conveyed no sense of climax or release. The judge pronounced the two sentences of life imprisonment with no more than the customary comment that this was a mandatory sentence provided by law. He rose without fuss and the court rose with him. The spectators shuffled out of the public gallery, casting last looks behind them as if reluctant to believe that the entertainment was over. The lawyers stuffed their papers and books into briefcases and conferred. The clerks bustled about the court, minds already occupied with the next case. It had been as undramatic and ordinary as the ending of a parish council meeting. Once there would have been a black cap, not a proper cap, but a small square of black cloth which the clerk would have placed grotesquely on top of the judge's wig. Once there would have been a gowned chaplain and the sonorous 'Amen' after the sentence of death. He had felt the need of some such bizarre and histrionic end to this formal celebration of reason and retribution. Something memorable should have been said or done, more worthy of the corporate ritual than the foreman's carefully expressionless voice pronouncing the word 'guilty' in response to the clerk's two questions, the judge's dispassionate judicial tone. For one wild second he had been tempted to leap to his feet and to cry out that it wasn't over, that it couldn't be over. It had seemed to him that the trial had been less a judicial process than a comforting formality through which all participants except himself had been purged or justified. It was over for them. It was over for the jury and the judge. It was over for Julie. But for him and for Mavis it had just begun.

The station clock jerked away the minutes and the hours. By eleven o'clock he was thirsty and would have liked to buy himself a coffee and a bun at the buffet, but he was afraid to leave his seat, to take his eyes off the entrance. But when at last he saw her, just after eleven-forty, he wondered how he could ever have doubted that he would know her again. He recognized her at once, and with such a physical shock that he instinctively turned away, terrified that she would feel across the concourse the surging power of his presence. It was impossible to believe that she could be here within yards of him, yet not be struck by the shock waves from that moment of recognition. Surely not even love could cry out so loudly for a response. He saw that she was carrying a small case, but apart from that he was aware of nothing about her, only of her face. The years dropped away and he was once again in that wood-cladded court gazing fixedly at the dock, but seeing her now with a dreadful knowledge which then he hadn't had; that he could never escape her as she could never escape him, that both of them were victims. He moved behind a rack of paperbacks in front of the station bookstall, bending like a man in a spasm of pain, hugging the rucksack to his body as if his wrapping arms could stifle the potent signals of the knife. Then he became aware that a man carrying an official briefcase was glancing at him with concern. He straightened up and made himself look again at the murderess. It was then that he noticed the girl. In that moment of recognition there was nothing about Mary Ducton that was hidden from him. The girl was a blood relation. He knew with absolute certainty, even without noting the imprint of the murderess on this younger, more glowing face, without consciously deducing that the girl was too young to be her sister and unlikely to be her niece, that this was Mary Ducton's daughter.

The girl proffered one ticket at the barrier together with a slip of paper, perhaps some kind of travelling warrant. The murderess stood back, her eyes fixed ahead like an obedient child under escort. He followed them through the gate and on to platform 8. There was a group of about twenty people waiting for the 11.40 train, and the murderess and her daughter walked some fifty yards further down the platform and stood alone, not speaking. He dared not make himself conspicuous by detaching himself from the main group. Now, with time to spare and nothing to do, they might well notice him. He opened his newspaper and with his back half-turned towards them, listened for the first vibrations of the approaching train. The first part of his plan was simple. He would move unhurriedly and unselfconsciously towards them as the engine drew in, and get into the same compartment. It was important to travel together if he were not to risk losing them at King's Cross. He was glad that the modern inter-city trains had long open carriages. The old-fashioned corridor trains with their single compartments would have been a difficulty. Apart from the fear that the murderess might recall his face even after all these years, the prospect of having to sit opposite them, almost knee to knee, to feel their eyes straying to his face, momentarily intrigued, perhaps, by his ugliness, his insignificance, was intolerable.

The train drew in on time. Prudently he stood back to let a family with young children enter before him, but the two corn-coloured heads were plainly in sight. They had moved down the compartment and had seated themselves side by side facing the engine. He slipped into a vacant window seat just inside the door, kept his rucksack on the table in front of him, and took refuge again behind his paper. Once he was seated their faces were out of sight, but, over his paper, he kept a watchful eye on the far door in case they should, after all, decide on a different carriage. But the door was blocked with incoming passengers and they didn't move.

Almost at once he realized that it had been a mistake to take a window seat. Just before the guard blew his whistle, a family of three, a fat, perspiring couple and their moonfaced teenage son, pushed through the door and settled themselves with grunts of satisfaction into the three empty seats. He shifted himself imperceptibly, disagreeably aware of the warm bulk of the woman urging his thighs nearer to the window. As soon as the train got up speed she opened a bulging plastic bag, took out a Thermos flask and three disposable cups and a plastic sandwich box, and began distributing cheese and pickle sandwiches to her husband and son. A powerful reek of vinegar and cheese hung over the table. He had no room to spread his paper, but he folded it small and pretended an interest in the list of births and deaths on the last page. He hoped he wouldn't need to visit the lavatory. The prospect of asking this hulk of a woman to shift herself intimidated him. But worse was the worry that he might be trapped at the end of the journey, that the murderess and her daughter might slip out of their seats and be gone before he could free himself.

He was hardly aware of the passing of time. For the first hour he sat stiffly, half fearing that the woman would hear the thudding of his heart, would sense the excitement that kept him rigid in his seat. For most of the time he stared out of the window at the bleak landscape of the Midlands, the rain-soaked fields and dripping trees, the alien towns with their blackened back-to-back houses and the villages, like rejected outposts of a deserted civilization, while beside the track the glistening wires rose and fell. After about an hour the rain stopped and the sun came out, hot and bright, drawing from the sodden fields faint puffs of vapour like a crop of thin cotton wool. Once, by a trick of light, the carriage was reflected in the windows, and he saw a row of ghostly travellers borne through the air, sitting immobile as dummies, their faces cavernous and grey as the faces of the dead. Only once was his attention keenly caught. The train stopped momentarily outside Doncaster and in the brief unnatural calm he saw, in the grass verge, tall strong stalks of cow parsley, bearing their delicate white blossoms like a foam. The flowers reminded him of the Methodist Sunday school to which he had been sent every Sunday afternoon, he supposed to get him out of his mother's way. Every August they had held a Sunday school anniversary service, and the children, by tradition, had decorated the church with wild flowers. It was an ugly Victorian building, its ponderous dark stone eclipsing the fragile beauty of the flowers. He saw again an earthenware jar of buttercups wilting against the pew end, and the cow parsley shedding its white dust over his new Sunday-best shoes. He had sat very still, huddled in his seat lest God should notice him, a Crippen sitting among the blessed, distancing himself from what he had no right to share, terrified he might be seeming to claim it. Sunday school had left him with nothing except that, for the rest of his life, at moments of stress and crisis, biblical texts, not always apposite, would slip unbidden into his mind. Remembering those long-drawn-out, anxiety-filled afternoons, it had never seemed to him a fair exchange.

Once during the journey he turned his eyes from the window and saw the girl coming down the compartment. She passed him without glancing at his table and tugged open the door. For the first time he took note of her and wondered how her existence might affect his plans. He wished her no particular harm. She was, he judged, some two to three years younger than Julie would have been. Julie was dead, she was alive. No other comparison between them was important in the face of that irrevocable alienation. But he doubted whether his gentle, timid daughter would have held herself with such assurance, would have surveyed the world with eyes so calmly confident in their own judgement. He watched her receding back, the tight corduroy trousers taut over her thighs, the casually worn jacket, the leather and canvas travelling bag slung over her shoulder, the thick pigtail of hair. The sheen of the corduroy curving over her inner thighs, the front zip which emphasized the flatness of the stomach and pointed to the gently swelling mound beneath it, had evoked in him as she passed a small prick of sexuality, so long dormant that the gentle disturbance released for a brief moment all the forgotten uncertainties and half-shameful excitements of adolescence.

The girl puzzled him. Try as he would he couldn't remember ever having heard of her at the time of the trial. But then, neither he nor Mavis had been interested in the members of that family except for the rapist and the murderess. They alone existed and the fact of their existence was an abomination which would one day be purged. He wondered what had been happening to the daughter in the intervening years. She looked well-nourished, prosperous. There was nothing of deprivation in that proud carriage, that assured walk. She had presumably kept in touch with her mother since they were here together; but they didn't look intimate. During the time he had observed them they had hardly spoken. Perhaps this journey was no more than a filial duty to be gratefully relinquished when the murderess was safely delivered at her final destination. Her unexplained and unexpected presence was a slight complication, but no more. But as she passed him on her return journey to her seat, balancing two covered plastic mugs and a pork pie, he noticed that there was a small identity tag attached by a narrow strap to the end of her travelling bag. It was just large enough to hold a visiting card, but the name was covered by a curling leather flap. Suddenly it occurred to him that if he could get close enough to her without attracting attention, perhaps in the crush when they were leaving the train, it might be possible gently to bend back the tag and get a sight of the name. The thought excited him. He spent the rest of the journey staring sightlessly out of the window imagining how it might be done.

It was two-fifteen before the train drew into King's Cross, one minute late. As soon as it slowed he stood up and reached for his raincoat and case. The fat woman grudgingly made way for him and he was one of the first out of his seat. He saw that the murderess and her daughter were making for the door closest to them at the other end of the compartment. He edged his way down the carriage, obstructed now by standing passengers reaching for their bags and struggling into their coats. By the time the two women had reached the doorway he was immediately behind them. There was the usual delay as passengers manoeuvred their luggage through the door and clambered down the platform, and the women patiently waited their turn. Neither of them looked round. It was far easier than he had hoped. He let his rucksack rest for a moment on the floor then bent down and fumbled with his shoe lace. As he rose his eyes were on a level with the dangling tag. It was the work of a second to lift the covering flap with his small cunning hands. The light was poor but it didn't matter. The name wasn't in small print on a visiting card but written by hand in a black elegant script. P. R. Palfrey.

He hoped that the next stage wouldn't be by taxi. It would be too risky to stand in the queue immediately behind them and, even if he did, he was unlikely to hear their directions. In the library books he remembered from his boyhood the hero leapt into the next cab shouting to the driver to follow the one in front. He couldn't see himself doing that, nor did it seem a practicable ruse in the tangle of traffic outside a major London terminus. But to his relief, the girl led the way down the steps to the Underground. This was what he had hoped. He followed about twenty feet behind them, feeling in his pocket for his loose change. There must be no delay at the booking office. With luck he might get close enough to hear their destination. At worse he would be able to watch the machine from which they got their tickets. But as long as he again travelled with them all would be well. He felt a surge of confidence and excitement. So far it had been easier than he had dared to hope.

But suddenly the entrance tunnel was clamorous with shouting and the clatter of rushing feet. Another train must have disgorged its passengers, and a crowd of youths had hurled themselves down the steps and were shouting and jostling their way past him, forcing him against the wall of the tunnel and momentarily obstructing his view. Desperately he pushed his way forward and saw again the two pale bobbing heads. They passed the entrance to the Northern and Bakerloo lines and, walking on, eventually turned right down the wide steps leading to the concourse of the Metropolitan and Circle lines. The crowd had swollen here and there was a long queue at the ticket office. The girl didn't join it, nor did she attempt to press through the jabbering crowd of travellers at the ticket machines. Instead hc saw with horror that she had bought two tickets in advance and that she and the murderess were calmly making their way through the barrier. And the ticket collector was meticulously looking at every ticket. There was no chance of forcing his way through and to try would only draw attention to himself. He almost fought his way to the first machine. His tenpenny piece seemed to stick in his fingers. His hand was trembling as he pushed it home. There was a clatter as the coin, rejected, fell into the waiting receptacle. He pushed it in again, and this time the machine delivered his ticket. But the air was already loud with the clatter of an approaching train, and as he pushed his way through the crowd at the barrier, the noise stopped. He dashed to the westward platform, the one they had taken, just in time to see the doors of the Circle line train close in his face. Apart from two turbaned Indians, and a tramp laid out asleep on a bench, the platform was empty. Even as he looked up, the train moved, the words 'Circle Line' disappeared from the indicator and the Hammersmith train was signalled.

TWO

Only when he reached Liverpool Street was he aware of hunger. He bought himself a coffee and roll before catching the train home. It was nearly four before he put his key in the latch. The silence of the house received him conspiratorially as if it had been watching for his return and was waiting to share his failure or success. Although it was still early, he felt very weary and his legs ached. But this positive tiredness was a new sensation, different in kind from the lassitude which had dragged his homeward footsteps at the end of each working day, and had made the half-mile trudge from the station into a small daily tribulation. He made himself a high tea of sausages and baked beans, followed by a jam tart from a packet of four in the refrigerator. He supposed that he was hungry, certainly he was rapacious for the food. The sausages split and burned under the grill and the gas flared under the saucepan of beans. He ate voraciously, yet he hardly tasted the meal, aware only of a physical need that demanded satisfaction. As he made a pot of tea in a small back kitchen, taking down the blue and white teapot with its patterned base of roses which he and Mavis had bought together on their honeymoon, he felt for the first time some affection for the house, and a tinge of regret that he must leave it. This struck him as odd. Neither he nor Mavis had ever been at home in it. They had bought it because it was the sort of house they were used to at a price they could afford, and because they needed to leave Seven Kings with all its memories and 19 Alma Road had been available. In the suburbs you could buy anonymity by moving three stations down the line, by changing your job. He remembered how they had first been shown over it, Mavis passing listlessly from room to room while the house agent, desperately trying to evoke some response, had extolled its advantages. At the end of the inspection she had said tonelessly: 'It'll do. We'll take it.' The man must have been amazed at so easy a sale. They had done little to it in the last eight years, some repainting, new paper in the seldom-used front sitting-room, the minimum structural repairs necessary to preserve their small investment in it. Mavis had worked conscientiously, though without interest, but it had always looked clean. Something about it repelled dust and wear as it repelled intimacy, happiness, love. How strange it was that only now was he beginning to feel that he belonged here, that he would leave something of himself behind its prim laurel hedge. The sense of the house's participation in his enterprise grew so strong that he found himself wondering whether he dared leave it, whether the strangers who would unpack their kettles and saucepans in this kitchen would pause in temporary unease and imbibe from the very air some secret knowledge that here murder had been planned. But he knew that he had to go. The quarry was in London, and in London would be run to earth. And he needed to be free, free even of this new sentience between him and the house, free of personal belongings, however meagre, free to begin his search, moving unrecognized and rootless amongst strangers.

And he knew now where he must look. When he had drunk his tea, he opened his map of London and the chart of the Underground and placed them side by side on the table. They had travelled westward on the Circle line. He counted up the stations. St James's Park was about half way, so that for any station beyond that it would have been more sensible to travel in the opposite direction. Victoria was out. They would have taken the Victoria line direct. Similarly, he could eliminate South Kensington and Gloucester Road since both were on the Piccadilly line and could be reached direct from King's Cross. That meant that they had almost certainly got out at one of the eight stations between King's Cross and High Street Kensington. It was possible, of course, that they had alighted at Baker Street or Paddington and changed lines or taken a British Rail train out of London. But the thought didn't worry him. He didn't believe for one moment they were in the country. It was in the vast anonymity of the capital that the hunted felt most secure. London, which asked no questions, kept its secrets, provided in its hundred urban villages the varied needs of ten million people. And the girl was no provincial. Only a Londoner would have strode with such confidence through the complexities of King's Cross Underground Station. And she had bought the tickets in advance. That meant, surely, that she had travelled up to York early that morning. No, they were in London all right.

On his larger map he traced the route of the Circle line. Bloomsbury, Marylebone, Bayswater, Kensington. The districts were unfamiliar to him, but he would get to know them. And the day hadn't been unsuccessful after all. He knew now that she had a daughter, and he knew the name of the daughter. She had changed it to Palfrey from Ducton by deed poll, adoption or marriage. But she hadn't, he remembered, been wearing a wedding ring. He had been thwarted by one small piece of ill-luck, the fact that she had troubled to buy the Underground tickets in advance. Unless they were in a hurry, and they hadn't walked as if they were in a hurry, that could only mean that she wanted to spare her mother thc possible trauma of being crushed among crowds while she waited at the ticket office. If so, it suggested a concern that he hadn't expected. And if the girl were concerned for the murderess, then they might stay together, at least for a time. That surely increased his chances of finding them. If all else failed, the daughter might yet lead him to the mother. He wrote the names of the eight stations in his diary in his careful copper-plate, then stared at them as if they were a conundrum and he could will the letters to move and shuffle and, at last, click into place and spell out the address he sought.

Tomorrow he would move into the next phase of the enterprise. He would make a direct effort to trace the murderess through her daughter. Even if they weren't still together, to know where the daughter lived would be a definite gain. He went into the hall and dragged out the L-R London telephone directory. There was no Palfrey, P. R., listed, but that wasn't particularly significant. If she had been adopted the number would be shown under her father's initials. The first step would be to telephone all the seven Palfreys listed in the London directory. It was an obvious ploy, more sensible than perpetually riding the Circle line or walking the squares of Bloomsbury or Kensington; but he would have to think of a plausible excuse, a reason for ringing those seven strangers which wouldn't sound suspicious. Suppose the girl herself came to the telephone, what was he to say? It was vital that the murderess shouldn't suspect that she was hunted. If he frightened her into flight, into changing her name, he might spend a lifetime in tracing her only to fail at last. He was twenty years older than she was. Death had robbed Mavis of revenge, it might even rob him.

And then, as he sat in the quietness of the kitchen, his hands cradling the cup of tea, the idea came to him. It fell into his mind like a minor act of creativity, as if it had always existed in its simplicity, its rightness, awaiting the moment until it could slip into his mind. The more he examined it, the more faultless it seemed. He was surprised that he hadn't thought of it earlier. He went to bed impatient for the morning.

THREE

Her mother walked into the room and stood still. She seemed afraid to speak, only her eyes moved. The room seemed to have shrunk since Philippa left it. The newly stained wooden boards, the faded rugs, the unmatched chairs, did they look too makeshift, too cheap a compromise? Had she glorified them in her own eyes?

'You like it?' She was irritated to hear the note of anxiety in her voice. She had done her best with the place. Presumably it was better than a shared room in a hostel. And it was only for two months.

'Very much.' Her mother smiled, a different smile from the one with which she had greeted Philippa that morning. This time it reached her eyes.

'It's lovely. I didn't expect that it would be as attractive as this. You were clever to find it. And you must have worked hard.'

Her voice shook, and Philippa saw that her eyes were too bright. And she looked very tired. The journey, the pressure of people must have been a strain. Terrified that the unshed tears would fall, she said quickly:

'I enjoyed myself. It was fun rummaging around the market. The greengrocer, George, helped me up with some of my finds. The picture is the only thing I've got from Caldecote Terrace, a Henry Walton. He was an eighteenth-century painter. Some of his work is too sentimental for my taste – almost Victorian – but I like that picture. I thought that it would look good in that light and against the wallpaper. But you don't have to keep it there.'

'I should like it to stay, unless you want it in your room. Where are you?'

'Here, next to the kitchen. I've got the quietest room and the better view. You've got the sun but more noise. We can change if you'd rather.'

They went into the back room. Her mother walked to the window and stared out over the patch of yard and the narrow strips of cluttered gardens. After a few minutes she turned and looked round the room.

'It doesn't seem fair for me to have the larger room. We could spin a coin.'

'But I've had the larger room for the last ten years. It's your turn now.'

She wanted to ask: 'Do you think you can be happy here?' But the question seemed a presumption with its implication that she – Philippa – had happiness within her gift. It was new to her, this carefulness with words, this sensitivity to their power to wound. It should have caused a constraint between them, but it didn't. She said:

'Come and see the kitchen. I've put the television there. We can carry our easy chairs in there if we want to watch.'

Hilda had said, resentfully:

'You'll have to hire a colour telly. She'll have got used to that in prison. Lifers get these extra privileges. She won't be satisfied with black and white.'

They went back together into the front room. Philippa said:

'I thought we might take about ten days' holiday before we start thinking of a job. We could look at London, or have some days in the country if you prefer.'

'I'd like both. Only there's one thing, I don't think I'll be much good going about on my own for a week or so. At least not in crowds.'

'You don't have to be on your own.'

'And could we buy some clothes first? I've only got what I'm wearing and one pair of pyjamas. I thought I could spend about fifty pounds of my two hundred. Then I could get rid of these things in the case. I don't want anything here which I had in prison.'

'That'll be fun. I like buying clothes. The sales are still on in Knightsbridge and we might get something good quite cheaply. We can get rid of what you've got in Mell Street market.'

They could get rid of the case there too, although Philippa doubted whether any of the stallkeepers would give more than a few pence for it. Better still, they could chuck it in the canal. It was a cheap fibre case, already scruffy at the corners. Her mother placed it on the floor, then, kneeling, opened it. She took out a pair of white cotton pyjamas and placed them on the bed. The only other objects in the case were a draw-string toilet bag and a manilla envelope. She handed it to Philippa, looking up into her face.

'This is the account I wrote in prison of what happened to Julie Scase. Don't read it now, wait a day or two. And I don't want to know when you've read it. While we're living together I know that you've a right to ask questions about the crime, about me, about your past. But I'd rather that you didn't. Not yet, anyway.'

Philippa took the envelope. Maurice had said:

'Lifers, murderers, have to justify themselves. I'm not talking about political murderers, terrorists, they don't have to waste mental energy fabricating excuses. They get their justification like their political philosophy, second-hand and ready made. I'm talking about the ordinary lifer, and most of them are ordinary. Murder is the one crime for which there can't be any reparation for the victim. We're all conditioned to regard it with particular abhorrence. So murderers, unless they're psychopaths, have to come to terms with what they've done. Some of them persist in claiming that they're innocent, wrongly convicted. Some probably believe it.'

She had said:

'Some may be innocent.'

'Of course. That's the irrefutable argument against capital punishment. A fair number take refuge in religious confession, officially recognized contrition if you like. There's a beautiful simplicity in claiming that you're assured of God's forgiveness, it puts your fellow humans at a moral disadvantage if they obstinately persist in unforgiveness. And of course there are plenty of eminent people happy to assist you in your emotional wallowings. I'd probably opt myself for conversion in the circumstances. Then there are the excuses based on mental instability, provocation, deprived background, drunkenness, the common stuff of any defending counsel's plea in mitigation. A few of the more robust spirits probably claim justifiable homicide, the victim got no more than he deserved. Your mother has survived ten years in prison on the one charge that the other women there can't ever forgive. That means she's tough. She's probably intelligent. Whatever story she decides to tell you will be plausible and, once she's met you, I've no doubt it will be tailored to what she decides are your particular psychological requirements.'

'Nothing she tells me can alter the fact that she's my mother.'

And he had said:

'So long as you remember that that is probably the least important fact about her.'

She put Maurice out of her mind. There was no hurry about questions. She could begin to learn who she was without an inquisition. After all, they were to have two months together. She said:

'I haven't any rights. We're here together because that's what we both want. It suits us both. You're not demanding to know what my life has been during the last ten years.'

She added, with deliberate lightness:

'There are no obligations except those which sharing a flat necessarily implies, cleaning the bath after use, doing one's share of washing-up.'

Her mother smiled.

'From that point of view I'll probably suit. Otherwise I think you could have chosen more wisely.'

But there was no question of choice. While her mother went to wash Philippa took the envelope into her bedroom and shut it in her bedside drawer. She had been asked to wait before reading it. She would wait, but not for long. She felt triumphant, almost exulted. She thought: 'You're here because you're my mother. Nothing in life or death can alter that. It's the only thing about myself I can be sure of. In your uterus I grew. It was your muscles that forced me into the world, your blood which first bathed me, and it was on your belly where I first took my rest.' Her mother liked the room, was glad to be with her. It was going to be a success. She wouldn't have to return to Maurice and confess failure. He would never be able to say 'I told you so'.

FOUR

The only post next morning was a letter from the house agent to say that the young couple had obtained their mortgage and that contracts were being drawn up. He read its turgid professional jargon without surprise or particular gratification. The house had to go. Apart from the fact that he needed more money than he had been able to save from a modest salary, he couldn't imagine himself returning to it after the murder. There was nothing in the house that he wanted, not even a photograph of Julie. Mavis had destroyed them all after her death. He would take with him enough clothes to fill one suitcase. The rest of his belongings and the furniture he would sell through one of those firms which advertised that they cleared houses. He supposed that they were called in after the deaths of the old and lonely to dispose of the detritus of unregarded lives and to save the executors trouble. It pleased him to think of moving thus unencumbered into his unknown future, so much alone that if he fell under a bus there would be no one in the world with any responsibility for him, no one who need assume the obligations of grief. He would lie, shrouded and docketed in the public mortuary while the police searched for a next of kin, someone to authorize the disposal of this embarrassingly redundant corpse. To move into this nothingness seemed to him a promise of an intoxicating and limitless freedom. As he boiled his breakfast egg and stirred powdered coffee into his cup of hot milk, it occurred to him that he had become more interesting to himself since he had started out on his enterprise. Before Mavis's death he had been like a man treadmilled on a moving staircase, walking but not advancing, while on each side of him bright images of a synthetic world, blown-up photographs, montages of life moved steadily in the opposite direction. As they passed he was programmed to perform certain actions. At daybreak he would get up and dress. At half-past seven he ate breakfast. At eight o'clock he set out to work. At eight-twelve he caught his train. At midday he ate his sandwiches at his desk. Home again in the evening, he would eat his supper in the kitchen with Mavis, then sit watching television while she knitted. The evenings had been dominated by the television programmes. For some of her favourites through those bleak years, 'Upstairs Downstairs', 'Dixon of Dock Green', 'The Forsyte Saga', she had even taken some trouble with her appearance. She no longer changed to please him or to go out with him, but she put on a different dress and even applied make-up for these bright ephemeral images. On those evenings they would have supper on a tray. It hadn't been an unhappy life. He hadn't felt any emotion as positive as unhappiness. But now, on the shoulders of the dead, he had hoisted himself into a different air, and although it stung his nostrils, at least it gave him the illusion of living.

Sitting in the train as it flashed through the incongruously-named stations of the eastern suburbs, his rucksack on his shoulder, he reflected that it was an odd and interesting quirk of his new character that he should need to make this particular journey at all. His plan stood an equal chance of success if he stayed at home and rang the Palfrey numbers from the anonymity of his front hall. The lie he was proposing to tell wouldn't be more believable because it would be supported by contrived verisimilitude, yet he knew that every detail would have to be right if he were to succeed. No one was going to challenge him, no one would check up on his story, or demand confirmation, yet he was compelled to act, as if by meticulous attention to every small part he could somehow confer the authority of truth on the whole.

From Liverpool Street he took the Central line to Tottenham Court Road and walked down Charing Cross Road. He had decided that Foyle's Bookshop would be the best for his purpose because it was the largest. The book he chose had to be valuable enough to be worth taking trouble about, but not so valuable that an honest finder would naturally take it to a police station. Non-fiction, he reasoned, would be more appropriate than fiction, and after some thought he selected from the shelves Pevsner's first volume on the buildings of London. The girl at the cash desk seemed hardly to look at him as she gave him his change.

Then he walked to Shaftesbury Avenue and took a number 14 bus to Piccadilly Circus. He gave the conductor a pound note for his fare since he knew he would need plenty of small change. At Piccadilly he shut himself up in one of the telephone booths. In the address pages of his pocket diary he wrote in pencil the initials and telephone numbers of all the subscribers listed under the name Palfrey, grateful that the girl had such an uncommon name. None of the Palfreys were shown as 'Miss' but that didn't surprise him. He had read somewhere that to advertise that you were a woman was to invite obscene telephone calls. When the eight numbers had been listed he printed in pencil the words 'Miss P. Palfrey' on the bookshop bag. No one would ever see it, yet he took care to form the letters in large uneven strokes, as different as possible from his own hand. Then, before raising the receiver, he rehearsed mentally the words he was to say:

'Excuse me for troubling you, but my name is Yelland. I've found a book left on a bench in St James's Park. It was bought at Foyle's and it's got the name "Miss P. Palfrey" written on the bag. I thought it was worth telephoning to try and trace the owner.'

The first call was answered by a gruff male voice which told him peremptorily that there was no Miss Palfrey at that address. 'Drop it in at a police station,' it commanded, and promptly rang off. He knew that his first attempt hadn't been altogether successful; even to his own ears his voice had sounded false and strained. Perhaps the listener had thought that he was a new breed of con man or was hoping for a reward. He put a cross against the name and dialled the second number.

He was almost relieved when there was no reply. He put a query against the number and dialled again.

The third call was answered by a woman, presumably a maid or an au pair, who spoke in a strong foreign accent and told him that 'Madam is shopping at 'arrods.' He explained that he wanted a Miss Palfrey, not Mrs Palfrey, only to be told again: 'Madam is not at 'ome. She is at 'arrods. Please to ring later.' He put a query against this number too, although he had little doubt that it wasn't the one he was seeking.

The next number rang for twenty seconds, and he had almost given up when the receiver was at last lifted, and he heard a harassed female voice raised to make itself heard against the shrieking of a young child. The sound was as piercingly sustained as a train's whistle. Obviously she was holding the child in her arms. He sensed her impatience with his story, and when he was half way through she broke in to say briefly that her daughter was only six and wasn't yet buying books, let alone leaving them on park benches. 'Nice of you to bother, though,' she added, and hung up.

He dialled the next number. The call was frustrating. It was answered by yet another female voice, but this had the high monotonous pitch and the quaver of extreme old age. It took a long time before she comprehended his message, then he had to hang on, putting in extra coins, while she held long conversations with her sister who was called Edith and who was presumably deaf since the conversation was carried on in shouts. Edith disclaimed any knowledge of the book, but her sister was reluctant to ring off, feeling, apparently, that she now had some personal responsibility in the matter.

His stock of small change was getting low. The next name was listed as Palfrey, M. S. The address was 68 Caldecote Terrace, S.W.1. Once again a woman answered. The voice sounded tentative, apprehensive even. She repeated the number carefully as if it were unfamiliar. He said his piece and almost at once he knew that this was it. He ended:

'Perhaps I could have a word with Miss Palfrey?'

'She isn't here. I mean, my daughter isn't at home at present.'

This time there could be no doubt of it. The voice held the breathy rising cadence of fear. He felt a surge of confidence, almost of exhilaration. He said:

'If you could give me her address, I could write or telephone.'

'Oh, I couldn't do that! And they're not on the phone. But I'll tell her about the book if I see her. Only I don't think I shall be seeing her. What did you say it was called?'

He repeated the title.

'It sounds like Philippa. I mean, she does like books about buildings. Perhaps you could post it here and I'll send it on. Only there's the postage. I know she would send the money to you if you enclosed your address. But then it may not belong to her.'

There was a silence. After a few seconds he said:

'Perhaps I'd better return it to Foyle's. They may know who it belongs to. And perhaps your daughter will think to inquire there first.'

'Oh yes, yes! That would be best. If Philippa telephones or calls in I'll tell her what you've done. Thank you for taking so much trouble. I think she's probably showing her – her friend – round London. She may need the book. I'll send her a postcard and tell her about your call.'

Relief made her sound suddenly effusive. He replaced the receiver and stood for a moment with his hand pressed down on it. The feel of the instrument, warm and sticky, conveyed an almost physical certainty. He knew now where her daughter lived. He knew that she was adopted. He knew that they were still together since the woman had used the plural tense. He knew what the girl's name was. Philippa Palfrey. Philippa R. Palfrey. Somehow the fact of knowing the name seemed more significant than anything he had learned so far.

FIVE

His map showed him that Caldecote Terrace lay on the fringes of Pimlico, south-west of Victoria and Eccleston Bridge, and he walked there from Victoria Underground down a side road flanking the main station. In distance it wasn't far from his old office, but it was the other side of the river and could have been a different city. It was a cul-de-sac of converted but unspoilt late eighteenth-century terraced houses which lay off the wider and busier Caldecote Road. He walked into it resolutely but uneasily aware that this was not a street in which he could safely loiter, that the tall, immaculately curtained windows might conceal watching eyes. He felt like an interloper entering a private precinct of orderliness, culture and comfortable prosperity. He had never lived in such a street and knew no one who did; yet he indulged his preconceptions on how such people lived. They would affect to despise the smartness of Belgravia; would enthuse about the advantages of a socially mixed society, even if the mixing didn't actually extend to sending their children to local schools; would patronize as a duty the small shopkeepers in Caldecote Road, particularly the dairy and the delicatessen; and would haul off their friends to drink at the weekend in the saloon bar of the local pub where they would be heartily affable to the barman and resolutely matey to the other customers.

He made himself walk down one side of the street and then up the other. The sense of being a trespasser was so strong that he felt he walked in an aura of guilt. But no one challenged him, no front door opened, the curtains didn't move. The street struck him as being peculiarly different from others; then he realized that it was because no cars were parked at the kerb and there were no residents' parking signs. So these desirable homes must have garages at the rear where once the mews had stabled horses. Momentarily the thought depressed him. It would be impossible to watch two exits to number 68, and if Mrs Palfrey customarily drove rather than walked or took public transport, he didn't see how he would be able to tail her. He hadn't thought of a car. But optimism reasserted itself. Single-mindedness, he had discovered, brought with it stamina and self assurance; it also brought luck. He was here. It was right that he should be here. He knew where the girl lived and where her family lived. Sooner or later she or they would lead him to Mary Ducton.

As he gained confidence in his right to be walking down the terrace he observed the houses more closely. The street had an impressive uniformity; the houses were identical except for variations in the patterns of the fanlights and in the wrought-iron tracery of the first-floor balconies. The front railings guarding the basements were spiked and ornamented at the ends with pineapples. The doors, flanked with columns, were thoroughly intimidating, the brass letter-boxes and knockers gleamed. Many of the houses were festive with window boxes; geraniums flared in discordant pinks and reds and trails of variegated ivy curled against the stone façades.

He reached the end of the terrace and crossed the road to the even-number houses. Number 68 was at the top end of the street. It was one of the few houses without window boxes or tubs before the door, uncompromising in its elegance. The door was painted black. The basement kitchen was brightly lit. He walked slowly past, glancing down, and saw that it was occupied. A woman was sitting at the table eating her lunch. There was a tray in front of her with a plate of scrambled eggs, and she was glancing as she ate at the flickering image of a black and white television set. So the Palfreys had a maid. He wasn't surprised to see her. He would have expected that girl in the train to have come from a home where they kept a maid, to have lived in just such a house as this, that golden girl who had walked past him down the swaying carriage of the train with the arrogant sexuality which spoke to him, to all the old, the poor, the unattractive: 'Look at me, but don't touch. I'm not for you.'

He returned to Caldecote Road, his mind still occupied with the problem of keeping a watch on the Palfreys' house. The road was in marked contrast to the terrace, a disorderly muddle of shops, cafés, pubs and the occasional office, typical of an inner London commercial street from which any glory had long since departed. It was a bus route, and small disconsolate groups of shoppers, laden with their baskets and trolleys, waited at the stops on either side of the road, while the number of cars and lorries adding to the congestion suggested that this was a popular route to the Lambeth and Vauxhall bridges. Here, if not in Caldecote Terrace, he could loiter in safety.

Then he noticed the two hotels. They were on the opposite side of the road, facing down the terrace, two large stuccoed Victorian houses which had survived change, war, decay and demolition and now stood alone, shabby, the stucco peeling, but still grandiosely intact between a car salesroom and the vulgarly ostentatious fascia of a supermarket. From any of the front upper windows he would be able to train his binoculars on the door of number 68; here he would be able to sit in comfort and watch and wait. Here he would have time to think and plan his strategy, freed from the fear of discovery, the tedium and exhaustion of perpetually loitering in the street.

The names might have been chosen to emphasize that neither hotel had any connection with the business next door. The left-hand one was called Hotel Casablanca, its neighbour the Windermere Hotel. The first, less reassuringly named, looked the cleaner and more prosperous and would, he judged, give a slightly better view down Caldecote Terrace. The outer door was open and he stepped into a porch with a framed Underground map on the left wall and a mirror advertising ale on the right. He pushed through an inner door, patterned with overblown facsimiles of credit cards, and was met by the concentrated smell of food, cigarettes and furniture polish. There was no one on duty and the hall was empty except for a young woman seated at a small telephone switchboard behind the reception desk. A brown smooth-haired bitch was sleeping at her feet, its slack pimpled belly flopped over the chequered tiles, its paws gently curving. It took no interest in Scase's arrival except to peer at him briefly through a slitted eye before closing it again and nudging its head closer to the girl's chair. A white guide-dog harness was slung on a hook on the side of the switchboard. She turned as soon as she heard the swing of the inner door, and her sightless eyes, blinking rapidly, seemed to search the air above his head. In one socket the eyeball, retracted and upward-turned, was only half-visible under the lid. The other eye was covered with a milky film. She was slight with a gentle eager face, her straight light brown hair drawn back and fastened behind her ears by two circular blue slides. He wondered irrelevantly why she had chosen blue, how such a decision could be made, what it must mean to be deprived of the petty vanities of choice. He said:

'I'm looking for a room. Do you know if there are any vacancies?'

She smiled, but in the absence of any kindling light or warmth from the dead eyes the undirected smile seemed fatuous, meaningless. She said:

'Mr Mario will be here in a moment, if you will ring the bell, please.'

He had seen the push-button bell on the counter, but hadn't liked to press it since she might have thought that he was impatient for a service which she was powerless to give. It gave out a strident ring. A minute later a short swarthy man in a white jacket appeared through the door to the basement stairs. Scase said:

'I wondered if you'd got a vacant room, one at the front. I don't like being at the back. I've retired and I'm selling my house in the suburbs and looking for a flat in this area.'

This explanation was received with total uninterest. Presumably, if he had explained that he was an IRA terrorist looking for a safe hideout there might have been some response. Mario ducked under the counter hatch and flipped open a grease-stained register. After a brief pretence at consulting it, he said in a voice which was almost entirely Cockney:

'There's a top front single. Ten pounds a night, bed and breakfast, payment in advance. Dinner extra. We don't do lunches.'

'I'll have to go home for my things.'

He had read somewhere that hotels were suspicious of guests who arrived without luggage. He said:

'Could I take it from tomorrow?'

'It'll be gone by then. This is the busy season, see? You're lucky to get a vacancy.'

'Could I see it, please?'

The request was obviously regarded by Mario as eccentric, but he took a key from the board and pressed the lift button. They were slowly carried up together in cranking, claustrophobic proximity to the top floor. He unlocked the door, then left abruptly, saying, 'See you downstairs at the desk, then.'

As soon as the door closed behind him, Scase went over to the window. He saw with relief that the room was ideal for his purpose. The view from a lower floor would have been constantly obstructed by buses and lorries; here at this meanly proportioned window under the eaves he was high enough to look down unimpeded over the traffic into Caldecote Terrace. Mario had taken the key away with him but there was a bolt on the door. He shot it, then took the binoculars from his rucksack. The door of number 68 trembled, opaque as if seen through a heat haze. He steadied his hands, adjusted the focus and the image leaped at him, gleaming, sharp edged and so close that he felt that he could stretch out his hands and stroke the glistening paintwork. The binoculars ranged over the façade of the house from window to window, each secretive behind the white veil of its drawn curtains. On the balcony there was a twist of paper, blown up, perhaps, from the street. He wondered how long it would lie there before someone found it and swept it away, that single flaw on the house's perfection.

He put away the binoculars and explored the room. He supposed that he ought not to linger too long; it might seem suspicious. Then he told himself that Mario was unlikely to worry. What, after all, was there to steal or damage in this bleak, impersonal, comfortless cell? He didn't wonder that Mario had left him so promptly, avoiding explanation and excuses.

The floor was covered with a scrappy fawn carpet on which all the previous occupants seemed to have deposited their mark; a spatter of tea or coffee by the bed, more sinister-looking stains under the wash-basin. In one corner a larger area of dampness mirrored a similar stain on the ceiling where the roof must have leaked. The bed had a plain wooden headboard, presumably so that the occupant shouldn't be tempted to strangle himself with his tie from the bedrail. A large wardrobe stood unsteadily against one wall, its door swinging ajar. An over-sized dressing table in veneered walnut with a spotted mirror occupied the darkest corner. There were some compensations. The bed, when he sat on it, was comfortable enough; a glance showed that the sheets, although crumpled, were clean. He turned on the hot tap and after some minutes of gurgling and erratic flow the water spurted hot. These were small bonuses. He was glad of them but they weren't important. He would have slept as well on a hard bed and been happy to wash in cold water. The room had all that he asked, the view from the window.

And then he noticed the bedside locker. It was a sturdy oblong box in polished oak with one shelf and a cupboard underneath and with a wooden roller at one side for a towel. He recognized it. He had seen one before. It was an old hospital locker, probably part of a job lot, sold off by some hospital management committee when the wards were upgraded. What could more appropriately find a place in this room for human rejects, furnished with rejects? When he opened the cupboard the smell of disinfectant rose up strongly, working like a catalyst on memory. His mother, dying at last and knowing that she was dying, twisting her head restlessly on the pillow, the dyed hair, that last vanity, grey at the roots, the sinews of her wasted neck stretched like cords, her fingers sharp as claws scraping the coverlet. He heard again her querulous voice:

'I've had no bloody luck in my life, by God I haven't. No bloody luck at all.'

He had tried to make some gesture of comfort by straightening the pillow, but, impatiently, she had pushed his hand aside. He had known that he was part of the bad luck, that even on her deathbed nothing he did or said could please her. What, he wondered, would she think if she could see him here now, could know why he was here. He could almost hear her scorn.

'Murder! You? You wouldn't have the guts. Don't make me laugh.'

He left the room, closing the door carefully and quietly behind him as if her wasted body, uncomforted, lay there on the bed. He wished that the hotel had provided a different type of bedside locker. But otherwise the room would do very well indeed.

SIX

Philippa had always thought that if one were forced to share a flat it would be easier with a stranger than with a friend. And this stranger was so orderly, so quiet, so undemanding, was accommodating without being subservient, was capable about the flat without being obsessional. It was extraordinary how easily they established their shared routine. Philippa awoke now to sounds and smells that quickly became so familiar that it was difficult to believe that they were new. Her day began with the soft rustle of her mother's dressing-gown, with a cup of tea silently placed on her bedside table. Maurice had occasionally brought up her morning tea at Caldecote Terrace. But that was in another country and, besides, that wench was dead. She prepared their breakfast of cereal and boiled egg while her mother cleaned the flat, and then they sat together over their coffee, map spread, planning each day's excursions. It was like showing London to a foreign visitor, but one from a different culture, even a different dimension of time, an intelligent, interested tourist whose eyes surveyed the sights presented for her edification with pleasure, sometimes with delight, but who seemed to be looking beyond them, attempting to reconcile each new experience with an alien, half-remembered world. She was a tourist who was wary of the natives; anxious not to draw attention to herself by any solecism of taste; sometimes confused about the currency, mixing the tenpenny and fifty-pence piece; momentarily disconcerted by space and distance. Watching her, Philippa thought: she's like a woman who suffers simultaneously from claustrophobia and agoraphobia. And she was a visitor whose native country must be thinly populated since she was so frightened of crowds. London was packed with tourists, and although they set out early and avoided the most popular tourists' resorts, it was impossible to avoid the crush of bodies at bus stops and tube-station platforms, in shops and subways. Either they lived as hermits, or they contributed to and endured the hot, chattering, polluting pressure of humanity, breathed air which, on the warmer airless days, seemed to have been exhaled from a million lungs.

She discovered that her mother liked and had an instinctive appreciation of pictures; it was a discovery, too, for her mother. It pleased her to believe that her own pleasure in painting was inherited, enhanced by, but not the result of Maurice's careful tutelage. They became almost obsessive tourists during their first week together, setting out early with a packed lunch to be eaten on park seats, on river steamers, on the top deck of a bus, in the secret squares and gardens of the city.

She thought that she knew the exact moment when her mother had voluntarily taken upon herself the burden of happiness. It was the evening of their third day together when they threw the things she had brought with her from Melcombe Grange into the Grand Union Canal. In the morning they had taken a bus to Knightsbridge and had fought their way into one of the sales. Watching her mother's face as the horde of bodies pressed upon them, Philippa surprised in herself an emotion too close to sadism to be comfortable. They could have shopped perfectly well in Marks and Spencer in Edgware Road, getting there at nine-thirty before the crowd of tourists arrived. Had it been entirely because of a wish to see her mother in expensive clothes that she had led them to this mêlée? Hadn't it been in part deliberate, a test of her mother's courage, perhaps even the half-shameful pleasure of observing with detached interest the physical manifestations of pain and endurance? At the worst moment, the crush at the foot of the escalator, looking at her mother's face, she had been suddenly afraid that she was going to faint. She had taken her mother by the elbow and urged her forward; but she hadn't held her hand. Not once, not even in that bleak sitting-room at Melcombe Grange had there been a touching of each other's fingers, a meeting of flesh.

But she had been pleased with their bargains; a pair of fawn linen slacks, a jacket to match in fine wool, two cotton shirts. Trying them on again once they were home, her mother had turned to her with a curious look, half rueful, half resigned, which seemed to ask: 'Is this what you want? Is this how you see me? I'm attractive, intelligent, still young. I have to live the rest of my life without a husband, without a lover. So what are these clothes for? What am I for?'

Afterwards she had sat on the bed and watched while her mother packed her case. Everything that she had brought with her from prison went in; the suit in which she had travelled to London, her gloves, her underclothes, her shoulder-bag, even her toilet articles and pyjamas. It was an extravagance thus to relinquish even the small necessities of living, all of which would have to be replaced; but Philippa didn't check her. It was an extravagance necessary to both of them.

They set out for the canal half an hour before the tow-path was due to be closed to the public, and walked in silence, her mother carrying the case, until they reached an unfrequented stretch of the path overshadowed by trees. It was a warm, heavy evening of low cloud. The canal, rich and sluggish as treacle, slipped undisturbed under the low bridges and seeped into the moist fringes of the bank. A crowd of midges danced above the water, and single leaves, dark green, still glossy with the patina of high summer, floated slowly past on the sluggish stream. The air was rich with a rank river smell overlaid with loamy earth and spiced with the drifting scent of lawn cuttings and roses from the high gardens above the canal. The birds were silent now, except for the occasional distant cry, plaintive and alien, from the zoo aviary.

Still without speaking, Philippa took the case from her mother and hurled it into the middle of the stream. She had first glanced each way to make sure that the tow-path was empty, but even so the splash as the case hit the water sounded so like a falling body that they simultaneously glanced at each other, frightened that someone from the road must have heard. But there were no calling voices, no running footsteps. The case rose slowly, slid along the greasy surface of the water then reared itself like a sinking ship, toppled and was gone. The circle of ripples died.

She heard her mother give a little sigh. Her face, stained by the green shadows, was extraordinary peaceful. She looked like a woman in a moment of mystical exultation, even of religious ecstasy. Philippa felt an almost physical relief, as if she had flung away something of herself, of her past, not the past which she knew and recognized, but the formless weight of unremembered years, of childhood miseries which were not less acute because they lurked beyond the frontier of memory. They were gone now, gone for ever, sinking slowly into the mud. She needn't bother any more to try to recall them, nor fear that they might leap out of her subconscious to confuse and terrorize her. She wondered what her mother was thinking, she whose past, seared on so many memories, documented between the buff covers of official files, could not so easily be flung away. They stood in silence at the water's edge. Then the spell broke. Her mother turned to her. Her face relaxed into a smile like a woman released from pain into peace. It was almost a grin of pleasure. But all she said was:

'That's done. Let's go home.'

SEVEN

That night she decided that she had waited long enough; it was time to read her mother's account of the murder. But now that the moment had come she found herself reluctant to take the manuscript from her drawer. Almost she wished that her mother hadn't handed it to her, that she could have been spared this new moment of decision. She wished it read; yet dreaded to read it. There was nothing to prevent her from destroying it, but that was unthinkable. It was here; she had to know what it said. She asked herself what was holding her back. Her mother had told her the bare facts on that first visit to Melcombe Grange. Nothing in that waiting foolscap envelope could alter those facts, nothing could extenuate or excuse them.

The night was warm and she lay rigidly under a single blanket staring at the pale haze of the open window. Her mother's window must be open too. She could hear the faint rumble of traffic along Lisson Grove and the occasional shouts and laughter of revellers outside the Blind Beggar. Through her own window there wafted a warm summer smell of flowers and earth as if there lay outside all the richness of a country garden.

There was no sound from her mother's room but she waited to put on her bedside light until the last shouts from the pubs had died away and the street was finally quiet. It seemed to her important that she shouldn't begin reading until she could be sure that her mother was asleep. Then she switched on the lamp and slowly drew the envelope from the drawer. The manuscript was written in her mother's firm, upright but rather difficult hand on heavy, closely lined paper with a red-lined margin. Her mother had written only on alternate lines. The careful handwriting, the official-looking, very clean paper and the red margin gave the manuscript the look of an affidavit or of an examination script. It was written in the third person:

After she had been in Holloway for five years a new prisoner, a woman who had run a prostitution and extortion racket, standing beside her at the library shelf and looking at her with slant-eyed malice, had whispered:

'You're one of the Ductons, aren't you? I read about you in a book I got from the public library: *Fifty Years of Murder 1920–1970*. It was a kind of encyclopaedia of murder, the most notorious cases. You were under D in the Child Killer section. The Ductons.'

It was then that she realized that she wasn't a person any more. She was a Ducton, categorized by crime, partner in an unholy alliance, indissolubly linked by infamy. But she was surprised that the compiler had thought them worth including. They hadn't seemed notorious at the time, only a commonplace pair of bunglers, putting up a particularly poor fight in a trial which hadn't attracted much publicity, hadn't been able to compete with the suicide of a pop star or the sexual indiscretions of a minister of the Crown. The author must have had to scrape the barrel to pad out his chapter on child killers. She could guess what he had written under their entry. She herself had browsed through just such an encyclopaedia of death.

'Martin and Mary Ducton, who were convicted in May 1969 of the murder of twelve-year-old Julie Mavis Scase, both came from respectable, upper-working-class parents. Ducton was a clerk at the time of the murder, and his wife worked as a hospital medical records clerk. She was studying in her spare time for an external university degree and had some pretensions to culture. She is generally considered to have played the leading part in the child's death.'

She had other pretensions too, to happiness, to achievement, to a different life for them both. And it was true that she took the lead. She always took the lead, even in their joint destruction.

After that meeting she decided to write the truth about the crime, except that the truth was as shifting as her feelings, as unreliable as memory. It was like a butterfly. You could catch it and kill it and pin it down on a board with every delicate detail, every nuance of colour displayed. But then it wasn't a butterfly any more. She thought that imagery was pretentious; but then she had pretensions.

At the trial she had sworn to tell the truth, the whole truth and nothing but the truth. She had nearly added 'So help me God' but that wasn't written on the card. Only in fiction, apparently, did witnesses speak those words. There had been a little pile of holy books on the ledge of the box. The clerk, who was gowned like a verger, had handed her the Bible. She wondered what would happen if he gave her the wrong one, the Koran perhaps. Would she have to give her evidence all over again? The Bible was black and she took it with distaste because it was contaminated with the sweat of murderers' hands and she knew that they hadn't bothered to disinfect it. That was almost all she remembered of the trial. These facts are the truth.

She remembered coming home a little later that evening because the gynaecological clinic at the hospital where she worked had been busier than usual and she wasn't free until after six. It was very cold even for January. A thin fog writhed round the street lamps and crept into the front gardens truncating the trees so that they seemed to move uprooted in majestic inconsequence, surpliced in white mist. As soon as she opened the front door she heard the child crying. It was a high desolate wailing, not loud but continuous and piercing. At first she thought that it was a cat. But that was ridiculous. She was the last woman to mistake the cry of a child.

And then she saw her husband. He was standing half way up the stairs looking down at her. She could remember everything about that moment, the thin wailing of the child, the warm familiar smell of the hall, the patterned wallpaper and the break at the join where she hadn't managed to match it accurately, her husband's eyes. She remembered most his look of shame. There had been terror there, too, and a desperate appeal. But what she remembered was the shame. She could never afterwards remember what they said. Perhaps they didn't speak. It wasn't after all, necessary. She knew.

There is no rehearsal for a murder trial. You have to get it right first time. There are no explanations, only deceptively innocent questions to which the most dangerous response can be the truth. She could only recall one question to her in the witness box from the prosecuting counsel and her reply to that had been fatal.

'And what had you in mind when you went upstairs to the child?'

She supposed that she could have said: 'I wanted to see that she was all right. I wanted to tell her that I was there and that I'd take her home. I wanted to comfort her.' None of the jury would have believed her, but some of them might have wished to believe her. Instead she told them the truth.

'I had to stop her crying.'

Childhood is the one prison from which there's no escape, the one sentence from which there's no appeal. We all serve our time. She was eleven when she realized the truth, that her father didn't beat her and her brother because he was drunk; he got drunk because he enjoyed beating them and that was how he found the courage to do it. When he came back at night her brother would begin crying even before they heard his heavy feet on the stairs and she would slide into bed with him trying to stifle the noise in her arms, hearing the lurching feet, her mother's expostulatory whine. She learned at the age of eleven that there was no hope, only endurance. She endured. But for the rest of her life she couldn't bear to hear a child crying.

Murderers often excuse themselves by claiming that they can't remember exactly what happened. Perhaps it's true. Perhaps the mind mercifully erases what it can't bear to recall. But she could remember so much horror. Why then should this particular moment be a blank? She must have lost her temper with this wailing stupid girl who hadn't, after all, been seriously hurt, who surely had been warned that she shouldn't go with strange men, who hadn't even the sense to stop crying and get out of the house and keep quiet. At the trial the pathologist described the post-mortem findings. Death had been by throttling; the neck was bruised with the marks of human hands. They must have been her hands. Who else's could they have been? But she couldn't remember touching the child, nor could she remember the moment when what she was shaking was no longer a child.

After that, memory was like a film rolling on with only a few moments when the picture was lost or no longer in focus. Her husband was in the kitchen. She saw that there were two cups and the teapot and milk jug on the kitchen table. For one moment she had a ridiculous thought, that he was restoring them with tea. She said:

'I've killed her. We must get rid of the body.'

He accepted the brutal statement as if he already knew, as if she was telling him the most commonplace of facts. Perhaps he was so petrified by horror that no new horror could touch him.

He whispered:

'But her parents. We mustn't hide her. We can't let them go on hoping, wondering, praying that she's all right.'

'They won't be left hoping for long. We won't take her very far, just to the edge of Epping Forest. The body will be found soon enough. But it mustn't be found here.'

'What are you going to do?'

Fear sharpened her wits. It was like fabricating a plot. All the details had to be right. She considered, discarded, contrived. They would use the car. The body would be put in the boot. But it would have to be wrapped. If they were suspected, the car would be searched by forensic scientists. They would find traces of the child, hair, dust from her shoes, a thread of cloth. A sheet would do to cover her, a clean, ordinary, white terylene and cotton sheet from her airing cupboard. She always washed them at the launderette. There would be no laundry mark to betray them. But it would be difficult to dispose of a sheet; they would have to bring it back in the car for washing. Plastic would be better, that long plastic bag in which her winter coat had come back from the cleaners. No one would be able to trace it to her, and after they had disposed of the body it could be screwed up and left in any public litter basket. But they would need an alibi for the time of death and that meant speed. They must start now, at once. She said:

'We'll take back our library books. I'll ask for the new Updike; it's still on the reserve list. That means that the girl will remember us if the police check up. Then we'll go to the cinema at Manse Hill. We'll have to do something there to make the box-office girl notice us. I'll find I haven't enough money and ask you for some. We'll argue about it. No, better still, I'll accuse her of cheating me over the change. That means paying with a five-pound note. Have you got one?'

He nodded.

'I think so.'

He tried to take out his wallet. His hands were shaking as if he were palsied. She put her own hand into his jacket pocket and found it. In the note compartment there was a new five-pound note and a couple of crumpled pound notes. She said:

'We only stay in the cinema for about half an hour. Once we're through the foyer we'll take our own tickets and separate. If the police do suspect us they'll be asking people if they saw a couple leaving. They won't expect us to be apart. And we'd better sit at the end of different rows, not next to anyone. It shouldn't be difficult. There won't be many people there on a night like this. But you must keep your eyes on me. As soon as I get up to leave slip out after me. We'll go out by the side entrance, the one that leads straight on to the car park. Then we'll drive to the forest.'

He said:

'I don't want to sit away from you. I don't want us to be parted. Don't leave me.'

He was still shaking. She couldn't be sure that he had understood. She wished that she could do it all alone, that she could help him to bed, tuck him in with a hot water bottle, cosset him like a grieving child. But that wasn't possible. He, more than she, must have an alibi. She couldn't leave him alone in the house.

They had to be seen together. Then she remembered the brandy, the miniature bottle she had won at the hospital Christmas party. She had been saving it for some unspecified emergency. She hurried to the pantry and poured the brandy into a glass. When she smelled it she knew how much she needed it. But there were only a couple of mouthfuls in the bottle, not enough to do good to two of them. She took it to him. She switched on the third bar of the electric fire.

'Drink this, darling. Try to get warm. Stay here, I'll call you when I'm ready.'

She was amazed at how clearly her mind was working. Before she went upstairs she put the front door on the latch. She went outside and unlocked the boot of the car. The road was deserted. The nearest street light, ten yards away, was a yellow haze in the freezing mist. All the curtains of number 39 were drawn; behind them the dark and empty rooms waited for their new owners. At number 43 only the front downstairs room was lit. Here too, the curtains were drawn but they couldn't muffle the gusts of laughter from the television comedy show. The Hicksons, inveterate viewers, were settled for the evening.

She took the plastic bag from the hanger in the cupboard under the stairs. Her coat still smelled of cleaning fluid. She wondered whether this familiar pungent smell would always be associated for her with this night. Then she thought of gloves. There was a pair of thin washing-up gloves hung over the taps of the kitchen sink. She hated to work in thick gloves. She put them on. Then she went upstairs.

The bedside lamp was on beside the double bed, the curtains were drawn. It was as if she saw the child for the first time. She lay sprawled on the bed, her left arm flung out, the fingers curving. Her blue knickers were down to her knees. She looked very peaceful. Her spectacles had been shaken off and lay separately on the counterpane. They looked ridiculously small, a delicate contraption of glass and wire. The woman picked them up and felt in the pocket of the child's coat for the case. It wasn't there. She felt a moment of panic as if it were vitally important that the spectacles were kept safe. The she noticed a small black shoulder bag on the floor. She picked it up. It was made of cheap plastic and looked very new. Perhaps it had been bought specially to go with her Guide's uniform. Inside was a handkerchief, still folded, a Girl Guide diary, a pencil, a small purse containing a few coins, and a red spectacle case. The woman folded the spectacles into the case. Then she opened the diary, the hand was childish, printed letters linked with straight lines. Julie Mavis Scase, 104 Magenta Gardens. She wondered why the child had taken this long way home. Surely it would have been quicker to go across the recreation ground. And if she had gone across the recreation ground she wouldn't be lying here dead. They were a full mile from Magenta Gardens. It might be a day or two after the body was found before the police started their door-to-door inquiries here, and every day would make them safer.

She took the child's coat and the Girl Guide beret and placed them on the body. Gently she pulled up the knickers. Then she drew the long plastic bag carefully over the child, twisting it above her head. Seen through the transparent sheeting her face, unspectacled, the lids closed, was transformed, delicate, beautiful even, but unreal. The lips were slightly parted showing the moist gleam of her thin metal braces across the teeth. A blob of saliva hung on it like a pearl. She looked like a doll gift-wrapped for Christmas, a present for a good girl. When the woman lifted the body in her arms she could feel its warmth through the thin plastic. The child was heavier than she had expected. The weight dragged at her arms and stomach muscles. It would have been easier to have slung the burden over her shoulder. Wasn't that how they taught you to carry an unconscious person from a burning house? But she found she couldn't do it. She had to carry the child in her arms gently, as if this were a sick and sleeping baby who must not be awakened. Words came into her mind. She is not dead, but sleeping. She wanted to pray: 'Oh God, help us, please help us. Please make it all right.' But that wasn't possible. She had put herself beyond the power of prayer. No one, not even God, could make it all right for them ever again.

Their car was a red second-hand Mini. They had only had it for six months. They had been able to save up for it because she worked. Even so, their Sunday trips to the sea with Rosie had

had to be rationed. She was an unpractised driver, unused to fog. She drove very slowly, knowing what it could mean if they were in an accident, were stopped by the police. He sat beside her, propped up like a corpse, eyes staring ahead through the windscreen. She had wound his thick scarf round his neck, half obscuring his face: but she couldn't hide his eyes. Neither of them spoke. Sometimes she murmured foolish sibilant reassurances as one might to a fractious horse. From time to time she took her left hand from the wheel and laid it on his. But she had made him wear his gloves and she didn't know whether those stiff wool-encased fingers were aware of her touch.

The lights of the library windows shone through the fog. Although this was a branch she often used, she hadn't driven there before and was unsure where to leave the car. She turned carefully to a side road and saw two cars parked at the kerb. She stopped the Mini carefully behind them. Then she told him what to do. He nodded. She didn't know if he had understood. She pushed open the library door and was met by the familiar warm effluence of books and floor polish underlaid by the sour smell emanating from the adjacent reading-room where the old men, swathed in their decaying overcoats, sat all day slumped over the newspapers, taking refuge from loneliness and the cold. She could see through the glass partition that three of them were still there. She envied them because they were alive and Martin was dead. That was the only moment during the night in which she was for a second disorientated, the child forgotten, thinking that it was his body huddled there in the boot of the car. But he was walking dead at her side.

She went up to the counter with the three books she had brought with her to return. He remembered her instructions and went over to the nearest fiction shelf. She called out to him:

'There's no time to choose new books, darling, if we're going to get there in time for the big film. I'll just put in my card for the Updike.'

He seemed not to have heard. He stood there stiffly facing the shelves like a dummy in a shop window. There was only one person in front of her, a determinedly bright middle-aged woman apparently returning library books for her invalid mother. The girl librarian listened impassively as she sorted out the tickets while the woman gabbled on about the books she was returning, her mother's health, the books she hoped to take out. She must have been a frequent visitor. Perhaps returning library books was the only chance she got of a little freedom. The librarian said 'Thank you, Miss Yelland' as she handed over the three tickets.

And now it was the woman's turn. She asked to be placed on the waiting list for the Updike and filled up the card with her name and address in bold capitals. She was surprised that her hand could be so steady. She took a lot of trouble over forming the letters, bold and black against the white card. If the police did check up, surely no one could believe that these firm letters had been penned by anyone under stress. Then she went over to her husband. He seemed rooted to the ground and she had almost to lead him to the door and out to the car.

And here, again, the film ceased to roll, the pictures were lost. The worst part of the drive must have been circling the roundabout where five roads met at Manse Hill. But she must have managed that without incident because the next thing she remembered was parking the car in front of the cinema. The car park was more crowded than she had expected, but that was a good thing. It meant that the cinema would be fairly full, that their departure would be less likely to be noticed. She was able to find a parking space close to one of the side exits. When she switched off the engine the silence was almost frightening. They sat together in the fog-shrouded car and she told him again what to do. She said: 'Darling, do you understand?' He nodded, but he didn't speak. They got out of the car and she closed his door for him. The fog was thicker now. It rose and fell like a malignant gas, spilling in glutinous dollops from the high street lamps. They waded through it, knee-deep, to the foyer.

The last programme must have begun. There were only two people in front of them at the box office. When her turn came she asked for eight-and-sixpennies and handed over the five-pound note. She took her change and propelled him a little ahead of her letting one of the four one-pound notes drop from her hand. Then she turned and went back to the box office. She said:

'I think I'm a pound short. There are only three here.'

The woman said solidly:

'I gave you four, madam. You saw me count them out.'

'There are only three here.'

The woman repeated:

'You saw me count them out, madam,' and turned to the next customer.

She moved away from the box office, then said loudly:

'I'm sorry, I must have dropped it. It's here on the floor.'

The whole episode struck her even at the time as unreal, artificial. The woman in the box office shrugged her shoulders. They moved together across the foyer to the entrance to the stalls. She tried to hand him his ticket, but he wouldn't take it, pretending not to notice her nudging hands. But she knew that he couldn't face sitting apart from her. They would have to stay together.

They stepped into what seemed an immensity of warm-scented blackness. Only the screen was alight, blazing with colour and noise. It was a James Bond film and it must just have begun. She followed the pinpoint of light from the usherette's torch down the centre gangway, one hand behind her clutching at his coat. They were shown into two seats at the end of a row. This wouldn't do. She wanted to slip out from the side entrance, not to walk again up the centre aisle. After they had sat for about ten minutes she whispered to him and took his hand. Together they slipped out of their seats and she led him forward towards the screen until her eyes, more accustomed now to the darkness, could discern a sparsely occupied row. There were only three couples, all seated near the central gangway. They pushed their way past them muttering apologies and took their seats at the far end of the row, almost immediately opposite the red exit sign.

She made herself wait nearly half an hour before she gave him the sign. It was an exciting point of the film; the background music was rising to a crescendo, the screen was full of hurling cars and screaming mouths. In the rows in front of her every face was turned to the screen. She gave a pull on his hand and half rose to her feet. He followed her and they were out through the door. There was a short flight of concrete steps, then she was pushing at the bar of the final door, the cold fog swirled in their faces, and they were in the car park. She felt in her coat pocket for the keys. They weren't there. And instantly she knew. She had left them in the car. Clutching his hand she dragged him with her as she raced through the fog to where she had parked the Mini; but she knew what she would find. The two painted white lines enclosed emptiness. The Mini had gone.

And after that the film of memory broke again. They must have walked for three hours, hand in hand, trudging onwards through the fog towards the forest. Her next memory was of a narrow road stretching straight and unlit between the trees.

The night was icy cold and very still. On each side of the road the forest stretched ahead of them, shrouded in mist. She thought she could hear from it a gentle persistent dripping, slow and portentous as drops of blood. In her imagination it stretched for ever, exuding its black miasma, dropping terror from the tangled bushes, the high leafless boughs, oozing a slow contagion from the slimy trunks. She could see their breath, small puffs of white smoke, leading them onwards. There was no other sound, only the endless ring of their feet on the tarmac. Occasionally they would hear the purr of an approaching car. Instinctively they would step into the darkness of the trees until it passed in a sweep of light, carrying ordinary people, perhaps on their way to a party or driving home late after a long day, happy people with nothing to worry about except mortgages and sickness, their children, their marriages, their jobs.

And then, suddenly, he stopped. He said, his voice dull, utterly defeated:

'I'm tired. Come with me into the forest and we'll find somewhere to sleep. I'll cuddle you. You won't feel the cold. We'll be together. We need never wake up ever again.'

But she failed him. She wouldn't go with him. In the end he pleaded, almost cried, but still she refused. She made him turn with her, defeated, and begin the slow trudge home. Ever since earliest childhood she had been terrified of the forest. It wasn't the forest of primary-school fairy tales, the wail of a hunting horn calling through dappled glades, paths regal with stags. This was a mush of corruption, the place where her father had threatened to lose her if she screamed, the dumping ground for murdered bodies. In her childish imagination the sluggish streams ran with blood.

And it wasn't only the terror of the forest. She didn't share – she never had shared – his pessimism. Life for him was fundamentally tragic, a series of days to be somehow got through, not a privilege to be rejoiced in but a burden to be endured. He was always surprised by joy. The thought of death held no anguish for him; it was life which called for courage. But she was different. Nothing but intolerable pain or utter despair could make her kill herself. The heart of her personality was buoyant with optimism, all her life she had been nourished by hope. She hadn't survived the miseries of her childhood to die so easily now. She told herself that all might yet be well. The car thieves might never open the boot; why should they? The car wasn't worth stealing for its own sake. That meant that they wanted it just for the ride and would abandon it when they had finished with it. In time the police would find it and examine it. But tracing the car to them didn't make her a murderess. The rapist – anyone – could have stolen it from outside their door. All they had to do now was to make their way home, wait for the morning, and report it missing.

But in her heart she knew that the hope was false. Once the car was found they would be the chief suspects. They would be asked about their movements that evening; the call at the library, the argument over the cinema tickets. They would be asked how they had travelled to the cinema without the car. There was no direct or easy bus route. And they couldn't reply that their car had been stolen from outside the cinema. Why hadn't they reported the theft before they left the house? She knew that Martin wouldn't be able to stand up to this early and probing questioning. She had banked on having several days before the police got around to him and, even then, with nothing to connect them with the crime, it would only have been a routine door-to-door visit. Nothing was known against him. Now everything was changed. The plastic bag would be traced to the local dry-cleaners. Her recent visit there would be discovered.

And so they trudged home together to the waiting police cars standing already outside the house, to the watching eyes from the houses across the road, to the knowledge that, never again, would they be alone together.

The terrors of the forest were imaginary. All the terrors to come would be real. If she had cared enough she could surely have taken his hand and let him lead her into the darkness under the trees. She could have conquered panic in his arms. Always she had been the stronger. It was to her he had looked for support, for comfort, for reassurance. Wasn't that, after all, why she had married him, because he was a man who had none of the qualities which her father had taught her belonged to manliness? Now, and for the first time, he had asked her to trust to him. He had wanted it that way, wanted to lie in the darkness with her, comforting her into death. But because of her childhood terrors she failed him. She withheld from him the right to die with dignity in his own way and in his own time. She condemned him to the trial, the dock, the torture of those eighteen months in prison before death released him. She had heard what prisoners did to child molesters. She had lived through those eighteen months separated from him, unable to comfort him, unable to tell him that she was sorry. The child's death hadn't been willed; she told herself that she couldn't have prevented that act of violence. The child had been murdered by the child she had once been. But this desertion of him at the end had been voluntary.

I should have died with him that night. He was right, there was nothing else for us to do. That was the real sin, the failure of love. 'Perfect love casteth out fear.' It didn't need a perfect love not to fail him then. It only needed a little kindness, a little courage.

And there the manuscript broke off. When she had finished reading Philippa turned off the light and lay very still, her heart pounding. She felt sick and at the same time faint. She got up and sat on the edge of her bed for a moment then made her way over to the window and leant out, breathing great gulps of the sweet-smelling air. She didn't ask herself how much of the story she believed. She didn't judge it as writing or as description. She couldn't distance herself from it any more than she could distance herself from the woman who had written it. She knew that that she wouldn't tell her mother that she had read it and that her mother wouldn't ask. This was all that she would ever be told about the murder, all she would ever know or need to know. After ten minutes of silently gazing at the night sky she put the manuscript back in her drawer and went back to bed. Only then did she wonder where she had been that night.

EIGHT

He returned that same evening and took possession of his command post. Next morning he breakfasted as soon as the dining-room was open at half-past seven, and by eight o'clock he had begun his watch. He sat at the window on the one chair, the binoculars resting on the ledge, the door bolted. At his side he placed the open rucksack ready to slip the binoculars inside and to hurry downstairs once Mrs Palfrey was sighted. It would take too long to go down by lift; he would have to move fast if he were to keep her in sight.

At nine-fifteen precisely a tall, dark-haired man carrying a briefcase left number 68. This, presumably, was Mr Palfrey. He had the businesslike air of a man with his morning planned, and Scase didn't believe that it included calling on the murderess or her daughter. His first conviction had never wavered; it was the woman whose frightened voice he had heard over the telephone who would eventually lead him to them.

At nine-forty-five the maid appeared, bumping a shopping trolley up the basement steps. Then no one left or arrived until she returned two hours later, pulling its laden weight after her and manoeuvring it carefully down the basement steps. He went out and lunched on coffee and sandwiches at a coffee bar down a side street within fifty yards of the hotel, and was back at his post at a quarter to two. All the afternoon he kept watch but no one appeared. The man returned home shortly after six and let himself in at the front door.

He broke off his watch again at eight o'clock for dinner, but was back at the window by nine, and stayed there until the light faded, the street lights came on and, at last, it was eleven o'clock and then midnight. The first day was over.

And this was the routine of the next three days. The man left at nine-fifteen precisely in the morning. The maid, usually with her trolley, was out of the house by ten. It was on the following Monday, tempted by the sun, by the need for exercise and by frustration, that he decided to follow her. He had some idea that he might get into conversation, might at least learn whether Mrs Palfrey was at home, might even think of some excuse for asking her where the girl had gone. He didn't know how he would approach her, or what he would say, but the instinct to follow her was suddenly so immediate, so strong, that he was down the stairs and in the street almost as soon as she had reached the corner of Caldecote Terrace.

The first shop she visited was a local newsagent to pay the paper bill. And here the newsagent greeted her by name, and he knew who she was. He was irritated with himself; the facile assumption which had taken her for a maid had wasted three days. Glancing at her as he pretended to hesitate over his choice of newspaper it was difficult to associate this slight, depressed figure, this anxious face with the confident girl he had seen in the train, or to see her as mistress of number 68. When she had settled the bill, he bought a *Daily Telegraph*, then followed her at a careful distance to her next call, the butcher. Here there was ham on the bone on display in the window, and he decided to buy a quarter of a pound and lunch on it in his room. He joined the queue behind her and waited patiently while she selected a shoulder of lamb. For the first time he saw her animated. The joint was displayed for her inspection and she and the butcher, confederates in expertise, contemplated it with loving care. She asked for it to be boned and he bore it off willingly, leaving his assistant to serve the queue while he obliged this discriminating customer.

After he had bought the ham he followed her through squares of stuccoed Victorian houses to a street market. Here she moved slowly from stall to stall, eyeing the produce with what seemed to him excessive anxiety, surreptitiously pressing the tomatoes and pears. Lastly she visited a delicatessen. He stood on the pavement, pretending an interest in the shrivelled fingers of dried sausages while she bought smoked salmon, watching while the shopkeeper laid his long knife against the pink flesh, and held drooping over the blade the first rich transparent slice for her inspection. Scase had never tasted smoked salmon and the price on the half fish displayed in the refrigerated window appalled him. They ate well, the Palfreys. The Ducton girl had done well for herself. On impulse he followed Mrs Palfrey into the shop and bought two ounces. He would eat them before dinner in his room and discover what this unknown delicacy tasted like, knowing that her tongue would experience the same sensation, that these two slivers of veined flesh would bind them closer together.

And this was the pattern of his life for the next ten days. Pimlico was her village, and it became his, bounded by Victoria Street and Vauxhall Bridge Road, two flowing thoroughfares like unnavigable rivers over which she never ventured to pass. Twice a week she would walk to the Smith Street branch of the Westminster Library to change her books. He would go into the reading-room and pretend to occupy himself with periodicals while he watched her through the glass partition moving from shelf to shelf. He wondered what books she bore back to solace her in that basement kitchen. It seemed to him that she carried with her a climate of anxiety and loneliness, but it didn't affect him. He couldn't recall any recent time in his life more free from strain. She was easy to trail. Her preoccupations were personal and secret; she seemed hardly to notice the life around her except as it related to shopping and food. But he had no sense of hurry or of time wasted. He knew that this was where he was meant to be. In the end, before long, she would lead him to them.

The weather became warmer, the sun less fitful. On these high summer days she would take a sandwich and fruit to eat on one of the benches in the Embankment Gardens where the boughs of the plane trees dragged to sweep the water with their leaves. He had got into the habit of carrying a packed lunch himself, bought from a delicatessen in Caldecote Road, to be eaten either in a park or at the window of his room. They would sit distanced by twenty or thirty yards on their separate benches and he would watch as she stared over the parapet at the gritty fringes of the Thames, plumed with gulls, at the great barges as they grunted upstream, slapping the tide against the embankment wall. After she had eaten she would feed the sparrows, crouching patiently for as long as fifteen or twenty minutes with the crumbs on her outstretched palm. Once he did the same, and smiled when, after a few minutes of patient waiting, the sparrow fluttered down and he felt the commotion of its frantic wings and the scrape of its tiny claws on his palm. One warm turbulent morning when the high tide heaved in the throes of a spent and distant storm, she brought with her a bag of crusts to feed the gulls. He watched while she stood at the parapet, hurling the bread with stiff ungainly jerks of her arm. The rushing air was suddenly white with wings, spiked with beaks and claws, clamorous with high, desolate screams.

He was surprised how quickly he came to feel at home at the Casablanca. The hotel had few comforts, but it had no pretensions. There was a small and over-crowded bar in a room off the dining-room and most evenings he would take a single dry sherry before his dinner. The meals were predictable: eatable, but only just. But occasionally the standard varied. It was as if the cook were engaged in a private game, judging when the customers were on the point of revolt and then confounding them with a dinner of unexceptionable excellence. But usually little cooking had been done. Scase was familiar with the taste of all the soups; he had opened these tins himself. The prawn cocktail consisted of tinned prawns, hard and salty, smothered with the cheapest of bottled dressing and reposing on a limp lettuce leaf; the pâté maison was commercial liver-sausage; the potatoes were invariably served mashed since they were reconstituted from a packet. All his senses were sharpened since he had set out on his enterprise; he noticed these things now, but they didn't bother him.

The Mario who had booked him in seemed to run the place. Scase saw no one else in authority. The other staff were part-time, including Fred, an elderly cripple who spent all night dozing in an armchair behind the counter and whose job it was to let in guests who arrived back after twelve-thirty. The regular clientele were mostly commercial travellers. With some of them Mario was friendly, joining them, white-jacketed, at their table for long intimate conferences. Their common interest was apparently betting. Lists and evening papers were consulted and money changed hands. But most of the trade was foreign package-tours from

Spain. With the weekly arrival of the morning coach the hotel came alive. Mario, galvanized into frantic activity, immediately became Spanish in speech and gesture; the hall was blocked with luggage and chattering tourists; the lift invariably broke down and Coffee, the bitch, quivered with excitement.

The hotel was ideal for his purpose. No one bothered about him, no one was curious. The only way in which a visitor could attract interest at the Hotel Casablanca was by failing to settle the bill weekly in advance and in cash. If he felt the need for conversation, a brief craving for the sound of a human voice directed at himself, he would stop to chat to the blind girl. He learned that her name was Violet Hedley and that she was an orphan who had been educated in a residential school for the blind and now lived with a widowed aunt in a council flat off the Vauxhall Road. In exchange he told her nothing about himself except that his wife and only child were dead. She was the only person to whom he felt he could safely talk. Whatever her private imaginings of him might be, he knew that all his secrets, his past, his present purpose, even his ugliness and his pain, were safe from any probing by those sightless eyes.

On Friday morning, 25th August, he was led by Mrs Palfrey across the newly created piazza and into the cool, incense-sweet immensity of Westminster Cathedral. He saw that she didn't dip her fingers in the stoup of holy water; that she hadn't apparently come to pray. This visit was just one more way of killing time. He followed her, attaching himself unobtrusively to a party of French-speaking tourists, as she wandered between the great square marble pillars, paused to survey each of the side chapels, bent to stare with repugnant fascination at the silver-encased body of St John Southworth, small as a child in his glass case.

He had never before been in the Cathedral and its red-brick-bounded Byzantine exterior hadn't prepared him for the wonder which lay beyond the west door. The rough unadorned bricks climbed upwards from great pillars of smooth marble, green, yellow, red and grey, to the black curving immensity of the domed roof. It hung suspended above him, darkness and chaos given a form and substance, and he felt that he crawled crab-like beneath its mystery. The completed Lady Chapel, gleaming with gold mosaics, pretty and sentimental, meant nothing to him. Even the smooth beauty of the marble pillars served only to draw the eye upwards to that curving wonder of the roof. He hadn't expected to be so excited by any building. When the act was done, he would come back and walk here again. He would look up at that dark void and find a comfort which he would gain from no lighted candles, no stained glass. There would be other buildings to explore, perhaps even other cities to visit. There could be a life, solitary though it might be, that was more than mere existence. But now even to experience this wonder pricked him with guilt. He remembered the prick of the sparrow on his palm. That, too, had been a moment very close to joy. But to feel joy while Mary Ducton was still alive was a betrayal of the dead. Already he felt that he was being seduced by routine into a complacent lethargy. He would wait for only one more week. If in that time he hadn't been led to the murderess, if the girl Philippa still hadn't returned to Caldecote Terrace, then he would have to think of a plan, however desperate, to trick Mrs Palfrey into betraying to him where they were.

NINE

When the ten days of freedom which they had promised themselves were up and it was time to look for a job, they avoided the Government Job Centre in Lisson Grove, which was too intimidatingly a reminder of officialdom and searched instead in the evening papers and on the display boards outside newsagents. They found advertisements for kitchen staff/waitresses at Sid's Plaice off Kilburn High Road pinned to a board outside a stationer's shop at the north end of the Edgware Road. The advertisement said helpfully 'take 16 bus and alight Cambridge Avenue'. It added that the wages were one pound an hour plus food. They calculated that if they worked six hours a day for five days their living expenses should be comfortably covered. One free fish meal a day would be a bonus.

Sid's Plaice was a double-fronted fish and chip shop with café attached, and looked and smelled reassuringly fresh. Sid himself, whom Philippa had pictured as small, swarthy and greasy, was discovered to be a blond, ruddy-faced, amateur boxer. He himself worked behind the counter, simultaneously directing operations on both sides of his establishment, crashing down the lid of the fish-fryer, plunging the wire baskets of chips into the sizzling fat, joking with customers at the counter as he wrapped their orders in greaseproof and newspaper, bawling demands at the kitchen staff and slapping fish and chips on plates to be shoved at the waitresses who regularly pushed their heads through the serving hatch and yelled out their orders. The din, to which Sid and his staff were apparently impervious, was constant and appalling. Philippa early decided that customers needed strong nerves although not necessarily a strong stomach to dine at Sid's Plaice.

Sid's girls took it in turn to wait at the tables, if taking the plates from the hatch and dumping them in front of the customers at the formica-topped tables could be described as waitress service. The job was preferred to washing-up, since there were the tips. Sid explained that most customers left something, and there was always the hope of unintended generosity from a visitor or recently arrived immigrant confused about the value of English money. This flexible use of his female labour, which saved him the expense of employing two categories of worker, was described by Sid as 'mucking in together like one big happy family'.

He took on Philippa and her mother with alacrity, and if he were surprised that two apparently educated women were actually seeking work in his shop, he didn't show it. Philippa told herself that this was a place of work where she could be in no possible danger of meeting anyone from her past life, and where no questions would be asked. She was wrong in that; questions were perpetually asked by her fellow workers, but no one cared whether the answers were true.

There were three other washers-up on the evening shift: Black Shirl, Marlene and Debbie. Marlene's hair, spiked and dyed bright orange, looked as if it had been hacked off by shears. Two moons of bright red decorated each cheek, but Philippa was relieved to see that she had apparently jibbed at piercing her ear lobes with safety pins. Her forearm was covered with tattoos, two intertwining hearts pierced with an arrow and surrounded by a garland of roses, and a sixteenth-century galleon in full sail. It fascinated Debbie who was happy to wipe up dishes for Marlene all evening so that she could see it sinking and rising in the detergent.

'Make it sink. Go on, Marl! Make it sink,' she would plead, and Marlene would plunge her arms in the detergent foam and let the bubbles froth around the little craft.

In the damp and ill-equipped kitchen behind the café, with its two sinks, they worked in pairs. They talked incessantly, usually about the previous night's television, their boy friends, shopping up West. They were given to extraordinary swings of mood and terrifying bursts of temper. They walked out frequently, demonstrating a pathetic and fiercely guarded if illusory independence, and walked in again a few days later. They complained about Sid behind his back, and were alternately surly and outrageously flirtatious to his face. They discussed his alleged sexual inadequacies in anatomical detail and at length, although it was obvious to Philippa that all Sid's energies were spent on the business, his occasional amateur boxing bouts, racing his greyhound and keeping Mrs Sid happy. This lady, of a formidable smartness and vulgarity, appeared briefly once a day in the chippie, apparently to remind Sid and warn the others that she existed. Poor Sid, thought Philippa. He would probably have been afraid of his female helots if they had had enough sense to organize a united confrontation. But they waged their war of attrition with cunning and some success. They regularly stole small quantities of food from him, bread, butter, sugar and tea, and he knew they did. Perhaps this was regarded by both sides as one of the perks of the job; but Philippa saw that he took no chances with his till, which was closely guarded.

Debbie, waif-like, with pale transparent skin, looked as if her life were subcutaneously draining away. Her nose and fingers were perpetually pink-tipped, her anxious eyes swam in red pools and even the ridges of her ears, ragged as if they had been nibbled, looked about to ooze blood. She spoke in whispers and crept about the kitchen bestowing indiscriminately her sweetly inane smile. But it was Debbie who was the most violent. Sharing a sink with Philippa, Black Shirl said:

'She knifed her ma when she was twelve.'

'You mean she killed her?'

'Bloody near thing. They put her in care. But she's all right now as long as you don't let her near your feller.'

'You mean she'd knife him?'

Black Shirl roared with laughter.

'Naw. She'd fuck 'im. She's terrible she is. Lord, that girl, she's terrible!'

Mechanically taking plate after plate from Shirl's hands, Philippa thought that if her father had encountered Debbie instead of Julie Scase, he would be alive now. There would have been no rape, no murder, no adoption. His only problem would have been to get rid of her, to stop another visit, but ten shillings and a bag of sweets would probably have done the trick. It was his bad luck to have met instead Julie Scase, that dangerous mixture of innocence and stupidity.

All three treated her mother with wary respect, perhaps because she was older, perhaps because there was something inhibiting about her quiet composure. Unlike Philippa, she seemed undisturbed by the irrational explosions of violence. Once when Debbie, washing a carving knife, suddenly pointed it at Marlene's throat, she succeeded in persuading the girl to hand it over with no more than a quiet, 'Give it to me, Debbie.' But they were curious about her. One night, when her mother was on waitress duty and Marlene and Philippa were sharing a sink, Marlene said:

'Been in the bin, has she, your ma? You know, a mental hospital?'

'Yes, she has. Why did you ask?'

'You can allus tell. My auntie was the same. You can tell by the eyes, see. All right now, is she?'

'Oh, yes, she's fine. The doctor said she mustn't be under any strain. That's why we took this job. It isn't exactly stimulating, but at least you can put it behind you when you go home.'

This was accepted in silence. They all had excuses for lowering themselves by condescending to take Sid's job. Black Shirl, sloshing suds at the next sink, said, belligerent, suspicious:

'Why do you speak posh?'

'It's not my fault. My uncle looked after me when I was a kid, after my dad died. He and my aunt were particular. That's why I ran away. That and my uncle trying to get into bed with me.'

Marlene said:

'My uncle did that to me, too. I didn't mind. He was all right. Used to take me up West Saturday nights.'

Black Shirl said:

'Went to a posh school then, did you?'

'I ran away from that too.'

'Got a place have you? You and your ma?'

'Oh yes, just a room. But we won't be stopping there long. My boy friend is buying a flat for us.'

'What's his name, your boy friend?'

'Ernest. Ernest Hemingway.'

The name was received in a disparaging silence. Marlene said:

'You wouldn't get me going out with a feller called Ernest. My granddad was Ernest.'

'What's he like?' asked Black Shirl.

'The outdoor type really. He shoots and hunts a lot. And he likes bulls. Actually, he's getting rather a bore.'

She enjoyed fabricating the lies and soon learnt that they were infinitely credulous. Either nothing was too egregious to be unbelievable, or they didn't greatly care. Their own lives were made tolerable by fantasy; they had none of the pettiness which would grudge it to others. What did worry them, as it obviously did Sid, was the fact that she and her mother had presented their National Insurance cards for stamping. All the girls working in the chippie were drawing unemployment benefit. They felt vaguely threatened by this orthodoxy. Philippa found it necessary to explain:

'It's my probation officer. He knows I'm working. I can't put anything across on him.'

They looked at her pityingly. Probation officers were admittedly less gullible than local authority social workers, but this unreasonable docility lowered her in their eyes. Not by such naïvety did one survive in the urban jungle. Often she smiled to herself, remembering that Gabriel believed, or claimed to believe, that the weak, the sick and the ignorant preyed on the strong, the healthy and the intelligent. He could have found evidence enough at Sid's Plaice. But Philippa bent over the sink, her back aching, her skin sodden with steam, told herself that Gabriel's world could well survive the pathetic depredations of Marlene, Debbie and Black Shirl.

Two vivid and contrasting mental pictures came frequently into her mind: Gabriel calling for her one bright Saturday morning in the summer term, swinging himself out of his Lagonda, running up the steps of number 68, his cashmere sweater slung from his shoulders; Black Shirl humping to a corner of the kitchen the great bag of washing for her five children which she would wheel in a pram to the launderette on her way home. Perhaps Maurice's mind was patterned with equally vivid images, contrasts which had made him a Socialist and which, even now, kept him one, despite the knowledge, which surely he shared, that his creed would merely transfer the Lagonda to an owner equally, if differently, privileged and that there was no economic system in this world which would transfer the Lagonda to Shirl and the washing and the five children to Gabriel.

Once, when walking to the late-night bus, her mother asked:

'You don't think we exploit them?'

'How? Considering we get through twice the washing-up at our sink that they do at theirs, you could argue that they exploit us.'

'I suppose I mean that we pretend to be friendly, to be one of them, but back home we talk and laugh about them as if they're objects, interesting specimens.'

'But they are interesting specimens, more amusing and interesting than any we'd meet in the typical office. If they don't know how we talk about them does it matter?'

'Perhaps not to them. It might to us.'

After a few seconds silence, she said:

'Are you going to write about them?'

'That hadn't occurred to me. That isn't why we took the job. I suppose I'll file them in the subconscious until I need them.'

She half-expected her mother to ask, 'Will you file me there too?' But she said nothing, and for a little time they walked together in silence.

In the bus, her mother asked:

'How long do you suppose we ought to stay at Sid's?'

'As long as we're happy to live on fish and chips. I admit I sometimes wonder if they've any vacancies for washers-up at L'Ecu de France.'

'Is that where you used to eat?'

'Only on special occasions. That and the Gay Hussar and Mon Plaisir are Maurice's favourites. Bertorelli's was for every day. I used to meet him there for lunch sometimes. I love Bertorelli's.'

She wondered whether Maurice still ate there, and if Signor Bertorelli ever asked for her in that other world. Her mother said tentatively:

'We could stay for another week or so, perhaps, if you're not too tired or bored. I don't mind the fish. I rather like it.'

'I'm not in the least bored. And we can change jobs as soon as we are. We've got our cards nicely stamped up, and I suppose Sid would give us a reference if we twisted his arm. He doesn't give many bills, have you noticed? Two-thirds of his business is on a cash, no-tax basis. I daresay we'd only have to whisper that and he'd happily give us a year's pay in lieu of notice.'

'I don't think we ought to do that. He's been decent to us.'

'Anyway, we're free to go when we like. That's the fun of it. Just let me know when you're tired of fish.'

TEN

Their freedom did, indeed, seem to be limitless, stretching out in concentric waves from those three small rooms above Monty's Fruit and Veg to embrace the whole of London. The freedom of the city, of the lumpy grass under the elms of St James's Park where they would search for a spare length of grass among the knapsacks of the prone tourists, and lie on their backs, staring up through a dazzle of shivering green and silver and listening to the midday band concert. There would be a circle of deck chairs round the bandstand and here the regulars would sit having taken their seats early: large ladies from the suburbs and the provinces with their sandwiches, their summer hats, their plump, ringed fingers guarding bulging handbags on comfortable laps. When the drizzle began they would rummage in their bags and spread mackintoshes over their knees, unfold a concertina of thin plastic to cover their hats. Having paid their money for a deck chair, the vagaries of an English summer couldn't cheat them of their forty minutes of crashing brass, the red-braided uniforms, the conductor's brisk salute.

But for Philippa and her mother, despite these almost daily excursions, the core of their joint life lay in Delaney Street and Mell Street. Philippa told herself that she couldn't have found a better part of London in which to be anonymous. The district had a life of its own, but it was one in which the sense of community was fostered by seeing the same familiar faces, not by inquiring into their business. Delaney Street was a quiet cul-de-sac inhabited chiefly by the middle-aged or elderly living above their small family shops. It had something of the atmosphere of a self-sufficient, ancient and sleepy village, a sluggish backwater between the great surging rivers of the Marylebone Road and the Edgware Road. Many of its occupants, like Mr and Mrs Tookes at the junk shop, and the two eccentric Miss Peggs who spent their time perambulating in Mell Street, leading a string of small discouraged dogs, had been born in the street as had their parents before them. They formed a select and secretive coterie, much given to standing in each other's doorways, apparently wordlessly communicating, seeming to huddle themselves against the cold even on the warmest day, and viewing with dispassionate, amused or ironic eyes the casual visitors or newcomers like natives viewing the arrival of yet another wave of credulous and soon to be disillusioned settlers. Their chief preoccupation was the rumour and threat of a local authority development which would sweep their world away. They stared across at the corrugated fence of the wasteland with hard but troubled eyes. Philippa, always curious, got to know a little about them by casually discreet questions to George. She might have learned more had she and her mother drunk in the Blind Beggar, but they thought it prudent to keep apart; one could not patronize the local pub for long and remain private. But they felt accepted in the street. Their neighbours were always polite and sometimes friendly. They watched, occasionally they smiled, but they asked no questions.

Saturday was market day in Mell Street. By nine o'clock the police van had arrived, the barriers had been dragged out and were in place and the street was closed to through traffic. It was a small, intimate, bustling market, cosmopolitan but at the same time very English. The bargaining was carried out with humour and good nature, and occasionally in the old money. Early in the morning the seller of second-hand rugs and carpets wheeled up his great wooden barrow and patterned the road with his wares. Unregarding and unrebuked, the shoppers walked over them. The tarmac itself became festive. Later the market took on something of the atmosphere of an eastern souk when the brass-seller arrived to set out his jangling pots, and a Pakistani who sold cheap jewellery hung across his stall a swinging curtain of wooden beads. On the material stall lengths of brightly patterned cloth were spun from the great bales; the vendors of fruit and vegetables, fish and plants, meat and kitchenware bawled out their wares; the air was sickly with the smell from the hot-dog stall; and at a corner of the street a thin gentle-faced boy wearing a button, 'Jesus loves me', patiently held out his pamphlets to the unregarding crowd. Cats looped among the wooden trestles and stretched themselves in a rigid similitude of death on the woollen jumpers which spilled from the second-hand clothes stall while, outside the shops, the bright-eyed dogs quivered with excitement or crouched gently groaning, their eyes half closed against the sun. Philippa and her mother rummaged among the clothes stalls for hand-knitted woollens, some of them too worn to be used. Her mother would later unpick, then skein and wash the wool. There seemed always to be crinkled loops of wool drooping across the bath to dry. The boxes of odds and ends placed at the sides of the stalls yielded their treasures, including a tea-cloth of hand embroidered linen which they mended, washed and starched and used ceremoniously for Saturday afternoon tea.

Behind the stalls were the small shops; the old-fashioned draper where one could still buy woollen combinations and sleeved vests, and where the pink lace-up corsets hung in the window, their strings dangling; the Greek delicatessen smelling of syrup and sharp Mediterranean wine; the small general store, clean, sweet-smelling, perpetually dark, with a bell on the door where old Mrs Davies shuffled in from the shadows to serve them with milk, butter and tea; the larger of the half-dozen junk shops whose cluttered interior they would penetrate through to a back yard piled with old furniture and fitted along one wall with racks where a miscellany of crockery, pans and pictures offered the chance of a find. Here it was they uncovered two uncracked cups, one early Worcester, one Staffordshire, with chipped but matching saucers, and an agreeably shaped grime-covered dish which, after washing, was revealed as blue and white seventeenth-century Swansea pottery. It was like playing at housekeeping; the re-enactment of the innocent childhood games which neither of them had known.

Philippa had still learned almost nothing of her mother's past. From time to time they would talk briefly about her mother's life in prison, but nothing about the crime and nothing about their earliest and shared years. Philippa asked no questions. She told herself that L. P. Hartley was right; the past was another country and they could choose whether to visit there. Her mother didn't choose and she had no right to compel her, vulnerable as she was to travel that stony road. She had been given the account of the murder, she told herself that, for the present, it must be enough. She couldn't use her possession of the flat, her companionship, her defence against the noisy intrusions of this new world to purchase a confidence which wasn't freely offered. There was no commitment and that meant no commitment on either side. But she found that she was visualizing less and less a future in which they would be completely apart. She had virtually compelled her mother to share a flat with her because she needed to discover her own identity. She was discovering it, and in ways which she had neither expected nor planned. Discovering her mother's identity was another matter and it could wait. There was no hurry to explore the past; experiencing the present was interesting enough, and they had, after all, their whole lives before them.

ELEVEN

After ten days her mother's probation officer came to the flat. Philippa knew that the visit was inevitable, a condition of her mother's licence, yet she prepared herself to dislike him. He had written to say when he would arrive, and she arranged to take their sheets to the launderette, ostensibly so that her mother and he could talk in private, but really in the hope of avoiding an introduction. But when she returned and put the key in the lock she could hear her mother's voice, clear, ordinary, even animated.

He was in the kitchen, drinking tea from a mug. She found herself shaking hands with a mild-eyed, stocky young man with a russet, tangled beard and balding head. He wore blue jeans and a fawn sweat-shirt. His sandalled feet were brown and surprisingly clean. Everything about him was clean. Some of Maurice's colleagues dressed with just such informality, but with them it was an ostentation, a desire to demonstrate their solidarity with their students. She felt that this man dressed to suit himself. Her mother introduced him but her mind blocked the words from her consciousness. She wanted none of him, not even his name.

He had brought with him an African violet which he had grown himself from a cutting. Watching him help her mother to pot it, she knew that she resented him, resented her mother's docile acceptance of this mild but degrading surveillance, resented his intrusion on their privacy. And she knew herself to be jealous. She was looking after her mother. They were looking after each other. They didn't need the bureaucratic, carefully rationed caring of the State. Later during the visit, when he and her mother had been discussing the pots of herbs growing on the kitchen window, and her mother had gone to find a pencil and paper to write down some of the names, she said:

'Don't you think that after ten years society could leave my mother alone? She isn't a danger to anyone; you must know that.'

He said gently:

'Licence has to be the same for everyone. The law can't make fish of one and fowl of the other.'

'But what good do you hope to do? Not to my mother; I know the answer there. What good do you do for your more ordinary clients? You do call them clients, don't you? I mean, you are a kind of emotional bank manager.'

He ignored the last question and answered the first.

'Not much. It's more a question of not doing them harm, trying to help them not to do themselves harm.'

'But what exactly do you do?'

'The Statute says, "advise, assist and befriend".'

'But you can't befriend someone by Act of Parliament. How could anyone, even the most deprived, be satisfied with or deceived by that kind of friendship, a spurious second-best?'

'Second-best is all that most people ever have. People manage with very little; friendship as well as money. I rely on their good will more than they do on mine. Your parsley's doing very well. It won't grow for us. Did you start this from seed?'

'No. It's a root we got from the health-food shop in Baker Street.'

She picked a small bunch for him, glad to give an exchange for the violet. That way they needn't feel under an obligation to him. He took the parsley, and washing his handkerchief under the hot tap of the kitchen sink, rinsed it with cold water and folded the leaves carefully inside it. His hands were large, snub-fingered. He used them, gently, unfussily. When he bent over the sink his sweat-shirt rode up to reveal a few inches of smooth flesh, brown and speckled as an egg. She felt a sudden desire to touch it, and found herself wondering what he would be like in bed. Gabriel had made love as if he were a ballet dancer, narcissistically preoccupied with his body, every movement an exercise in control. He performed as if thinking, 'This is a necessary, unaesthetic business; but see how I contrive to give it grace.' She thought that this man would be different, gentle but direct, free of pretence, free of guilt. After he had wrapped the parsley, he said:

'Mara will be glad of that. Thanks.'

She supposed that Mara was his wife or girl friend. She knew that if she had asked he would have told her; but he never volunteered information. He seemed to view himself and his world with commonsense detachment, accepting kindness at its face value, as if kindness was a common currency of life, answering questions simply, as if unaware of the devious motives from which they sprang. Perhaps in his job it was necessary for survival to take people at their face value too. He hadn't reacted to her obvious antagonism, yet he didn't give her the impression that he was exercising any particular control. She thought that his attitude could be summed up: 'We're all of the same blood, and we're in the same shipwreck. Recriminations, explanations, panic are all a waste of time. Safety requires only that we act towards each other with love.'

She was glad when, at the end of the visit, he said to her mother:

'In about a month's time then. Perhaps you'd rather drop in at the office. I'm out visiting or in court most days, but you'll find me there Tuesdays and Fridays, nine to twelve-thirty.'

She was glad that he wasn't coming back, that the flat would once again be their own. Apart from George, when he had helped her lug up some furniture, and Joyce Bungeld's brief visit, he was the only other person who had set foot in it. She felt, too, that she wasn't ready yet to cope with someone who might – intriguing and unsettling thought – be naturally good.

TWELVE

In the evenings at weekends, or on Mondays when they didn't work, they often watched television together, carrying the two basket chairs from their bedrooms into the kitchen. Watching television was something of a novelty for Philippa. Working for her O- and A-levels and the Cambridge Scholarship had taken most of her time, and the television at Caldecote Terrace was seldom switched on. Maurice, like a number of pundits who never refused an invitation to appear, affected to despise all but a few minority-taste programmes. Now she and her mother became mildly addicted to the risible awfulness of a family drama series in which the characters apparently physically and mentally unscathed by the traumas of the last episode, were resurrected weekly, freshly coiffured, their wounds healed and scarless, for yet another emotional and physical blood-bath. Such a convenient ability to live for the moment with its subliminal message that the past could literally be put behind one had much to recommend it. There ought, she thought, to be a word coined to describe the frank enjoyment to be had from the reassuring second-rate. And that was how, switching the set on too early, they caught the last ten minutes of Maurice's encounter with the Bishop.

Maurice looked relaxed, perfectly at home in this milieu, swivelling gently in the aggressively modern chair of chrome and black leather, one leg thrown lightly over the other. Philippa recognized the pattern of his socks, the discreet arrow pointing the ankle, the gleam of hand-made leather shoes. He was particular about his clothes. The Bishop, stiffly upright in the twin chair, looked less comfortable. He was a large man. His pectoral cross, insignificant in thin silver, rested crookedly against the episcopal purple. She despised him for this timid affirmation of faith. A talisman, if one went in for these things, should be heavy, beautiful and worn with panache. He had obviously been trapped into fighting on his weakest ground and his heavy face wore the embarrassed, slightly ashamed and conciliatory half-smile of a man who knows that he is letting down the side, but hopes that no one but himself will have noticed it.

Maurice was in excellent form. She anticipated each of the well-remembered mannerisms, the sudden twitch of the left shoulder, the lift of the head away from his opponent, the sudden clasp of his bony hands over the right knee and the hunching of the shoulders as if he were bending his mind to the nub of the argument. None of these antics had anything to do with nervousness. They were the extrovert pantomime of the interaction of mind and body, both too restless to be confined within this trendy contraption of steel and leather, the enclosing cardboard walls with their carefully designed title for the series, 'Dissent'. His voice was reedier than normal, a pedant's voice.

'Well, let's just recapitulate what you're asking us to believe. That God, who you say is a spirit, which I take to mean is incorporate – doesn't one of your creeds say without shape, form or passions? – has created man in His own image. That man has sinned. I won't hold you to that fable of some celestial Kew Garden and forbidden Cox's Orange Pippin – let's use your own words, that he's fallen short of the glory of God. That every child coming into the world is contaminated with this primeval sin through no fault of his own. That God, instead of demanding in expiation a bloody sacrifice from man, sent His only son into the world to be tortured and done to death in the most barbaric fashion in order to propitiate His Father's desire for vengeance and to reconcile man to his creator. That this son was born of a virgin. Incidentally, you told us last week that sex was somehow sacred because ordained by God, and I confess to finding it curious that He despised the orthodox method of procreation which He Himself devised and presumably approves. We are asked to believe that this miraculously born, God-made man lived and died without sin to atone for man's first disobedience. Now we may not have a great deal of historical evidence about the life of Jesus of Nazareth, but we do know quite a lot about Roman methods of capital punishment. Neither you nor I, I'm happy to say, have witnessed a crucifixion, but we can agree that as a method of execution it was agonising, degrading, slow, bestial and bloody. If you or I actually saw a victim being hauled on to that cross and could get him down – provided, of course, that we didn't risk anything by interfering – I don't think we could prevent ourselves from trying to save him. But the God of Love was apparently content to let it happen, indeed, willed it to happen, and to His only son. You can't ask us to believe in a God of Love who behaves less compassionately than would the least of his creatures. I no longer have a son, but that is hardly my idea of parental love.'

Her mother got up and, without speaking, turned down the sound. She said:

'What does he mean, he no longer has a son?'

'He did once, but Orlando was killed in a road accident with his mother. That's why Maurice and Hilda took me on.'

It was the first time that her adoptive parents had been mentioned between them and she waited, curious to see if this was the moment when their silence would be broken, whether her mother would ask about those lost ten years, whether she had been happy at Caldecote Terrace, where she had gone to school, what kind of life she had led. But she only said:

'Is that how he brought you up, as an atheist?'

'Well, he told me when I was about nine that religion was nonsense and that only fools believed it and then made it clear that I must think its tenets out for myself and make up my own mind. I don't think he has ever been a believer.'

'Well, he believes now, or why does he hate God so much? He wouldn't be so vehement if the Bishop were inviting him to believe in pixies or the theories of the flat-earthers. Poor Bishop! He could only win by saying things that he'd be too embarrassed to utter and which neither the BBC nor the viewers – especially the Christians – would in the least wish to hear.'

What things? she wondered. She said:

'Do you believe?'

Her mother answered:

'Oh, yes, I believe.' She glanced towards the screen where Maurice, still articulating, had been reduced to a silent and ridiculously posturing cypher. 'The Bishop doesn't know for certain, but loves what he thinks he believes. Your father knows and hates what he knows. I believe, but I can't love any more. He and I are the unlucky ones.'

Philippa wanted to ask: 'What do you believe? What difference does it make?' She felt the mixture of excitement, curiosity and apprehension of someone putting a first tentative foot on dangerous and uncertain ground. She said:

'But you can't believe in hell.'

'You can once you've been in it.'

'But I thought anything is forgivable. I mean, isn't that the whole point of it? You can't place yourselves beyond the mercy of God. I thought Christians only had to ask.'

'You have to believe.'

'Well, you do believe, you've just said so. That's lucky for you. I don't.'

'There has to be contrition.'

'What's so difficult about that? Feeling sorry. I should have thought that was the easiest part.'

'Not sorry because you did something and the results have been unpleasant for you. Not just wishing that you hadn't done it. That's easy. Contrition means saying "I did that thing. I was responsible."'

'Well, is that so difficult? It seems a fair exchange if you can get instant forgiveness and eternal life thrown in for good measure.'

'I can't spend ten years explaining to myself that I wasn't responsible, that I couldn't have prevented myself doing what I did, and then when I'm free, as free as I'll ever be, when society thinks I've been punished enough, when everyone has lost interest, then I can't decide that it would be pleasant to have God's forgiveness as well.'

'I don't see why not. Remember Heine's last words: "*Dieu me pardonnera, c'est son métier.*"'

Her mother didn't reply. Her face had the closed withdrawn

look of someone who finds the conversation painful or distasteful. Philippa went on.

'Why don't you like talking about religion?'

'You've managed very well without it so far.'

She glanced towards the television set, then suddenly rose and switched it off. The Bishop's benign, embarrassed face dissolved into a diminishing square of light. Then another and more personal thought fell into Philippa's mind. She asked:

'Was I christened?'

'Yes.'

'You never told me.'

'You never asked before.'

'What did you call me?'

'Rose, after your father's mother. Your father called you Rosie. But you know that your name is Rose. It's on your birth certificate. Before your adoption you were Rose Ducton.'

'I'll make the coffee.'

Her mother seemed about to speak, then changed her mind. She went out of the kitchen and into her own room. Philippa took down the two mugs from the kitchen shelf. Her hands were shaking. She put them on the table and tried to fill the kettle. Of course she had known that her name was Rose, had known it as soon as she had opened that innocuous-looking official envelope and had taken out her birth certificate. But then it had been just another label. She had hardly taken it in, except to notice that Maurice, in relegating it to second place, had nevertheless allowed her to retain something from her past. The edge of the kettle rattled against the tap. Carefully she placed it on the draining board and stood bent, clasping the cold edge of the sink as if fighting nausea. Rose Ducton. Rosie Ducton. Philippa Rose Palfrey. A row of books with Rose Ducton on the spine. It was a trisyllabic cypher, having nothing to do with her. I baptize you in the name of the Father and of the Son and of the Holy Ghost. A trickle of water running over her forehead. It could hardly have been of any real importance since Maurice could wipe it away with a stroke of his pen. Where, she wondered, had she been christened; in that dull suburban church in Seven Kings under the stunted travesty of a spire? Rose. It didn't even suit her. It was a name in a catalogue; Peace, Scarlet Wonder, Albertine. She had thought that she had got used to the knowledge that nothing about her was real, not even her name. Why, then, was she so shaken now?

She had control of the trembling now and, careful as a child entrusted with an unfamiliar task, she filled the kettle. Rose. It was strange that her mother hadn't once called her by that name, hadn't once inadvertently let it slip, the name which, after all, she had chosen, or at least had accepted for her baby, the name which she had used for eight years, the name which she must have had in mind during the last ten years of solitude and survival. If she believed in God, that strange eccentricity which she Philippa – she Rose – would have to explore, she must have used that word in her prayers, if she did pray. God bless Rosie. It must have taken a disciplined effort from their first meeting always to remember to call her Philippa. Every time she spoke that new Maurice-bestowed name she was playing a part, being less than honest. No, that wasn't fair. And it was stupid to mind so much. What did it matter? But she wished that her mother had, just for once, forgotten to be careful and had called her by her right name.

THIRTEEN

The loneliness descended on him soon after breakfast, as dragging and exhausting as a physical weight. It was the more disturbing because it was so unexpected. Loneliness was a state he had got used to since Mavis's death and he hadn't expected to feel it again as a positive emotion nor to be visited by its sad aftermath of restlessness and boredom. By eleven o'clock Mrs Palfrey hadn't appeared and he thought it now unlikely that she would. It had been the same last Sunday. Perhaps this was the day when they went out together, leaving by car from the carriage road at the back of the terrace which his investigations had shown led to a row of garages. Without her to follow there was little chance of shaking off this weight of ennui. His life had become so linked with hers, his routine tied to her daily perambulations that, when she didn't appear, he felt deprived as if of her actual company.

The hotel was full; a new package-tour of Spaniards had

arrived on Saturday evening and service for the rest of the guests was perfunctory. The dining-room was a jabber of excited voices, the hall obstructed with their luggage. Mario gabbled, gesticulated, rushed frantically from reception desk to dining-room. Glad to get away from the crush, Scase had settled himself early at his bedroom window with his binoculars trained on number 68, but with no real hope of seeing her. It was a morning of alternate rain and sunshine. Fierce and sudden squalls slashed at the window, then as suddenly ceased; the nudging clouds parted and the pavement steamed as the sun reappeared, hot and bright. By half-past eleven restlessness got the better of him and he went downstairs in search of coffee. Violet was at the switchboard as usual, the dog at her feet. Needing to hear a human voice, he said something to her about the pleasure of seeing the sun, then stopped appalled at his tactlessness. He should have said feeling the sun. She smiled, her sightless eyes seeking the echo of his voice. Then to his surprise he heard himself say:

'I thought of going to Regent's Park this afternoon to look at the roses. You go off duty at midday on Sunday, don't you? Would you and Coffee care to come?'

'That would be nice. Thank you. We'd both like it.'

Her hand found the dog's head and pressed it. The animal stirred and pricked its ears, bright eyes fixed on her face.

'And would you like to have some dinner first? Lunch I mean?'

She flushed and nodded. She seemed pleased. He saw that, under her fawn woollen cardigan, she was wearing what looked like a new summer dress in blue cotton. After he had spoken she stroked the skirt gently with both hands and smiled as if glad that she had taken the trouble to put it on. He told himself that having committed one folly, he had now embarked on a second. But it was too late now to draw back and he didn't really want to. Then he wondered where he would take her for luncheon. There was a small sandwich bar off Victoria Street which he used occasionally during the week but he wasn't sure whether it would be open on a Sunday. It was very clean but not at all smart. Then he remembered that the shabbiness of its cramped partitions wouldn't matter since she couldn't see them, and was ashamed that the thought had entered his mind. It was wrong to cheat her just because she was blind. He must try to make the occasion special for her. After all, she would be doing more for him than she knew. And she would be the first woman other than Mavis whom he had taken out since the day of his marriage. Admittedly she was blind. But then, if she hadn't been blind, she wouldn't have accepted his invitation. He remembered that there was an Italian restaurant fairly close to the station. Perhaps that would be open on Sunday. At least Coffee wouldn't be any problem. Children, he had noticed, were seldom welcomed, but nobody minded a dog.

The day brightened for him. It was time he took a day off, time too that he walked and talked with another human being. He made arrangements with her to call for her at the desk just before twelve and went back to his room. As he unlocked his room door it struck him that there would be little point this morning in taking with him his rucksack with the accoutrements of murder and he wondered whether it would really be safe to leave it in his locked room. But the rucksack had become almost part of him. He felt that he would walk strangely without its familiar weight on his right shoulder. And why shouldn't he take it? It occurred to him that he had by impulse chosen the best possible person as companion on his walk. She wouldn't wonder what he was carrying in the rucksack. She wouldn't ask. And after the killing, if things did go wrong and the police traced him to the Casablanca, she was the one person they wouldn't ask to identify him.

FOURTEEN

After breakfast, on 27th August, their second Sunday together, her mother said abruptly:

'Do you mind if we go to church?'

Philippa, surprised, managed to respond as if this were the most usual of requests. She had gone through a phase of sermon tasting and felt herself as well qualified to recommend a church for its service and music as she was to discuss its architecture. She inquired what her mother had in mind: the ordered ceremonial and beautifully balanced choir of Marylebone parish church?

High Anglican Mass at All Saints', Margaret Street, in a dazzle of mosaics, gilded saints and stained glass? The Baroque splendours of St Paul's? Her mother said that she would like somewhere quiet and close, so they went to the eleven o'clock Sung Eucharist in the cool, uncluttered interior of Sir Ninian Comper's St Cyprian's where an all-male choir sang the liturgy in plainsong from the balcony, a gentle-voiced priest preached an uncompromisingly Catholic sermon and the incense rose pungent and sweet, clouding the high altar. Philippa sat throughout the prayers, but with her head slightly bowed since she had, after all, chosen to be there and politeness dictated at least a token compliance. They hadn't compelled her in; why make an offensive parade of unbelief when neither belief nor disbelief mattered. And it was, after all, no hardship to listen to Cranmer's prose, or as much of it as the revisers had left unmutilated. From these sonorous, antiphonal cadences Jane Austen, on her deathbed, receiving the sacrament from her brother's hands, had taken comfort. That fact alone was enough to silence irreverence. Watching her mother's bent head and clasped hands, she wondered what communication she was making to her god. Once, she thought, 'Perhaps she's praying for me' and the idea was obscurely gratifying. But although she herself couldn't pray, she liked to sing the hymns. The sound of her soaring voice always surprised her. It was a rich contralto, deeper than her speaking voice, unrecognizable as her own, the expression, it seemed, of a part of her personality unrestrained and unpredictable, only released by poor metric verse and cheerfully nostalgic school-assembly tunes.

Her mother didn't move forward to the altar when the time came for the faithful to eat and drink their god, and she slipped out, Philippa following, during the last hymn. That way, as Philippa realized, there could be no risk that the priest or members of the congregation would introduce themselves, or try to make the strangers feel welcome. Whatever this strange, unsacramental, religious life meant to her mother, it could never include coffee in the parish room, or cosy valedictory gossip in the porch; and for that, at least, she could be grateful. Closing the porch door behind them softly as the last hymn drew to its close, they decided not to bother with cooking lunch, but to stay out as long as possible while the weather was fine. They would find themselves somewhere cheap to eat in Baker Street, then spend the afternoon in Regent's Park.

Although they lived so close, it was the first time that they had visited the park. The early morning rain had stopped and high sunlit clouds drifted imperceptibly across a sky of clear blue which deepened to mauve over a cluster of distant trees across the lake. The geraniums and ivy planted each side of the metal bridge trailed down to the water and the rowers laughed, rocking their skiffs as the fronds brushed their faces. The park was coming to life after the rain. Deck chairs, stacked under the trees for shelter, were brought out again. Their legs sank into the moist grass as little family groups settled into them to contemplate rose beds, distant vistas and the comforting proximity of toilets and the coffee house. Staid Sunday promenaders paced with their leashed dogs between the lavender and the delphiniums, and the queue at the coffee-house lengthened. In Queen Mary's rose garden the roses, plumped by the rain, held the last drops between delicate streaked petals, pink Harrinny, bright yellow Summer Sunshine, Ena Harkness and Peace.

While her mother wandered among the bushes, Philippa sat on one of the benches under a great swag of small white roses and took from her shoulder-bag the pocket edition of Donne's poems picked up for ten pence from a stall in the market. The roses swung gently above her head, thick as May blossom, dropping their sweetness and an occasional shower of small white petals and golden stamens on to the clovered grass. The sun was warm on her face, inducing a gentle lethargic melancholy. She couldn't remember when last she had visited Queen Mary's rose garden, perhaps never. Maurice preferred buildings to nature, even nature as disciplined, organized and formally displayed as Regent's Park. There was one rose garden which she could remember, but that had been at Pennington and her imagined father had been there, coming towards her through the enclosing circle of green. Odd that so clear a memory, scent, warmth and mellow afternoon light, recalled with peculiar intensity, almost with pain, should be nothing but a childish fantasy. But this garden, this park were real enough, and Maurice was right about architecture. Nature needed the contrast, the discipline of brick and stone. The colonnades and pediments of John Nash's terraces, the eccentric outline of the zoo, even the technical phallus of the Post Office Tower soaring above the hedges, contributed to the park's beauty, defined it and set its limits. It would, she thought, be intolerable to contemplate this lush perfection stretching to infinity, a never-ending, corrupted Garden of Eden.

She lowered her eyes from contemplating the swinging roses to watch her mother. She was always watching her mother, who had, she supposed, exchanged one kind of surveillance for another. She was smelling an orange-red rose, cupping the flower gently in her hand. Most of the rose worshippers closed their eyes to savour the scent; she opened hers wider. She had a look of intense concentration, the facial muscles drawn and taut as if racked with pain. She was standing a little apart, quite motionless, oblivious of everything except the rose resting in her palm.

It was then that Philippa saw the man. He had come up the sloping path from the lake, a small, spectacled, grey-haired man solicitously accompanying a blind woman with a coffee-coloured guide dog. His glance fell on her, their eyes met and instinctively, and out of the lazy pleasure of the moment, she smiled at him. The result was extraordinary. He stood transfixed, eyes widened, in what seemed a second of incredulous terror. Then he turned abruptly away and, taking the woman by the elbow, almost forced her back down the path and towards the lake. Philippa laughed aloud. He was a plain little man, ordinary but not repulsive, and surely not so plain that no woman before had ever spontaneously smiled at him. Perhaps he thought that she was trying to pick him up, a summer temptress lurking under the swinging roses. She watched the odd couple out of sight, wondering about their relationship, whether he was the girl's father, what excuse he was giving her for so abruptly hurrying her away. Then she thought that she might have seen him somewhere before, but the memory was elusive. His, after all, was hardly a memorable face. But the feeling that she ought to have recognized him was frustrating. She bent her eyes again to her book and put him resolutely out of her mind.

FIFTEEN

Violet Hedley said, her voice sharp with anxiety:

'What is it? What happened? Are you all right?'

His grip must have tightened painfully on her elbow. Or was it that she had smelled the sudden reek of excitement and fear? People said that the blind had an extra sense. He slackened his pace.

'I'm sorry. Nothing's wrong. It's just that I saw someone unexpectedly, a man I used to work with in the accounts office. I didn't want to have to talk to him.'

She was silent. It occurred to him that she might think that he was embarrassed to be seen with her, and he added quickly:

'I've never liked him. He was rather officious, a bit of a bully. You know the kind. I didn't want him to see me. I didn't want to have to speak to him.'

She said gently:

'He must have made you very unhappy.'

'Not really. Not too unhappy. But it was a shock seeing him so unexpectedly. I thought that part of my life was behind me for good. There are some rather nice yellow roses in this bed. I'll find the label and tell you what they're called.'

She said:

'They're called Summer Sunshine.'

It had been hard to keep his voice steady. He felt sick with disappointment. They were there together. He had seen the murderess bending over one of the rose bushes in that second as he turned abruptly away. He had found them at last and he was helpless, tied, prevented from following them. And it was an ideal opportunity. Like the girl, he could have found a seat and sat there innocently in the sun watching them. The park was getting more crowded every minute. When at last they decided to leave for home nothing would have been easier than to tail them, one anonymous man among the crowd. He could have used his binoculars if necessary. Many of the tourists wore them and trained them occasionally on the more exotic water fowl. Time, place, chance were all in his favour and he had to let them go. For a moment he toyed with the idea of deserting Violet, making some excuse, planting her on a seat and promising to return. But he couldn't do it, and he was ashamed of the impulse. And after all, he had to return to the hotel and so did she. She would expect some explanation of his desertion and there was none he could give. But, worst of all, Philippa Palfrey had seen him, had actually smiled at him, might recall his face if she saw him again.

The smile, in its spontaneity, its openness, its frank asexual comradeship, had appalled him. It had seemed too like an invitation to a shared happiness in the warmth of the day, the scent of the rose-drenched air, the physical joy of living; an acknowledgement of a common humanity, a kinship of pleasure which he repudiated, most of all from her. But had it been as simple as that? As they made their slow way back to the hotel, not speaking, he tried to recall that moment from which he had turned away with such instinctive horror. Surely he couldn't have been mistaken? It had been a smile of spontaneous pleasure, nothing more. She couldn't have known who he was, couldn't have guessed his purpose. Surely it was madness to persuade himself even for a moment that what he had seen had been a smile of complicity, of shared knowledge?

But one thing was certain. It had spoilt the day for Violet Hedley. It had started so well. She had enjoyed her meal and they had been happy together in the park. He had found himself talking to her without strain. But that was over. Even Coffee lurched along beside them, dejected, tail drooping. And he had learned his lesson. From now on he must learn to bear his loneliness. To move, however cautiously, into the ordinary world of friendship, of caring, of shared confidences, could be fatal. He was totally alone and that was how it must be. He must keep himself unencumbered for the task in hand.

SIXTEEN

And then, at last, on Thursday 31st August, she led him to them. The day had started like any other with himself at his room window, binoculars trained on the door of number 68. Mr Palfrey left as usual at quarter-past nine. He noted the time on his wristwatch. It wasn't important, but he had grown into this habit of timing every move as if he were a fictional spy. Three minutes later he saw the woman. At once it struck him that there was something different about her, and he saw that she wasn't carrying her string shopping bag or trundling the trolley. All she had with her was a large old-fashioned handbag. She wore a fawn-coloured coat, undistinguished in cut, and a little too long for fashion, instead of her usual cardigan, and her face was obscured by an immense headscarf patterned in blue and white. There was only a gentle humming wind and the day wasn't cold; perhaps she wanted to keep her hair tidy. Most surprisingly, she was wearing fawn gloves, a touch of formality which reinforced his impression that this outing was different, that some attempt had been made at smartness.

He grabbed his rucksack and followed quickly. She was only fifty yards ahead and he saw that she was making her way towards Victoria. As he followed her across Eccleston Bridge and down the side of the station he worried in case she intended to join the queue for taxis at the front entrance and was relieved when she turned instead down the entrance to the Underground. She took a ticket from the thirty-five-pence machine. He found that he hadn't a fivepenny piece and there were two young tourists, rucksack laden, who, pushing ahead of him, had already inserted ten pence and were taking their time over finding the necessary coins. But he had two tenpenny pieces ready in his hand. He inserted them quickly in the next machine and was able to follow a few yards behind her through the barrier and down to the Victoria line.

He kept as close behind her on the escalator as he dared, afraid that she might just catch a train; but he heard with relief a receding rumble before either of them reached the platform. The next came quickly, and the carriage was only half-full. He took a seat close to the door, but distanced from her. She sat very still, unrelaxed, her eyes fixed on the opposite advertisements, feet together, gloved hands in her lap. She looked tense, preoccupied. Was it his imagination that she was bracing herself for some ordeal, rigid with the self-absorption of a victim on her way to a dreaded medical examination or a crucial interview?

She changed at Oxford Circus and he followed her on the long track to the northbound Bakerloo line. Never once did she glance behind her. She got out at Marylebone and he followed her up the escalator clutching the fifty-pence piece in his hand and suddenly worried that the collector might be desultory in giving him change for the outstanding fare. But all went well. The thirty-five pence were speedily and nonchalantly pressed into his hand and he was through the barrier before she was half way across the concourse of Marylebone Station. Again, to his relief, she ignored the queue of three or four people at the taxi rank and made her way north towards Marylebone Road.

Here he let himself fall back a little. The crossing lights were against her and a solid stream of vehicles in both directions blocked her way. He guessed that it might be some time before the lights changed and he didn't want to stand close to her, the two of them alone at the crossing signal. But it was important to cross when she did. If he lost the lights there might be several minutes in which she could be lost in the criss-cross of streets south of the great divide of Marylebone Road. But again, all went well. He was only a few yards behind her as they crossed together, but she seemed unaware of his presence. She turned into Seymour Place.

And here was her destination, an imposing stone building with an elaborately carved coat of arms above the cornice. A name plate told him that this was the Inner London Juvenile Court. Mrs Palfrey disappeared through the open double green door through which there came a babble of childish voices as piercingly discordant as a school playground. He walked on pondering his next move. Obviously she was neither a delinquent nor the mother of one. He knew that she didn't work here. That meant that she must be either a witness or a juvenile magistrate. The latter seemed to him unlikely, but in either case he had no way of knowing when she would emerge. At last he went resolutely inside and asked the policeman on duty if he could watch the proceedings. The answer was a polite no; the general public were not admitted to a juvenile court. He said:

'A friend of mine, a Miss Yelland, is one of the witnesses. I forget the name of the case, but I said I'd meet her here when it was over. When are they likely to finish?'

'Depends on the list, sir. And there's more than one juvenile bench sitting. If it is a defended case she could be here a long time. But they should all be through by mid to late afternoon.'

He returned to the Marylebone Road. There was a seat beside the bus stop and he sat there to consider his next step. Would there be any point in killing time until Mrs Palfrey left at the end of the day? On reflection he decided that this was what he must do. After all, if what he believed were true, and the murderess and the girl were living together in this area, somewhere near to Regent's Park, Mrs Palfrey was reasonably close to them for the first time since he had been trailing her. There was always the chance that she would visit them on her way home. He would return in the late afternoon and wait for her to come out. It wouldn't be an easy doorway to keep watch on. There were no convenient bookshops opposite in which he could pretend to browse. He would have to return in good time and then walk slowly up and down Seymour Place, never out of sight of the courtroom entrance, yet never loitering so close that his presence would arouse interest. The slow parade, the need for constant watchfulness, would be tedious, but it shouldn't be too difficult to avoid suspicion. This was no village street with peering eyes behind the curtains. As long as he kept quietly walking, crossing the road from time to time at the traffic lights, it was unlikely that his comings and goings would be noticed. And what if they were? He told himself that he was getting unnecessarily careful. There were only three people from whom he must keep his presence secret and one of them was inside that building. In the meantime he decided to spend a couple of hours in the public library on Marylebone Road – the girl was someone who bought books and might even turn up there – and then walk in Regent's Park and revisit the rose garden. There was sure to be a place in upper Baker Street where he could buy a sandwich and coffee for lunch. He looked at his wrist-watch. It was now nearly ten o'clock. Shifting his rucksack more firmly on his shoulder he turned right towards Baker Street.

SEVENTEEN

She had never really wanted to sit on the juvenile Bench, but

Maurice had suggested with the persuasive force of a command that she ought to have what he described as 'some interest outside the kitchen,' and the wife of one of his colleagues, herself a magistrate, had suggested the juvenile Bench and had put her name forward. Maurice had said:

'You ought to be able to make a useful contribution. The Bench is stolidly upper middle class, self-perpetuating. They need shaking out of some of their comfortable misconceptions. And most of them haven't an idea what sort of lives their clients lead. You'll bring to the job a different experience.'

He meant, she knew, that she could bring to the job the experience of living in a small terraced house in the poorest part of Ruislip, of a comprehensive school education, of being the only child of working class parents who hung their window curtains patterned side outward because what determined conduct and comfort was what the neighbours thought, whose highest ambition for her had been a job as a bank clerk, who saved up to take their annual holiday in the same boarding house at Brighton.

Sitting on the left of the chairman under the royal coat of arms, none of it seemed particularly relevant. Lady Dorothy, with whom she usually sat, brought to the job the experience of living in Eaton Square with weekends in a converted seventeenth-century rectory in Norfolk. Yet Lady Dorothy, if she didn't share the lives of the children and parents who stood before her in varying attitudes of resignation, sullenness or fear, seemed to have no difficulty in sharing their feelings. She dealt with them with a brisk common sense, tempered with more sensitivity than her heavy tweed-clad body and gruff arrogant voice would suggest. Scanning the social inquiry report with its mention of a common law husband in prison, of too many children and too little of everything else, she would lean forward and say briskly to the mother of the boy before her:

'I see your husband's not at home at present. That must make it hard for you with four boys. And this office cleaning job you're doing at Holborn; that's a long journey for you. How do you go, on the Central line?'

And the woman, apparently sensing an interest and compassion which the voice certainly didn't convey to Hilda, would crouch forward eagerly on the edge of her chair and pour it all out as if the courtroom had suddenly emptied and there was no one there except herself and Lady Dorothy: how that, yes, it had been hard, and that Wayne was a good boy at home only he missed his dad and had got in with the Billings gang, and how he wouldn't go to school because of the bullying and she'd tried taking him but it meant losing an hour's pay because she was supposed to start work at eight o'clock and, anyway, he only ran off again after the roll had been taken, and how her journey was all right except that she had to change at Oxford Circus and it was expensive because the tube fares had gone up and it was no use going by bus because they weren't all that reliable in the mornings.

Lady Dorothy would nod as if she had spent all her life changing at Oxford Circus to get to her cleaning job at Holborn. But some communication passed between them. An impulse of sympathy, if unspoken, was acknowledged and understood. The woman felt better at the end of it, and so, she supposed, did Lady Dorothy. Hilda remembered having overheard the words of a fellow justice:

'She treats them all as if they were wives of her father's gamekeepers, but it seems to work.'

But what made every sitting of the juvenile court a long-drawn-out purgatory for Hilda was not her inadequacy as a Justice – she was used to inadequacy by now – but her terror of blushing. It was worse some days than others, but she could never hope entirely to escape its anguish. At some stage in the proceedings, early or late, she knew that it was going to happen, that nothing could stop it; not willpower, not desperate prayer, and not the pathetic expedients she had devised to try to conceal it: the hand casually held up to shield her forehead as if in deep thought, the studious examination of her papers so that the hair hung over her cheeks, a paroxysm of simulated coughing, her handkerchief held to her face. She would feel first the clutch of fear at the heart, as physical as pain, and then it would begin, the burning flush spreading over her neck, mottling her face and forehead, a scarlet deformity of shame. She felt that every eye in the courtroom was fixed on her. The child with his parents, fidgeting in his chair, the clerk lifting his head from the court register to stare in wonder, the social workers watching with their pitying professional eyes, the chairman briefly pausing to glance at her before averting his eyes in embarrassment, the attendant police, stolidly gazing at her with their dead, controlled faces. And then the red pulsating tide would recede, leaving her momentarily as cold and cleansed as a wave-scoured beach.

Today she had managed to get through the morning session without too much trauma. The court rose at one and it was then the custom for the three magistrates to lunch together at a small Italian restaurant in Crawford Street. This morning her fellow magistrates were Group Captain Carter and Miss Belling. The Group Captain was a grey-haired, stiff-moving punctilious man who treated her with an old-fashioned courtesy which she could sometimes mistake for kindness. Miss Belling, forthright and keen-eyed behind her immense horn-rimmed spectacles, was the senior English mistress at one of the outer London comprehensive schools. She made Hilda feel like a not particularly bright fourth-former, but as this accorded with her private view of herself she didn't resent it. Neither of them was particularly frightening and she might almost have enjoyed her lasagne and beaujolais if she hadn't been worried in case the Group Captain, always punctilious in inquiring about her family, should ask what Philippa was doing.

But the first case on the afternoon list had only been in progress for about twenty minutes when she felt the quickening drum of her heart and immediately the scarlet tide surged over her neck and face. She was holding her handkerchief in her lap and now she raised it to smother her mouth and nose, pretending to stifle an irritating spasm of coughing. During the morning session and in the intervals at lunch her restless hands had tangled the handkerchief to a moist rag. Now it smelled rankly of sweat, meat sauce and wine. As she hacked away, the simulated cough sounding unnatural even to her own ears, the social worker giving evidence hesitated, glanced at the Bench, then went on speaking. Miss Belling in the chair, without glancing at Hilda, pushed across the carafe of water. Hilda reached for the glass, her hands shaking. But as the water, stale and lukewarm, slid over her tongue she knew that the worst was over. This had been a mild attack. The scarlet tide was receding. She would be all right now until the session ended, all right until the next time.

Crumbling the handkerchief into her lap, she looked up and

found herself staring into a pair of terrified eyes. At first she thought that the girl sitting alone two feet from the bench was the juvenile defendant. Then she remembered. This was a care case based on allegations of ill treatment and the girl was the baby's mother. She was a wan-faced, lanky teenager with blonde straggling hair and a sharp narrow nose above a mouth whose top lip was full and curved, the lower slack and almost bloodless. She wore no make-up except for a smudged black line round her eyes. The eyes themselves were remarkable, large, grey and wide-spaced. They looked into Hilda's with a desperate appeal.

For the first time Hilda noticed the incongruity of her dress. Someone must have advised her to wear a hat to court. Perhaps the wide-brimmed straw with the bunch of cherries with crushed and faded leaves drooping from the side of the brim had originally been bought for her wedding. She wore a faded fawn cotton top faintly patterned with some slogan which had been washed out, above a short black skirt. On the top was pinned a metal brooch in the shape of a rose. It dragged at the thin cotton. Her legs were bare, the knees scabbed and knobbly as a child's. On her feet she wore sandals with thick cork soles and plastic straps wound round her ankles. She was nursing a bulging black handbag, old-fashioned in shape and very large, clutching it desperately to her chest as if afraid that one of the magistrates might leap from the bench and snatch it from her. And still her eyes gazed unwaveringly at Hilda. The fixed stare conveyed nothing but a wordless cry for help, but Hilda was aware of a more complicated and personal communication, an impulse of painful pity. She yearned to lean over the bench and stretch out her hands to the girl, to get out from her seat and fold the rigid body in her arms. Perhaps in that impossible embrace both of them would receive comfort. She too was under judgement, officially deemed incompetent, bereft of her child. Her lips cracked in an inadmissible smile. It wasn't returned. The girl – she looked little more than a child – was too petrified to respond even to so timid and suspect an attempt at friendship.

She seemed not to be listening as the local authority social worker continued her evidence. Her child, a ten-week-old boy, was now in a home under a place-of-safety order and the local authority were applying for a second interim care order while they prepared their case for the final hearing. At the end of the submission Miss Belling turned first to Group Captain Carter and then to Hilda. She whispered:

'We renew the interim care order then, for another twenty- eight days. That should give the local authority time to prepare their case.'

Hilda didn't reply. Miss Belling said again:

'We make an interim care order, then?'

Hilda found herself saying:

'I think we ought to talk about it.'

With no sign of irritation, Miss Belling informed the court that the magistrates would retire. Surprised, the court shuffled to its feet as Miss Belling led her colleagues out.

Hilda knew that there was nothing she could do or say which would make any difference, that this sick confusion of pity and outrage was futile. They had to protect the baby. The machinery of justice, majestic, well meaning, fallible, would roll inexorably onward and there was nothing that she could do or say to halt it. And if it were stopped, then perhaps the baby might be harmed again, might even die. In the dull claustrophobic retiring room her fellow justices were patient with her. After all, she hadn't given them any trouble before. Group Captain Carter attempted to explain what she already knew.

'We're only proposing a twenty-eight-day interim care order. The local authority won't be ready with their case for another three or four weeks. We must continue to protect the baby in the meantime. Then it will be for the court to decide what order to make.'

'But they took her baby away from her six weeks ago! Now she's got to wait another four weeks. And suppose they don't let her have him back then?'

Miss Belling said with surprising gentleness:

'It's the court that will decide that. It's us, not some anonymous they. The child is being protected under a place-of-safety order. That expires tomorrow. I don't think we can just ignore the local-authority application for a second interim order; in effect that would mean sending the baby home. It's too big a risk. You heard the medical evidence, the round burns on the inside of the thighs suggestive of cigarette burns, the healed broken rib, the bruises to the buttocks. Those weren't caused accidentally.'

'But the social worker said that the husband had left home. He's walked out on them. If he's the one responsible then the baby will be all right now.'

'But we don't know whether he was the one responsible. We don't know who ill-treated the baby. It isn't our job to establish that in law. We aren't an adult criminal court. It's our job to consider the welfare of the child. We must continue to protect him until the substantive care proceedings.'

'But then she'll lose her baby completely, I know she will. He's only ten weeks old and they've been parted for six weeks. And who's going to talk for her?'

Miss Belling said:

'That's what worries me about these cases. Until the Government implements section sixty-four of the Children Act 1975 there's no chance of a mother in her situation having a lawyer from legal aid to look after her interests. The child gets the lawyer, not the parent. It's a scandal that section sixty-four hasn't been implemented. There ought to be some procedure for looking at Acts of Parliament which are never brought into force, or which are delayed as long as this. But that's not our concern. There's nothing we can do about it. What we have to do now is decide whether there is sufficient evidence to justify us making an interim order. I don't think we have any real choice. We can't prevent the husband from returning home any time he chooses; presumably the girl wants him to come home. And even if she didn't ill-treat the child herself, she was obviously powerless to prevent him from ill-treating it.'

Hilda whispered:

'I wish I could take her and the baby home with me.'

She thought of Philippa's room, so clean and empty. Philippa hadn't wanted it, had rejected it, but the girl would be safe and happy there. They could put the cot under the south window where it would get the sun. The girl looked as if she needed feeding up; it would be lovely to cook for someone who was really hungry. She heard Miss Belling say:

'You must try and remember what you were told when you

were trained. The juvenile court isn't a welfare tribunal. The local authority has the job of looking after the child. We must act judiciously, within the law, within the rules.'

When they had resettled themselves on the Bench and Miss Belling had briefly announced the expected decision, Hilda didn't again meet the girl's eyes. She was only aware that one moment the skinny figure clutching the outsized bag was standing like a condemned prisoner to receive sentence, and the next moment was gone. For the rest of the afternoon she made herself attend assiduously to every case. They passed before her, the sad procession of the inadequate, the criminal, the dispossessed. She read each social inquiry report with its catalogue of poverty, fecklessness, misery and failure and felt the increasing weight of her own powerlessness, her own inadequacy. After the session had ended, and as she stood alone in the sun outside the court house, she felt a sudden and overwhelming need to find Philippa, to see that she at least was all right. She wanted to speak to her. She knew that this wasn't possible. Philippa had made it so plain that the break, however temporary, had to be complete. But she knew where they were, and Delaney Street was so very close. It wouldn't hurt just to have a look at the outside of their flat, find out exactly where they were.

She walked as usual with her eyes down, carefully avoiding the lines between the paving stones. She had known since early childhood that to step on the line was bad luck. She wondered whether this might be an unpropitious time to risk visiting Delaney Street. If they were both working, and surely they were, they might be coming home about now. It would be dreadful if she ran into them. Philippa would think that she was spying. She had been so insistent that she wanted to be private. No one was to be told where they were, no one was to call. She had only given Hilda the address so that her letters could be sent on, and so that they could contact her in an emergency. What kind of emergency, Hilda wondered. How ill would Maurice have to be before that counted as an emergency? She didn't believe that she herself would ever count. She prayed: 'Please God, don't let them see me.' Her life was punctuated by such desperate and irrational petitions. 'Please God, make the crème brûlée a success.' 'Please

God, help me to understand Philippa.' 'Please God, don't make me blush this session.' 'Please God, make Maurice love me again.' The crème brûlée was invariably a success, but she could have managed that on her own. The other petitions, those extravagant demands for love, went unheard. It didn't surprise her. She had stopped going to church after her marriage and she could hardly expect her prayers to be answered when it was so apparent that she feared Maurice more than she feared God.

She made her way towards Marylebone Road without noticing the silent watcher about twenty yards down on the opposite pavement who hurried his footsteps so that he caught the traffic lights, crossed the road with her and followed her at a careful distance past Marylebone Station, across Lisson Grove, and up Mell Street.

EIGHTEEN

So he had found them at last. He stood looking down Delaney Street, outwardly composed, the mild eyes blinking behind his spectacles, but he could have reared his arms and shouted in exultation. A part of him, some memory of that boy who had knelt in the Methodist Chapel at Brighton, wanted to kneel now, to feel his knees pressing the hard pavement. He had been right, they were in London. They were here, within yards of where he stood, living in a flat above a greengrocer's shop at number 12. Here less than ten minutes ago he had seen Mrs Palfrey loiter, look up, walk quickly past the shop, retrace her steps, look up again. If she had been an *agent provocateur* paid to lead him to his quarry, she couldn't have improved on that mime of betrayal. After about two minutes of this pacing she had bought two oranges from the stall, her eyes slewing up to the flat windows, afraid perhaps that they might appear. He wondered why she was so nervous. Had the girl perhaps insisted on privacy? What exactly was the relationship between her and her adoptive parents, if adopted she had been? But of course she had been adopted. There could be no doubt that she was the murderess's daughter, and no doubt either that her name was now Palfrey. Perhaps her adoptive parents had disapproved of her leaving home.

He felt a surge of fresh excitement when it occurred to him that this tentative visit by Mrs Palfrey might be the first step to a reconciliation. If the girl went back to Caldecote Terrace and abandoned the murderess to live alone here then his task would be easy.

After buying the oranges she had walked more quickly than usual up Mell Street to the Edgware Road and had stood in the queue for the 26 bus to Victoria. She was on her way home. He need follow no longer. He had almost run back to Delaney Street, terrified that he might miss the sight of them, the confirmation that they were really here. But, standing at the corner of the street and looking down its drab length, he had no doubt. The intoxication of triumph and fear was familiar. He felt again the sick excitement of the ten-year-old boy standing on the wet sands under Brighton pier with the roar of the sea in his ears, and holding in his small hands the spoils of his latest theft. Then, as now, he felt no guilt. It was extraordinary that during the years of innocence he had lived under a perpetual burden of guilt; paradoxically, only when he became a thief had that weight lifted. It was the same with Julie's death. He knew that when he drove the knife into Mary Ducton's throat he would drive out guilt from his mind for ever. He had no way of telling if he could free Mavis's spirit; he only knew how he could free his own.

And then they appeared. The sight of them was less traumatic than when he had seen them in Regent's Park, and he was better able to control himself. The girl shut the front door, saying something to her mother, and they both turned towards Mell Street. They were casually dressed, both wearing slacks and jackets, the girl had her travelling bag slung over her shoulder. He turned quickly to the right up Mell Street, judging that they would be on their way to Baker Street and the West End. But, glancing back, he saw that they were taking the same path and were only about forty yards behind him. He turned quickly down a side street and loitered there until he had seen them pass.

Back in Delaney Street he surveyed it like a strategist. Now that he knew they weren't there to observe him he could take his time. The problem was to know where without attracting attention to himself he could safely keep watch. The pub, the Blind Beggar, was an obvious possibility, quickly rejected. In a small

London pub all the regulars were known to the publican and each other; a new and frequent customer would be noticed. They wouldn't force themselves on him; nowhere would he be safer from intrusion. But when the body was discovered he would be bound to be among the suspects. If he had the kill here on the murderess's home ground, the police would come with their photographs and questions. And depending on whether the publican and his customers had reason to oblige the police, someone sooner or later would talk. Besides, he drank very little and the prospect of sitting there in the fumes of tobacco and beer under the curious glances of the regulars, trying to make his pint last, repelled him. And it wouldn't really do as a vantage point. Like all Victorian pubs, he saw that little could be glimpsed of the interior from outside. Short of standing up and peering over the ornately painted glass, he would see nothing.

The bookshop next to the pub and the junk shop adjacent to the greengrocer's both afforded an opportunity to browse and loiter. But, here again, he would be noticed and remembered if he became too frequent a visitor. Perhaps the launderette was the best bet. The prospect of burdening himself with his small supply of spare clothes for frequent and unnecessary washings was a disadvantage; but then he told himself that he needn't wash anything. Once the launderette was reasonably busy, he had only to sit there patiently like the others with his plastic bag and newspaper, and it would be assumed that his washing was either being pounded in one of the washing machines, or was revolving in a drier. During Mavis's illness he had taken their sheets to the local launderette. He knew that it was common practice for people to come and go, shopping or visiting the pub until their washing was ready. But here too he would have to be careful. It was a less likely place for the police to make their inquiries, but he couldn't sit there day after day. It was a place though, where the woman herself or her daughter might well come. Surely they would use a launderette so conveniently close.

More and more it seemed to him that he ought to try and get access to the flat. He walked slowly but purposefully down that side of the road and noticed the lock. It was a simple Yale, one of the easiest to break open. The greengrocer's shop occupied what had obviously been the front room of the original house. He saw that there was a door at the side of the shop which must lead into the downstairs hall and that this, too, was fitted with a Yale.

He went across to the second-hand booksellers and began to look through the four trays of paperbacks set out on trestles. Suddenly it occurred to him to wonder why he was here, why he hadn't followed the murderess and her daughter. He had his knife with him. What had prevented him from following them and seizing his opportunity? It had been done before. He had read about it in newspapers often enough, the crowded pavement, the press of bodies at the tube station entrance, the silent attacker slipping in his knife and making his escape before the onlookers, embarrassed, then puzzled and finally horrified, realized what had happened. It was partly, he decided, that it had all been too sudden, too unexpected. Psychologically he wasn't yet ready for the kill. His mind had been preoccupied with the problem of tracking them down; he had not yet turned his thoughts to the deed itself. But there was something more important; that wasn't how it was meant to be, a sordid street crime, public, hurried, clumsy, perhaps even botched. That wasn't how he saw it. In his imaginings he and the murderess were alone together. She was lying on a bed asleep, her neck stretched out, the pulse beating. The execution, the plunge of the knife into her throat, would be unhurried, ceremonious, a ritual of justice and expiation.

The bookshop was a good place to loiter. A small part of the window obscured from within by the back of a bookcase acted as a mirror. Lifting his eyes from the grubby copy of *A Farewell to Arms* which he was pretending to study, he saw that the greengrocer was closing his shop, lugging the sacks of onions and potatoes to the back, piling up the boxes of tomatoes and lettuces, demolishing the careful pyramids of apples and oranges, and dragging the green artificial grass from the front trestle table. Scase put down his book and sauntered across the road to the junk shop. Here part of the pavement was piled with the cheaper items, a wood-topped desk with all the drawers missing, two cane-bottomed chairs with the seats sagging and split, a tin bath piled with cracked crockery. On the desk was a cardboard box almost filled with a tangle of old spectacles. He rummaged among them, picking out one or two pairs to hold before his eyes, as if testing the vision. Through a distorted haze he saw the greengrocer take off his fawn working coat and replace it by a blue denim jacket from a peg at the back of the shop. Then he disappeared for a second and came back with a pole with a hook on the end and clanged down the metal front to the shop.

A few seconds later he came out of the front door, shut it firmly behind him and made his way up Delaney Street. So he didn't live above the shop. But he would still need a key to the Yale lock on the front door since the shop front had been locked from the inside and there was no other way he could get in to open up the premises except through the front door. He would keep the key on him, perhaps on a ring with others, perhaps in the pocket of his jacket. He had been wearing tight-fitting jeans with two back pockets, both lying flat against the curve of the buttocks. There had been no key there. Almost automatically Scase picked up one pair of spectacles after another and turned them over in his hands. Perhaps it might be worthwhile buying a pair or two if he could find some which weren't too distorting to the vision. A change of spectacles would alter his appearance. He had never before thought of disguise, since it seemed an art beyond his capacity. But there was one skill he knew he had. It was many years since he had exercised it but then it had never once let him down. He didn't think it would let him down now. He could pick pockets.

The exhilaration of knowing that he had found them at last was so intoxicating that he could hardly bear to leave Delaney Street. But the door of number 12 was locked against him, there was nowhere he could safely conceal himself and he needed to get back to the safety and anonymity of his attic room, needed time to rest and think and plan. Before leaving he walked for the last time down the street, surveying the possibilities. It was then he noticed the narrow passage which led down the side of the Blind Beggar, and which was flanked by the grimy brick wall of the pub and by the corrugated-iron fence about seven feet high which surrounded the acre of weed-infested wasteland. He saw that the panels which faced Delaney Street, rusting, the concrete supports no longer firmly upright, had sagged apart in places producing slits from which it would be possible to keep watch on the street. The problem was to gain access to the wasteland and to check that there were no high windows in surrounding buildings from which the vantage point could be observed.

He glanced quickly up and down the street, then stepped into the passageway. If challenged he would have a credible excuse ready; he would say apologetically that he was looking for a lavatory. He quickly saw that this explanation would have more plausibility than he had realized. The passage led to a small yard smelling strongly of beer and less strongly of urine and coal dust. To the right was the back door of the pub and in front of him an outside coal store, now disused, and a wooden door with a slit at the top and bottom on which the word 'gents' had been crudely painted.

He darted into the lavatory and shut the bolt. Through the top slit he could see one dingy and heavily curtained upstairs window at the back of the pub, and could examine the fence. Here it was even less secure than in the front, and the gap between two of the panels was, he thought, sufficiently wide to enable a slim man to force his way through. After dark it could probably be done with some safety, despite the old-fashioned lamp which projected on brackets at the corner of the pub wall. But this was late summer, a miserably cold and disappointing summer but the light still lasted well into the evening. Unless there were no upper windows overlooking the wasteland, his time of observation might have to be restricted to the hours of darkness.

The huge wooden seat almost engulfed him. It must have been here as long as the pub itself. He slid his thin buttocks to its edge and crouched there, keen as a cornered animal, all his senses alert. There were no voices from the house. He could hear no footfalls, no shouts from Delaney Street and even the rumble of traffic passing down Mell Street was muted. The reek of disinfectant was pungent as a gas. A thin drizzle had begun to fall and the wind was rising, blowing a mist through the slit of the door, obscuring his spectacles. He took out his handkerchief to wipe them and saw that his hand was shaking. He thought it strange that this particular moment, closeted as he was in safety, unobserved, should be so traumatic. Perhaps it was a delayed reaction to the shock of finding them at last.

It was time to go. Having made up his mind he left the shed swiftly and with his shoulder pressed against the most vulnerable panel of the fence. It gave slightly. With his hand he pulled the second panel forward, aware of the sharp edge of the metal biting into his hand. The gap widened. He slipped through.

It was like stepping into a garden. As he worked his way round in the shadow of the fence the weeds were almost waist-high. They looked so fragile with their small pink flowers, yet they had forced their way through this impacted earth, in part splitting the concrete. Where they were highest he paused to survey the waste-land. It was better for his purpose than he had dared to hope. There was only one gate. This faced Delaney Street and he could see that it was barred and padlocked. Once there had been a row of houses there, now demolished, he supposed, for redevelopment and in front of him was a blank windowless wall where the neighbouring house had been sliced away. There were no windows in the side wall of the Blind Beggar and the area was bounded on the fourth side by a glass and concrete building which looked like a school. He might possibly be seen from its upper windows, but the building would be empty after school hours unless, of course, it was used for evening classes. But surely not in summer? He would have to find out.

Then he realized that it might not be necessary. He could be in luck. Two decrepit vehicles, a battered van and the chassis of a car, wheel-less and with its left door hanging loose, had been parked or dumped within a few yards of the Delaney Street boundary. They could shield him from any prying eyes from the school if only they were in the right place, standing against a part of the fence where the panels weren't completely joined. Even so, vision would be restricted. Ideally he needed to be exactly opposite the door to number 12. He worked his way towards them, still keeping close to the iron fence as if its height and corrugated surface could somehow confuse an onlooker and make him invisible.

He quickened his pace as he approached the van, the first of the abandoned vehicles, resisting the urge to run for its comforting cover. When at last he reached it, he stood panting with relief, eyes closed, back pressed against the fence. After a few seconds he made himself open his eyes and look round the wasteland. It was still deserted but more desolate now as the drizzle turned to a slanting rain and the clumps of weeds strained against the fretful, changeable wind. Then he turned to examine the fence. It was as he had hoped; there was a gap just below eye-level. It wasn't exactly opposite the greengrocer's shop, but it was close enough and the gap sufficiently wide to give him an uninterrupted view.

He stood there, legs slightly bent, arms wide, fingers clutching at the curve of the iron, staring at the closed door of number 12, watching and waiting. The rain fell steadily soaking his shoulders, running in rivulets under his jacket collar. He tried to wipe his streaming spectacles but his handkerchief was quickly soaked. The street lamp at the corner of Delaney Street was switched on, laying a shivering gleam on the wet pavement. Somewhere a church clock struck the quarters, the half-hours, the sonorous chimes of nine, ten and eleven o'clock. The swish of passing cars down Mell Street became less frequent. The noise from the pub grew, became raucous, then faded with a clatter of departing feet and the last valedictory shouts. And still they didn't come. From time to time he stretched himself upright to ease the intolerable ache of shoulders and legs, but bent his eyes again to the gap whenever he heard a footfall. It was half-past eleven before they returned home. He watched them, both it seemed drooping a little with tiredness, as the girl felt in her bag for her keys. They spoke together easily, casually, as she pushed the door open. And then they were inside and it closed behind them. A few seconds later the two windows on the first floor became oblongs of pale light. Only then, so cramped that he could hardly move, aware for the first time of hunger, of his jacket and shirt like a wet poultice against his back, he forced himself once more through the gap in the fence and made his painful way to Baker Street station and took the Circle line to Victoria.

NINETEEN

When Maurice got home late that afternoon the kitchen, although lit, was empty. He found Hilda in the garden. She was standing at the wrought-iron table arranging a cut-glass bowl of roses. It was a shallow, crudely shaped bowl and it took a second or two before he could remember how they had come by it. Her parents had given it to them as a wedding present. He could picture them conferring anxiously over it, spending more money than they could afford. He remembered, too, that his mother had owned one very like it. He had never been trusted to help wash it up. She had made trifle in it for Sunday tea, a layer of bought sponge cakes covered with jelly and topped with thick synthetic custard. This bowl was filled with crumpled wire to hold the roses. As Hilda forced in each stem the wire scraped against the glass, setting his teeth on edge. The roses had been picked too late and over-handled. Surely Philippa, when she did flowers for the drawing-room, always cut them early in the day and left them in the cool, standing in water. These lay in a flabby heap on the table, their heads already drooping, their stems lax. Suddenly he decided that he didn't like roses. It was a surprising discovery to make at this particular moment and after so many years. They were an over-praised flower, soon blowzy, their beauty dependent on scent and poetic association. One perfect bloom in a specimen vase placed against a plain wall could be a marvel of colour and form, but flowers ought to be judged by how they grew. A rose garden always looked messy, spiky recalcitrant bushes bearing mean leaves. And the roses grew untidily, had such a brief moment of beauty before the petals bleached and peeled in the wind, littering the soil. And the smell was sickly, the stuff of cheap scent. Why had he ever imagined that it gave him pleasure?

Hilda, dissatisfied with her arrangement and pulling out the stems to start again, had pricked herself. There was a bead of blood on her thumb. 'Died of a rose in aromatic pain.' Browning or Tennyson? Philippa would have known. While his mind was tracing the source of the quotation, she said pettishly:

'I miss Philippa doing the flowers. It's too much, cooking the meal and trying to make the table look nice.'

'Yes, Philippa had a pleasant decorative sense. Are those for tonight?'

Immediately she looked up at him, defensive, worried.

'Won't they do?'

'Isn't the arrangement too large? People need to be able to see each other over the flowers. You can't talk to someone you can't see.'

'Oh, talking!'

'Talking is what a dinner party's about. And they smell too strong. We want to smell the food and wine. Roses on the dinner table confuse the senses.'

She said with the note of sulky truculence which he found particularly irritating and which he had heard more frequently since Philippa's departure:

'I don't seem to be able to do anything right.'

'Right? Right for whom?'

'Right for you. I don't know why you married me.'

As soon as the words were out of her mouth she stared at him appalled, or so it seemed to him, as if there were words between which their minds could formulate, but which it would be fatal to speak aloud. He picked up one of the roses. The blossom drooped over his palm. He said, hearing the coldness in his voice:

'I married you because I was fond of you and because I thought we could be happy together. If you aren't happy you must try to tell me what's worrying you.'

It was paradoxical that the truth could sound so false, could be so much less than the truth. If he had loved her enough he could have made himself lie and say 'Because I loved you.' But if he had loved her enough the lie wouldn't have been necessary. She muttered:

'You needn't talk to me as if I'm one of your students. I know you think I'm stupid, but you don't have to patronize me.'

He didn't reply, but stood watching her as she forced the last rose stem through the crumpled wire, grazing its stem. But the arrangement was top-heavy and the entangled wire keeled over on to the table spilling rose petals, pollen and dollops of water. She gave a little moan and began dabbing at the water with her handkerchief. She said:

'Philippa leaving, you blamed me for that. I know what you thought. I couldn't give you a child of your own and I couldn't even make the adopted one stay with me.'

'That's ridiculous, and you must know that it is. I could have stopped Philippa leaving, but I wasn't prepared to pay the price. Philippa must find her own way back to reality.'

She said, so quietly that he could only just catch the words:

'It would have been different if I'd been able to have a baby.'

He felt a tremor of pity, transitory, but strong enough to make him unwise. He heard himself speaking:

'That reminds me, there's something I meant to tell you. I went to see Dr Patterson last week. There's nothing wrong, it was only a check-up. But he got out my records and confirmed what I half guessed when we saw the specialist together twelve years ago. I'm the one who's infertile. It's nothing to do with you.'

She stared at him, rose in hand. She said:

'But you had Orlando!'

He said sharply:

'It's nothing to do with Orlando. It happened after he was born. The doctor puts it down to an attack of mumps I had when he was six weeks old. These things aren't uncommon. There's nothing to be done about it.'

She stared at him; her full unwinking gaze was unnerving. He wanted to turn away, dismissing the inconsequent detail of his infertility with a nonchalant shrug, a wry smile at the perversity of fate. But his eyes were held by that dumb unwinking stare. He cursed himself for his folly. Because of a bowl of ruined roses, because of a moment of futile compassion, he had blurted it out. Not the whole truth, he had never imagined himself telling that, but a part of the truth, the essential truth. A secret he had kept for twelve years, a part of him which he had become fond of, as one might a slightly disreputable friend, was his no longer. He had reacted to his particular guilty secret as he supposed the majority of his fellow men did to theirs. Most of the time he had been able to forget it, not by any conscious effort of will, but because it was as much part of him as his digestion, unintrusive unless it gave trouble. Occasionally it would come into his mind and he would cogitate upon it as an interesting and intriguing complication of his personality which repaid study, much as he might cogitate about the complexities of a student's style. Sometimes he had even enjoyed it. A guilty secret is, nevertheless, a secret and can be relished with at least some of the innocence of childhood conspiracies. Sometimes, but increasingly rarely, it had intruded into his waking thoughts and provoked disagreeable sensations of distress and worry, even slight physical manifestations of quickened breath which he would have diagnosed as guilt and shame if those were words which he had ever cared to use. And now it was no longer his secret. He had borne its weight for twelve years and now he would have to shoulder the burden of her reproach, her renewed disappointment. Self-pity took hold of him. Why should she stare at him like that with those amazed unbelieving eyes? He was the one who was entitled to understanding. It was he, not she, who was maimed. She said:

'You've known all the time, haven't you? It isn't true that you've been to Dr Patterson. You knew when we first had those tests, when you said that you didn't want to go on with them any longer, that you'd had enough. And you let me think it was my fault that we couldn't have a child. All those years, you let me think it was me.'

'It's no one's fault. It's not a question of fault.'

He must have been mad to think for one moment that all that was lacking between them was truth. The tragedy of his marriage – except that tragedy was too grand a word for such a commonplace misfortune – was not that she always made the wrong response to his needs; it was that there was no right response which it was within her power to make. She said accusingly:

'I could have had a child if I hadn't married you.'

'You might have had. That supposes that you would have married someone else, that he wanted a child, that both of you were capable of parenthood.'

She had dropped her eyes at last. Clumsily gathering up the roses, she whispered sulkily:

'There were other men that liked me. George Bocock liked me.'

Who in God's name was George Bocock, he wondered. The name struck a chord. Of course, that pimply youth who had been a clerk in the university admissions office. So he had been competing with George Bocock. If that didn't puncture his self-esteem, nothing would.

At dinner she was more withdrawn than usual, less, he thought, from her customary shyness, than because she was preoccupied with her private thoughts. They had guests, and it wasn't until they were alone together in the bedroom that they had an opportunity to talk. Then she said, forcing out the words belligerently as if half expecting him to remonstrate:

'I want to give up the juvenile Bench.'

'Resign your commission. Why?'

'I'm not any good at it. I don't help anyone. And I don't like it. I'll finish this three-month stint, but I won't do any more.'

'If you feel like that, then there's no point in going on. You'd better write to the Lord Chancellor's office. But I suggest you try to think of some less childish reason.'

'Not doing any good, not being able to help anyone isn't a childish reason.'

'What will you do with the extra time? Do you want me to talk to Gwen Marshall about the possibility of school-care work? They're always looking for suitable people.'

'Why should I be any better at that? I can fill up my time.'

She paused, and then said:

'I want a dog.'

'In London? Is that fair? It won't be easy to exercise him.'

'There are places, the Embankment Gardens, St James's Park.'

'I should have thought there were enough dogs fouling the public parks. But if you're sure, you'd better decide what breed you want and we'll find some reputable kennels. We could do it this weekend.'

His magnanimity surprised him. And perhaps it wasn't such a bad idea. She and Philippa hadn't exactly been companions, but the house probably seemed empty without her. A dog needn't inconvenience him if the animal were properly trained. They could drive to the kennels that weekend, make an excursion of it.

She said:

'I don't care about the breed. I want a stray from the Battersea Dogs' Home.'

He said irritably:

'Really Hilda, if you're determined on a dog, at least get a good-looking animal.'

'I don't care about good looks. You and Philippa do, but I don't. I want a stray, a dog no one has claimed, one who'll have to be destroyed if they can't find it a home.'

She turned from the dressing table and spoke for the first time with animation, almost pleadingly:

'He won't make a mess in the garden. I know how you feel about the roses. I'll see he doesn't get on the flower beds. I could train him. He can live in a basket in the kitchen. And he won't be expensive. We waste a lot of food he could eat, and Mr Pantley would be obliging with bones for him. I'm a good customer.'

He said:

'It's all right I suppose, as long as you take responsibility for him.'

It was like humouring an importunate child. She said sadly:

'Oh yes, I'll do that. I'll look after him. That's one thing I can do.'

'If in making your choice, you contrive to be attracted to one of the smaller and less-yapping varieties, you would oblige me.'

She knew then that it was going to be all right. She remembered that Philippa had once said that when Maurice spoke like a character in a Jane Austen novel it meant that he was in a good mood. The literary allusion meant nothing to her, but she had learnt to recognize the tone. She would be able to have her dog. She pictured him, bright eyed, head cocked up at her, tail quivering. It was no good naming him before she'd chosen him. She would have to see what he looked like. But she rather liked the name Scamp. Maurice and Philippa would say that it was too ordinary, too common, but that was the kind of dog she wanted. Lying down in the single bed in which Maurice so seldom joined her she felt a surge of confidence, almost of power. She wasn't barren after all. It was his fault, not hers. She needn't spend her life making up to him for a deprivation which was nothing to do with her. And after this three-month stint she need never sit on the Bench again.

BOOK THREE

Act of Violence

ONE

And now he moved with a mounting sense of excitement away from his settled routine at Pimlico and into a new world, their world. And the act itself was no longer hidden in an unknown future; the time had come to prepare himself physically and mentally for the deed. But he perceived a difference in himself. Shadowing Mrs Palfrey, he, the follower, had nevertheless felt himself to be in control. She led and he shadowed, but the invisible cord between them had reined her to his controlling hands. It seemed to him that he had followed her in a state of gentle euphoria, unstressed by anxiety, certain that in the end she would lead him to his prey. Her loneliness, the sad futility of her life, the inevitability of her betrayal, had even bred in him a sense of pity and comradeship.

It was different now; he was on enemy ground. He was shadowing two women, not one, and the girl had seen him and would recognize him again. He still remembered that moment in the rose garden with a mixture of shame and horror. And she was younger, keener-eyed, swifter, almost certainly more intelligent. His task had become infinitely more difficult and the risk of discovery greater. He would have to take his time, move with more cunning. The first task must be to watch from his hiding place on the waste-ground and try to get some idea of their daily routine.

It took him a week to discover where they went when they set out every evening at five o'clock. For three days he followed them at a distance up Mell Street then watched from the shelter of a chemist's doorway until they mounted a number 16 bus going north up the Edgware Road. The next day he secreted himself closer to the bus stop until they arrived, then mounted the bus after them. They took seats on the lower deck, so he went quickly up the stairs. He took a ticket to the terminus to avoid giving a destination, then watched from the window at every stop to see where they got off. When at last, after a twenty-minute drive, he saw them alight at Cricklewood Broadway he made his way down the stairs, jumped off at the first red traffic light, and hurried back. But he was too late, they were nowhere in sight.

The next evening he again took the bus, hurrying out of his hiding place to join it once they were safely aboard and again taking a seat on the top deck. But this time he was ready to alight, and he didn't lose them. He was thirty yards behind them as they entered a fish and chip restaurant, Sid's Plaice. He strolled past and joined a queue at the next bus stop, waiting to see if they emerged. After about ten minutes he strolled past the shop and looked through the glass window at the rows of formica-topped tables. They were nowhere to be seen. It didn't surprise him; he had hardly supposed they would travel so far for an evening meal. So this was where they worked. The choice surprised him; but then he understood. They needed to take a job where the daughter would be in no danger of meeting people she knew, could be sure that no one would ask questions.

After that he knew that he could relax his watch every evening between five o'clock and eleven. He couldn't kill her during their bus journeys, nor while she was at work. But what about that late lonely walk down Mell Street? He pictured himself waiting for them one night, straining himself against the door to avoid being seen, knife ready. Then the lunge at her throat, the one word 'Julie' spoken so low that only she would hear, the vicious double twist, the tearing flesh as the knife was wrenched free, and then his feet pounding down Delaney Street to the shelter of – where? It wouldn't work; nothing about it rang true. That quick withdrawing knife, suppose it stuck, twisted in her muscles, was caught behind a bone? He would need time to force it out. He couldn't leave the knife in the wound. Surely the blood must flow freely if she were to die. And the girl would be there, younger, stronger, swifter than he. How could he hope to get away?

Never once during the first week of his surveillance did he see them apart. They were together all day and, more important, they stayed together all night. Since he had rejected the idea of an attack on the murderess in the street, his plan depended on knowing when the girl had left her alone in the flat. He would have to find an excuse for calling, particularly after dark, but that shouldn't be difficult. He would say that he had an urgent message from Caldecote Terrace for Philippa Palfrey. The fact that he knew the girl's name and previous address would ensure that the murderess would at least let him in. And that was all he needed. It would be better if he could kill her while she slept, cleaner, more certain, less horrible, more seemly. But all he needed was to come face to face with her in that flat, and alone.

He followed them on their daily excursions. Not because he expected an opportunity to kill, but because he was restless when they weren't in sight. It was simple enough to trail them on the Underground. They usually went from Marylebone, the nearest station. He supposed that, on that first journey from King's Cross, the girl had chosen Baker Street or Edgware Road on the Circle line to save them the time and trouble of a change of line. He would walk behind them at a safe distance, linger in the entrance tunnel while they stood on the platform, then enter a different compartment and stand at the door throughout the journey so that he could watch when they got off. After that it became more difficult. Sometimes prudence made him hang back and lose them. Occasionally they walked along the lonelier reaches of the river, through remote Georgian squares in Islington or the City, where any follower would have been conspicuous. Then he would stand and watch them through his binoculars over the parapet of a bridge, or from the shelter of a church porch or shop doorway, motionless until the two golden heads were out of sight.

It had become less important to trail them, to keep them in sight, than to share their lives, to experience vicariously their interests and pleasures. He had become obsessed with them, itchy with restlessness when he was parted from them, terrified, despite the evidence of their settled way of life, that he might arrive one morning at Delaney Street to find them gone. He noted with obsessive concern the small details of their shared life, that it was the girl who seemed to be in control, who organized their lunching arrangements, taking the oblong plastic picnic box from her shoulder-bag and handing it, opened, to her mother; that it was the girl who bought the tickets, who carried the map. He no longer thought of them apart and this, when it occurred to him, was worrying. One night he even had a confused nightmare in which it was the girl whom he killed. She was lying on his bed at the Casablanca, naked, and the wound in her throat was bloodless but gaping, like moistly parted lips. He turned round, the dripping knife in his hand, appalled at his mistake, to find his mother and the murderess standing together in the doorway and clutching at each other, screaming with laughter. The terror stayed with him next day and, for the first time since he had found them, it took an effort of will to leave the shelter of his room.

He was bound to them by hate; he was bound to them, too, by envy. He never saw them touch, they didn't often talk together; when they smiled it was the spontaneous smile of two people who laugh at the same things. They were like friends, undemonstrative, companionable, uneffusive, sharing their days because there was, at present, no other person with whom they preferred to be. So might he have walked and smiled and been companionable with his daughter.

He might have gone on like that for weeks, following them during the daytime, returning to the hotel for his dinner, then waiting behind the iron fence at night, until at last he heard their returning footsteps, the door of number 12 close behind them, and saw the twin oblongs of light shine out from their windows. He hardly knew what he was hoping for, crouching there in the darkness. The girl was hardly likely to leave her mother alone in the flat so late at night. But until the light was finally extinguished he could not bear to leave. And then, on the morning of Saturday 9th September everything changed.

They were shopping in Mell Street market, as they had on the previous Saturday, and he was shadowing them, anonymous in the milling crowd, watching from the shelter of the antique supermarket, from behind the bric-à-brac stalls, stepping back if their heads turned his way to conceal himself among the swinging hangers of cotton shirts, summer dresses and long printed Indian skirts. It was a bright, warm morning after an early mist and Mell Street was crowded. He was standing at the stall which sold mangoes and huge bunches of unripe bananas to the West Indian women, listening to their high staccato jabber and looking across the road to where the murderess and her daughter were rummaging in a cardboard carton of old linen. They seemed to be searching for pieces of lace. On the edge of the stall was an Australian bushranger's hat, broad brimmed, turned up at the side. Suddenly the girl took it and perched it on her head. Her unbraided golden hair was flowing loose, a swinging curtain of gold. The strap of the hat hung under her chin. She turned on her heel towards her mother and tipped back the brim of the hat in a gesture defiant and debonair. Then she began searching in her shoulder-bag for the money. She had bought it, that gallant, ridiculous hat. And the murderess laughed! Across the width of the road, above the rich West Indian voices, above the shouts of the buskers, the hysterical barking of the dogs, he could hear the laughter, a peal of joyous, spontaneous mirth.

She was laughing. Julie was dead, Mavis was dead, and she was laughing. He was shaken not by anger, which he could have borne, but by a terrible grief. Julie was rotting in her grave. Her life had been choked out of her almost before it had begun. This woman was laughing, opening her throat to the sun. He had no child. She had her daughter alive, healthy, exulting in her candescent beauty as if nourished vampire-like by Julie's blood. They walked in freedom. He slunk behind them like a scavenging animal. They sat companionably together in their shared home and smiled, talked, listened to music. He crouched alone in the cold, night after night, peering like a sexual voyeur through that slit in the wall. He heard again the voice of his Auntie Gladys, dead now like his mother, like Mavis, like Julie. She, being dead, yet speaketh: 'That boy gives me the willies. He creeps round the place like a sodding animal.' Is thy servant a dog that he should do this thing? He might as well cock his leg against the door of the derelict car that sheltered him and void his inadequacy, his self-disgust. The voice of his mother, as clear as if the words had once actually been spoken: 'Murder! You! Don't make me laugh.'

He found that he was crying, soundless, wordless, unassuageable tears. They poured over his face, seeped like salty rain into his quavering mouth, splashed over his unavailing hands. He walked on through the crowds, seeing nothing. There was nowhere he could go, nowhere he could hide. There was no place in London where a man could cry in peace. He thought of Julie, anxious eyes behind the steel National Health spectacles, the brace on her teeth, a thin face armoured with metal. He so seldom admitted that shadowy face into his mind. The greatest horror of murder was that it degraded the memory of the dead. If Julie had died in illness, been killed in a road accident, he could have thought of her now with sadness, but with a measure of acceptance and in peace. Now all memories of his child were corrupted by anger, by a half-salacious horror, by hate. All pictures of her childhood had superimposed on them like faulty print the horror and humiliation of her dreadful end. The murderers had robbed him even of the common tribute which humanity pays to its dead. He seldom remembered, because it was too uncomfortable to remember. If both of them had hanged, would that have cleansed his thoughts or added a new dimension of horror to her death?

He found that he had walked the length of Mell Street and now trembled on the very edge of the pavement where the stream of traffic flowed down the Edgware Road. He found himself longing for what he now thought of as home, that small high room at the Casablanca. But he had made a decision. This was the end of trailing after them like an animal twitching at the end of its string. If nothing could separate them, then he would have to get access to their flat. He would have to creep in at night when the murderess would be sleeping alone. And that meant that the time had come to steal the keys.

TWO

Since they had tacitly agreed that it was not yet time to talk about the lost years of their separation, they talked a great deal about books. With the past outlawed and the future uncertain, English literature was at least a shared experience which they could discuss without embarrassment or constraint, the safest of subjects. It was the more ironic that it should be a minute of commonplace literary chat over breakfast on Friday 15th September that led them directly to Gabriel Lomas.

Philippa asked:

'What did you read inside as well as Shakespeare?'

'The Victorian novelists mostly. The library was better than you'd think. There are two main requirements for cell literature: inordinate length and the writer's ability to create a distinctive and alternative world. I'm the prison-service authority on three-volume novels about intelligent, masochistic women who perversely marry the wrong man or no man at all; you know, *Portrait of a Lady*, *Middlemarch*, *The Small House at Allington*.'

Philippa asked:

'Weren't the books spoilt for you, reading them in prison?'

'No, because, while I was reading them, I wasn't in prison. *Middlemarch* kept me sane for six weeks. There are eighty-six chapters and I rationed myself to two a day.'

Middlemarch was first published in 1871. They would have hanged her mother then, but not in public. Surely public executions were stopped three years earlier. Maurice would know. She said:

'I don't think I'd have had that amount of self-control. *Middlemarch* is a marvellous novel.'

'Yes, but it would be more marvellous if the sexual conventions had let George Eliot be more honest. A novel must be flawed if one of its main themes is the story of a marriage and we can't even be told whether the marriage is consummated. Do you think Casaubon was impotent?'

'Yes, don't you? All the evidence is there.'

'But I don't want to have to deduce facts from evidence in a realistic novel. I want to be told. I know that the Victorians couldn't be explicit, but surely they needn't have been quite so timid.'

Philippa said:

'Timid is about the last adjective I'd associate with George Eliot. But if you're feeling critical about Victorian writing, why not indulge yourself with Victorian art? It might be fun to go to the exhibition of great Victorian paintings at the Royal Academy this morning. I think it closes on the seventeenth. Afterwards we could go on as planned to the Courtauld Institute, if that won't be a surfeit of painting.'

'I don't think I could have a surfeit of anything now, not even of pleasure.'

And so, at last, they met someone from Philippa's past. That didn't, in itself, matter. She had always known that it was inevitable. What did matter was that it should be Gabriel Lomas.

He came up behind them quietly while they were in the inner gallery, standing in front of Alma-Tadema's *The Baths of Caracalla* and studying the catalogue note. He was alone, which was surprising; but it was surprising that he should be there at all. There was no way in which Philippa could have avoided the introduction and she had no intention of trying. She touched her mother's arm and said:

'This is a friend of mine, Gabriel Lomas. Gabriel, my mother. She's in London and we're spending the day together.'

He hid his surprise admirably. For a second – no more – his arrogant mobile face froze and his hands tightened on the catalogue. Then he said easily:

'How pleasant for you both. But why not tear yourselves away from these glittering eyeballs and recover with lunch at Fortnum and Mason? Afterwards I thought of going to the Tate. The Henry Moore exhibition is finished, but one doesn't need an excuse for visiting the Tate.'

His mouth smiled, his voice held exactly the right mixture of interest and pleasure, but his eyes, carefully avoiding too keen a scrutiny of her mother, were the eyes of an inquisitor. Gazing steadily at his face, Philippa said:

'No thank you, Gabriel. We're going on to the Courtauld Galleries and lunching later. We've planned rather a full day.'

He would, she knew, be both too well bred and too proud to insist or to force his company on them. He said:

'I telephoned your adoptive mother a couple of weeks ago. She told me that you'd gone to earth. She was intriguingly mysterious.'

'She needn't have been. Didn't she explain that I'm spending three months in London on my own? I'm trying to find out if I can support myself in anything approaching the manner Maurice has accustomed me to. And I'm gaining experience for a book.'

That second explanation sounded pretentious and it was one she would have preferred not to make. But unlike the first, it rang true. Half the upper sixth were probably even now picking up experience for a first novel, as if experience lay like litter on the comfortable surface of their lives.

He said:

'What about Paris, Rome, Ravenna? I thought you said you'd be saving to embark on the Grand Tour before Cambridge.'

'Not so grand. The mosaics at Ravenna will wait. I have a lifetime to see them. But this experiment is now or never.'

'Why not take an evening off from it and come to the ballet – both of you?'

The flick of his eyes towards her mother was amused, inquisitive. She said:

'No thank you, Gabriel. I'm seeing no one. The whole thing will lose its point if I see friends whenever I'm lonely or go home as soon as I'm uncomfortable.'

'You don't look at all comfortable now. On the other hand you're obviously not lonely.'

Her mother had moved a little apart, ostensibly studying her catalogue, dissociating herself from them. He glanced at her; this time with overt curiosity and something like contempt. He said:

'Until Cambridge, then.'

'Until Cambridge.'

'Can I drive you up?'

'Oh Gabriel, I don't know! It all seems so far ahead. Perhaps I'll be in touch.'

'Ah well, *abiit*, *excessit*, *evasit*, *erupit*. Give my love to the Sisley.'

'What Sisley?'

'*Snow at Lucienne*. That is, if you're really on your way to the Courtauld. And good luck with the experiment.'

He raised his eyebrow and made a small rueful grimace which might have been intended to express regret, but in which she thought she detected a hint of complicity. Then he turned and bowed to her mother and was gone. Philippa went up to her and said:

'I'm sorry about that. I thought he was out of London. Actually he's the last person I should have expected to find here and alone. He affects to despise Victorian art. But we were bound to run across someone I knew sooner or later. I don't mind if you don't.'

'I mind your not being able to invite them home.'

Invite them home. The words conjured up suburban teatime in the front room, home-made scones on doilies, fishpaste sandwiches, the best tea service brought out so that she wouldn't be disgraced by the family in front of this unknown, eligible young man. Since she had never sat in such a room, it was odd that she knew precisely how it would be. She said:

'But I don't want to. We're perfectly cosy on our own. I shall have three years of Gabriel at Cambridge. You're not bored are you?'

'No. Not bored. Never that.'

'What did you think of him?'

'He's very good-looking, isn't he? Good-looking and confident.'

'He can afford to be. Nothing has ever happened to him to dislodge him from the centre of his universe.'

But one small thing had happened. She felt a twinge of anxiety. Had he really accepted that sexual failure philosophically? Wasn't he a man who would need his small revenge? As if echoing her thoughts, her mother said:

'I think he could be dangerous.'

'He'd be flattered to hear you say so; but he's no more dangerous than any other young male animal, and he's not dangerous to us. No one can be.'

Donne's words came into her mind, but she did not speak them aloud: 'Who is so safe as we where none can do Treason to us, except one of we two.'

She wondered whether her mother had read Donne. She said:

'Forget him. He hasn't spoilt the day for you, has he?'

'No, he couldn't do that. No one could.' She paused as if wondering whether to speak, and then added:

'Do you like him?'

'We don't seem able to stay apart from each other for long. But I don't think that what we have in common has anything to do with liking. Forget Gabriel. Let's fight our way into the coffee bar before it gets too crowded, and then go on to the Courtauld. I want to show you some real pictures.'

THREE

That evening, just after half-past six, the strident ring of the telephone set Hilda's heart jumping. She had never liked answering it and during the day it seldom rang. Most of Maurice's colleagues telephoned him at the university and he or Philippa would answer it when they were at home, taking it for granted, she supposed, that the call wouldn't be for her. But since Philippa had left she had grown to dread that insistent, broken summons. She was tempted to take off the receiver, but then there might be a call from the court about one of her sittings, or Maurice might ring to say that he would be late home or was bringing a colleague back for dinner. She could think of no possible excuse why he should find the number continually engaged.

It was difficult to forget that the telephone was there. The house seemed infected with instruments. There was one on the table in the hall and another by their bed. Maurice had even had an extension fitted to the wall in the kitchen. Occasionally she would let it ring unanswered, standing stock-still, hardly daring to breathe, as if the instrument held its own secret, sinister life and could detect her presence. But the accusing silence after the final ring, the niggling guilt at her own inadequacy and weakness, were harder to bear than the fear of what she might hear. She hardly knew what it was she dreaded. She only knew that some catastrophe lay waiting in the future and that it would be heralded by this imperious ring.

Now she wiped her hands on her apron and took off the receiver and heard at the other end, the coin being shot home. Her palms were moist and she felt the receiver slipping through her fingers. She steadied it with her other hand and spoke the number. To her relief it was a voice she knew.

'Mrs Palfrey? It's I, Gabriel Lomas.'

As if she knew a dozen Gabriels; and anyone less pedantic would have said 'It's me'. She had always been a little in awe of him. He had taken too much trouble with her, confusing her with his easy charm. Sometimes his eyes had met hers in a mocking conspiracy, as if to say: 'You know that you're not worth bothering about, I know it, so what are we both up to, my dear, delightful, dull Mrs Palfrey?' But at least this was a familiar voice, a lively voice, not the voice of a stranger, mysterious, heavy with imagined malice. She said:

'How are you, Gabriel?'

'Fine. Look, I've seen Philippa and her mother. I met them at the Arts Council exhibition of great Victorian pictures at the Royal Academy. They were looking at those two Abraham Solomon oils *Waiting for the Verdict* and *The Acquittal.* I oughtn't to have been surprised to meet her there. Philippa has always been fascinated by the Victorians. I must say I adore the peculiar awfulness of high Victorian art. Every picture tells a story. And what a story! A positively decadent feast of colour, my dear. Imperial confidence, pathos, Victorian eroticism and dreadful warnings about the horrid fate which awaited unfaithful wives. Have you seen the exhibition?'

'No, not yet.'

He must have known that she didn't go to exhibitions. Maurice fitted in those that he wished to see during his lunch break and on the way home. Philippa went on her own or with her friends. Sometimes she had gone with Gabriel. Only once, in an effort to interest Hilda in art, she had taken her to an exhibition of paintings from the Prado. It hadn't been a success. There had been an uncomfortable crush of people. The pictures had seemed to Hilda very dark. She remembered only the long, gloomy Spanish faces, the dark heavy robes. It had been difficult to simulate interest. None of the pictures had, she felt, any relation to her or to her life. She strained to hear Gabriel's voice which seemed suddenly to have got fainter. Then she heard it:

'It was unnerving. The pictures, I mean, not the encounter. Although that was unnerving too, in its way.'

'How did she seem, Gabriel? Was she happy?'

'Philippa? Who can tell? No one is better at disguising emotion. She wanted to talk, but we only had about five seconds. Her mother moved tactfully away; at least I thought she was being tactful, giving us the chance for a private word, but now I'm not so sure. It may have been embarrassment. Anyway, she moved to the other wall and began rather ostentatiously studying Ford Madox Brown's *The Last of England.* Well, if one had to look at any picture that was the one most worth attention. It's an extraordinary situation, isn't it? Philippa and her mother, I mean.'

Puzzled and confused, Hilda asked:

'Did Philippa tell you?'

'Oh yes, just the essentials. We only had a second. She wants me to visit her on Thursday at their place. Apparently the mother is going out. She said that there were things she wanted to talk over.'

Hilda was aware of a transitory pain that Philippa should have confided her secret so casually, after all her careful and insistent instructions that no one was to be told under any circumstances. No one. But perhaps Gabriel was special. She had sometimes felt that he might be. But how much had she told? And what was that he had said earlier about a verdict and acquittal? She said:

'What things? Is she all right?'

'She isn't ill, if that's what you mean. A bit strained, perhaps, but that might have been a touch of the Alma-Tademas. They were on their way out when we met. As I said, there really wasn't time for confidences other than the main one, where her mother had been all these years.'

So she had told him, he did know. Confused, she said:

'She told you that?'

'Well, I more or less guessed. There is a certain wariness about the eyes. I took one look and thought: either hospital or prison. I'm not sure that taking her to view high Victorian art is exactly calculated to adjust her to contemporary London. I did try to lure them to the Tate, but I got the impression from her mother that my company wasn't exactly welcome.'

'How did they seem to you? Are you sure that Philippa's all right?'

'I'm not altogether sure that the experiment is working, if that's what you mean. I take it that that's what she wants to see me about.'

'Gabriel, try to persuade her to come home. I don't mean permanently if she doesn't want to. Just to come and talk to us.'

'That's what I had in mind. It's silly cutting herself off. It's this thing she has about the biological tie. It's completely irrational. You're her mother in any real sense of the word.'

He didn't believe that. She didn't believe it. And it wasn't important anyway. Why should he need to tell her lies? Why did they all lie to her; obvious, commonplace, childish lies which they didn't even take the trouble to make convincing. But at least he had seen Philippa. At least she would be getting some news. Then she heard his voice again.

'I'm supposed to be there next Thursday at six. The trouble is that I've lost the address. I scribbled it down on the back of my catalogue and now I can't lay my hands on it. The name too.'

'Ducton. The name's Ducton. And they're at 12 Delaney Street, north west one. It's off Mell Street.'

'I remembered Mell Street and the number of the house. And of course, she introduced her mother as Ducton. It was Delaney Street I couldn't remember. Have you any message for her?'

'Just my love. Give her my love. Perhaps you'd better not say that we've spoken, but Gabriel, try to persuade her to come home.'

'Don't worry,' he said. 'She'll come home all right.'

When she had put down the receiver Hilda's heart was lightened. She felt something very like happiness. After all, if they were visiting exhibitions, things couldn't be too bad. They would hardly be looking at pictures together if life were intolerable for them. And at least Philippa had got in touch with a friend, one of her own age-group. Gabriel would ring her back and give her the news. She wouldn't tell Maurice that he had rung. She knew that he was anxious about Philippa, but she knew too, that it wasn't an anxiety he was willing to discuss. But, after next Thursday, she would get some news. Perhaps Philippa was ready to come home. Perhaps everything was going to be all right after all.

As she rinsed and dried her hands and went back to chopping the onions, she wondered briefly and totally without anxiety why Gabriel had troubled to telephone from a public box.

FOUR

His plan was basically simple, although he knew that carrying it out would be trickier. He would lift the key ring from Monty's jacket pocket while, at the same time, dropping from his hand a bunch of keys roughly equal in size. Monty would be aware, even if only subconsciously, of the weight and jangle of the keys against his thigh. Simply to steal them would mean almost immediate discovery. Once the keys were in his possession he would have to get the two Yales copied as quickly as possible, preferably somewhere close but where there were plenty of customers so that one face might not be particularly remembered. Then the genuine keys would have to be returned and the substitutes recovered. It would mean two appearances at the shop within a comparatively short time. And there would be other customers, he would have to choose his moment carefully. But first he must get a close look at the key ring and the number and weight of the keys.

On the first day, Monday 11th September, he stationed himself at his watching post on the wasteland at eight-forty-five, binoculars at the ready. The greengrocer arrived on his bicycle at three minutes past nine, felt in the pocket of his close-fitting denim jacket and unlocked the door. But his back was firmly towards the street and it was impossible for Scase to get a glance at the keys. Two minutes later the shop front was cranked open and Monty began the business of dragging forward the crates of fruit and vegetables from the back of the shop, and arranging his display. He had exchanged his blue jacket for the shabby fawn working coat which he wore open. It had two large side-pockets, the left-hand one slightly ripped at the seam. The door between the shop and the ground-floor passage of the house was open.

Shortly after ten past nine a small van stopped outside the shop and the driver and a lad clambered down from the cabin and began lugging crates of fruit and vegetables on to the pavement. The street door was closed. Monty's hand went into his left pocket and he pressed something into the boy's palm. Then he began helping the driver to unload while the lad unlocked the door, wedged it open with a net of Spanish onions and began to hump in the crates of fresh produce. For a few seconds the key was left in the door, the bright ring of metal and the pendant keys hanging against the wood. But the driver, carrying a box of apples, moved across obscuring the view. Then the boy's hand fastened on the keys and he tossed them back to Monty. Scase glimpsed nothing but the flash of metal and Monty's hand snatching at the air.

For the next three days the routine was the same. Scase stayed all day at his post, fortified at mid-morning with sandwiches, but was still unable to get a close look at the keys. Monty worked alone. At midday he went over the road to the Blind Beggar and brought back a brimming pint-mug of beer, then dragged an upturned crate from the back of the shop and sat beside the stall drinking the beer and eating an immense roll of what looked like cheese and tomato. Occasionally during the morning he would go over to the pub. When this happened the wizened little man from the junk shop temporarily took over the stall. Scase guessed that they had this arrangement; that Monty would keep an eye on the junk from time to time while his neighbour covered his visits to the Blind Beggar. During the whole of the three days the connecting door between the shop and the rest of the house was left ajar, except when Monty was about to leave when he would firmly close it. Focusing his binoculars with some difficulty through the slit in the fence, Scase was able to see that this door, too, had a Yale lock and he guessed that Monty would be equally punctilious about closing the connecting door before finally leaving at night.

By Friday morning, frustrated, he knew that he must get closer, must be there early in the morning to watch while the door was unlocked. There was no reason why he shouldn't; someone had to be the first customer. It would mean that he was noticed; it added to the risk that he would be remembered. But that couldn't be helped. He would worry about that later when the time came to fabricate an alibi. Now all his thoughts were fixed on getting possession of that bunch of keys.

The timing was tricky. Monty invariably arrived between nine o'clock and nine-five in the morning. The murderess and her daughter left their apartment between nine-fifteen and nine-twenty. Provided Monty were on time and the other two didn't decide to leave early, he should be all right. But he couldn't safely loiter in Delaney Street before nine o'clock. Neither the junk shop nor the second-hand bookshop opened much before half-past nine, and his presence, unoccupied and aimlessly sauntering in the deserted street, might well be noticed from the window of number 12.

That afternoon he bought a canvas shopping basket from Woolworth's in Edgware Road and next morning began walking slowly down Mell Street towards the junction of Delaney Street just before nine o'clock. At two minutes past nine Monty appeared, cycling from the direction of Lisson Grove, and turned into Delaney Street. Scase quickened his steps and caught him up just before he dismounted. He said:

'Good morning. Are you opening up now?'

'That's right. Take me about three minutes. You in a hurry?'

'I am rather. I'll just pop round the corner to the station bookstall for a newspaper and then come back.'

As he spoke, Monty, still with one hand on the bar of his cycle, inserted a Yale key into the lock. Scase kept his eyes fixed on the key ring, memorizing its size, its probable heaviness, the shape and number of the keys. It was a large ring and there hung on it two Yales, a small flat key about the size of a car key, and one heavier, solid Chubb about two inches long.

He bought his paper at Marylebone Station and sat reading it in the waiting-room, concealing his face behind it until half-past nine. Then, when he could be sure that the murderess and her daughter would have left Delaney Street, he returned to Monty's stall and bought four oranges, a pound of apples and a bunch of grapes. He could lighten his load by eating them during the day. Then he walked quickly to Woolworth's and bought a large key ring. It had a tag attached bearing an ornamental initial, but this, without much difficulty, he was able to prise away.

He spent the rest of the morning searching for substitute keys in the junk shops and antique markets of Mell Street and Church Street. His first find was a substitute for the smallest key; this he took from the lock of a battered tea caddy. A Yale was discovered in a tobacco jar containing screws and pipe cleaners. The heavy Chubb proved more elusive and, in the end, he was forced to steal a key similar in weight and size from the top drawer of an old chest which was standing inside one of the shops. It pleased him that his fingers could act with speed and cunning. He found the second Yale in an old tin box of nails, screws, spectacles and broken pieces of electrical equipment stuck under the table outside the junk shop in Delaney Street. By the end of the morning he had succeeded in putting together a key ring which in appearance and weight was as close to Monty's as he could hope to find.

For the rest of the day he walked again the very streets of his childhood, euphoric, borne on a tide of excitement and terror, half-pleasurable, wholly familiar. The concrete underpass at Edgware Road echoed with the distant thunder of the sea. He had only to close his eyes against the sun to feel again the gritty sand creeping between his toes, and to see once more the brightly patterned shore. The raucous voices of children calling to each other down the side streets jolted his heart with half-forgotten playground menace and the smell of the pavement after a squall of summer rain was the smell of the sea. Now, as then, he knew exactly what he had to do, knew the necessity, the inevitability of the act. Now, as then, he was torn between the longing to get it over and the half-shameful hope that he still might have a choice, that it was within his power to stop now, to decide that the risk was too great. With part of his mind he wished that he had returned to the stall as soon as the key ring was complete, and had tried his luck then, carried forward on a tide of optimism and success. But he knew that it could have been fatal. He had yet to prove that the old skills remained to him.

He spent the whole of Sunday and Monday practising. He locked his room and hung his jacket over the corner of a chair. He hooked the new key ring over the little finger of his left hand and insinuated his hand under the flap of the pocket. With his thumb he gently lifted his own key ring at the same time as he slid the substitute ring from his finger. He performed the procedure over and over again, sometimes using his thumb, sometimes his middle finger, watching for the slightest movement of the jacket pocket, counting out the seconds to time himself. Speed meant safety. When he felt that he was proficient he started again, only this time using the fingers of his right hand. He had to be ambidextrous in skill. He couldn't be sure until the moment came, until he was close enough to Monty to press his hands against the jacket, which of the pockets would hold the keys. For two days he hardly left his hotel room except to buy sandwiches, hurrying through the hallway, almost oblivious to Violet's greeting as she recognized his footsteps and her dead eyes searched for him, grudging every moment away from his task. And by Monday evening 18th September he felt that he was ready.

FIVE

The next day he collected together two pairs of underclothes and a couple of shirts and stuffed them into a plastic shopping bag. He went first to the Delaney Street launderette, arriving soon after nine o'clock. Once his washing was swirling in the machine he moved to a chair next to the open door from where he could watch number 12. One possibility worried him, that the murderess and her daughter might choose this morning to visit the launderette themselves. But he told himself that the risk of an encounter was small. If they came out with a bag which might contain clothes, he would simply walk out before they arrived and return later to empty his machine.

But all was well. He saw them emerge as usual by nine-forty-five, carrying nothing but their shoulder-bags. He moved away from the window, but they passed on the other side of the street and without glancing his way. One or two pensioners, always the earliest out in the mornings, had made their way to Monty's door but business was slack, the street had not yet come alive. When the third customer, an elderly woman, had shuffled away with her load of potatoes, he judged that the moment had come. He picked up the empty bag and moved across the road to the stall. His right hand deep in his jacket pocket fingered the dummy set of keys. The metal grew warm and moist under his touch. It irritated him that his hands were sweating with fear until he remembered that the moistness would help, the keys would slip the more easily from his fingers. And at least his hands weren't trembling. Even at the height of childhood delinquency his hands had never trembled.

Monty, temporarily without a customer, was burnishing Cox's Orange Pippins on his sleeve and arranging them in a line across the front of the stall. Pretending to be interested in a carton of avocado pears, Scase brushed past him, his left hand briefly pressing against Monty's right-hand pocket. It felt padded; something was there, a handkerchief perhaps, or a rag. But he could detect nothing hard or metallic. So the keys, if they were on him at all, must be in the other pocket. He retreated from the back of the stall, and asked for four oranges, holding open his bag. Monty picked them out and dropped them in. Then Scase demanded and received four of the Cox's Orange Pippins. Lastly he asked for two bananas, not too ripe, and pointed to a couple which formed part of a bunch slung from a rail at the back of the stall. It was the most inaccessible bunch, and Monty had to stretch over to reach them, steadying himself by grasping the rail with his left hand. Scase moved close to him, his eyes fixed on the bananas. He hooked his little finger into the bunch of dummy keys, closed his fist round them, then insinuated his hand into Monty's coat pocket and felt with a surge of triumph the hard tangled coldness of the keys. He strengthened his middle finger and lifted the bunch, at the same time gently relinquishing the dummy ring. After the practice of the last few days and with no occluding pocket-flap to hinder him, the ploy was surprisingly easy. He judged that it took less than three seconds. By the time Monty had straightened himself to tear the two selected bananas from the bunch and had tossed them into the pan of his scales, Scase was standing meekly by his side, stretching wide his shopping bag to receive them.

He made himself walk unhurriedly down Delaney Street, but as soon as he turned the corner into Mell Street, his steps quickened. He was lucky, there were two taxis waiting outside Marylebone Station. He took the first to Selfridges and went to the key-cutting counter in the basement. Even at this early hour there were two people before him, but it was only minutes before he was prising the two Yale keys from Monty's bunch and handing them over. He asked for two copies of each, knowing that sometimes a newly-cut Yale would be defective. He left the store by the front entrance and, as he had hoped, had no difficulty in getting a taxi. They were arriving in a steady stream, dropping tourists for their morning shopping. He asked for Marylebone Station and, after paying off the cab, actually walked on to the concourse in case the driver should be watching. Within two minutes he was back in Delaney Street. His plan was to transfer his washing to the drying machine, then to watch the greengrocer's shop from the window until it seemed a propitious moment to change back the keys. But as he approached the stall his heart sank. Monty was no longer wearing the fawn working coat. The day had become hotter, the stall busier and he was serving now wearing nothing but his blue jeans and a singlet. The coat was nowhere to be seen.

He left Delaney Street and sat on a bench in Marylebone Station waiting for the clock to show five minutes to twelve. Monty invariably went across to the Blind Beggar for his beer just after the hour. The thirty-minute wait seemed interminable. He sat in a fever of anxiety and impatience which drove him every few minutes to pace up and down the concourse. It was unlikely that Monty would want the keys until it was time for him to shut up the shop at night. Even then he wouldn't need them; the locks were both Yales and all that was necessary was for him to close both the shop and street doors after him. He might not discover that he had a substitute set of keys until he tried to open the street door next morning. But there would be no possible chance of making the substitution after nightfall. It had to be done now.

He walked back to Delaney Street at eight minutes to twelve and pretended to browse in the bookshop. At twelve o'clock Monty called to his neighbour and, a second or two later, appeared from the back of the shop wearing his denim jacket and went across to the Blind Beggar. The old man from the junk shop settled himself on the upturned crate, lifted his face for a moment to the sun, then opened his newspaper. It had to be now. It might be only a couple of minutes, perhaps less, before Monty reappeared with his beer. And the only hope of success lay in boldness. He walked briskly across the road and into the recesses of the shop, so quickly that the old man hardly had time to raise his eyes as he brushed past. All was well. The fawn working coat hung on the nail above two sacks of potatoes piled against the wall. As his fingers met the smooth metal of the keys his heart leaped in triumph.

The old man was standing in the space between the wall and the counter. Before he could speak Scase said:

'I've left a Marks and Spencer bag somewhere where I've been shopping. I've only been here, over the road at the bookshop and to the dairy in Mell Street and it isn't there. I thought Monty might have found it and put it on one side for me.'

The sharp little eyes were suspicious. But Scase hadn't been anywhere near the cash register. He wasn't helping himself to anything, hadn't been in the shop long enough to steal. What, anyway, was there worth stealing at the back of the counter? He said grumpily:

'Monty? He's not Monty. Been dead twenty year, Monty has. That's George. And he never said nothing to me.'

'It's not at the back, and there's nowhere else he would have put it. It looks as if I must have left it in the launderette and someone's taken it. Thank you.'

He walked briskly away, crossing the road and stepping on to the kerb outside the Blind Beggar as Monty – it was difficult to think of him as George – emerged, carefully carrying a brimming pint in each hand.

The relief, the excitement, the exultation were greater than any he had experienced in childhood after the lesser, more innocent delinquencies. His heart sang a paean of undirected praise. If the keys had been strung on a ring he would have needed to spin them in a flashing arc, to have tossed and caught them like a toy. But none of this triumph showed in his face. As George passed he smiled at him. There must have been something strange about the smile. As he turned into Mell Street his last memory was of George's astonished face.

SIX

He had carefully matched the two sets of keys and had strung them on different lengths of string. One set would open the front door, the second the door leading from the hall into the shop. Until he tried them in the lock he couldn't know which was which. He hoped luck would be with him and that he would get it right first time. The longer he lingered or fumbled at the door, the greater the chance that he would be seen. He watched from his usual vantage point on the wasteland until the murderess and her daughter had left for work, then waited another forty minutes in case they should have forgotten something and return unexpectedly. From the narrow slit in the corrugated iron he had a very restricted view of Delaney Street, but he put his ear against it and listened until he could hear no footfalls. Then he edged his way quickly across the wasteland and slid through the gap in the fence as he had so many times. Delaney Street was deserted. Above the closed shops he could see a row of lit upstairs windows where he could imagine people eating an early supper or settling down to an evening's television. To his left the launderette shone brightly with light, but he could see only one customer, an elderly woman with a basket on wheels dragging her tangled linen from one of the machines.

He took one set of the keys from his pocket and concealed them in his clenched palm, then he walked quickly but deliberately across the street and inserted the key in the lock. It didn't turn. His lips moved. Silently he said to himself: gently, gently, gently. He felt for the second string of keys and this time the key turned without difficulty and he stepped into the hall, closing the door behind him.

And then there came a moment of atavistic horror. The house had shuddered at his entrance. He stood transfixed, holding his breath. Then he relaxed. The vibration was only the rumble of a passing tube train, presumably in the tunnel between Marylebone and Edgware Road. The noise receded, and the house settled into calmness. He closed the door and stood motionless, listening to the silence. The hall held the earthy heavy smell of potatoes, with a trace of a lighter, sharper scent, perhaps of apples. At the end of the passage he could see a faint haze where a door with two panels of opaque glass led to a garden or back yard. He switched on his torch and followed the pool of light down the passage. The door was bolted, both at the top and at the bottom. That meant that the yard offered no sanctuary, no place to hide. The murderess and her daughter would almost certainly check those locks before they finally went to bed.

He shone his torch on the stairs and made his way up, testing each stair with his foot before he put his full weight on it. There was a small half landing. He paused, then made his way up the second short flight. Their door was on the left. He shone the torch full on it, and the pool of bright light illumined a security lock.

Disappointment rose in his throat like a hard core of bile which he had to resist the temptation to vomit away. He didn't beat his hands against the door in frustration, but he rested his head against it for a moment, fighting down nausea. Then came anger and a sense of self-betrayal. How stupid of him not to have known that the door would be locked. But he had thought of the premises as the single house which once they had been, with one front door, one lock. And this was no Yale lock. Unless he could again steal a set of keys – and how could he? – he could only force his way through this barrier by breaking down the door.

He had intended to explore the flat in detail, to discover where the murderess slept, so that he could go unhesitatingly to her room and make his escape afterwards without blundering through the wrong door. This was now impossible. He had to change his plan. But there were things that he could do, preparations that he could make. He could begin by familiarizing himself with the house. He knew that the women weren't due back until midnight, but he walked on tip-toe, the torch beam sheltered by his left palm, his ears keen for the slightest sound. Gently and very quietly he pushed open the door to the bathroom, standing to one side as if expecting to find it occupied. The window was wide open at the top, and the air rushed at him, cool and strong as a wind, billowing the curtains. They were drawn back and he dared not switch on his torch, but the garish London sky, streaked with purple and crimson, showed him the outline of the gas boiler, the delicately-linked hanging chain with its bulbous handle, the great white bath. There was no cupboard, no curtained recess, nowhere here where he could conceal himself.

He spent the next five minutes mounting and descending the stairs, testing them for creaks. The fifth and ninth were particularly noisy; he would have to remember not to tread on them. Most of the others creaked under his tread but it was possible, by keeping close to the wall, to reduce all but the slightest sound.

Lastly, he took the second set of keys from his pocket and unlocked the door leading into the shop. As he pushed it open, the rich smell of earth, the zest of lemons and oranges, met him so strongly that it caught at his breath. The darkness was absolute. No chink of light from the street lamps shone through the metal shutters, and if there were a window at the rear of the shop it must have been boarded up. No drawn curtains could so effectively exclude the sky. He leaned back against the door, staring into the blackness, breathing freely for the first time since he had entered the house. Even if the women returned early, they would have no key to this room. Here he could be sure of safety. Emboldened, he switched on his torch and swept it slowly over the shop, over the stall of potatoes and fruit, the folded trestle table, the rolled mat of synthetic grass, the piled boxes of tomatoes, apples and lettuces waiting for the morning, the sacks of potatoes and the meshed bags of onions humped against the wall. At the rear and under the shuttered window was an old porcelain sink; one of the taps was missing, from the other a continuous bead of water formed, then fell. He had to resist the urge to turn it off, to stop the regular soft dripping. To one side his torch illumined a wooden table with a formica top on which was a gas ring, a kettle, and a brown stained teapot. Underneath the table was an orange box turned on its side, containing two blue-rimmed mugs, a tin marked 'sugar' and a tea caddy with a coronation picture of King George V and Queen Mary.

He propped his torch against one of the boxes. Then, illumined by the single beam of light, he put on the long mackintosh and the gloves, drawing them up over the tucked-in cuffs of the sleeves. Lastly he took the knife from the bottom of the rucksack. He squatted against the strong wooden upright at the back of the stall, knees bent under his chin, his thin buttocks hard against the unyielding floor, holding the sheathed knife in his hand. It wouldn't happen tonight. He knew that with complete certainty, although he was unable to say why. But he felt obscurely that the mackintosh and the gloves were some protection against leaving a trace of himself for Monty to find, and it was right that he should thus formally garb himself for his task, should be prepared in case, by some miracle, the murderess returned alone. He sat on in the darkness, waiting, counting the regular dripping of the tap, smelling the warmth of the plastic mackintosh superimposed on the loamy scent of the shop, holding his white-gloved hands before him, palm to palm, like the hands of a priest.

It was just before midnight when at last they returned and he heard the firm closing of the front door. He thought he could detect a low murmur of voices and the creaking of the stairs, but he wasn't sure. But then they were overhead. The house had not been built as two flats and there were only the joists and the wooden floor between them. The timbers creaked loudly as their feet struck them, and occasionally the wood cracked like a shot. Then his heart would leap and he would stare, petrified, at the ceiling, as if afraid that a foot would descend through the boards. He could hear every move. It seemed impossible that his presence, the very smell of him, the warmth of his spent breath, should not penetrate through to them. He could identify the two sets of footsteps, one lighter than the other. That would be the murderess; the girl was taller and walked with more confidence. Then the footsteps separated; they were moving about in different rooms. The quieter footfalls were in the front of the house; so the murderess must sleep in the bedroom overlooking the street. After about five minutes he heard her footsteps across the ceiling and, a few minutes later, there was the flush of the lavatory cistern and the muffled roar of the gas boiler. So the murderess was in the bathroom. This, if all else failed, could give him his chance. But he needed to know whether, with no one in the house at night except another woman, she would bother to lock the door, whether the door to the flat itself was propped open or closed when either of them went to the bathroom. Perhaps it would be instinctive to close both doors. If, in the end, he had to kill her in the bathroom, these were the facts it would be important to know.

By half-past twelve the last sounds had died away, but still he sat on, the wood of the upright hard against his backbone. The loamy smell of freshly turned earth from the sacks of potatoes was stronger than ever. He found himself trying to hold his breath against memory. But it was no use. Suddenly he was standing again with Mavis by the covered heap of red earth at the edge of Julie's grave in that vast east London cemetery, watching the small white coffin jerking slowly downwards into darkness. They had been the only two mourners; Mavis had insisted on a private funeral. They had always kept themselves to themselves; why should they be generous in grief? Why now should they expose themselves to the avid, salacious eyes of their neighbours? Their own minister had been ill and the young substitute had worn unpolished shoes. Mavis had kept her eyes on them throughout the words of committal. Listening to her complaints afterwards he had said:

'But he took the service very nicely dear, I thought he spoke very well.'

And she had replied in the grudging, obstinate voice with which he was to grow so familiar:

'He should have cleaned his shoes.'

He fixed his mind on the murderess sleeping overhead. Within a few days she would be dead. Perhaps he and the girl would be dead too. In that moment it seemed to him not to be important if they also died. There might be a necessity which he couldn't yet foresee or understand, but which, when the time came, he would be powerless to prevent. That the three of them should die together even had a certain rightness, a completion, an avoidance of future complications which he could almost welcome. For himself, he feared death less than he feared imprisonment. Perhaps it was the possibility of his own imminent death, which he faced now for the first time, more than the certainty of hers, which drove his thoughts back to the past. On his mind there clicked a series of bright, disjointed images, like pictures flashed on a screen. The tinsel Christmas tree on the bar of the Goat and Compasses, glimpsed through the open door; the seaweed hanging in swathes from the girders of the pier, moving in slimy tentacles beneath the green onrushing tide, the grating dampness of the sand as he scuffed it over a stolen purse; Mr Micklewright, holding a knight between his first and second fingers and sliding it towards him across the board; Eli Watkin spooning out the cat food and hissing endearments at his squawking brood; Julie in her new Girl Guide uniform; Julie sleeping in her pram under the apple tree on the lawn of Magenta Gardens; Mavis glancing at him across the scarred desk of the local secondary school where they had first met at evening classes in French. Why, he wondered, had they chosen French? Neither had ever been to France, neither had ever had any particular wish to go. But that had been the beginning. Nothing that had happened between them afterwards had ever persuaded him that he was lovable; only that, by some miracle of chance, Mavis had found him so.

From time to time he dozed, then woke and stretched his cramped legs. At last, before the dawn, he got slowly to his feet, took off his gloves and mackintosh and replaced them with the sheathed knife in his rucksack. His vigil was over; this was a new day. He wouldn't return that evening; it was important to stay at the Casablanca on alternate nights, to ensure that he kept his senses fresh and alert, that he didn't go too short of sleep. But he would come back on Thursday and on alternate nights after that until his chance came. Optimism had been reborn. He knew that the wait wouldn't be long.

He closed the shop door with infinite care, then crept down the few yards of the passage. There was still the front door to shut, but he didn't fear that that quiet click would wake the sleepers overhead. Even if the murderess still lay awake or stirred in her sleep, so small a sound would hardly disturb her. This was an old house; old houses were full of mysterious nocturnal noises. And by the time she switched on the light and got to the window he would be out of sight. The door closed behind him and he set off for Baker Street Station to wait for the first Circle line train.

SEVEN

It was mid-afternoon on Thursday 21st September, and Philippa was sitting in the basket chair at the open window of her room. She and her mother had just returned from a visit to Brompton Oratory to see the Mazzuoli Marbles and there was an hour before they needed to set out for work. Her mother had said that she would make the tea. From the kitchen Philippa could hear small noises like the scrapings of a secretive domestic animal, delicate tinklings, an occasional soft footfall. The sounds were extraordinarily pleasurable. The door of her mother's room was open, but Thursday was early-closing and no sounds came up from the street. The voices which drifted in through her own window seemed far-away shouts of joy from another world. It had been a hot oppressive day with the threat of thunder, but in the last half-hour the sky had lightened and now the room was filled with the strong mellow light which comes before the dusk.

Philippa sat absolutely still in the silence, and there began to flow through her a sense of tingling delight, entrancing in its strangeness. Even the inanimate objects in the room, the air itself, were suffused with this iridescent joy. She fixed her eyes on the geranium on the window sill. Why had she never before realized how beautiful it was? She had seen geraniums as the gaudy expedient of municipal gardeners to be planted in park beds, massed on political platforms, a useful pot plant for the house, since it throve with so little attention. But this plant was a miracle of beauty. Each flowerlet was curled like a miniature rosebud on the end of its furred, tender stem. Imperceptibly but inevitably as her own breathing they were opening to the light. The petals were a clear, transparent pink, faintly striped with yellow, and the fan-like leaves, how intricately veined they were, how varied in their greenness, each with its darker penumbra. Some words of William Blake fell into her mind, familiar but new. 'Everything that lives is holy. Life delights in life.' Even her body's flux, which she could feel as a gentle, almost controlled, flow, wasn't the inconvenient and disagreeable monthly discharge of the body's waste. There was no waste. Everything living was part of one great wholeness. To breathe was to take in delight. She wished that she knew how to pray, that there was someone to whom she could say: 'Thank you for this moment of happiness. Help me to make her happy.' And she thought of other words, familiar but untraceable to their source: 'In whom we live and move and have our being.'

She heard her mother calling her from the front room. There was a smell of cut lemons and freshly brewed China tea, and the pot with their two special cups, the Worcester and the Stafford-shire, were on a papier maché tray on the bedside table. Her mother was smiling and holding out to her a tissue-wrapped package. She said:

'I made it for you.'

Philippa took it and shook out from its folds a polo-necked jumper in a variety of soft browns and fawns, and with two oblongs of apple green, carefully placed above the right breast and at the back. The jumper had been constructed from every kind of knitting stitch, and the variety of textures between the panels, the subtle blending of colours, gave its basic simplicity such distinction that Philippa, tugging it over her head, exclaimed aloud with pleasure:

'It's lovely! Lovely! You are clever, but when did you knit it?'

'In my room, late at night. I didn't want you to see it until it was finished. It's quite simple really. The sleeves are just oblongs grafted on to the dropped shoulders. Of course, it's too warm to be worn now, but come the autumn in Cambridge you will be glad of it.'

'I'm glad of it now. I'll always be glad of it. It's beautiful. Everyone will wonder where I bought it. I shall like saying that my mother knitted it for me.'

They looked at each other, two faces transformed with pleasure. 'I shall like saying that my mother knitted it for me.' She had spoken the words spontaneously, without embarrassment. She couldn't remember in her private, self-conscious, fabricated life when she had been able to speak so simply what was in her heart. She tugged her mane of hair free from the rolled collar and shook it free. Stretching both arms widely, she spun round in pleasure. In the oval glass which she had set between the two windows, she watched her spinning image, gold and fawn and brown and flashing green, and behind her the still flushed face of her mother, bright-eyed and alive.

The peal of the front doorbell, strident and peremptory, broke their mood. Philippa stopped spinning and they gazed at each other with surprised and anxious eyes. No one had rung that bell since the probation officer's last visit. Her mother said:

'Perhaps George has come back for something and has forgotten his key.'

Philippa went to the door. She said:

'You stay here. I'll go.'

The bell had rung again before she reached the bottom of the stairs. And with that second ring she knew that this was trouble. She opened the door.

'Miss Palfrey? I'm Terry Brewer.'

The voice was cautious, almost apologetic. He was proffering a card. He must have had it ready in his hands as he heard her coming down the stairs. She didn't look at it. The police had cards too. There was a card for every purpose: warrants, authorizations, identity cards, licences, passes. They said: 'Let me in. I exist. I am authorized, safe, respectable.' She didn't need a card to know what business he was in. She kept her eyes on his face.

'What do you want?'

He was very young, not much older than she was, with strong, tightly curled hair low on his forehead, a heart-shaped face with a neatly cleft chin, jutting cheek-bones and a delicate, moistly pouting mouth. His eyes were large and luminous, pale brown speckled with green. She made herself look into them.

'Just a chat. I'm a feature writer, a freelance. I've been asked to do an article for the *Clarion*. About lifers and their readjustment to the world outside prison. Nothing sensational. You know the *Clarion*. They're not interested in morbid sensationalism. What I'm after is the human interest, how you discovered who your mother was, what it's like living together after all these years, how she survived her time in prison. I'd like to interview you both. Of course, the name will be changed. I shan't mention Ducton.'

It was hopeless to try to close the door in his face. Already his foot was jammed against the wood. She said:

'I don't know what you're talking about and I don't want to see you.'

'Oh, but I don't think you've got much choice, have you? Better me than a dozen others. One interview, exclusive, and I leave you strictly alone. No address printed. No names. The others might not be so accommodating. You don't need me to tell you that.'

It was a lie about being a feature writer or a freelance. She doubted whether he were even a reporter. More likely he was a trainee journalist or had some minor job on the *Clarion* and he saw this as his first big chance. But someone must have tipped him off and there could be only one person. She asked:

'How did you find us?'

'I've got friends.'

'One friend particularly. Gabriel Lomas?'

He didn't answer, but she knew at once that the guess had been correct. His muscles were too undisciplined, the face too mobile for dissembling. So Gabriel must have telephoned Caldecote Terrace, choosing his time so that Hilda would be likely to be there alone. Maurice would have sniffed danger and deceit over the line, but Hilda, silly, innocent Hilda, was a predestined victim. She wondered by what guile Gabriel had extracted the truth from her and how much of it he had learned. He would have lied about their meeting, of course; even if it weren't strictly necessary he couldn't have resisted at least one lie. And then he would have done his research. He was to read history at Cambridge. He would have been meticulous about ascertaining the facts. And it wouldn't have been so very difficult. There weren't many crimes for which a woman would be imprisoned for nearly ten years. He would only have to study the press cuttings for 1968 and '69. She was surprised that it had taken him as long as a week to discover who her mother was. But, then, he might have had more important matters on his mind. Perhaps this small betrayal hadn't been given top priority.

Watching Brewer's predatory, ingratiating smile, she could understand why Gabriel had been attracted. Singularity and strangeness in a face had always drawn him. Why else, at first, had he bothered with her? He picked people over like bric-à-brac on a street stall. She had seen him at parties momentarily entranced by the fall of light on a turning cheek, a flash of unsuspected wit, the confident turn of a head. And, like bric-à-brac, people could be discarded if he made a bad buy. This face would have intrigued him. The farouche good looks, the hint of corruption and danger, the spurious vulnerability. He was trying to look deprecatory, harmless, but she could almost smell his excitement. He was rather too carefully dressed and not altogether at ease in his clothes. This must be his best suit, kept for job interviews, weddings, seductions, blackmail. It was a little too well-cut, the lapels too wide, the cloth, more synthetic than wool, already creasing. It was odd that Gabriel hadn't done something about his clothes. But he held himself well, he fancied himself, this common little pouf with his false, ingratiating smile.

'Look you'd better let me in. Get it over with. I'll only be back. And I don't want to discuss it here. I don't want to start shouting. After all, someone from the street might hear us. They think your mother is called Palfrey, I suppose? Better keep it that way.'

Her mother had appeared at the top of the stairs. She whispered:

'Let him in.'

Philippa stepped aside and he slid through the door. Her mother was standing at the open door of the flat and he pushed past her and moved into the front room as confidently as if he had been there before. They followed, side by side, and stood in the doorway regarding him. How eagerly he had pranced up those narrow shabby stairs, despising their poverty, their vulnerability! Now he was frankly surveying the room, keen-eyed as a creditor pricing their few possessions, his glance resting at last on the Henry Walton. The picture, which even to Philippa's eyes looked suddenly out of place, seemed momentarily to confuse him.

It was an abomination that he should be there. Anger flowed through her. She was lifted exhilaratingly on a tide of passionate rage in which inspiration and action flowed together.

'Wait,' she said. 'Wait.'

She ran into the kitchen and dragged the toolbox from the cupboard under the sink. Grasping the largest and strongest chisel, she walked past the front room with only a glance at Brewer's face, stupid and vacant with astonishment, then went out shutting the door of the flat behind her. Then she inserted the blade of the chisel in the narrow gap between the lock and the door-jamb and worked away at the lock. She had no energy to waste on wondering what was happening inside the flat; all her strength, all her mind were concentrated on the task in hand. The lock didn't break. It had been made to resist any such crude assaults. But the door itself was more fragile. It had never been intended as a front door and it had been there for over eighty years. She worked away, grunting with effort, and soon she heard the first creaks, saw the first splintering of the wood. After about two minutes it finally cracked and broke away. She gave a little moan and the door burst open under her hands. And now she was in the front room facing him, breathless, the chisel in her hand. When she could speak her voice was perfectly controlled.

'Right. Now get out. If you write a word, I'll complain to your paper and to the Press Council that you forced your way in here, broke down the door and threatened to betray us to everyone in the neighbourhood unless we gave you an exclusive story.'

He backed against the wall, his eyes fixed on the chisel. His voice shook. He said in a hoarse whisper:

'You crazy bitch! Who's going to believe you?'

'More people than will believe you. Can you afford to take the risk? I'm eminently respectable, remember. Are you? And do you think a reputable newspaper will welcome that kind of publicity? My mother may be beyond compassion, but I'm not. I'm the dutiful daughter, risking my future to help her. Cambridge scholar in backstreet hideout. "She's my mother," says Mary Ducton's daughter. That's the kind of emotional muck you had in mind, isn't it? I qualify for pity. Do you seriously believe that anyone will believe that I broke down that door myself?'

'It isn't my chisel! Why should I come here with a chisel?'

'Why indeed, except perhaps to force open a door. It's a perfectly ordinary chisel. New, as you see. No distinguishing marks. Prove it isn't yours if you can. And remember, it's two against one. You seem to know who my mother is, what she did. Do you suppose a lie would stick in her throat? Not if it's going to destroy your career it won't.'

He said, with a kind of wonder:

'Christ, I believe you'd do it!'

'I'm her daughter. If this didn't succeed and you got away with it, how long do you think I'd let you last?'

There could be no doubt now of his terror. She could smell it, rancid as vomit. He backed towards the door as she advanced, chisel in hand, the point at his throat. Then he was gone and they heard the clatter of his frantic feet on the stairs.

Her mother moved along from the wall, feeling it with outstretched hands like a blind woman. Philippa went to her and led her to the bed. They sat side by side, their shoulders touching. Her mother whispered:

'You frightened him.'

'I did, didn't I? They won't print anything, and he won't write anything. Not yet anyway. Even if he tells, they'll check with their lawyers first.'

'Couldn't we go away? Not for long, just for a few days so that he'll think he's scared us off. We could go to Ventnor, in the Isle of Wight. I went there once for a Sunday School treat when I was nine. There are cliffs and sand and little Victorian coloured houses. Once he finds we've gone he won't keep coming back.'

'He won't come back at all. He won't dare. He knows that I wasn't bluffing. The *Clarion* is the last paper to print the kind of sentimental muck he had in mind. Even if they did print a story, they wouldn't identify either of us or print the address. They have their liberal conscience to preserve. They won't see it as their business to hunt you down. After all, as a lifer out on licence, in their eyes you're practically a protected species.'

She was surprised that her mother was so shaken. She had seemed so strong when she first came out of prison. But perhaps nothing had mattered very much to her then. Perhaps it was only when she had stood on the canal bank in the green watery twilight, watching that shabby case finally topple out of sight that she had laid herself open to the pain of living. She moved closer to her mother and put her arm round the shaking shoulders. She laid her cheek against her mother's cheek, flesh against colder flesh. Then she kissed her. It was all so easy, so beautifully easy. Why had it taken her so long to learn that there was nothing to be afraid of in loving? She said:

'It's going to be all right. Nothing dreadful is going to happen. We're together and no one can touch us.'

'But suppose he goes to another paper?'

'He won't, not while he's working for the *Clarion*. And if he does, we'll destroy his career. All you have to do is to confirm what I tell them. If you seem frightened – well that would be natural. All it needs is the capacity to lie.'

'I don't think I'd be very good at lying.'

'I don't see why you should worry about lying. Telling the truth didn't do you much good. But you won't have to lie. I tell you, he's not coming back.'

'The door. How can we lock it?'

'I'll buy a bolt tomorrow and we can use that at night until I can get a new lock fixed. That isn't important, it's the least of our worries. He won't come back, and there's nothing worth stealing except the picture. A professional thief wouldn't bother with this kind of place. He certainly wouldn't take the Henry Walton. We were burgled once at Caldecote Terrace. What they like to pick up are small, the easily disposable valuables. There's nothing here that anyone could want.'

She watched her mother's hands restlessly moving together. Her own fingers, long, bony, the nails strong and narrow, but on her mother's hands. Wringing her hands. It wasn't an expression one would ever write, too trite, too imprecise; but apparently it did happen except that 'wringing' wasn't the right word for this rhythmic pressing together of the palms. The hands seemed to be comforting each other. She was staring fixedly ahead, apparently oblivious of those kneading palms. Perhaps she was recalling the heavy smoothness of a sea-washed stone rolled between her hands, seeing in memory the layered sea, stretching to infinity, the mottled wave curving to crash in shingled foam against her naked feet. Then her eyes blinked again into the present. She said:

'How did he know?'

'Gabriel Lomas told him. Gabriel can smell out scandal, secrets, fear; it's a talent he has. He couldn't resist telling him. I can understand that. It was too important to him. Like me and the pregnant wife. In the end we think of no one but ourselves.'

'What pregnant wife?'

'No one you know. Someone I did down. Someone who needed this flat.'

'He seems a strange friend for Gabriel Lomas, a different class.'

'Oh Gabriel has a personality like a hexagon. People need touch only one side for an illusion of closeness. Forget about him. Perhaps it would be a good idea to get out of London for a time. Ventnor is as good a place as any, but you mustn't expect to find it the same. No place ever is. And we'll need some money. I've something left in the bank but we must keep a small reserve for when this lease runs out. It won't be easy to find work in the Isle of Wight, not immediately, not at the end of the season.'

Her mother turned to her with the eyes of a pleading child.

'I'm sure you'll like it there. And we needn't be away long.'

Philippa said:

'And you could change your name you know. It would make things easier.'

Her mother shook her head.

'No, I couldn't do that. That would be defeat. I have to know who I am.'

Philippa got up from the bed.

'We'll go tomorrow, just as soon as I've got the door mended and a new lock fixed. But first I have to go to Caldecote Terrace. I won't be away long, not more than an hour. Will you be all right?'

Her mother nodded. She said, trying to smile:

'I'm sorry I'm being so stupid. Don't worry. I'll be all right.'

Philippa slung her bag over her shoulder and made for the door. Suddenly her mother called her back. She said:

'Rose! You won't take anything that isn't yours?'

'Don't worry,' she answered. 'I shan't take anything that they don't owe us.'

EIGHT

The things to take were the silver caddy spoons. They were small, portable, easily disposed of; silver was fetching a high price. Maurice had over a hundred in his collection. About half were kept in the wall safe in his dressing-room and the others on display in an eighteenth-century rosewood cabinet in the drawing-room. The cabinet was always kept locked, but she knew that the key was in the safe, and she knew, too, the combination. From time to time he would change the ones on display although, once they were arranged on the purple velvet, he seldom looked at them again. As a child she had enjoyed helping him to set them out, had liked the feel of their smooth bowls, their delicate balance in her fingers. He had taught her to recognize the hallmarks, handing the spoons to her as he took them from the box and asking her to guess their date and the name of the silversmith. Yes, it was right that she should take the caddy spoons. And it wouldn't be difficult. If Maurice hadn't changed the combination of his wall safe, and she thought this unlikely, there wouldn't even be a need to break the cabinet lock. It was a pretty object. It would have been a hurtful necessity to have had to damage it. It never once occurred to her to make the theft look like a burglary. She would take as many spoons as she needed to sell to keep herself and her mother without working for about a month. Maurice would know that it was she who had taken them, and one day she would tell him why. She knew which were the rarest and which, therefore, the most valuable. Even quite ordinary ones in Church Street market were fetching thirty pounds. She need only take twenty of the best and their immediate problems would be over. There wouldn't be any difficulty in getting rid of them provided she offered them singly and in the right shops. She wouldn't get what they were worth, but she would get enough.

Because she was in a hurry to get the job done and return to her mother, she decided on the extravagance of a cab from Marylebone Station. She paid it off at the corner of Caldecote Road, an instinctive precaution which, as soon as the taxi moved away, struck her as silly and unnecessary. The basement kitchen was in darkness, as she knew it would be. This was Thursday, Hilda would be in court. But she turned the key in the lock and shut the door behind her with extreme care, holding her breath, as if afraid to wake an echo in the white, clean-smelling hall. She was a stranger here, and it seemed to her that the house knew it. Then she ran lightly upstairs to the front bedroom. As she put her hand on the door, the second before she turned the knob, she knew instinctively and with absolute certainty that she wasn't alone. She stopped dead in the doorway, then slowly pushed the door open.

They were both on the bed, Maurice and the girl, half reclining, transfixed by that first sound of her footsteps on the landing. They had finished making love. The rumpled bed, the spread towel, told their own story, and she thought she could sniff in the air the unmistakable, doughy smell of sex. Maurice was wearing only his pants, but the girl was naked. She shoved herself clumsily from the bed and with a little cry began gathering up her clothes from the chair. Philippa stood at the door, half-aware of Maurice's unembarrassed, ironic gaze, while the girl, scarlet-faced, diminished by shame, tried to cover herself with her skirt, and bent in an ungainly display of buttocks to scrabble under the bed for her shoes. Philippa knew that she had met her before, but for a moment she couldn't recall when or where. Absolute nakedness was intrusive, confusing to the senses. Paradoxically it both revealed and diminished identity. She made herself stare at the girl's face, and then remembered. She was one of Maurice's students. The name came to her a second later. Sheila. Sheila Manning. Eighteen months ago she had come to dinner; it was an evening when Gabriel had also been invited. She had been an uncomfortable guest, voluble in her nervousness, alternately aggressive and aggrieved, treating them to a rehashed version of Maurice's latest seminar on the cycle of disadvantage. Gabriel had taken trouble with her, resisting the frequent temptation to wit or sarcasm, steering the conversation from Marxist dogma to such innocuously boring subjects as food and holidays. It hadn't, Philippa thought, been done through kindness. Like most men, he reserved kindness for women who, beautiful or successful, had the least need of it. She had decided that he was acting either to disoblige her, or in obedience to some nursery dictate that it was the responsibility of a guest to attempt to rescue from social disaster even the most unpropitious dinner party. The girl, as had been painfully apparent, was in love with Maurice even then. Had it really taken her eighteen months to get into his bed?

Now they were face to face, and she stood silently to one side to let the girl pass. She was clutching a bundle of clothes to her chest. Encountering Philippa's disparaging stare she dropped her shoes; scarlet-faced she scrabbled for them, letting slip the rest of the bundle. Philippa noticed the strong body, curiously disproportionate to the etiolated neck and the thin face. Her breasts were as heavy as a nursing mother's, the nipples jutting like miniature udders from their brown concave aureoles. How could he have chosen to take them into his mouth? She thought complacently of her own high tight breasts, the delicately furled nipples, only slightly raised. She was glad she approved of her body, even if, as yet, she hadn't taught it how to give her pleasure.

She came into the room and closed the door. She said:

'I would have thought you'd have had more pride than to bring her here, to fuck her on your own bed.'

'Whose bed are you suggesting I should more properly use? Don't be predictable, Philippa. Do you have to react like a character in a second-rate TV soap opera?'

'But it's that kind of situation, isn't it? Commonplace. Farcical.' And so, she thought, is this conversation. Like everything we say to each other, it's contrived.

He sat on the bed and began knotting his tie. She was surprised that he hadn't first reached for his trousers. To be trouserless was surely to be vulnerable, ridiculous, the stock butt of bedroom farce. His pants were very short, white and narrowly striped with blue. She had seen Hilda pulling them out of the washing machine often enough. A tangle of male clothes. He was fastidious. Everything was clean every day. He said:

'It might seem farcical and commonplace – but doesn't it occur to you that I might be fond of her, might love her?'

'No. You're like me. We don't know how.'

Once she had been afraid that she would never learn, but not now, not any more. She watched him dress. How long had it been going on, she wondered. Weeks, months, years? Had it perhaps started as soon as Hilda was appointed to the Bench? It must have seemed an ideal opportunity, the same day with the house free every week for three months. How many girls? A new one for each academic year? They would have to avoid arriving together, but that wouldn't be difficult. He could come home through the mews service road leading to the garden door, then open the front door to her ring. The street was very quiet in the afternoon; but it wouldn't greatly matter if she were seen. After all, he was a lecturer, he had students to supervise. She asked:

'Where is she now?'

'I haven't the least idea. In the bathroom, I imagine.'

'As long as she isn't drowning herself. That would take some explaining away.'

'Oh, I don't think she's suicidal. Insecure and emotionally a bit intense, but not suicidal. But you'd better go and find out if you're worried.'

'She's your responsibility, not mine. She's rather wet isn't she? I shouldn't have thought that she was your type. Is she really the best you can find?'

'Don't underrate her.'

'That would be difficult, judging by her dinner conversation. She was so stupid with her talk about property and theft.

Second-hand jargon and third-hand ideas. I got tired of waiting for her to make an original or amusing remark. No wonder you're reduced to fucking her. Anything would be less boring than listening to her conversation.'

He had finished dressing now and was putting on his jacket, carefully transferring odd items from the dressing table into his pockets. He said:

'Oddly enough, it was after that evening that we became lovers. I felt sorry for her. With me that's always dangerous.'

'Is that why you married Hilda?'

As soon as the words were out she regretted them. But all he said was:

'No, that was because she was sorry for me.'

She waited for him to explain, but he said no more. And suddenly, she thought of Orlando. She had never spoken his name to Maurice, but now she was filled with a sympathy which had to find expression. She said:

'I forgot about Orlando. I always do forget. I suppose it's because you've never talked about him, never even shown me a photograph. And I've never told you that I'm sorry he died. Until now I don't think I was particularly sorry. If he hadn't died I wouldn't be here. And I never knew him: if one can ever know a child. But you've lost him more completely than my mother was ever in danger of losing me. At least she'd have known that I was alive somewhere.'

He didn't reply, but his hands ceased their careful busyness with his jacket. She looked at his face. In one second it had become as vacant as the face of a spent actor's in repose, all emotion, even the lines, smoothed away. Then there passed over it a look so momentary that she almost missed it, of pain, regret, of the rueful acceptance of defeat. She had seen that look once before. The picture came vividly to her mind, limned with the colour of blood. The screech of tyres followed immediately by a crash like an explosion. The young motor-cyclist, helmetless, lying on the kerb at the junction of Oxford Street and Charing Cross Road. The wheels of his motor cycle spinning in the air. A second of eerie silence, absolute, the air holding its breath. Then the babble of voices, cries. A woman with a face like lard, a cardigan stretched across her bolster of a chest, yelling in anger and remembered pain.

'He was coming too fast! He was too bloody fast! Oh Christ, those fucking machines!'

He was lying there, dying so publicly, and her railing voice was the last sound he heard on earth. Involuntarily she had stepped towards him and his eyes had met hers. She had seen in them that same look, the rueful acceptance of a terrible knowledge. Afterwards she had hurried home to write it down, an exercise in the creative recollection of trauma. She had torn up the passage. She always did tear up such exercises. Her life was encumbered enough, the wasteland between imagination and reality already too nebulous. But she wished that she hadn't recalled it now. This was a moment of small triumph, a time for planning and action. She hadn't wanted to think about death.

They were simultaneously aware that Sheila Manning had come into the room. She was dressed and was carrying a jacket and a heavy, old-fashioned hand-bag. Ignoring Philippa, she spoke directly to Maurice:

'You promised that it would be safe. You said no one would be here.'

She was making a brave attempt at dignity, but she couldn't keep from her voice the note of querulous reproach. She sounded, thought Philippa, like Hilda when Maurice was late home for dinner. He wouldn't welcome that peevish reminder of small delinquencies. There was only one way for her to carry off this débâcle successfully, with humour and panache, but these weren't in her armoury. And whatever she said, this would be the end of the affair. The girl was as humiliated and inept as a child caught out in her first sexual experimenting. This room, this moment, most of all this man would be remembered only with self-disgust. She knew that she herself was part of the humiliation, sitting there calmly on the bed by Maurice's side in possession of more than herself.

She said:

'I'm sorry. It was unintentional.'

She sounded insincere to her own ears. She would have despised anyone who believed her, and the girl didn't.

'It doesn't matter. You've done what you wanted to do.'

She turned away. Watching the drooped head, Philippa wondered whether she had started to cry. Maurice at once got up from the bed and went to her. He put an arm round her shoulders and said gently:

'It was horrible for you. I'm so sorry. Please don't worry. These things aren't important, you know. In a few weeks you'll be able to laugh about it.'

'It has never been important, not to you anyway. I shan't come back.'

Perhaps she hoped, pathetically, that the threat would provoke some response from him; pain, anger, reproach. Instead he said, punctilious as a host:

'I'll see you out. Are you sure you've got everything?'

She nodded. They went out together, his arm still round her shoulder, and a minute later Philippa heard the closing thud of the front door. She waited for him in the bedroom, still sitting on the edge of the dishevelled bed. He stood at the door silently regarding her for a moment, then began to pace up and down the room. He said:

'You are enjoying yourself? You look happy and you look well.'

'Yes. Yes I am. I suppose it's the first time in my life that I've been able to feel important to another human being.'

'Indispensable, you mean. There's nothing so intoxicating to the ego as the knowledge that happiness is in one's gift. It's the foundation of every successful marriage. The other person has to be capable of being made happy, of course, and that capacity is rarer than one might imagine. I take it that your mother is?'

'For most of the time, yes.'

'I suppose there are moments when she wonders whether she has the right to live.'

She said:

'Why should she? The world is full of people who've killed a child: a wartime bomb released, a bullet in Belfast which hits the wrong target, a stamp on the car accelerator in a fit of impatience. And what about the drunken drivers, the incompetent doctors? They don't spend their days wondering whether they've a right to live. And she has survived nearly ten years in prison. If anyone has the right to live, she has.'

'And how do you spend your days? I take it you're enjoying the pleasure of patronage, giving her the benefit of your education.'

She thought: 'You should know about that. You enjoyed teaching me.' She said:

'We look at pictures. And I'm showing her London.'

'Didn't she know London already? She and Ducton lived close enough.'

'I don't know. We never talk about the past. She doesn't want to.'

'That's very wise of her. What, incidentally, have you come home for? It wasn't a particularly propitious moment to choose, but I take it that this *démarche* wasn't planned.'

'I came to get some money. The Press have found out where we are. We've got to get away, at least for a time. I don't think they'll be back, but my mother's too upset to stay in Delaney Street. We're going to the Isle of Wight.'

'So the running has started and she's dragging you with her.'

'Not dragging. Never dragging. I'm going because I want to be with her.'

'For God's sake why the Isle of Wight?'

'We think we'd like it there. She went there once as a girl, some kind of Sunday school treat.'

'There are cheaper bolt holes. I suppose you intended to help yourself from the safe. What I keep in there will just about get you across the Solent.'

'There are other things here I could take and sell. I thought of the caddy spoons. We only want enough cash for the first week or two. Then we can both get a job. That shouldn't be difficult even at the end of the season. We're not fussy what we do.'

'How did the Press discover where you where?'

'We met Gabriel Lomas at the Royal Academy exhibition. I think he put his boy friend on to us. But first he must have phoned Hilda and got the address out of her. That wouldn't be difficult, not for Gabriel.'

'You might have expected it from that decadent Tory with his high talking and squalid morality. Well, at least you've learned that betrayal isn't the prerogative of the extreme left.'

'I never thought it was.'

'So now you've got a choice between blackmail and theft. Why don't you sell the Henry Walton, by the way? You've got it. It's yours.'

'We like it. We're taking it with us. Besides, you owe us something.'

'Not any longer. You're eighteen, you're of age. When I adopted you I owed you a home, food, education, a reasonable standard of care. I owed you conscientious affection. Anything more isn't within my gift. I don't think there's anything on the slate.'

'I'm not thinking about me. I'm thinking about my mother. You owe her my purchase price. You didn't have to adopt me. You could have fostered me, become my legal guardian. You could have given me a home and education without taking me away from her for ever. The experiment would have been the same – nearly the same anyway. You would still have been able to say: "Look what I've done. Look what I've made of this odd, difficult, uncommunicative child, the daughter of a rapist and a murderer." It's not as if you ever cared about abstractions like justice or retribution. It's not as if you really worried about what she'd done. And you've never had a high regard for criminal justice, have you? Magistrates' courts, the Crown court; a formal system for ensuring that the poor and incompetent know their place, that the dispossessed don't get their grubby hands on the spoils. The petty thief ends in prison, the financier who makes his fortune dealing in currency ends up in the Lords. I've heard you often enough. Slice through society – you even know the precise socio-economic point at which the cut should be made – and the top half sits in judgement under the Royal Arms, the bottom half stands in the dock. The rich man in his castle, the poor man at his gate, law makes them high and lowly and orders their estate. So why didn't she qualify for your kind of mercy? She was poor enough, disadvantaged, under-educated, all the things you preach excuse crime. So why not excuse her?'

He said calmly:

'I'm not in the habit of confusing petty recidivism with murder and rape.'

'But you know nothing about her! You don't know what pressures drove her to kill that child. You never bothered to find out. You only knew that she had something you wanted – experimental material – me. Scarce experimental material, no, unique. A child who might have been specially bred for your purpose, to demonstrate that man is the creature of his environment. And there were incidental advantages, a child to keep your wife occupied while you fucked your students. No wonder you had to get your hands on me. But what about my mother? If she'd been hanged, if it had all happened before the death penalty was abolished, the hangman would have been more just. At least he'd have left her something. You were going to take me away for ever. She would have come out of prison and we'd never have known each other, never even have met. By what right did you do that to us? And then you say that you don't owe her anything!'

'Is this what she's told you?'

'No. It's what I've worked out for myself.'

He came over to her, but he didn't sit beside her on the bed. Instead he stood over her, looking down. When he spoke his voice was harder. He said:

'Is that what you've really felt all these last ten years, that you were experimental material? No, don't answer hastily. Think about it. Be honest. Your generation make such a fetish of honesty. The more hurtful it is to others, the more necessary you appear to find it. When Hilda's excellent food slipped down your gullet, did you really see yourself as an experimental animal being fed its nicely calculated ration of protein, vitamins and minerals?'

'Hilda is different. I wish I could love Hilda.'

He said:

'I daresay we both wish that we could love Hilda.' He added: 'She misses you.'

She wanted to cry out: 'But what about you? Do you miss me?' Instead she said:

'I'm sorry, but I'm not coming back.'

'And what about Cambridge?'

'I'm beginning to think that Cambridge isn't as important as I thought it was.'

'Do you mean you'll delay going up, wait a year?'

'Or not go up at all. After all, I'm going to be a novelist. A university education isn't essential for a writer. It could even be a disadvantage. There are better ways of spending the next three years.'

'You mean with her?'

'Yes,' she said simply. 'With her.'

He went across to the window and stood for a minute, parting the curtains, looking down into the street. What, she wondered, was he expecting to see? What inspiration did he hope for from those brightly painted doors, the elegant fanlights, the brass-bound tubs and window boxes of the opposite terrace? After a moment he turned and began pacing between the two tall windows, eyes on the ground. Neither of them spoke. Then he said:

'There's something I've got to tell you. No, that's not strictly true. I don't have to tell you. Until this afternoon I didn't intend to tell you. But it's time you stopped living in a fantasy world and faced reality.'

She thought: 'He's trying to sound reluctant, concerned, but what he's really feeling is excitement, triumph.' Something of the excitement communicated itself to her and she felt, too, a spasm of fear. But it passed quickly. There was nothing he could say now which could harm her or her mother. Her eyes followed his careful pacing. Never before had she been so aware of his physical presence, of every breath he drew, of every bone of his head and hands, of every contraction of muscle; the air between them drummed with his heartbeat. And because of this intensity of awareness there was something else she knew, something that she couldn't explain. If now he wanted to hurt her, it had nothing to do with Sheila Manning. How lightly he had taken that humiliation! What had changed him had been that blurted out sympathy for the loss of Orlando. This moment was to do with her and him; but it was to do with Orlando too. She waited without speaking for him to begin. If he wanted to make a pretence of embarrassment, of reluctance, she wasn't going to help him. He said:

'You've assumed that Hilda and I adopted you after the murder, that your mother let you go because she was serving a life sentence, had no real choice. I thought when you started living together that she might have told you the truth. Obviously she hasn't. Your adoption order went through exactly two weeks before Julie Scase was killed, and we'd had you as a foster child for six months before then. The truth is quite simple: your mother let you go, because she didn't want you.'

She wished that he'd stop his slow regular pacing, that he'd come over to her, sit beside her, look into her face, do anything except touch her. Instead he glanced at her, an artful, almost conspiratorial glance, so swift that she wondered whether she had imagined that slit-eyed momentary regard. Something, perhaps a speck of dust, was irritating his left eye. He took his handkerchief from his jacket pocket and rubbed it, then stood blinking. Satisfied, he started again on his slow perambulation. He said:

'I don't know what went wrong originally. She was pregnant when she married and it might have been that. I was told that she had a long and painful labour after a difficult pregnancy. That's one of the diagnostic pointers to child abuse. Anyway, there was no bonding of mother and child. I gather that you weren't easy. You were difficult to feed, an unresponsive, perpetually-crying baby. She hardly slept at night for your first two years.'

He paused, but she didn't speak. His voice was as cool and controlled as if this were a dissertation before his students, an exposition that he had given so many times before that he knew it by heart. He went on:

'Things didn't improve. The screaming baby became an unloving child. Both of you had violent tempers, but you, of course, were too young to injure her except psychologically. She, unfortunately, could do more damage. One day she struck out at you and gave you a black eye. After that she became frightened. She decided she wasn't cut out for motherhood, so she went back to work and placed you with foster parents. I understand that it was a weekly arrangement; you came home for the weekends. She could stand you for two days a week.'

Philippa said quietly:

'I remember. I remember Auntie May.'

'There were, no doubt, a succession of spurious aunties of various degrees of suitability and of responsibility. In June 1968 one of them brought you down to Pennington; it was supposed to be a treat for you, a day in the country. It was just before the house was sold and the woman was visiting her sister who was the pastry cook there. She's retired now, of course. All the old servants have gone. I had to go down to Pennington to arrange about some of Helena's things before the sale, and Hilda and I met you and your foster parent in the garden. Hilda talked to her. She was a relief, I suppose, from the people in the house. And that's how we heard about you. Beddows was her name, Mrs Gladys Beddows. She wanted to stop fostering you – you weren't the easiest of children – but she was worried about letting you go back full time to your parents. She wasn't very bright and she didn't even like you but she had some sense of responsibility.

'After that meeting I couldn't get you out of my mind. The thought of you was like an irritation, something I would rather not have known but wasn't able to forget. I didn't want to get involved. I told myself that you were no concern of mine. I wasn't even thinking then about adopting a child. Hilda had mentioned the possibility, but it wasn't an idea that appealed to me. Certainly, I wasn't looking for a child. I told myself that it would do no harm to find out what had happened to you. It was easy enough to trace Mrs Beddows through her sister. She told me that you were back full time with your mother. I nearly left it at that. But I was in the neighbourhood; it would do no harm to call. I didn't even bother to concoct an excuse for the visit, which was unlike me. I don't usually go into new situations unprepared. It was early evening by then and your mother had just come home from work. You weren't there. You had been admitted two days earlier to King George V Hospital, Ilford, with a suspected fracture of the skull. And that was the most dangerous and the last time that your mother lost her temper with you.'

She said through bloated lips, not realizing what tense she was using:

'Is that why the child could never remember anything that happened before she was eight?'

'The amnesia was partly the result of the injury, partly, I imagine hysterical, the mind's natural reluctance to recall the unbearable. Neither Hilda nor I have ever attempted to cure it. Why should we?'

'And then what happened to her?'

'Your parents agreed that we should foster you when you came out of hospital, with a view to adoption if it worked out all right. There wasn't a prosecution. The hospital apparently accepted your mother's explanation that you'd fallen downstairs and cracked your head on the bottom banister. Those were the days before the Maria Colwell case and the authorities were less ready than now to suspect deliberate ill-treatment. But she told me the truth, she told me everything that June evening. I think she was glad to have someone, a stranger, to whom she could talk. You came to us straight from hospital and six months later we adopted you. Your parents both gave their consent without, I may say, any apparent reluctance. And that is the mother for whom you now propose to give up Cambridge, become a thief, and spend God knows how many years dragging after her from one watering place to another. The Scase murder, of course, is hardly relevant. She didn't murder you after all, although I gather it was a pretty close thing.'

She didn't cry out in vehement protest that he was lying, that it wasn't true. Maurice only lied about important things, and then only when he could be certain that he wouldn't be found out. This wasn't important to him, and the truth could easily be proved. But she didn't need to check. She knew that it was the truth. She wished that she didn't feel so cold. Her face, her limbs, her fingers, were icy. He ought to have seen that she was shaking. Why didn't he tug a blanket from Hilda's bed and fold it round her? Even her lips were swollen with cold, stiff and numbed as if she had been given a dental injection. It was difficult to form words and her voice, when it came, sounded slurred.

'Why didn't you tell me?'

'I should like to believe that it was because I didn't want to hurt you. Perhaps it was. There are some cruelties which take courage. Mine are on a meaner scale. I did try to warn you. I told you to find out the facts, to read the Press accounts of the trial. Those would have told you the date of the murder. You already knew your date of adoption. It might also have struck you as odd that the Press reports made no mention of a child. But then you didn't want to know the facts, didn't want to talk to us about it; it seemed you were wilfully determined to be blind. It's odd that over something so important you never once used your intelligence, you who have always relied on intelligence, have had such a respect for your own mind.'

She wanted to cry out: 'What else have I had to rely on? What else had I on offer?' Instead she said:

'Thank you for telling me now.'

'It needn't make any difference. It's an irrelevance. After all, you're not concerned with conduct or responsibility or nurture. If the blood tie is all that matters to you, well that at least is intact. But I did have you for ten years. I may not be entitled to make any claims on you, but at least I've a right to express a view about your future. And I'm not letting you give up Cambridge without a struggle. The chance of those three years won't come again, not now, not when you're young which is when they matter.'

He added drily:

'I've also the right to my own Georgian silver. If you need money for her, sell the Henry Walton.'

She said as humbly as a servant at the end of an interview:

'Is there anything else you want to tell me before I go?'

'Only that this is your home if you want it. This is where you belong. I've got an adoption order to prove it. And if that legalistic conveyance of possession lacks the emotional charge of the blood tie; hasn't your family had enough of blood?'

At the door she turned and looked back at him. She said:

'But why did you do it? Why me?'

'I told you. I couldn't put you out of my mind. And I was afraid of what might happen to you. I hate waste.'

'But you must have hoped for something: gratitude, diversion, interest, the gratification of patronage, companionship for your old age, the ordinary things?'

'It didn't seem so at the time, but I suppose I did. My demands have always been presumptuous. Perhaps what I hoped for was love.'

Three minutes later he stood at the window watching her leave. There was something different about her, a sense of brightness dulled, of limbs uncoordinated. Perhaps it was the hunch of the shoulders, diminishing height, foreshowing how she might look as an old woman, or the way in which she scurried from the front door, furtive as an interloper surprised. At the end of the terrace she broke into a run, swerving from the pavement into the path of a taxi. He gasped; his heart skidded. When he could bear to open his eyes he saw that she was safe. Even from this distance he could hear the screech of brakes, the shouted abuse. Then, without a backward glance, she had half-run, half-shambled out of sight.

He wasn't sorry that he had told her, nor was he seriously concerned about her. She had survived those first seven years; she would survive this. And, after all, she wanted to be a writer. Someone had said – he couldn't remember who – that an artist should suffer in childhood as much trauma as could be borne without breaking. And she wouldn't break. Others would break, but not she. There would be tatters and torn flesh enough on the barbed wire guarding that untender heart. But he was aware of a nag of anxiety, irritating because he guessed that it might be difficult to rationalize away, and because, like all his anxieties, it was allied to guilt. He wondered what she would say to her mother. Whatever the nature of the tie between them, he didn't suppose that she loved her mother in any sense in which he understood that ubiquitous word. After all, they had only been together for five weeks. She had lived with him and Hilda for ten years, undisturbed, apparently, by any need to love. He wondered what she would have said, how she would have looked, if sitting there on the bed in his post-coital depletion, he had spoken at least a part of the truth about Sheila Manning.

'I took her from egotism, boredom, curiosity, sexual conceit, pity, perhaps even from affection. But she's only a substitute. They're all of them substitutes. When she was in my arms I was imagining that she was you.'

He saw that the bedcover was crooked and he smoothed it. That was the kind of detail that Hilda, obsessive housewife that she was, would notice. Then he went into the bathroom to check that Sheila had left no trace of herself there. He needn't worry that there would be an echo of her scent lingering in the bedroom. Before he had brought her to Caldecote Terrace for the first time he had warned her not to wear scent. She had replied:

'I never do.'

He remembered her face, blotched with embarrassment and hurt, that he shouldn't have noticed that. The warning, revealing as it had a calculation of risk, born perhaps of previous embarrassments and discoveries, had denigrated their love in her eyes, reduced their first time together to a commonplace, sordid intrigue. It hadn't been that; but for him it hadn't been much more. Why, he wondered, was he driven into these petty expedients of lust? Boredom? The ennui of the male menopause? A compensation for his sterility? The need to reassure himself that he was still virile, still attractive to younger women? A search, which he knew in advance to be hopeless, for the lost enchantments of love?

He felt physically and emotionally drained. He needed to cosset himself. He fetched a glass, a bottle of Niersteiner and the ice bucket and went to sit in the garden. The air was as heavy and oppressive as a sweaty blanket and he thought he could sniff the far-off metallic smell of thunder. He wished that the blanket would burst and the rain would fall, that he could lift up his face and feel the great cool sheets of it drenching his skin. He wondered why Hilda was so late, then remembered that she had said something at breakfast about late shopping in Oxford Street. He supposed that meant that they were to make do with a cold supper.

He wasn't distressed about Sheila Manning. Hilda was due to give up the juvenile Bench in two weeks' time, and he had planned to use that as an excuse for ending the affair. This evening's fiasco had saved him the protracted and emotionally wearing strategies, the appeals and reproaches, which usually accompanied the death of desire. The problem about wanting women who evoked his pity was that these were precisely the women who were the most difficult to get rid of. He wished he could be like some of his colleagues and take a succession of the guilt-free, experienced and cheerfully randy young who would ask nothing more of him than the occasional good dinner and the brief exchange of pleasure.

He supposed he would have to let Hilda know about Philippa's visit. He would tell the truth, merely editing out Sheila Manning. He could be confident that Philippa would never tell her, and it seemed to him not of immense importance if she did. Philippa would be coming home now and that should please Hilda. Life would go on as it had before. He supposed that that was what he wanted. He let his mind slip free of worry and guilt and closed his eyes. And in that moment of almost disembodied peace, the smell of wine and roses fused and he was back again, walking between the high hedges into the great circular rose garden at Pennington on a June day ten years ago. He was seeing Philippa for the first time.

NINE

He had never seen a child like her. She stood very still, a little apart from her keeper, a shapeless ungainly woman, querulous in the heat, and regarded him gravely with those extraordinary luminous green eyes under the curving brows. Her skin absorbed the mellow afternoon light, the shadowed green of the high hedge, so that it was like seeing her through water. Her hair was plaited corn drawn across her forehead in a mature, old-fashioned style which added to the contrast between the sixteenth-century Renaissance head held so proudly, and the childish body. He guessed that she was about seven. She was wearing a kilt too heavy for summer and reaching almost to her calves, with an immense safety-pin bunching it on one side. Her pale arms, downy and glinting in the sun, stuck out from a shirt so thin that it clung to her bony chest, brittle as a bird's. He could see her nipples, two pink delicate tags of flesh.

Hilda began talking to the woman, learning that her name was Gladys Beddows, that she was at Pennington to visit her sister. He spoke to the child:

'Isn't it dull for you here? What would you like to do?'

'Have you any books?'

'Lots, in the library. Would you like to see them?'

She nodded and they began walking across the lawn together, the two women following. She walked at his side, but distanced, her hands held in front of her, the palms folded together in a curiously formal, unchildish gesture. A few yards behind them Mrs Beddows seemed to be confiding her difficulties to Hilda. That type of woman usually did. Hilda, herself uncommunicative, gauche, somehow invited confidences, or lacked the assurance and ruthlessness to reject them. Whenever he entered the kitchen on the two days a week when the daily help was there he would find the two women drinking coffee together, Hilda's head docilely bowed under a spate of domestic disgruntlement. Now the whine of resentment came clearly to them, carried on the warm, rose-scented air.

'Not as if they pay much. And I have her all day, some nights as well. She's a difficult child. Never get a thank you out of her. And talk about temper! Screaming tantrums some of the time. Nightmares too. Not surprised her mother can't cope. Not what you'd call pretty, is she? Odd-looking child. Clever, mind you. Always got her head in a book. Oh, she's sharp, that one! So sharp she'll cut herself one of these days.'

He glanced at the child. She must have heard. How could she help hearing? But she gave no sign. She walked on in her unchildish, hieratic dignity, but carefully, as if holding something precious between the clasped hands.

The woman was right. She wasn't a pretty child. But the fine bone structure of the face, the green eyes, gave promise of a spectacular if eccentric beauty. And she was intelligent, courageous and proud. These were the qualities he respected. Something could be made of such a child. He wanted to say to her: 'I don't think you're plain. And I like clever children. Never be ashamed of being clever.' But glancing again at her set face he said nothing. Pity would be an impertinence to this proud, self-absorbed child.

The southern aspect of Pennington stretched out before them, golden and serene, the great orangery shooting shafts of light so that his eyes dazzled. This was the view of the house he had seen when he had first visited Pennington with Helena. That, too, had been in high summer; but then he had been in love, intoxicated with the smell of roses and gillyflowers, with the wine they had drunk with their picnic on the drive down, with happiness, with the immensity of his prize. They had been coming to Pennington together to tell her father that they were to be married. Now walking that same lawn, the child's shadow moving with his like a ghost, he could look back almost dispassionately, with pity as well as with contempt, to that poor deluded fool frolicking in a dead summer which now seemed to have held the concentrated sweetness of all summers, invincibly arrogant in the high renaissance of the heart. And so they walked across the lawn together, the child with her pain, he with his.

The library was dark and cool after the glare of the sun. The books had been sold separately from the house, and already the archivists and workmen were there checking and packing the volumes. It should have pleased him that yet another aristocrat was reneging on his responsibilities, that this great house would no longer be the seat of a family, passing from father to son in the primogeniture of privilege, but would become institutionalized, debased. Instead, looking up at the fine stuccoed ceiling, and at the gorgeous Grinling Gibbons carvings on the bookcases, he was aware of a gentle nostalgic melancholy. If this room had belonged to him, he would never have let it go.

The child stood at his side, both of them looking in silence. Then he led her across the room to the chart table where a miscellany of Helena's books had been collected for him.

He said:

'How old are you? Can you read?'

Her voice rebuked him:

'I'm eight. I could read before I was four.'

'Then let's see how you do with this.'

He picked up the Shakespeare, opened it and handed it to her. He was behaving like a pedant with no particular intention. The afternoon was hot, he was bored, the child intrigued him. She took the book into her hands with difficulty and began to read. He had opened it at *King John*.

> 'Grief fills the room up of my absent child,
> Lies in his bed, walks up and down with me,
> Puts on his pretty looks, repeats his words,
> Remembers me of all his gracious parts,
> Stuffs out his vacant garments with his form.'

She read to the end of the speech, faultlessly. She didn't, of course, speak it in the cadence of blank verse. But she knew that it was poetry and she spoke it carefully in her childish, unemphatic voice, wary of unfamiliar words. It was the more poignant. He felt the tears stinging his eyes for the first time since he had learned that Orlando wasn't his son.

And that was how it had begun. It seemed to him that those two moments, so curiously linked by the memory of Orlando, the first in which he had watched the tears start from Hilda's eyes, the second in which the child's clear voice had brought tears to his, had been the only times in his life which had been free from self-regard. The one had resulted in his second marriage; the other in the adoption of Philippa. He wasn't asking himself now if they had led to disappointment. He wasn't sure what his expectations had been. The absence of expectation had been part of the purity of the moments, had brought them close to what he supposed some people might call goodness. He had almost forgotten the anguish of grief. Now it returned to him, less keen but more diffuse, embracing in one nostalgic melancholy the loss of Orlando, the unborn children he could never father, the stripped library at Pennington, and the child in her ridiculous skirt walking with him across the lawn in the mellow sunlight of a dead June day ten years ago.

TEN

For Philippa the journey from Caldecote Terrace to Delaney Street was a blank. Time was blotted out completely as if her mind were anaesthetized and her body was obeying some programmed instructions. Afterwards she could remember only one incident; running for the bus at Victoria and grasping the slippery rail, a moment of panic, and then the jerk of her armpit as a passenger on the platform caught her and hauled her aboard. Delaney Street was very quiet. The rain had begun to fall steadily in slivers of silver against the street lamps, and behind the patterned glass of the Blind Beggar the lights of the bar shone red and green. She turned her key in the Yale lock, closed the front door quietly behind her and walked up the stairs calmly without switching on the light. In the darkness she pushed the flat door, feeling under her palm the sharpness of the splintered wood. Her mother heard her and called out from the kitchen. She must be preparing supper, mixing the salad dressing; there hung in the air the sharp tang of vinegar. It was the same smell that had greeted her on her return to Caldecote Terrace, after her visit to Seven Kings and the two moments fused together, the old pain reinforcing the new. Her mother's voice sounded happy, welcoming. Perhaps she was getting over her panic. Perhaps she had decided that they needn't move after all. She walked into the kitchen. Her mother turned, smiling, to greet her. Then the smile died, and Philippa watched as the face, so different yet so like her own, drained of blood. Her mother whispered:

'What is it? What's happened? What's happened, Philippa?'

She said:

'Why don't you call me Rose? You called me Rose earlier this evening. You had me christened Rose. I was Rose when you nearly killed me. I was Rose when you decided you didn't want me. I was Rose when you gave me away.'

There was a moment of silence. Her mother felt for a chair and sat down. She said:

'I thought you knew. When you first came to Melcombe Grange I asked if you knew about your adoption. You said you did.'

'I thought you meant did I know about the murder. I thought you were reminding me why it was that you had to give me up. You must have known that's what I thought.'

Her mother went on as if she hadn't spoken:

'And afterwards, because I was so happy here, I said nothing. I told myself that the past wasn't our past. They were two different people in a different story. I thought I might let myself have just these two months. Whatever happened afterwards, I should have something worth remembering. But I meant to tell you. I would have told you in the end.'

'When you could be sure that I'd got used to having a mother. When I didn't want to let you go. My God, you're clever! Maurice warned me that you were clever. At least I've learned one thing about myself, where I get my scheming intelligence. And what about my father? Did he hate me too? Or was he too ineffective to stop you, too timid to do anything except rape a child? What did you do to him that he needed that act to prove his manhood?'

Her mother looked up at her as if there was something which had to be explained, which could be explained.

'You mustn't blame your father. He wanted to keep you. I persuaded him to let you go. I was the one who thought it was better for you. And it *was* better for you. Where would you be now if you'd stayed with us?'

'Was I such a nuisance, so much trouble? Couldn't you have tried with me a little longer? Oh God, why did I ever find you!'

'I did try. I wanted to love you. I wanted you to love me. But you didn't respond, ever. You cried endlessly. Nothing I could do comforted you. You wouldn't even let me feed you.'

Philippa cried out:

'Are you telling me that I rejected you?'

'No, only that it seemed like it to me.'

'How could I, a new-born child? I had no choice. I had to love you in order to survive.'

Her mother asked with a humility which Philippa found almost unbearable:

'Do you want me to leave at once?'

'No, I'll go. I'll find somewhere. It's easier for me. I don't have to go back to Caldecote Terrace. I've got friends in London. You can stay here until the lease runs out. That'll give you time to find another place. I'll send for the picture. You can have the rest.'

She heard her mother's voice. She spoke so softly that Philippa hardly caught the words:

'Is what I did to you so much more difficult to forgive than what I did to that child?'

She didn't reply. She snatched up her shoulder-bag and made for the door. Then she turned and spoke to her mother for the last time:

'I don't want to see you ever again. I wish they'd hanged you ten years ago. I wish you were dead.'

ELEVEN

She controlled her crying until she was out of Delaney Street. Then it burst out in a scream of agony. Hair flying loose, she ran wildly through the rain, her shoulder-bag bumping against her side. Instinctively, she turned up Lisson Grove seeking the dark solitude of the canal tow-path. But the gate had long since been closed for the night. She pounded against it, but she knew that it wouldn't yield. On she ran, her face streaming with mingled tears and rain. Seeing no one, careless now which way she ran, almost howling with pain. Suddenly a spasm of cramp twisted like a knife in her side. Doubled up, she gasped, gulping in the streaming air like a drowning woman. She clutched at some nearby railings, waiting for the pain to pass. Beyond the railings were tall trees and, even through the rain, she could smell the canal. She checked her crying and listened. The night was full of small secretive noises. And then there came a howl, alien and eerie, louder and wilder even than her own misery, answering pain with pain. It was the cry of an animal; she must be close to the Regent's Park zoo.

She was calmer now. Her tears were still flowing but in a gentle, unbroken stream. She walked on through the night. The city was streaked with light, bleeding with light. The headlamps of the cars dazzled on the road and the crimson pools of the traffic lights lay on the surface like blood. The rain was falling in a solid wall of water, drenching her clothes, plastering her hair against her face and eyes; she could taste it on her lips as salty as the sea.

It seemed to her that her mind was a black and seething dungeon, too many thoughts fighting for air, pressing each other down, tortuous elongated thoughts writhing in rank darkness. And from that dense confusion rose the thin misery of a child's cry. It wasn't the peevish complaint one heard in supermarkets; this was a desolation of terror and anguish not to be comforted with a packet of sweets at the check-out. She told herself that she mustn't panic; to panic would be to go mad. She must sort out her thoughts, arrange them, impose order on chaos. But first she had to stop that dreadful crying. She put her hands up to her throat and squeezed, strangling the child into silence, and when she released her hands the crying had stopped.

They hadn't, in all their weeks together, once spoken of the dead child. They hadn't talked about the child's parents. How much had they cared? How long had they grieved? Perhaps they now had other children and this long-dead, violated child was only a painful, half-rejected memory. Grief fills the room up of my absent child. The child was dead. That fact had been less important to her than whether her mother had kept the kitchen clean. Her mother had killed a child, had clamped her small hand to a pram and dragged her faster and faster, until she fell under the spinning wheels. But that was a different child, another place. She had killed the child's father, too. He had come across the lawn in the summer sunshine, beautiful as a god, to where they used to meet in the rose garden at Pennington. And now he, too, was dead. She had buried him in the moist drifts of the forest. But that was someone else's father. Hers was under quicklime in an anonymous grave in a prison yard. Or was that only how they buried executed murderers? What did they do with the bodies of felons who died in prison? Did they carry them out secretly at night, cheaply coffined, to be disposed of at the nearest crematorium, without any comfortable words, the furnace flaring like the flames of hell? And what did they do with the ashes? That neatly packaged residue of ground bone must have been buried somewhere. She had never thought to ask, and her mother had never told her. Parthenophil is lost, and I would see him for he is like to something I remember a great while since, a long long time ago.

Suddenly there shone before her the glowing sign of Warwick Avenue Underground Station. The wide road, lined with its Italianate houses and stuccoed villas, ran with liquid light. As she half ran, half walked down the deserted pavement, the overhanging bushes in the front gardens rained a shower of white sodden petals and torn leaves over her hair. And here, at last, was the canal and she was standing on the elegant wrought-iron bridge which spanned the dividing waterway. At each corner of the bridge the high nineteenth-century lamps, each on its pedestal, cast a trembling light over the canal basin, the leafy island, the painted longboats moored at the canal wall, the long dark length of tree-shadowed water. Where the lamps shone brightest the plane trees seemed to burn with flickering green flames and below her, where the rain spurted from the roof of a longboat, there gleamed a brightly painted enamel jug filled with storm-tossed Michaelmas daisies.

Behind her the unceasing wheels of the cars swished past, slicing through the running gutters and hurling fountains of spray against the bridge. There were no pedestrians in sight and the avenues on each side of the canal were deserted. From the houses the lights shone out from balconied windows, illuminating the plane trees and laying a shivering path of light over the sluggish water.

She was still wearing the jumper her mother had knitted for her. It was sodden and weighted with rain, the high collar cold against her neck. She pulled it over her head then, reaching up, she held it out and let it gently drop over the parapet and into the canal. For a minute it lay on the surface of the water illumined by the lamp-light, looking as frail and transparent as gossamer. The two sleeves were stretched out; it could have been a drowning child. Then, almost imperceptibly, it floated out of the path of light, sinking slowly as it moved, until her swollen watching eyes could only imagine its pattern on the dark water.

With the jumper gone she felt a physical sense of release. She was wearing nothing now but her trousers and a thin cotton shirt. The rain drenched it so that it clung to her like a second skin. And so, unencumbered, she walked on, under the great concrete arches of the Westway and south towards Kensington. She had no awareness of time, no sense of direction; all that mattered was that she should keep walking. She hardly noticed when the rain changed to slow, ponderous drops, then finally stopped, when the noisy bus routes gave way to quiet squares.

But at last she walked herself into exhaustion. It hit her suddenly, as unexpected and violent as a body blow. Her legs sagged and she tottered to the side of the pavement and grasped at a row of iron railings which surrounded the garden of a wide square. But the weariness which cramped her body had released her mind; thought was once again coherent, disciplined, rational. She leaned her head against the railings and felt the iron, parallel red-hot rods, branding her forehead. There was a privet hedge behind the railings, its pungent greenness filled her nostrils and spiked her cheeks. The wave of exhaustion flowed through her, leaving in its wake a gentle tiredness which was almost pleasurable.

Consciousness slipped away. She was jerked back to awareness by a high-pitched yell. The night was suddenly loud with running feet and raucous voices. From the far corner a gang of youths erupted into the square and reeled in a disorderly stream across the road to the garden. They were obviously drunk. Two of them, clutched together, were bawling a plaintive, discordant song. The others shouted meaningless staccato chants, slogans and tribal battle cries in a hoarse, broken cacophony of menace. Terrified that they would see her, that her shoulder-bag, she herself, would present too easy a spoil, Philippa strained back against the railings. The gang had no clear purpose or direction. It was possible that they would stagger again into the road and miss seeing her.

But the voices grew louder. They were coming her way. One of them flung a toilet roll. It spun over the railings and into the garden, just missing her head. Its pale, undulating tail, transparent as a stream of light, floated and turned on the night breeze then came to rest on the surface of the hedge, light as a cobweb. And still they came, heads bobbing above the privet. She began to walk quickly away from them, still keeping close to the railings, but as soon as she moved they saw her. They gave a great shout, the jarring, unrelated voices raised in the united bellow of triumph.

She broke into a run, but they pounded after her, more purposeful and less drunk than she had expected. She forgot her tiredness in her fear, but she knew that she couldn't sustain the pace for long. She sped across the wide street and down a road of tall, decaying houses. She could hear her feet slapping the pavement, could see from the corner of her eyes the flashing railings, could feel the wild rhythmic drumming of her heart. They were still behind her, shouting less now, reserving energy for the chase. Suddenly she came to another road turning off to the left. She swerved down it and saw with a gasp of relief that a gate in the railings was open. She almost threw herself down the steps and into the dark, evil-smelling area, almost colliding with three battered dustbins. She squeezed herself behind them and crouched in the narrow space under the flight of steps leading to the front door. Bent almost double she folded her arms over her chest, trying to stifle the pounding of her heart. How could they fail to be drawn to that insistent drumming? But the running feet hesitated, then clattered past, then died. From down the street she heard their bay of frustrated anger. Then they broke again into the disorganized shouts and singing. There was to be no search. They probably thought that she lived in the street and had gained the safety of her own home. More probably they were too drunk to think clearly. Once the quarry had gone to earth their interest died.

She stayed there long after their voices had faded away, crouched under the curve of the brick roof. She felt herself confined in a dark stinking cell, breathing dust and the spent breath of long-dead captives, bereft of the sky. The three malodorous dustbins, their shape imagined rather than seen, blocking her escape as effectively as a bolted door. There came to her in the darkness no blinding revelation, no healing of the spirit, only a measure of painful self-knowledge. From the moment of her counselling she had thought of no one but herself. Not of Hilda, who had so little to give but asked so little in return and needed that little so much. Hilda, who might reasonably have expected a greater return for those difficult years of caring than occasional help with the dining-room flowers. Not of Maurice, as arrogant and self-deceiving as herself, but who had done his best for her, had given with generosity even if he couldn't give with love, had somehow found the kindness to shield her from the worst knowledge. Not of her mother. What had she been but a purveyor of information, the living pattern of her own physical life, the victim of her patronage and self-love? She told herself that she had to learn humility. She was not sure that the lesson lay within her competence, but this stinking corner of the sleeping city into which she had crept like a derelict was as good a place as any in which to begin. She knew, too, that what bound her to her mother was stronger than hate, or disappointment or the pain of rejection. Surely this need to see her again, to be comforted by her, was the beginning of love; and how could she have expected that there could be love without pain?

After a time she eased herself out of the area and again breathed the cool night air and saw the stars. She walked on, almost light-headed with tiredness, searching for the names of streets. They told her nothing except that she was in the west ten district. She found herself in another square lying quiet and secret under the surging sky. In her mind the city seemed to stretch for ever, a silent half-derelict immensity, palely illumined by the recurrent moon. It was a dead city, plague-ridden and abandoned, from which all life had fled except for that band of scavenging louts. Now they too would have staggered into some filthy area, huddled together in death. She was completely alone. Behind the peeling stucco, the tall balustrades, lay the rotting dead. The stench of the city's decay rose like a miasma from the basement areas.

And then she saw the woman walking quickly but lightly across the square towards her on high-arched elegant feet. She wore a long pale dress and a stole. Her yellow hair was piled high. Everything about her was pale, the floating dress, her hair, her night-bleached skin. As they came abreast, Philippa asked:

'Could you please tell me where I am? I'm trying to get to Marylebone Station.'

The voice that answered her was pleasant, cheerful, cultured.

'You're in Moxford Square. Walk down this street for about a hundred yards. Take the first turning on the left and you'll find yourself at Ladbroke Grove Underground. I think you'll have missed the last train but you might pick up a late-night bus or a taxi.'

Philippa said:

'Thank you. If I can get to Ladbroke Grove I know my way.'

The woman smiled and walked on across the square. The encounter had been so unexpected and yet so ordinary that Philippa found herself wondering whether her tired brain had conjured up an apparition. Who was she and where was she going, this confident walker of the night? What friend or lover had deposited her here, unescorted, in the early hours? From what party had she come or was she escaping? But the woman's directions proved correct. Five minutes later Philippa found herself at Ladbroke Grove and began walking southwards towards home.

Delaney Street was silent and empty, sleeping as quietly as a village street beneath the unthreatening sky. The rain-washed air smelled of the sea. The windows of all the houses were dark except where number 12 showed a faint haze of light behind the drawn curtains. It wasn't bright enough for the ceiling light. Her mother must be still awake, or if she had fallen asleep, must have done so before she remembered to switch off the bedside lamp. She hoped that she would still be awake. She wondered what they would say to each other. She knew that she wouldn't be able to say that she was sorry, not yet; she had never said that in all her life. But perhaps it was a beginning that she could feel it. Perhaps, too, her mother would understand without the need of words. She would hold out the key of the front door to her and say:

'I must have meant all the time to come back. I didn't remember to leave you the key.'

She would stand there in her mother's doorway, and the fact that she was there would be enough. It would say:

'I love you. I need you. I have come home.'

TWELVE

The bedside lamp was on and in its pool of softened light her mother lay on her back asleep. But there was someone else in the room. Sitting slumped forward at the foot of the bed, hands between his knees, was a man, white-robed, shimmering with light. He didn't move or look up as she walked over to the bed. Her mother's face was perfectly calm. But something strange had happened to her neck. An animal had her by the throat, a small white, slug-like beast with its pink snout buried in her flesh. Something was eating her alive, burrowing away, tearing out the sinews, voiding its leavings on her white skin. But still she didn't stir. Philippa turned to the man; and this time she saw in his dangling hands the blood-stained knife. And then she both saw and understood.

He looked so grotesque that her first thought was he was the creature of delirium born of her exhaustion and the phantasmagoria of the night. But she knew that he was real. His being there by her mother's side was as inevitable as was her death. He was wearing a long raincoat of white transparent plastic, so thin that it clung to him like a film. On his hands were plastic gloves, surgeons' gloves, clinging to the pale flesh. They were too large for his tiny hands. At the end of each finger the plastic had gummed together and hung in pale flaps as if the skin itself were peeling away. Hiroshima hands. She said:

'Take off your gloves, they disgust me. You disgust me.'

Obediently he peeled them off.

He looked up at her, simply as a child craving reassurance:

'She won't bleed. She won't bleed.'

She moved closer to the bed. Her mother's eyes were closed. It was considerate of her to die with her eyes closed, but was that something one could choose to do? She tried to recall the pictured dead. It wasn't difficult; there were so many of them. The minds of her generation were patterned like nursery wallpaper with images of death; violence lay around their cradles. The corpses of Belsen piled like skinned rabbits in ungainly heaps, spike-bellied children of Ethiopia and India carrying their hunger like a monstrous foetus, the denuded bodies of soldiers sprawled in the clumsy dishevelment of death, all open-eyed. 'Tis a fine deceit to pass away in a dream. Indeed I've slept with mine eyes open a great while. But her mother's eyes were closed. Had she gone so gently into her goodnight? She turned to the man and said fiercely:

'Have you touched her?'

He didn't reply. He made a movement of his bent head. It could have meant yes or no. There was an envelope propped against a small tablet bottle on the bedside table. The flap hadn't been stuck down. She read:

'If God can forgive her death then he will forgive mine. These five weeks have been worth every day of the last ten years. Nothing is your fault. Nothing. This is the better way for me, not just for you. I can die happy because you are alive and I love you. Never be afraid.'

She put the note down on the table and looked again at the man. He was sitting on the edge of the bed, head bowed, the knife drooping from his hands. She took it from him and put it on the table. His hands were small, like a child's hands, a hamster's claws. He was beginning to shake and the bed shook with him. Her mother's body might have been shaking with laughter. She was afraid that the barely closed eyes would jolt open and that she would have to look on death. What was so terrible about grief was not grief itself, but that one got over it. It was strange to learn this truth even before the grieving had begun. She said, more gently:

'Come away from her. She won't bleed. The dead don't bleed. I got to her before you.'

She took hold of his shoulder and, half lifting him from the bed, led him over to the basket chair. The two-bar electric fire was off, as if her mother had remembered that they needed to save electricity. She switched on a single bar and turned it towards him. She said:

'I know who you are. I saw you in Regent's Park and somewhere else too, somewhere before that. Did you always plan to kill her?'

'My wife did, from the moment our daughter died.' Then he added, 'We planned it together.'

He seemed to need to explain.

'I came late tonight, but you hadn't left. The light in the front room was still on. I sat in the shop and listened and waited. But you didn't leave. There were no footsteps overhead, no sounds. At midnight I crept upstairs. The door was smashed and open. I thought she was asleep. She looked as if she was asleep. I didn't notice until I drove in the knife that her eyes were open. Her eyes were wide open and she was looking at me.'

She said:

'You'd better go. You did what you came for. It wasn't your fault that she escaped you in the end.' Death of one person can be paid but once and that she hath discharged. What thou wouldst do is done unto thy hand.

She said more loudly, shaking him gently by the shoulder:

'I shall have to call the police. If you don't want to be here when they come you'd better go now. There's no need for you to get involved.'

He didn't move. He was staring at the bar of the fire. He muttered something. She had to bend her head to hear him:

'I didn't know it would be like this. I want to be sick.'

She supported him into the kitchen and held his head while he retched over the sink, surprised that she could touch him without revulsion, could be so aware of the curiously silken texture of his hair, sliding over the hard skull. It seemed to her that her hand experienced simultaneously every single hair and the soft moving mass. She wanted to say: 'She didn't mean to kill. It was a burst of anger which she couldn't control. She never wanted your child dead in the way that you and I wanted her dead, willed her death.' But what was the use? What did it matter? His child was dead. Her mother was dead. Words, explanations, excuses, were an irrelevance. About that final negation there was nothing new to be thought, nothing new to be said, nothing that could be put right.

Everything in the kitchen was the same. As his head shuddered between her hands and the stink of vomit rose to her nostrils, she gazed round at the familiar objects, marvelling that they were unchanged. The teapot and two cups on the round papier mâché tray; the glistening pellets of coffee beans in their glass jar, how erotically beautiful they were, freshly-ground coffee had been one of their extravagances; the row of herbs in their pots on the window ledge. The north-facing window wasn't the best light for them, but still they had thrived. Tomorrow they had planned to snip the first chives for a herb omelette. The dressing her mother had made was still there in a jug on the table, the tang of vinegar still in the air. She wondered if she would be able to smell it in the future without thinking of this moment. She looked at the carefully folded tea towels, the two mugs on their hooks, the saucepans with their handles carefully aligned. How excessively neat they had been, imposing order and permanence on their insubstantial and precarious lives.

He was still retching but now it was only bile. The worst of the sickness was over. She handed him a towel and said:

'The bathroom's on the half landing if you want it.'

'Yes, I know.' He wiped his face and his mild eyes met hers. 'Won't you get into trouble? With the police, I mean.'

'No. She killed herself. The knife wound was made after death. Doctors can prove that. You saw yourself that she didn't bleed. I don't think there is a criminal offence of mutilating the dead. Even if there is, I don't suppose they'll charge me. All anyone will want is to get the whole unsavoury affair neatly tidied up. You see, no one cares about her. No one will mind that she's dead. She doesn't count as a human being. They think that she should have been killed nine years ago. She should have been hanged, that's what they'll all say.'

'But the police might think you killed her.'

'There's a suicide note to prove I didn't.'

'But suppose they think that you forged it.'

How extraordinary that he should get that idea. What a sophistical mind he must have. She looked into the meek, anxious eyes. Behind them a clever little brain must be scheming away. He ought to be writing thrillers. He had the mind of a thriller writer, obsessive, guilt-ridden, preoccupied with trivia. He had lived too long with thoughts of death. She said:

'I can prove that she wrote it. I've got a long specimen of her handwriting, a story she wrote in prison, a story about a rapist and his wife. Look, you'd better go. There's no point in letting the police find you unless you like the idea of seeing your face in all the newspapers. Some people do; is that what you want?'

He shook his head. He said:

'I want to go home.'

'Home?' she asked. She hadn't thought of him as having a home, this nocturnal predator with his finicky hands that could do so much damage, his stink of vomit. She thought he whispered something about Casablanca being home, but that was surely absurd.

He asked:

'Shall we see each other again?'

'I don't suppose so. Why should we? All we have in common is that we both wanted her dead. I don't see that as a basis for social acquaintance.'

'Are you sure you'll be all right?'

'Oh yes,' she said. 'I'll be all right. There'll be plenty of people to make sure that I'm all right.'

There was a rucksack on the floor beside the door. She hadn't noticed it before. He took off his mackintosh, rolled it, and stuffed it inside. It was, she thought, something he had done many times before. But when he reached for the knife, she said:

'Leave it. Leave it where it is. I'll see that it has my fingerprints on it.'

They went down the stairs together as if he were a dilatory visitor whom she was managing to see off at last. He walked quickly up Delaney Street without a backward glance, and she watched him out of sight. She returned to the bedroom. She couldn't look at her mother, but she made herself take up the knife and hold it for a moment in her hand. Then she ran out of the flat to Marylebone Station to telephone Maurice.

The entrance to the concourse was deserted, the row of telephone booths empty, except for one figure. A young man was huddled in the furthest booth. She couldn't tell whether he was drunk or asleep. Perhaps he might even be dead. But she recognized him. She had seen him before, patiently trying to hand out texts in Mell Street market.

She found a tenpenny piece in her purse, dialled the seven familiar digits, then pushed the coin home as Maurice's voice repeated the number. He had answered at once. But then, the telephone was by his bed. She said:

'It's Philippa. Please come. My mother's dead. I wanted her to kill herself and she has.'

He said:

'Are you sure she's dead?'

'I'm sure.'

'Where are you ringing from?'

'Marylebone Station.'

'I'll come straight away. Wait where you are. Don't talk to anyone. Do nothing until I come.'

The streets were almost empty in the calm of the early hours, but, even so, he must have driven very fast. It seemed only a matter of minutes before she heard the Rover.

She walked towards him and into his arms. Suddenly they

were round her, fierce and stiff, a clasp of possession not a gesture of comfort. Then, as suddenly, he let her go and she tottered and nearly fell. She felt his fingers gripping her shoulder, propelling her towards the car. He said:

'Show me.'

The Rover slid to a stop outside the door of number 12. He took his time over locking it, looking up and down the street, calm and unhurried as if this were a late social visit and he would prefer on the whole not to be observed. She turned the key in the Yale lock and he followed her upstairs. Their climbing feet echoed in the hall. If he noticed the smashed lock on the flat door, he said nothing. She led the way to her mother's room and stood aside, waiting and watching while he walked over to the bed and looked down. He read the suicide note, his face expressionless. He picked up the empty bottle and studied the label, then tipped out on to his palm the one white bullet-shaped pellet. He said:

'Distalgesic. Considerate of her to have left this. It'll save the analyst time and trouble. I wonder how she got hold of it. Distalgesic is on prescription; you can't just buy it across the counter. Someone must have smuggled it into prison for her if she didn't steal it from the hospital wing or have it prescribed for her. That's probably something we'll never know. She's not the first person to have mistaken the strength of this stuff. It's got paracetamol in it; but that isn't the danger. It contains an opium-type compound. An overdose kills very quickly. She was planning the usual histrionic gesture and misjudged the strength.'

Philippa wanted to reply: 'She didn't misjudge anything or anyone. She killed herself because she meant to kill herself, because she knew that's what I wanted her to do. You might at least give her the credit of knowing what she did.' But she said nothing. He bent his head slightly and looked at the savaged throat intently, like a doctor. Then he frowned. It was a frown of worried distaste, as if he were faced with a technical problem and had encountered an unexpected snag. He said:

'Who did this?'

'I did. At least I suppose I did.'

'You suppose you did?'

'I can remember wanting to kill her. I can remember going into the kitchen and getting the knife. That's all.'

'When you talk to the police, forget the first sentence. You didn't kill her, so what you intended or wanted isn't relevant. Did you break down the door, too?'

So he had noticed. But of course he had. She said:

'After I got back from Caldecote Terrace we quarrelled. I ran out of the flat. I didn't intend to come back. But then I did come back. We've only one pair of keys and I'd forgotten to take them. I banged on the door but she wouldn't let me in, so I broke it down. I had a chisel with me from the tool chest. I'm not sure why. I think I might have been threatening her with it before I ran out, but I can't remember now.'

He said:

'If you didn't take the keys with you, how did you get in at the street door? Aren't they on the same ring?'

She had forgotten that. She said quickly:

'There's only a Yale there. I slipped the latch up. I got used to doing that if I went out briefly at night.'

'Where is the chisel, the one you used on the door?'

'I put it back in the tool box.'

The inquisition had ended. He moved from the bed and said:

'Come away from here. Is there another room or somewhere comfortable?'

'No, not very comfortable. There's only my room and the kitchen.'

He placed his arm round her shoulders and pushed her gently into the passage. They went into the kitchen. He said.

'I'm going to ring the police now from Marylebone Station. Do you want to come with me, or are you all right here?'

'I'll come with you.'

'Yes, that would be best. Get your coat. It's cold.'

He made her wait in the car while he telephoned. It didn't take long. When he came back to the car he said:

'They'll be here very quickly. When they come just tell them what you told me. You can't remember anything between going to the kitchen drawer for the knife and running out to telephone me.'

The police came quickly too. There seemed a lot of them for so unimportant a death. She was put to wait in her own room. They lit the gas fire. They brought her tea. She wanted to explain that it was the wrong cup, her mother's cup. There was a policewoman with her, blonde, pretty, almost as young as herself. She looked attractive in her dark blue, well-cut uniform. Her face, disciplined of pity, watchful, was carefully neutral. Philippa thought:

'She isn't sure whether she's guarding a victim or a villain. Normally she would have put a consoling hand round my shoulders. But then, there is that slit in my mother's throat.' When the detective came in to question her Maurice was with him, and another man whom she recognized as Maurice's solicitor. He introduced him formally.

'Philippa, I don't think you've ever met Charles Cullingford. This is my daughter.'

She stood up and shook hands. It was as punctilious and ordinary, as if they were meeting in the drawing-room at Caldecote Terrace. He kept his eyes rather too carefully from looking round the bleak little bedroom. The police brought in two chairs from her mother's room. They introduced the inspector to her but she didn't take in his name. He was dark and fitted rather too well into his clothes and his eyes had no kindness in them. But he questioned her gently and Maurice was at her side.

'Has anyone else been here this evening?'

'No. Only us.'

'Who broke in the door?'

'I did it. I did it with the chisel in the kitchen drawer.'

'Why did you take the chisel with you when you left the flat?'

'In case she tried to lock me out.'

'Had your mother ever done that before?'

'No.'

'Why did you think she might lock you out tonight?'

'We had a quarrel after my father had told me that she'd given me away.'

'Your father says that you ran out of the flat and walked for about three hours. What happened when you came back?'

'I found that the door was locked and she didn't answer, so I broke in with the chisel.'

'Did you know when you found her that she was dead?'

'I think so. I can't remember what I felt. I can't remember what happened after I broke down the door. I think I wanted to kill her.'

'Where did you get the knife?'

'From the kitchen drawer.'

'But before that? It's new isn't it?'

'My mother bought it. We wanted a sharp knife. I don't know where she got it.'

They went away again. There was a knock at the door, loud voices, confident feet. Her door was ajar. The policewoman got up and closed it. The feet were moving more slowly now, half-shuffling down the passage. They were taking her mother away. When she realized this she sprang up with a cry, but the policewoman was quicker. She felt her shoulder seized in a surprisingly strong grip and, gently but firmly, she was forced back into her chair.

The blur of voices came through the door, disconnected words – '. . . clearly dead when she stuck the knife in. You didn't need to pull me out of bed to tell you that. I suppose you've got a charge somewhere which fits the case if you want to find one, but it can't be homicide.'

Maurice's voice:

'This place is pathetic. God knows what these six weeks have been like for her. I couldn't stop her . . . she's of age . . . my fault. I should never had told her that her mother battered and then abandoned her.'

She thought she heard someone say:

'It's all for the best.' But perhaps that was imagination. Perhaps that was only what they were all thinking. Then Maurice was standing over her.

'We're going home now, Philippa. It's going to be all right.'

But of course it would be all right. Maurice would arrange it all. He would dispose of the flat, selling the last few weeks of the lease, get rid of all that was left of their life together. She would never see any of their belongings again. The Henry Walton would be replaced on her wall at Caldecote Terrace. That was too expensive to be discarded. But it was spoilt for her. She would look at it now with different eyes, seeing behind the elegance and order the prison hulks lying off Gravesend, the flogging-block, the public hangman. But there had to be some limit to the indulgence of sensitivity. She would be expected to go on living with the Walton. But everything else would go. The rest would be treated as the rubbish it was. His lawyers would silence the publicity, would gentle her through the further questioning, the inquest, the publicity. Only there wasn't likely to be much publicity. Maurice would see to that too. Everyone, police, coroner, Press, would be sympathetic. When they remembered that ravaged throat they would fight down repulsion or dislike, remembering whose daughter she was. They would be sorry for her; but they would be a little frightened too. Had she only imagined the inspector's final words, bluff, almost humorous:

'You can take her home now, sir. And for God's sake keep her away from knives.'

Afterwards, he would take her away, perhaps to Italy since an Italian visit had always been his personal therapy. They would see together the cities she had planned one day to see with her mother. How long would it be before he could look into her eyes without wondering whether she was, after all, her mother's daughter, without asking himself whether she would have plunged that knife into a living throat. Perhaps the thought would excite him; people were excited by violence. What, after all, was the sexual act but a voluntarily endured assault, a momentary death?

And now they were alone. Before they left together, she went to her room and came back with her mother's manuscript. She held it out to him.

'I want you to read this, please. It's her account of the murder. She wrote it in prison long before she met me.'

'Is that what she told you? Look at the colour and newness of the paper. Feel it. This hasn't lain about in a cell for years. This was written recently. Didn't that strike you?'

He took it over to the fireplace, then paused. He didn't smoke and carried no matches. While she watched he went into the kitchen and came back with a box. He held up the manuscript and the flame bit, crept in a widening circle across the writing, then burst into flame. He held the paper almost until his fingers were burnt, then dropped it into the grate.

Suddenly she was aware of her tiredness, the stains and filth on her shirt, her trousers grimed with coal dust where she had crouched behind the bins in that distant area. She felt a gout of blood discharge and roll down her leg. He looked at her and said gently:

'Go to the bathroom. I'm waiting for you.'

When she came back five minutes later he had taken down the oil painting and had in his arms one of the blankets from her bed. He put it round her shoulders. Without speaking they went together down the stairs and out of the flat.

The drive home seemed very short through the deserted streets. No one had seen them go. Tomorrow George would open his shop and wonder why they were so silent, where they had gone. No one would miss them for long.

At Caldecote Terrace there was a light on in the hall and in the drawing-room but the kitchen was in darkness. The door opened to them before Maurice had time to fit his key in the lock. Hilda stood there, anxious-eyed, wearing her blue quilted dressing-gown. Maurice said to her quietly:

'She's all right. Don't worry. Everything's all right. Her mother's dead. Suicide.'

She was smothered in Hilda's padded arms. She heard her say:

'Your room's still waiting for you, darling,' as if it might have taken off and vanished during her absence. And then she heard a dog barking and Hilda's face was suddenly tender with concern.

'You've woken Scamp. I'd better go down to him.'

At the bottom of the stairs he took the blanket from her shoulders and tossed it aside. When she came down next morning it would be gone. Even an old blanket from Delaney Street wouldn't be allowed to contaminate memory. He followed her upstairs; his footsteps firm behind her faltering ones. She felt like a prisoner under escort. But the room to which her feet weakly but unhesitatingly led her was white and peaceful and the single bed looked comfortable. It had nothing to do with her; she didn't belong here. But she thought that the girl who did wouldn't mind if she used it. She peeled off her dirt-stained shirt and filthy trousers, let herself drop face downwards on the bed grasping the pillows with her hands and felt Maurice drawing the blankets over her shoulders. She hadn't bathed; but that didn't matter, she didn't think the girl would mind. Just before she fell asleep she remembered that there was someone for whom she needed to weep. But she had no tears left, and she had never found it easy to cry. And that didn't matter either. She had a lifetime ahead of her in which to learn how.

BOOK FOUR

Epilogue

ONE

Sunday afternoon evensong was over. The packed congregation, released from their role of silent participants in the music, joined with cheerful abandon in the concluding hymn. The boy choristers, their calm candle-lit faces rising translucent as flowers from their ruffs, had closed their books and were filing from their stalls. Philippa rose from her knees, shook free her hair, twitched the pleated cotton more comfortably on her shoulders and joined the small band of similarly white-gowned members of college who were following the procession out through the carved screen and into the cool, light-filled immensity of the ante-chapel.

She saw him almost immediately, but then she would have recognized this insignificant little man anywhere in the world. He was standing in his neat over-pressed suit at the end of the first row, diminished under the marvel of Westell's surging vault, but with his own small human dignity. His hands, those well-remembered hands, were resting on the back of the chair in front of him. As she came within touching distance, the knuckles tightened into shining pebbles. Their eyes met and he looked steadily at her with what she thought was a mute appeal that she shouldn't escape him. It never occurred to her to try; nor did she believe for one moment that this encounter was by chance. After she left the chapel she lingered at the south porch until he came up quietly beside her. They didn't greet each other but turned, as if by mutual consent, and began pacing the sunlit path beside Gibb's Building. She said:

'How did you find me? But I'd forgotten; you're an expert at tracking people down.'

'It was your book. I read the reviews and two of them said that you were a student at King's. You published it under your name, Philippa Ducton.'

'Ducton's my name. I dropped the Rose. It didn't suit me. I thought I was entitled to one small personal preference of identity. But you didn't come here, surely, to congratulate me on the novel. Did you read it?'

'I asked for it at the library.'

She laughed, and looking at her he flushed and said:

'Is that the wrong thing to say to a writer? I suppose I ought to have bought it.'

'Why should you? And you couldn't have welcomed it – the name Ducton on your shelves. Did you enjoy it?'

She could see from his face that he wasn't sure whether she was teasing him. At last he said, surprisingly:

'It was clever, of course. Some of the critics said that it was brilliant. But I thought that it was harsh, unfeeling.'

'Yes it was. That's just what it was, unfeeling. But you didn't take all this trouble to track me down just so that we could have a literary discussion.'

Looking at his face, she said quickly:

'I'm not sorry to see you. You had to leave suddenly when we last met. I've had that feeling, too, that there's unfinished business between us. I've wondered from time to time about you, what you were doing, where you were.'

She wanted to add: 'And whether you were happier knowing that my mother was dead.' But looking at his calm, untroubled face, that was a question which she didn't need to ask. Perhaps that was why revenge was so satisfying; it worked.

He answered her eagerly, as if he were glad to be telling her.

'I left London after the inquest on your mother and travelled about England and Wales for about eighteen months. I stayed at cheap boarding-houses in the summer and moved into better-class ones in the autumn and winter. You get special rates out of season. I spent my time looking at places, buildings, thinking about myself. I wasn't unhappy. Six months ago I returned to London and went back to the Casablanca. That's the hotel where I took a room when I was tracking you down. I'm not sure why I went back, except that I felt at home there. It was just the same; the blind telephonist, the one you saw me with in Regent's Park, was still there. Her name's Violet Hedley. We started going out together on her free afternoons. We're going to get married.'

So this was why he had come. She said:

'And you don't know how much you ought to tell her?'

'She knows about Julie, of course. And I told her that both the Ductons were dead. But I'm not sure whether I ought to tell her what I tried to do. There's no one in the world but you I can talk to about it, no one else to consult. I had to find you.'

She said:

'If you're marrying a blind woman, I shouldn't advise you to tell her that you once twisted a knife in another woman's throat. It could be unsettling.'

The shock and the hurt on his face were as palpable as if she had struck him. Even the physical manifestation was the same. He flushed, and then became very pale, except for one scarlet lash on his cheek. She said more gently:

'I'm sorry. I'm not a kind person. I try to be sometimes, but I'm not very good at it yet.' She nearly added: 'And the person who could have taught me how is dead.' She went on:

'It's your bad luck that you're stuck with me as a confidante. But the advice is still sound. We none of us know another human being so well that we can be absolutely sure about him. I can't see what you gain by telling. Why distress her?'

'But I love her. We love each other. Doesn't that mean that I ought to be honest with her?'

She said:

'This conversation between us is honest as far as I can make it so. That doesn't mean that either of us likes it the better. You have the whole of your past life to be honest about. One incident in it isn't important.'

'It was an important incident to me. And it brought us together. I wouldn't have been at the Casablanca, wouldn't have met Violet, if I hadn't tried to kill your mother.'

She could have replied that his child and her mother would both have been alive if he had kept his daughter at home on a foggy January night twelve and a half years ago. But what point was there in tracing back the long concatenation of chance. She said, interested:

'How are you going to manage? Have you a job?'

'I've lived simply during the last two years. I've got about twelve thousand pounds left from the sale of the house. That will be enough to put down on a cottage somewhere. And my local-authority pension starts in a few months' time. We should be all right. We don't want a large place, just somewhere with a garden.

Violet loves the smell of roses. She became blind when she was eight; before that she could see, so she has some memories, and if I describe things to her carefully, buildings, the sky, flowers, it helps. I have to look at things differently now, more carefully, so that I can remember them. We're so happy together, I can't believe it.'

She wondered if the happiness included going to bed together. Probably it did. He wasn't sexually repulsive, this poor little murderer manqué. And even Crippen had had his Ethel Le Neve. The unlikeliest couples found their way to that irrational joy. She remembered the feel of his hair under her hand, silkier than her own. And his skin was soft, unblemished. Besides, his Violet wouldn't have to see him. It must be strange to be blind, making love always with one's eyes shut. She caught a glance at his smile, secret, reminiscent, almost lubricious. He had come to her with his anxieties, but that wasn't one of them. Remembering the girl she had seen in the park, she wondered whether his Violet was young enough to have a child. As if his mind had flowed with hers, he said:

'She's much younger than I am. If she has a baby I could help look after him. There's nothing we can't manage together.'

He turned to her.

'Do you ever feel that you don't deserve happiness? The time I first went out with her, the day you saw us in the rose garden, I was exploiting her, making use of her blindness. I was lonely and she was the only person I could feel safe with, because she couldn't see.'

How early he must have learned that primeval lesson, the distrust of joy. Touch wood, cross fingers, light a candle, please God don't notice that I'm happy. She wanted to say:

'I used my mother to avenge myself on my adoptive father. We all use each other. Why should you expect to be less corrupt than the rest of us.' Instead she said:

'Why not learn to be gentle with yourself, to accept the possibility of happiness? Forget about my mother and me. That's over.'

'But suppose Violet found out? She'd find it hard to forgive, the deception or what I did.'

'There's nothing for her to forgive. It wasn't her throat. Besides, we can forgive anything as long as it isn't done to us. Haven't you learned that? And how could she find out? You needn't worry about me. I shan't ever tell.'

'But you're a writer; you might want to use it one day.'

She nearly laughed aloud. So that was what was worrying him. He must have borrowed her novel from the library in trepidation. What, she wondered, had he been expecting? Some lurid Gothic romance with himself as a pathetic Eumenides? But he would hardly be expecting a dissertation on the nature of the creative imagination. She said:

'Some writers can only write about their own direct experience. That's not the kind of writer I am or want to be. I said that we all use each other, but I hope to use people with rather more subtlety than that.'

He said, tentatively, as if venturing on dangerous ground:

'Do they know about your mother here? After all, you do call yourself Ducton.'

'Some of them know and some of them guess. It's hardly a subject that comes up naturally in conversation.'

'And does it make any difference, to you I mean?'

'Only, perhaps, to make them a little afraid of me. For someone who values privacy that's no bad thing.'

They had reached the bridge over the Cam. Philippa paused and gazed down at the water. He stood beside her, his tiny hands grasping the parapet. And then he asked:

'Do you miss her?'

She thought: 'I shall miss her every day of my life.' But she said:

'Yes. I'm not sure that I really knew her. We only lived together for five weeks. She didn't say very much. But when she was there she was more there than anyone I've ever known. And I was there too.'

He seemed to understand what she meant. They walked on, again in silence, and then he said:

'I've wondered about you. I'm grateful to you for what you did for me. I'm frightened of authority, frightened of being locked up. If you'd called the police that night I know I would never have been able to cope. And I would never have met Violet again. I've wondered many times how things were with you, what happened after I left you, whether your mother – I mean Mrs Palfrey – is well.'

He could have been asking after any casual acquaintance. She said:

'She's very well. She has a dog now. His name is Scamp. And nothing very much happened to me. My adoptive father arranged everything; he's a great fixer. Afterwards he took me on a long holiday to Italy. We went to see the mosaics at Ravenna.'

She didn't add: 'And in Ravenna I went to bed with him.' She wondered how he would have looked, what he would have said, if she had responded to his confidence with that gratuitous news. And it wasn't, after all, important. What, she wondered, had it meant exactly, that gentle, tender, surprisingly uncomplicated coupling; an affirmation, a curiosity satisfied, a test successfully passed, an obstacle ceremoniously moved out of the way so that they could again take up their roles of father and daughter, the excitement of incest without its legal prohibition, without any more guilt than they carried already? That single night together, the windows open to the smell of cypresses, to the warm Italian night, had been necessary, inevitable, but it was no longer important. She said:

'My mother insured her life for five hundred pounds so that she could pay her share of the flat. There wasn't a suicide prohibition in the policy – I don't suppose they bothered with so small a sum – so I got the money. She must have arranged it secretly soon after we started living together, perhaps when she went to see her probation officer. No one knows for certain how she got hold of the distalgesic but she must have been secreting those tablets away for months. I tell myself that it shows that she was thinking of killing herself even before she came out of prison, that her death had nothing to do with me. There are so many expedients for getting rid of guilt. You'll find one for yourself in time.'

He said nothing more. He seemed satisfied. Suddenly he stopped and held out his hand. She shook it. The gesture seemed to be important to him. Then he walked on alone down the avenue in the spring sunshine, under the tender green of chestnuts, beeches and lime trees, between the bright grass patterned with gold and purple crocuses. Just before he reached a turn in the avenue he paused and looked back, not, she thought, at her, but at the chapel, as if to fix it in his mind. She stood watching him until he was out of sight. If it is only through learning to love that we find identity, then he had found his. She hoped one day to find hers. She wished him well. And perhaps to be able to wish him well with all that she could recognize of her unpractised heart, to say a short untutored prayer for him and his Violet, was in itself a small accession of grace.

THE SKULL BENEATH THE SKIN

CONTENTS

Even the most diligent search of maps and charts will fail to discover Courcy Island or its Victorian castle lying off the coast of Dorset, since both have their reality only in the imaginations of the writer and her readers. Similarly, the events past and recent of Courcy's bloodstained history and the characters who took part in them have no relation to actual events or living people.

Webster was much possessed by death
And saw the skull beneath the skin;
And breastless creatures under ground
Leaned backward with a lipless grin.

Daffodil bulbs instead of balls
Stared from the sockets of the eyes!
He knew that thought clings round dead limbs
Tightening its lusts and luxuries.

from T. S. ELIOT, 'Whispers of Immortality'

PART ONE

Call to an Off-shore Island

CHAPTER ONE

There could be no doubt about it, the new name-plate was crooked. Cordelia had no need to adopt Bevis's expedient of dodging through the mid-morning traffic which cluttered Kingly Street and squinting at it through a dazzle of grinding delivery vans and taxis to recognize stark mathematical fact; the neat bronze oblong, so carefully designed and so expensive, was half an inch out of true. Lopsided as it was, it looked, she thought, despite the simplicity of its wording, both pretentious and ridiculous, a fitting advertisement of irrational hope and ill-advised enterprise.

Pryde's Detective Agency
(Third Floor) *Prop:* Cordelia Gray

Had she been superstitious, she might have believed that Bernie's unquiet spirit was protesting against the new plaque with the deletion of his name. And indeed, it had seemed at the time symbolic, the final obliteration of Bernie at her hands. She had never considered changing the name of the Agency; while it remained in being it would always be Pryde's. But it had become increasingly irksome to be asked by her clients, disconcerted as much by her sex as by her youth, 'But I thought I would be seeing Mr Pryde.' They might as well know from the start that there was now only one proprietor and she a female.

Bevis rejoined her at the door, his pretty, mobile face a parody of desolation, and said:

'I measured it carefully from the ground, honestly, Miss Gray.'

'I know. The pavement must be uneven. It's my fault. We should have bought a spirit level.'

But she had been trying to limit expenditure from the petty cash, ten pounds a week kept in the battered cigarette tin inherited from Bernie with its picture of the battle of Jutland, from which money seemed to drain away by a mysterious process unrelated to actual expenditure. It had been only too easy to accept the assurance of Bevis that he was handy with a screwdriver, forgetting that, for Bevis, any job was preferable to the one he was actually supposed to be doing. He said:

'If I close my left eye and hold my head like this it looks all right.'

'But we can't rely on a succession of one-eyed, wry-necked clients, Bevis.'

Glancing at Bevis's face, which had now fallen into an extreme of despair which would not have been inappropriate to the announcement of an atomic attack, Cordelia felt an obscure desire to comfort him for his own incompetence. One of the disconcerting aspects of being an employer of staff, a role for which she increasingly felt herself almost wholly unsuited, was this over-sensitivity to their feelings coupled with a vague sense of guilt. This was the more irrational since, strictly speaking, she didn't directly employ either Bevis or Miss Maudsley. Both were hired from Miss Feeley's employment agency on a weekly basis when the Agency's case-load warranted it. There was seldom competition for their services; both were invariably and suspiciously available when asked for. Both gave her honesty, conscientious timekeeping and a fierce loyalty; both would, no doubt, have also given her an efficient secretarial service if that had lain in their power.· Both added to her anxieties, since she knew that the failure of the Agency would be almost as traumatic for them as for her. Miss Maudsley would suffer the more. She was a gentle, sixty-two-year-old, rector's sister, eking out her pension in a bed-sitting-room in South Kensington, whose gentility, age, incompetence and virginity had made her the butt of the countless typing-pools through which she had drifted since her brother's death. Bevis, with his facile, slightly venal charm, was better equipped to survive in the London jungle. He was supposed to be a dancer working as a temporary typist while resting, an inappropriate euphemism when applied to such a restless boy, perpetually fidgeting in his chair or pirouetting on tiptoe, fingers splayed, eyes widened and alarmed as if poised for flight. He was certificated to type thirty words a minute by an obscure secretarial school long since defunct, but Cordelia reminded herself that even they hadn't guaranteed his proficiency to undertake minor jobs as a handyman.

He and Miss Maudsley were unexpectedly compatible, and a great deal more chat went on in the outer office between the bouts of inexpert typing than Cordelia would have expected from two such discordant personalities, denizens, she would have thought, of such alien worlds. Bevis poured out his domestic and professional tribulations liberally laced with inaccurate and occasionally scurrilous theatrical gossip. Miss Maudsley applied to this bewildering world her own mixture of innocence, High Anglican theology, rectory morality and common sense. Life in the outer office became very cosy at times, but Miss Maudsley had old-fashioned views on the proper distinction to be made between employer and employed and the inner room where Cordelia worked was sacrosanct.

Suddenly Bevis cried out:

'Oh God, it's Tomkins!'

A small black and white kitten had appeared at the doorway, shaken one exploratory paw with deceptive insouciance, stretched its tail rigid, then shivered with ecstatic apprehension and darted under a Post Office van and out of sight. Bevis, wailing, fled in pursuit. Tomkins was one of the Agency's failures, having been repudiated by a spinster of that name who had employed Cordelia to find her missing black kitten with a white eye patch, two white paws and a striped tail. Tomkins precisely fulfilled the specification, but his putative mistress had immediately known him for an impostor. Having rescued him from imminent starvation on a building site behind Victoria station they could hardly abandon him and he now lived in the outer office with a dirt tray, cushioned basket, and access to the roof via a partly opened window for his nightly excursions. He was a drain on resources, not so much because of the rising cost of cat food – although it was a pity that Miss Maudsley had encouraged an addiction to tastes beyond their means by providing the most expensive tin on the market for his first meal and that Tomkins, although in general a stupid cat, could apparently read labels – but because Bevis wasted too much time playing with him, tossing a ping-pong ball or drawing a rabbit's foot on string across the office floor with cries of:

'Oh look, Miss Gray! Isn't he a clever leaping beastie?'

The clever leaping beastie, having caused chaos among the traffic in Kingly Street, now streaked into the rear entrance of a pharmacy with Bevis in noisy pursuit. Cordelia guessed that neither kitten nor boy was likely to reappear for some time. Bevis picked up new friends as obsessively as others pick up litter, and Tomkins would be a great introducer. Oppressed by the realization that Bevis's morning was now fated to be almost entirely unproductive, Cordelia was aware of a lethargic disinclination for any further effort herself. She stood against the jamb of the doorway, closed her eyes and lifted her face to the unseasonable warmth of the late September sun. Distancing herself by an effort of will from the grind and clamour of the street, the pervading smell of petrol, the clatter of passing feet, she played with the temptation, which she knew she would resist, to walk away from it all, leaving the lopsided plaque as a memorial to her efforts to keep faith with the dead Bernie and his impossible dream.

She supposed that she ought to be relieved that the Agency was beginning to make a reputation for something, even if it were only for finding lost pets. Undoubtedly there was a need for such a service – and one in which she suspected they had a monopoly – and the clients, tearful, desperate, outraged by what they saw as the callous indifference of the local CID, never haggled at the size of the bill, and paid more promptly than Cordelia suspected they might have done for the return of a relative. Even when the Agency's efforts had been unsuccessful and Cordelia had to present her account with apologies, it was invariably paid without demur. Perhaps the owners were motivated by the natural human need at a time of bereavement to feel that something had been done, however unlikely that something, to achieve success. But frequently there were successes. Miss Maudsley, in particular, had a persistence in door-to-door inquiries coupled with an almost uncanny empathy with the feline mind that had restored at least half a dozen cats, damp, half-starved and feebly mewing, to their ecstatic owners, while occasionally exposing the perfidy of those animals who had been living a double life and had transferred more or less permanently to their second home. She managed to conquer her timidity when in pursuit of cat thieves, and on Saturday mornings walked purposefully through the rowdy exuberance and half-submerged terrors of London's street markets as if under divine protection, which no doubt she felt herself to be.

But Cordelia wondered from time to time what poor, ambitious, pathetic Bernie would have thought about the debasement of his dream-child. Lulled into a trance-like peace by the warmth and the sun, Cordelia recalled with startling clarity that confident, over-loud voice: 'We've got a gold-mine here, partner, if once we get started.' She was glad that he couldn't know how small the nuggets and how thin the seam.

A voice, quiet, masculine and authoritative, broke into her reverie.

'That name-plate's crooked.'

'I know.'

Cordelia opened her eyes. The voice was deceptive: he was older than she had expected, she guessed a little over sixty. Despite the heat of the day he was wearing a tweed jacket, well tailored but old with leather patches on the elbows. He wasn't tall, perhaps no more than five feet ten inches, but he stood very upright with an easy, confident stance, almost an elegance, which she sensed concealed an inner wariness, as if he were tensed for a word of command. She wondered if he had once been a soldier. His head was held high and fixed, the grey and somewhat sparse hair brushed smoothly back from a high, creased forehead. The face was long and bony with a dominant nose jutting from cheeks reddened and crossed by broken veins, and a wide, well-shaped mouth. The eyes which scrutinized her (not, she felt, unbenignly) were keen under the bushy eyebrows. The left brow was held higher than the right and she saw that he had a habit of twitching his brows and working the corners of the long mouth; it gave his face a restlessness which was singularly at variance with the stillness of his body and which made it slightly embarrassing for her to meet his eyes. He said:

'Better get the job done properly.'

She watched without speaking while he put down the briefcase he was carrying, took from a pocket a pen and his wallet, found a card, and wrote on the back of it in an upright, rather schoolboyish hand.

Taking the card, Cordelia noted the single name, Morgan, and the telephone number, then turned it over. She read:

Sir George Ralston, Bt., DSO, MC.

So she was right. He had been a soldier. She asked:

'Will he be expensive, this Mr Morgan?'

'Less expensive than making a nonsense. Tell him I gave you his number. He'll charge what the job's worth, no more.'

Cordelia's heart lifted. The lopsided name plaque, gravely surveyed by the critical eye of this unexpected and eccentric knight errant, suddenly seemed to her irresistibly funny, no longer a calamity but a joke. Even Kingly Street was transformed with her mood and became a glittering, sunlit bazaar, pulsating with optimism and life. She almost laughed aloud. Controlling her trembling mouth she said gravely:

'It's very kind of you. Are you a connoisseur of name-plates or just a public benefactor?'

'Some people think I'm a public menace. Actually, I'm a client, that is, if you're Cordelia Gray. Don't people ever tell you . . .'

Cordelia, unreasonably, was disappointed. Why should she have supposed that he was different from other male clients? She finished the sentence for him:

'That it's an unsuitable job for a woman? They do, and it isn't.'

He said mildly:

'I was going to say, don't they ever tell you that your office is difficult to find? This street's a mess. Half the buildings aren't properly numbered. Too much change of use, I suppose. But the new plate should help when it's properly fixed. Better get it done. Gives a poor impression.'

At that moment Bevis panted up beside them, his curls damp with exertion, the tell-tale screwdriver protruding from his shirt pocket. Holding a richly purring Tomkins against one flushed cheek, he presented his charming delinquency to the newcomer. He was rewarded by a curt, 'A botched job that' and a look which instantly rejected him as officer material. Sir George turned to Cordelia:

'Shall we go up then?'

Cordelia avoided Bevis's eyes, which she guessed were rolling heavenward, and they climbed the narrow, linoleum-covered stairs in single file, Cordelia leading, past the single lavatory and washroom which served all the tenants in the building (she hoped that Sir George wouldn't need to use it) and into the front outer office on the third floor. Miss Maudsley's anxious eyes looked up at them over her typewriter. Bevis deposited Tomkins in his basket (where he at once began washing away the contamination of Kingly Street), gave Miss Maudsley a wide-eyed, admonitory look, and mouthed the word 'client' at her. Miss Maudsley flushed, half rose from her chair, then subsided again and applied herself to painting out an error with a shaking hand. Cordelia led the way into her inner sanctum.

When they were seated she asked:

'Would you like some coffee?'

'Real coffee or ersatz?'

'Well, I suppose you'd call it ersatz. But best quality ersatz.'

'Tea, then, if you have it, preferably Indian. Milk please. No sugar. No biscuits.'

The form of the request was not meant to be offensive. He was used to ascertaining the facts, then asking for what he wanted.

Cordelia put her head outside the door and said 'Tea please' to Miss Maudsley. The tea, when it arrived, would be served in the delicate Rockingham cups which Miss Maudsley had inherited from her mother and had lent to the Agency for the use of special clients only. She had no doubt that Sir George would qualify for the Rockingham.

They faced each other across Bernie's desk. His eyes, grey and keen, inspected her face as if he were an examiner and she a candidate, which in a way she supposed she was. Their sudden, direct and glittering stare, in contrast to the spasmodically grimacing mouth, was disconcerting. He said:

'Why do you call yourself Pryde's?'

'Because the Agency was set up by an ex-Metropolitan policeman, Bernie Pryde. I worked for him for a time as his assistant and then he made me his partner. When he died he left the Agency to me.'

'How did he die?'

The question, sharp as an accusation, struck her as odd, but she answered calmly.

'He cut his wrists.'

She didn't need to close her eyes to see again that remembered scene, garish and sharply outlined as a cinema still. Bernie had lain slumped in the chair in which she now sat, his half-clenched right hand close to the open cutthroat razor, his shrunken left hand, with its scored and gaping wrist, resting palm upwards in the bowl like some exotic sea anemone glimpsed in a rock pool, curling in death its pale and wrinkled tentacles. But no rock pool had ever been so brightly pink. She could smell again the sickly-sweet insistent odour of freshly spilt blood.

'Killed himself, did he?'

His tone lightened. He might have been a golfing partner congratulating Bernie on a well-placed putt, while his quick glance round the office suggested that the action had been in all the circumstances entirely reasonable.

She had no need to see either room through his eyes. What she saw through her own was depressing enough. She and Miss Maudsley had redecorated her office together, painting the walls pale yellow to give an impression of greater light and cleaning the faded carpet with a proprietary liquid; it had dried patchily so that the final impression reminded her of diseased skin. With its newly washed curtains, the room at least looked clean and tidy, too tidy since the absence of clutter suggested no great pressure of work. Every surface was crammed with plants. Miss Maudsley had green fingers and the cuttings she had taken from her own plants and lovingly tended in a variety of oddly shaped receptacles picked up during her forays in the street markets had flourished despite the poor light. The resulting rampant greenery suggested that it had been cunningly deployed to conceal some sinister defect in the structure or décor. Cordelia still used Bernie's old oak desk, could still imagine that she could trace the outline of the bowl in which he had bled away his life, could still identify one particular stain of spilt blood and water. But then there were so many rings, so many stains. His hat, with its upturned brim and grubby ribbon, still hung on the curved wooden coat-stand. No jumble sale would take it and she found herself unable to throw it away. Twice she had taken it as far as the dustbin in the back yard but had been unable to drop it in, finding this final symbolic rejection of Bernie even more personal and traumatic than the exclusion of his name from the name-plaque. If the Agency did finally fail – and she tried not to think what the new rent would be when the lease came up for renewal in three years' time – she supposed that she would still leave the hat hanging there in its pathetic decrepitude for unknown hands to toss with fastidious distaste into the waste-paper basket.

The tea arrived. Sir George waited until Miss Maudsley left. Then, measuring milk carefully into his cup, drop by drop, he said:

'The job I'm offering is a mixture of functions. You'd be part bodyguard, part private secretary, part investigator and part – well, nursemaid. A bit of everything. Not everyone's cup of tea. No knowing how it may turn out.'

'I'm supposed to be a private investigator.'

'No doubt. Shouldn't be too purist in these times. A job's a job. And you could find yourself involved in detection, even in violence, although it doesn't seem likely. Unpleasant but not dangerous. If I thought there was any real risk to my wife or to you I wouldn't be employing an amateur.'

Cordelia said:

'Perhaps you could explain what, exactly, you want me to do.'

He frowned into his tea as if reluctant to begin. But when he did his account was lucid, concise and unhesitating.

'My wife is the actress Clarissa Lisle. You may have heard of her. Most people seem to know of her although she hasn't worked much recently. I am her third husband and we married in June 1978. In July 1980 she was employed to play Lady Macbeth at the Duke of Clarence Theatre. On the third night of the advertised six-month run she received what she saw as a death threat. These threats have continued intermittently ever since.'

He began sipping his tea. Cordelia found herself gazing at him with the anxiety of a child hoping that her offering is acceptable. The pause seemed very long. She asked:

'You said that she *saw* the first note as threatening. Are you implying that its meaning was ambiguous? What form exactly do these threats take?'

'Typewritten notes. Variety of machines by the look of it. Each communication surmounted by a small drawing of a coffin or a skull. All are quotations from plays in which my wife has appeared. All the quotations deal with death or dying: the fear of death, the judgement of death, the inevitability of death.'

The reiteration of that numinous word was oppressive. But surely it was in her imagination that he twisted it on his lips with mordant satisfaction? She said:

'But they don't specifically threaten her?'

'She sees this harping on death as threatening. She's sensitive. Actresses have to be I suppose. They need to be liked. This isn't friendly. I have the notes here, the ones she kept. The first ones were thrown away. You'll need the evidence.'

He unclicked the briefcase and took out a stout manilla envelope. From it he spilled a heap of small sheets of paper and began spreading them over the desk. She recognized the type of paper at once; it was a popular, medium-quality, white writing-paper sold in three sizes with envelopes to match over thousands of stationery counters. The sender had been economical and had selected the smallest size. Each sheet bore a typed quotation surmounted by a small drawing about one inch high of either an up-ended coffin with the initials RIP on the lid or a skull with two crossbones. Neither had required much skill; they were emblems rather than accurate representations. On the other hand, they were drawn with a certain sureness of line and decorative sense which suggested some facility with the pen or, in this case, with a black-tipped ball-point. Under Sir George's bony fingers the white slips of paper with their stark black emblems shifted and rearranged themselves like the cards for some sinister game – hunt the quotation, murderer's snap.

Most of the quotations were familiar, words which would readily come to the mind of anyone reasonably well read in Shakespeare and the Jacobeans who chose to ponder on references in English drama to death and the terror of dying. Even reading them now, truncated and childishly embellished as they were, Cordelia felt their potent and nostalgic power. The majority of them were from Shakespeare and the obvious choices were there. The longest by far – and how could the sender have resisted it? – was Claudio's anguished cry from *Measure for Measure:*

Ay, but to die, and go we know not where
To lie in cold obstruction and to rot;
This sensible warm motion to become
A kneaded clod; and the delighted spirit
To bathe in fiery floods; or to reside
In thrilling region of thick-ribbed ice;
To be imprisoned in the viewless winds,
And blown with restless violence round about
The pendant world! . . .
The weariest and most loathed worldly life
That age, ache, penury and imprisonment
Can lay on nature, is a paradise
To what we fear of death.

It was difficult to interpret that familiar passage as a personal threat; but most of the other quotations could be seen as more directly intimidating, hinting, she thought, at some retribution for real or imagined wrongs.

He that dies pays all debts.

Oh, thou weed!
Who art so lovely fair and smell'st so sweet
That the sense aches at thee, would thou hadst ne'er been born!

Some care had been taken in the choice of illustration. The skull adorned the lines from *Hamlet*,

Now get you to my lady's chamber, and tell her, let her paint an inch thick, to this favour she must come.

as it did a passage which Cordelia thought might be from John Webster, although she couldn't identify the play.

Being heretofore drown'd in security,
You know not how to live, nor how to die;
But I have an object that shall startle you,
And make you know whither you are going.

But, even allowing for the sensitivity of an actress, it would take a fairly robust egotism to wrench these familiar words from their contexts and apply them to oneself; that, or a fear of dying so strong as to be morbid. She took a new notebook from her desk drawer and asked:

'How do they arrive?'

'Most come by post in the same type of envelope as the paper and with the address typed. My wife didn't think to keep any of the envelopes. A few were delivered by hand either at the theatre or at our London flat. One was pushed under the dressing-room door during the run of *Macbeth*. The first half-dozen or so were destroyed – best thing to do with them all in my view. These twenty-three are all we now have. I've numbered them in pencil on the back in the order of receipt as far as my wife can remember and with information about when and how each was delivered.'

'Thank you. That should be helpful. Your wife has played a great deal of Shakespeare?'

'She was a member of the Malvern Repertory Company for three years after she left drama school and played a fair amount then. Less in recent years.'

'And the first of these – which she threw away – came when she was playing Lady Macbeth. What happened?'

'The first one was upsetting, but she told no one about it. Thought it was an isolated bit of malice. She says she can't remember what it said, only that it had the drawing of a coffin. Then a second came and a third and fourth. During the third week of the season my wife kept breaking down and had to be continually prompted. On the Saturday she ran off the stage during the Second Act and her understudy had to take over. It's all a matter of confidence. If you think you're going to dry up – drying is the theatrical jargon I believe – then you dry. She was able to return to the part after a week but it was a struggle to get through the six weeks. After that she was due to appear at Brighton in a revival of one of those thirties murder mysteries, the sort where the *ingénue* is called Bunty, the hero is Clive and all the men wear long tennis flannels and keep dashing in and out of french windows. Curious affair. Not exactly her kind of part, she's a classical actress, but there aren't a lot of opportunities for middle-aged women. Too many good actresses chasing too few parts, so they tell me. Same thing happened. The first quotation appeared on the morning the play opened and they came at regular intervals thereafter. The play came off after four weeks and my wife's performance may have had something to do with it. She thought so. I'm not so sure. It was a stupid plot, couldn't make sense of it myself. Clarissa didn't act again until she accepted a part in Webster's *The White Devil*, at Nottingham, Victoria something or other.'

'Vittoria Corombona.'

'Was that it? I was in New York for ten days and didn't see it. But the same thing happened. The first note arrived again on the day the play opened. This time my wife went to the police. Not much joy. They took the notes away, thought about them and brought them back. Sympathetic but not very effective. Made it obvious that they didn't take the death threat seriously. Pointed out that if people are serious about killing, they do it, they don't just threaten. Must say, that was rather my view. They did discover one thing, though. The note which arrived while I was in New York was typed on my old Remington.'

Cordelia said:

'You still haven't explained how you think I can help.'

'Coming to that. This weekend my wife is to play the leading role in an amateur production of *The Duchess of Malfi*. The play is to be given in Victorian dress and will take place on Courcy Island about two miles off the Dorset coast. The owner of the island, Ambrose Gorringe, has restored the small Victorian theatre which was first built by his great grandfather. I understand that the original Gorringe, who rebuilt the ruined medieval castle, used to entertain the Prince of Wales and his mistress, the actress Lillie Langtry, and the guests used to amuse themselves with amateur theatricals. I suppose the present owner is trying to restore past glories. There was an article in one of the Sunday papers about a year ago describing the island, the restoration of the castle and theatre. You may have seen it.'

Cordelia couldn't recall it. She said:

'And you want me to go to the island and be with Lady Ralston?'

'I hoped to be there myself but that won't be possible. I have a meeting in the West Country which I can't miss. I propose to motor down to Speymouth with my wife early Friday morning and take leave of her at the launch. But she needs someone with her. This performance is important to her. There's to be a revival of the play at Chichester in the spring and if she can regain her confidence she might feel that she can do it. But there's more to it than that. She thinks that the threats may come to a head this weekend, that someone will try to kill her on Courcy Island.'

'She must have some reason for thinking that.'

'Nothing that she can explain. Nothing that would impress the police. Not rational, perhaps. But that's what she feels. She asked me to get you.'

And he had come to get her. Did he always procure for his wife whatever she wanted? She asked again:

'What precisely am I being employed to do, Sir George?'

'Protect her from nuisance. Take any telephone calls which come for her. Open any letters. Check the set before the performance if you get the chance. Be on call at night; that's when she's most nervous. And bring a fresh mind to the question of the messages. Find out, if you can in just three days, who is responsible.'

Before Cordelia could respond to these concise instructions there came again that disconcerting pierce of grey from under the discordant brows

'D'you like birds?'

Cordelia was temporarily nonplussed. She supposed that few people, except those afflicted with a phobia, would admit to not liking birds. They are, after all, one of the most graceful of life's fragile diversions. But she supposed that Sir George was covertly inquiring whether she could recognize a marsh-harrier at fifty yards. She said cautiously:

'I'm not very good at identifying the less common species.'

'Pity. The island's one of the most interesting natural bird sanctuaries in Great Britain, probably the most remarkable of those in private hands, almost as interesting as Brownsea Island in Poole Harbour. Very similar, come to think of it. Courcy has as many rare birds; the blue-eared and Swinhold pheasants as well as Canada geese, black godwits and oyster catchers. Pity you're not interested. Any questions – about the case I mean?'

Cordelia said tentatively:

'If I'm to spend three days with your wife, ought she not to interview me before any decision is made? It's important that she feels she can trust me. She doesn't know me. We haven't even met.'

'Yes you have. That's how she knows she can trust you. She was having tea with a Mrs Fortescue last week when you returned the Fortescue cat – Solomon I think the brute's called. Apparently you found him within thirty minutes of beginning the search so your bill was correspondingly small. Mrs Fortescue is devoted to the animal. You could have charged treble. She wouldn't have queried it. That impressed my wife.'

Cordelia said:

'We're rather expensive. We have to be. But we are honest.'

She remembered the drawing-room in Eaton Square, a feminine room if femininity implies softness and luxury; a cluttered, cosy repository of silver-framed photographs, an over-lavish tea on a low table in front of the Adam fireplace, too many flowers conventionally arranged. Mrs Fortescue, incoherent with relief and joy, had introduced her guest to Cordelia as a matter of form but her voice, muffled in Solomon's fur, had been indistinct and Cordelia hadn't caught the name. But the impression had been definite. The visitor had sat very still in her armchair beside the fireplace, one thin leg thrown over the other, heavily ringed hands resting on the arms. Cordelia recalled yellow hair intricately piled and wound above a tall forehead, a small, bee-stung mouth, and immense eyes, deep-set but with heavy, almost swollen, lids. She had seemed to impose on the lush conformity of the room a hieratic and angular grace, a distinction which, despite the plainness of the formal suede suit, hinted at some histrionic or eccentric individuality. She had gravely bent her head and watched her friend's effusions with a half-mocking smile. Despite her stillness there had been no impression of peace. Cordelia said:

'I didn't recognize your wife but I remember her very well.'

'And you'll take the job?'

'Yes, I'll take it.'

He said without embarrassment:

'Rather different from finding lost cats. Mrs Fortescue told my wife what you charge per day. This will be higher, I suppose.'

Cordelia said:

'The daily rate is the same whatever the job. The final bill depends on the time taken, whether I have to use either of my staff, and the level of expenses. These can sometimes be high. But as I'll be a guest on the island, there will be no hotel bills. When do you want me to arrive?'

'The launch from Courcy – it's called *Shearwater* – will be at Speymouth jetty to meet the nine thirty-three from Waterloo. Your ticket's in this envelope. My wife has telephoned to let Mr Gorringe know that she's bringing a secretary-companion to help her with various odd jobs during the weekend. You'll be expected.'

So Clarissa Lisle had been confident that she would take the job. And why not? She had taken it. And she was apparently equally confident of being able to get her way with Ambrose Gorringe. Her excuse for including a secretary in the party was surely rather thin and Cordelia wondered how far it had been believed. To arrive for a country-house weekend accompanied by one's private detective was permissible for royalty, but in any less elevated guest showed a lack of confidence in one's host, while to bring one incognito might reasonably be regarded as a breach of etiquette. It wasn't going to be easy to protect Miss Lisle without betraying that she was there under false pretences, a discovery which would hardly be agreeable for either her host or fellow guests. She said:

'I need to know who else will be on the island and anything you can tell me about them.'

'There's not much I can tell. There'll be about one hundred people on the island by Saturday afternoon when the cast and invited audience arrive. But the house party is small. My wife, of course, with Tolly – Miss Tolgarth – her dresser. Then my wife's stepson, Simon Lessing, will be there. He's a seventeen-year-old schoolboy, the son of Clarissa's second husband who was drowned in August 1977. He wasn't happy with the relatives who were his guardians so my wife decided to take him on. I'm not sure why he's invited, music's his interest. Clarissa probably thought it was time he met more people. He's a shy boy. Then there's her cousin, Roma Lisle. Used to be a schoolmistress but now keeps a bookshop somewhere in north London. Unmarried; aged about forty-five. I've only met her twice. I think she may be bringing her partner with her but, if so, I can't tell you who he is. And you'll meet the drama critic Ivo Whittingham. He's an old friend of my wife. He's supposed to be doing a piece about the theatre and the performance for one of the colour magazines. Ambrose Gorringe will be there, of course. And there are three servants: the butler, Munter, and his wife and Oldfield, who is the boatman and general factotum. I think that's all.'

'Tell me about Mr Gorringe.'

'Gorringe has known my wife since childhood. Both their fathers were in the diplomatic. He inherited the island from his uncle in 1977, when he was spending a year abroad. Something to do with tax avoidance. He came back to the UK in 1978 and has spent the last three years restoring the castle and looking after the island. Middle-aged. Unmarried. Read history at Cambridge I believe. Authority on the Victorians. I know no harm of him.'

Cordelia said:

'There's one last question I have to ask. Your wife apparently fears for her life, so much so that she is reluctant to be on Courcy Island without protection. Is there any one of that company whom she has reason to fear, reason to suspect?'

She could see at once that the question was unwelcome, perhaps because it forced him to acknowledge what he had implied but never stated, that his wife's fear for her life was hysterical and unreal. She had demanded protection and he was providing it. But he didn't think it was necessary; he believed neither in the danger nor in the means he was employing to reassure her. And now some part of his mind was repelled by the thought that his wife's host and her fellow guests were to be under secret surveillance. He had done what his wife had asked of him, but he didn't like himself any the better for it. He said curtly:

'I think you can put that idea out of your head. My wife has no reason to suspect any of the house party of wishing to harm her, no reason in the world.'

CHAPTER TWO

Nothing more of importance was said. Sir George looked at his watch and got to his feet. Two minutes later he said a curt goodbye at the street door, neither mentioning nor glancing at the offending name-plate. As she climbed the stairs, Cordelia wondered whether she could have managed the interview better. It was a pity that it had ended so abruptly. There were questions which she wished she had thought to ask, in particular whether any of the people she was to meet on Courcy Island knew of the threatening messages. She would have to wait now until she met Miss Lisle.

As she opened the office door, Miss Maudsley and Bevis looked up over their typewriters with avid eyes. It would have been heartless to deny them a share in the news. They had sensed that Sir George was no ordinary client and curiosity and excitement had virtually paralysed them. There had been a suspicious absence of clacking typewriters from the outer office during his visit. Now Cordelia told them as little as was compatible with telling them anything worth hearing, emphasizing that Miss Lisle was looking for a companion-secretary who would protect her from an irritating but unimportant poison-pen nuisance. She said nothing about the nature of the threatening messages nor of the actress's conviction that her life was seriously threatened. She warned them that this assignment, like all jobs, even the most trivial, was to be treated as confidential. Miss Maudsley said:

'Of course, Miss Gray. Bevis understands that perfectly well.'

Bevis was passionate in his assurances.

'I'm more reliable than I look. I won't utter, honestly. I never do, not about the Agency. But I'll be no good if anyone tortures me for information. I can't stand pain.'

Cordelia said:

'No one's going to torture you, Bevis.'

By general consent they took an early lunch-hour. Bevis fetched sandwiches from the Carnaby Street delicatessen and Miss Maudsley made coffee. Sitting cosily in the outer office they gave themselves over to happy speculation about where this interesting new assignment might lead. And the hour wasn't wasted. Unexpectedly, both Miss Maudsley and Bevis had helpful information to give about Courcy Island and its owner, pouring out a spate of antiphonal chat. It wasn't the first time this had happened. Their more orthodox skills might be suspect, but they not infrequently provided a bonus in the way of useful gossip.

'You'll enjoy the castle, Miss Gray, if you're interested in Victorian architecture. My brother took the Mothers' Union to the island for their summer outing the month before he died. Of course, I'm not a full member, I couldn't be. But I usually went on the outings, and this one was so interesting. I particularly enjoyed the pictures and the porcelain. And there's one delightful bedroom which is almost a museum to the Victorian arts and crafts movement; De Morgan tiles, Ruskin drawings, Mackmurdo furniture. It was quite an expensive outing, I remember. Mr Gorringe, he's the owner, only allows parties once a week during the season and he restricts the numbers to twelve at a time, so I suppose he has to charge rather a lot to make it worth while. But no one grumbled, not even Mrs Baggot who was always, I'm afraid, rather inclined to complain at the end of the day. And the island itself, so beautiful and varied, and such peace. Low cliffs, woods, fields and marshes. It's like England in miniature.'

'Darlings, I was actually in the theatre when she dried, Clarissa Lisle, I mean. It was ghastly. It wasn't just that she forgot the lines, though I don't see how anyone can forget Lady Macbeth, the part practically speaks itself. She dried completely. We could hear the prompter positively shrieking at her from where Peter – he was my friend – and I were sitting. And then she gave a kind of gasp and ran offstage.' Bevis's outraged voice recalled Miss Maudsley from her happy recollection of Orpen portraits and William Morris tapestries.

'Poor woman! How terrible for her, Bevis.'

'Terrible for the rest of the cast. For us, too. Altogether shame-making. After all, she is a professional actress with something of a reputation. You don't expect her to behave like a hysterical schoolgirl who's lost her nerve at her first amateur performance. I was amazed when Metzler offered her Vittoria after that *Macbeth*. She started all right and the notices weren't that bad, but they say that things got pretty dodgy before it folded.'

Bevis spoke as one who had been privy to all the negotiations. Cordelia had often wondered at the assurance which he assumed whenever they spoke of the theatre, that exotic world of fantasy and desire, his promised land, his native air. He said:

'I'd love to see the Victorian theatre on Courcy Island. It's very small – only a hundred seats – but they say it's perfect. The original owner built it for Lillie Langtry when she was mistress to the Prince of Wales. He used to visit the island and the house party would amuse themselves with amateur theatricals.'

'How do you get to know these things, Bevis?'

'There was an article about the castle in one of the Sundays soon after Mr Gorringe had completed the restoration. My friend showed it to me. He knows I'm interested. The auditorium looked charming. It even has a royal box decorated with the Prince of Wales feathers. I wish I could see it. I'm madly envious.'

Cordelia said:

'Sir George told me about the theatre. The present owner must be rich. It can't have been cheap, restoring the theatre and the castle and collecting the Victoriana.'

Surprisingly, it was Miss Maudsley who replied:

'Oh, but he is! He made a fortune out of that bestseller he wrote. *Autopsy*. He's A. K. Ambrose. Didn't you know?' Cordelia hadn't known. She had bought the paperback, as had thousands of others, because she had got tired of seeing its dramatic cover confronting her in every bookshop and supermarket and had felt curious to know what it was about a first novel that could earn a reputed half a million before publication. It was fashionably long and equally fashionably violent and she remembered that she had indeed, as the blurb promised, found it difficult to put down, without now being able to remember clearly either the plot or the characters. The idea had been neat enough. The novel dealt with an autopsy on a murder victim and had told at length the stories of all the people involved, forensic pathologist, police officer, mortuary attendant, family of the victim, victim and, finally, the murderer. You could, she supposed, call it a crime novel with a difference, the difference being that there had been more sex, normal and abnormal, than detection and that the book had attempted with some success to combine the popular family saga with the mystery. The writing style had been nicely judged for the mass market, neither good enough to jeopardize popular appeal nor bad enough to make people ashamed of being seen reading it in public. At the end she had been left dissatisfied, but whether that was because she had felt manipulated or because of a conviction that the pseudonymous A.K. Ambrose could have written a better book had he chosen, it was hard to say. But the sexual interludes, cunningly spaced, all written with undertones of irony and self-disgust, and the detailed description of the dissection of a female body certainly had a salacious power. Here at least the writer had been himself.

Miss Maudsley was anxious to disclaim any implied criticism in her question.

'It's not surprising that you didn't know. I wouldn't have known myself, only one of the members on the summer outing had a husband who keeps a bookshop and she told us. Mr Ambrose doesn't really like it to be known. It's the only book he's written I believe.'

Cordelia began to feel a lively curiosity to see the egregiously talented Ambrose Gorringe and his off-shore island. She sat musing on the oddities of this new assignment while Bevis collected the coffee cups, it being his turn to wash up. Miss Maudsley had fallen into a pensive silence, hands folded in her lap. Suddenly she looked up and said:

'I do hope you won't be in any danger, Miss Gray. There's something wicked, one might say evil, about poison-pen letters. We had a spate of them once in the parish and it ended very tragically. They're so frighteningly malevolent.'

Cordelia said:

'Malevolent, but not dangerous. I'm more likely to be bored by the case than frightened. And I can't imagine anything very terrible happening on Courcy Island.'

Bevis, precariously balancing the three mugs, turned around at the door.

'But terrible things have happened there! I don't know what exactly. The article I read didn't say. But the present castle is built on the site of an old medieval castle which used to guard that part of the Channel, so it's probably inherited a ghost or two. And the writer did mention the island's violent and bloodstained history.'

Cordelia said:

'That's just a journalistic platitude. All the past is bloodstained. That doesn't mean that its ghosts still walk.'

She spoke entirely without premonition, glad of the chance of a real job at last, happy at the thought of getting out of London while the warm autumnal weather still lasted, seeing already in her mind the soaring turrets, the gull-loud marshes, the gentle uplands and woods of this miniature England, so mysterious and beautiful, lying waiting for her in the sun.

CHAPTER THREE

Ambrose Gorringe now visited London so rarely that he was beginning to wonder whether the subscription to his town club was really justified. There were parts of the capital in which he still felt at home, but too many others in which he had previously walked with pleasure now seemed to him grubby, despoiled and alien. When business with his stockbroker, agent or publisher made a visit desirable, he would plan a programme of what he described to himself as treats, an adult re-enactment of school holidays, leaving no portion of a day so unprovided for that he had time to ponder on his stupidity in being where he was. A visit to Saul Gaskin's small antique shop near Notting Hill Gate was invariably in his programme. He bought most of his Victorian pictures and furniture at the London auction houses, but Gaskin knew and partially shared his passion for Victoriana and he could be confident that there would be, awaiting his inspection, a small collection of the trivia which was often so much more redolent of the spirit of the age than his more important acquisitions.

In the unseasonable September heat the cluttered and ill-ventilated office at the back of the shop smelt like a lair in which Gaskin, with his white, pinched face, precise little hands and grubby moleskin waistcoat scurried around like a tenacious rodent. Now he unlocked his desk drawer and reverently laid before this favoured customer the scavengings of the last four months. The Bristol blue decanter engraved with a design of grapes and vineleaves was attractive, but there were only five glasses and he liked his sets complete, while one of a pair of Wedgwood vases designed by Walter Crane was slightly chipped. He was surprised that Gaskin, knowing that he demanded perfection, had bothered to keep them for him. But the ornately trimmed menu for the banquet given by the Queen at Windsor Castle on 10th October 1844 to celebrate the appointment of King Louis Philippe of France as a Knight of the Garter was a happy find. He played with the idea that it would be amusing to serve the same meal at Courcy Castle on the anniversary, but reminded himself that there were limits both to Mrs Munter's culinary skills and to the capacity of his guests.

But Gaskin had saved the best until last. He now brought out, with his customary grave air of serving some secular Mass to a devotee, two heavy mourning brooches, beautifully wrought in black enamel and gold, each with a lock of hair intricately twisted into whorls and petals; a widow's black peaked bonnet, still in the hatbox in which it was delivered, and a marble carving of a baby's plump truncated arm reposing on a purple velvet cushion. Gorringe took the cap in his hands stroking the goffered satin, the streamers of ostentatious woe. He wondered what had happened to its owner. Had she followed her husband to an untimely grave, desolated by grief? Or had the bonnet, an expensive contraption, merely failed to please? Both it and the brooches would be an addition to the bedroom in Courcy Castle which he called Memento Mori and where he kept his collection of Victorian necrophilia; the death masks of Carlyle, Ruskin and Matthew Arnold, the black-edged memorial cards with their weeping angels and sentimental verses, the commemorative cups, medals and mugs, the wardrobe of heavy mourning garments, black, grey and mauve. It was a room Clarissa had only once entered with a shudder and now pretended didn't exist. But he had noted with pleasure that those of his guests who were lovers, acknowledged or furtive, liked occasionally to sleep there rather, he thought, as eighteenth-century whores had copulated with their clients on the flat tops of tombs in London's East End graveyards. He watched with a sardonic and slightly contemptuous eye this symbiosis of eroticism and morbidity, as he did all those human foibles which he happened not to share.

He said:

'I'll take these. And probably the marble too. Where did you find it?'

'A private sale. I don't think it's a memorial piece. The owner claimed that it was a duplicate of one of the marble limbs of the royal children at Osborne carved for Queen Victoria. This one is probably the arm of the infant Princess Royal.'

'Poor Vicky! What with her formidable mother, her son and Bismarck, not the happiest of princesses. It's almost irresistible, but not at that price.'

'The cushion is the original. And if it is the arm of the Princess, it's probably unique. There's no record as far as I know of any duplicates of the Osborne pieces.'

They entered into their usual amicable pattern of bargaining, but Gorringe sensed that Gaskin's heart wasn't in it. He was a superstitious man and it was apparent to Gorringe that the marble, which he seemed unable to bring himself to touch, both fascinated and repelled him. He wanted it out of his shop.

Hardly had the business concluded than there was a ring on the locked street door. As Gaskin left to answer it, Gorringe asked if he might use the telephone. It had occurred to him that with some slight hurry he could catch an earlier train. As usual, it was Munter who answered the ring.

'Courcy Castle.'

'Gorringe, Munter. I'm ringing from London. I find that I shall, after all, be able to catch the two thirty train. I should be at the quay by four forty.'

'Very good, sir. I will instruct Oldfield.'

'Is all well, Munter?'

'Quite well, sir. Tuesday's dress rehearsal was hardly a success but I understand that this is considered propitious for the actual performance.'

'The lighting rehearsal was satisfactory?'

'Yes, sir. If I may say so, the company is more fortunate in the talent of its amateur electricians than in its actors.'

'And Mrs Munter? Have you been able to get all the help she needs for Saturday?'

'Not quite all. Two of the girls from the town have defaulted but Mrs Chambers is bringing her granddaughter. I have interviewed the girl and she seems well intentioned if untrained. If the Courcy play is to be an annual event, sir, we may have to reconsider our staffing needs, at least for this one week of the year.'

Gorringe said calmly:

'I don't think that either you or Mrs Munter need assume that the play will be an annual event. If you feel the need to plan for twelve months ahead, it would be safer to assume that this is the last performance which Lady Ralston will give on Courcy.'

'Thank you, sir. I should tell you that Lady Ralston telephoned. Sir George has an unexpected meeting to attend and is unlikely to arrive before Saturday afternoon and, possibly, not until after the performance. Lady Ralston proposes to solace marital deprivation by inviting a secretary-companion, a Miss Cordelia Gray. She will arrive with the rest of the party on Friday morning. Lady Ralston appeared to think that she need not speak to you personally about this arrangement.'

Munter's disapproval came over the line as clearly as his carefully controlled irony. He was adept at judging just how far he could safely go, and since his veiled insolence was never directed against his employer, Gorringe was indulgent. A man, particularly a servant, was entitled to his small recalcitrant bolsterings of self-respect. Gorringe had noted early in their relationship how Munter's persona, modelled as it was on Jeeves and his near namesake Bunter, became markedly closer to parody when any of his carefully contrived domestic arrangements was upset. During Clarissa's visits to the castle he became almost intolerably Bunterish. Relishing his manservant's eccentricities, the contrast between his bizarre appearance and his manner, totally uncurious about his past, Gorringe now hardly bothered to wonder whether a real Munter existed and, if so, what manner of man he might be.

He heard him say:

'I thought that Miss Gray could be companionable in the De Morgan room, subject to your agreement.'

'That would seem suitable. And if Sir George does arrive for Saturday night he can have Memento Mori. A soldier should be inured to death. Do we know anything about Miss Gray?'

'A young lady, I understand. I take it that she will eat in the dining-room.'

'Of course.'

Whatever Clarissa thought she was up to, it would at least even the numbers at his dinner-table. But the thought of Clarissa with a secretary-companion, and a woman at that, was intriguing. He hoped that her addition to the party wouldn't make the weekend more complicated than it already promised to be.

'Goodbye, Munter.'

'Goodbye, sir.'

When Gaskin returned to the office he found his customer sitting contemplatively holding the marble arm. He gave an involuntary shiver. Gorringe replaced the marble on its cushion and watched while Gaskin busied himself finding a small cardboard box and lining it with tissue paper.

He said:

'You don't like it?'

Gaskin could afford to be frank. The limb was sold and Mr Gorringe had never yet rejected a piece once the price was agreed. He lowered the arm into its box taking care to touch only the cushion.

'I can't say I'm sorry to see it go. I usually do very well with those porcelain models of the human hand which the Victorians were so fond of, ring stands and so on. I had a nice one in last week but the wrist frill was chipped. It wouldn't have interested you. But a child's arm! And cut off like that! I call it brutal, almost morbid. It's just a feeling I have about the piece. You know how I am. It reminds me of death.'

Gorringe took a final look at the brooches before they were wrapped and boxed.

'Less rationally, surely, than should the jewellery and the widow's cap. I agree with you; I doubt whether this is a memorial marble.'

Gaskin said firmly:

'They're different. They don't worry me, memorials never have. But this is different. To tell you the truth, I took against it as soon as it came into the shop. Whenever I look at it, I keep imagining that it's oozing blood.'

Gorringe smiled.

'I must try it on my house guests and watch their reactions. The Courcy play next weekend is *The Duchess of Malfi*. If this were a full-sized male hand we could use it for one of the props. But even the Duchess in her extremity could hardly mistake this for the dead hand of Antonio.'

The allusion was lost on Gaskin who had never read Webster. He murmured:

'No indeed, sir,' and smiled his sly, sycophantic smile.

Five minutes later, he saw his customer and his parcels formally off the premises, congratulating himself with premature satisfaction – for despite his carefully nurtured sensitivity he had never claimed to be a clairvoyant – that he had seen and heard the last of the arm of the dead Princess.

CHAPTER FOUR

Less than two miles away, in a Harley Street consulting-room, Ivo Whittingham slipped his legs over the edge of the examination couch and watched Dr Crantley-Mathers shuffle back to his desk. The doctor, as always, was wearing his old but well-tailored pinstripe suit. Nothing so clinical as a white coat ever intruded into his consulting room, and the room itself with its patterned Axminster carpet, its Edwardian carved desk holding the silver-framed photographs of Sir James's grandchildren and distinguished patients, its sporting prints and the portrait of some solidly prosperous ancestor holding pride of place above the carved marble mantelshelf, looked more like a private study than a consulting room. No apparent effort was made to keep infection at bay; but then, thought Whittingham, germs would know better than to lurk in the well-upholstered armchair in which Sir James's patients awaited his advice. Even the examination couch looked unclinical, being covered with brown leather and mounted by way of elegant eighteenth-century library steps. The assumption was that, although a number of Sir James's guests might wish for some private whim to take off their clothes, that eccentricity could have nothing to do with the state of their health.

Now he looked up from his prescription pad and asked:

'That spleen troubling you?'

'As it must weigh twenty pounds and I look and feel like a lopsided pregnant woman, yes, you could say that it's troubling me.'

'The time may come when it's better out. No hurry, though. We'll have another think in a month's time.'

Whittingham went behind the painted oriental screen where his clothes were folded over a chair and began to dress, drawing his trousers up over the heavy belly. It was, he thought, like carrying one's own death, feeling it drag at the muscles, a foetus-like incubus which never stirred, reminding him with its dead weight, by the deformity which he saw in his mirror every time he bathed, what it was he bore within him. Looking over the screen, he said, his voice muffled by his shirt:

'I thought you explained that the spleen is enlarged because it's taken over the manufacture of the red blood corpuscles which my blood's no longer producing.'

Sir James didn't look up. He said with careful unconcern, 'That's more or less what's happening, yes. When one organ ceases to function, another tends to take over.'

'So would it be tactless to inquire which organ will obligingly take over the job when you've whipped out the spleen?'

Sir James guffawed at this witticism. 'Let's cross that bridge when we come to it, shall we?' He had never, thought Whittingham, been a man for originality of speech.

For the first time since his illness began Whittingham would have liked to ask his doctor directly how much time remained for him. It wasn't that there were affairs that he needed to put in order. Divorced from his wife, alienated from his children, and living now alone, his affairs, like his obsessively tidy flat, had been depressingly in order for the last five years. The need to know was now little more than a mild curiosity. He would be glad to learn that he was to be spared another Christmas, his most disliked time of the year. But he realized that the question would be in the worst of taste. The room itself had been designed to make it unsayable; Sir James was adept at training his patients not to ask questions which they knew it would distress him to have to answer. His philosophy – and Whittingham wasn't altogether in disagreement with it – was that patients would realize in their own good time that they were dying and that, by then, physical weakness would ensure that the realization would be less painful than a sentence of death pronounced when the blood still ran strongly. He had never believed that the loss of hope did anyone any good, and besides, doctors could be wrong. This last assertion was a conventional gesture to modesty. Sir James did not privately believe that he personally could be wrong, and indeed he was a superb diagnostician. It was hardly his fault, thought Whittingham, that the ability of the medical profession to diagnose is so far in advance of its ability to cure. Slipping his arms through his jacket sleeves he spoke aloud Brachiano's words from *The White Devil*:

'On pain of death, let no man name death to me:
It is a word infinitely terrible.'

It was a view Sir James obviously shared. It was surprising, supposing him to know them, that he hadn't carved the words over his door lintel.

'I'm sorry, Mr Whittingham. I didn't quite catch what you said.'

'Nothing, Sir James. I was merely quoting Webster.'

Escorting his patient to the consulting-room door at which an exceedingly pretty nurse was waiting to see him finally on his way, the doctor asked:

'Are you going out of London this weekend? It's a pity to waste this weather.'

'To Dorset, actually. To Courcy Island, off Speymouth. An amateur company with some professional support is putting on *The Duchess of Malfi* and I'm doing a piece for one of the colour supplements.' He added, 'It's chiefly about the restoration of the Victorian theatre on the island and its history.' Immediately he despised himself for the explanation. What was it but a way of saying that dying he might be but he wasn't yet reduced to reviewing amateurs?

'Good. Good.' Sir James boomed out a note of approval which might have sounded excessive even for God on the seventh day.

When the imposing front door had closed behind him Whittingham was tempted to hire the taxi which had just drawn up, presumably to deposit another patient. But he decided he might manage a mile of the walk to his Russell Square flat. And there was a new coffee house in Marylebone High Street where the young couple who owned it ground the beans freshly and made their own cakes, and where a few chairs under umbrellas gave the locals the illusion that the English summer was suitable for eating out. He might rest there for ten minutes. It was extraordinary how important these trivial self-indulgences had become. As he resigned himself to the accidie of mortal illness he was beginning to acquire some of the foibles of old age, a liking for small treats, a fussiness about routine, a reluctance to bother with even his oldest acquaintances, an indolence which made even dressing and bathing a burden, a preoccupation with his bodily functions. He despised the half-man he had become, but even this self-disgust had some of the querulous resentment of senility. But Sir James was right. It was difficult to feel regret about losing a life so diminished. By the time this sickness had finished with him, death would be no more than the final disintegration of a body from which the spirit had already seeped away, worn out by pain, by weariness and by a malaise which went deeper than physical weakness, some brittle-armed traitor of the heart who had never mustered the will to fight.

As he made his way down Wimpole Street through the mellow autumn sunlight he thought of the great performances he had seen and reviewed and mentally spoke the names like a roll call: Olivier's Richard the Third, Wolfit playing Malvolio, Gielgud's Hamlet, Richardson's Falstaff, Peggy Ashcroft's Portia. He could recall them, could remember the theatres, the directors, even some of the most quoted extracts from his reviews. It was interesting that, after thirty years of play-going, it was the classics which had lasted longest for him. But he knew that, even if he were this night to take his accustomed seat in the third row of the stalls, formally dressed as he always was for a first night, listening to that anticipatory hum which is unlike any other sound in the world, nothing that happened when the curtain rose would move or excite him beyond a mild, detached interest. The glory and the wonder had departed. Never again would he feel that tingle between the shoulder blades, that almost physical surge of the blood which, for all his youth, had been his response to great acting. It was ironic that now, all passion spent, he was about to review his last play, and that an amateur production. But somehow he would find the energy for what he had to do on Courcy Island.

The island was reputed to be beautiful and the castle an interesting example of high Victorian panache. Seeing them would probably be worth the effort of the journey, which was as close as he could now get to enthusiasm. But he was less sure about the company. Clarissa had mentioned that her cousin, Roma Lisle, was to be there with a friend. He hadn't met Roma, but had had to listen to Clarissa's caustic disparagement of her for too many years to relish being under the same roof as them both, while the careful omission of the friend's name hadn't been reassuring. And the boy was to be with them, apparently. Clarissa's decision to take on the son of her drowned husband, Martin Lessing, had been one of her more spectacular impulses; he wondered who was regretting it more, benefactress or victim. On the three occasions on which he had met Simon Lessing, two at the theatre and one at a party at Clarissa's Bayswater flat, he had been struck by the boy's *gaucherie* and by a sense of deep personal wretchedness which he thought had less to do with adolescence than with Clarissa. There had been something dog-like in his servility, a desperate need to win her approval without the least idea what it was she wanted of him. Whittingham had seen that same look in his father's eyes; the prick of memory hadn't been comfortable. Simon was supposed to be a talented pianist. Probably Clarissa had seen herself splendidly cantilevered in one of the front boxes at the Royal Festival Hall while her prodigy, adoring eyes glancing upwards, took his triumphant bow. It must be disconcerting for her to be faced instead with the moodiness and the physical gracelessness of adolescence. He found himself possessed of a slight interest in seeing how the two of them were making out. And there would be other minor satisfactions; not the least would be watching how Clarissa Lisle was coping with her own neurosis. If this were to be his last performance there was some satisfaction in knowing that it might well be hers. She would know that he was dying. She had the use of her eyes. But he wouldn't grudge her any pleasure she could get from observing the process of his physical disintegration. There were subtler pleasures than that; watching mental disintegration might, he suspected, be among them. He was discovering that even hatred died a little at the end. But it still lasted longer than desire, longer even than love.

Walking slowly in the sunshine and thinking of the weekend ahead, he smiled at the realization that what was most alive in him now was the capacity for mischief.

CHAPTER FIVE

In the basement of a small shop in a passageway off the north end of Tottenham Court Road, Roma Lisle was on her knees unpacking and sorting a box of second-hand books. The room, which had originally been a kitchen and which still contained an old porcelain sink, a row of wall-mounted cupboards and a disconnected gas cooker so heavy that the combined efforts of Colin and herself had been unable to shift it, was oppressively hot despite the tiled floor. Outside, the accumulated heat of the dying summer seemed to have concentrated in the area beneath the iron railings, pressing against the one small window like a sweaty, fume-soaked blanket, cutting off air as well as light. Above her the single pendant light threw shadows rather than illumination; it was ridiculous to have to be using expensive electricity on such a day. She must have been mad ever to have thought that this hole could be transformed into an intimate, invitingly cosy second-hand books department, a browser's delight.

The books, she now saw, were a poor lot. She had bid for them and bought them cheaply at a country-house sale. Now the first real inspection revealed that it hadn't been cheap enough. The best had been on the top. The rest were a motley collection of Victorian sermons, reminiscences of retired generals, biographies of minor politicians as undistinguished in death as they had been in life, novels which provoked no interest except a wonder that anyone should have chosen to publish them.

Her knees were numb against the tiles, her nostrils choked with the smell of dust, of mouldering cardboard and rotting paper. In her imagination it was to have been so different; Colin kneeling beside her, the happy rummaging, the exclamations of pleasure as each treasure came to light, the laughter, the planning, the fun. She remembered their last day at Pottergate Comprehensive, the farewell party with its cheap sherry, and inevitable crisps and cheese savouries; the barely concealed envy of their colleagues that she and Colin were getting out, setting up business together, saying goodbye to timetables, mark sheets, examinations, the daily dispiriting struggle to impose order on a class of forty in an inner city comprehensive where teaching had always to be subordinated to the struggle to maintain some semblance of discipline.

And that was only nine months ago! Nine months in which everything they had bought, everything they needed had become more expensive, in which the shop had been as dead as if boarded up and bankrupt. Nine months of overwork and dwindling returns, of fading hope and half-acknowledged panic. Nine months – could it be? – of the slow death of desire. She almost cried out in protest, shoving her strong hands against the box as if the thought and its pain could be physically pushed from her mind. And then she heard his step on the stairs. She turned her face to his, making herself smile. He had hardly spoken over luncheon. But that was three hours ago. Sometimes his moods didn't last. His first words destroyed hope.

'My God, this place stinks.'

'It won't, once we get it cleaned up.'

'And how long will that take? It needs an army of cleaners and decorators. And even then, it'll still look what it is, a basement slum.'

He slumped down on an unopened box of books and began turning over the pile she had unpacked, letting them drop with careful disdain in an untidy heap. In the dim light his handsome, petulant face looked lined with weariness. Why? she wondered. It was she who had been doing the work. She held out her hand and after a moment he took it in a limp grasp.

She thought:

'Oh God, I love you! We love each other. Don't take that away from me.'

He slid his hand from hers almost furtively and began to pretend an interest in one of the books. As he opened it, a small sheet of thick and faded paper fluttered out.

She said:

'What's that?'

'Some kind of old woodcut by the look of it. I shouldn't think it has any value.'

'We could ask Ambrose Gorringe when we get to Courcy Island. He knows about these things even if they aren't his period.'

They peered at it together. It was certainly old, early seventeenth-century she guessed from the antiquated spelling, and it was in remarkably good condition. The paper was headed with a crude woodcut of a skeleton holding in its right hand an arrow and in its left an hourglass. Beneath was the title, 'The Gt Meffenger of Mortality', followed by the verse. She read the first four lines aloud:

Fair lady lay your costly robe afide,
No longer may you glory in your pride,
Take leave of all your carnal vain delight,
I'm come to fummon you away tonight.

The undated subscription gave the printer's name as John Evans of Long Lane, London.

Roma said:

'It reminds me of Clarissa.'

'Of Clarissa? Why?'

'I don't know. I don't know why.'

He pressed her, sounding irritably insistent, as if it mattered, as if she had intended something.

'It's just something I said, something that came into my mind. It didn't mean anything. Put the paper by the sink, on the draining-board. We'll show it to Ambrose Gorringe.' He did so and returned moodily to his box. He said:

'It was a mistake, buying this junk. We should have stuck to the new stock. London seems to have a surfeit of bookshops. And God knows why I let you talk me into buying all that left-wing stuff upstairs. No one wants it. The left wing already have enough cosy haunts in this neighbourhood and it only repels the other buyers. Those pamphlets are just gathering dust. I must have been mad.' She knew that he wasn't referring only to the left-wing literature. The injustice stung her into anger. She knew even as she spoke that it was folly. He needed to be cajoled, humoured, comforted. The quarrels which he seemed increasingly to provoke only left him sulky and resentful and herself exhausted. But she had had enough.

'Look, you didn't take on this place to oblige me. You were just as keen to get out of Pottergate. You loathed teaching. Remember? I was fed up with it, I admit, but I wouldn't have resigned if you hadn't made the first move.'

'You mean, it's all my fault.'

'All! What all? It isn't anyone's fault. We both did what we wanted.'

'Then what are you complaining about?'

'It's just that I'm tired of being made to feel as if I'm some kind of encumbrance, worse than a wife, as if you're only keeping on the shop because of me.'

'I'm keeping it – we're keeping it on – because there's no alternative. Pottergate wouldn't take us back even if we applied.'

And where else could they apply? He didn't need her to tell him about the unemployment in the teaching profession, the expenditure cuts, the desperate search for jobs even by the best qualified. She said, knowing even as she spoke that argument was folly, that it would only fuel his irritation:

'If you do chuck it, it'll please Stella. I suppose that's what she's been waiting for. She can say "I told you so" and hand you over, neatly trussed, a sacrificial victim to dear Daddy and the family business. My God, she must be praying for our bankruptcy! It's a wonder she doesn't lurk outside counting the customers.'

His protest was sulky rather than vehement. It was, after all, an argument they had had before. 'She knows I'm worried, obviously. She's worried herself. She has a right to be. Half of the money I put in here was hers.'

As if that needed saying. As if she didn't know exactly how much cash from Daddy's generous allowance Stella had graciously handed over. And that was generous of her, generous or stupid or cunning. Or all three. Because she must have known that Colin was going into partnership with his mistress, she wasn't that blind. Oh, she'd known all right! She couldn't understand what he saw in Roma – she wasn't unique in that – but she'd known the score. And had this been her revenge, the money to set up a partnership which was bound to fail, given their inexperience, their small capital, their self-delusions; a failure that would draw him back, suitably chastened, to the place where he belonged, the place, come to think of it, that he'd never really left? And then what would there be for him but Daddy's business, the store in Kilburn which sold cheap plywood furniture on hire purchase to customers too ignorant to know when they were being cheated or too proud in their poverty to rummage round the street markets and buy good solid oak, second-hand. The stuff he dazzled them with, cocktail cabinets, room dividers, ornate suites would fall or be kicked to pieces long before they'd finished paying for it. Was that what Colin wanted to do with his life? Had he left teaching for that? And had Stella thought all this out for herself or had Daddy a hand in it? The money she had lent them, hadn't it been carefully calculated, enough to make the enterprise possible but not enough to enable them to succeed? She was sharp enough. She had a shrewd little mind to go with those sharp painted nails, those white, childlike teeth. And she had other weapons, Justin and Joanna. Possessiveness and acquisitiveness had been sanctified by maternity. She had the twins. And, by God, she knew how to use them! With every childhood infection, every school speechday, every dental appointment, every family holiday, every Christmas demanding his presence at home, it was as if she were saying: 'He may sleep with you, play at keeping shop with you, imagine that he's in love with you, confide in you. But he'll never give you children. And he'll never divorce me to marry you.' Appalled at her thoughts, at what was happening to them, she cried:

'Look, darling, don't let's quarrel. We're tired, we're hot and it's a bloody day. On Friday we shut the door on the whole scene and take off for Courcy Island. Three days of peace, sunshine, good wines, first-class food and the sea. The island's only three miles by two-and-a-half, so Clarissa says, but there are marvellous walks. We can get away from the rest of the party. Clarissa will be busy with the play. I don't suppose Ambrose Gorringe will care a damn what we do. No creditors, no people, just peace. And, my God, don't I need it.'

She was going to add, 'And I need you, my darling. More and more. Always.' But then she looked up and saw his face.

It wasn't an unfamiliar look, that mixture of shame, irritation, embarrassment. She had seen it before. This, after all, had been the pattern of their lives, the plans so confidently, so happily made, the last-minute cancellations. But never before had it mattered so desperately. Tears scalded her eyes. She told herself that she had to stay calm, that she mustn't break down, but when she could speak the note of angry recrimination was unmistakable even to her own ears and she saw the look of shame harden into defiance.

'You can't do this to me! You can't! You promised! And I've told Clarissa I'm bringing my partner. It's all arranged.'

'I know and I'm sorry. But Stella's father telephoned at breakfast to say that he's coming for the weekend. I've got to be there. I've told you what he's like. He was pretty fed up about my leaving teaching. We've never got on. He thinks I don't appreciate her enough; you know how it is with an only child. He's not going to be pleased if he finds I'm away for a long weekend leaving her to cope with the kids. And he won't believe the story about attending a book sale. I don't think even Stella does.'

So that was it. Daddy was arriving, Daddy who paid the twins' school fees, provided the car, the annual holiday, the luxuries which had become necessities. Daddy who had his own ideas about his son-in-law's future.

She said in a voice that was almost a wail:

'What is Clarissa going to think?'

'Well, isn't it rather what she'd think if I did come? She knows I'm married. I mean, you must have let that drop. Wouldn't it look rather odd, the two of us arriving together? And it's not as if we could have shared a room or anything like that.'

'By anything like that I suppose you mean that we couldn't have slept together. Why not? Clarissa isn't exactly a model of purity and I don't suppose Ambrose Gorringe creeps down his corridors at night checking that his guests are in their own rooms.'

He muttered:

'It's not that. I explained. It's Stella's father.'

'But this weekend might have freed you from him and her. I thought we could have spoken to Clarissa, told her about the shop, asked if she couldn't help. That's why I wangled the invitation. After all, a third of her money comes to me if she dies without a child. It's all in Uncle's will. It wouldn't harm her to part with some when it's most needed. We'd only be asking for a loan.'

She tried not to see the hope brightening in his face. Then it faded. He said sulkily:

'I couldn't ask a woman for money.'

'You wouldn't have to. I'd do the asking. What I thought was that she'd meet you, like you. She'd be seeing you under the best possible conditions. Then I could speak to her when the time seemed right. It's worth a try, darling. Even twenty thousand would mean all the difference.'

'What would you get if she died?'

'I'm not sure. About eighty thousand I think. It could be more.'

He turned away. 'And that's about what we'd need if I were to leave Stella, get a divorce. But Clarissa isn't going to die just to convenience us. Twenty thousand might just save the shop. But that's about all it would do. And why should she part with it? Anyone with an ounce of financial sense would see that it would be throwing good money after bad. It's no use. I can't come this weekend.'

Above them the floor creaked. Someone had come into the shop. He said quickly, gratefully:

'Sounds like a customer. Look, I'll close promptly at five if there's nothing doing and give you a hand down here. We'll get this room together somehow.'

When he had gone she went over and stared out of the window, standing rigidly, grasping the edges of the sink so tightly that her knuckles were white. Her eyes were unfocused, staring beyond the railings, the crumbling stucco on the basement wall, to where the brightly patterned reds, greens and yellows of the fruit stall on the opposite pavement fused and shivered. From time to time feet passed, voices called, the narrow street broke momentarily into life. And still that silent figure at the window stood unmoving. Then she gave a little sigh. The taut shoulders relaxed, the fingers loosened their grip. She took up the woodcut from the draining-board and studied it as if she hadn't seen it before. Then she opened her shoulder-bag and folded it carefully away.

CHAPTER SIX

Simon Lessing stood at the open window of his study at Melhurst and gazed out over the wide lawns to where the river cut its slow stream between the horse chestnuts and the limes. In his hand he held Clarissa's still unopened letter. It had arrived by the morning post, but there had been an excuse for not opening it then. He had had an early practice period. And that had been followed by the sixth-form seminar. He had told himself that he would wait until break. But the morning had passed and now it was the lunch-hour. In less than five minutes the bell would sound. He couldn't delay indefinitely. It was ridiculous and humiliating to be so afraid, to stand like a first-former holding a dreaded school report, knowing that, however long and cunningly deferred, the moment of truth must come at last.

He would wait until the bell actually sounded, and then he would read it, quickly, uncaring and with his mind on luncheon. And at least he could do so in peace. From the middle school upwards, every boy at Melhurst had his own study. The importance of a daily period of silence and privacy was one of the more enlightened precepts of the school's pious seventeenth-century founder and, largely because it had been incorporated into the almost monastic architecture, had endured through three hundred years of changing educational fashion. It was one of the things about Melhurst which Simon most valued, one of the privileges which Clarissa's patronage, Clarissa's money, had procured for him. Neither she nor Sir George had ever considered another choice of school, and Melhurst had made no difficulty about finding a place for the stepson of one of its more distinguished alumni. Its motto, in Greek rather than the more usual Latin, extolled the virtues of moderation, and for three hundred years, in obedience to Theognis' dictum, the school had been moderately famous, moderately expensive and moderately successful. No school could have suited him better. He recognized that its traditions and occasionally bizarre rituals, which he quickly learned and sedulously observed, were designed as much to discourage too personal a commitment as to promote a corporate identity. He was tolerated but left alone, and he asked nothing more. Even his talents were acceptable to the ethos of the school, which, perhaps because of a strong personal antipathy between a nineteenth-century headmaster and Dr Arnold of Rugby, by tradition eschewed muscular Christianity and almost all manifestations of the team spirit and espoused High Anglicanism and the cult of the eccentric. But music was well taught; the school's two orchestras had a national reputation. And swimming, the only physical skill at which he excelled, was one of the more acceptable sports. Compared with the Norman Pagworth Comprehensive, Melhurst seemed to him a haven of civilized order. At Pagworth he had felt like an alien set down without a phrase book in a lawless, ill-governed and alien country whose language and customs, crudely harsh as the playground in which they were born, were terrifyingly incomprehensible. The prospect of having to leave Melhurst and return to his old school had been one of his worst terrors since he began to sense that things were going wrong between himself and Clarissa.

It was strange that fear and gratitude should be so mixed. The gratitude was genuine enough. He only wished that he could experience it as it surely ought to be experienced, a graciousness, a reciprocal benison, free of this dragging load of obligation and guilt. The guilt was the worst to bear. When its weight became almost too much for him he tried to exorcise it by rational thought. It was ridiculous to feel guilty, ridiculous and unnecessary even to feel too oppressive an obligation. Clarissa owed him something after all. It was she who had destroyed his parents' marriage, enticed away his father, helped kill his mother through grief, left him an orphan to endure the discomforts, the vulgarities, the suffocating boredom of his uncle's house. It was Clarissa, not he, who should feel guilt. But even to let this thought creep traitorously into his mind only increased his burden of obligation. He owed her so much. The trouble was that everyone knew just how much. Sir George, who was seldom there, but who, when he was, presented himself to Simon as a silent, accusing personification of all those masculine qualities which he knew were alien to his own personality. He sometimes sensed in Clarissa's husband an inarticulate goodwill which he would have liked to have put to the test if only he could summon the courage. But most of the time he imagined that Sir George had never really approved of Clarissa taking him on and that their secret marital conversations were punctuated with the phrases: 'I told you so. I warned you.' Miss Tolgarth knew; Tolly whose eyes he dared not meet for fear of encountering one of those judgemental gazes in which he thought he detected dislike, resentment and contempt. Clarissa knew it, probably to the last penny. Increasingly he had come to feel that Clarissa repented of a generosity which at first had held all the charm of novelty, the magnificent gesture, superbly theatrical at the time in all its eccentricity but which she now saw had lumbered her with a spotty, inarticulate adolescent, ill at ease with her friends; with school bills, holiday arrangements, dental appointments, with all the minor irritations of motherhood and none of its essential compensations. He sensed that there was something she required of him which he could neither identify nor give, some return, unspecified but substantial, which would one day be demanded of him with all the brutal insistence of a tax-collector.

She seldom wrote to him now, and when he did see in his cubby hole that tall, curved hand – she disapproved of personal letters being typed – he had to steel himself to open the envelope. But the apprehension had never before been as bad as this. The letter seemed to have stuck to his hand, to have grown heavy with menace. And then the one o'clock bell clanged out. With sudden vehemence he tore at the corner of the envelope. The pale-blue, linen-based paper which she always used was tough. He wrenched in his thumb and tore a jagged slit through envelope and letter, rough as a lover who cannot wait to know his fate. He saw that the letter was short and his immediate reaction was a moan of relief. If she were throwing him out, if there was to be no last term at Melhurst, no chance of a place at the Royal College of Music, no more allowance, surely the excuse, the justification would require more than half a page. But the first sentence did away with his worst fears.

> This is to let you know the arrangements for next weekend. George will drive Tolly and me down to Speymouth before breakfast on Friday but it will be best if you arrive with the

rest of the house party in time for lunch. The launch will meet the nine thirty-three from Waterloo. Be at the harbour at Speymouth by eleven-forty. Ivo Whittingham and my cousin Roma will be on the train and you'll also meet a girl, Cordelia Gray. I shall need some extra help during the weekend and she is a kind of temporary secretary, so there will be someone young on the island for you to practise talking to. You should also be able to get some swimming so you won't need to be bored. Bring your dinner-jacket. Mr Gorringe likes to dress in the evenings. And he knows something about music so you may as well select some of your best pieces, the ones you know, nothing too heavy. I've written to your housemaster about the extra day's leave. Did Matron give you that acne lotion I sent last month? I hope you've been using it.

Love,
Clarissa

It was odd how soon relief could change to a new and different anxiety, even to resentment. Reading the letter for the second time he wondered why he should have been invited to the island. It was Clarissa's doing, of course. Ambrose Gorringe didn't know him and would hardly be likely to include him among his guests if he did. He remembered vaguely having heard about the island, the restored Victorian theatre, the plans to stage the Webster tragedy, and he sensed that the performance was important to Clarissa, amateur production though it might be. But why should he be there? He was expected to keep out of her way, not to make a nuisance of himself; that much was evident. He could disport himself in the sea or the pool. He supposed that there would be a pool and pictured Clarissa, pale and golden, stretched out in the sun and beside her this new girl, this Cordelia Gray with whom he was supposed to practise making conversation. And what else did Clarissa want him to practise? Making himself agreeable? Paying compliments? Knowing what jokes women like and when to make them? Flirting? Showing himself to be a susceptible heterosexual male? The prospect made his mouth dry with terror. It wasn't that he disliked the idea of a girl. He had already created in his mind the girl he would like to be with on

Courcy Island – on any island; sensitive, beautiful, intelligent, kind and yet wanting him, wanting him to do to her those terrifyingly exciting and shameful things which would no longer be shameful because they loved each other, acts which would reconcile for him in sweet responsive flesh, finally and for ever, that dichotomy which so occupied his day-dreaming hours, between romanticism and desire. He didn't expect to meet this girl, on Courcy or anywhere else. The only girl with whom he had so far had anything to do had been his cousin Susie. He hated Susie, hated her bold contemptuous eyes, her perpetually chewing mouth, her voice which alternately whined or yelled, her dyed hair, her grubby, beringed fingers.

But even if this girl were different, even if he liked her, how could he get to know her when Clarissa would be watching them, marking him for articulacy, attraction, wit, checking up on his social performance as she and this Ambrose Gorringe would be checking up on his musicianship? The reference to his music made his cheeks burn. He was insecure enough about his talent without having it diminished by this coy reference to his 'pieces' as if he were a child showing off to the neighbours at a suburban tea party. But the instruction was clear enough. He was to bring with him something showy or popular or both, something he could play with practised bravado so that she wouldn't be disgraced by any nervous misfingerings and she and Ambrose Gorringe would together decide whether he had enough talent to justify a final year at school, a chance to try for a place at the Royal College or the Academy.

And suppose the verdict went against him? He couldn't return to Mornington Avenue, to his aunt and uncle. Clarissa couldn't do that to him. After all, it was she who had brought the order of release. She had arrived unannounced on a warm afternoon during the summer holidays, when he had been in the house alone as usual, reading at the sitting-room table. He couldn't remember how she had announced herself, whether he had been told that the silent upright man with her was her new husband. But he remembered how she had looked, golden and effulgent, a cool, sweet-smelling miraculous vision who had immediately taken hold of his heart and his life as a rescuer might pluck a drowning child from the water and set him firmly on a sunlit rock. It had been too good to last, of course. But how marvellous in memory shone that long-dead summer afternoon.

'Are you happy here?'

'No.'

'I don't see how you could be, actually. This room's pretty gruesome. I've read somewhere that a million copies of that print have been sold but I didn't realize people actually hung it on their walls. Your father told me that you were musical. Do you still play?'

'I can't. There isn't a piano here. And they only teach percussion at school. They have a West Indian steel band. They're only interested in music where everyone can join in.'

'Things which everyone can join in usually aren't worth doing. They shouldn't have put two different papers on the walls. Three or four might have been bizarre enough to be fun. Two are just vulgar. How old are you? Fourteen, isn't it? How would you like to come and live with us?'

'For always?'

'Nothing is for always. But perhaps. Until you grow up, anyway.'

Without waiting for his reply, without even looking into his face to watch his initial response she turned to the silent man at her side.

'I think we can do better than this for Martin's boy.'

'If you are sure, my dear. Not a thing to decide quickly. Shouldn't make an impulse buy of a child.'

'Darling, where would you be if I hadn't made an impulse buy? And he's the only son I'm ever likely to give you.'

Simon's eyes were turning from one face to the other. He remembered how Sir George had looked, the features stiffening as if the muscles were bracing themselves against pain, against vulgarity. But Simon had seen the hurt, visible, unmistakable, before Sir George had turned silently away.

She had turned to him.

'Will your aunt and uncle mind?'

The misery, the grievances, had spilled out. He had had to prevent himself from clutching at her dress.

'They won't care! They'll be glad! I take up the spare room and I haven't any money. They're always telling me how much it costs to feed me. And they don't like me. They won't mind, honestly.'

And then, on impulse, he had done the right thing. It was the only time he had done exactly the right thing where Clarissa was concerned. There had been a pink geranium in a pot on the window-ledge; his uncle was a keen gardener and grew cuttings in the lean-to greenhouse at the side of the kitchen. One of the flower heads was small and delicate as a rose. He had broken it off and handed it to her; looking up into her face. She had laughed aloud and taken it from him and slipped it into the belt of her dress. Then she had looked at her husband and had laughed again, a peal of happy triumph.

'Well that seems to have decided itself. We'd better stay until they come home. I can't wait to see the owners of this wallpaper. And then we'll take you to buy some clothes.'

And so, with such promise, in such an exhilaration of surprised joy, it had all begun. He tried now to recall when the dream had faded, when things had first started to go wrong. But, apart from the first meeting, had they ever really gone right? He sensed that he was worse than a failure, that he was the last of a series of failures, that earlier disappointments had reinforced her present discontent. He was beginning to dread the holidays although he saw little either of Clarissa or of Sir George. Their official life together, such as it was, was lived in the London flat overlooking Hyde Park. But they were seldom there together. Clarissa had a flat in a Regency square in Brighton, her husband a remote flint cottage on the marshes of the east coast. It was there that their real lives were lived, she in the company of her theatrical friends, he in bird-watching and, if rumour were correct, in right-wing conspiracy. Simon had never been invited to either place although he often pictured them in those other secret worlds, Clarissa in a whirl of gaiety, Sir George conferring with his mysterious, hard-faced and nameless confederates. For some unexplainable reason, these imaginings, which occupied a disproportionate part of his holiday hours, were in the guise of old films. Clarissa and her friends, dressed in the waistless shifts of the twenties, hair shingled and flourishing long cigarette-holders, flung out their legs in a hectic Charleston while Sir George's friends arrived at their rendezvous in veteran cars, trench-coated, their wide-brimmed trilbies pulled down over secretive eyes. Excluded from both these worlds, Simon spent the holidays in the Bayswater flat, looked after occasionally by an almost silent Tolly or coping on his own, eating his dinner each night, by arrangement, in a local restaurant. Recently the meals had become poorer, dishes he chose were no longer available although they were served to others, he was shown to the worst table and kept waiting. Some of the waiters were almost openly offensive. He knew that Clarissa was no longer getting value for money, but he dared not complain. Who was he, so expensively bought and maintained, to talk about value for money?

It was time to go if he wanted any luncheon. He crumpled the letter in his hand and stuffed it into his pocket. Shutting his eyes against the brightness of grass and trees and shimmering water, he found himself praying, petitioning the God in whom he no longer believed, with all the desperate urgency, all the artless importunity of a child.

'Please let the weekend be a success. Don't let me make a fool of myself. Please don't let the girl despise me. Please let Clarissa be in a good mood. Please don't let Clarissa throw me out. Oh God, please don't let anything terrible happen on Courcy Island.'

CHAPTER SEVEN

It was ten o'clock on Thursday night and in her top-floor flat off Thames Street in the City Cordelia was completing her preparations for the weekend ahead. The long, uncurtained windows were fitted with wooden-slatted blinds but these were still up and as she moved from the single large sitting-room to her bedroom she could see spread below her the glittering streets, the dark alleyways, the towers and steeples of the city, could glimpse beyond them the necklace of light slung along the Embankment and the smooth, light-dazzled curve of the river. The view, in daylight or after dark, was a continual marvel to her, the flat itself a source of astonished delight.

It had only been after Bernie's death and at the end of her own first traumatic case that she had learned that her father's small estate had at last been wound up. She had expected nothing but debts and it had been a surprise to discover that he had owned a small house in Paris. It had, she imagined, been purchased years before when he had been comparatively well off to provide a safe house and occasional refuge for the comrades and himself; such a dedicated revolutionary would surely otherwise have despised the acquisition of even so dilapidated and insalubrious a piece of real estate. But the area had been zoned for development and it had sold surprisingly well. There had been enough money, when the debts were paid, for her to finance the Agency for another six months and to begin her search for a London flat cheap enough to buy. No building society had been interested in a sixth-floor apartment at the top of a Victorian warehouse with no lift and the barest amenities, nor in an applicant with an income as uncertain as it was erratic. But her bank manager, apparently to his surprise as much as hers, had been sympathetic and had authorized a five-year loan.

She had paid for the installation of a shower and for the fitting out of the small kitchen, narrow as a galley. She had done the rest of the work herself and had furnished the flat from junk shops and suburban auctions. The immense sitting-room was in white with one wall covered by a bookcase made from painted planks resting on columns of bricks. The dining and working table was scrubbed oak and the heating was provided by an ornate wrought-iron stove. Only the bedroom was luxurious, an intriguing contrast to the spartan bareness of the sitting-room. As it was only eight feet by five Cordelia had felt justified in extravagance and had chosen an expensive and exotic hand-printed paper with which she had covered the ceiling and cupboard door as well as the walls. At night, with the window which occupied almost one wall, wide open to the sky, she would lie, warmly cocooned in eccentric luxury, feeling that she was drawn up in her bright capsule to float under the stars.

She guarded her privacy. None of her friends and no one from the Agency had ever been in the flat. Adventures occurred elsewhere. She knew that if any man shared that narrow bed for her it would mean commitment. There was only one man she ever pictured there and he was a Commander of New Scotland Yard. She knew that he, too, lived in the City; they shared the same river. But she told herself that the brief madness was over, that at a time of stress and frightening insecurity she had only been seeking for her lost father-figure. There was this to be said for a smattering of amateur psychology: it enabled one to exorcize memories which might otherwise be embarrassing.

A narrow ledge with a parapet ran outside all the windows, wide enough for rows of pots of herbs and geraniums and for a single deckchair in summer. Underneath were warehouses and offices, mysterious businesses symbolized rather than identified by a double row of ancient name-plates. By day the building had a secretive, many-tongued and sometimes raucous life. But by five o'clock this began to seep away and, at night, it held a vast, almost unbroken silence. One of the tenant firms imported spices. To Cordelia, climbing up to her flat at the end of the day, that pungent, alien smell permeating the stairs represented security, comfort, her first real home.

The most onerous part of the preparation for this new case was deciding which clothes to pack. In her more puritanical moments Cordelia despised women who spent an inordinate amount of time and money on their appearance. Such a total preoccupation with externals must, she felt, argue a need to compensate for some deficiency at the heart of personality. But she was quick to recognize that her own interest in clothes and make-up, although spasmodic, was intense while it lasted and that she had never known the state of not in the least caring how she looked. In this, as in all matters, she preferred to travel light and the whole of her wardrobe could be comfortably accommodated within one cupboard and three drawers which were fitted along the wall of her bedroom. She opened them now and considered what would be necessary for a weekend which, apart from detection, might offer anything from sailing and rock-climbing to amateur theatricals. The creamy-fawn pleated skirt in fine wool and the matching cashmere two-piece, both bought at Harrods in the July sale, should, she felt, take care of most occasions; the cashmere's understated extravagance might, with luck, inspire confidence in the Agency's prosperity. If the warm weather held, her brown corduroy knickerbockers might be warm for sleuthing or walking but they were tough and she liked the jerkin and jacket, either of which looked good with them. Jeans and a couple of cotton tops were an obvious choice as was her Guernsey. The evenings were more difficult. Few people now dressed for dinner but this was a castle, Ambrose Gorringe might well be an eccentric, and anything was possible. She would need something cool and reasonably formal. In the end she packed her only long dress, in Indian cotton in subtle shades of pink, red and brown, and a pleated cotton skirt with matching top.

She turned with relief to the more straightforward business of checking her scene-of-crime kit. It was Bernie who had first devised it, basing it, she knew, on the kit issued to the Murder Squad of New Scotland Yard. His had been less comprehensive but all the essentials had been there: envelopes and tweezers for the collection of specimens, dusting powder for the detection of fingerprints, a Polaroid camera, a torch, fine rubber gloves, a magnifying glass, scissors and a sturdy penknife, a tin of plasticine for taking impressions of keys, test tubes with stoppers for the collection of blood samples. Bernie had pointed out that, ideally, these should hold a preservative and anti-clotting agent. Neither had ever been necessary then or now. Rescuing lost cats, shadowing errant husbands, tracing runaway teenagers had required persistence, good feet, comfortable footwear and infinite tact rather than the esoteric lore which Bernie had so enjoyed teaching her, compensating, in those long summer sessions in Epping Forest of stalking, tracking, physical combat and even gun lore, for his own professional failure, trying to recreate through Pryde's Agency the lost hierarchical and fascinating world of the Metropolitan CID.

She had made only a few alterations to the kit since Bernie's death, dispensing with the original case and using instead a canvas shoulder-bag fitted with inner pockets which she had bought in a store which sold ex-army equipment. And since her first case she had included an additional item, a long leather belt with a buckle, the belt with which that first victim had been hanged. She had no wish to dwell on the case which had promised so much and had ended so tragically, one which had left her with its own legacy of guilt. But the belt had once saved her life and she recognized an almost superstitious attachment to it, justifying its inclusion with the thought that a length of strong leather always came in useful.

Lastly she took a manilla envelope file and wrote the name CLARISSA LISLE in capitals on the cover, taking care to make the letters neat and even. She had often thought that this was the most satisfying part of a new investigation, a moment of hope spiced with anticipatory excitement, the pristine folder and crisp lettering themselves symbolic of a fresh beginning. She glanced through her notebook before adding it to the folder. Except for Sir George and his briefly seen wife, her companions on the island were still only names, a roll-call of putative suspects: Simon Lessing, Roma Lisle, Rose Tolgarth, Ambrose Gorringe, Ivo Whittingham; sounds written on paper but holding the promise of discovery, of challenge, of the fascinating variety of human personality. And all of them, Clarissa Lisle's stepson, her cousin, her dresser, her host, her friend, circling like planets round that central golden figure.

She spread out the twenty-three quotations on the table to study them before filing them in the case folder in the order of their receipt by Miss Lisle. Then she took from her shelf her two volumes of quotations, the paperback *Penguin Dictionary of Quotations* and the second edition of the *Oxford Dictionary*. As she had expected, all the passages appeared in one or the other, all but three in the paperback. Almost certainly that had been the dictionary used; it could be bought in almost any bookshop and its size would make it easy to conceal and light to carry about. To select the quotations would take no great trouble or time, merely a look at the index under death or dying or a quick read through the forty-five pages devoted to the plays of Shakespeare, the two which covered Marlowe and Webster. And it would not be too difficult to discover which plays Clarissa Lisle had appeared in. She had been a member of the Malvern Repertory Company for three years and Shakespeare and the

Jacobean dramatists were its forte. Any programme note covering her career, then or later, would list her main appearances. But it was a safe bet that, given the exigencies of a Shakespearean production with the resources of a medium-sized repertory company, she would have had at least a walking-on part in all the plays.

Only two of the quotations which she had tentatively identified as Webster were not in the *Penguin Dictionary*. But these could be found by studying the texts. All the quotations were familiar; she herself had had no difficulty in recognizing most of them even if she wasn't always sure of the play. But typing them accurately from memory was another matter. In each passage the lines were set out correctly and the punctuation was faultless; another reason for concluding that the typist had worked with the *Penguin Dictionary* at his or her elbow.

Next she studied them under her magnifying glass, wondering as she did so how much scientific attention the Metropolitan Police had thought it worth while to give them. As far as she could judge only three were typed on the same machine. The quality as well as the size of the letters varied; some were uneven, others faint or partly broken. The typing wasn't particularly expert; the work of someone who was used to a machine, perhaps for his own correspondence, but didn't type professionally. She thought that none had been typed on an electric typewriter. And who would have access to twenty different machines? Obviously someone who dealt in second-hand typewriters or someone who owned or worked in a secretarial school. It was unlikely to be a secretarial agency; the quality of the machines wasn't good enough. And it needn't necessarily be a secretarial school. Probably most modern comprehensives taught shorthand and typing; what was to prevent any member of the staff, whatever his or her subjects, from staying after school hours and making private use of the machines?

And there was another way in which the messages could have been produced and one which she thought the most likely. She had bought cheap second-hand machines for her own Agency, visiting the shops and showrooms where they were chained on display and trying them out, moving unhindered and unregarded from machine to machine. Anyone armed with a pad of paper and the *Dictionary of Quotations* could have provided himself – or herself – with a sufficient supply to keep the menace going, making a series of short visits to a variety of shops in districts where he was unlikely to be recognized. A reference to the Yellow Pages of the telephone directory would show him where to find them.

Before filing the messages in the folder she looked closely at the one which Sir George had told her had been typed on his machine. Was it her imagination that the skull and crossbones had been drawn by a different, a more careful, less assured hand? Certainly the heads of the two crossing bones were differently shaped and slightly larger than in the other examples, the skull more broad. The differences were small, but she thought significant. The drawings of the other skulls and the coffin were practically identical. And the quotation itself, typed with erratic spacing of the letters, had no venom in its admonition:

On pain of death let no man name death to me:
It is a word infinitely terrible.

It wasn't a quotation known to her and she couldn't find it in the *Penguin Dictionary*. Webster, she thought, rather than Shakespeare; perhaps *The White Devil* or *The Devil's Law Case*. The punctuation looked accurate enough although she would have expected a comma after the first word 'death'. Perhaps this quotation had been remembered not looked up; certainly it had been typed by a different and less expert hand. And she thought she knew whose.

The remaining quotations varied in the degree of their menace. Christopher Marlowe's bleak despair,

Hell hath no limits, nor is circumscribed
In one self place; for where we are is hell,
And where hell is, must we ever be

could only doubtfully be described as a death threat although its stark contemporary nihilism might well be unwelcome to a nervous recipient. The only other Marlowe quotation, received six weeks earlier,

Now hast thou but one bare hour to live,
And then thou must be damned perpetually!

was direct enough but the threat had proved baseless: Clarissa had lived out more than her hour. But it seemed to Cordelia that, since these earlier messages, the quotations had increased in menace, had been selected to build up to some kind of climax from the sinister threat typed underneath a coffin;

I wish you joy o' the worm

to the brutally explicit lines from *King Henry VI*:

Down, down to hell; and say I sent thee thither.

Seen together, the sonorous reiteration of death and hatred was oppressive, the silly childish drawings limned with menace. She began to understand what this carefully organized programme of intimidation might do to a sensitive and vulnerable woman, to any woman come to that, darkening the mornings, making terrible such ordinary events as the arrival of the post, a letter on the hall salver, a note pushed under the door. It was easy to advise the victim of a poison pen to flush the messages down the lavatory like the rubbish they were. But in all societies there was an atavistic fear of the malevolent power of a secret adversary, working for evil, willing one to failure, perhaps to death. There was a horrible and rather frightening intelligence at work here, and it wasn't pleasant to think that the person responsible might be one of that small group who would be with her on Courcy Island, that the eyes which would meet hers over the dining-table could be hiding such malignancy. For the first time she wondered whether Clarissa Lisle could be right, whether there really was a threat to her life. Then she put the thought aside, telling herself that the messages were beginning to exercise their malevolence even on her. A murderer did not advertise his intention over a period of months. But was that necessarily true? To a mind consumed with hatred, might not the act of killing be too swift, too momentary in its satisfaction? Could Clarissa Lisle have an enemy so bitter that he needed to watch her suffer, to destroy her slowly with terror and failure before he moved in for the kill?

She shivered. The warmth of the day was already dissipating, the night air, drifting through the open window, even in this city eyrie held the taste and tang of autumn. She put away the last message and closed the folder. Her own instructions had been clear, to safeguard Clarissa Lisle from any worry or distress before Saturday's performance of *The Duchess of Malfi* and, if possible, to discover who was sending her the messages. And that, to the best of her ability, she would do.

PART TWO

Dress Rehearsal

CHAPTER EIGHT

Victorian Speymouth, which to the surprise of its citizens had converted its street lamps to gas without explosion or other disaster, had seen no reason to reject the new railway or, while accepting its inevitability, to banish it as had Cambridge to an inconvenient distance from the town. The charming little station was only a quarter of a mile from the statue of Queen Victoria which marks the centre of the promenade and when Cordelia stepped out into the sunlight, bag in one hand and portable typewriter in the other, she found herself gazing down over a jumble of brightly painted houses to a stone-enclosed harbour, tiny as a pool, and beyond it to the stunted pier and the shimmering sea. She was almost sorry to leave the station. With its gleaming white paint and its curved roof of wrought iron, delicate as lace, it reminded her of the summer issues of her weekly childhood comic where the sea had been always blue, the sand a bright yellow, the sun a golden ball and the railway a highly coloured toy-town welcome to these imagined joys. Mrs Wilkes, the poorest of all her foster mothers, had been the only one to buy her a comic, the only one whom Cordelia remembered with affection. Perhaps it was a happy augury that she should think of her now.

There was already a small queue waiting for the taxis but she saw no reason to join it. The road was downhill and the quay clearly in sight. She stepped out, almost oblivious of the weight of her luggage in the pleasure of the day. The little town was bathed in sunshine and the rows of Georgian terraced houses, simple, unpretentious and dignified with elegant façades and wrought-iron balconies looked as charmingly artificial and as brightly lit as a stage-set. In the bay the grey shape of a small warship rested stiffly immobile as a child's cut-out toy. She could almost imagine putting out her hand and plucking it from the water. As she made her way down a steep, cobbled street, terraces of fawn, pink and blue houses curved upwards towards a glimpse of distant hills, while below the brightly painted statue of Queen Victoria, majestically robed, pointed her sceptre imperiously towards the public lavatories.

And everywhere there were people, jostling on the pavements, spilling from the Esplanade on to the beach, laid in sunburned rows on the gritty sand, lumped in sagging deck-chairs, queuing at the ice-cream kiosk, peering from the windows of the cars in search of a parking place. She wondered where they had all come from on this mid-September weekday when the holiday season was surely over, the children back at school. Were they all truants from work or schoolroom, drawn out from autumn's hibernation by this resurgence of summer, with their mottled red faces above white necks, their glistening chests and arms, recently covered against September's chills, revealing again the unlovely evidence of harsher suns? The day itself smelt of high summer, of seaweed, hot bodies and blistering paint.

The busy little harbour was a confusion of rocking dinghies and furled sails but the launch with *Shearwater* painted on its bow was soon identified. It was about thirty feet long with a central, low-roofed cabin and a slatted seat in the stern. One wizened seaman seemed to be in charge. He was squatting on a bollard, his thin legs clamped, wearing seaboots and a blue jumper with Courcy Island emblazoned across the chest. He looked so like Popeye that Cordelia suspected that the pipe, which he slowly took from his apparently toothless gums on seeing her approach, was sucked for effect rather than solace. He touched his hat and grinned when she gave her name but didn't speak. Taking the typewriter and her bag he stowed them in the cabin, then turned to offer her his hand. But Cordelia had already jumped on board and had seated herself in the rear. He resumed his seat on the bollard and, together, they waited.

Three minutes later a taxi drew up at the mouth of the quay and a boy and a woman got out. The woman paid the fare – not, it seemed, without some argument – while the boy stood uneasily to one side, then loitered to the edge of the quay to stare down at the water. She joined him and they moved together to the launch, he a little behind her like a reluctant child. This, thought Cordelia, must be Roma Lisle with Simon Lessing in tow, neither apparently pleased with the chance that had forced them into sharing a taxi. Cordelia observed her as she allowed herself to be handed aboard. Superficially, she had nothing in common with her cousin except the shape of the lower lip. She too was fair, but it was an ordinary Anglo-Saxon blondness in which the strong sun already revealed the glint of grey. Her hair was short and expensively shaped to her head. She was taller than her cousin and moved with a certain assurance. But her face, with its lines scored across the forehead and from nose to mouth, had a look of brooding discontent and there was no peace in the eyes. She was dressed in an extremely well-tailored fawn trouser-suit with blue braid facing the collar and a high-necked sweater striped in fawn and pale blue, an outfit which seemed to Cordelia to combine superficial suitability for a holiday weekend with an inappropriate smartness, perhaps because she was wearing it with high-heeled shoes which made the descent into the launch less than graceful. The colour, too, was unflattering to her skin. It was impossible not to recognize that here was a woman who cared about clothes without having any clear idea what suited either her or the occasion. About the young man there was less chance to make a judgement, sartorial or otherwise. He glimpsed Cordelia in the stern, blushed and scuttled into the cabin with an alacrity which suggested that he was unlikely to add to the gaiety of the weekend. Miss Lisle seated herself in the bow while the boatman again took his seat on the bollard. They waited in silence while the launch gently rocked against the fender of old tyres slung against the stones of the quay and small boats gently edged past them on the way to the open sea. After a few minutes Miss Lisle called out:

'Oughtn't we to be moving off? We're expected for lunch.'

'One more acomin'. Mr Whittingham.'

'Well, he couldn't have been on the nine thirty-three. He'd have been here by now. And I didn't recognize him at the station. Perhaps he's driving down and has got delayed.'

'Mr Ambrose said he'd be acomin' by train. Said to wait for him.'

Miss Lisle frowned and gazed fixedly out to sea. Two more minutes passed. Then the boatman called out:

'Here he be. He's acomin' now. That'll be Mr Whittingham.' The triple assurance given he rose, and began making ready to move off. Cordelia looked up and saw through a distorting dazzle of sun what seemed at first like a death's head on stilts jerking across the quay towards her, its skeleton fingers grasping a canvas holdall. She blinked and the picture composed itself, moved into focus, became human. The skull clothed itself in flesh, stretched and grey over the fineness of the bones, but still human flesh. The sockets moistened into eyes, keen and a little amused. The figure was still the thinnest and most desperately sick man she had ever seen moving on his own feet but the voice was firm, and the words were easy and comfortable.

'Sorry to hold you up. I'm Ivo Whittingham. The quay looked deceptively close. And having started walking I couldn't, of course, find a taxi.'

He brushed aside Oldfield's proffered arm, but without impatience, and lowered himself into a seat in the bow, wedging his bag between his legs. No one spoke. The final end of rope spilled free from the bollard and was wound aboard. The engine shuddered into life. Almost imperceptibly the launch crept away from the quay and made for the harbour mouth.

Ten minutes later they seemed no closer to the island towards which crabwise they were edging, although the shore was visibly receding. The fishermen on the end of the pier shrank into matchstalk men with fairy wands, the bustle of the town was swallowed up in the noise of the engine and finally shaken off, the royal statue became a coloured blur. The horizon was a pale purple curdling into low clouds from which there separated great islands of creamy whiteness which rose to float almost motionless against a clear azure blue. The small waves seemed to be leaping with light, absorbing it from the bright air and reflecting it back to the paler blue of the sky. Cordelia thought that the sea and the distant shore were like a Monet painting, bright colour laid in streaks against bright colour, light itself made visible. She leaned over the edge of the boat and plunged her arm into the leaping wake. The cold made her gasp, but she held her arm under the water, spreading her fingers so that three small wakes spouted into the sunlight, watching the hairs on her forearm catch and hold the shining drops. Suddenly her mood was broken by a woman's voice. Roma Lisle had made her way round the cabin and come up beside her. She said:

'It's typical of Ambrose Gorringe just to send Oldfield and leave his guests to introduce themselves. I'm Roma Lisle, Clarissa's cousin.' They shook hands. Her fingers were firm and pleasantly cool. Cordelia gave her name. She said:

'But I'm not a guest. I'm going to the island to work.'

Miss Lisle's glance went to the typewriter. She said:

'Good Lord, Ambrose isn't writing another blockbuster is he?'

'Not as far as I know. I'm employed by Lady Ralston.' It might, thought Cordelia, have been more accurate to say that she was employed by Sir George but she sensed that this might only lead to complications. But sooner or later some explanation of her presence would have to be given. It might as well be now. She prepared for the inevitable questions.

'By Clarissa! Doing what, for God's sake?'

'Dealing with her correspondence. Making telephone calls. Generally easing things along while she concentrates on the play.'

'She's got Tolly to ease things along. What does she think of this – Tolly I mean?'

'I haven't the least idea. I haven't met her yet.'

'I can't see her liking it.' She gave Cordelia a look in which suspicion mingled with puzzlement.

'I've read of those stage-struck oddballs, without talent themselves, who try to buy themselves into the club by attaching themselves to one of their idols, cooking, shopping, running errands, acting as a kind of poodle. They either die of overwork or end up with nervous breakdowns. You're not one of that pathetic breed are you? No, I can see that you aren't. But don't you find your job well . . . odd?'

'What do you do? And is your job any less odd?'

'I'm sorry. I was being offensive. Put it down to the fact that I'm a failed schoolteacher. At present I work in a bookshop. It may sound pretty orthodox but I assure you it has its moments. You'd better meet Clarissa's stepson. Simon Lessing. He's probably nearer your age than anyone else on this benighted weekend.'

Hearing his name, the boy came out of the cabin and blinked in the sun. Perhaps, thought Cordelia, he preferred a voluntary appearance to being dragged out by Miss Lisle. He held out his hand and she shook it, surprised that his clasp should be so firm. They murmured a conventional greeting. He was better looking than a first glimpse had suggested, with a long, sensitive face and widely spaced grey eyes. But his skin was pitted with the scars of old acne with a fresh outcrop along the forehead, and his mouth was weak. Cordelia knew that with her wide brow, high cheekbones and cat-like face she looked younger than her age but she couldn't imagine any time when she wouldn't have felt older than this shy boy.

And then there was a fresh voice. The last passenger was making his way astern to join them. He said:

'When the Prince of Wales came to Courcy Island in the eighteen nineties, puffing across the bay in a steam launch, old Gorringe used to have his private band waiting on the quay to play him ashore. They were dressed, for some reason not recorded, in Tyrolese costume. Do you suppose that Ambrose's love affair with the past extends to laying on a similar welcome for us?'

But before anyone had a chance to respond, the launch had turned the eastern edge of the island and the castle itself came suddenly into sight.

CHAPTER NINE

Although Cordelia wasn't aware that she had consciously thought about the architecture of Courcy Castle, it had, nevertheless, formed itself in her mind as a grey-stoned, massive, crenellated sham, over-ornate in its Victorian solidity, an unsatisfactory compromise between domesticity and grandeur. The reality, suddenly presented to her in the clarity of the morning sunlight, made her catch her breath with wonder. It stood on the edge of the sea, almost as if it had risen from the waves, a castle of rose-red brick, its only stonework the pale, flush lines and the tall, curved windows which now coruscated in the sun. To the west soared a slender round tower topped with a cupola, solid yet ethereal. Every detail of the matt-surfaced walls, the patterned buttresses and the battlements was distinct, unfussy, confident. The whole was compact, even massive, yet the high sloping roofs and the slender tower gave an impression of lightness and repose which she hadn't associated with high Victorian architecture. The southern façade overlooked a wide terrace – surely wave-swept in winter – from which two flights of steps led down to a narrow beach of sand and shingle. The proportions of the castle seemed to her exactly right for its site. Larger and it could have looked pretentious; smaller and there would have been a suggestion of facile charm. But this building, compromise though it might be between castle and family house, seemed to her brilliantly successful. She almost laughed aloud at the pleasure of it.

She was unaware that Ivo Whittingham had come up beside her until he spoke.

'This is your first visit, isn't it? What do you think of it?'

'It's remarkable. And unexpected.'

'You're interested in Victorian architecture?'

'Interested, but not at all knowledgeable.'

'I shouldn't tell Ambrose that. He'll devote the whole weekend to educating you in his passions and prejudices. I've done my homework so I'll forestall him by telling you now that the architect was E. W. Godwin who worked for Whistler and Oscar Wilde and was associated with the aesthetes. What he aimed for – so he tells us – was the careful adjustment of solids and voids. Well, he's achieved that here. He did some perfectly awful town halls including one at Northampton – not that Ambrose would admit to its awfulness – but I think that he and I will agree about this achievement. Are you taking part in the play?'

'No, I'm here to work. I'm Miss Lisle's secretary, her temporary secretary.'

His quick glance was surprised. Then his lips curved in a smile.

'So I should imagine. Clarissa's relationships tend to be temporary.'

Cordelia said quickly:

'Do you know anything about the play? I mean, which company is acting in it?'

'Didn't Clarissa explain? They're the Cottringham Players, said to be the oldest amateur company in England. They were started in 1834 by the then Sir Charles Cottringham, and the family have more or less kept them going ever since. The Cottringhams have been mad about acting for over three generations, their enthusiasm invariably in inverse proportion to their talent. The present Charles Cottringham is playing Antonio. His great-grandfather used to take part in the revels here until he was imprudent enough to cast a lascivious eye on Lillie Langtry. The Prince of Wales made his displeasure known, and no Cottringham has spent the night under the castle roof ever since. It's a convenient tradition for Ambrose. He need only entertain the leading lady and a few private guests. Judith Cottringham has a house party for the producer and the rest of the cast. They'll all come over tomorrow by launch.'

'Where did they act before Mr Gorringe offered the castle?'

'It was offered, I imagine, by Clarissa rather than by Gorringe. They gave an annual performance in the old assembly rooms at Speymouth, an occasion more social than cultural. But tomorrow shouldn't be too discouraging. A Speymouth butcher, appropriately enough, is playing Bosola and he's reputed to be good. Ferdinand is taken by Cottringham's agent. Hardly Gielgud; but Clarissa tells me that he knows how to speak verse.'

The sound of the engine died to a gentle shudder and the launch slowly edged towards the jetty. The stone quay curved from the terrace in two arms to form a miniature harbour. At intervals, steep steps festooned with seaweed led down to the water. At the end of the eastern, longer arm was a charming folly, a circular bandstand of delicate wrought iron, painted white and pale blue with slender pillars supporting a curved canopy. Beneath this stood the welcoming party, a group of two men and two women, as immobile and carefully positioned as a tableau. Clarissa Lisle was a little to the front, her host attendant at her left shoulder. Behind them, waiting with the impassive, careful non-involvement of servants, stood a dark-clad man and woman, the man out-topping the group in height.

But the dominant figure was Clarissa Lisle. The immediate impression, whether by chance or design, was of a goddess of classical mythology with her attendants. As the launch drew alongside the quay Cordelia saw that she was wearing what looked like shorts and a sleeveless top in closely pleated cream muslin with, over it, a loose-fitting, almost transparent shift in the same material, wide-sleeved and corded at the waist. Beside this deceptively simple, cool flowing elegance Roma Lisle in her trouser-suit seemed to exude a sweaty and eye-dazzling discomfort.

The waiting group, as if under instruction, held their poses until the launch gently bumped the landing steps. Then Clarissa fluted a small cry of welcome, spread batwings of fluttering cotton and ran forward. The pattern was broken.

During the chatter which followed the formal introductions and while Ambrose Gorringe was supervising the unloading of luggage and the humping ashore of boxes of supplies from a locker in the stern, Cordelia studied her host. Ambrose Gorringe was of middle height with smooth black hair and delicate hands and feet. He gave an impression of spry plumpness, not because he carried excess fat but because of the feminine softness and roundness of his arms and face. His skin gleamed pink and white, the circular flush on each cheekbone looked almost artificial. His eyes were his most striking feature. They were large and sparkling bright as black, sea-washed pebbles, the surrounding whites clear and translucent. Above them the brows curved in a strong arch as tidily as if they had been plucked. The ends of the mouth curved upwards in a fixed smile so that the whole face held the shining humorous animation of a man enjoying a perpetual internal joke. He was wearing brown cotton trousers and a black short-sleeved singlet. Both were highly suitable for the weather and the occasion, yet to Cordelia they seemed incongruous. Something more formal was needed to define and control the latent strength of what she guessed was a complex and, perhaps, a formidable personality.

In his way the manservant, now supervising the loading of the luggage and crates of supplies on to a small motorized truck, was equally remarkable. He must, thought Cordelia, be well over six feet in height and with his dark suit and heavy white lugubrious face had the spurious gloom of a Victorian undertaker's mute. His long, rather pointed head sloped to a high and shiny forehead topped with a wig of coarse black hair, which made absolutely no pretensions to realism. It was parted in the middle and had been inexpertly hacked rather than trimmed. Cordelia thought that such a bizarre appearance could hardly be inadvertent and she wondered what perversity or secret compulsion had led him to contrive and present to his world a persona so uncompromisingly eccentric. Could it be revulsion against the tedium, the conformity or the deference demanded of his job? It seemed unlikely. Servants who found their duties frustrating or uncongenial nowadays had a simple remedy. They could always leave.

Intrigued by the man's appearance she scarcely noticed his wife; a short, round-faced woman who stood always at her husband's side and didn't speak during the whole course of the disembarkation.

Clarissa Lisle had taken absolutely no notice of her since their arrival but Ambrose Gorringe came forward, smiled and said:

'You must be Miss Gray. Welcome to Courcy Island. Mrs Munter will look after you. We've put you next to Miss Lisle.' Cordelia waited until the Munters had finished unloading the launch. As the three of them walked together behind the main party, Munter handed his wife a small canvas bag with the words:

'Not much post this morning. The parcel from the London Library hasn't come. That means Mr Gorringe probably won't get his books until Monday.'

The woman spoke for the first time. 'He'll have plenty to do this weekend without new library books.'

At that moment Ambrose Gorringe turned and called to Munter. The man moved forward, changing his quick steps to a stately unhurried walk which was probably part of his act. As soon as he was out of earshot Cordelia said:

'If there's any post for Miss Lisle it comes first to me. I'm her new secretary. And I'll take any telephone calls for her. Perhaps I'd better take a look at the post. We're expecting a letter.'

Rather to her surprise, Mrs Munter handed over the bag without demur. There were only eight letters in all, held together in a rubber band. Two were for Clarissa Lisle. One, in a stout envelope, was obviously an invitation to a dress show. The name, but not the address, of the prestigious designer, was engraved on the flap. The second, an ordinary white envelope, was addressed in typing to:

The Duchess of Malfi,
c/o Miss Clarissa Lisle,
Courcy Island,
Speymouth,
Dorset

She walked a few steps ahead. She knew that it would be wise to wait until she reached the privacy of her room, but restraint was impossible. Controlling her excitement and curiosity she slipped her finger under the flap. It was loosely gummed and came apart easily. She guessed the communication would be short and it was. Inside, on a small sheet of the same paper was a neatly drawn skull and crossbones and typed underneath just two lines which she instinctively knew rather than recognized were from the play.

Call upon our dame aloud,
And bid her quickly don her shroud!

She put the message back into the envelope and slipped it quickly into her jacket pocket, then lingered until Mrs Munter had caught up with her.

Cordelia saw that the main rooms opened on to the terrace with a wide view of the Channel, but that the entrance to the castle was on the sheltered eastern side away from the sea. They passed through a stone archway which led to a formal walled garden, then turned down a wide path between lawns and finally through a high arched porch and into the great hall. Pausing at the doorway, Cordelia could picture those first nineteenth-century guests, the crinolined ladies with their furled parasols, followed by their maids, the leather, round-topped trunks, the hatboxes and gun-cases, the distant beat of the welcoming band as that heavy Germanic prince carried his imposing paunch before him under Mr Gorringe's privileged portals. But then the great hall would have been ostentatiously over-furnished, a lush repository of sofas, chairs and occasional tables, rich carpets and huge pots of palms. Here the house party would congregate at the end of the day before slowly processing in strict hierarchical order through the double doors to the dining-room. Now the hall was furnished only with a long refectory table and two chairs, one on each side of the stone fireplace. On the opposite wall was a six-foot tapestry which she thought was almost certainly by William Morris; Flora, rose-crowned with her maidens, her feet shining among the lilies and the hollyhocks. A wide staircase, branching to left and right, led to a gallery which ran round three sides of the hall. The eastern wall was almost entirely taken up by a stained-glass window showing the travels of Ulysses. Motes of coloured light danced in the air, giving the great hall something of the quiet solemnity of a church. She followed Mrs Munter up the staircase.

The main bedrooms opened out of the gallery. The room into which Cordelia was shown was charming with a lightness and delicacy which she hadn't expected. The two windows, high and curved, had curtains of a lily-patterned chintz which was used also for the bed-cover and the fitted cushion of the mahogany cane-backed bedside chair. The simple stone fireplace had a panelled frieze of six-inch tiles, their patterns of flowers and foliage echoed in the larger tiles, which surrounded the grate. Above the bed was a row of delicate watercolours, iris, wild strawberry, tulip and lily. This, she thought, must be the De Morgan room of which Miss Maudsley had spoken. She glanced round with pleasure and Mrs Munter, noting her interest, assumed the role of guide. But she recited the information without enthusiasm, as if she had learned the facts by rote.

'The furniture here is not as old as the castle, Miss. The bed and chair were designed by A. H. Mackmurdo in 1882. The tiles here and in the bathroom are by William De Morgan. Most of the tiles in the castle are by him. The original Mr Herbert Gorringe, who rebuilt the castle in the eighteen sixties, saw a house that he'd done in Kensington and had all the original tiles here ripped out and replaced by De Morgan. That mahogany and pine cabinet was painted by William Morris and the paintings are by John Ruskin. What time would you like your early tea, Miss?'

'At half-past seven, please.'

After she had left, Cordelia went through to the bathroom. Both rooms faced west and any broad view of the island was blocked by the tower which rose immediately to her right, a phallic symbol in patterned brick, soaring to pierce the blue of the sky. Gazing up at its smooth roundness she felt her head swim and the tower itself reeled dizzily in the sun. To her left she could just glimpse the end of the southern terrace and, beyond it, a wide sweep of sea. Beneath the bathroom window a wrought-iron fire escape led down to the rocks, from which, presumably, it was possible to reach the terrace. Even so, the escape route seemed to her precarious. In a high storm one would surely feel trapped between fire and sea.

Cordelia had started to unpack when the communicating door between her room and the adjoining one opened and Clarissa Lisle appeared.

'Oh, here you are. Come next door, will you? Tolly will see to your unpacking for you.'

'Thank you, but I'd rather do my own.'

Apart from the fact that the few clothes she had brought could be hung up in minutes and she preferred to do these things for herself, Cordelia had no intention of letting other eyes see the scene-of-crime kit. She had already noticed with relief that the bottom drawer of the cabinet had a key.

She followed Clarissa into her bedroom. It was twice as large as her own and very different in style; here opulence and extravagance replaced lightness and simplicity. The room was dominated by the bed, a mahogany half-tester with canopy, cover and side curtains of crimson damask. The head and footboard were elaborately carved with cherubs and swags of flowers, the whole surmounted by a countess's coronet. Cordelia wondered whether the original owner, thrusting his way upwards through the Victorian social hierarchy, had commissioned it to honour a particularly important guest. On either side of the bed was a small, bow-fronted chest and across its foot a carved and buttoned *chaise longue*. The dressing-table was set between the two tall windows from which, between the looped curtains, Cordelia saw only an expanse of blue, untroubled sea. Two ponderous wardrobes covered the opposite wall. There were low chairs and a screen of Berlin woolwork before the marble fireplace in which a small pile of sticks had already been laid. Ambrose Gorringe's chief guest was to have the luxury of a real fire. She wondered whether some housemaid would creep in in the early hours to light it, as had her Victorian counterpart when the long-dead countess stirred in her magnificent bed.

The room was very untidy. Clothes, wraps, tissue paper and plastic bags were flung across the *chaise longue* and the bed, and the top of the dressing-table was a jumble of bottles and jars. A woman was walking about, calmly and uncensoriously gathering up the clothes over her arm. Clarissa Lisle said:

'This is my dresser, Miss Tolgarth. Tolly, meet Miss Cordelia Gray. She's come to help with my correspondence. Just an experiment. She won't be in anyone's way. If she wants anything done, look after her, will you?'

It wasn't, thought Cordelia, an auspicious introduction. The woman neither smiled nor spoke, but Cordelia didn't feel that the steady gaze which met her own held any resentment. It didn't even hold curiosity. She was a heavily busted, rather sturdy woman with a face that looked older than her body, and with remarkably elegant legs. Their shape was enhanced by very fine stockings and high-heeled court shoes, an incongruous touch of vanity which emphasized the plainness of the high-necked black dress, its only ornament a gold cross on a chain. Her dark hair, parted in the middle and drawn back into a bun at the nape of the neck, was already streaked with grey and there were lines deep as clefts across the forehead and at the ends of the long mouth. It was a strong, secretive face not, Cordelia thought, the face of a woman willingly subservient. When she had disappeared into the bathroom, Clarissa said:

'I suppose we'll have to talk, but it can't be now. Munter has set lunch in the dining-room. It's ridiculous on a day like this. We ought to be in the sun. I've told him that we shall eat on the terrace, but that means he'll see that we don't get it until one thirty so we may as well make a quick tour of the castle. Is your room comfortable?'

'Very, thank you.'

'I suppose I'd better give you some letters to type just to allay suspicion. There are one or two that need answering. You may as well do some work while you're here. You can type, I suppose?'

'Yes, I can type. But that's not why I'm here.'

'I know why you're here. I was the one who wanted you. And I still want you. But we'll talk about that tonight. There won't be a chance until then. Charles Cottringham and the other principals are coming across after lunch for a run-through of one or two scenes and they won't be gone until after tea. You've met my stepson haven't you, Simon Lessing?'

'Yes, we were introduced on the boat.'

'Find him, will you, and tell him there's time for him to have a swim before lunch. There's no point in his trailing round the castle with us. You'll probably find him hiding in his room. It's two down from your own.'

Cordelia thought that the message could more suitably have come from Clarissa. But she reminded herself that she was supposed to be a secretary-companion, whatever that meant, and that the job probably included running errands. She knocked on Simon's door. He didn't call out but, after what seemed an inordinate delay, the door slowly opened and his apprehensive face appeared. He blushed when he saw who it was. She gave him Clarissa's message, suitably edited, and he managed a smile and a whispered, 'Thank you' before quickly closing the door. Cordelia felt rather sorry for him. It couldn't be altogether easy, having Clarissa as a stepmother. She wasn't sure that it would be any easier having her as a client. For the first time she felt some of her euphoria drain away. The castle and the island were even lovelier than she had pictured. The weather was glorious and no change threatened in this balmy resurgence of summer. It promised to be a weekend of comfort, even of luxury. And, above all, the envelope in her pocket confirmed that the job was real, that she would pit her brain and her wits against a human adversary at last. Why then should she have to struggle against a sudden and overwhelming conviction that her task was doomed to disaster?

CHAPTER TEN

'And now,' announced Clarissa leading the way down the staircase and across the great hall, 'we'll end with a visit to Ambrose's private Chamber of Horrors.'

The tour of the castle had been hurried and incomplete. Cordelia sensed that the sun-warmed terrace beckoned and that the thoughts of the party were less on Ambrose's treasures than on their pre-luncheon sherry. But there were treasures, and she promised herself that if she had the chance she would enjoy later and at leisure what was a small but comprehensive museum of the artistic achievements and spirit of Victoria's long reign. The tour had been too rushed. Her mind was a confusion of form and colour; porcelain, pictures, glass and silver jostled for place: pottery exhibited at the Great Exhibition of 1851, jasper, Grecian ware, terracotta, majolica; cabinets of painted Wedgwood dishes and delicate *pâte-sur-pâte* made by M.-L Solon for Minton; part of a Coalport dinner-service presented by Queen Victoria to the Emperor of Russia and decorated with English and Russian Orders surrounding the Russian royal crown and eagles.

Clarissa had floated on ahead waving her arms and producing a stream of doubtfully accurate information. Ivo had lingered when he was allowed to and had said little. Roma stumped behind them with an expression of careful uninterest and from time to time made an acid comment about the misery and exploitation of the poor represented by these glittering monuments to wealth and privilege. Cordelia felt some sympathy with her. Sister Magdalen, who had taught nineteenth-century history at the Convent, hadn't shared the views of some of the sisters that since the pleasures of the world were to be rejected so might some of its vicarious sorrows, and had attempted to instil a social sense into her privileged pupils. Cordelia couldn't see a picture of that pudding-faced matriarch with her plain, discontented-looking children around her without seeing also the wan, aching-eyed seamstresses working their eighteen-hour day, the factory children half-asleep at their looms, the bobbin lace-makers bent double over their cushions, and the steaming tenements of the East End.

Cordelia had found more to interest her than to admire in Ambrose's collection of pictures. Everything that she most disliked in high Victorian art was here, the strained eroticism, the careful naturalism which had nothing to do with nature, the vapid anecdotal pictures and the debased religiosity. But he did have a Sickert and a Whistler. As they passed along the gallery Roma said to her:

'There's a William Dyce in my room called "The Shell Gatherers". Not badly painted, rather good, in fact. A crinolined group of ladies examining their finds on a Kentish beach. But what's the reality? A group of over-fed, over-clad, bored and sexually frustrated upper-class females with nothing to do with their time but collect shells to make their useless shell-boxes, paint insipid water-colours, entertain the gentlemen after dinner at the pianoforte, and wait for a man to give status and purpose to their lives.'

It was while she and Roma were standing in front of a Holman Hunt, neither of them finding anything to say, that Ambrose had come up to them.

'Not perhaps one of his best. The Victorians may have got their money from the dark satanic mills but they had a passionate craving for beauty. It was their tragedy that, unlike us, they understood only too well how far they fell short of achieving it.'

The tour was now almost at an end. Clarissa led them down a tiled passageway to Ambrose's business room. Here, apparently, was the promised Chamber of Horrors.

It was a smaller room than most in the castle and looked out over the lawn which faced the eastern entrance. One wall was hung with a framed collection of Victorian popular gallows literature, the crudely printed and illustrated broadsheets which were sold to the mob after a notable trial or execution. Roma seemed particularly interested in them. Murderers, looking remarkably slim and elegant in their breeches, sat penning their last confessions under the high-barred window of the condemned cell, listened in the chapel at Newgate to their last sermons with their coffins placed at hand, or dropped from the rope end as the robed Chaplain stood, his book in hand. Cordelia disliked the pictures of hanging and moved to join Ambrose and Ivo who were examining a wall shelf of Staffordshire figures. Ambrose identified his favourites.

'Meet my notorious murderers and murderesses. That pair are the infamous Maria and Frederick Manning, hanged in November 1847 in front of Horsemongers Lane Gaol before a riotous crowd of fifty thousand. Charles Dickens saw the execution and he wrote afterwards that the behaviour of the crowd was so indescribable that he thought he was living in a city of devils. Maria wore black satin for her part in the entertainment, a choice which did absolutely nothing for its subsequent fashionable appeal. The gentleman appropriately clad in a shooting-jacket is William Corder aiming his pistol at poor Maria Marten. Notice the Red Barn in the background. He might have got away with it if her mother hadn't repeatedly dreamed that her daughter's body was buried there. He was hanged at Bury St Edmunds in 1828, also in front of a large and appreciative audience. The lady next to him in the bonnet and carrying a black bag is Kate Webster. The bag contains the head of her mistress whom she beat to death, cut into pieces and boiled in the kitchen boiler. She is said to have gone round the local shops offering cheap dripping for sale. She was turned off, as they used to say, in July 1879.'

Leaving the business room, they paused at two elegant rosewood display cases which stood one each side of the door. The left-hand one contained a clutter of small objects which were all neatly labelled; a doll and a solitaire set with small coloured marbles, both of which had belonged to the Queen as a child; a fan, early Christmas cards, scent bottles in crystal, silver gilt and enamel, and a collection of small silver objects, waist hook, chatelaine, prayer-book and posy-holder. But it was the right-hand case which drew their eyes. Here were less agreeable mementoes, an extension of Ambrose's museum of crime. He explained:

'That tag end of rope is part of the executioner's rope which hanged Dr Thomas Neill Cream, the Lambeth poisoner, in November 1892. The stained linen nightdress with the broderie anglaise frills was worn by Constance Kent. It's not the nightdress she had on when she slit the throat of her small stepbrother but it has a certain interest all the same. That pair of handcuffs with the key were used on young Courvoisier who murdered his master, Lord William Russell, in 1840. The spectacles are a pair which belonged to Dr Crippen. As he was hanged in November 1910 he's really nine years out of my period but I couldn't resist them.'

Ivo asked:

'And the marble of a baby's arm?'

'That hasn't any criminal interest as far as I know. It should be in Memento Mori or in the other cabinet but I hadn't time to rearrange the exhibits. But it doesn't look out of place among the props of murder. The man who sold it to me would approve. He told me that he kept imagining that the limb was oozing blood.'

Clarissa hadn't spoken and, glancing at her, Cordelia saw that her eyes were fixed on the marble with a mixture of fear and revulsion which none of the other exhibits had evoked. The arm, a chubby replica in white marble, lay on a purple cushion bound with cord. Cordelia herself thought it an unpleasant object, sentimental and morbid, useless and undecorative, and to that extent not untypical of the minor art of its age. Clarissa said:

'But it's perfectly hateful! It's disgusting! Where on earth did you pick it up, Ambrose?'

'In London. A man I know. It may be the only extant copy of one of the limbs of the royal children made for Queen Victoria at Osborne House, said to be by Mary Thornycroft. This one could be poor Pussy, the Princess Royal. It's either that or a memorial piece. And if you dislike it, Clarissa, you should see the Osborne collection. They look like the remnants of a holocaust, as if the Prince Consort had descended on the royal nursery with a machete, as he may well have been tempted to do, poor man.'

Clarissa said:

'It's repulsive! What on earth possessed you, Ambrose? Get rid of it.'

'Certainly not. It may be unique. I regard it as an interesting addition to my minor Victoriana.'

Roma said:

'I've seen the Osborne pieces. I find them repulsive too. But they throw an interesting light on the Victorian mind, the Queen's in particular.'

'Well, this throws an interesting light on Ambrose's mind.'

Ivo said quietly:

'As a piece of marble, it's rather well done. It's the association you find unpleasant, perhaps. The death or mutilation of a child is always distressing, don't you think, Clarissa?'

But Clarissa appeared not to have heard. She turned away and said:

'For God's sake don't start arguing about it. Just get rid of it, Ambrose. And now I need a drink and my lunch.'

CHAPTER ELEVEN

Half a mile from the shore Simon Lessing stopped his slow and regular crawl stroke, turned on his back and let his eyes rest on the horizon. The sea was empty. Faced with that shuddering waste of water, it was possible to imagine that there was emptiness also behind him, that the island and its castle had gently subsided under the waves, silently and without turbulence, and that he floated alone in a blue infinity of sea. This self-induced sense of isolation excited but didn't frighten him. Nothing about the sea ever did. Here was the element in which he felt most at peace; guilt, anxiety, failure washed away in a gentle and perpetual baptism of redemption.

He was glad that Clarissa hadn't wanted him tagging along behind her on the tour of the castle. There were rooms he would be interested to see, but there would be time enough to explore on his own. And it would give him another excuse to keep out of her way. He couldn't swim more than twice a day at most without it seeming odd and deliberately unsociable but it would seem perfectly natural to ask if he might wander off to explore the castle. Perhaps the weekend might not be so terrifying after all.

He had only to thrust himself upright to feel the bite of the cold undercurrent. But now he floated, spread-eagled under the sun, feeling the sea creeping over his chest and arms as softly warm as a bath. From time to time he let his face submerge, opening his eyes on the thin film of green, letting it wash lightly over his eyeballs. And deep down there was the knowledge, unfrightening and almost comforting, that he only had to let himself go, to give himself up to the power and gentleness of the sea and there need never again be guilt or anxiety or failure. He knew that he wouldn't do it; the thought was a small self-indulgence which, like a drug, could be safely experimented with as long as the doses were small and one stayed in control. And he was in control. In a few minutes it would be time to turn and strike for the shore, to think about luncheon and Clarissa and getting through the next two days without embarrassment or disaster. But now there was this peace, this emptiness, this wholeness.

It was only at moments like this that he could think without pain of his father. This was how he must have died, swimming alone in the Aegean on that summer morning, finding the tide too strong for him, letting himself go at last without a struggle, without fear, giving himself up to the sea he loved, embracing its majesty and its peace. He had imagined that death so often on his solitary swims that the old nightmares were almost exorcized.

He no longer awoke in the darkness of the early hours as he had in those first months after he had learned his father's death, sweating with terror, desperately tearing at the blankets as they dragged him down, living every second of those last dreadful minutes, the stinging eyes, the agony as he glimpsed through the waves the lost, receding, unattainable shore. But it hadn't been like that. It couldn't have been like that. His father had died secure in his great love, unresisting and at peace.

It was time to turn back. He twisted under the water and began again his steady powerful crawl. And now his feet found the shingle and he pulled himself ashore, colder and more tired than he had expected. Looking up, he saw with surprise that there was someone waiting for him, a dark-clad, still figure standing like a guardian beside his pile of clothes. He shook the water from his eyes and saw it was Tolly.

He came up to her. At first she didn't speak but bent and picked up his towel and handed it to him. Panting and shivering he began patting dry his arms and neck, embarrassed by her steady gaze, wondering why she was there. Then she said:

'Why don't you leave?'

She must have seen his incomprehension. She said again:

'Why don't you leave, leave this place, leave her?' Her voice, as always, was low but harsh, almost expressionless. He stared at her, wild-eyed under the dripping hair.

'Leave Clarissa! Why should I? What do you mean?'

'She doesn't want you. Haven't you noticed that? You aren't happy. Why go on pretending?'

He cried out in protest.

'But I am happy! And where can I go? My aunt wouldn't want me back. I haven't any money.'

She said:

'There's a spare room in my flat. You could have that for a start. It isn't much, a child's room. But you could stay there until you found something better.'

A child's room. He remembered hearing that she had once had a child, a girl who had died. No one ever spoke about her now. He didn't want to think about her. He had thought enough about dying and death. He said:

'But how could I find somewhere? What would I live on?'

'You're seventeen, aren't you? You're not a child. You've got five O-levels. You could find something to do. I was working at fifteen. Most children in the world start younger.'

'But doing what? I'm going to be a pianist. I need Clarissa's money.'

'Ah yes,' she said, 'you need Clarissa's money.'

And so, he thought, so do you. That's what this is all about. He felt a surge of confidence, of adult cunning. He wasn't a child to be so easily fooled. Hadn't he always sensed her dislike of him, caught that contemptuous glance as she set down his breakfast on those days when she and he were alone in the flat, watched the silent resentment with which she gathered up his laundry, cleaned his room. If he weren't there she wouldn't need to come in except twice a week to check that all was well. Of course she wanted him out of the way. Probably she expected to be left something in Clarissa's will; she must be ten years younger even if she didn't look it. And she was only a servant after all. What right had she to upset him, to criticize Clarissa, to patronize him, offering her sordid little room as if it were a favour. It would be as bad as Mornington Avenue; worse. The small, seductive devil at the back of his mind whispered its enticement. However difficult things might be at times he would be crazy to give up the patronage of Clarissa, who was rich, to put himself at the mercy of Tolly, who was poor.

Perhaps something of this reached her. She said almost humbly but with no trace of solicitation:

'You'd be under no obligation. It's just a room.' He wished she would go. Yet he couldn't walk away, couldn't start dressing while that dark, oppressive figure stood there seeming to block the whole beach. He drew himself up and said as stiffly as his shivering body would permit:

'Thank you, but I'm perfectly happy as I am.'

'Suppose she gets tired of you like she did your father.' He gaped at her, clutching his towel. Above them a gull shrieked, shrill as a tormented child. He whispered:

'What do you mean? She loved my father! They loved each other! He explained to me before he left us, mother and me. It was the most marvellous thing that had ever happened to him. He had no choice.'

'There's always a choice.'

'But they adored each other! He was so happy.'

'Then why did he drown himself?'

He cried:

'It isn't true! I don't believe you!'

'You don't have to if you don't want to. Just remember it when your turn comes.'

'But why should he do it? Why?'

'To make her feel sorry, I suppose. Isn't that usually why people kill themselves? But he should have known. Clarissa doesn't understand about guilt.'

'But they told me that there was an inquest. They found that it was accidental death. And he didn't leave a note.'

'If he did they didn't see it. It was Clarissa who found his clothes on the beach.'

His eyes fell to where his own trousers and jacket were jumbled under a stone. A picture came unbidden into his mind, so clear that it might have been memory. The gritty sand, hot as cinders, an alien sea layered in purple and blue to the horizon, Clarissa standing with the wind billowing in her sleeves, the note in her hand. And then the tattered scraps of white, fluttering down like petals, briefly littering the sea before floating and dissolving in the surf. It had been three weeks before his father's body, what was left of it, had been washed up. But bones and flesh, even when the fish have finished with it, lasted longer than a scrap of paper. It wasn't true. None of it was true. As she had told him, there was always a choice. He would choose not to believe.

He looked down so that he need not meet her eyes, that compelling stare which was much more convincing than any words she could speak. There was a swathe of seaweed wound round his calf, brown as a gash on which the blood had dried. He bent and plucked at it. It tightened, a slimy ligature. He knew that she was watching him. Then she said:

'Suppose she died. What would you do then?'

'Why should she die? She isn't sick, is she? She never said anything to me about being sick. What's wrong with her?'

'Nothing. Nothing's wrong with her.'

'Then why are you talking about dying?'

'She thinks she's going to die. Sometimes when people think that strongly enough they do die.'

His heart surged with relief. But that was ridiculous! She was trying to frighten him. Everything was plain to him now. She had always been jealous of him just as she had been jealous of his father. He picked up his jacket and tried to sound dignified through the chattering of his teeth.

'If she does die I'm sure you'll be remembered. I shouldn't worry if I were you. And now perhaps you'll let me get dressed. I'm cold and it's time for luncheon.'

As soon as the words were out he felt ashamed. She turned away without another word. And then she looked back and their eyes met for the last time. He knew what she must see in his, the shame, the fear. He was prepared to encounter anger and resentment. But what he hadn't expected to see was pity.

CHAPTER TWELVE

A long arcade, brick-built but with columns and arches of patterned stonework, led from the west side of the castle, past a rose garden and formal pool, to the theatre. Making his solitary way, rather late, to watch part of the final run-through, Ivo could picture the slow after-dinner procession of Victorian guests passing under the arches, pale arms and necks above the richness of satin and velvet, jewels sparkling on bosoms and in the intricately piled hair, the white shirt fronts of the men gleaming in the moonlight. The theatre itself surprised him, less by the perfection of its proportions, which he had expected, than by its contrast to the rest of the castle. He wondered whether it was the work of a different architect; he would have to ask Ambrose. But if Godwin had been responsible, it was apparent that his client's insistence on opulence and ostentation had prevailed over any inclination he himself might have had for lightness or restraint. Even now, with only half the house lights lit, the theatre glowed with richness. The deep red velvet of the curtains and seats had faded but was still remarkably well preserved. The candle lighting had been replaced by electricity – the conversion must have given Ambrose a pang – but the delicate convolvulus light-shades were still in use and the original crystal chandelier still glittered from the domed ceiling. Everywhere there was ornament, sumptuous, florid, occasionally charming, but always splendid in its craftsmanship. Across the front of the boxes gilded, plump-buttocked cherubs held swags of flowers or lifted trumpets to pouting mouths, while the richly carved royal box with its Prince of Wales feathers and twin seats, regal as thrones, must have satisfied even the most ardent monarchist's view of what was owing to the heir apparent. Ivo had settled himself at the end of the fourth row of the stalls with no intention of staying for more than an hour. He was anxious to disabuse the cast of any idea they might have that he was on the island primarily to review their performance and this casual appearance to watch the final rehearsal would remind them that he was less interested in what they managed to make of Webster's tragedy than in the glories, scandals and legends of the theatre itself. He was glad that the seats, designed for broad Victorian rumps, were so luxuriously comfortable. The afternoon was always the worst time for him when his luncheon, however frugal, lay heavily on his distorted stomach and the monstrous spleen seemed to grow and harden under his supporting hands. He twisted himself more comfortably into the velvet plush, aware of Cordelia sitting silent and upright further along the row, and tried to fix his attention on the stage.

The cast had obviously been instructed by De Ville, a director more at home with the moderns, to concentrate on the sense and let the verse look after itself, a ploy which would have been disastrous with Shakespeare but which succeeded well enough with Webster's rougher metre. And at least it made for pace. Ivo had always believed that there was only one way to direct Webster, as a highly stylized drama of manners, the characters, mere ritual personifications of lust, decadence and sexual rapacity, moving in a stately pavane towards the inevitable orgiastic triumph of madness and death. But De Ville, half sunk in lugubrious disgust at finding himself actually directing amateurs, was obviously aiming at some semblance of realism. It would be interesting to see how he dealt with the more gratuitous horrors. He would be lucky to get away with the proffered severed hand and the gaggle of madmen without a suppressed giggle or two. Revenge tragedy was hardly a genre for the inexperienced; but then, what classic was? Certainly this charnel-house poet, heaping horror on horror until the appetite sickened, and then suddenly piercing the heart with lines of redeeming beauty, demanded more than the present enthusiastic bunch of play-actors. Still, De Ville only had to get one performance out of them. It wasn't what you could raise yourself to on one night but what you could continue to do, night after night and two matinées a week, for three months or more, that marked the professional from the amateur. He had known that the play was to be done in Victorian costume. The idea had seemed to him an eccentric, slightly ludicrous conceit. But he could see that it had its uses. The stage and the small auditorium fused into one claustrophobic cockpit of evil, the high-necked dresses and the bustles hinted at a sexuality which was the more lascivious because covert, overlaid with Victorian respectability. And there was some wit in the decision to dress Bosola as a kilted Highlander although it was hard to imagine Victoria's good old Brown in this complex creature of nihilism and thwarted nobility.

The four principals had been rehearsing now for nearly fifty-five minutes. De Ville had been leaving them pretty much to themselves, his heavy, frog-like face expressing nothing but a settled gloom. Probably he had resented being dragged away from his post-prandial nap and subjected to yet another sea trip merely to indulge Clarissa's wish for a final run-through in costume of her more important scenes. Ivo glanced at his watch. Boredom was taking hold of him as he knew it would, but the effort of moving seemed too great. He glanced along the row and watched Cordelia's face, upturned to the stage, the firm yet delicate chin, the sweet curve of the throat. He thought: two years ago I should have been mildly agonizing over her, scheming how I might get into her bed before the weekend was out, fretting at the possibility of failure. He recalled his past exploits, less with disgust than with a detached wonder that so much time and thought and energy should have been expended on such petty expedients against boredom. The trouble had been so disproportionate to the satisfaction, the desire less urgent than the need to prove himself still desirable. What, after all, would getting into bed with her have meant but a small fillip to the ego, ranking only a little higher than the quality of the food and wine and the wit of the after-dinner conversation as an index of the success of the weekend. Always he had aimed to conduct his affairs on the level of a civilized, uncommitted exchange of pleasure. And always they had ended in rows, recriminations, in messiness and disgust. It had been no different with Clarissa except the rows had been more bitter, the disgust more lasting. But then, with Clarissa he had made the mistake of letting himself become involved. With Clarissa, at least for those first six months when he had been cuckolding Simon's father, he had known again the agonies, the ecstasies, the uncertainties of love.

He made himself look again at the stage. They were playing the second scene of Act Three. Clarissa, dressed in a voluminous, lace-trimmed dressing-gown was seated at her looking-glass with Cariola in attendance, hairbrush in hand. The dressing-table, like all the props, was authentic, borrowed, he supposed, from the castle. There was more than one advantage in staging the play in the eighteen nineties. The scene was being played with the accompaniment of a musical-box which had been placed on the dressing-table and which tinkled out a medley of Scottish airs. That too was probably another of Ambrose's pieces of Victoriana, but he suspected that the idea was Clarissa's. The scene began well enough. He had forgotten how Clarissa could take on an almost luminous beauty, the power of that high, slightly cracked voice, the grace with which she used her arms and body. She wasn't a Suzman or a Mirren, but she did manage to convey something of the high erotic excitement, the vulnerability and the rashness of a woman deeply in love. That wasn't surprising; it was a part she had played often enough in real life. But to produce such conviction with a leading man who obviously saw Antonio as an English country gentleman sinning above his station was something of an achievement. But Cariola was a disaster, nervous and skittish, tripping across the stage in her goffered cap like a soubrette in a French farce. When she had stumbled for the third time over her lines De Ville called out impatiently:

'You've only to remember three lines, God help you. And cut

out the coyness. You're not playing *No, No, Nanette.* All right. Take it from the beginning of the scene.'

Clarissa protested:

'But it needs pace, lightness. I lose the impetus if I have to keep going back.'

He reiterated:

'Take it from the beginning.'

She hesitated, shrugged, then sat silent. The cast glanced at each other furtively, shuffled, waited. Ivo's interest suddenly rekindled. He thought:

'She's losing her temper. With her, that's halfway to losing her nerve.'

Suddenly she took the music-box and slammed down the lid. The crack was as sharp as a gunshot. The tinkling little tune stopped. It was followed by absolute silence as the cast seemed to hold their breath. Then Clarissa came forward to the footlights:

'That bloody box is getting on my nerves. If we have to have background music in this scene, then surely Ambrose can find something more suitable than those damn Scottish tunes. They're driving me mad, so God knows what they'll do to the audience.'

Ambrose called quietly from the back of the auditorium. Ivo was surprised to hear him and wondered how long he had been silently sitting there.

'It was your idea, as I remember.'

'I wanted a musical-box but not a bloody Scottish medley. And do we have to have an audience? Cordelia, can't you find something useful to do? God knows, we're paying you enough. Tolly could do with some help ironing the costumes, unless you propose to sit on your ass all afternoon.'

The girl got to her feet. Even in the half-light, Ivo could detect the flush rising on her throat, could see her mouth half open in protest, then close resolutely. Despite those candid almost judgemental eyes, the disconcerting honesty, the impression of controlled competence, she was at heart a sensitive child. Anger rose in him, satisfyingly strong and uncomplicated. He rejoiced that he could feel it. With difficulty, he pulled himself erect. He was aware that all eyes had turned towards him. He said calmly:

'Miss Gray and I will take a walk. The performance hasn't been exactly riveting so far and the air outside will be fresher.'

When they were outside, their going silently watched by the cast, she said:

'Thank you, Mr Knightley.'

He smiled. Suddenly he felt well, extraordinarily well, his whole body mysteriously lighter.

'I'm afraid I'd make a poor dancer in my present state, and if I had to cast you as any character in *Emma* it certainly wouldn't be poor Harriet. You must excuse Clarissa. When she's nervous, she's apt to become rude.'

'That may be her misfortune but I don't find it particularly excusable.'

He added:

'And public rudeness provokes in me the kind of childish retort which is only satisfying for the second after it's spoken. She'll apologize very prettily when she next sees you alone.'

'I'm sure she will.'

Suddenly she turned to him and smiled:

'Actually I should like a walk if you won't find it too exhausting.'

She was, he thought, the only person on the island who could say that to him without making him feel either irritated or embarrassed. He said:

'What about the beach?'

'I'd like that.'

'It'll be slow going, I'm afraid.'

'That doesn't matter.'

How very sweet she was, with that gentle, self-contained dignity. He smiled and held out his hand to her.

'"Upon such sacrifices, my Cordelia, the Gods themselves throw incense." Well, shall we go?'

CHAPTER THIRTEEN

They trudged slowly side by side along the very edge of the tide where the firmer sand made the going easiest. The beach was narrow, cut by rotting breakwaters and bounded by a low stone wall beyond which rose the tree-covered, friable cliffs. Much of the bank must once have been planted. Between the beeches and the oaks were clumps of laurel, old rose bushes twined among the thicker foliage of rhododendrons, woody geraniums distorted by the wind, hydrangeas in their autumn shades of bronze, lime-yellow and purple, so much more subtle and interesting, thought Cordelia, than the gaudy heads of high summer. She felt at peace with her companion and wished for a moment that she could confide in him, that her job needn't impose such a weight of deception. For ten minutes they walked in undemanding silence. Then he said:

'This may be a stupid question. Gray isn't an uncommon name. But you're not by any chance related to Redvers Gray?'

'He was my father.'

'There's something about the eyes. I only met him once, but his was a face one didn't forget. He had a great influence on my generation at Cambridge. He had the gift of making rhetoric sound sincere. Now that the rhetoric and the dream are not only discredited, which is discouraging, but unfashionable, which is fatal, I suppose he is almost forgotten. But I should like to have known him.'

Cordelia said:

'So should I.'

He glanced down at her.

'It was like that, was it? The revolutionary idealist dedicated to mankind in the abstract but not much good at caring for his own child. Not that I can criticize. I haven't done too well with mine. Children need you to talk to them, play with them, give time to them when they're young. If you can't be bothered it isn't surprising if, when they're adolescents, you find that you don't much like each other. But then, by the time mine were adolescents I didn't much like their mother either.'

Cordelia said:

'I think I could have liked him if we'd had time. I did spend six months with him and the comrades in Germany and Italy. But then he died.'

'You make death sound like a betrayal. And so, of course, it is.'

Cordelia thought of those six months. Half a year of cooking for the comrades, shopping for the comrades, carrying messages, sometimes not without danger, finding rooms, propitiating landladies and shopkeepers, sewing for the comrades. They and her father believed implicitly in equality for women without troubling to acquire the basic domestic skills which would have made that equality possible. And it was for that precarious nomadic existence that he had taken her from the Convent, made it impossible for her to take up her place at Cambridge. She no longer felt any particular resentment. That period of her life was passed, finished. And she hoped that they had given something to each other, if only trust. She had early dropped Redvers from her name telling herself that it was an unnecessary piece of cabin luggage. She had been reading Browning at the time. Now she wondered if it had been a more significant rejection, even a small revenge. The thought was unwelcome and she thrust it away. She heard him say:

'And what about your education? One was always seeing pictures of him being dragged off by the police. That's all very admirable in youth no doubt. In middle age it begins to look embarrassing and ridiculous. I don't remember hearing about a daughter, or of a wife for that matter.'

'My mother died when I was born.'

'And who looked after you?'

'I was placed with foster parents for most of the time. Then when I was eleven, I won a scholarship to the Convent of the Holy Child. That was a mistake, not the scholarship but the choice of school. They muddled my name with another C. Gray, who was a Roman Catholic. I don't think father much liked it, but by the time he bothered to reply to the Education Officer's letter I was settled and they didn't like to move me. And I wanted to stay.'

He laughed. 'Redvers Gray with a convent-educated daughter! And they didn't succeed in converting you? That would have taught Papa, dedicated atheist, to answer his letters more promptly.'

'No, they didn't convert me. But then they didn't try. I didn't believe but I was happy in my invincible ignorance. It's rather an enviable state. And I liked the Convent. I suppose it was the first time I felt secure. Life wasn't messy any more.'

She had never before spoken so freely of her time at the Convent, she who was so slow to confide. She wondered whether this unusual frankness was possible only because she knew he must be dying. The thought seemed to her ignoble and she tried to put it from her. He said:

'You agree with Yeats. "How but in custom and in ceremony are innocence and beauty born?" I can see that it must have been reassuring, even one's sins neatly categorized into venial and mortal. Mortal sin. I like the expression even if I reject the dogma. It has a note of splendid finality. It dignifies wrongdoing, almost gives it form and substance. One can imagine oneself saying, "What have I done with my mortal sin? I must have put it down somewhere." One could carry it around, neatly packaged.'

Suddenly he stumbled. Cordelia put out her hand to steady him. His palm in hers was cold, the dry skin sliding over the bones. She saw that he looked very tired. The walk over the shingle had not, after all, been easy. She said:

'Let's sit for a while.'

There was a kind of grotto above them cut out of the cliff, with a mosaic terrace, now fractured and almost overgrown, and a curved marble seat. She helped pull him up the slope, watching as his feet found convenient clumps of grass and half hidden stone steps. The back of the seat, warmed by the sun, still struck a little chill through her thin shirt. They sat side by side, untouching, and lifted their faces to the sun. Above them hung a beech tree. Its trunk and boughs had the tender luminosity of a girl's arm, its leaves, just beginning to turn with their autumn gold, were veined marvels of reflected light. The air was very still and quiet, the silence pierced only by the occasional cry of a gull, while below them the sea hissed and withdrew in its everlasting restlessness.

After a few minutes, his eyes still closed he said:

'I suppose a mortal sin has to be something special, something more original and momentous than the expedients, the meannesses, the small delinquencies which make up everyday living for most of us?'

Cordelia said:

'It's a grievous offence against the law of God, which puts the soul at risk of eternal damnation. There has to be full knowledge and consent. It's all laid down. Any RC will explain it to you.'

He said:

'Something evil, if the word means anything to you, if you believe in the existence of evil.'

Cordelia thought of the Convent chapel, altar candles flickering fitfully, her own bowed lace-covered head among the ranks of muttering conformists. 'And deliver us from evil.' For six years she had repeated these words at least twice a day long before she had ever asked herself what it was from which she craved deliverance. It had taken her first case, after Bernie's death, to teach her that. She could still recall, in sleeping and waking dreams, the horror which she had not in fact actually seen; a white elongated neck, a boy's disfigured face drooping from the noose, the twisting feet pointing to the floor. It was when she had finally stared into the face of his murderer that she had known about evil. She said:

'Yes, I believe in the existence of evil.'

'Then Clarissa once did something which you might dignify as evil. I don't know whether the good sisters would designate it as mortal sin. But there was knowledge and consent. And I've a feeling that, for Clarissa, it could prove mortal.'

She didn't speak. She wouldn't make it easy for him. But there was no self-control in her silence. She knew he would go on.

'It happened during the run of *Macbeth* in July 1980, Tolly – Miss Tolgarth – had had an illegitimate daughter four years earlier. There was no particular secret about it, most of us in Clarissa's set knew about Viccy. She was a sweet child. Grave-faced, rather silent, intelligent I think, as far as one can judge at that age. Sometimes, but only rarely, Tolly would bring her to the theatre, but most of the time she kept her private and working lives separate. She paid a child-minder to look after Viccy while she was working and it must have been convenient having mainly an evening job. She wouldn't take any money from the father. I think she was too possessive about Viccy to want to share even the cost of her food. Then two days before Clarissa opened in *Macbeth* it happened. Clarissa was at the theatre – there was a final rehearsal – and the minder was in charge of Viccy. The child had slipped out into the street and was playing with something in the gutter behind a parked lorry. It was the usual tragedy. The driver didn't see her and reversed. She was horribly injured. They rushed her to hospital and operated and she stood that very well. We thought that she'd make it. But on the first night of *Macbeth* the hospital telephoned at nine forty-five to say that there had been a relapse and to ask Tolly to go at once. Clarissa took the call. She had just come offstage for her costume change before the Third Act. She was appalled at the thought of losing her dresser at that moment. She took the message and put down the receiver. Then she told Tolly that the hospital wanted her to visit but that there was no hurry, after the performance would be all right. When Tolly wanted to ring back she wouldn't let her. And shortly after the performance ended, the hospital rang again to say that the child was dead.'

'How do you know this?'

'Because I took the trouble to get in touch with the hospital and ask about that first message. And because I was there in Clarissa's dressing-room when it came. You could say I was in something of a privileged position at the time. I wasn't with them when Clarissa finally told Tolly that she couldn't leave. I'd have stopped that; at least I hope I would. But I was there when the call came through. Then I went back to my seat. When the play ended and I went backstage to take Clarissa out to supper, Tolly was still there. And fifteen minutes later the hospital telephoned to say the child was dead.'

'And when you learned what had happened, was that when you stopped being a privileged person?'

'I should like to be able to tell you that it was. The truth is less flattering. She became my mistress for two reasons; firstly because I'd gained some reputation and Clarissa has always found power an aphrodisiac, and secondly because she imagined that a fuck a week would ensure her good notices. When she discovered her mistake – like most men I'm capable of betrayal but not of that particular betrayal – the privileges ceased. There are some favours it is unwise to pay for in advance.'

'Why are you telling me this?'

'Because I like you. Because I don't want to have this weekend spoilt by watching yet another person I respect being seduced by her charm. She has charm even if she hasn't bothered yet to exercise it on you. I don't want to see you behaving like all the others. I suspect that you may be possessed of that divine common sense which is impervious to the blandishments of egotism, whether sexual or otherwise, but who can be sure? So I am committing one more small act of betrayal to strengthen you against temptation.'

'Who was the child's father?'

'No one knows, except presumably Tolly, and she isn't saying. The question is, who did Clarissa think he was?'

Cordelia glanced at him.

'Not her husband?'

'Poor besotted Lessing? Possible I suppose, but hardly probable. He and Clarissa had only been married a year. Admittedly, she was already giving him hell, but I can't see him choosing that way of revenge. My guess is that it was De Ville. His only requirements are that the woman is comely and willing and not an actress. He's reputed to be impotent with anyone who holds an Equity card, but that may be only his device for keeping his professional and private lives separate.'

'The man who is directing the Webster? The one who's here now? Do you think that Clarissa was in love with him?'

'I don't know what Clarissa means by that word. She may have wanted him if only to prove that she could get him. One thing's certain; if he wouldn't play then she wouldn't easily forget an affair with her own dresser.'

'Why do you think he's here? He's famous, he doesn't have to bother with an amateur production, particularly out of London.'

'Why are any of us here? He may see the island as a future dramatic Glyndebourne, a world-famous centre for experimental drama. This may just be a way of getting his foot in the door. After all, he's not exactly sought-after now. His tricks were much admired in their day, but there are some clever young dogs coming along now. And Ambrose, if he's prepared to spend money, could make something of his Courcy Festival. Not commercially, of course; a theatre which only seats a hundred comfortably can hardly be that, particularly when it could always be cut off by a storm on the first night. But he could have some fun with it once he's got rid of Clarissa.'

'And does he want to get rid of Clarissa?'

'Oh, yes,' said Ivo easily. 'Hadn't you noticed that? She's trying to take him over, him and his theatre and his island. He likes his private kingdom. Clarissa is a particularly persistent invader.'

Cordelia thought of the child, lying alone on her high, aseptic hospital bed behind the drawn curtains. Had she been conscious? Had she known that she was dying? Had she perhaps cried out for her mother? Had she gone frightened and alone into that last goodnight? She said:

'I don't see how Clarissa can live with that memory.'

'I'm not sure that she can. When a person is terrified of dying it could be because with one part of their minds they feel that they deserve it.'

'How do you know she's terrified?'

'Because there are some emotions which even an actress as experienced as Clarissa can't altogether hide.'

He turned to her, saw the expression of her face, upturned to the glitter of shuddering green and gold, and said quietly:

'There are, perhaps, excuses one should make for her. And if not excuses, explanations. She was about to make an important costume change. She couldn't have managed it herself, and there wasn't another dresser available.'

'Did she even try to find one?'

'I don't suppose so. You see, from her point of view, she wasn't in the world of hospitals and sick children. She was Lady Macbeth. She was at Dunsinane Castle. I doubt whether she would have left the theatre to go to her own dying child, not at that moment. It didn't occur to her that someone else might want to.'

Cordelia cried:

'But you can't excuse it! You can't explain it. You don't really believe that a play, any play, any performance is more important than a dying child!'

'I don't suppose for one moment that she really believed the child to be dying, assuming that she gave the matter thought.'

'But is that what you believe? That a performance, any performance, could be more important?'

He smiled:

'Now we're edging towards that old philosophical minefield. If the building's on fire and you can only rescue a syphilitic old tramp or a Velasquez which, or who, gets incinerated?'

'No, we aren't. We're talking about a dying child wanting her mother, balancing that need against a performance of *Macbeth*. And I get tired of that old burning building analogy. I should throw the Velasquez out of the window and start lugging the tramp to safety. The real moral choice is when you find that he's too heavy. Do you escape alone or keep trying and risk getting incinerated with him?'

'Oh, that's easy. Obviously you escape alone and without leaving the decision too conscientiously to the last possible moment. About the child; no, I don't believe that any performance could be more important, certainly none that Clarissa is capable of giving. Does that satisfy you?'

'I don't understand how Miss Tolgarth can go on working for her. I couldn't.'

'But you will? I confess I'm intrigued about your precise function here. But presumably you won't throw in your hand?'

'But that's different; at least I shall persuade myself that it is. I'm just a temporary employee. But Tolly believed Clarissa when she was told that there was no immediate danger; she trusted her. How can she stay with her now?'

'They've been together almost all their lives. Tolly's mother was Clarissa's nurse. The family with a small 'f' served the Family with a large 'F' for three generations. They're born to be served, she was born to serve them. Perhaps, given the habit of subservience, a dead child here or there doesn't make any difference.'

'But that's horrible! It's ridiculous, and degrading. It's Victorian!'

'Don't you believe it! The instinct for worship is remarkably persistent. What else is religious belief? Tolly's lucky to have her God walking the earth with shoes that need cleaning, clothes that need folding, hair that needs brushing.'

'But she can't want to go on serving. She can't like Clarissa.'

'What has liking to do with it? Though she slay me yet shall I trust her. It's a perfectly common phenomenon. But I admit I do sometimes wonder what would happen if she faced the truth about her own feelings. If any of us did, come to that. It's getting colder, isn't it? Don't you feel it? Perhaps it's time we were getting back.'

CHAPTER FOURTEEN

They hardly spoke on the way back to the castle. For Cordelia, the sunlight had drained out of the day. The beauty of sea and shore passed unregarded by her desolated heart. Ivo was obviously very tired by the time they reached the terrace and said that he would rest in his room; he wouldn't bother with tea. Cordelia told herself that it was her job to stay close to Clarissa however unwelcome that might be to both of them. But it took an effort of will before she could make her way back to the theatre, and it was a relief to find that the rehearsal still wasn't over. She stood for a minute at the back of the auditorium, then made her way to her own room. The communicating door was open and she could see Tolly moving from bathroom to bedroom. But the thought of having to speak to her was intolerable and Cordelia made her escape.

Almost on impulse she opened the door next to her own which gave access to the tower. A circular staircase of elaborately decorated wrought iron curved upwards into semi-darkness lit only by occasional slit windows less than a brick in width. She could see there was a light-switch, but preferred to climb steadily upwards in the gloom in what seemed an endless spiral. But at last she reached the top and found herself in a small, light-filled circular room with six tall windows. The room was unfurnished except for one cane armchair with a curved back and was obviously used to store acquisitions for which Ambrose hadn't yet found a place or which he had inherited from the previous owner; chiefly a collection of Victorian toys. There was a wooden horse on wheels, a Noah's ark with carved animals, three china dolls with bland faces and stuffed limbs, a table of mechanical toys including an organ-grinder with his monkey, a set of cat musicians on a revolving platform, gaudily dressed in satin and each with his instrument, a grenadier toy soldier with his drum, a wooden musical-box.

The view was spectacular. The whole island, seen as if from an aircraft, was a neatly patterned coloured map precisely placed in a crinkled sea. To the east was a smudge which must be the Isle of Wight. To the north the Dorset coast looked surprisingly close; she could almost make out the stunted pier and the coloured terraces. She gazed down over the island, at the northern marshes fringed with white gulls, the central uplands, the fields, small patches of green amid the many-hued curdle of autumnal trees, the brown cliffs sliding down to the shore, the spire of the Church rising amid the beeches, the roof of the arcade leading to a toy theatre. From his cottage in the stable block the foreshortened figure of Oldfield crept, a bucket in either hand, and, as she watched, Roma emerged from the copse of beech trees which lined the lawn and made her way, hands hunched in her pockets, towards the castle. Across the grass a peacock stalked, dragging his tattered tail.

Here, slung between earth and sky in a brick-enclosed eyrie, the sound of the sea was a low moan almost indistinguishable from the sighing of the wind. Suddenly Cordelia felt immensely lonely. The job which had promised so much seemed now a humiliating waste of time and effort. She no longer cared who was sending the messages or why. She felt that she hardly cared whether Clarissa lived or died. She wondered what was happening at Kingly Street, how Miss Maudsley was coping, whether Mr Morgan had come to see to the name-plate. And thinking of him reminded her of Sir George. He had paid her to do a job. She was here to protect Clarissa, not to judge her. And there were only two more days to be got through. By Sunday it would all be over and she would be free to get back to London; need never hear Clarissa's name again. She recalled Bernie's words when he had once rebuked her for being over-fastidious:

'You can't make moral judgements about your clients in this job, mate. Start that and you may as well shut up shop.'

She turned from the window and, on impulse, opened the musical-box. The cylinder slowly revolved and the delicate metal filaments plucked out the tune 'Greensleeves'. Then one by one she set the other mechanical toys in motion. The grenadier thumped his drum; the cats revolved, mouths grinning, jerking their satined arms; cymbals clashed; the plaintive 'Greensleeves' was lost in the discordant din. And thus, in a gentle cacophony of childish sounds, which couldn't entirely shut out from her mind the image of a dying child but which helped to release some tension in her, Cordelia stared down over Ambrose's coloured kingdom.

CHAPTER FIFTEEN

Ivo had been wrong. Clarissa didn't apologize for her behaviour at the rehearsal but she did exert herself to be particularly charming to Cordelia over tea. It was a boisterous and protracted feast of sandwiches and over-rich cake, and it was after six before the launch bearing De Ville and the other principals back to Speymouth finally drew away from the quay. Clarissa spent the hour before it was time to dress for dinner playing Scrabble in the library with Ambrose. She played noisily and badly, constantly calling out to Cordelia to look up challenged words in the dictionary or to support her against Ambrose's allegations that she was cheating. Cordelia, happily engrossed with old copies of the *Illustrated London News* and the *Strand Magazine*, in which she could read the Sherlock Holmes stories as they had originally appeared, wished that she could have been left in peace. Simon was apparently to entertain them with music after dinner and the distant sound of Chopin from the drawing-room where he was practising was pleasantly restful and evocative of her schooldays. Ivo was still in his room and Roma sat in silence with the weekly journals and *Private Eye*. The library, with its barrel roof and carved brass-fronted bookcases set between the four tall windows, was one of the most beautifully proportioned in the castle. The whole of the southern wall was taken up with one immense window decorated with round panes of coloured glass. In the daytime the window framed nothing but a view of sea and sky. But now the library was in darkness except for the three pools of light from the desk lamps, and the great window rose like a sheet of rain-washed marble, blue-black and smudged with a few high stars. It was a pity, thought Cordelia, that, even here, Clarissa was incapable of occupying herself in peaceable silence.

When it was time to dress they went up together and Cordelia unlocked both rooms and made a check on Clarissa's bedroom before she went in. All was well. She dressed quickly, put out the light, then sat quietly at her window looking out at the distant clumps of trees, black against the night sky, and the faint shimmer of the sea. Suddenly a light flashed from the south. She watched. In three seconds it flashed again and then for a third and last time. She thought that it must be some kind of signal, perhaps in answer to one from the island. But why and from whom? But then she told herself that the thought was childish and melodramatic. It was probably some solitary sailor on his way back to Speymouth harbour casually flashing a light over the quay. But there remained something discomforting and almost sinister about that threefold flash as if someone was signalling that the cast was assembled, the leading lady ensconced in splendour under the castle roof, that the drawbridge could be drawn up and the play begin. But this was a castle without a drawbridge, its moat the sea. For the first time since her arrival, Cordelia was touched by a sense of claustrophobic unease. Here their only lifelines were the telephone and the launch, both easily put out of commission. She had been drawn to the mystery and loneliness of the island; now she missed the solid reassurance of the mainland, of towns and fields and hills ranged at her back. It was then that she heard Clarissa's door close and Tolly's departing footsteps. Clarissa must be ready. Cordelia went through the communicating door and they made their way together to the hall.

The dinner was excellent, artichokes followed by *poussin* and spinach *au gratin*. The south-facing room still held the warmth of the day and the wood fire had been lit more for its sweet-smelling and comforting glow than because it was needed. The three tall candlesticks threw a steady light on the epergne of coloured glass and Parian, the rich gold, green and rose of the Davenport dinner-service and the engraved table-glasses. Above the fireplace was an oil painting of the two daughters of Herbert Gorringe. Their poses were awkward, almost angular, and the faces with their bright, exophthalmic eyes under the strong Gorringe brows and the moist, half-open mouths looked flushed and feverish while the reds and deep blues of the evening dresses shone as brightly as if the paint had recently dried. Cordelia found it difficult to keep her eyes from the picture which so far from being tranquil or domestic seemed to her charged with a hectic sexual energy. Watching her gaze, Ambrose said:

'It's by Millais, one of the comparatively few social portraits which he did. The dinner-service we're using was a wedding gift to the elder daughter from the Prince and Princess of Wales. Clarissa insisted that I bring it out for tonight.'

It seemed to Cordelia that there was a great deal which Clarissa insisted on at Courcy Castle. She wondered if she also proposed to supervise the washing-up.

It should have been a festive meal but the pleasure didn't match the food or the excellence of the wines. Beneath the glittering surface and the easy social chat flowed a current of unease, which from time to time spurted into antagonism. No one but Simon and herself with their youthful appetites did justice to the food, and he shoved it in furtively, watching Clarissa from the corner of his eye like a child allowed up for his first dining-room meal and expecting any minute to be banished to the nursery. Clarissa, elegant in her high-necked dress of blue-green chiffon, began by teasing her cousin about the absence of her partner who had apparently been expected for the weekend, a topic which she seemed reluctant to let go.

'But it's so odd of him, darling. Surely we didn't frighten him away? I thought you wanted to show him off? Isn't that why you schemed for an invitation? Who are you ashamed of, us or him?'

Roma's face was an unbecoming pink above the harsh blue of her taffeta dress.

'We're expecting an American customer to drop into the shop this Saturday. And Colin has got behind with the accounts. He's hoping to get them finished before Monday.'

'On a weekend? How conscientious of him. But I'm relieved to hear that you have some accounts worth doing. Congratulations.'

Cordelia, finding that she could make little headway with Simon, who seemed afraid to speak, withdrew her interest from her fellow guests and concentrated on her meal. When she next took notice it was to hear Roma's belligerent voice. She was addressing Ambrose across the table, clutching her fork as if it were a weapon.

'But you can't opt out of all responsibility for what's happening in your own country! You can't just say that you're not concerned, not even interested!'

'But I can. I didn't collude in the depreciation of its currency, the spoliation of its countryside, the desecration of its towns, the destruction of its grammar schools or even the mutilation of the liturgy of its Church. For what am I personally expected to feel a responsibility?'

'I was thinking of aspects which some of us see as more important. The growth of Fascism, the fact that our society is more violent, less compassionate and more unequal than it has been since the nineteenth century. And then there's the National Front. You can't ignore the Front!'

'Indeed I can, together with Militant Tendency, the Trots and the rest of the rabble. You'd be surprised at my capacity for ignoring the ignorable.'

'But you can't just decide to live in another age!'

'But I can. I can live in any century I wish. I don't have to choose the dark ages, old or new.'

Ivo said quietly:

'I'm grateful that you don't reject modern amenities or modern technology. If I should enter into the final process of dying during the next few days and need a little medical help to ease the way, I take it you won't object to using the telephone.'

Ambrose smiled round at them and raised his glass:

'If any of you decide to die in the next few days, all necessary measures will be taken to ease you on your way.'

There was a short, slightly embarrassed silence. Cordelia looked across at Clarissa, but the actress's eyes were on her plate. For a second, the long fingers trembled and were still.

Roma said:

'And what happens to Eden when Adam, solaced with no Eve, finally returns to the dust?'

'It would be pleasant to have a son to follow one here, I admit, almost worth marrying and breeding for. But sons, even supposing they came to order and if the process of getting them, deceptively simply physiologically, wasn't so fraught with practical and emotional complications, are notoriously unreliable. Ivo, you're the only one here with experience of children.'

Ivo said:

'It's unwise, certainly, to look to them for vicarious immortality.'

'Or anything else, wouldn't you say? A son might easily convert the castle to a casino, lay down a nine-hole golf course, make the air hideous with speedboats and water skiing and hold pretentious Saturday hops for the locals, eight-fifty a head, three-course dinner included, evening dress obligatory, no extras guaranteed.'

Clarissa looked across at Ivo:

'Talking of children, what's the news of your two, Ivo? Is Matthew still living in that Kensington squat?'

Cordelia saw that Ivo's chicken had been pushed almost untouched to the side of his plate and that although he was forking his spinach into shreds, little of it was reaching his mouth. But he had been drinking steadily. The claret decanter was on his right hand and he reached for it again, adding to a glass which he seemed not to realize was already three-quarters full. He looked across at Clarissa, eyes bright in the candlelight.

'Matthew? I suppose he's still with the Children of the Sun or whatever they call themselves. As we don't communicate I'm not in a position to say. Angela, on the other hand, writes a filial letter at boring length every month. I have two granddaughters now, she informs me. Since Angela and her husband refuse to visit a country where they might find themselves sharing a dining-table with a black and I have a distaste for sharing a table with my son-in-law, I am unlikely to make their acquaintance. My ex-wife, in case you meant to inquire, is with them in Johannesburg, which she calls Jo'burg, and is said to be enchanted with the country, the climate, the company and the kidney-shaped swimming pool.'

Clarissa laughed, a small bell note of triumph.

'Darling, I wasn't asking for a family history.'

'Weren't you?' he said easily. 'Oh, I rather thought you were.'

The table fell into a silence which, to Cordelia's relief, lasted with few interruptions until the meal was at last over and Munter opened the door for the women to follow Clarissa into the drawing-room.

CHAPTER SIXTEEN

Ivo wanted neither coffee nor liqueur but he carried the decanter of claret and his glass with him into the drawing-room and settled himself in an armchair between the fire and the open french windows. He felt no particular social responsibility for the rest of the evening. The dinner had been sufficiently grim, and he had every intention of getting quietly but thoroughly drunk. He had listened too much to his doctors. Throw physic to the dogs, I'll none of it. Obviously, what he needed was to drink more, not less; and if it could be wine of this quality and at Ambrose's expense, so much the better. Already his self-disgust at allowing Clarissa to provoke him into that spurt of angry revelation was fading under the influence of the wine. And what was taking its place was a gentle euphoria in which his mind became supernaturally clear, while the faces and words of his companions moved into a different dimension so that he watched their antics with bright sardonic eyes as he might actors on a stage.

Simon was preparing to play for them, arranging his music on the stand with uncertain hands. Ivo thought: Oh God, not Chopin followed by Rachmaninov. And why, he wondered, was Clarissa draping herself over the boy, ready to turn the pages? It wasn't as if she could read music. If this was to be the start of her usual system of alternate kindness and brutality she would end by driving the boy out of his wits as she had his father. Roma, in the taffeta dress which would have looked too young on an *ingénue* of eighteen, was sitting rigidly on the edge of her chair like a parent at a school concert. Why should she care how the boy performed? Why should any of them care? Already his nervousness was communicating itself to his audience. But he played better than Ivo expected, only occasionally attempting to disguise the misfingerings by too fast a tempo and the over-use of the sustaining pedal. Even so, it was too like a public performance to be enjoyable, the pieces chosen to show off his technique, the occasion made more important than anyone wanted. And it went on too long. At the end Ambrose said:

'Thank you, Simon. What are a few wrong notes between friends? And now, where are the songs of yesteryear?'

The decanter was now less than a quarter full. Ivo stretched himself more deeply in the chair and let the voices come to him from an immense distance. They were all round the piano now, roaring out sentimental Victorian drawing-room ballads. He could hear Roma's contralto, invariably late and slightly off-key, and Cordelia's clear soprano, a convent-trained voice, a little unsure but clear and sweet. He watched Simon's flushed face as he bent over the keys, the look of intense, exultant concentration.

He was playing with more assurance and sensitivity now than he had alone. For once, the boy was enjoying himself.

After about half an hour Roma drifted away from the piano and walked over to look at two oils by Frith, crowded anecdotal canvases showing rail-travellers going to the Derby by first class and third class. Roma walked from one to the other studying them intently as if to check that no detail of social or sartorial contrast had been neglected by the artist. Then Clarissa suddenly dropped her hand from Simon's shoulder, swept past Ivo, her chiffon floating against his knee, and went out on the terrace alone. Cordelia and Ambrose were left singing together. The three of them at the piano were linked by their enjoyment, seemingly unaware of their audience, transposing and consulting, choosing and comparing and collapsing into laughter when a piece proved beyond their range or competence. Ivo recognized only a few of the songs; Peter Warlock's Elizabethan pastiches, Vaughan Williams's 'Bright is the Ring of Words'. He was listening now with the nearest he had come to happiness since his illness had been diagnosed. Nietzsche was wrong; it wasn't action but pleasure which bound one to existence. And he had become afraid of pleasure; to admit even the possibility of joy to his shrivelled senses was to open the mind to anguish and regret. But now, listening to that sweet voice blending with Ambrose's baritone and floating past him out and over the sea, he lay back, weightless, in a dreamy contentment which was without bitterness and without pain. And gradually his senses began to tingle into life. He was aware of the cool stream of air from the window on his face, nothing as inconvenient as a draught, but a barely perceptible sensation like a stroking finger; of the sharp red of the wine glowing in the decanter and its softness against his tongue; of the smell of the wood fire, evocative of lost boyhood autumns.

And then his mood was broken. Clarissa stormed into the room from the terrace. Simon heard her and stopped playing in mid-bar. The two voices sang on for a few notes then broke off. Clarissa said:

'I'll have enough of amateurs before the weekend's finished without you three adding to the boredom. I'm going to bed. Simon, it's time you called it a day. We'll go together; I want to see to your room. Cordelia, ring for Tolly will you and tell her

I'm ready for her, then come up in fifteen minutes, I want to discuss arrangements for tomorrow. Ivo, you're drunk.'

She waited with a shiver of impatience until Ambrose had opened the door for her, then swept out, merely pausing briefly to offer him her cheek to kiss. He bent forward but was too late and his pursed lips pecked ludicrously at the air. Simon bundled up his music with shaking hands, looked round as if for help, and ran after her. Cordelia went across to where the embroidered rope hung by the side of the fireplace. Roma said:

'Black marks all round. We should have realized that we're here to applaud Clarissa's talent not to demonstrate our own. If you plan to make a career as secretary-companion, Cordelia, you'll have to learn more tact.'

Ivo was aware of Ambrose bending over him, of his flushed face and the black eyes bright and malicious under the strong half circles.

'Are you drunk, Ivo? You're remarkably quiet.'

'I thought I was, but I seem not to be. Sobriety has overtaken me. But if you would open another bottle I could begin the agreeable process again. Good wine is a good familiar creature, if it be well used.'

'But shouldn't you keep your mind clear for the task of tomorrow?'

Ivo held out the empty decanter. He was surprised to see that his hand was perfectly steady. He said:

'Don't worry. I shall be sober enough for what I have to do tomorrow.'

CHAPTER SEVENTEEN

Cordelia waited exactly fifteen minutes, refused Ambrose's offer of a nightcap, then made her way upstairs. The communicating door between her room and Clarissa's was ajar and she went through without knocking. Clarissa, in her cream satin dressing-gown, was sitting at the dressing-table. Her hair was tugged back from her face and tied with a ribbon at the nape of the neck; her hairline was bound with a *crêpe* band. She was scrutinizing her face in the glass and didn't look round.

The room was lit only by one bright light on the dressing-table and the softer glow of the bedside lamp. A thin wood fire crackled in the grate and threw leaping shadows over the richness of damask and mahogany. The air smelt of woodsmoke and perfume and the room, dim and mysterious, struck Cordelia as smaller and more luxurious than in its daytime brightness. But the bed was more than ever dominant, glowing under its scarlet canopy, sinister and portentous as a catafalque. Cordelia was certain that Tolly must have been there before her. The sheets were turned back and Clarissa's nightdress had been laid out, its waist pinched. It looked like a shroud. In the shadowed half-light it was easy to imagine that she stood in the doorway of a bedroom in Amalfi with Webster's doomed duchess bright-haired at her toilet, while horror and corruption stalked in the shadows and beyond the half-open window a tideless Mediterranean lay open to the moon.

Clarissa's voice broke into her mood. 'Oh, here you are. I've sent Tolly away so that we can talk. Don't just stand there. Find yourself a chair.' On each side of the fireplace was a low, spoon-backed chair with carved arms and feet. Cordelia slid one forward on its casters and seated herself to the left of the dressing-table. Clarissa peered at herself in the glass then unscrewed a jar of cleansing pads and began wiping off her eye-shadow and mascara. Thin black-stained scraps of tissue crept over the polished mahogany. The left eye, wiped clean of make-up, looked diminished, almost lifeless, giving her suddenly the mask of a lopsided clown. She peered at the denuded lid, frowned, then said:

'You seem to have enjoyed yourself this evening. Perhaps I should remind you that you were hired as a detective not an after-dinner entertainer.'

It had been a long day and Cordelia couldn't summon the energy for anger.

'Perhaps if you were honest with them and told them why I'm here they'd be less likely to treat me as a fellow guest. Private detectives aren't expected to sing, at least I wouldn't think so. They probably wouldn't even want to eat with me. A private eye is hardly a comfortable dining companion.'

'What good would that do? If you don't mix with them, how

can you watch them? Besides, the men like you. I've seen Ivo and Simon looking at you. Don't pretend that you don't know it. I hate that kind of sexual coyness.'

'I wasn't going to pretend anything.'

Clarissa was busy now with an immense jar of cleansing cream, smearing dollops of the cream over face and neck and wiping it off with strong upward sweeps of cotton wool. The discarded greasy balls were added to the mess on the dressing-table. Cordelia found herself studying Clarissa's face with as much intensity as did its owner. The eyes were a little too far apart, the skin was thick, unluminous, but almost without lines; the cheeks were flat and wide; the mouth with its pouting lower lip too small for beauty. But it was a face that could take on loveliness at Clarissa's will and even now, bandaged, unenhanced and sunk in repose, it held the assurance of its latent, eccentric beauty.

Suddenly, she asked:

'What do you think of Simon's playing?'

'I'm not really qualified to judge. Obviously, he has talent.'

She was about to add that he might make a more successful accompanist than solo performer, then thought better of it. It was perfectly true: she wasn't competent to judge. And she had the feeling that ignorant though she was, some kind of decision might depend on her answer.

'Oh, talent! That's common enough. One doesn't invest six thousand pounds or so in mere talent. The thing is, has he the guts to succeed? George thinks not, but that he may as well be given his chance.'

'Sir George knows him better than I do.'

Clarissa said sharply:

'But it isn't George's money is it? I'll consult Ambrose, but not until after the play. I can't worry about anything until then. He'll probably damn the poor boy. Ambrose is such a perfectionist. But he does know something about music. He'd be a better judge than George. If only Simon had taken up a stringed instrument, he might eventually try for a place in an orchestra. But the piano! Still, I suppose he could always work as an accompanist.'

Cordelia wondered whether she should point out that the job of a professional accompanist, so far from being an easy option, required a formidable combination of technical ability and musicality, but she reminded herself that she hadn't been employed to advise on Simon's career. And this talk of Simon was wasting time. She said:

'I think we should discuss the messages and our plans for the weekend, especially tomorrow. We ought to have spoken earlier.'

'I know, but there hasn't really been time what with the rehearsal and Ambrose showing off his castle. Anyway, you know what you're here for. If there are any more messages, I don't want to receive them. I don't want to be shown them. I don't want to be told about them. It's vital that I get through tomorrow. If I can only get back my confidence as an actress, I can face almost anything.'

'Even the knowledge of who is doing this to you?'

'Even that.'

Cordelia asked:

'How many of the people here know about the messages?'

Clarissa had finished cleaning her face and now began removing the varnish from her nails. The smell of acetone overlaid the smell of scent and make-up.

'Tolly knows. I haven't any secrets from Tolly. Anyway she was with me in my dressing-room when some of them were brought in by the doorman, the ones sent by post to the theatre. I expect Ivo knows; there's nothing happens in the West End that he doesn't get to hear about. And Ambrose. He was with me in my dressing-room at the Duke of Clarence when one was pushed under the door. By the time he'd picked it up for me and I'd opened it, whoever it was had gone. The corridor was empty. But anyone could have got in. Backstage at the Clarence is like a warren and Albert Betts used to drink and wasn't always on the door when he should have been. They've sacked him now, but he was still working there when the note was delivered. And my husband knows, of course. Simon doesn't, unless Tolly has told him. I can't think why she should.'

'And your cousin?'

'Roma doesn't know and, if she did, she wouldn't care.'

'Tell me about Miss Lisle.'

'There's not much to tell and what there is, is boring. We're first cousins, but George has told you that. It's quite a common story. My father made a sensible marriage and his younger brother ran off with a barmaid, left the Army, drank and made a general mess of his life, then expected Daddy to help out. And he did, at least as far as Roma was concerned. She was always staying with us when I was a child, particularly after Uncle died. Poor Little Orphan Annie. Glum, badly dressed and perpetually miserable. Even Daddy couldn't stand her for long. He was the most marvellous person, I adored him. But she was such a bore, and so plain, worse than she is now. Daddy was one of those people who really couldn't bear ugliness, particularly in women. He loved gaiety, wit, beauty. He just couldn't make himself look at a plain face.'

Cordelia thought that Daddy, who sounded like a self-satisfied humbug, must have spent most of his life with his eyes shut, depending, of course, on his standard of ugliness. Clarissa added:

'And she wasn't a bit grateful.'

'Should she have been?'

Clarissa seemed to feel that the question deserved serious thought, or as much as she could spare from the business of filing her nails.

'Oh, I think so. He didn't have to take her in. And she could hardly expect him to treat her the same as me, his own child.'

'He could have tried.'

'But that's not reasonable, and you know it. You wouldn't behave like that so why expect him to. You really must guard against becoming just a bit of a prig. Men don't like it.'

Cordelia said:

'I don't much like it myself. Someone once told me that it's the result of having an atheist father, a convent education and a non-conformist conscience.'

There was silence between them, not uncompanionable. Then Cordelia said on impulse:

'These notes – could Miss Tolgarth have anything to do with them?'

'Tolly! Of course not. Whatever put that idea into your head? She's devoted to me. You mustn't be put off by her manner. She's always been like that. But we've been together since I was a child. Tolly adores me. If you can't see that you're not much of a detective. Besides, she can't type. The messages are typed in case you hadn't noticed.'

Cordelia said gravely:

'You should have told me about her child. If I'm to help I need to know anything that might be relevant.' She waited, apprehensive, for Clarissa's response. But the hands, busy with their self-ministrations, didn't falter.

'But that isn't relevant. It was all a mistake. Tolly knows that. Everyone knows it. I suppose Ivo told you. That's typical of his malice and disloyalty. Can't you see that he's sick? He's dying! And he's eaten up with jealousy. He always has been. Jealousy and malice.'

Cordelia wondered whether she could have asked the question more tactfully, whether it had been wise to ask it at all. Ivo hadn't asked her not to betray their conversation but presumably he had hoped for discretion. And the weekend promised to be difficult enough without setting two of the guests at each other's throats. Direct lying had never been easy for her. She said cautiously:

'No one has been disloyal. Obviously I did some tactful research before I arrived here. These things do get talked about. I have a friend in the theatre.' Well that was true enough anyway even if poor Bevis was more often out than in. But Clarissa was uninterested in putative theatrical friends.

'I'd like to know what right Ivo has to criticize me. Do you realize how many careers he's ruined by his cruelty? Yes, cruelty! I've seen actors – actors mind you – in tears after one of his reviews. If he could have resisted the impulse to be clever he might have been one of the great British critics. He could have been a second Agate or a Tynan. And what is he now? Dying on his feet. He's no right to come here looking as he does. It's like having a death's head at table. It's indecent.'

It was interesting, thought Cordelia, the way in which death had replaced sex as the great unmentionable, to be denied in prospect, endured in a decent privacy, preferably behind the drawn curtains of a hospital bed, and followed by discreet, embarrassed, uncomforted mourning. There was this to be said about the Convent of the Holy Child; the views of the Sisters on death had been explicit, firmly held and not altogether reassuring; but at least they hadn't regarded it as in poor taste.

She said:

'Those first messages, the ones that came when you were playing Lady Macbeth, the ones you threw away. Were they the same as the later ones, typed on white paper?'

'Yes, I suppose so. It was a long time ago.'

'But you can't have forgotten?'

'They must have been the same, mustn't they? What does it matter? I don't want to talk about it now.'

'It's the only chance we may get. I haven't been able to see you alone today and tomorrow isn't going to be any easier.'

Clarissa was on her feet now, pacing between the dressing-table and the bed.

'It wasn't my fault. I didn't kill her. She wasn't properly cared for. If she had been she wouldn't have had the accident. What's the point of having a child – a bastard too – if you don't look after it?'

'But wasn't Tolly at work, looking after you?'

'The hospital had no right to phone like that, upsetting people. They must have known that it was a theatre that they were calling, that West End curtains rise at eight, that we'd be in the middle of a performance. She couldn't have done anything if I had let her go. The child was unconscious, she wouldn't have known her. It's sentimental and morbid, this sitting by the bedside waiting for people to die. What good does it do? And I had three changes in the Third Act. Kalenski designed the banquet costume himself; barbaric jewellery, a crown set with great dollops of red stones like blood, a skirt so stiff I could hardly move. He meant me to be weighed down, to walk stiffly like an over-encumbered child. "Think of yourself as a seventeenth-century princess," he said, "wonderingly loaded with inappropriate majesty." Those were his words, and he made me keep moving my hands down the sides of the skirt as if I couldn't believe that I was actually wearing so much richness. And of course it made a marvellous contrast with the plain cream shift in the sleep-walking scene. It wasn't a nightgown, they used to sleep naked apparently. I used it to wipe my hands. Kalenski said, "Hands, darling, hands, hands, that's what this part is all about." It was a new interpretation, of course, I wasn't the usual kind of Lady Macbeth, tall, domineering, ruthless; I played her like a sex-kitten but a kitten with hidden claws.'

It was, thought Cordelia, a novel interpretation of the part, but surely not altogether consonant with the text. But perhaps Kalenski, like other Shakespearean directors whose names came to mind, didn't let that bother him. She said:

'But was it true to the text?'

'Oh, my dear, who cares about the text? I don't mean that exactly, but Shakespeare's like the Bible, you can make it mean anything, that's why directors love him.'

'Tell me about the child.'

'Macduff's son? Desmond Willoughby played him, an intolerable child. A vulgar Cockney accent. You can't find a child actor now who knows how to speak English. Too old for the part too. Thank God I never had to appear with him.'

One biblical text came into Cordelia's mind, brutally explicit in its meaning, but she didn't speak it aloud:

> Whoso shall offend one of these little ones which believe in me, it were better that a millstone were hanged about his neck, and that he were drowned in the depth of the sea.

Clarissa turned and looked at her. Something in Cordelia's face must have pierced even her egotism. She cried:

'I'm not paying you to judge me! What are you looking like that for?'

'I'm not judging you. I want to help. But you have to be honest with me.'

'I am being honest, as honest as I know how. When I first saw you, that day at Nettie Fortescue's, I knew I could trust you, that you were someone I could talk to. It's degrading to be so afraid. George doesn't understand, how could he? He's never been afraid of anything in his life. He thinks I'm neurotic to care. He only went to see you because I made him.'

'Why didn't you come yourself?'

'I thought you might be more likely to accept the job if he asked you. And I don't enjoy asking people for favours. Besides, I had a fitting for one of my costumes.'

'There wasn't any question of a favour. I needed the job. I probably would have taken almost anything if it wasn't illegal and didn't disgust me.'

'Yes, George said that your office was pretty squalid. Well, pathetic rather than squalid. But you aren't. There's nothing squalid or pathetic about you. I couldn't have put up with the usual kind of female private eye.'

Cordelia said gently:

'What is it that you're really afraid of?'

Clarissa turned on Cordelia, her softly gleaming, cleansed, uncoloured face looking for the first time, in its nakedness, vulnerable to age and grief, and gave a sad, rather rueful smile. Then she lifted her hands in an eloquent gesture of despair.

'Oh, don't you know? I thought George had told you. Death. That's what I'm afraid of. Just death. Stupid isn't it? I always have been: even when I was a young child. I don't remember when it began, but I knew the facts of death before I knew the facts of life. There never was a time when I didn't see the skull beneath the skin. Nothing traumatic happened to start it off. They didn't force me to look at my Nanny, dead in her coffin, nothing like that. And I was at school when Mummy died and it didn't mean anything. It isn't the death of other people. It isn't the fact of death. It's my death I'm afraid of. Not all the time. Not every moment. Sometimes I can go for weeks without thinking about it. And then it comes, usually at night, the dread and the horror and the knowledge that the fear is real. I mean, no one can say "Don't worry it may never happen." They can't say "It's all your imagination, darling, it doesn't really exist." I can't really describe the fear, what it's like, how terrible it is. It comes in a rhythm, wave after wave of panic sweeping over me, a kind of pain. It must be like giving birth, except that I'm not delivering life, it's death I have between my thighs. Sometimes I hold up my hand, like this, and look at it and think: Here it is, part of me. I can feel it with my other hand, and move it and warm it and smell it and paint its nails. And one day it will hang white and cold and unfeeling and useless and so shall I be all those things. And then it will rot. And I shall rot. I can't even drink to forget. Other people do. It's how they get through their lives. But drink makes me ill. It isn't fair that I should have this terror and not be able to drink! Now I've told you, and you can explain that I'm stupid and morbid and a coward. You can despise me.'

Cordelia said:

'I don't despise you.'

'And it's no good saying that I ought to believe in God. I can't. And even if I could, it wouldn't help. Tolly got converted after Viccy died so I suppose she believes. But if someone told Tolly that she was going to die tomorrow she'd be just as unwilling to go. I've noticed that about the God people. They're just as frightened as the rest of us. They cling on just as long. They're supposed to have a heaven waiting but they're in no hurry to get there. Perhaps it's worse for them; judgement and hell and damnation. At least I'm only afraid of death. Isn't everyone? Aren't you?'

Was she? Cordelia wondered. Sometimes, perhaps. But the fear of dying was less obtrusive than more mundane worries; what would happen when the Kingly Street lease ran out, whether the Mini would pass its MOT test, how she would face Miss Maudsley if the Agency no longer had a job for her. Perhaps only the rich and successful could indulge the morbid fear of dying. Most of the world needed its energies to cope with living. She said cautiously, knowing that she had no comfort to offer:

'It doesn't seem reasonable to be afraid of something which is inevitable and universal and which I shan't be able to experience, anyway.'

'Oh, those are just words! All they mean is that you're young and healthy and don't have to think about dying. To lie in cold obstruction and to rot. That was in one of the messages.'

'I know.'

'And there's another for you to add to the collection. I've been keeping it for you. It came by post to the London flat yesterday morning. You'll find it at the bottom of my jewel case. It's on the bedside table, the left-hand side.'

The instruction as to the side was unnecessary; even in the subdued light and amid the clutter of Clarissa's bedside table, the softly gleaming casket was an object that caught the eye. Cordelia took it in her hands. It was about eight inches by five, with delicately wrought clawed feet, the lid and sides embossed with a representation of the judgement of Paris. She turned the key, and saw that the inside was lined with cream quilted silk.

Clarissa called:

'Ambrose gave it to me when I arrived this morning, a good luck present for the performance tomorrow. I took a fancy to it when I saw it six months ago but it took a time before he got the message. He has so many Victorian baubles that one less can't make any difference. The casket we're using in Act Three is his, well, most of the props are. But this is prettier. More valuable too. But not as valuable as the thing I'm keeping in it. You'll find the letter in the secret drawer. Not so very secret, actually. You just press the centre of one of the leaves. You can see the line if you look carefully. Better bring it here. I'll show you.'

The box was surprisingly heavy. Clarissa pulled out a tangle of necklaces and bracelets as if they were cheap costume jewellery. Cordelia thought that some of the pieces probably were, bright beads of coloured stone and glass intertwined with the sparkle of real diamonds, the glow of sapphires, the softness of milk-white pearls. Clarissa pressed the centre of one of the leaves which decorated the side of the box and a drawer in the base slid slowly open. Inside Cordelia saw first a folded cutting of newsprint. Clarissa took it out:

'I played Hester in a revival of Rattigan's *The Deep Blue Sea*, at the Speymouth Playhouse. That was in 1977, Jubilee Year, when Ambrose was abroad in his year's tax exile. The theatre's closed now, alas. But they seemed to like me. Actually, that's probably the most important notice I ever had.'

She unfolded it. Cordelia glimpsed the headline. 'Clarissa Lisle triumphs in Rattigan revival.' Her mind busied itself for only a second on the oddity of Clarissa's attaching so much importance to the review of a revival in a small provincial town and she noticed, almost subconsciously, that the cutting was oddly shaped and larger than the space taken by the notice. But her interest fastened on the letter. The envelope matched the one handed to her by Mrs Munter from the morning postbag but the address had been typed on a different and obviously older machine. The postmark was London, the date two days earlier, and like the other it was addressed to the Duchess of Malfi but at Clarissa's Bayswater flat. Inside was the usual sheet of white paper, the neat black drawing of a coffin, the letters RIP. Underneath was typed a quotation from the play.

Who must despatch me?
I account this world a tedious theatre
For I must play a part in't 'gainst my will.

Cordelia said:

'Not very appropriate. He must be getting to the end of suitable quotations.'

Clarissa tugged off her hairband. In the glass, her reflection gazed back at them both, a ghost face, hung about with pale dishevelled hair, the huge eyes troubled under their heavy lids.

'Perhaps he knows that he won't need many more. There's only tomorrow. Perhaps he knows – who better? – that tomorrow will be the end.'

PART THREE

Blood Flies Upwards

CHAPTER EIGHTEEN

Cordelia slept more deeply and for longer than she had expected. She was awoken by a quiet knock at the door. Instantly she was fully conscious and, throwing her dressing-gown round her shoulders, she went to open it. It was Mrs Munter with her early-morning tea. Cordelia had meant to be up well before she arrived. It was embarrassing to be discovered sleeping behind a locked door as if she were confusing Courcy Castle with a hotel. But if Mrs Munter was surprised at this eccentricity she gave no sign but placed the tray on the bedside table with a quiet 'Good morning, Miss,' and left as unobtrusively as she had arrived.

It was half-past seven. The room was filled with the smudged half-light of dawn. Going to the window, Cordelia saw that the eastern sky was just beginning to streak into brightness and that a low mist hung over the lawn and curled like smoke between the tree tops. It was going to be another lovely day. There was no sign of any bonfire, yet the air held the smoky wood-fire smell of autumn and the great mass of the sea heaved, grey and silver, as if it exuded its own mysterious light.

She crept to the communicating door and opened it very gently. It was heavy, but it swung open without a creak. The curtains were drawn across the windows but there was enough light from her own room to show her Clarissa, still sleeping, one white arm curved round her pillow. Cordelia tiptoed up to the bed and stood very still listening to the quiet breathing. She felt a sense of relief without knowing exactly why. She had never believed that there was a real threat to Clarissa's life. And their precautions against mischief had been thorough. Both the doors to the corridor had been locked with the keys left in the locks. Even if someone had a duplicate there was no way in which he could have got in. But she needed the reassurance of Clarissa's untroubled breathing.

And then she saw the paper, a pale oblong gleaming against the carpet. Another message had been delivered, pushed under the door. So whoever was responsible was here, on the island. She felt her heart jolt. Then she took hold of herself, angry that she hadn't thought of the possibility of a missive under the door, resenting her own fear. She crept across to pick up the paper and took it into her own room, shutting the door behind her.

It was another passage from *The Duchess of Malfi*, eleven short words surmounted by a skull.

Thus it lightens into action,
I am come to kill thee.

The form was the same, but the paper was different. This message was typed on the back of an old woodcut headed 'The Gt Mef-fenger of Mortality'. Beneath the title was the crude figure of death bearing an hourglass and arrow followed by four stanzas of verse.

She gulped down her tea, pulled on her trousers and shirt and went in search of Ambrose. She had hardly hoped to find him so early but he was already in the breakfast room, coffee cup in hand, gazing out over the lawn. It was one of the rooms which she had seen on Friday's quick tour of the castle, the furniture and fittings all designed by Godwin. There was a simple refectory table with a set of fretwork-backed chairs while one long wall was entirely covered by a set of cupboards and open shelves, charmingly carved in light wood and surmounted by a tiled frieze in which orange trees in bright blue pots alternated with highly romanticized scenes from the legend of King Arthur and the Round Table. At the time Cordelia had thought it an interesting example of the architect's move towards the simplicities of the Aesthetic Movement, but now its self-conscious charm was lost on her.

Ambrose turned at her entrance and smiled.

'Good morning. It looks as if we're going to be lucky in the weather. The guests should arrive in sunshine and get back without risk of parting with their supper. The crossing can be treacherous in bad weather. Is our leading lady awake?'

'Not yet.'

Cordelia made a sudden resolution. It could do no harm to tell him. The woodcut almost certainly came from his house. Clarissa had told her that he already knew about the poison-pen messages. And Clarissa was his guest. Above all, she wanted to see his reaction to the paper. She held it out and said:

'I found this pushed under Clarissa's door this morning. Does it belong to you? If so, someone has mutilated it for you. Look on the back.'

He studied it briefly, then turned it over. For a moment he was silent. Then he said:

'So the messages are still coming. I did wonder. Has she seen this?'

There was no need to ask whom he meant.

'No. And she won't.'

'Very wise of you. I take it that weeding out this kind of nuisance is one of your duties as secretary-companion?'

'One of them. But does it belong to you?'

'No. It's interesting, but not my period.'

'But this is your house. And Miss Lisle is your guest.'

He smiled and wandered over to the sideboard.

'Will you have coffee?' She watched while he went over to the hotplate, poured her cup and refilled his own. Then he said:

'I accept the implied criticism. One's guests certainly have the right not to be harassed or menaced while under one's roof. But what do you suggest I can do? I'm not a policeman. I can hardly interrogate my other house guests. That, apart from its certain lack of success, would only result in six aggrieved persons instead of one. I doubt whether Clarissa would thank me. And, forgive me, aren't you taking this a little too seriously? I admit that it's a practical joke in poor taste. But is it any more than a joke? And surely the best response to this kind of nonsense is a dignified silence, even a certain amused contempt. Clarissa is an actress. She should be able to simulate one response or the other. If there is someone on the island who is trying to spoil her performance he – or more likely she – will soon give up if Clarissa demonstrates a total unconcern.'

'That's what she will do, at least until after the play. She won't see this. I can trust you not to tell her?'

'Of course. I have a strong interest in Clarissa's success, remember. You didn't put the thing there yourself by any chance?'

'No.'

'I thought not. Forgive my asking, but you see my difficulty. If it wasn't you, it was presumably her husband – except that he isn't here at the moment – her stepson, her cousin, her faithful dresser, or one of her oldest friends. Who am I to start probing these family and long-standing relationships? Incidentally, that woodcut belongs to Roma.'

'To Roma! How do you know?'

'You do sound fierce, quite like a schoolmistress. Roma used to teach you know. Geography and games, Clarissa tells me. A strange combination. I can't quite picture Roma, whistle at the lip, panting down the hockey field exhorting the girls to greater efforts or plunging into the deep end of the swimming pool. Well, perhaps I can believe that. She has aggressively muscular shoulders.'

Cordelia said:

'But the woodcut?'

'She told me that she found it in a second-hand book and thought I might be interested in seeing it. She showed it to me yesterday, just before the rehearsal, and I left it on the blotter on my desk in the business room.'

'Where anyone could have seen and taken it?'

'You sound like a detective. As you say, where anyone could have seen and taken it. It looks, incidentally, as if the message were typed on my machine. That, too, is kept in the business room.'

The typesetting, at least, would be easy enough to check. She might as well do it now. But before she could make the suggestion Ambrose said:

'And there's another thing. Forgive me if I find it rather more annoying than Clarissa's poison pen. Someone has broken the lock of the display cabinet outside the business room and taken the marble arm. If, during your duties as secretary-companion you should happen to learn who it is, I'd be grateful if you would suggest that he or she put it back. I admit that the marble's not to everyone's taste but I have a fondness for it.'

Cordelia said:

'The arm of the Princess Royal? When did you notice that it had gone?'

'Munter tells me that it was in the display case when he locked up last night. That was at ten minutes past midnight. He unlocked this morning shortly after six but didn't look at the display case although he thinks that he might have noticed if the arm had gone. But he can't be sure. I myself saw that it was missing, and that the lock had been forced, when I went to the kitchen to make tea just before seven.'

Cordelia said:

'It couldn't have been Clarissa. She was asleep when I got up this morning. And I doubt whether she'd have the strength to break a lock.'

'Not much strength was required. A strong paper-knife would have done the trick. And, conveniently enough, there was a strong paper-knife on the desk in the business room.'

Cordelia asked:

'What are you going to do?'

'Nothing, at least until after the play. I can't see how it affects Clarissa. It's my loss, not hers. But I take it you would prefer her not to know?'

'I think it's vital that she doesn't know. The least thing could upset her. We'll just have to hope no one else notices that the arm has gone.'

He said:

'If they do, I suppose I can say that I've removed it since Clarissa found it so displeasing. It's humiliating to have to lie when there's no need, but if you think it important that Clarissa isn't told . . .'

'I do. Very important. I'd be grateful if you'd say and do nothing until after the play.'

It was then they heard the footsteps, firm, quick, clanging on the tiled floor. Both turned simultaneously and gazed at the door. Sir George Ralston appeared, tweed-coated and holding a grip. He said:

'I got through the meeting late yesterday. Drove most of the night and slept in a lay-by. Thought Clarissa would like me to put in an appearance if I could make it.'

Ambrose said:

'But how did you get to the island? I didn't hear a launch.'

'Found a couple of early fishermen. They put me ashore in the small bay. Got my feet wet but nothing worse. I've been on the island a couple of hours. Didn't like to disturb you. Is that coffee?'

A jumble of thoughts ran through Cordelia's mind. Was she still wanted? She could hardly ask Sir George directly with Ambrose present. She was supposed to be on the island as Clarissa's secretary, a job that was unlikely to be affected by his sudden appearance. And what about her room? Presumably he would wish to move next door to his wife. She was uncomfortably aware that she must look less than pleased to see him and that Ambrose was glancing at her with a sardonic, wryly amused look which recognized her discomfiture. Murmuring an excuse she slipped away.

Clarissa was stirring although Tolly hadn't yet brought in the early tray. Cordelia drew back the curtains and unlocked the door. She stood by the bed until Clarissa opened her eyes, then said:

'Your husband has just arrived. Apparently the meeting ended sooner than he expected.'

Clarissa heaved herself up from her pillows.

'George? But that's ridiculous! He isn't expected until late tonight at the earliest.'

'Well, he's here.'

Cordelia thought that it was as well she had warned Clarissa. Sir George could hardly have been gratified at her reception of the news. She sat up and stared straight ahead, her face expressionless. Then she said:

'Tug on that bell-rope, will you? The one by the fireplace. It's time Tolly brought in my tea.'

Cordelia said:

'I wondered whether you'll still want me.'

Clarissa's voice was sharp, almost frightened.

'Of course I still want you! What possible difference does this make? You know what you're here to do. If someone's out to get me, they aren't going to stop because George has arrived.'

'I could move out of the next-door room if you like.'

Clarissa swung her legs out of bed and made for the bathroom.

'Oh, don't be so bloody naïve, Cordelia! Stay where you are. And tell George I'm awake if he wants to see me.'

She disappeared. Cordelia decided to wait in the bedroom until Tolly arrived with the tea. If she could help it, there would be no time between now and the rise of the curtain when Clarissa would be left unguarded.

Clarissa returned from the bathroom and climbed back into bed.

Cordelia said:

'Before Miss Tolgarth arrives, could you tell me what the programme is today?'

'Oh, don't you know? I thought I'd explained it all. The curtain is due to rise at three thirty. Ambrose is arranging an early lunch, about midday, and I shall rest up here alone from one until two forty-five. I don't like to spend too long in my dressing-room before a performance. You can call me at two forty-five and we'll decide what, if anything, I want you to do during the play. The launch will fetch the Cottringham party from Speymouth. They should arrive at two thirty or shortly afterwards. There is a larger hired launch for the guests and that is due at three. We have tea in the interval at four thirty, set out under the arcade if it's warm enough, and supper at seven thirty in the great hall. The launches are ordered for nine.'

Cordelia said:

'And this morning? What is planned for the three hours between breakfast and luncheon? I think we should try to stay together.'

'We shall all stay together. Ambrose has suggested that we might like a trip round the island in *Shearwater* but I've told him that we're not a party of his five-pounds-a-day summer trippers. I've thought of a better plan. There are sights on Courcy that he hasn't shown us yet. I don't think you need worry about being bored. We'll start with a visit to the skulls of Courcy.'

Cordelia said:

'The skulls of Courcy? Do you mean real skulls, here in the castle?'

Clarissa laughed.

'Oh, they're real enough. In the crypt of the Church. Ambrose will recite the famous legend. They should put us all nicely in the mood for the horrors of Amalfi.'

Tolly with the tea-tray and Sir George arrived simultaneously. He was received very prettily. Clarissa held out a languid arm.

He raised her hand to his lips then bent with a stiff, graceless movement and briefly laid his face against hers. She cried, her voice high and brittle:

'Darling, how lovely! And how clever of you to find someone to bring you across.'

He didn't look at Cordelia. He said gruffly:

'You're all right?'

'Darling, of course. Did you think I wasn't? How touching! But, as you see, here I am, Duchess of Malfi still.'

Cordelia left them. She wondered whether Sir George would find an opportunity of speaking to her privately and, if so, whether she should tell him about the woodcut pushed under the door. It was, after all, he who had employed her. But it was Clarissa who had sent for her, Clarissa who was her client, Clarissa she was paid to protect. Some instinct urged her to keep her counsel, at least until after the play. And then she remembered the missing marble. In the surprise of Sir George's arrival it had slipped from the front of her mind. But now its pale image gleamed in her imagination with all the sinister force of an omen. Ought she at least to warn Sir George that it was missing? But warn him against what? It was only the carved replica of a baby's limb, the limb of a long-dead princess. How could it harm anyone? Why should it hold in its chubby fingers such a weight of portentous power? She couldn't even explain to herself why she thought it so important that Clarissa wasn't told about the loss, except that the marble had repelled her and that any mention of it would be upsetting. Surely she had been right in asking Ambrose to say nothing, at least until after the play? So why tell Sir George? He hadn't even seen the limb. It would be time enough for them all to be told when Ambrose started inquiring and looking for it after the play. And that would be this evening. There was only today to be got through. She was aware that she wasn't thinking very clearly. And one thought in particular surprised and fretted her. Surely the presence of Clarissa's husband on Courcy Island ought to make her job easier? She should be feeling relieved at a sharing of responsibility. Why then should she see this unexpected arrival as a new and unwelcome complication? Why should she feel for the first time that she was caught in a charade in which she stumbled blindfold, while unseen hands spun her round, pushed and pulled at her, in which an unknown intelligence watched, waited and directed the play?

CHAPTER NINETEEN

Breakfast was a long-drawn-out meal to which the members of the house party came singly, ate at leisure and seemed reluctant to finish. The food would have done justice to Herbert Gorringe's Victorian notions of a proper start to the day. As the lids of the silver dishes were raised, the discordant smells of eggs and bacon, sausages, kidneys and haddock filled the breakfast room, stifling appetite. Despite the early promise of another warm day Cordelia sensed that the party was ill at ease and that she wasn't the only one present who was mentally counting the hours to nightfall. There seemed to be an unspoken conspiracy not to upset Clarissa, and when she announced her plan to visit the Church and the crypt the murmur of agreement was suspiciously unanimous. If anyone would have preferred a trip round the island or a solitary walk no one admitted it. Probably they were well aware how precarious was her control before a performance and no one wanted to risk being held responsible if that control broke. As they walked in a group along the arcade, past the theatre and under the shadow of the trees which led to the Church, it seemed to Cordelia that Clarissa was surrounded by the solicitous care afforded to an invalid or – and the thought was disagreeable – to a predestined victim.

Sir George was the one most at ease. When they entered the Church and the rest of the party gazed round with the air of people resolved to find something positive to say, his reaction was immediate and uncompromising. He obviously found its nineteenth-century fusion of religious enthusiasm with medieval romanticism unsympathetic and viewed the richly decorated apse with its mosaic of Christ in glory, the coloured tiles and the polychromatic arches with a prejudiced eye.

'It looks more like a Victorian London Club – or a Turkish bath come to that – than a Church. I'm sorry, Gorringe, but I can't admire it. Who d'you say the architect was?'

'George Frederick Bodley. My great-grandfather had quarrelled with Godwin by the time he came to rebuild the Church. His relationships with his architects were always stormy. I'm sorry you don't like it. The paintings on the reredos are by Lord Leighton, by the way, and the glass is by William Morris's firm who specialized in these lighter hues. Bodley was one of the first architects to use the firm. The east window is considered rather fine.'

'I don't see how anyone could actually pray in the place. Is that the War Memorial?'

'Yes. Put up by my uncle from whom I inherited. It's the only architectural addition he ever made to the island.'

The memorial was a plain stone slab set in the wall to the south of the altar which read:

> In memory of the men of Courcy Island
> who fell on the battlefields of two world wars
> and whose bones lie in foreign soil.
> 1914–1918
> 1939–1945

This at least met with Sir George's approval.

'I like that. Plain and dignified. Wonder who put the wreath there. Been there some time by the look of it.' Ambrose had come up behind them. He said:

'There'll be a fresh one on 11th November. Munter makes them from our own laurels and hangs one up each year. His father was killed in the war, in the Navy I think. Anyway, he was drowned. He told me that much.'

Roma asked:

'And do you assist at this charade?'

'No, he hasn't asked me. It's a purely private ceremony. I'm not sure I'm even supposed to know that it happens.'

Roma turned away.

'It throws a new light on Munter though. Who would suspect him of that streak of romanticism? But I wouldn't have thought that the memorial was particularly appropriate. His father didn't live or work on the island, did he?'

'Not to my knowledge.'

'And if he drowned, his bones won't be buried in any soil, foreign or otherwise. It all seems rather pointless. But then, Remembrance Day is pointless. No one seems to know any longer what it's supposed to be for.'

Sir George said:

'It's for remembering the good chaps who've gone. Once a year. For two minutes. You wouldn't think that was too much to ask. And why degrade it into a sentimental mass love-in? At our last Parade the padre preached a sermon about the Third World and the World Council of Churches. I could see that some of the older chaps in the Legion were getting restless.'

Roma said:

'I suppose he thought his sermon had something to do with world peace.'

'Armistice Day isn't to do with peace. It's to do with war, and remembering one's dead. A nation that can't remember its dead will soon cease to be worth dying for. And what's so peaceful about the Third World?'

He turned quickly away and for a moment Cordelia thought that his eyes were moist. But then she saw that it was just a trick of the light and was embarrassed at her naïvety. He might be remembering his own good chaps and the lost, forgotten and discredited causes for which they had died. But he was remembering without tears. He had seen so many bodies, so many deaths. Could any death now, she wondered, be more to him than a single statistic?

A door in the vestry led down to the crypt. To make their way down narrow stone steps lit by Ambrose's torch was to descend into a different world, a different time. Here alone was there any trace of the original Norman building. The roof was so low that Ivo, the tallest of them, could hardly stand upright, and the squat, heavy pillars strained as if bearing on their capitals the weight of nine centuries. Ambrose put out his hand to a wall switch and the claustrophobic chamber sprang into harsh unflattering light. They saw the skulls at once. One whole wall was patterned with them, a grinning parade of death. They had been ranged on rough oak shelves and were so tightly wedged that Cordelia judged that it would be impossible to separate them except by hacking them apart. Little care had been taken in the arrangement. In some places cement had been poured over them fixing mouth to mouth in the parody of a kiss. In others, the grit of the years had seeped between them binding them into cohesion; blocking the nasal cavities, collecting in the eye sockets and laying over the smooth domes a patina of dust like a shroud.

Ambrose said:

'There's a legend about them of course: there always is. In the seventeenth century the island was held by the de Courcy family; they had, in fact, been here since the fourteen hundreds. The de Courcy at that time was a particularly unpleasant representative of his breed. Someone must have told him about Tiberius' little doings on Capri – I don't suppose he could himself read – and he started to emulate them here. You can imagine the kind of thing; local maidens from the mainland abducted, *droit de seigneur* exercised on a scale which even the most compliant tenants found unreasonable, mutilated bodies brought in on the tide to the general disapproval of the locals. Speymouth was a small fishing village then. The town only reached any size or importance in the Regency – a sort of West Country Brighton. But the word got around. No one did anything, of course. The story is that the father of one of the abducted girls, whose tortured body floated ashore three weeks later, laid information against him with the local magistrate. De Courcy was subsequently tried at the Assizes but acquitted. One supposes it was managed in the usual way, a venal judge, perjured witnesses, bribed jurymen, a mixture of subservience and fear. And, of course, there was no direct evidence. At the end of the trial the father – he was an immensely powerful man according to the legend – rose up in court and cursed de Courcy and all his clan in the customary dramatic terms of dead first-born, revolting diseases, the castle falling into ruins, the line extinct. Everyone must have enjoyed that part immensely. And then, in 1665 came the Plague.'

Cordelia thought that Ambrose's pause, if intended for dramatic effect, was unnecessary. The little group ranged round him were gazing at him with the rapt attention of foreign tourists whose guide, for once, is giving value for money. Ambrose went on.

'The Plague raged particularly fiercely on this coast. It was said to have been brought here by a family from Cheapside who had relations in the village and fled here for safety. One by one the local families fell victim. The parson and his family died early and there was no one to say the rites over the dead. Soon there was only one old man willing to bury them. Anarchy reigned. The island felt itself to be safe and de Courcy threatened death to anyone who landed. The story is that a boatload of women and children with one adult male to manage the boat did try. But if they were hoping to arouse de Courcy's compassion they were disappointed. He was behaving perfectly reasonably in this instance, of course. The only way to escape the pestilence was quarantine. It wasn't quite as reasonable to drive holes in the planks in the bottom of the boat before forcing it out to sea so that the human cargo drowned before they could reach shore, but that may be only a gloss on the story. About those seventeenth-century boat people, I think we ought to give him the benefit of the doubt. And now for the climax.'

Ivo murmured:

'This story has everything but costumes by Motley and incidental music by Menotti.' But Cordelia saw that he was as interested as any of them.

'I don't know whether you know about the bubonic plague, the symptoms I mean. The victims would first have the sensation that they could smell rotting apples. After that came the dreaded pink rash on the forehead. The day came when the father of the murdered girl smelt the smell, saw in his glass the mark of death. It was a summer night but unruly, the sea turbulent. He knew that he hadn't long to live, the Plague killed swiftly. He launched his boat and set sail for the island.

'De Courcy and his private court were at dinner when the door of the great hall opened and he appeared, his great shambling sea-drenched figure, stumbling towards his enemy, eyes blazing. There was a moment when they were all too astounded for action. And in that moment he reached de Courcy, flung his great arms around him and kissed him full on the mouth.'

No one spoke. Cordelia wondered whether they would break into polite applause. The story had been well told and it had, in its simplicity, its terror, its almost symbolic confrontation of innocence with evil, a remarkable power.

Ivo said:

'That story would make an opera. You've got the scenario. All you need is a Verdi or a second Benjamin Britten.'

Roma Lisle, gazing at the skulls in fascinated distaste, asked:

'And did the curse come true?'

'Oh yes. De Courcy and all his people here caught the Plague and were wiped out. The line is now extinct. It was four years before anyone came here to bury them. But then a kind of superstitious awe surrounded the island. The landsfolk averted their eyes from it. Fishermen, remembering the old religion, crossed themselves when they sailed in its shadow. The castle crumbled. It remained a ruin until my great-grandfather bought the place in 1864, built himself a castle in the modern style, reclaimed the land, cleared the undergrowth. Only the ruins of the old Church remained standing. De Courcy and his islanders hadn't been buried in the churchyard. The locals hadn't thought that they merited Christian burial. As a result Herbert Gorringe kept turning up the skeletons when planting his pleasure garden. His men collected the skulls and arranged them here, a nice compromise between Christian disposal and tossing them on the bonfire.'

Roma said:

'There's something carved above the top shelf, words and numbers. The carving's a bit crude. It could be a biblical reference.'

'Ah, that's a personal comment by one of the Victorian workmen who thought that the setting up of this row of Yoricks might be an opportunity to point a moral and adorn a tale. No, I shan't identify it for you. Look it up for yourselves.'

Cordelia didn't need to look it up. A convent-born knowledge of the Old Testament and a lucky guess led her unerringly to the text.

'Judgement is mine saith the Lord. I will repay.'

It was, she thought, an inappropriate comment on a vengeance which, if Ambrose's story were true, had been so singularly, so satisfyingly human.

It was very cold in the crypt. Conversation had died. They stood in a ring looking at the row of skulls as if these smooth domes of bone, the ragged nasal orifices, the gaping sockets, could be made to yield the secret of their deaths. How unfrightening they were, thought Cordelia, these age-long symbols of mortality, set up like a row of grinning devils to frighten children at a fairground and, in their denuded anonymity, stripping human pretensions to the risible evidence that what lasted longest in man were his teeth.

From time to time during Ambrose's story she had glanced at Clarissa, wondering what effect this recital of horrors might have on her. It seemed to her strange that the crudely drawn caricature of a skull could produce such fear while the reality provoked no more than an exaggerated *frisson* of distaste. But Clarissa's refined sensibilities were apparently capable of sustaining any amount of assault provided the horrors were anaesthetized by time and there were no threats to herself. Even in the harsh, draining glare of the crypt her face looked flushed and the immense eyes shone more brightly. Cordelia doubted whether she would be happy to visit the crypt alone but now, feeling herself the centre of the company, she was enjoying a thrill of vicarious dread like a child at a horror movie who knows that none of the terror is real, that outside is the familiar street, the ordinary faces, the comfortable world of home. Whatever Clarissa feared, and Cordelia couldn't believe that the fear was faked, she had no sympathy with these long-dead tormented souls, no dread of a supernatural visitation in the small hours. She was expecting that, when her fate came and in whatever guise, it would still wear a human face. But now excitement had made her euphoric. She said to Ambrose:

'Darling, your island's a repository of horrors, charming on the surface and seething underneath. But isn't there something closer in time, a murder which really did happen? Tell us about the Devil's Kettle.'

Ambrose avoided looking at her. One of the skulls was unaligned with its fellows. He took the white ball between his hands and tried to grind it back into place. But it couldn't be shifted and, suddenly, the jaw bone came apart in his hands. He shoved it back, wiped his hands on his handkerchief and said:

'There's nothing to see. And the story is rather beastly. Only interesting really to those who relish in imagination the contemplation of another's pain.'

But the warning and the implied criticism were wasted on her. She cried:

'Darling, don't be so stuffy! The story's forty years old at least and I know about it anyway. George told me. But I want to see where it happened. And I've got a personal interest. George was here on the island at the time. Did you know that George was here?'

Ambrose said shortly:

'Yes, I know.'

Roma said:

'Whatever it is, you may as well show us. Clarissa won't give you any peace until you do and the rest of us are entitled to have our curiosity satisfied. It can hardly be worse than this place.'

No one else spoke. Cordelia thought that Clarissa and her cousin were unlikely allies even in persuasion and wondered whether Roma was genuinely interested or merely hoped to get the story over with so that she could get out of the crypt. Clarissa's voice assumed the wheedling note of an importunate child.

'Please, Ambrose. You promised that you would some time or other. Why not now? After all, we're here.'

Ambrose looked at George Ralston. The look seemed to invite consent, or at least comment. But if he were hoping for support in resisting Clarissa, he was disappointed. Sir George's face was impassive, its restlessness for once stilled.

Ambrose said:

'All right, if you insist.'

He led them to a low door at the west end of the crypt. It was made of oak, almost black with age and with strong bands of iron and a double bolt. Beside it on a nail hung a key. Ambrose shot back the bolts then inserted the key in the lock. It turned easily enough but he needed all his strength to pull open the door. Inside he reached up and switched on a light. They saw before them a narrow vaulted passage only wide enough for two to walk abreast. Ambrose led the way with Clarissa at his shoulder. Roma walked alone followed by Cordelia and Simon with Sir George and Ivo at the rear.

After less than twenty feet, the passage gave way to a flight of steep stone steps which curved to the left. At the bottom it widened but the roof was still so low that Ivo had to stoop. The passage was lit by unshaded but protected light bulbs hung from a cable and the air, although fusty, was fresh enough to breathe without discomfort. It was very quiet and their footsteps echoed on the stone floor. Cordelia estimated that they must have covered about two hundred yards when they came to a turn in the passage and then a second flight of steps, steeper than the first and rougher, as if hewn out of the rock. And it was then that the light failed.

The shock of instantaneous and total blackness after the artificial brightness of the tunnel made them gasp and one of the women – Cordelia thought that it was Clarissa – gave a cry. She fought against a moment of panic, calming by an act of will her suddenly pounding heart. Instinctively she stretched out her hand into the darkness and encountered a firm warm arm under thin cotton, Simon's arm. She let go but almost immediately felt her hand grasped by his. Then she heard Ambrose's voice.

'Sorry, everyone, I'd forgotten that the lights are on a time switch. I'll find the button in a second.'

But Cordelia judged that it must have been fifteen seconds before the light came on. They blinked at each other in the sudden glare, smiling a little sheepishly. Simon's hand was immediately withdrawn as if scalded and he turned his face from her. Clarissa said crossly:

'I wish you'd warn us before playing silly tricks.' Ambrose looked amused.

'No trick I assure you. And it won't happen again. The chamber above the Devil's Kettle has an ordinary light system. Only another forty yards to go. And you did insist on this excursion, remember.'

They went down the steps with the aid of a looped rope which had been threaded through rings bolted into the rock. After another thirty yards the passage widened to form a low-roofed cave. Ivo asked, his voice sounding unnaturally loud:

'We must be forty feet below ground. How is it ventilated?'

'By shafts. One of them comes up into the concrete bunker built in the war to guard the southern approach to the island. And there are a number of others. The first of them is believed to have been installed by de Courcy. The Devil's Kettle must have had its uses for him.'

In the middle of the floor was an oak trapdoor furnished with two strong bolts. Ambrose drew them back and pulled open the flap. They crowded round and six heads bent to peer down. They saw an iron ladder leading down to a cave. Below them heaved sea water. It was difficult to tell which way the tide was running but they could see the light streaming in from an aperture shaped like a half moon and they heard for the first time the faint susurration of the sea and smelt the familiar salty seaweed tang. With each wave the water gushed almost silently into the cave and swirled around the rungs of the ladder. Cordelia shivered. There was something remorseless, almost uncanny, about that quiet, regular spouting. Clarissa said:

'Now tell!'

Ambrose was silent for a minute. Then he said:

'It happened in 1940. The island and the castle were taken over by the Government and used as a reception and interrogation centre for foreign nationals of the Axis powers trapped in the United Kingdom by the war, and others, including a number of British citizens who were suspected, at worst, of being enemy agents or at best of being Nazi sympathizers. My uncle was living in the castle with only his one manservant and they were moved out to the cottage in the stable block now occupied by Oldfield. What went on in the castle was, of course, top secret. The internees were only kept here for a relatively short time and I've no reason to suppose that their stay was particularly uncomfortable. A number were released after interrogation and clearance, some went on to internment on the Isle of Man, some I suppose eventually came to less agreeable ends. But George knows more about the place than I do. As Clarissa says, he was stationed here as a young officer for a few months in 1940.'

He paused, but again there was no response. He had spoken as if Sir George were no longer with them. Cordelia saw Roma glance at Ralston, surprised, a little wary. She half opened her mouth then thought better of it. But she kept her gaze on him with a stubborn intensity rather as if she were seeing him for the first time.

Ambrose went on:

'I don't know any of the details. Someone does, I suppose, or as much of the truth as came out. There must be an official record of the incident somewhere although it was never published. All I know is what my uncle told me on one of my rare visits and that was mostly rumour.'

Clarissa permitted herself a display of nicely judged impatience. It was, thought Cordelia, as artificial as the simulated moue of distaste with which she had first regarded the shelf of skulls. Clarissa had no need of impatience; Clarissa knew exactly what was coming.

Ambrose spread plump hands and shrugged, as if resigned to a recital he would prefer to have avoided. But he could have avoided it, thought Cordelia, if he had really tried. And for the first time she wondered whether the conversation, even the visit to the crypt, had been the result of collusion.

He said:

'In March 1940 there were about fifty internees on Courcy and, among them, a hard core of dedicated Nazis most of whom were Germans trapped in Britain at the outbreak of war. They suspected one of their number, a boy of twenty-two, of having betrayed their secrets to the British authorities during interrogation. Perhaps he did. On the other hand, he may have been a British under-cover agent who had infiltrated their group. All I know are rumours, and second-hand rumours at that. What does seem beyond dispute is that the group of Nazis convened a secret court in the crypt of the Church, convicted their comrade of treason and condemned him to death. Then they gagged him, bound his arms and brought him down the passageway to this cave, the Devil's Kettle. As you can see it has a narrow opening which leads to the east cove but the cave is always flooded at high tide. They bound their victim to that iron ladder and left him to drown. He was a very tall young man. He died slowly in the darkness, and he died hard. Later one of them crept back to untie him and let the body float out to sea. When it was washed up only two days later the wrists were cut through almost to the bone. One of his fellow internees told a story of the young man's mounting depression and it was suggested that he had bound his wrists to prevent himself from swimming and had leapt into the sea. None of his judges or executioners ever spoke.'

Roma asked:

'Then how was the story ever known?'

'Someone talked eventually, I suppose, but not until after the war. Oldfield was living in Speymouth at the time and was employed here by the Army. He may have heard rumours. He doesn't admit it now, but someone on the island must have suspected. Someone may even have condoned what happened, or at least closed his eyes. After all, the Army were in charge here. Yet the gang got their hands on the keys to the crypt and the secret passage and managed to return them undetected. That suggests, well, let's say a certain degree of official carelessness on someone's part.'

Clarissa turned to her husband.

'What was he called, darling, the boy who died?'

'His name was Carl Blythe.'

Clarissa turned to the company. Her voice was as out of key as an hysteric:

'And the most extraordinary thing is that he was English – well, his father was anyway, his mother was German – and George was at school with him, weren't you, darling? They were both at Melhurst. He was three years older and rather a horrid boy, cruel really, one of those bullies who make other boys' lives a torment to them, so he and George weren't exactly friends. In fact George hated him. And then to find him here and at his mercy. Wasn't it odd?'

Ivo said easily:

'Not particularly. The British public schools produced their share of Nazi sympathizers and this is where you'd expect to find them in 1940.'

Cordelia stared down at the iron ladder. The light in the passage, fierce and garish, did nothing to mitigate the horror; rather it intensified it. In the old days, the cruelty of man to man was decently shrouded in darkness; the mind dwelt on airless unlit dungeons, on light filtering through the slits of narrow windows. But the modern interrogation rooms and torture chambers were ablaze with light. The technocrats of pain needed to see what they were at. Suddenly the place became intolerable to her. The chill of the passageway intensified. She had to tauten her arms and clench her fists to prevent herself visibly shaking. In her imagination the tunnel behind them stretched to infinity and they were doomed to rush down its contracting brightness like terrified rats. She felt a bead of sweat roll down her forehead and sting her eyes and knew that it had nothing to do with the cold. She made herself speak, hoping that her voice didn't betray her.

'Can't we get out of here? I feel like a voyeuse.'

Ivo said:

'And I feel cold.'

Taking her cue promptly, Clarissa shivered. Then Sir George spoke for the first time. Cordelia wondered whether it was her confused senses or the echo from the low roof which made his voice sound so different.

'If my wife has satisfied her curiosity perhaps we might go.'

Then he made a sudden jerk forward. Before they could guess what was coming he put his foot behind the open trapdoor and pushed. It crashed down. The walls seemed to crack and the passage shook under their feet. They must all have cried out, their voices thin screams in the echoing, reverberating roar. When it had faded no one spoke. Sir George had already turned on his heel and was making his way towards the entrance.

Cordelia found herself a little ahead of the others. Fear, and a deadening sense of misery which was stronger than fear and which added to her claustrophobia, urged her forward. Even the crypt with its neatly disposed ossuary was preferable to this horrible place. She stooped to pick up the neatly folded oblong of paper almost instinctively and without curiosity, without even turning it over to see if it were addressed. In the harsh light of the single bulb the neatly drawn skull and the typed quotation were starkly clear and she realized that she had known from the first what it must be.

Thy death is plotted; here's the consequence of murder.
We value not desert nor Christian breath,
When we know black deeds must be cur'd with death.

It was not, she thought, completely accurate. Surely the first word should be 'My' not 'Thy'. But the message was plain enough. She slipped it into her shirt pocket and turned to wait for the rest of the party. She tried to recall where they had all been standing when the lights went out. Surely it had been at about this spot where the tunnel curved. It would have taken only a few seconds for one of them to dart back under cover of the darkness, someone who had the message ready, someone who didn't care, might even have been pleased, that Clarissa would know that her enemy was one of this small party. And if anyone other than she had seen it first, or if the group had been together, then it must have been placed in Clarissa's hands. It was addressed to her in the same typed letters. Ambrose was perhaps the most likely culprit. That light had failed very conveniently. But any of the others could have done it, any except Simon. She had felt his hand firmly in hers.

And then they came into view. She stood under the light and scanned their faces. But none betrayed anxiety, none showed any surprise, no eyes dropped to the ground. Joining them she felt that she fully understood for the first time why it was that Clarissa was so afraid. Until now the messages had seemed little more than a childish persecution which no intelligent woman would think worth more than a moment's real anxiety. But they were a manifestation of hatred, and hatred, whatever else it was, could never be petty. They were childish, but there was an adult and sophisticated malice behind the childishness and the danger they threatened might, after all, be real and imminent. She wondered whether she was right in keeping this message and the earlier ones from Clarissa, whether it might not be safer to put her on increased guard. But her instructions had been clear; to save Clarissa from any anxiety or annoyance before the performance. There would be time enough after the play to decide what else should be done. And there were less than four hours now before the curtain rose.

While they were passing the row of skulls, this time without a glance, Cordelia found herself walking with Ivo. His speed, whether by necessity or design, was slower than the others and she kept pace with him. He said:

'That was an instructive episode, don't you think? Poor Ralston! I take it that the whole episode and his subsequent moral scruples were an offering of conjugal unreserve. What did you think of it all, oh wise Cordelia?'

'I thought that it was horrible.'

And both of them knew that she wasn't thinking only of that poor renegade's last agony, his lonely and terrible death. Roma came alongside them. Cordelia saw that, for once, she looked animated, her eyes brightly malicious. She said:

'Well that was an unedifying performance. For those of us fortunate enough to be unmarried it makes holy matrimony seem a pretty unholy estate. Almost terrifying.'

Ivo said:

'Marriage is terrifying. At least I've found it so.'

Roma was unwilling to let the matter rest.

'Does she always need to psych herself up with an exhibition of cruelty before a performance?'

'She's nervous certainly. It takes people different ways.'

'But this is only an amateur performance, for God's sake! The theatre can't hold more than eighty or so. And she's supposed to be a professional. What do you think George Ralston was feeling back there?'

The note of satisfaction was unmistakable. Cordelia wanted to say that one had only to have looked at his face to have seen what Sir George was thinking. But she didn't speak. Ivo said:

'Like most professional soldiers, Ralston is a sentimentalist. He takes the great absolutes, honour, justice, loyalty, and binds them to his heart with hoops of steel. I find it rather appealing. But it does make for a certain . . . rigidity.'

Roma shrugged.

'If you mean that he's abnormally controlled, I agree. It will be interesting to see what happens if ever the control snaps.'

Clarissa turned and called to them, her voice happily imperious:

'Come on, you three. Ambrose wants to lock the crypt. And I want lunch.'

CHAPTER TWENTY

The contrast between the sun-warmed terrace where, once again, luncheon was set out on a linen-covered trestle table, and the dark, rank-smelling pit of the Devil's Kettle, was so great that

Cordelia felt disorientated. That brief descent into the hell of the past could have happened in a different place and time. Looking out across the light-flecked sea to where the canvases of the Saturday sailors curved to catch the breeze, it was possible to imagine that it hadn't happened at all, that de Courcy's plague-ridden court, Carl Blythe's agony as he struggled against the horror of his long dying were the remnants of a nightmare which had no more reality than the caricatures of a horror comic.

It was a light meal, a watercress and avocado salad followed by salmon soufflé, chosen perhaps to soothe a nervous digestion. But even so, no one ate with appetite or evident enjoyment. Cordelia took one glass of the cool Riesling and forced down the salmon, knowing rather than tasting that it was delicious. Clarissa's brittle euphoria had given way to a silent preoccupation which no one liked to disturb. Roma crouched on the step at the end of the terrace, her unregarded plate in her lap, and gazed moodily out to sea. Sir George and Ivo stood together but neither spoke. But all of them, except Clarissa and herself, drank steadily. Ambrose said little but moved among them refilling the glasses, his bright eyes amused and indulgent as if they were children behaving predictably under stress.

Unexpectedly, Simon was the liveliest of the party. He was drinking heavily, apparently unnoticed by Clarissa, swilling the wine down as if it were beer, his hand a little unsteady, his eyes bright. At about ten to one, he suddenly announced loudly that he would go for a swim, looking round at them rather as if he expected them to take an interest in this news. No one did, but Clarissa said:

'Not so soon after a meal, darling. Take a walk first.'

The endearment was so unexpected that they all looked up. The boy blushed, gave them a stiff little bow, and disappeared. Shortly afterwards, Clarissa put down her plate, looked at her watch and said:

'Time to rest. No coffee, thank you, Ambrose. I never take it before a performance. I thought you knew that. Will you ask Tolly to bring up the tea-tray at once? China tea. She knows the kind I have. George, would you come up in five minutes? I'll see you later, Cordelia. Better make it ten past one.'

She made her slow way across the terrace with the graceful deliberation of a stage exit. For the first time, she seemed to Cordelia to be vulnerable, almost pathetic in her lonely, self-absorbed fear. She felt an impulse to follow, but knew that it would only arouse Clarissa's fury. And she had no fear of Clarissa finding another message thrust under the door. Cordelia had checked the room immediately before coming down to lunch. She knew now that the person responsible had been one of the small party who had visited the Devil's Kettle and all of them had been under her eye throughout the meal. Only Simon had left early. And she did not believe for one moment that the culprit was Simon.

Suddenly Roma struggled to her feet and hurried out after her cousin, almost running from the terrace. The eyes of Ambrose and Ivo met but neither spoke, inhibited perhaps by the presence of Sir George. He walked to the end of the terrace, his back to them, coffee cup in hand. He seemed to be counting the minutes. Then he glanced at his watch, replaced his cup on the table and made for the french windows. Looking round, foot on the step, he asked:

'What time does the curtain rise, Gorringe?'

'At three thirty.'

'And we change before then?'

'That's what Clarissa expects. There won't be time afterwards, anyway. Supper is at seven thirty.' Sir George nodded and was gone. Ivo said:

'Clarissa organizes her helots with the brutal precision of a military commander. Ten minutes before you need report for duty, Cordelia. Time surely for a second cup of coffee.'

When Cordelia unlocked her bedroom and went through the communicating door, Sir George was with his wife standing by the window looking out over the sea. The round silver tea-tray with its single cup and saucer, its elegant matching pot, was on the bedside chest as yet untouched. Clarissa, still in her Bermuda shorts and shirt, was pacing up and down, her colour high.

'She asked me for twenty-five thousand, came out with it, red-faced, as if she were a child asking for an increase in pocket money. And now of all times! She couldn't even wait until after the performance. Talk about crass stupidity! Is she deliberately trying to upset me or something?'

Sir George spoke without turning.

'Important to her, I expect. Couldn't bear the suspense of waiting. Had to know. It's not easy to get you alone.'

'She never had any sense of timing, even as a child. If there was a wrong moment for anything, trust Roma to pick it. Part of her general insensitivity. By God, she's chosen the wrong moment now!'

The voice from the window said quietly:

'Would there have been a right one?'

Clarissa seemed not to have heard.

'I told her that I wasn't prepared to hand over capital to support a lover who hadn't even the guts or decency to come and ask for it himself. I gave her some advice. If you have to buy yourself a man, he's not worth having. And if you can't get sex without buying it, buy cheaper. She's madly in love with him, of course. That's what this shop of theirs is all about, a ploy to get him away from his wife. Roma in love! I could almost feel sorry for him if he wasn't such a fool. When a plain virgin of forty-five falls in love for the first time and gets her first taste of sex, God help the man.'

'My dear, is that our concern?'

She said sharply:

'The money's my concern. Apart from anything else, they haven't a chance of making a go of it. No capital, no experience, no sense. Why should I throw good money after bad?'

She turned to Cordelia:

'You'd better go and get yourself dressed. Then lock your room and come out this way. I don't want you fussing about next door while I'm resting. I suppose you'll be wearing that Indian thing again. It shouldn't take long to get into that.'

Cordelia said:

'None of my clothes takes long to get into.'

'Nor to get out of, no doubt.'

Sir George swung round, his voice low:

'Clarissa!'

She smiled, gratified, and going up to him gently tapped his cheek.

'Dear George. Always so gallant.'

She might have been patting a dog.

Cordelia said:

'I wondered whether you'd like me to stay next door while you rest. The communicating door could be open or locked as you like. I wouldn't make any noise.'

'I've told you! I don't want you next door, or anywhere near me for that matter. I might want to speak some of the verse and I can't do that when I know someone's listening. With the three doors locked and no telephone in the room I suppose I can hope to be left in peace.' Suddenly she called out:

'Tolly!'

Tolly came out of the bathroom, dark-clad, expressionless as ever. Cordelia wondered how much if anything she had heard. Without being asked she went to the wardrobe and brought out Clarissa's satin robe and folded it over her arm. Then she went and waited silently beside her mistress. Clarissa unbuttoned her shirt and let it fall. Tolly made no move to pick it up but unhooked the back of Clarissa's brassière. That too fell away and was plucked off by Clarissa, held out and let drop. Lastly Clarissa unbuttoned the front of her shorts and eased them off together with her pants letting them fall together over her knees to the floor. She stood there for a moment immobile, her pale body dappled in the sunlight; the full, almost heavy breasts, the narrow waist, the jutting angular hips and smudge of corn-gold hair. Without haste Tolly unfolded the dressing-gown and held it out for Clarissa's waiting arms. Then she knelt, collected the bundle of discarded clothes and returned to the bathroom. Cordelia thought that it had been a ritualistic display of almost innocent sensuality, less vulgar than she would have expected, narcissistic rather than provocative. A conviction came to her as certain as it was irrational, that this was the image of Clarissa that she would remember all her life. And, whatever its motive, Clarissa's moment of frank exultation in her beauty seemed to have calmed her. She said:

'Don't take any notice of me, darlings. You know what it is before a performance.'

She turned to Cordelia:

'Just get anything you want from your room and let me have

both the keys. I'll set the alarm for two forty-five so come up about then and I'll let you know if there's anything I want you to do during the performance. And don't rely on being able to watch up front. I may want you backstage.'

Cordelia left them still together and went into her room by the communicating door. As she substituted her long cotton dress for shirt and jeans, she thought about Roma's extraordinary request. Why hadn't she done the obvious thing and waited until after the performance when she might have hoped to catch her cousin in the euphoria of success? But perhaps she had seen this as the most propitious, perhaps the only possible time. If the performance were a fiasco Clarissa would be unapproachable; it was possible that she might even leave the island without waiting for a celebratory party. But surely Roma must have known her cousin well enough to see that whatever moment she chose, hers was a hopeless cause. What was she hoping for; that Clarissa would once again indulge in the grand generous gesture as she obviously had with Simon Lessing, that she wouldn't be able to resist the insidiously gratifying role of patron and deliverer? Cordelia thought that two things were certain. Roma must be in desperate need of the money; and Roma, for one, wasn't betting on Clarissa's success.

She brushed her hair vigorously, gave a final look at herself in the glass without enthusiasm, and locked her bedroom door leaving the key in the lock. Then she knocked at the communicating door and went through. The key to that door was in the lock on Clarissa's side. Sir George and Tolly had left and Clarissa was seated at the dressing-table brushing her hair with long firm strokes. Without looking round she said:

'What have you done with your key?'

'Turned it and left it in the lock. Shall I lock the communicating door now?'

'No. I'll see to it. I want to check that you've locked your outside door.'

Cordelia said:

'I'll stay within call. If you want me I'll be at the end of the corridor. I can perfectly well get a chair from my room and sit there with a book.'

Clarissa's anger flared:

'Can't you understand English? What are you trying to do, spy on me? I've told you! I don't want you next door and I don't want you pussyfooting up and down the corridor. I don't want you, or anyone, near me. What I want now is to be left in peace!'

The note of hysteria was new and unmistakable. Cordelia said:

'Then will you roll up one of your towels tightly and wedge it against the door? I don't want any notes delivered to you by hand.'

Clarissa's voice was sharp.

'What do you mean? Nothing has happened since I arrived, nothing!'

Cordelia said soothingly:

'I just want to ensure that it stays that way. If whoever is responsible should land on Courcy Island, he might make one last attempt to get a message to you. I don't in the least think that it will happen. I'm sure it won't. The notes have probably stopped for good. But I don't want to take any risks.'

Clarissa said ungraciously:

'All right. It's not a bad idea. I'll block the bottom of the door.'

There seemed nothing else to say. As Cordelia went out, Clarissa followed her, firmly closed the door on her and turned the key. The scrape of metal, the small click were faint but Cordelia's keen ears heard them distinctly. Clarissa was locked in. There was nothing more that she could do until two forty-five. She looked at her watch. It was just one twenty.

CHAPTER TWENTY-ONE

There was only an hour and a half to be got through, but Cordelia found herself possessed of an irritable restlessness which made the slow minutes stretch interminably. It was a nuisance that her room was barred to her and that, before locking it, she had forgotten to pick up her book. She went to the library hoping to pass an hour with old bound copies of the *Strand Magazine*. But Roma was there, not reading but sitting upright close to the telephone, and the look she gave Cordelia was so unwelcoming that it was obvious she was expecting or hoping for a call and wanted to take it in private. Closing the door, Cordelia thought with envy of Simon, probably even now enjoying his solitary swim and of Sir George, striding out with his binoculars at the ready. She wished that she could be with him, but her long skirt was unsuitable for walking and, in any case, she felt that she shouldn't leave the castle.

She made her way to the theatre. The house lights were already on and the crimson and gold auditorium with its rows of empty seats seemed to be waiting in a hushed, portentous, nostalgic calm. Backstage, Tolly was checking the main women's dressing-room, setting out boxes of tissues and a supply of hand towels. Cordelia asked if she needed any help and received a polite but definite refusal. But she remembered that there was something she could do. Sir George, when he was at Kingly Street, had mentioned checking the set. She wasn't sure what he had had in mind. Even if the poison pen managed to secrete a missive on the set or among the props, Clarissa would hardly open and read it in the middle of a performance. But Sir George had been right. It was a sensible precaution to check the set and the props and she was glad to have something definite to do.

But all was well. The set for the first scene, a Victorian garden outside the palace, was simple: a blue backcloth, bay trees and geraniums in stone urns, a highly sentimental statue of a woman with a lute, and two ornate cane armchairs with cushions and footrests. At the side of the stage stood the props table. She checked over the assortment of Ambrose's Victoriana assembled for the indoor scenes; vases, pictures, fans, glasses, even a child's rocking-horse. A suede glove stuffed with cotton wool was placed ready for the prison scene and did, indeed, look unpleasantly like a severed hand. The musical-box was here, as was the silver-bound jewel chest for the Second Act. Cordelia opened it, but no missive lurked in its rosewood depths.

There was nothing else she could usefully do. There was still an hour before she was due to wake Clarissa. She walked for a time in the rose garden, but the sun was less warm here on the westerly side of the castle and, in the end, she returned to the terrace and sat in the corner of the bottom step leading to the beach. It was a small sun trap; even the stones struck warm to her thighs. She closed her eyes and lifted her face to the sun, relishing the soft air on her eyelids, the smell of pines and seaweed, and soothed by the gentle hiss of the waves on the shingle.

She must have dozed briefly, but was roused by the arrival of the launch. Ambrose and both the Munters were there to receive the cast, Ambrose already changed and wearing a voluminous silk cloak over his dinner-jacket, which gave him the appearance of a Victorian music-hall conjurer. There was a great deal of excited chatter as the cast, some of the men already in Victorian costume, jumped ashore and disappeared through the archway which led to the eastern lawn and the main entrance to the castle. Cordelia looked at her watch. It was two twenty; the launch was early. She settled down again but didn't dare risk closing her eyes. And twenty minutes later, she set off through the french windows to call Clarissa.

She paused outside the bedroom door and glanced at her watch. It was two forty-two. Clarissa had asked to be called at two forty-five but a few minutes could hardly matter. She knocked, quietly at first, and then more loudly. There was no reply. Perhaps Clarissa was already up and in the bathroom. She tried the door and to her surprise it opened and, looking down, she saw that the key was in the lock. The door opened easily with no obstructing wedge of towel. So Clarissa must have already got up.

For some reason which she was never able afterwards to understand, she felt no premonition, no unease. She moved into the dimness of the room calling gently:

'Miss Lisle, Miss Lisle. It's nearly two forty-five.'

The lined and heavy brocade curtains were drawn across the windows, but brightness pierced the paper-thin slit between them, and even their heavy folds couldn't entirely exclude the afternoon sun which seeped through as a gentle diffusion of pinkish light. Clarissa lay, ghost-like, on her crimson bed, both arms gently curved at her sides, the palms upwards, her hair a bright stream over the pillow. The bedclothes had been folded down and she was lying on her back, uncovered, the pale satin dressing-gown drawn up almost to her knees. Lifting her arms to draw back the curtains, Cordelia thought that the subdued light in the room played odd tricks; Clarissa's shadowed face looked almost as dark as the canopy of the bed, as if her skin had absorbed the rich crimson.

As the folds of the second curtain swung back and the room sprang into light she turned and saw clearly for the first time what it was on the bed. For a second of incredulous time her imagination whirled crazily out of control, spinning its fantastic images; Clarissa had applied a face mask, a darkening, sticky mess which had even seeped into the two eye-pads; the canopy was disintegrating, dripping its crimson fibres, obliterating her face with its richness. And then the ridiculous fancies faded and her mind accepted the stark reality of what her eyes had seen. Clarissa no longer had a face. This was no beauty mask. This pulp was Clarissa's flesh, Clarissa's blood, darkening and clotting and oozing serum, spiked with the brittle fragments of smashed bones.

She stood at the side of the bed, shaking. The room was full of noise, a regular drumming which filled her ears and pounded against her ribs. She thought: I must get someone, I must get help. But there was no help. Clarissa was dead. And she found that her limbs were rooted, only her eyes could move. But they saw things clearly, too clearly. Slowly she turned them from the horror on the bed and fixed them on the bedside chest. Something was missing, the silver jewel casket. But the small round tray of tea was still there. She saw the shallow cup, delicately painted with roses, the pale dregs of tea with two floating leaves, the smear of lipstick on the rim. And beside the tray there was something new: the marble limb, thick with blood, resting on top of a sheet of white paper, the chubby blood-stained fingers seeming to pin it to the polished wood. The blood had seeped over the paper, almost obliterating the familiar skull and crossbones, but the typed message had escaped that insidious stream and she could read it clearly:

Other sins only speak; murder shrieks out:
The element of water moistens the earth,
But blood flies upwards and bedews the heavens.

And then it happened. The alarm clock on the other bedside

cabinet rang making her leap with terror. Her limbs were galvanized into life. She dashed round the bed and tried to silence it, grabbing it with hands so shaking that the clock clattered on the polished wood. Oh God! Oh God! Would nothing stop it? Then her fingers found the button. The room was silent again, and in the echo of that dreadful ringing she could hear once again the thudding of her heart. She found herself looking at the thing on the bed as if terrified that the din had woken it, that Clarissa would suddenly jerk up stiff as a marionette and confront her with that faceless horror.

She was calmer now. There were things she must do. She must tell Ambrose. Ambrose would have to ring the police. And nothing must be touched until the police arrived. She found herself looking round the room, noticing all the details with great intensity: the balls of cotton wool smeared with make-up on the dressing-table, the bottle of eye lotion still unstoppered, Clarissa's embroidered slippers neatly placed on the hearth-rug, her make-up box open on a fireside chair, her copy of the script fallen by the bed.

As she turned to the door it opened and she saw Ambrose with Sir George behind him, his binoculars still round his neck. They stared at each other. No one spoke. Then Sir George pushed past Ambrose and moved up to the bed. Still without a word he stood gazing down at his wife, his back rigid. Then he turned. His face was taut; all its restlessness stilled, the skin almost green. Then he swallowed and put his hand to his throat as if he were about to retch. Cordelia made an instinctive movement towards him and cried:

'I'm sorry! I'm so very sorry!'

The words in all their futile banality appalled her as soon as she had uttered them. And then she saw his face, a mask of astonished horror. She thought: Oh, God, he thinks I'm confessing! He thinks I killed her.

She cried:

'You employed me to look after her. I was here to keep her safe. I should never have left her.'

She watched the horror drain from his face. He said calmly, almost crisply:

'You couldn't have known. I didn't believe she was in any danger, no one did. And she wouldn't have let you stay with her, you or anyone. Don't blame yourself.'

'But I knew that the marble had been taken! I should have warned her.'

'Against what? You couldn't have expected this.' He said again, sharply as if he were giving a command: 'Don't blame yourself, Cordelia.'

It was the first time he had used her Christian name.

Ambrose was still at the door. He said:

'Is she dead?'

'See for yourself.'

He moved up to the bed and looked down at the body. His face flushed a deep red. Watching him, Cordelia thought that he looked more embarrassed than shocked. Then he turned away.

He said:

'But this is incredible!' Then he whispered, 'Horrible! Horrible!'

Suddenly he darted to the communicating door and turned the knob. It was unlocked. They followed him into Cordelia's room and through into the bathroom. The window to the fire escape was open as she had left it. Sir George said:

'He could have got out this way and down the fire escape. We'd better organize a search of the island. The castle too, of course. How many men can we muster including those in the play?'

Ambrose made a rapid calculation.

'About twenty-five of the players and six of us including Oldfield. I don't know whether Whittingham will be much use.'

'That's enough for four search parties, one for the castle, three to cover the island. It needs to be systematic. You'd better ring the police at once. I'll get the men organized.'

Cordelia could imagine the disruption that thirty or more people tramping over the house and island would cause. She said:

'We mustn't touch anything. Both these rooms must be locked. It's a pity that you handled the door knob. And we'd better prevent the audience from landing. About the search, mightn't it be better to wait for the police?'

Ambrose looked uncertain. Sir George said:

'I'm not prepared to wait. That's not possible. It's not possible, Gorringe!'

His voice was fierce. His eyes looked almost wild. Ambrose said soothingly:

'No, of course not.'

Sir George asked:

'Where's Oldfield?'

'In his cottage, I imagine. The stable block.'

'I'll get him to take out the launch and patrol the Channel between here and Speymouth. That'll block any escape by sea. And then I'll join you in the theatre. Better warn the men that I'll be wanting them.'

He was gone. Ambrose said:

'It's best that he has something to do to keep him busy. And I don't suppose they'll do any harm.'

Cordelia wondered what Oldfield was supposed to do if he did intercept a boat leaving the island. Board it and tackle a murderer single-handed? And did either Ambrose or Sir George seriously expect to find an intruder on Courcy? Surely the significance of that bloody hand couldn't have escaped them.

Together they checked the door in Cordelia's room leading to the corridor. It was locked from the inside with the key still in place. So the murderer couldn't have left by that route. Next they closed and locked the communicating door. Finally they locked Clarissa's room behind them and Ambrose pocketed the key. Cordelia said:

'Are there any duplicate keys?'

'No, none. The spare bedroom keys were missing when I inherited and I've never bothered to have others made. It wouldn't have been easy, anyway. The locks are complicated; these are the original keys.'

As they turned from the door they heard footsteps and Tolly appeared round the corner of the gallery. Acknowledging them with only a nod she went up to Clarissa's door and knocked. Cordelia's heart thumped. She looked at Ambrose, but he seemed bereft of speech. Tolly knocked again, this time more loudly. Then she turned to Cordelia.

'I thought you were supposed to call her at two forty-five. She should have left it to me.'

Cordelia said, through lips which were so dry and swollen that she thought they would crack:

'You can't go in. She's dead. Murdered.'

Tolly turned and knocked again.

'She's going to be late. I have to go to her. She always needs me before a performance.'

Ambrose took a step forward. For a moment Cordelia thought that he was going to lay a hand on Tolly's shoulder. Then his arm dropped. He said in a voice which seemed unnaturally harsh:

'There isn't going to be a performance. Miss Lisle is dead. She's been murdered. I'm just about to ring the police. Until they arrive no one can go into that room.'

This time she understood. She turned and faced him, her face expressionless but so white that Cordelia, thinking she would faint, put out a hand and grasped her arm. She felt Tolly shudder, a small spasm of rejection, almost of revulsion which was unmistakable, as shocking as a blow in the face. Quickly she withdrew her hand. Tolly said:

'The boy. Does the boy know?'

'Simon? Not yet. No one knows except Sir George. We've only just discovered the body.'

His voice held a trace of aggrieved impatience, like an overworked servant. Cordelia almost expected him to protest that he couldn't see to everything at once. Tolly still fixed her eyes on him. She said:

'You'll break it gently, sir. It will be a shock to him.'

Ambrose said curtly:

'It's a shock for us all.'

'Not for one of us, sir.'

She turned and left them without another word.

Ambrose said:

'Extraordinary woman! I've never understood her. I doubt whether Clarissa did. And why this sudden concern for Simon? She's never shown any particular interest in the boy. Oh, well, we'd better get on with telephoning the police.'

They made their way down the stairs and through the great hall. Here preparations for the buffet supper were already under way. The long refectory table was covered with a cloth and rows of wine glasses were ranked at one end. The door to the dining-room was open and Cordelia could see Munter pulling the chairs from the table and putting them in line, presumably before carrying them into the hall. Ambrose said:

'Wait here a moment, will you.'

A minute later he was back. He said:

'I've told Munter. He'll get down to the quay and prevent the launches from tying up.'

They went together into the business room. Ambrose said:

'If Cottringham were here, he'd probably insist on speaking to the Chief Constable personally. But I suppose the Speymouth police are the ones to ring. Ought I to ask for the CID?'

'I should just ring the Speymouth Station and leave it to them. They'll know the procedure.'

She looked up the number for him and waited while he got through. He gave the facts succinctly and without emotion, mentioning that Lady Ralston's jewel box was missing. Cordelia was interested that he had noticed its absence; nothing had been said while they were in the bedroom. There was a certain amount of delay from the other end of the line and then the crackle of a voice. She heard Ambrose say:

'Yes, we've already done that,' and, later: 'That is what I propose doing as soon as I get off the line.' Shortly afterwards he put down the receiver and said:

'Much as you expected. Lock the rooms. Don't touch anything. Keep people together. Don't let anyone land. They're sending a Chief Inspector Grogan.'

In the theatre the house lights were already on. A door to the left of the proscenium led backstage. From the open doors of the two main dressing-rooms came laughter and a confusion of voices. Most of the cast had already changed and were now making up with a great deal of giggling advice from their friends. The atmosphere was reminiscent of an end-of-term frolic. Ambrose knocked on the closed doors of the two rooms reserved for the principals, then called out loudly:

'Will you all come on stage please, immediately.'

They tumbled out in an unruly bunch, some clutching their clothes around them. But one glance at his face silenced them and they trooped on to the stage subdued and expectant. Partly costumed and half made-up as they were, their faces white except for the garish patches of rouge, they looked, thought Cordelia, like the clients and inmates of some Victorian bawdy-house pulled out by the police for interrogation. Ambrose said:

'I'm afraid I have some very shocking news for you. Miss Lisle is dead. It looks very much like murder. I've telephoned the police and they'll be here shortly. In the meantime, they've asked that you all stay together here in the theatre. Munter and his wife will bring you all some tea and coffee and anything else you need. Perhaps, Cottringham, you'd take charge here. There are still people I have to tell.'

One of the women, a blonde, pert-faced girl dressed as a parlour-maid in a frilled apron and goffered cap with long streamers said:

'But what about the play?'

It was a question born of shock which Cordelia thought she would probably remember with shame all her life. Someone gasped, and she blushed scarlet. Ambrose said curtly:

'The performance is cancelled.'

Then he turned on his heel and left. Cordelia followed. She said:

'What about the search parties?'

'I'll leave that to Ralston and Cottringham to sort out. I've told the cast to stay together. I can't cope with trying to enforce police instructions against the determination of the bereaved husband to demonstrate his competence. Where, do you suppose, are the rest of the party?'

He sounded almost peevish. Cordelia said:

'I suppose Simon is swimming. Roma was in the library, but she's probably dressing by now. I imagine that Ivo is in his room, resting.'

'See them, will you, and break the news. I'll go and find Simon. Then we'd better stay together until the police arrive. I suppose it would be courteous if I kept company with my guests in the theatre but I'm not in the mood to cope with a gaggle of agitated women all hurling questions at me.'

Cordelia said:

'The less they're told until the police arrive, the better.'

He glanced at her with his sharp bright eyes.

'I see. You mean we should keep quiet about the actual cause of death?'

'We don't know the actual cause of death. But yes, I think we should say as little as possible to anyone.'

'But surely the cause of death was obvious. Her face had been battered in.'

'That may have been done after death. There was less blood than one would expect.'

'There was more than enough blood for me. You're remarkably knowledgeable for a secretary-companion.'

'I'm not a secretary-companion. I'm a private detective. There's no point in carrying on the charade any longer. Anyway, I know that you'd already guessed. And if you're going to say that I've been useless, I know that too.'

'My dear Cordelia, what more could you have done? No one could have expected murder. Stop blaming yourself. We're going to be stuck here together at least until the inquest, and it will be boring enough being grilled by the police without having you sunk in lugubrious self-reproach. It doesn't suit you.'

They had reached the door which led from the arcade into the castle. Glancing round, they saw Simon in the distance, towel slung round his shoulders, making his way down the long grass slope which led upwards from the rose garden between the avenue of beeches to the crown of the island. Without speaking, Ambrose went to meet him. Cordelia stood in the shadow of the doorway and watched. Ambrose didn't hurry; his walk was little more than a leisurely stroll. The two figures came together and stood in the sun, their heads bent, their shadows staining the bright grass. They didn't touch. After a moment, still distanced, they began walking slowly towards the castle. Cordelia passed into the great hall. Coming down the staircase was Ivo with Roma at his side. He was in his dinner-jacket, Roma was still wearing her trouser-suit. She called down to Cordelia:

'Where is everyone? The place is dead as a morgue. I've just been telling Ivo I've no intention of changing, and I'm not coming to the play. You two can do what you like but I'm damned if I'll climb into an evening dress in the middle of a warm afternoon just to watch a bunch of amateurs make fools of themselves and pander to Clarissa's megalomania. You all indulge her nonsense as if you're terrified of her. Someone should put a stop to Clarissa.'

Cordelia said:

'Someone has.'

They froze on the stairway, gazing down at her.

She said:

'Clarissa's dead. Murdered.'

And then her control broke. She gave a gasp and felt the hot tears coursing down her face. Ivo ran down to her and she felt his arms, thin and strong as steel rods, pulling her towards him. It was the first human contact, the first sympathetic gesture which anyone had made since the shock of finding Clarissa's body, and the temptation to give way and cry like a child against his shoulder was almost irresistible. But she gulped back her tears, fighting for control, while he held her gently without speaking. Looking up over his shoulder she saw, through her tears, Roma's face hanging above her, a streaked amorphous pattern of white and pink. Then she blinked and the features came into focus: the mouth, so like Clarissa's, hanging loose, the eyes staring wide, the whole face blazing with an emotion which could have been terror or triumph.

She wasn't sure how long they stayed there, she locked in Ivo's arms, Roma staring down at them. Then she heard footsteps behind her. She broke free murmuring over and over again, 'I'm sorry. I'm sorry. I'm sorry.' Ambrose spoke:

'Simon's gone to his room. He's very shocked and he wants to be alone. He'll be down as soon as he feels ready.'

Ivo asked:

'What happened. How did she die?'

Ambrose hesitated and Roma cried out:

'You've got to tell us! I insist that you tell us!'

Ambrose looked at Cordelia. He gave a shrug of resigned apology. 'Sorry, but I'm not prepared to do the work of the police. They have a right to know.' He looked up at Roma. 'She was battered to death. Her face has been smashed to pulp. It looks as if the weapon used was the limb of the dead princess. I haven't told Simon how she was killed and I think it better that he doesn't know.'

Roma sank down on the stairs and grasped the banister. She said:

'Your marble? The killer took your marble? But why? How did he know it was there?'

Ambrose said:

'He, or she, took it from the display cabinet some time before seven o'clock this morning. And I'm afraid that the police are only too likely to take the view that he knew it was there because, yesterday before luncheon, I myself showed it to him.'

CHAPTER TWENTY-TWO

Ten minutes later Roma, Ivo and Cordelia stood at the drawing-room window and looked down over the terrace to the landing stage. All three of them were now outwardly calm. The first shock had been replaced by a restlessness, almost an unhealthy, prurient excitement which they recognized in themselves and each other and which was as shaming as it was unexpected. They had all resisted the temptation to take alcohol, perhaps feeling that it would be unwise to face the police with its smell on their breath. But Munter had served strong coffee in the drawing-room and it had been almost as effective.

Now they watched as the two heavily loaded launches rocked dangerously at the quayside, the passengers in their evening clothes crowding to one side like a gaudily clad cargo of aristocratic refugees fleeing from some republican holocaust. Ambrose was talking to them, with Munter standing at his shoulder like a second line of defence. There was a great deal of gesticulating. Even at this distance, Ambrose's pose, the slightly bent head, the spread hands, conveyed regret, distress and some embarrassment. But he was standing firm. The sound of chattering came to them, faint but high like the squeaking of distant starlings. Cordelia said to Ivo:

'They look restless. I expect they want to stretch their legs.'

'Want to pee I expect, poor dears.'

'There's someone standing up on the gunwale taking photographs. If he's not careful, he'll go overboard.'

'That's Marcus Fleming. He's supposed to be taking the pictures to illustrate my article. Oh well, he'll be able to phone a scoop of sorts to London if they don't capsize with excitement before they reach shore.'

'The fat lady seems very determined, the one in mauve.'

'That's Lady Cottringham, the formidable dowager. Ambrose had better watch her. If she gets one foot on the quay there'll be no holding her. She'll dash in to give poor Clarissa the once-over, subject us all to third-degree and solve the crime before the police get here. Ah, victory for Ambrose! The launches are pulling away.'

Roma said quietly:

'And here come the police.'

Round the corner of the island came four bright wings of spray. Two sleek, dark-blue launches were approaching, their long wakes feathering the paler blue of the sea. Roma said:

'Odd that one feels so apprehensive. Stupid, too. It's like being a schoolgirl again. One always felt and looked most guilty when one was totally innocent.'

Ivo said:

'Totally? That's an enviable state. I've never managed to achieve it. But I shouldn't worry. The police have a formula for these occasions. The suspects are ranked in strict order of priority; first, the husband, then the heirs, then the family, then close friends and acquaintances.'

Roma said dryly:

'As I'm both an heir and a relation, I can hardly find that reassuring.'

They watched in silence as the two brightly laden launches drew clumsily away and those sleek blue hulls came rapidly closer.

PART FOUR

The Professionals

CHAPTER TWENTY-THREE

Sergeant Robert Buckley was young, good-looking and intelligent and well aware of these advantages. Less commonly, he was also aware of their limitations. He had gained three A-level subjects with respectable grades at the end of his two years in the sixth, an achievement which would have justified going on to university in company with friends similarly qualified. But it wouldn't have been the university of his choice. He suspected that his intelligence, although keen, was superficial, that he couldn't compete with real scholars, and he had no intention of joining the over-educated unemployed at the end of another three years of mildly boring academic grind. He judged that success would come quickest in a job for which he was over- rather than under-qualified and where he would be competing with men who were less rather than better educated than himself. He recognized in himself a streak of sadism which found a certain mild satisfaction in the pain of others without necessarily needing actively to inflict it. He was an only child of elderly parents who had begun by doting on him, moved on to admiring him and had ended by being a little afraid of him. That, too, he found agreeable. His choice of career had been natural and easy, the final decision made while he was loping with long, easy strides over the Purbeck hills, watching the earth move in streaks of fawn and green. There had only been two possibilities, the Army or the Police, and he had quickly rejected the first. He was aware of some social insecurity; there were traditions, mores, a public school ethos about the Army for which he felt a wary distrust. This was an alien world which might expose him, even reject him, before he had had a chance to master it. The Police, on the other hand, given what he had to offer, ought to be pleased to have him. And to do them justice, they had been pleased.

Sitting now in the bow of the launch, he felt satisfied with the world and with himself. He made a practice of concealing his enthusiasm as he did his imagination. Both were like fascinating but wayward friends, to be enjoyed rarely and with caution since they had about them the taint of treachery. But as he watched Courcy Island steadily taking form and colour across a dazzle of sea, he was aware of a heady mixture of exultation and fear. He exulted at the promise that here, at last, was the murder case of which he had dreamed since he had gained his sergeant's stripes. He feared that it might yet collapse; that they would be met at the jetty with those depressingly familiar words:

'He's waiting for you upstairs. We've got someone watching him. He's in a terrible state. He says he doesn't know what came over him.'

They never did know what came over them, those self-confessed murderers, as pathetic in defeat as they were incompetent in their killing. Murder, the unique and ultimate crime, was seldom the most interesting forensically or the most difficult to solve. But when you did get a good one there was no excitement like it; the heady combination of a man-hunt with a puzzle, the smell of fear in the air, strong as the metallic smell of blood, the sense of randy well-being, the fascinating way in which confidence, personality, morale subtly changed and deteriorated under its contaminating impact. A good murder was what police work was about. And this promised to be a good one.

He glanced across to where his chief sat, his red hair glinting in the sun. Grogan looked as he always did before a case, silent and withdrawn, the eyes hooded but wary, the muscles tensed under the well-cut tweed, the whole of that powerful body gathering its energies for action like the predator he was. When Buckley had been introduced to him three years earlier he had been at once reminded of pictures in his boyhood comics of an Indian brave and had mentally crowned that carved and ruddy head with ceremonial feathers. But the comparison had in some subtle way been inaccurate. Grogan was too large a man, too English and too complicated for so uncompromisingly simple an image. Buckley had only once been invited briefly into the stone cottage outside Speymouth where, separated from his wife, Grogan lived alone. It was rumoured that he had a son and that there was some trouble with the boy; what exactly no one seemed to know. The cottage had revealed nothing. There were no pictures, no mementoes of old cases, no photographs of family or colleagues, few books apart from what looked like a complete set of the Famous Trials series, little but bare stone walls and a bank of expensive stereo equipment. Grogan could have packed his bags and been out of it in half an hour leaving nothing of himself behind. Buckley still didn't understand him although after two years of working under him he knew what to expect; the alternate taciturnity and volubility during which he would use his sergeant as a sounding-board; the occasional sarcasm, the ruthlessness and the impatience. He only partly resented being used as a combination of clerk, shorthand writer, pupil and audience. Grogan did too much of the work himself. But you could learn from him; he got results; he wasn't tainted with failure and he was fair. And he was nearing retirement; only two years to go. Buckley took what he wanted from him and bided his time.

There were three figures waiting for them on the jetty, motionless as statues. Buckley guessed who two of them must be before the launches had chugged to a stop: Sir George Ralston standing almost at attention in his old-fashioned shooting-jacket. Ambrose Gorringe more relaxed but incongruously formal in his dinner-jacket. Both of them watched the arrivals disembark with wary formality like the commanders of a besieged castle awaiting the armistice negotiators and watching with undeluded eyes for the first hint of treachery. The third man, dark-clad and taller than the other two was obviously some kind of servant. He stood a little behind them and gazed stolidly past them out to sea. His stance conveyed that certain guests were welcome on Courcy but that the police were not among them.

Grogan and Gorringe made the introductions. Buckley noticed that his chief expressed no sympathy, spoke no words of formal regret to the widower. But then, he never did. He had once explained why: 'It's offensively insincere, and they know it. There's enough duplicity in police work without adding to it. Some lies are insulting.' And if Ralston or Gorringe noticed the omission, neither made a sign.

Ambrose Gorringe did all the talking. As they moved between wide lawns towards the castle entrance, he said:

'Sir George has organized a search of the castle and the island. The castle has been searched but the three groups covering the island aren't back yet.'

'My men will take that over now, sir.'

'So I supposed. The rest of the cast are in the theatre. Sir Charles Cottringham would be glad of a word with you.'

'Did he say what about?'

'No. Merely a matter, I imagine, of letting you know that he's here.'

'I know that already. I'll see the body now and then I'd be grateful for the use of a small and quiet room for the rest of the day and, possibly, until Monday.'

'I thought that my business room would be the most suitable. If you will ring from Miss Lisle's room when you're ready, I'll show you where it is. And Munter will get you anything you need. My guests and I will be in the library when you want us.'

They moved through a large hall and up the staircase. Buckley noticed nothing of his surroundings. He walked with Sir George immediately behind Grogan and Ambrose Gorringe and listened while Gorringe gave his chief a succinct but remarkably comprehensive account of the events leading up to Miss Lisle's death: how she came to be on the island; brief particulars of the rest of the house party; the threatening letters; the fact that she had thought it necessary to bring her own private detective with her, Miss Cordelia Gray; the loss of the marble limb; the discovery of the body. It was an impressive performance, as carefully impersonal and factual as if it had been rehearsed. But then, thought Buckley, it probably had.

Outside the door, the party paused. Gorringe handed over three keys. He said:

'I locked all three doors after the discovery of the body. These are the only keys. I take it you don't want us to come in?'

Sir George spoke for the first time:

'When you need me, Chief Inspector, I'll be with my wife's stepson in his room. Boy's upset. Natural in the circumstances. Munter knows where to find me.' He turned abruptly and left them.

Grogan answered Gorringe's question.

'You've been very helpful, sir. But I think we can manage here on our own.'

She was an actress even in death. The scene in the bedroom was extraordinarily dramatic. Even the set had been cleverly designed for melodrama in the grand manner, the props glittering and ostentatious, the dominant colour red. And there she lay sprawled under the crimson canopy, one white leg carefully raised to show an expanse of thigh, her face plastered with artificial blood, while director and cameraman stepped round her, contemplating the best angles, careful not to touch or disturb that artfully provocative pose. Grogan stood at the right of the bed and looked down at her frowning, as if wondering whether the casting director had been right in choosing her for the role. Then he leaned down and sniffed at the skin of her arm. The moment was bizarre. Buckley thought: 'Is thy servant a dog that he should do this thing?' Almost he expected her to shudder with outrage, sit up and stretch out groping hands, demand a towel to wipe the mess from her face.

The room was overcrowded but the experts in death, investigating officers, fingerprint officers, photographer and scene-of-crime searchers, were adept at keeping out of each other's way. Grogan, as Buckley knew, had never reconciled himself to the use of civilian scene-of-crime officers, which was odd when you considered that he had come from the Met where the employment and training of civilians had gone about as far as it could go. But these two knew what they were about. They moved as delicately and confidently as a couple of cats prowling their familiar habitat. He had worked with both of them before but he doubted whether he would recognize them in the street or the pub. He stood back out of the way and watched the senior of them. It was always their hands that he watched, hands sheathed in gloves so fine that they looked like a second glistening skin. Now those hands poured the remnants of the tea into a collecting flask, stoppered, sealed and labelled it; gently eased the cup and saucer into a plastic bag; scraped a sample of blood from the marble limb and placed it in the specially prepared tube; took up the limb itself, touching it only with the tips of the fingers and lowered it into a sterile box; delicately picked up the note with tweezers and insinuated that gently into its envelope. At the bed his colleague was busy with magnifying glass and tweezers, collecting hairs from the pillow, seemingly oblivious of that shattered face. When the Home Office pathologist had completed his examination, the bedclothes would be bundled into a plastic bag, sealed and added to the other exhibits.

Grogan said:

'Doc Ellis-Jones is visiting his mother-in-law at Wareham, conveniently for us. They've sent an escort. He should be here within the next half-hour. Not that there's much he can tell us that we can't see for ourselves. And the time of death is fixed within pretty tight limits anyway. If you reckon the loss of body heat on this kind of day at about one and a half degrees an hour for the first six hours, he's unlikely to be able to put it any closer than we already know, some time between twenty past one when the girl left her alive, so Ambrose Gorringe tells us, and two forty-three when the same girl found her dead. To be the last one to see the victim and the one to find the body suggests that Miss Cordelia Gray is either careless or unfortunate. We may be able to judge which when we see her.'

Buckley said:

'From the appearance of the blood, sir, I'd say that she died sooner rather than later.'

'Yes. My guess would be within about thirty minutes of being left. That quotation under the marble limb. You recognized it, Sergeant?'

'No, sir.'

'I'm relieved to hear it. From *The Duchess of Malfi*, so Ambrose Gorringe informs us, the play in which Miss Lisle was cast in the title role. "Blood flies upwards and bedews the heavens." I applaud the sentiment even if I couldn't identify the source. But it isn't particularly apposite. The blood didn't fly upwards, or not to any great extent. This systematic destruction of the face was done after death. And we know the possible reasons for that.'

It was rather like a *viva-voce* examination, thought Buckley. But this question was an easy one.

'To conceal identity. To obscure the real cause of death. To make absolutely sure. An explosion of anger, hatred or fear.'

'And then, after that brainstorm of violence, our literary-minded murderer calmly replaces the eye pads. He has a sense of humour, Sergeant.'

They moved together into the bathroom. Here was a compromise between period opulence and modern functionalism. The great bath was marble and encased in a mahogany surround. The seat of the lavatory was mahogany, too, with a high flush. The walls were tiled, each tile painted in blue with a different posy of wild flowers, and there was a cheval-glass, its frame decorated with cherubs. But the towel-rail was heated, there was a bidet, a shower had been installed above the bath and a shelf over the hand-basin held a formidable assortment of bath essences, powder and expensive wrapped soaps.

Four white towels were untidily hung over the rail. Grogan sniffed each of them and rumpled them in his huge hands. He said:

'It's a pity about that heated rail. They're completely dry. And so are the bath and hand-basin. There's no way of telling whether she had time to bath before she was killed, not unless Doc Ellis-Jones can isolate traces of powder or bath essence from her skin, and even that wouldn't be conclusive. But the towels look as if they've been recently used and they're slightly scented. So is the body and it's the same smell. My guess is that she did have time. She drank her tea, took off her make-up and bathed. If Miss Gray left her at twenty past one, that would bring us to about twenty minutes to two.'

The senior scene-of-crime officer was waiting at the door. Grogan stood aside for him then went back into the bedroom and stood at the window looking out to where a hairline of purple separated the darkening sea from the sky. He said:

'Have you heard of the Birdhurst Rise Poisonings?'

'In Croydon, wasn't it, sir? Arsenic.'

'Three members of the same middle-class family murdered with arsenic between April 1928 and March 1929; Edmund Duff, a retired Colonial Civil Servant, his sister-in-law and her widowed mother. In each case the poison must have been administered in food or medicine. It could only have been a member of the household, but the police never made an arrest. It's a fallacy to suppose that a small circle of suspects, all known to each other, makes a case easier to solve. It doesn't; it only makes failure indefensible.'

Failure wasn't a word which Buckley could remember having

heard before on Grogan's lips. His euphoria gave way to a small weight of anxiety. He thought of Sir Charles Cottringham even now cooling his heels in the theatre, of the Chief Constable, of Monday's publicity. 'Baronet's wife battered to death in island castle. Well-known actress slain.' This wasn't a case which any officer ambitious for his future could afford to lose. He wondered what it had been about this room, this victim, this weapon, perhaps the air of Courcy Island itself, which had evoked that depressing note of caution.

For a moment neither of them spoke. Then there was a sudden roar and a speedboat rounded the eastern tip of the island and swept a wide curving wake towards the quay. Grogan said:

'Doc Ellis-Jones is making his usual dramatic appearance. Once he's told us what we already know, that she's a female and she's dead, and has explained what we can work out for ourselves, that it wasn't accident or suicide and it happened between one twenty and two forty-three, we can get down to the business of finding out what our suspects have to say for themselves, beginning with the baronet.'

CHAPTER TWENTY-FOUR

It was nearly half-past four and Ambrose, Ivo, Roma and Cordelia were standing together on the jetty looking out to sea as *Shearwater*, taking the cast back to Speymouth, moved beyond the eastern tip of the island and out of sight. Ambrose said:

'Well, they may have been done out of their moment in the spotlight but they can't complain that the day has been dull. Clarissa's murder will be all over the county by dinner-time. That means we can expect a press invasion by dawn.'

Ivo said:

'What will you do?'

'Prevent anyone from landing, although not with the brutal effectiveness of de Courcy at the time of the Plague. But the island is private property. And I'll instruct Munter to refer all telephone inquiries to the police at Speymouth. They've presumably got a public relations department. Let them cope.'

Cordelia, still in her cotton dress, shivered. The bright day was beginning to fade. Soon would come that transitory and lovely moment when the setting sun shines with its last and brightest rays, intensifying the colour of grass and trees so that the air itself is stained with greenness. Now the shadows lay long and heavy over the terrace. The Saturday sailors had turned for home and the sea stretched in an empty calm. Only the two police launches rocked gently against the quay, and the smooth bricks of the castle walls and turrets, which for a moment had glowed with a richer red, darkened and reared above them, ponderous and forbidding.

As they passed through the great hall, the castle received them into an unnatural silence. Somewhere upstairs the police were busy with their secret expertise of death. Sir George was either being questioned or was with Simon in his room. No one seemed to know and no one liked to ask. The four of them, still awaiting their formal questioning, turned by common consent into the library. It might be less comfortable than the drawing-room, but at least it offered plenty of material for those who chose to pretend that they wanted to read. Ivo took the only easy chair and lay back with his eyes turned to the ceiling, his long legs stretched. Cordelia sat at the chart table and slowly turned the pages of the 1876 bound copy of the *Illustrated London News*. Ambrose stood with his back to them, looking out over the lawn. Roma was the most restless, regularly pacing between the bookshelves like a prisoner under compulsory exercise. It was a relief when Munter and his wife brought in the tea, the heavy silver teapot, the brass kettle with the wick burning under it, the Minton tea-service. Munter drew the curtains across the tall windows and put a match to the fire. It crackled into life. Paradoxically the library became at once cosier but more oppressive, enclosed in its shadowed hermetic calm. They were all thirsty. No one had much appetite but ever since the finding of the body they had craved the comfort and stimulus of strong tea or coffee, and busying themselves with cups and saucers at least gave them something to do. Ambrose settled himself beside Cordelia. Stirring his tea he said:

'Ivo, you have all the London gossip. Tell us about this man, Grogan. I confess that, on first acquaintance, I don't take to him.'

'No one has all the London gossip. London, as you very well know, is a collection of villages, socially and occupationally as well as geographically. But theatrical gossip and police gossip do occasionally overlap. There's an affinity between detectives and actors as there is between surgeons and actors.'

'Spare us the dissertation. What do you know about him? You've spoken to someone, I suppose?'

'I admit I did telephone a contact; from this room actually, while you were busy receiving Grogan and his minions. The story is that he resigned from the Met because he was disgusted with the corruption in the CID. That, of course, was before the latest purge. He is, apparently, a proper William Morris man: "No more now my knight, or God's knight any longer, you being than they so much more white, so much more pure and good and true." That should reassure you, Roma.'

'Nothing about the police reassures me.'

Ambrose said:

'I suppose I'd better be careful about offering him drink. It could be construed as an attempt to bribe or corrupt. I wonder if the Chief Constable, or whoever it is decides these things, sent him here to fail.'

Roma said sharply:

'Why should anyone do that?'

'Better the incomer than one of your own men. And he could very easily fail. This is a story-book killing: a close circle of suspects, isolated scene-of-crime conveniently cut off from the mainland, known *terminus a quo* and *terminus ad quem*. It should be perfectly possible to tie it up – that's the jargon, isn't it? – within a week. Everyone will expect it to be solved quickly. But if the killer keeps his head clear and his mouth shut I very much doubt whether he or she is in real danger. All he needs to do – let's be chivalrous and assume it's a man – is to stick to his story; never excuse, never embellish, never explain. It isn't what the police know or suspect; it's what they can prove.'

Roma said:

'You sound as though you don't want it solved.'

'Without having strong feelings on the matter, I should prefer to have it solved. It would be tedious to spend the rest of one's life as a suspected murderer.'

'It'll bring in the summer tourists though, won't it? People love blood and horror. You'll be able to show the scene of the crime – for an extra twenty pence, of course.'

Ambrose said easily:

'I don't pander to sensationalism. That's why summer visitors don't get shown the crypt. And this is a murder in poor taste.'

'But aren't all murders in poor taste?'

'Not necessarily. It would make a good parlour game, classifying the classical murder cases according to their degree of tastelessness. But this one strikes me as particularly bizarre, extravagant, theatrical.'

Roma had drained her first cup of tea and was pouring a second. 'Well that's appropriate enough.' She added:

'It's odd that we've been left here alone, isn't it? I thought that there'd be a plain-clothes underling sitting in and taking a note of all our indiscretions.'

'The police know the limit of their territory and of their powers. I've given them the use of the business room and, naturally, they've locked the two guest-rooms. But this is still my house and my library and they come in here by invitation. Until they decide to charge someone, we're all entitled to be treated as innocent. Even Ralston, presumably, although as husband he has to be elevated to chief suspect. Poor George! If he really loved her this must be hell for him.'

Roma said:

'My guess is he'd stopped loving her six months after the wedding. He must have known by then that she wasn't capable of fidelity.'

Ambrose asked:

'He never showed the least sign, did he?'

'Not to me, but then I hardly ever saw them. And what could he do, faced with that particular insubordination? You can hardly deal with an unfaithful wife as if she were a recalcitrant subaltern. But I don't suppose he liked it. But if he didn't kill her and I don't for one moment believe that he did, he's probably not entirely ungrateful to whoever did. The money will come in useful to subsidize that Fascist organization he runs. The Union of British Patriots, UBP. Wouldn't you know from the name that it's a Fascist front?'

Ambrose smiled:

'Well, I wouldn't expect it to be full of Trots and International Socialists certainly. It's harmless enough. A *Boys' Own Paper* mentality and a geriatric army.'

Roma slammed down her cup and began again her restless pacing. 'My God, you're good at deceiving yourselves, aren't you? It's nasty, it's embarrassing and most unforgivable of all, the people concerned actually take themselves seriously. They really believe in their dangerous nonsense. So let's all laugh at it, and perhaps it will go away. When the chips are down, who do you think this geriatric army are going to be defending? The poor bloody proles? Not likely!'

'I rather hope they'll be defending me.'

'Oh, they will, Ambrose, they will! You and the multi-national corporations, the establishment, the Press barons. Clarissa's money will do its bit towards keeping the rich man in his castle, the poor man at his gate.'

Ambrose said mischievously:

'But don't you get some of the money? And won't it come in useful to you?'

'Of course, money always does. But it isn't important. I'll be glad enough of it, I suppose, when it actually comes, but I don't need it. It certainly isn't important enough to kill for. Come to that, I don't know what is.'

'Oh, come on, Roma, don't be naïve! A cursory read of the daily papers will tell you what people find important enough to kill for. Dangerous and destructive emotions, to begin with. Love, for example.'

Munter was at the door. He coughed, rather, thought Cordelia, like a stock butler in a play, and said:

'The pathologist, Dr Ellis-Jones, has arrived, sir.'

Ambrose looked for a moment distracted as if wondering whether he was expected formally to greet the newcomer. He said:

'I'd better come, I suppose. Do the police know he's here?'

'Not yet, sir. I thought it right to inform you first.'

'Where is he, the pathologist?'

'In the great hall, sir.'

'Well, we can't keep him waiting. You'd better take him to Chief Inspector Grogan. I suppose there are things he may need. Hot water, for example.'

He looked vaguely around as if expecting a jug and basin to materialize from the air. Munter disappeared.

Ivo murmured:

'You make it sound like childbirth.'

Roma swung round, her tone was a mixture of the peevish and appalled. 'But surely he's not going to do the post-mortem here!' They all looked at Cordelia. She thought that Ambrose must surely know the procedure, but he too gazed at her with a look of bland, almost amused inquiry. She said:

'No. He'll just do a preliminary examination at what they call the scene-of-crime. He'll take the temperature of the body, try to estimate the time of death. Then they'll take her away. They don't like to move the body until the forensic pathologist has seen it and certified that life is extinct.'

Roma Lisle said:

'What a lot of curious information you have acquired for a girl who calls herself a secretary-companion. But of course, I forgot. Ambrose tells us that you're a private eye. So perhaps you'll explain why we've all had to have our fingerprints taken. I found it particularly offensive, the way they take hold of your fingers and press them down on the pad. It wouldn't be so repulsive if you were allowed to do it yourself.'

Cordelia said:

'Didn't the police explain the reason? If they find any prints in Clarissa's room they want to be able to eliminate ours.'

'Or identify them. And what else are they doing, apart from grilling George? God knows they've brought enough men with them.'

'Some of them are probably scientific officers from the forensic science laboratory. Or they may be what are called scene-of-crime officers. They'll collect the scientific evidence, samples of blood and body fluids. They'll take away the bedclothes and the cup and saucer. And they'll analyse the dregs of tea to find out if she was poisoned. She could have been drugged before she was killed. She was lying very peaceably on her back.'

Roma said:

'It didn't need a drug for Clarissa to lie peaceably on her back.'

Then she saw their faces. Her own went scarlet and she cried:

'I'm sorry! I shouldn't have said that. It's just that I can't really believe it; I can't picture her lying there, battered to death. I haven't that kind of imagination. She was alive. Now she's dead. I didn't like her and she didn't like me. Death can't alter that for either of us.'

She almost stumbled to the door.

'I'm going for a walk. I've got to get out of this place. If Grogan wants me he can come and find me.'

Ambrose refilled the teapot and poured himself another cup; then seated himself leisurely next to Cordelia.

'That's what surprises me about political commitment. Her cousin, the woman she was practically brought up with, is messily done to death and will shortly be carted off to be scientifically carved up by a Home Office pathologist. She's shocked, obviously. But basically she cares as little as if she'd been told that Clarissa was inconvenienced by a mild attack of fibrositis. But one mention of poor Ralston's Union of British Patriots and she's hysterical with outrage.'

Ivo said:

'She's frightened.'

'That's obvious, but what of? Not that pathetic bunch of amateur warriors?'

'They frighten me occasionally. I suppose she was right about the money and Ralston will get most of it. How much is that?'

'My dear Ivo, I don't know. Clarissa never confided the details of her personal finances, we weren't that close.'

'I rather thought you were.'

'And even if we had been, I doubt whether she would have told. That's one surprising fact about Clarissa. You won't believe this but it's true. She loved to gossip, but she could keep a secret when she wanted to. Clarissa liked hoarding, and that included nuggets of useful information.'

Ivo said lightly:

'How unexpected, and how very dangerous.'

Cordelia looked at them, at Ambrose's bright malicious eyes, at Ivo's barely covered skeleton angularly disposed in his chair, at the long bony hands drooping from wrists which looked too thin and brittle to hold them, at the putty-coloured face with its jutting bones turned upwards to the stuccoed ceiling. She was seized with a confusion of feelings; anger, a deep unfocused pity, and a less familiar emotion which she recognized as envy. They were so secure in their sardonic, half-humorous detachment. Could anything really touch their hearts or nerves except the possibility of their own pain? And even physical pain, that universal leveller, they would meet with wry disgust or derisive contempt. Wasn't that how Ivo was facing his own death? Why should she expect them to grieve because a woman neither of them had greatly liked was lying upstairs with her face smashed in? And yet it wasn't necessary to affirm Donne's overworked aphorism to feel that something was owed to a death, that something in their relationships, in the castle itself, in the very air they breathed, had been touched and subtly altered. Suddenly she felt very alone and very young. She was aware of Ambrose looking at her. As if he had read her thoughts he said:

'Part of the horror of murder is that it does the dead out of their rights. I don't suppose anyone in this room is personally desolated by Clarissa's death. But if she'd died a natural death, at least we'd be mourning her in the sense that we'd be thinking of her with that confused mixture of regret, sentimentality and sympathetic interest which is the normal tribute to the recently dead. As it is, all we're thinking of is ourselves. Well, aren't we? Aren't we?'

Ivo said:

'I don't think Cordelia is.'

The library enclosed them again in its silence. But their ears were abnormally alert to every creak and three heads jerked upwards simultaneously at the sound of muffled footfalls across the hall and the distant thud, faint but unmistakable, of a closing door. Ivo said quietly:

'I think they're taking her away.'

He moved silently behind one of the curtains and Cordelia followed. Between the wide lawns, frosted by moonlight, four dark and enlongated figures, shadowless as phantoms, bent to their task. Behind them paced Sir George, stiff-legged and erect, as if his sword clanked at his side. The small procession looked like a group of mourners surreptitiously burying their dead according to some esoteric and prohibited rite. Cordelia, drained by shock and tiredness, wished she could feel some personal and appropriate response of pity. But there came into her mind instead a whisper of atavistic horror, images of plague and secret murder, de Courcy's men disposing of his victims under the cloak of night. It seemed to her that Ivo had stopped breathing. He didn't speak but she sensed through the contact of his rigid shoulder the intensity of his gaze. Then the curtains parted and Ambrose stood behind them. He said:

'She arrived in the morning sun and leaves by moonlight. But I should be out there. Grogan should have told me they were ready to take her away. Really, that man's behaviour is becoming intolerable!'

And so it was, thought Cordelia, that Clarissa left on her final journey from Courcy Island, on that note of slightly peevish complaint.

An hour later the door opened and Sir George came in. He must have been aware of their inquiring looks, of the question which no one cared to ask. He said:

'Grogan was perfectly civil, but I don't think he's formed any theories. I suppose he knows his business. That red hair must be a disadvantage – disguise you know.'

Ambrose said gravely, controlling the twitching of his mouth:

'I think detection at this level is chiefly desk-work. I don't suppose he does much lurking in the undergrowth.'

'Must do some fieldwork, keep his hand in. He could dye it I suppose.'

He picked up the *Spectator* and settled himself at the chart table as much at ease as if he were in his London club. The others stood and regarded him in baffled silence. Cordelia thought: We're behaving like candidates at an oral examination who'd rather like to know what questions to expect but feel that it would be taking an unfair advantage actually to ask. The same thought must have struck Ivo. He said:

'The police aren't running a competition for their favourite suspect of the year. I confess to some curiosity about their strategy and technique. Reviewing Agatha Christie at the Vaudeville is a poor preparation for the real thing. So how did it go, Ralston?'

Sir George looked up from his journal and appeared to give the question serious thought. 'Much as you'd expect. Where exactly was I and what was I doing this afternoon? I told them I was bird-watching on the west cliffs. Told them, too, that I'd seen Simon coming ashore through my binoculars on the way home. Seemed to think that was important. Asked about Clarissa's money. How much? Who gets it? Grogan wasted twenty minutes asking me about bird-life on Courcy. Trying to put me at my ease, I suppose. A bit odd, I thought.'

Ivo said:

'Trying to catch you out more likely with cunning traps about the nesting habits of non-existent species. What about this morning? Are we expected to detail every waking moment of the day?'

His voice was carefully casual, but all four of them knew what it was he was asking and the importance of the reply. Sir George took up his journal again. Without looking up he said:

'Didn't say more than I needed. Told them about the visit to the Church and the Devil's Kettle. Mentioned the drowning but didn't give names. No point in confusing the investigation with old history. Not their concern.'

Ivo said:

'You reassure me. That's rather the line I propose to take. I'll have a word with Roma when the opportunity arises and you, Ambrose, might speak to the boy. As Ralston says, there's no point in confusing them with old, unhappy, far-off things and battles long ago.'

No one replied, but Sir George suddenly looked up over his journal:

'Sorry, I forgot. They want to see you now, Cordelia.'

CHAPTER TWENTY-FIVE

Cordelia could understand why Ambrose had offered the business room for the use of the police. It was appropriately furnished as an office, it wasn't too large and it kept them well out of his way. But as she seated herself in the mahogany and cane chair and faced Chief Inspector Grogan across the desk, she wished that Ambrose had chosen any room other than this private museum of murder. The Staffordshire figures on the wall shelf behind Grogan's head seemed to have grown, no longer quaintly fashioned antiques but real people, their bland, painted faces glowing and twisting into life. And the framed Victorian broadsheets with their crudely drawn scaffolds and death cells were intrusive in their horror, stark celebrations of the cruelty of man to man. The room itself was smaller than she remembered and she felt herself closeted with her interrogators in frightening and claustrophobic proximity. She was only half aware that there was a uniformed woman police officer sitting almost motionless in the corner by the window, watchful as a chaperone. Did they think that she would faint or accuse Grogan of assaulting her? She wondered briefly whether it was the same anonymous officer who had helped move her clothes and belongings from the De Morgan room to her new bedroom. She had no doubt that they had been thoroughly examined before being neatly arranged on the bed.

She found herself studying Grogan for the first time. He seemed even larger than the tall, broad figure she had first watched alighting from the police launch. The strong red-gold hair was longer than one would expect on a police officer; one swathe fell across his forehead and from time to time he would sweep it back with a huge hand. Despite its size, his face with its jutting cheekbones and deep-set eyes gave an impression of gauntness. Under each cheekbone, a brush of hair increased the sense of rough animality, an impression oddly at variance with the excellent cut of his formal tweed suit. His skin was ruddy so that his whole appearance was of redness; even the whites of his eyes seemed bloodshot. When he moved his head, Cordelia could glimpse, under his immaculate collar, the clear dividing line between the sunburnt face and his white neck. It was so marked that he looked like a man who had been decapitated and joined together again. She tried to imagine him, red-bearded, as an Elizabethan adventurer, but the image was subtly wrong. For all his strength, he wouldn't have been found among the men of action but secretly scheming in the closets of power. Might he perhaps have been discovered in that dreaded room at the Tower working the levers of the rack? But that was unfair. She thrust the morbid images out of her mind and made herself remember what he in fact was; a twentieth-century senior police officer, bound by Force regulations, restricted by Judges' Rules, doing a vital if disagreeable job and entitled to her cooperation. Yet she wished that she wasn't so frightened. She had expected to feel anxiety, but not this rush of humiliating terror. She managed to master it but was miserably aware that Grogan, experienced as he was, had recognized it and that it wasn't unwelcome to him.

He listened in silence while, at his request, she recounted the sequence of events between the arrival of Sir George at Kingly Street and her discovery of Clarissa's body. She had handed over the collection of messages and they were spread out on the desk before him. From time to time, as her quiet voice rose and fell, he shifted them about as if searching for some meaningful pattern. She was glad that she wasn't wired up to a lie machine. Surely the needle must have leapt as she came to those moments when, although she told no direct untruth, she carefully omitted the facts which she had decided not to tell; the death of Tolly's child, Clarissa's disclosure in the Devil's Kettle, Roma's unsuccessful appeal to her cousin for money. She didn't try to justify these suppressions by pretending that they wouldn't be of interest to him. She was too tired now to make up her mind about the morality of her decision. She only knew that, even when recalling Clarissa's battered face, there were things that she couldn't bring herself to tell.

He made her go over her story again and again, particularly pressing her about the locking of the bedroom doors. Was she absolutely certain that she had heard Clarissa turn her key? How could she be so sure that she had, in fact, locked her own door? Sometimes she wondered whether he were deliberately trying to confuse her as a counsel for the defence might, pretending to be obtuse, pretending that he hadn't quite understood. She was increasingly aware of her own tiredness, of his strong hand lying in the pool of light from the desk lamp, the ruddy hair gleaming on the back of his fingers, of the soft rustle as Sergeant Buckley turned the page. She must have been speaking for well over an hour before he finished the long interrogation and both their voices fell silent. Then he said suddenly, as if rousing himself from boredom:

'So you call yourself a detective, Miss Gray?'

'I don't call myself anything. I own and run a detective agency.'

'That's a nice distinction. But we haven't time to go into it now. You tell me that Sir George Ralston employed you as a detective. That's why you were here when his wife died. Suppose you tell me what you've detected so far.'

'I was employed to look after his wife. I let her be killed.'

'Now, let's get this straight. Are you telling me that you stood by and let someone kill her?'

'No.'

'Or killed her yourself?'

'No.'

'Or encouraged, or helped or paid anyone else to kill her?'

'No.'

'Then stop feeling sorry for yourself. Presumably you didn't think she was in any real danger. Nor did her husband. Nor did the Metropolitan Police apparently.'

Cordelia said:

'I thought that they might have had a reason for scepticism.'

His eyes were suddenly sharp.

'You did?'

'I wondered whether Miss Lisle sent one of the notes herself, the one typed on her husband's typewriter. He was in America at the time so he couldn't have posted it to her himself.'

'And why should she do that?'

'To try to exonerate Sir George. I think she was afraid that the police might suspect him. Don't they usually think of the husband first? She wanted to make sure that he was in the clear, perhaps because she didn't want the police to waste their time on him, perhaps because she genuinely knew that he wasn't guilty. I think the Metropolitan Police might have suspected that she sent the message herself.'

Grogan said:

'They did more than suspect it. They tested the saliva on the flap of the envelope. It belonged to a secretor with the same blood group as Miss Lisle, and that group is rare. They asked her to type an innocuous note for them, a message which had some of the same letters and in the same order as the quotation. On that evidence they suggested, tactfully, that she might have sent the note. She denied it. But you could hardly expect them to take the death threats very seriously after that.'

So she had been right. Clarissa had sent that one message. But she might be wrong about the reason. It had, after all, been clumsily done, and had it really exonerated Sir George? But it had ensured that the police took no further interest in what they must have seen as the time-wasting mischief of an attention-seeking and probably neurotic woman. And that would have suited the real culprit very well. Had anyone suggested to Clarissa that she should send that one note herself? And had it been the only one for which she had been responsible? Could the whole sequence of quotations be an elaborate conspiracy between herself and one other person? But Cordelia rejected that theory almost as soon as it came into her mind. Of one thing she was sure: Clarissa had dreaded the arrival of the messages. No actress could have simulated that fear. She had been convinced that she would die. And she had died.

Cordelia was aware that the two men were looking at her intently. She had been sitting silently, hands curved in her lap, eyes lowered, occupied with thought. She waited for them to break the silence and when the Chief Inspector spoke she thought she could detect a different note in his voice which could have been respect.

'Did you deduce anything else about these notes?'

'I thought that they might have been sent by two different people, apart from Miss Lisle, I mean. I wasn't shown the first half dozen which she received. I thought it possible that they might have been different from the later communications. And most of the ones I saw, the ones I've handed over to you, can be found in *The Penguin Dictionary of Quotations*. I think that whoever typed them had that book in front of him and typed from the text.'

'On different machines?'

'That wouldn't be difficult. They aren't new machines and the makes are different. There are numerous shops in London and the suburbs which sell new and reconditioned typewriters and which put out a machine or two for people to try. It would be almost impossible to trace a machine if one went from shop to shop and typed a few lines in each.'

'And who do you suggest did?'

'I don't know.'

'And what about the original anonymous correspondent, the one you might say who had the bright idea in the first place?'

'I don't know that either.'

That was as far as she was willing to go. She had told them enough, perhaps too much. If they wanted motives, let them grub around for themselves. And there was one motive for the poison pen that she would never divulge. If Ivo Whittingham had kept silent about Tolly's tragedy, then so would she.

And then Grogan was speaking again, leaning over the desk towards her so that the powerful body, the strong coarse voice surged towards her, palpable as a force.

'Let's get one thing straight, shall we? Miss Lisle was battered to death. You know what happened to her. You saw the body. Now, she may not have been a good or likeable woman. That has nothing to do with it. She had as much right to live her life to the last natural moment as you or I or any creature under the Queen's peace.'

'Of course. I don't see why that needs saying.'

Why did her own voice sound so small, almost peevish?

'You'd be surprised what needs saying in a murder investigation. It's the most powerful mutual protection society in the world, the trade union of the living. It's the living you'll be thinking about, wanting to protect, yourself most of all of course. My job is to think of her.'

'You can't bring her back.'

The words, torn out of her, fell between them in all their sad banality.

'No, but I can stop someone else from going the same way. No one is more dangerous than a successful murderer. I'm boring you with platitudes because I want you to get one thing straight. You may be too bright for your own good, Miss Gray. You're not here to solve this crime. That's my job. You're not here to protect the living. Leave that to their lawyers. You're not even here to protect the dead. They're beyond needing your condescension. *On doit des égards aux vivants; on ne doit aux morts que la vérité.* You're an educated young woman. You know what that means.'

'"We owe respect to the living; to the dead we owe only truth." It's Voltaire, isn't it? But I was taught a different pronunciation.'

As soon as the words were out she was ashamed. But to her surprise his only response was a bellow of laughter.

'I bet you were, Miss Gray. I bet you were. I taught myself with a primer and a key to phonetics. But think about it. There's no better motto for a detective, and that includes female private eyes who would like to help the police but still be able to lie abed with a good conscience. It can't be done, Miss Gray. It can't be done.'

She didn't reply. After a moment, Grogan said:

'What surprises me a little, Miss Gray, is how much you noticed and how carefully when you found the body. Most people, and not only young women, would have been in a state of shock.'

Cordelia thought that he was entitled to the truth, or as much as she herself understood of it.

'I know. That has surprised me too. I think what happened was that I couldn't bear to feel too much emotion. It was so horrible that it was almost unreal. My intellect took over and made it into a kind of detective puzzle because, if I hadn't concentrated on detaching myself from the horror, examining the room, noticing little things like the lipstick smear on the cup, it would have been unbearable. Perhaps that's how doctors feel at the scene of an accident. You have to keep your mind on procedures and techniques because, otherwise, you might realize that what you have lying there is a human being.'

Sergeant Buckley said quietly:

'It's how a policeman trains himself to behave at the scene of an accident. Or a murder.'

Without taking his eyes from Cordelia, Grogan said:

'You find that credible then, do you Sergeant?'

'Yes, sir.'

Fear sharpens perception as well as the senses. Glancing at Sergeant Buckley's handsome, rather heavy face, at the controlled self-satisfied smile, Cordelia doubted whether he had ever in his life needed such an expedient against pain and wondered whether he was trying to signal his sympathy or was colluding with his superior in some pre-arranged interrogatory ploy. The Chief Inspector said:

'And what exactly did your intellect deduce when it had so conveniently taken over from your emotions?'

'The obvious things: that the curtains had been drawn although they weren't when I left, that the jewel box was missing, that the tea had been drunk. And I thought it odd that Miss Lisle had cleaned the make-up from her face but that there was a lipstick stain on the cup. That surprised me. I think she has – she had – sensitive lips and used a creamy lipstick which does smear easily. So why hadn't it come off when she ate her lunch? It looked as if she must have made up her lips again before she drank her tea. But if so, why had she taken off the rest of her make-up? The balls of stained cotton wool were all over the dressing-table top. And I noticed that there wasn't as much blood as one would expect from a head wound. I thought it possible that she might have been killed some other way and the injuries to her face made afterwards. And I was puzzled about the pads over her eyes. They must have been put there after death. I mean, it wouldn't be possible for them to stay so neatly in place while her face was being destroyed.'

After she had finished there was a long silence. Then Grogan said, his voice expressionless:

'You're sitting on the wrong side of the desk, Miss Gray.'

Cordelia waited. Then she said, hoping that she wasn't doing more harm than good:

'There's one thing more I ought to tell you. I know that Sir George can't have killed his wife. I'm sure that you wouldn't suspect him, anyway, but there is something you should know. When he first arrived in the bedroom and I blurted out how sorry I was he looked at me with a kind of amazed horror. I realized that he thought for a moment that I'd killed her, that I was confessing.'

'And you weren't?'

'Not to murder. Only to failure to do what I was here for.'

He changed the tack of his questioning again.

'Let's go back to the Friday night, the time when you were with Miss Lisle in her room and she showed you the secret drawer in her jewel box. That review of the Rattigan play. Are you sure that that is what it in fact was?'

'Quite sure.'

'The paper wasn't a document or a letter.'

'It was a newspaper cutting. And I read the headline.'

'And at no time did your client – and she was your client, remember – ever give you the least indication that she knew or suspected who it was threatening her?'

'No, never.'

'And she had no enemies as far as you know.'

'None that she told me of.'

'And you yourself can throw no light on why and by whom she was killed?'

'No.'

It must, she thought, feel like this to be in the witness box, the careful questions, the even more careful answers, the longing to be released.

He said:

'Thank you, Miss Gray. You've been helpful. Not, perhaps, as helpful as I'd hoped. But helpful. And it's early days yet. We shall be talking again.'

CHAPTER TWENTY-SIX

After Cordelia had left, Grogan relaxed in his chair:

'Well, what do you think of her?'

Buckley hesitated, uncertain whether his chief wanted an assessment of the last interviewee as a woman or as a suspect. He said cautiously:

'She's attractive. Like a cat.' Since this evoked no immediate response he added: 'Self-contained and dignified.'

He was rather pleased with the description. It had, he thought, a certain cleverness while committing him to nothing. Grogan began doodling on the blank sheet in front of him, a complicated mathematical design of triangles, squares and precisely interlacing circles spread over the page and reminding Buckley of the more obscure of his school geometry problems. He found it difficult not to fix his eyes obsessively on isosceles triangles and bisecting arcs. He said:

'Do you think she did it, sir?'

Grogan began filling in his design.

'If she did, it was during those fifty-odd minutes when she claims she was taking the sun on the bottom step of the terrace, conveniently out of sight and sound. She had time and opportunity. We've only her word that she locked her bedroom door or that Miss Lisle actually locked hers. And even if both doors and the communicating one were locked, Gray is probably the only person Lisle would have let in. She knew where the marble was kept. She was up and about early this morning when Gorringe first discovered that it was missing. She has a locked cabinet in her room where she could have kept it safely hidden. And we know that the final message, like the one typed on the back of the woodcut, was typed on Gorringe's machine. Gray can type and she had access to the business room where it's kept. She's intelligent, and she can keep her head even when I'm trying to needle her into losing it. If she did have a hand in it, my guess is that it was as Ralston's accomplice. His explanation of why she was called in sounded contrived. Did you notice how she and Ralston gave almost identical accounts of his visit to Kingly Street, what he said, what she said? It was so neat it could have been rehearsed. It probably was.'

But Buckley could think of an objection and he voiced it.

'Sir George was a soldier. He's used to getting his facts right. And she has a good memory, particularly for important events. And that visit was important. He probably paid well, and it could have led to other jobs. The fact that they gave the same account, got the details right, speaks as much for innocence as guilt.'

'According to both of them, that's the first time they met. If they are conspirators, they must have got together before then. Whatever there is between them, it shouldn't be too difficult to grub it out.'

'They're an unlikely couple. I mean, it's difficult to see what they have in common.'

'Politics rather than bed I imagine. Although, when it comes to sex, nothing is too bizarre to be ruled out. Police work teaches you that if nothing else. She could have taken a fancy to being Lady Ralston. There must be easier ways of getting money than running a detective agency. And Ralston will have money, remember. His wife's, to be specific. And I don't suppose that will come before it's needed. He must be spending a packet on that organization of his – the UBP or whatever they call it. And that's an odd business if you like. I suppose you can argue a case for an amateur force trained and ready to support the civil power in an emergency, but isn't that what General Walker has in hand? So what exactly do George Ralston and his geriatric conspirators think they're up to?'

As Buckley didn't know the answer and had, in fact, hardly heard of the Union of British Patriots, he wisely kept silent. Then he said:

'Did you believe Gray when she said that Sir George thought that she was confessing?'

'What Miss Gray thought she saw in Sir George's face isn't evidence. And no doubt he did look amazed if he thought he heard her confessing to a murder he'd done himself.'

Buckley thought about the girl who had just left them; saw again that gentle, uplifted face, the immense and resolute eyes, the delicate hands folded like a child's in her lap. She was keeping something back, of course; but didn't they all? That didn't make her a murderess. And the idea of her and Ralston together was ludicrous and disgusting. Surely the Chief hadn't yet reached the age when he needed to start believing that pathetic old lie with which the middle-aged and the elderly deceived themselves, that the young find them physically attractive? What they can do, the old goats, he told himself, is to buy youth and sex with money and power and prestige. But he didn't believe that Sir George Ralston was in that market or that Cordelia Gray could be bought. He said stolidly:

'I can't see Miss Gray as a murderess.'

'It takes an effort of the imagination I grant you. But that's probably what Mr Blandy thought of Miss Blandy. Or L'Angelier of Miss Madeleine Smith, come to that, before she so unkindly handed him his cocoa and arsenic through the basement railings.'

'Wasn't there a verdict of not proven in that case, sir?'

'A fainthearted Glasgow jury who should have known better and probably did. But we're theorizing in advance of facts. We need the PM result and we need to know what, if anything, was in that tea. Doc Ellis-Jones will probably get her on the slab tomorrow, Sunday or no Sunday. Once he's got his hands on the body he's quick enough at his butchering, I'll say that for him.'

'And the lab, sir. How long are they likely to take?'

'God knows. It's not as if we've any idea what they're supposed to be looking for. There isn't an unlimited number of drugs which can put you out, or kill you, within a short time and with no obvious signs on the body. But there are enough to keep them busy for the next few days if this is the only murder on the stocks. We may get a clue from the PM of course. Meanwhile we get on with the London end. How well did any of these people know each other before they arrived on the island this weekend? What, if anything, do the Met know about Cordelia Gray and her agency? What did Simon Lessing really feel about his benefactress and how, exactly, did his father die? Is Miss Tolgarth quite the devoted dresser cum family retainer that we're supposed to believe? What sort of money is Sir George spending on his toy soldiers? How much exactly is Roma Lisle going to get under the will and how badly does she need it? And that's just for starters.'

And none of it, thought Buckley, was the kind of information people came running to give you with happy smiles. It meant talking to bank managers, lawyers, friends, acquaintances and colleagues of the suspects, most of whom would know to a word just how far they needed to go. In theory everyone wanted murderers caught, just as in theory they all approved of hostels for the mentally ill in the community, provided they weren't built at the bottom of their garden. It would be simpler for the police as well as reassuring to the house party at the castle if they did discover those convenient young burglars hiding terrified somewhere on the island. But he didn't believe that they existed and nor, he suspected, did anyone else. And it would be a tamely disappointing ending to the case. What glory would there be in pulling in a couple of terrified local villains who'd killed on impulse and wouldn't have the nous even to keep their mouths shut until they got a brief. There was an intelligence at work here. The case was exactly the kind of challenge he enjoyed and which police work so seldom provided.

'There are facts. There are suppositions. There are beliefs. Learn to keep them separate, Sergeant. All men die: fact. Death may not be the end: supposition. There's pie in the sky when you die: belief. Lisle was murdered: fact. She received anonymous communications: fact. Other people were there when they arrived. They threatened her life: supposition. They were a bloody sight more likely to put her off her stroke as an actress. They terrified her: supposition. That's what her husband tells us and what she told Miss Gray. But she was an actress, remember. The thing about actresses is that they act. Suppose she and her husband concocted the whole scheme, threatening messages, apparent terror and distress, breakdown in the middle of a play, calling in a private eye, the lot.'

'I don't see why, sir.'

'Nor do I, yet. Would any actress willingly humiliate herself on stage? God knows. Actors are an alien breed to me.'

'If she knew that she was finished as an actress, could she and her husband have concocted the messages to provide a public excuse for failure?'

'Over-ingenious and unnecessary. Why not just pretend that her health has failed? And she didn't make the messages public. On the contrary, she seems to have taken care to prevent the news getting out. Would any actress wish her public to know that someone hated her that much? Don't they crave to be loved by all the world? No, I was thinking of something rather more subtle. Ralston somehow persuades her into pretending that her life is threatened, and then kills her, having, as it were, seduced her into conniving at her own murder. My God, that would be neat. Too neat, perhaps.'

'But why take the risk of calling in Miss Gray?'

'What risk? She could hardly discover that the letters were faked, not in one short weekend. A very short weekend as far as Lisle was concerned. Employing Gray gave the final artistic touch to the whole plan.'

'I still think he'd have been taking a risk.'

'That's because we've seen the girl. She's intelligent and she knows her job. But Ralston wasn't to know that. Who was she, after all? The proprietor of a one-woman detective agency, apparently. After Lisle first met her at the house of that friend of hers – Mrs Fortescue wasn't it? – she probably suggested to Ralston that they call her in. That's why she never bothered to interview the girl herself. Why trouble when the whole thing was a ploy?'

'It's ingenious, sir, but it still begs the question why Lisle should have connived in it all. I mean, what possible reason could Ralston give to persuade her to pretend that her life was threatened?'

'What, indeed, Sergeant? Like Miss Gray, I'm in danger of being too clever for my own good. But one thing I'm sure of. The murderer spent the day under this roof. And I've a choice bunch of suspects. Sir George Ralston, baronet, something of a war hero and darling of the geriatric Right. A distinguished theatre critic, one even I have actually heard of. Seriously ill too, by the look of him, which means that he'll probably die on me under the gentlest interrogation. Interrogation. Odd how one dislikes that word. Too many echoes of the Gestapo and KGB I suppose. A best-selling novelist who not only owns the island but happens to be friendly with the Cottringhams who have the ear of the Lord Lieutenant, the Chief Constable, the MP and anyone else who matters in the County. A respectable bookseller ex-schoolteacher who's probably a member of the civil rights and women's lib lobbies and who will protest to her MP about police harassment if I raise my voice to her. And a school kid – and sensitive with it. I suppose I should be grateful that he's not a juvenile.'

'And a butler, sir.'

'Thank you for reminding me, Sergeant. We mustn't forget the butler. I regard the butler as a gratuitous insult on the part of fate. So let's give the gentry in the library a respite and hear what Munter has to tell us.'

CHAPTER TWENTY-SEVEN

Buckley noted with irritation that Munter, invited by Grogan to sit, managed in the mere act of lowering his buttocks on to the chair to suggest both that it was unseemly for him to seat himself in the business room and that Grogan had committed a social solecism in inviting him to do so. He couldn't remember ever having seen the man in Speymouth; his was certainly not an appearance one was likely to forget. Watching Munter's strong and lugubrious face on which the unease proper to his present situation was noticeably absent he found himself prepared to disbelieve everything he heard. It seemed to him suspicious that a man should want to make himself more grotesque than nature had intended and if this was Munter's way of cocking a snook at the world he had better not try it on with the police. Basically conforming and ambitious, Buckley had no resentment of those wealthier than himself; he had every intention of eventually joining them. But he despised and distrusted those who chose to earn their living by pandering to the rich and suspected that Grogan shared this prejudice. He watched them both with a wary and critical eye and wished that he was taking a more active part in the interrogation. Never had his chief's insistence that he sit silent unless invited to speak, watch carefully and take unobtrusive shorthand notes seemed more restrictive and demeaning. Morbidly sensitive to any nuance of condescension he felt that the glance Munter casually gave him conveyed a slight surprise that he should have been allowed into the house.

Grogan, seated at the desk, leaned back in his chair so strongly that its back creaked, twirled round to face Munter and splayed his legs wide as if to assert his right to feel perfectly at home. He said:

'Suppose you begin by telling us who you are, where you came from and what precisely is your job here.'

'My duties, sir, have never been precisely defined. This is not altogether an orthodox household. But I am in charge of all the domestic arrangements and supervise the two other members of staff, my wife and Oldfield, who is the gardener, handyman and boatman. Any additional help necessary when Mr Gorringe is entertaining or has house guests is obtained on a temporary basis from the mainland. I look after the silver and the wine and wait at table. The cooking is generally shared. My wife is the pastry cook and Mr Ambrose himself occasionally cooks a meal. He is fond of preparing savouries.'

'Very tasty, I'm sure. And how long have you been part of this unorthodox household?'

'My wife and I came into Mr Gorringe's service in July 1978 three months after his return from a year abroad. He had inherited the castle from his uncle in 1977. Perhaps you would wish for a brief *curriculum vitae.* I was born in London in 1940 and educated at Pimlico Primary and Secondary Schools. I then took a course in hotel catering and for seven years worked in hotels here and abroad. But I decided that institutional life was unsuited to my temperament and entered private services firstly with an American business gentleman living in London and then, when he returned home, here in Dorset with his lordship at Bossington House. I am sure my previous gentleman will speak for me if necessary.'

'No doubt. If I were looking for a manservant you'd do very nicely. But I'll be consulting a more objective character reference source, the Criminal Records Office. Does that worry you?'

'It offends me, sir. It doesn't worry me.'

Buckley wondered when Grogan would stop this needling and get down to the main inquiry, what Munter had been doing between the ending of lunch and the finding of the body. If these preliminaries were meant to provoke the witness they weren't succeeding. But Grogan knew his business, at least the Met had appeared to think so. He had come to Dorset burdened with something of a reputation. Now he stopped looking at Munter; his voice became conversational: 'This play. It was to be a regular event, was it? An annual drama festival perhaps?'

'I have no means of knowing. Mr Gorringe did not confide his plans to me.'

'Once was enough, I should think. It must have made a lot of extra work for you and your wife.'

Munter's slow and disapproving glance round the business room was an inventory of unwelcome change; the slight rearrangement of the furniture, Buckley's jacket slung over the back of his chair, the coffee-tray with the two stained cups, its surface crumbed with half-eaten biscuits. He said:

'The domestic inconvenience occasioned by Lady Ralston living was nugatory compared with the inconvenience of Lady Ralston murdered.'

Grogan held his pen in front of his face and peered at its tip, moving it backwards and forwards as if testing his eyesight.

'You found her a pleasant, likeable guest, easy to get on with?'

'That was not a question to which I addressed myself.'

'Address yourself to it now.'

'Lady Ralston seemed a very agreeable lady.'

'No trouble? No disagreements? No rows as far as you knew?'

'None, sir. A great loss to the English stage.' He paused and added woodenly:

'And, of course, to Sir George Ralston.'

It was impossible to judge whether the statement was ironic, but Buckley wondered whether Grogan, too, had caught the clear bite of contempt. Grogan rocked back in his chair, legs stretched, and stared consideringly at his witness. Munter gazed ahead with a look of patient resignation and, after a minute of silence, permitted himself a glance at his watch.

'Right! Let's get on with it. You know what we want, a full account of where you were, what you were doing and who you saw between one o'clock when lunch was over and two forty-three when Miss Gray found the body.'

According to Munter's account, he had spent the whole of that time on the ground floor of the castle chiefly moving between the dining-room, his pantry and the theatre. As he had been continually busy with preparations for the play and the supper party, it wasn't always possible to say where he had been or with whom at any particular moment in time, although he doubted whether he had ever been alone for more than a few minutes. He said in a voice which held no trace of regret, that he very much regretted not being able to be more precise, but he could not, of course, have known so detailed an account would subsequently be required. At first he had helped his wife clear away the luncheon and had then gone to check on the wine. There had then been three telephone calls to answer, one from a guest who was prevented by illness from attending the performance, a second inquiring about the time the launch would leave Speymouth, a call from Lady Cottringham's housekeeper to know whether they needed any extra glasses. He had been checking on the men's dressing-room when his wife had appeared backstage to ask him to look at one of the tea urns which she thought might not be working. It was unfortunate that they had to hire urns; Mr Gorringe had a strong dislike of them and complained that they made the great hall look like a meeting of the Women's Institute, but with an audience of eighty people and the cast to provide for, the use of the urns had been necessary.

At some time, he couldn't remember precisely when, he had remembered that Mr Gorringe had asked him to find a second musical-box for use in the Third Act of the play, Miss Lisle having expressed dissatisfaction with the one provided at the dress rehearsal. He had come here into the business room to fetch it from the walnut chiffonier. At this stage his eyes indicated what Buckley sourly thought could very well have been described as a cupboard. His Aunt Sadie had one like it, not as fancily carved on the doors or at the end of the shelves, but pretty much the same. She claimed it had been in the family for generations, kept it in the back parlour, and called it a dresser. She used it for the bits and pieces her kids brought back from holiday for her, cheap souvenirs from the Costa del Sol, Malta and, now, from Miami. He'd have to tell her that what she'd got was a chiffonier and she'd reply that he made it sound like a bloody ice-cream.

He turned the page of his notebook. Munter's resigned voice droned on. He had taken the second musical-box and placed it with the first one on the props table. Shortly afterwards, it could have been as late as two fifteen, Mr Gorringe had appeared and they had checked over the props together. By then it was time to go to the quay to meet the launch bringing the rest of the cast from Speymouth. He had gone with Mr Gorringe to receive them and had helped with the disembarkation. Mr Gorringe and he had escorted the gentlemen to their dressing-rooms and his wife and Miss Tolgarth had looked after the ladies. He had stayed backstage for about ten minutes and had then gone to his pantry where Mrs Chambers and her granddaughter were polishing glasses. He had had occasion to complain to the girl, Debbie, about a smeared glass and had supervised the arrangements to rewash them all. After that he had gone to the dining-room to collect the chairs together for the supper party, which was to be held in the great hall. He had been there when Mr Gorringe had put his head in to inform him of Miss Lisle's murder.

Grogan sat with his great head lowered, as if bowed with the weight of assimilating this succinct account. Then he said quietly:

'You are, of course, devoted to Mr Gorringe.'

'Yes indeed, sir. When Mr Gorringe broke the news to me I said: What, in our house?'

'Quite Shakespearean. The *Macbeth* touch. And no doubt Mr Gorringe could riposte with: "Too awful anywhere"?'

'No doubt he could have, sir. Actually what he said was that I should go to the landing stage and prevent the guests from landing. He would follow as soon as possible and explain the lamentable circumstances which necessitated the cancellation of the performance.'

'The launches were then at the quay?'

'Not at that time. I judged that they were three-quarters of a mile away.'

'So there was no particular hurry to warn them?'

'It was not a matter to be left to chance. Mr Gorringe was anxious that the police investigation should not be hampered by the presence on the island of another eighty people in a state of confusion or distress.'

Grogan said:

'In a state of highly enjoyable excitement, more likely. Nothing like a good murder for a thrill. Or wouldn't you know?'

'I wouldn't know, sir.'

'Still, it was considerate of your master – I suppose that's what you call him – to have as his first thought the convenience of the police. Highly commendable. What was he doing, do you know, while you were wasting a certain amount of time at the quay?'

'I suppose that he was telephoning the police and acquainting his guests and the cast of the play with the fact of Lady Ralston's death. I have no doubt he will inform you if asked.'

'And how exactly did he acquaint you with the fact of Lady Ralston's death?'

'He told me that she had been battered to death. He instructed me to inform the guests when they arrived that she had been killed by a blow to the head. There was no need to harrow them unnecessarily. In the event I was not required to tell them anything as Mr Gorringe had joined me by the time the launches arrived.'

'A blow to the head. You have seen the body?'

'No, sir. Mr Gorringe locked the door of Lady Ralston's room after the discovery. There was no occasion for any of the staff to see the body.'

'But you have, no doubt, formed some opinion as to how this blow to the head was inflicted. You permitted yourself a theory, a little natural curiosity? You went so far, perhaps, as to discuss it with your wife?'

'It did occur to me to wonder whether the assault was connected with the missing marble hand. Mr Gorringe will have told you that the display case was forced in the early hours of this morning.'

'So suppose you tell us what you know about that.'

'The object was brought back to the castle by Mr Gorringe on his return from London on Thursday night and placed by him in the showcase. The showcase is kept locked since groups of visitors are shown round the castle during the summer months on days which are announced in advance and Mr Gorringe's insurance company has insisted on this degree of security. Mr Gorringe himself placed the hand in position, watched by me, and we had some conversation on its possible provenance. He then locked the showcase. The keys to the display cabinets are not, of course, kept on the key board with the house keys but in the bottom left locked drawer of the desk at which you are now sitting. The showcase was undamaged and the marble arm in place when I saw it shortly after midnight. Mr Gorringe found it in its present state when he was on his way to the kitchen just before seven o'clock. He is an early riser and prefers to make his own morning tea and carry the tray either on to the terrace or into the library depending on the state of the weather. We inspected the damage together.'

'You saw no one, heard nothing?'

'No, sir. I was busy in the kitchen preparing the early morning tea-trays.'

'And they were all there when you took up the early tea-trays?'

'The gentlemen were. I understand from my wife that the ladies were also in bed. Lady Ralston's early tea was taken up later by her maid, Miss Tolgarth. At about seven thirty Mr Gorringe came to tell me that Sir George had arrived unexpectedly, put ashore in the small bay west of the headland by a local fishing boat. I did not myself see him until I set breakfast on the hotplate in the small breakfast room at eight o'clock.'

'But anyone could have got into the house at any time after six five when you opened up the castle?'

'The back door leading to the great hall was unlocked by me at six fifteen. At the time I looked out over the lawn and the path leading to the beach and the coastal walk. I saw no one. But anyone could have entered and done the damage between six fifteen and seven o'clock.'

The rest of the interview was unfruitful. Munter appeared to repent of his loquacity and his answers became shorter. He had no idea that Lady Ralston was receiving poison-pen communications and had no suggestions to offer as to their origin. Shown one of the messages he fingered the paper with fastidious distaste and said that it was the kind he and his wife commonly bought but in cream not white. The castle writing paper had an engraved address and was of a different quality as the Chief Inspector would be able to check by opening the top left-hand drawer of the desk. He had not known that Mr Gorringe had given Lady Ralston one of his Victorian jewel caskets nor had he been told that it was missing. He could, however, describe the casket in question since there were only two in the castle. It had been made by a silversmith of Hunt and Rosken in 1850 and was thought to have been among their pieces shown at the Great Exhibition of 1851. It had been considered for use as a prop in the Third Act of the play but the larger and less valuable if more showy casket had been thought the better choice.

Grogan frowned, irritated by this display of irrelevant knowledge. He said:

'There's been murder done here, bloody murder of a defenceless woman. If there's anything you know, anything you suspect, anything that later occurs to you bearing on this crime I expect to be told it. The police are here, and we're here to stay. We may not always be physically present but we'll be around, we'll be concerned with this island, concerned with what happens here, and that means concerned with you, until the murderer is brought to justice. Have I made myself clear?'

Munter got to his feet. His face was still impassive. He said:

'Perfectly, sir. May I say that Courcy Island is used to murder. And the murderers commonly haven't been brought to justice. Perhaps you and your colleagues will have better luck.'

After he had left, there was a long silence which Buckley knew better than to interrupt. Then Grogan said:

'He thinks the husband did it, or he wants us to think that the husband did it. No marks for originality. It's what we're bound to think anyway. D'you know the Wallace case?'

'No, sir.' Buckley told himself that, if he were to continue working with Grogan, it would be as well to get hold of a copy of *The Murderers' Who's Who*.

'Liverpool, January 1931. Wallace, William Herbert. Inoffensive little insurance agent trotting round door to door and collecting the odd bob weekly from poor sods terrified they wouldn't be able to pay for their own funerals. Taste for chess and the violin. Married a bit above himself. He and his wife Julia lived in genteel poverty, which is the worst poverty of the lot in case you didn't know, and kept themselves to themselves. Then on 19th January, when he's out looking for the address of a prospective customer who may or may not exist, Julia gets her head savagely bashed in in her own front sitting-room. Wallace stood trial for the murder and a sturdy Liverpool jury, who probably weren't entirely unbiased, convicted. The Court of Criminal Appeal subsequently made legal history by quashing the verdict on the grounds that it was unsafe having regard to the evidence. So they let him go and he died of kidney disease two years later a bloody sight more slowly and painfully than he would have done at the end of a rope. It's a fascinating case. Every piece of evidence can point either way, depending on how you choose to look at it' I can lie awake at night thinking about it. It ought to be compulsory study for every detective constable, a warning of how a case can go wrong if the police get it fixed in their minds that it has to be the husband.'

Which was all very well, thought Buckley, but in these cases if the criminal statistics were to be believed, it usually was the husband. Grogan might be keeping an open mind but he had no doubt whose name featured at the head of his list. He said:

'They've got a cosy little set-up here, the Munters.'

'Haven't they just? Nothing to do but fuss around Gorringe while he knocks up his little savouries, polish the antique silver and wait on each other. But he lied about at least one thing. Look back to that interview with Mrs Chambers.'

Buckley thumbed back through his notebook. Mrs Chambers and her granddaughter had been two of the first interviewed since the woman had demanded that she be returned to the mainland in time to cook her husband's supper. She had been voluble, aggrieved and pugnacious, viewing the tragedy as one more trick of fate designed to cause domestic inconvenience. What chiefly concerned her was the waste of food; who, she had demanded, was going to eat a supper prepared for over a hundred? Buckley had been interested, thirty minutes later, to watch her waddling down to the launch with her granddaughter both lugging a couple of covered baskets. Some of the food, at least, would find its way down the gullets of the Chambers family. She and her granddaughter, a cheerful seventeen-year-old, apt to giggle in moments of emotion, had been busy, for the most part together or with Mrs Munter, for the whole of the critical time. Buckley privately thought that Grogan had wasted too much time on them and had resented having to record the woman's spate of irrelevances. He found the page at last and began to read, wondering if the old man was checking up on the accuracy of his shorthand.

'It's disgusting, that's what it is! I always say there's nothing worse than being killed away from home and by strangers. There never was anything like this when I was a girl. It's them mods on their motor cycles, that's who it is. Great crowd of them came roaring into Speymouth last Saturday with their noisy smelly machines. Why don't the police do something about it, that's what I want to know? Why don't you take their machines away and chuck them off the end of the pier, and their trousers too? That'd put a stop to it fast enough. Don't you waste time interviewing decent law-abiding women. Go after them motorcycling mods.'

Buckley broke off.

'That's where you pointed out that even mods could hardly motorcycle to Courcy Island, and she replied darkly that they had their little ways, they were that cunning.'

Grogan said:

'Not that part. A little earlier when she was rabbiting on about the domestic arrangements.'

Buckley flipped back a couple of pages.

'I'm always happy to oblige Mr Munter. I don't mind coming to the island for the odd day and bringing Debbie if wanted. And it wasn't the girl's fault if the glasses were smeary. They've no right to send them out like that. And Mr Munter had no call to go on at Debbie like he did. It's always the same when Lady Ralston's here. He gets his knickers in a twist when she's about, no mistake. We were here last Tuesday for the dress rehearsal and you never heard such goings on. Asking for this, asking for the other, nothing quite to her ladyship's liking. And forty of the cast for lunch and tea if you please. Everything had to be just so even if Mr Gorringe wasn't here. Took himself off to London Mr Munter said and I don't know as I blame him. Anyone would think she was mistress here. I said to Mr Munter, I don't mind helping out this time but if you're going to be stuck with this palaver next year you can count me out. That's what I said. Count me out. And he said not to worry. He reckoned that this would be the last play Lady Ralston would appear in on Courcy Island.'

Buckley stopped reading and looked at Grogan. He told himself that he should have remembered that piece of evidence. He must have taken it down in a fugue of boredom. Black mark. His chief said quietly:

'Yes, that's it. That's the passage I wanted. I'll be asking Munter for an explanation of that remark when the time's right, but not yet. It's as well to keep a few unpleasant shocks in hand. I've no doubt that Mrs Munter will be equally discreet when she obligingly confirms her husband's story. But we'll let the lady wait. I think it's time to hear what Miss Lisle's host has to say for himself. You're a local man, Sergeant. What do you know of him?'

'Very little, sir. He opens the castle to visitors in the summer, but I imagine it's a ploy to get tax relief on the maintenance. He keeps himself to himself, discourages publicity.'

'Does he now? He'll get a bellyful of it before this case is finished. Put your head outside and ask Rogers to summon him with, of course, the usual compliments.'

CHAPTER TWENTY-EIGHT

Buckley thought that he had never seen a murder suspect as much at ease under questioning as Ambrose Gorringe. He sat back in the chair opposite Grogan, immaculate in his dinner-jacket, and gazed across the desk with bright, interested eyes in which Buckley, occasionally glancing up from his note-taking, thought he could detect a gleam of amused contempt. Admittedly Gorringe was on his own ground, sitting, in fact, in his own chair. Buckley thought it rather a pity that the chief hadn't deprived him of this psychological advantage by bundling the lot of them off to Speymouth station. But Gorringe was too calm for his own good. If the husband didn't kill her, then here for his money was a close runner-up.

Now being formally questioned for the first time, he repeated without discrepancies the facts he had first briefly told them when they arrived on the island. He had known Miss Lisle from childhood – both their fathers had been in the diplomatic service and had been stationed for a time at the same embassies – but they had lost touch in recent years and had seen very little of each other until he had inherited the island from his uncle in 1977. The next year they had met at a theatrical first night and she had been invited to the island. He couldn't now remember whether the suggestion had come from him or from Miss Lisle. From that visit and her enthusiasm for the Victorian theatre had flowed the decision to stage a play. He had known about the threatening messages since he had been with her when one of them was delivered but she hadn't confided that they were still arriving, nor had she told him that Miss Gray was a private detective although he had suspected that she might be when she had confronted him with the woodcut pushed under Miss Lisle's door. It had been their joint decision not to worry Miss Lisle either with that or with the news that the marble limb had been stolen. He admitted without apparent concern that he had no alibi for the crucial ninety-odd minutes between one twenty and the discovery of the body. He had lingered over his coffee with Mr Whittingham, gone to his room at about one thirty leaving Whittingham on the terrace, had rested for about fifteen minutes until it was time to change and had left his room to go to the theatre shortly after two. Munter had been backstage and they had checked over the props together and discussed one or two matters relating to the after-show supper party. At about two twenty they had gone together to meet the launch bringing the cast from Speymouth and he had been backstage in the male dressing-room until about two forty-five.

Grogan said:

'And the marble limb? That was last seen by you when?'

'Didn't I tell you, Chief Inspector? By me at about eleven thirty last night when I went to check the tide timetable. I was interested to estimate how long the launches would take on Saturday afternoon and returning to Speymouth that night. The water can run strongly between here and the mainland. Munter saw it in place just after midnight. I found that it was missing and the lock forced when I went to the kitchen at six fifty-five this morning.'

'And all the members of the house party had seen it and knew where it was kept.'

'All except Simon Lessing. He was swimming when the rest of the party were shown round the castle. As far as I know, he has never been near the business room.'

Grogan said:

'What is the boy doing here anyway? Shouldn't he be at school? I take it that Miss Lisle – Lady Ralston – was buying him a privileged education, that he isn't a day boy at the local comprehensive.'

The question could have sounded offensive, thought Buckley, if the carefully controlled voice had held a trace of emotion.

Gorringe replied, equally calmly.

'He's at Melhurst. Miss Lisle wrote for special weekend leave. She may have thought that Webster would be educational. Unfortunately, the weekend has proved educational for the boy in ways she could hardly have foreseen.'

'A proper little mother to him was she?'

'Hardly that. Miss Lisle's maternal sense was, I should have thought, undeveloped. But she genuinely cared for the boy within her capacity. What you must understand about the victim in this case was that she enjoyed being kind, as indeed most of us do provided it doesn't cost us too much.'

'And how much did Mr Lessing cost her?'

'His school fees primarily. About £4,000 a year I suppose. She could afford it. It all began I imagine because she had a conscience about breaking up his parents' marriage. If she did, it was quite unnecessary. The man had a choice presumably.'

'Simon Lessing must have resented the marriage, on his mother's account if not his own. Unless, of course, he thought a rich step-mama a good exchange.'

'It was six years ago. He was barely eleven when his father walked out on him. And if you're suggesting, without much subtlety I may say, that he resented it enough to bash in step-mama's face, then he waited long enough to do it and he chose a singularly inappropriate time. Does Sir George Ralston know that you suspect Simon? He probably considers himself as the boy's stepfather. He'll want to take steps to see that the boy's interests are safeguarded if you're going on with that somewhat ridiculous idea.'

'I never said that we suspected him. And, in view of the boy's youth, I have agreed with Sir George that he shall be present when I speak to the boy. But Mr Lessing is seventeen. He's no longer a juvenile in law. I find these concerted measures to protect him interesting.'

'As long as you don't find them sinister. He was extremely shocked when I broke the news to him. His own parents are dead. He was devoted to Clarissa. It's natural that we should wish to minimize his pain. After all, you're hardly here in the capacity of child-care officers.'

Grogan had scarcely glanced at his witness during this exchange. The unlined notepad which he preferred to the normal police issue was on the desk blotter in front of him and he was sketching with his fountain pen. A careful oblong shape with two doors and two windows took shape under the huge speckled hand. Buckley saw that it was a representation of Clarissa Lisle's bedroom, something between a plan and a drawing. The proportions of the room were carefully to scale but small objects were being inserted, over-large and carefully detailed as a child might draw them; the jars of cosmetics, a box of cotton-wool balls, the tea-tray, the alarm clock. Suddenly and still without looking up, he asked:

'What made you go to her room, sir?'

'Just after Miss Gray went to call her? Merely a chivalrous impulse. I thought that, as her host, it would be seemly if I escorted her to her dressing-room. And there were things to be carried. Her make-up case for one. As we haven't much dressing-room accommodation and she was having to share with Miss Collingwood who plays Cariola, Miss Collingwood had undertaken to be dressed and out before the star wanted the room, but Miss Lisle wasn't going to risk anyone borrowing her greasepaint. So I went to carry the box and to escort the lady.'

'In the absence of her husband who would normally perform that service.'

'Sir George had just come in to change. We met at the top of the stairs as I've already explained.'

'You seem to have taken a lot of trouble for Miss Lisle.' He paused and added, 'One way or another.'

'Walking her two hundred yards from her room to the theatre hardly counts as trouble.'

'But putting on the play for her, restoring the theatre, entertaining her guests. It must have been an expensive business.'

'I'm not a poor man, happily. And I thought that you were here to investigate a murder not to inquire into my personal finances. The theatre, incidentally, was restored for my satisfaction not Miss Lisle's.'

'She wasn't hoping that you might partly finance her next

professional appearance? What's the theatrical jargon, be her angel?'

'I'm afraid you've been gossiping to the wrong people. That particular angelic role has never attracted me. There are more amusing ways of losing money. But if you're trying tactfully to suggest that I may have owed Miss Lisle a favour, you're perfectly right. It was she who gave me the idea for *Autopsy*, my bestseller, in case you're one of the half-dozen who haven't heard of it.'

'She didn't write it for you, by any chance?'

'No, she didn't write it. Miss Lisle's talents were varied and egregious but they didn't extend to the written word. The book was fabricated rather than written, by an unholy triumvirate of my publisher, my agent and myself. It was then suitably packaged, promoted and marketed. No doubt there are sins to be laid to Clarissa's charge but *Autopsy* isn't one of them.'

Grogan let his pen drop from his hand. He leaned back in his chair and looked Gorringe full in the face. He said quietly:

'You knew Miss Lisle from childhood. For the last six months or so you've been intimately concerned with this play. She came here as your guest. She was killed under your roof. However she died, and we shan't know until after the post-mortem, the killer almost certainly used your marble to bash in her face. Are you sure that there is nothing you know, nothing you suspect, nothing she ever said to you that can throw any light on how she died?'

Put it any plainer, thought Buckley, and you'd have to be administering an official caution. He half expected Gorringe to reply that he would say nothing until he had seen his lawyer. But he spoke with the calm unconcern of a disinterested party who has been asked for his considered opinion and has no objection to giving it.

'My first thought – and it remains my theory – was that a trespasser had somehow gained access to the island knowing that my staff and I would be busy with preparations for the play and that the castle would be, as it were, undefended. He climbed up the fire escape, perhaps out of mischief or devilment and with no clear idea of what he meant to do. It could have been a young man.'

'The young usually hunt in gangs.'

'Several young men, then. Or a couple if you prefer it. One of them gets in with the general idea of a prowl round while the house is quiet. That supposes a local boy, one who knew about the play. He creeps into Miss Lisle's room – she had forgotten to lock the communicating door or had thought the precaution unnecessary – and sees her apparently asleep on the bed. He is about to make his exit, with or without the jewel case, when she takes the pads off her eyes and sees him. In a panic he kills her, seizes the box and makes his escape the same way as he came in.'

Grogan said:

'Having thoughtfully provided himself in advance with the marble hand, which according to your evidence, must have been taken from the display case between midnight and six fifty-five this morning.'

'No, I don't think he came provided with anything except a general intention of mischief. My theory is that he found the weapon ready to hand – forgive the atrocious pun – on the bedside chest together, of course, with the quotation from the play.'

'And who are you suggesting put them there? The door to that room was locked, remember.'

'I don't think there's much mystery about that surely. Miss Lisle did.'

Grogan said:

'With the object of frightening herself into hysteria or merely providing any potential murderer who might drop in with a convenient weapon?'

'With the object of providing herself with an excuse if she failed in the play. As I'm afraid she almost certainly would. Or she may have had more devious reasons. Miss Lisle's complex personality was something of a mystery to me as it was, I suspect, to her husband.'

'And are you suggesting that this young, impulsive, unpremeditating killer then replaced the pads over his victim's eyes? That argues we have two complex personalities to elucidate.'

'He could have done. You're the expert on murder, not I. But I could think of a reason if pushed. Perhaps she seemed to be staring up at him and his nerve broke. He had to cover those dead accusing eyes. The suggestion is a little over-imaginative perhaps, but not impossible. Murderers do behave oddly. Remember the Gutteridge case, Chief Inspector.'

Buckley's hand jerked on his shorthand pad. He thought: 'My God, is he doing it on purpose?' The small audacity must surely have been deliberate. But how could Gorringe have learned of the chief's habit of referring to old cases? He glanced up, not at Grogan, but at Gorringe and met only a look of bland innocence. And it was to him that Gorringe spoke:

'Long before your time, Sergeant. Gutteridge was the police constable shot by two car thieves in an Essex country lane in 1927. An ex-convict, Frederick Browne, and his accomplice William Kennedy were hanged for the crime. After killing him, one of them shot out both his eyes. It is thought that they were superstitious. They believed that the dead eyes of a murdered man, fixed on the killer's face, will bear his visage imprinted on the pupils. I doubt whether any murderer willingly looks into his victim's eyes. An interesting feature of an otherwise dull and sordid case.'

Grogan had finished his drawing. The plan of the room was complete. Now, wnile they watched him in silence, he drew on the great bed a small sprawled matchbox figure with wisps of hair over the pillow. Lastly and with care, he blocked in the face. Then he put his great hand over the drawing and ripped out the page, crumpling it in his fist. The gesture was unexpectedly violent, but his voice was quiet, almost gentle.

'Thank you, sir. You've been very helpful. And now, if you've nothing else to tell us, no doubt you'll be wanting to go back to your guests.'

CHAPTER TWENTY-NINE

When Ivo Whittingham came into the room, Buckley, embarrassed, looked quickly down and began flipping back the pages of his notebook, hoping that Whittingham hadn't caught his first look of horror and surprise. Only once before had he seen so gaunt a figure, and that was his Uncle Gerry in those last weeks before the cancer finally got him. He had felt as much affection for his uncle as he was capable of feeling and the protracted agony of his dying had left him with one resolution. If that was what the body could do to a man, then it owed something in return. From now on he would take his pleasures without guilt. He might have become a cheerful hedonist if ambition and the caution which went with it hadn't been stronger. But he hadn't forgotten either the bitterness or the pain. And Ivo Whittingham reminded him in another way. His uncle had looked at him with just such glittering eyes as if they burned with all that remained of life and intelligence. He glanced up as Whittingham seated himself stiffly, grasping the chair sides with his skeletal hands. But when he spoke his voice was surprisingly strong and relaxed.

'This is unpleasantly reminiscent of a summons to one's house-master. Good seldom came of it.'

It was an irreverent beginning which Grogan was unlikely to encourage. He said curtly:

'In that case I suggest that we make it as brief as possible. I take it that you knew Miss Lisle well.'

'You may take it that I knew her intimately.'

'Are you telling me, sir, that she was your mistress?'

'That hardly seems the right word for so spasmodic a liaison. Mistress suggests a certain permanence, even a measure of respectability. One is reminded of dear Mrs Keppel and her King. It would be more accurate to say that we were lovers for a period of about six years as opportunity and her whim dictated.'

'And did her husband know?'

'Husbands. Our relationship outlasted more than one marital episode. But I imagine that you're interested only in George Ralston. I never told him. I don't know whether she did. And if you're wondering whether he took his revenge the idea is ludicrous. Why should he wait until a higher power, or fate or luck, whatever you choose to believe in, is about to rid him of me permanently? Ralston isn't a fool. And if you would like to ask whether I sent the lady on before me, the answer is no. Clarissa Lisle and I had exhausted each other's possibilities on this bank and shoal of time. But I could have killed her. I had the opportunity; I was alone in my room conveniently close all the afternoon. In case you haven't already inquired, it's on the same floor as Clarissa, a mere fifty feet away overlooking the eastern front of the castle. I had access to the means since I had been shown the marble limb. I suppose I could have found the strength. And I think she might have opened her door to me. But I didn't kill her and I don't know who did. You'll have to take my word for it. I can't prove a negative.'

'Tell me what she was like.'

It was the first time Grogan had asked that question. And yet, thought Buckley, it was at the heart of every murder investigation, and, if it were possible to find the answer, most other questions would become superfluous. Whittingham said:

'I was going to say that you've seen her face, but, of course, you haven't. A pity. One needed to know the physical Clarissa to get any clue to what else there might have been to know. She lived intensely in and through her body. The rest is a list of words. She was egocentric, insecure, clever but not intelligent, kind or cruel as the mood took her, restless, unhappy. But she had certain skills which a gentlemanly reticence inhibits me from discussing but which weren't unimportant. She probably gave more joy than she caused misery. Since that can't be said of many of us, it's unbecoming of me to criticize her. I remember that I once sent to her the words of Thomas Malory, Lancelot speaking to Guinevere: "Lady, I take record of God, in thee I have had my earthly joy." I don't take them back, whatever she may have done.'

'Whatever she may have done, sir?'

'A form of words merely, Chief Inspector.'

'So you mourn her?'

'No. But I shan't forget her.'

There was a pause. Then Grogan asked quietly:

'Why are you here, sir?'

'She asked me to come. But there was another reason. One of the Sunday papers commissioned me to do a piece on the island and the theatre. What was wanted was period charm, nostalgia and salacious legend. They should have sent a crime reporter.'

'And that was enough to tempt a reviewer of your eminence?'

'It must have been, mustn't it, since here I am.'

When Grogan asked him, as he had the other suspects, to describe the events of the day, he showed signs of tiredness for the first time. The body sagged in its chair like a puppet jerked from its string.

'There isn't much to tell. We had a late breakfast and then Miss Lisle suggested we see the Church. There's a crypt with some ancient skulls and a secret passage to the sea. We explored both and Gorringe entertained us with old legends about the skulls and a reputed drowning of a wartime internee in the cave at the end of the passage. I was tired and didn't listen very closely. Then back to luncheon at twelve. Miss Lisle went to rest immediately afterwards. I was in my room by quarter past one and stayed there resting and reading until it was time to dress. Miss Lisle had insisted that we change before the play. I met Roma Lisle at the head of the staircase as she came down from her room and we were together when Gorringe appeared with Miss Gray and told us that Clarissa was dead.'

'And during the morning, the visit to the Church and the cave, how did Miss Lisle seem to you?'

'I think I would say, Chief Inspector, that Miss Lisle was her usual self.'

Lastly Grogan spilled out from the folder the sheaves of messages. One of them fluttered to the floor. He bent and picked it up, then handed it to Whittingham.

'What can you tell us about these, sir?'

'Only that I knew she was getting them. She didn't tell me, but one does tend to pick up bits of theatre gossip. But I don't think it was generally known. And here, again, I seem to be the natural suspect. Whoever sent these knew Miss Lisle and knew his Shakespeare. But I don't think I would have added the coffin and the skull. An unnecessarily crude touch, don't you think?'

'And that is all that you want to tell us, sir?'

'It's all that I can tell you, Chief Inspector.'

CHAPTER THIRTY

It was nearly seven o'clock before they got round to seeing the boy. He had changed into a formal suit and looked, thought Buckley, as if he were attending his stepmother's funeral instead of an interview with the police. He guessed that there was no more than eight years' difference in their ages, but it could have been twenty. Lessing looked as neatly pressed and nervous as a child. But he had himself well under control. Buckley felt that there was something vaguely familiar about his entrance, the care with which he seated himself, the serious expectant gaze which he fixed on Grogan's face. And then he remembered. This was how he had looked and behaved at his final interview to join the police. He had been advised then by his headmaster. 'Wear your best suit, but no fountain pen or fancy handkerchief peeping coyly out of the jacket pocket. Look them straight in the eye, but not so fixedly that you embarrass them. Be slightly more deferential than you feel; they're the ones with the job on offer. If you don't know an answer, say so, don't waffle. And don't worry if you're nervous, they prefer that to over-confidence, but show that you've got the guts to cope with nervousness. Call them "sir" or "madam" and thank them briefly before you leave. And for God's sake, boy, sit up straight.'

And as the interview progressed beyond the first easy questions designed, Buckley could almost believe, to put the candidate at his ease, he sensed something else, that Lessing was beginning to feel as he had done; if you followed the advice, the ordeal wasn't so bad after all. Only his hands betrayed him. They were broad and unpleasantly white with thick stubbed fingers, but narrow – almost girlish – nails cut very short and so pink that they looked painted. He held his hands in his lap and from time to time he would stretch and pull at the fingers as if he were routinely performing some prescribed strengthening exercise.

Sir George Ralston remained standing with his back to them looking out of the window through the partly drawn curtains. Buckley wondered whether the intention was to demonstrate that he wasn't influencing the boy by word or glance. But the pose looked perverse, the more so as there was nothing in that still darkness which he could possibly see. Buckley had never known such silence. It had a positive quality; not the absence of noise but a silence which sharpened perception and gave importance and dignity to every word and action. He wished, not for the first time, that they were at headquarters with the sound of passing feet, of doors closing, of distant voices calling, all the comfortable background noises of ordinary life. Here it wasn't only the suspects who were under judgement.

This time Grogan's doodle looked innocuous, even charming. He seemed to be redesigning his kitchen garden. Neat rows of chubby cabbages, climbing runner beans and fern-topped carrots grew under his hand. He said:

'So after your mother died you went to live with her brother and his family and you were there when Lady Ralston came to visit you in the summer of 1978 and decided to adopt you?'

'There was no formal adoption. My uncle was my guardian and he agreed that Clarissa would be . . . well, a kind of foster mother, I suppose. She took over the whole responsibility for me.'

'And you welcomed that arrangement?'

'Very much, sir. Life with my uncle and aunt wasn't really congenial to me.'

And that was an odd word for the boy to use, thought Buckley. It made it sound as if they'd taken the *Mirror* instead of *The Times* and he hadn't been able to get his after-dinner port.

'And you were happy with Sir George and his wife?' Grogan couldn't resist the small note of sarcasm. He added:

'Life was congenial to you?'

'Very, sir.'

'Your stepmother – is that how you thought of her, as a stepmother?'

The boy blushed and glanced sideways at the silent figure of Sir George. He moistened his lips and said:

'Yes, sir. I suppose so.'

'Your stepmother has been receiving some rather unpleasant communications during the last year or so. What do you know about that?'

'Nothing, sir. She didn't tell me.' He added, 'We don't . . . we didn't see a great deal of each other. I'm at school and she was often at the Brighton flat during the holidays.'

Grogan pulled one of the messages from his file and pushed it over the desk.

'That's a sample. Recognize it?'

'No, sir. It's a quotation, isn't it? Is it Shakespeare?'

'You tell me, lad. You're the one at Melhurst. But you've never seen one of these before?'

'No, never.'

'Right then. Suppose you tell us exactly what you did between one o'clock today and two forty-five.'

Lessing looked down at his hands, seemed to become aware of his nervous methodical stretching, and grasped both sides of his chair as if to prevent himself from springing to his feet. But he gave his account lucidly and with growing confidence. He had decided to swim before the play and had gone straight to his room after lunch where he had put on his swimming-trunks under his jeans and shirt. He had taken his jersey and towel and made his way across the lawn to the shore. He had walked on the beach for about an hour because Clarissa had warned him not to swim too soon after his meal. He had then returned to the small cove just beyond the terrace and had entered the water at about two o'clock or shortly after, leaving his clothes, towel and wrist-watch on the shore. He had seen no one either during his walk or his swim, but Sir George had told him that he had watched him coming ashore through his binoculars when he himself was returning to the castle after his bird-watching. Here he again glanced round at his stepfather as if inviting corroboration and again got no response. Grogan said:

'So Sir George Ralston has told us. And what then?'

'Well, nothing really, sir. I was on my way back to the castle when Mr Gorringe saw me and came to meet me. He told me about Clarissa.'

The last few words were almost a whisper. Grogan bent his ruddy head forward and asked softly:

'And what exactly did he tell you?'

'That she was dead, sir. Murdered.'

'And did he explain how?'

Again the whisper.

'No, sir.'

'But you asked, presumably? You betrayed some natural curiosity?'

'I asked him what had happened, how she had died. He said that no one could be sure until after the post-mortem.'

'He's right. There's nothing you need to know except the fact that she is dead, and that it must have been homicide. And now, Mr Lessing, what can you tell us about the arm of the dead princess?'

Buckley thought that Sir George gave an exclamation of protest; but he still didn't interrupt. The boy looked from face to face as if the police had gone mad. No one spoke. Then he said:

'You mean, in the Church? We visited the crypt to see the skulls this morning. But Mr Gorringe didn't say anything about a dead princess.'

'It wasn't in the Church.'

'You mean, it's a mummified arm? I don't understand.'

'It's a marble hand, a limb to be accurate. A baby's limb. Someone has taken it from Mr Gorringe's display case, the one outside this door, and we'd rather like to know who and when.'

'I don't think I've seen it, sir. I'm sorry.'

Grogan had completed his kitchen garden and was separating it from the lawn by a trellis and archway. He looked up at Lessing and said:

'My officers and I will be back here tomorrow. We'll probably be around for a day or two. If there's anything that occurs to you, anything that you remember which is the least unusual or likely to help, however small and unimportant it seems, I want you to get in touch. Understand?'

'Yes, sir. Thank you, sir.'

Grogan nodded and the boy got to his feet, glanced for the last time at the still back of Sir George and went out. Buckley almost expected him to turn at the door and ask whether he'd got the job.

Sir George turned at last:

'He's due back at school on Monday morning before midday. Special leave. I take it he can go.'

Grogan said:

'It would be helpful to us, sir, if he could stay until the Tuesday morning. It's just a question of convenience. If anything does occur to him or to us it would be helpful to be able to clear it up quickly. But obviously he can go early on Monday if you think it important.'

Sir George hesitated.

'Don't suppose a day will make much odds. Better for him, though, to be away from here, back at work. I'll get in touch with the school tomorrow or Monday. He'll need leave later for the funeral, but I suppose it's too early yet to think about that.'

'I'm afraid so, sir.'

Sir George was almost at the door when Grogan called softly:

'There's one other thing, sir, which I have to ask. Your relationship with your wife. Would you say that yours was a happy marriage?'

The slim upright figure paused for a second, hand on the doorknob. Then Sir George turned to face them. His face was twitching violently, like that of a man afflicted with a nervous spasm. Then he controlled himself.

'I find that question offensive, Chief Inspector.'

Grogan's voice was still gentle, dangerously gentle.

'In a murder investigation, we sometimes have to ask questions which people find offensive.'

'It's meaningless unless you ask both parties. Too late for that now. Not sure that my wife had the capacity for happiness.'

'And you, sir?'

He answered with great simplicity.

'I loved her.'

CHAPTER THIRTY-ONE

After he had gone, Grogan said with sudden vehemence:

'Let's pack up and get out of this place. It's getting claustrophobic. What time is the launch expected with Roper and Badgett?'

Buckley looked at his watch.

'It should be here within fifteen minutes.'

Detective Constables Roper and Badgett were to be on duty in the business room, but for one night only. Their presence was almost a formality. No one at the castle had asked for police protection, nor did Grogan believe that they were in need of it. He had few enough officers without wasting manpower. The whole of the island including the secret passage to the Devil's Kettle had been searched; if anyone still believed in the theory of the casual intruder it was apparent that he wasn't now on Courcy. Tomorrow the police inquiries on the island would be complete and the investigation moved to an incident room at the Speymouth station. It was likely, thought Buckley, to be a tedious and less than comfortable vigil for Roper and Badgett. Ambrose Gorringe had offered a bedroom and had said that the two officers should ring for Munter if there was anything they needed. But Grogan's instructions had been clear.

'You'll bring your own flasks and sandwiches, lads, and ring for no one. You'll be beholden to Mr Gorringe for nothing but his light and heating and the water that flushes his bog.'

He pulled the bellcord. It seemed to Buckley that Munter took his time in coming. Grogan said:

'Will you tell Mr Gorringe that we're now leaving.'

'Yes, sir. The police launch isn't yet sighted, sir.'

'I'm aware of that. We shall wait for it on the quay.'

When the man had gone, he said irritably:

'What does he think we propose to do? Walk on water?'

Ambrose Gorringe arrived within minutes to see them off his premises with formal courtesy. They might, thought Buckley, have been a couple of dinner guests, if not particularly welcome or agreeable ones. He said nothing about the event that had brought them to Courcy and made no inquiries about the progress of the investigation. Clarissa Lisle's murder might have been an embarrassing mishap in an otherwise not unsuccessful day.

It was good to be in the air again. The night was extraordinarily balmy for mid-September and there still seemed to rise from the stones of the terrace a genial warmth like the last breath of a summer day. Briefcases in hand, they strolled together along the eastern arm of the quay. Turning to retrace their steps, they could see in the distance a stream of light from the dining-room windows and dark figures moving to and fro on the terrace, joining then parting, pausing and then walking on as if taking part in a stately pavane. It looked to Buckley as if they had plates in their hands. Probably making do with the cold left-over party food he thought, and some irrelevant quotation about baked funeral meats came into mind. He didn't blame them for not wanting to sit together round a table, faced with one empty chair.

He and Grogan settled themselves under the canopy of the bandstand to wait for the first lights of the launch. The peace of the night was seductive. Here on the southern shore where the mainland couldn't be seen it was easy to imagine that the island was totally isolated in a waste of sea, that they were waiting and watching for the masts of some overdue relief ship, and that the figures gliding on the terrace were the ghosts of long-dead settlers, that the castle itself was a shell, hall and library and drawing-room open to the sky, the great staircase rising into nothingness, ferns and weeds pushing their way between the broken tiles. He wasn't normally imaginative, but now he deliberately indulged his tiredness, letting his mind elaborate the fantasy while he sat gently massaging his right wrist.

Grogan's voice broke harshly into the reverie. Neither the peace nor the beauty had touched him. His thoughts were still on the case. Buckley told himself that he should have known there would be no respite. He remembered the overheard comment of a detective inspector: 'Red Rufus treats a murder investigation like a love affair. Gets obsessed with his suspects. Moves into their lives. Lives and breathes with the case, edgy and restless and frustrated, until it climaxes at the arrest.' Buckley wondered if that was one of the reasons for his failed marriage. It must be disconcerting to live with a man who, for most of the night as well as the day, simply wasn't there. And when he spoke his voice was as vigorous as if the inquiry had just begun.

'Miss Roma Lisle, cousin of the deceased, aged forty-five, shopkeeper, ex-schoolmistress, unmarried. What struck you most about the lady, Sergeant?'

Buckley dragged his mind back to the interview with Roma Lisle.

'That she was frightened, sir.'

'Frightened, defensive, embarrassed and unconvincing. Consider her story. She admits that the woodcut is hers and says that she brought it to Courcy because she thought that Ambrose Gorringe would be interested in it and would be able to advise her about its age and value. As he doesn't claim to be an authority on early seventeenth-century manuscripts, the hope was optimistic. Still, we needn't read too much into that. She found the thing, she thought it was interesting and she brought it with her. And now for today. She tells us that she left her cousin's bedroom at about five minutes past one, went straight to the library and stayed there until half past two when she went up to her room. It's on the floor immediately above the gallery and she didn't have to pass Miss Lisle's room to get to it. She saw and heard no one. During the hour and twenty minutes when she was in the library she was alone. Miss Gray briefly put her head round the door at about twenty past one but didn't stay. Miss Lisle remained in the library expecting a private business call from her partner which didn't, in fact, come through. She tells us that she also wrote a letter. Asked to produce it as a small indication of verisimilitude – not that it greatly matters – she blushes with embarrassment and says that she decided not to send it after all and tore it up. When we gently point out that there are no fragments in the library waste-paper basket she becomes even redder and confides that she took the scraps with her when she went to her room and flushed them down the WC. All very curious. But consider something even odder. She was one of the last people to see her cousin alive; not the last, but one of the last. And she tells us that she followed Miss Lisle up to her room because she wanted to wish her good luck in the play. All very proper and cousinly. But when we point out that she'd left it rather late to get changed, she tells us that she'd decided to give the performance a miss. Would you care to propound a theory which would explain these intriguing eccentricities of behaviour?'

'She was expecting a telephone call from her lover, sir, not necessarily her partner. When it didn't come, she decided to write to him. Then she thought better of it and tore up the letter. She retrieved the fragments from the waste-paper basket because she didn't want us piecing them together and reading her private correspondence, however innocuous.'

'Ingenious, Sergeant. But you see where it leaves us. At the time when, according to her, she took those scraps upstairs she couldn't have known that the police would be here to poke their inquisitive noses into anyone's private correspondence, not unless she also knew by then that her cousin was dead.'

'And that last visit to Miss Lisle?'

Grogan said:

'My guess is that it was less friendly than she makes out.'

'But why tell us about the letter, sir? She didn't have to. Why not just say that she spent the time in the library, reading?'

'Because she's a woman who normally tells the truth. She made no pretence, for example, of liking her cousin or being particularly grieved by her death. If she is going to lie to the police, she prefers to lie as little as possible. That way she has fewer untruths to remember and is able to convince herself that, essentially, she isn't really lying at all. It's a sound enough principle as far as it goes. But we shouldn't read too much into that torn-up letter. She may merely have wanted to save the servants trouble, or have been afraid that they might have been curious enough to piece it together. And if Miss Roma Lisle's story is less than convincing, she's not the only one. Consider the curious reticence of the lady's maid. It sounds like the chapter heading for one of those snobbish thirties thrillers.'

Buckley thought back over the interview with Rose Tolgarth. Before she had come in, Grogan had said to him:

'You question the lady, Sergeant. She may prefer youth to experience. Give her a treat.'

Surprised, Buckley had asked:

'At the desk, sir?'

'That would seem the obvious place, unless you intend to prowl round her like a predator.'

Grogan himself had greeted her and invited her to sit with more courtesy than he had shown Cordelia Gray or Roma Lisle. If she were surprised to find herself facing the younger of the two officers she hadn't shown it. But then, she hadn't shown anything. She had gazed at him with her remarkable eyes, with their smudgy black irises, as if she were looking into . . . what, he wondered? Not his soul, since he didn't believe that he had one, but certainly into some part of his mind which wasn't intended to be public property. All his questions had been answered politely but with the minimum of words. She had admitted that she knew about the threatening messages but refused to speculate about who might have sent them. That job, she implied, was the responsibility of the police. It was she who had made and taken up Miss Lisle's tea before she settled for her usual pre-performance rest.

The routine was always the same. Miss Lisle drank Lapsang Souchong tea with no milk or sugar but with two thick slices of lemon put into the teapot before the boiling water was poured in. She had made the tea in the usual way in Mr Munter's pantry and Mrs Chambers and Debbie had been with her at the time. She had taken up the tray immediately and at no time had the teapot been out of her sight. Sir George had been in the bedroom with his wife. She had placed the tea tray on the bedside cabinet and had then gone into the bathroom where there was a certain amount of tidying to be done before Miss Lisle took her bath. She had returned to the bedroom to help her mistress undress and had found Miss Gray there. After Miss Gray had returned to her own room, Sir George had left his wife and she herself had followed almost immediately afterwards. She had spent the afternoon preparing the ladies' dressing-room backstage and helping Mrs Munter with the arrangements for the party. At two forty-five she had become concerned in case Miss Gray had forgotten to call Miss Lisle and had gone herself. She had met Sir George, Mr Gorringe and Miss Gray outside the bedroom and had then learned of Miss Lisle's death.

They had taken her up to the bedroom and asked her to look round carefully but without touching anything, and say whether the room was as she would expect to find it, whether there was anything which struck her as unusual. She had shaken her head. Before leaving she had stood for a moment gazing over the *chaise longue*, the stripped and empty bed with a look which Buckley couldn't fathom. Sadness? Speculation? Resignation? The right word eluded him. Her eyes were open but he thought he saw her lips moving. For a moment he had the extraordinary idea that she might be praying.

Back in the business room he had asked:

'You were happy working for Miss Lisle? You liked each other?'

And that was as tactful a way as he knew of asking whether she had hated her employer enough to bash in her skull.

She had replied quietly:

'We are used to each other. My mother was her nurse. She asked me to look after her.'

'And you can't think of a reason why anyone should want to kill her. All one big happy family, were they?'

The attempt at Grogan-like sarcasm had been unsuccessful. She had met it with a brand of her own.

'There's never a good reason for people to kill each other, even in happy families.'

He had had little more success with Mrs Munter. She, too, had been a polite but unrewarding witness, saying as little as possible, resisting all his blandishments to entice her into volubility or indiscretion. Ambrose Gorringe had concealed his secrets, if any, with a spate of apparently artless conjecture. Miss Tolgarth and Mrs Munter had concealed theirs with a silence and obstinacy which just avoided being overtly uncooperative. Buckley thought that Grogan could hardly have selected two more difficult witnesses for him to practise interrogation on. Perhaps that had been the idea. The impression they apparently wanted to convey was that murder, like most of the world's violence, was a male concern from which, as women, they were only too happy to be excluded. From time to time he had found himself staring at them with what he was uncomfortably aware must have been obvious frustration. But human beings weren't like school geometry problems. If you stared at them long enough, they didn't suddenly make sense. He said:

'Miss Tolgarth admits that she didn't leave Miss Lisle until after Sir George had gone and that accords with his evidence. Miss Gray was in her own room so nobody saw her leave. She could have returned to the bathroom, pretended to busy herself with preparations for the bath, come back into the bedroom when Gray had left, and killed her mistress then.'

'The timing would be very tight. Mrs Munter saw her downstairs in the pantry at one twenty.'

'So she says. I got the feeling, sir, that those two are standing together. I got precious little out of either of them, Rose Tolgarth in particular.'

'Except one highly interesting lie. Unless, of course, the lady is less sharp-eyed than I give her credit for.'

'Sir?'

'In the bedroom, Sergeant. Think. You asked her if everything looked as she would expect to find it. Her answer was a nod. But visualize that dressing-table. What among all that female clutter was missing, something which we would have expected to see, given the things which, in fact, we did see?'

But the launch bringing Roper and Badgett had actually touched the quay before Buckley was able to work out the answer to the conundrum.

CHAPTER THIRTY-TWO

And now, at last, the dreadful day was over. Soon after ten o'clock struck, one by one and with brief 'goodnights', they had crept silently to their beds. The casual night-time commonplaces had become unsayable – 'I'm terribly tired. It's been a long day. Sleep well. See you all in the morning,' – all bore a weight of innuendo, tactlessness or bad taste. Two women police officers had moved Cordelia's things from the De Morgan room, a touch of delicacy which would have amused her had she been capable of being amused. The new bedroom was on the same gallery floor but on the other side of Simon and overlooking the rose garden and the pool. As she turned the key in the lock and breathed the stuffy, scented air Cordelia thought that it might not often be used. It was small, dim and cluttered and looked as if Ambrose had furnished it strictly in period for the edification of his summer visitors. The lightness and delicacy which he had achieved in so much of the castle was absent. Every square inch of the walls was covered with pictures and ornaments and the ornate furniture, papier-mâché lined with mahogany, seemed to press in on her, dark and threatening. The room felt musty but when she opened wide the window the sound of the sea burst in, no longer soporific and comforting but a steady menacing roar. She lay wondering whether she could summon up the energy to get out of bed and half close the window. But that was her last conscious thought before weariness took over and she felt herself drifting unresistingly down the long stream of tiredness into sleep.

PART FIVE

Terror By Moonlight

CHAPTER THIRTY-THREE

At nine fifteen Cordelia went into the business room to ring Miss Maudsley, wondering as she lifted the receiver whether the police would be listening in. But monitoring private telephone calls, even from the scene of a murder, counted as phone tapping and for that the consent of the Home Secretary was surely necessary. It was strange how little she knew about a real police investigation despite Bernie's tutelage. It had already struck her that their legal powers were a great deal less extensive than a reading of detective fiction might suggest. On the other hand, their physical presence was far more frightening and oppressive than she would have believed possible. It was like having mice in the house. They might for a time be both silent and invisible but, once known to be there, it was impossible to ignore their secret and polluting presence. Even here in the business room the force of Inspector Grogan's rebarbative personality still lingered, although all trace of his brief occupation had been cleared away. It seemed to her that the police had left the room tidier than they had found it, and this in itself was sinister. As she dialled the London number it was difficult to believe that the call would go unrecorded.

It was a nuisance that Miss Maudsley in her cheap bed-sitting-room had no private telephone. The single instrument was in the darkest and most inaccessible corner of the hall at Mancroft Mansions and Cordelia knew that she might have to wait for minutes until one of the other residents, driven mad by its insistent ring, came out to silence it, and that she would then be lucky if he understood English and luckier still if he were willing to trudge up four flights to call Miss Maudsley. But this morning her call was answered almost immediately. Miss Maudsley confided that she had bought her usual Sunday paper on the way home from eight o'clock Mass and had been crouching on the bottom step of the stairs wondering whether to ring the castle or to wait for Cordelia's call. She was almost incoherent with anxiety and distress and the brevity of the press report hadn't helped. Cordelia thought how chagrined Clarissa would be to learn that her fame, even after a violent death, didn't justify top billing on a day when a spectacular parliamentary scandal, the death of a pop star from a drug overdose and a particularly brutal terrorist attack in Northern Italy had presented the editor with a surplus of candidates for the front page. Miss Maudsley, her voice breaking, said:

'It says that she was . . . well . . . battered to death. I can't believe it. And it's so horrible for you. Her husband, too, of course. That poor woman. But naturally one thinks of the living. I suppose it was some kind of intruder. The paper does say that her jewellery is missing. I do hope that the police won't get any wrong ideas.'

And that, thought Cordelia, was as tactful a way as any of saying that she hoped that Cordelia herself wasn't under suspicion.

Cordelia gave her instructions slowly, and Miss Maudsley made audible attempts to calm herself and listen.

'The police will be sure to check up on me and on the Agency. I don't know the procedure, whether someone will call from the Dorset CID or whether they'll get the Met to do it for them. But don't worry. Just answer their questions.'

'Oh dear, yes I suppose we must. But it's all so dreadful. Am I to show them everything? Suppose they ask to see the accounts? I did balance the petty cash on Friday afternoon, at least it didn't balance exactly I'm afraid. Mr Morgan, a delightful man, came to fix the name-plaque . . . He said that he'd leave the bill until you got back, but I sent Bevis for some biscuits for him to have with his coffee and he forgot how much they cost and we threw away the packet with the price on it.'

'They're more likely to ask about Sir George Ralston's visit. I don't think the police will be interested in the petty cash. But let them see anything they ask for except, of course, the clients' files. They're confidential. And Miss Maudsley, tell Bevis not to try to be clever.'

Miss Maudsley promised in a voice which had become calmer; she was obviously making efforts to convey her total reliability to deal with whatever crises Monday might bring. Cordelia wondered which would be the more damaging, Bevis's play-acting or Miss Maudsley's passionate protestations that in no possible circumstances could dear Miss Gray be capable of murder. Probably

Bevis would be intimidated by the physical presence of the law from the worst excesses of his histrionic talents unless, by some ill chance, he had happened recently to view one of those television documentaries devoted to exposing the corruption, brutality and racism of the police, in which case anything was possible. But at least she could be certain that, whoever visited Kingly Street, it wouldn't be Adam Dalgliesh. From the rarefied and mysterious heights of hierarchy which he now inhabited any such chore was unthinkable. She wondered whether he would read about the crime, whether he would learn that she was involved.

Nothing could have prepared Cordelia for the singularity of the rest of Sunday morning. As he was helping himself to his breakfast scrambled eggs Ambrose suddenly paused, spoon in hand.

'My God, I've forgotten to cancel Father Hancock! It's too late now. Oldfield will be on his way to fetch him.'

He turned to explain:

'He's an elderly Anglican priest who has retired to Speymouth. I usually invite him to take Sunday morning service when I have guests. People nowadays seem to feel the need of these ministrations. Clarissa liked him to come when she was here for a weekend. He amused her.'

'Clarissa!' Ivo gave a hoarse burst of laughter which shuddered his gaunt frame. 'He'll probably arrive at the same time as the police. So we explain to Grogan that we aren't at his disposal for an hour or so because we'll all be at Divine Service. I can't wait to see his face. Admit that you didn't cancel on purpose, Ambrose.'

'No, I assure you. It entirely slipped my mind.'

Roma said:

'He probably won't come. He'll have heard of the murder by now – it'll be all over Speymouth – and he'll assume that you don't expect him.'

'Don't you believe it. If we were reduced by mass homicide to two and Oldfield were available to fetch him, he'd come. He's nearly ninety and has his own priorities. Besides, he enjoys his sherry and luncheon. I'd better remind Munter.'

He went out, smiling his secretive complacent smile.

Cordelia said:

'I wonder if I ought to change out of trousers.'

Ivo seemed suddenly to have found an appetite. He spooned out a generous helping of egg.

'Unnecessary, surely? I don't suppose you've brought gloves and a prayerbook. Never mind, even if the props are missing we can still proceed to church in the approved Victorian fashion. I wonder whether the Munters and Oldfield will come to make a showing in the servants' pew. And what on earth will the old man find to preach about?'

Ambrose reappeared.

'Well, that's settled. Munter hadn't forgotten. Will you all be coming or have we any conscientious objectors?'

Roma said:

'I disapprove, but I don't mind putting in an appearance if the object is to irritate Grogan. We aren't expected to sing, are we?'

'Of course. There is the *Te Deum* and the responses and we have one hymn. Would anyone like to choose it?'

No one volunteered.

'Then I suggest "God moves in a mysterious way". We meet the launch at ten forty.'

And so the astonishing morning got under way. *Shearwater* beat the police launch to the jetty by five minutes and Ambrose received a frail figure in cloak and biretta who alighted with remarkable sprightliness and gazed on them benignly from moist and faded blue eyes. Before Ambrose could make the introductions he turned to him and said:

'I was sorry to hear of your wife's death.'

Ambrose said gravely:

'Yes, it was unexpected. But we weren't married, Father.'

'Were you not? Dear me! Forgive me, I hadn't realized. Drowned, I think they said. These waters can be very treacherous.'

'Not drowned, Father. She suffered a severe concussion.'

'I thought that my housekeeper said drowned. But perhaps I'm thinking of someone else. The war, perhaps. A long time ago, anyway. I'm afraid my memory is not what it was.'

The police launch shuddered to the quay and they watched

while Grogan, Buckley and two other plain-clothes officers alighted. Ambrose said formally:

'May I introduce Father Hancock who is here to take Morning Service according to the rites of the Church of England. It usually lasts an hour and a quarter. You and your officers are, of course, very welcome to attend.'

Grogan said curtly:

'Thank you, but I am not a member of your Church and my men make their own arrangements and in their off-duty time. I should be glad if we could again have access to all parts of the castle.'

'Of course. Munter will look after you. And I shall, of course, be available myself after luncheon.'

The Church received them into its archaic, multi-coloured silence. Simon was persuaded to seat himself at the organ and the rest of the party filed decorously into the high pew originally built for Herbert Gorringe. The organ was old, requiring to be pumped, and Oldfield was already there, hand at the ready. With the appearance of a surpliced Father Hancock the service got under way. Ambrose obviously took the view that his guests were dissenters, if not worse, who required a strong lead in the responses, and Ivo retained throughout an attentive gravity and showed a familiarity with the liturgy which suggested that this was his normal Sunday morning activity. Simon managed the organ competently enough, although Oldfield let it run out of wind at the end of the *Te Deum* and it produced a late, noisy and discordant amen. Roma forgot her resolve to remain silent and sang in a rich contralto only slightly out of tune. Father Hancock used the 1662 *Book of Common Prayer* without deletions or substitutions and his congregation proclaimed themselves miserable offenders who had followed too much the devices and desires of their own hearts and promised amendment of life in a slightly ragged but resolute chorus. It was only at the end of the petitions when, unexpectedly, he inserted a prayer for the souls of the departed that Cordelia heard a small concerted intake of breath and the air of the Church grew for a moment colder. The sermon lasted fifteen minutes and was a learned dissertation on the Pauline theology of the redemption. As they rose to sing the hymn Ivo whispered to Cordelia:

'That's all one asks of a sermon. No possible relevance to anything but itself.'

Before luncheon, Munter served dry and chilled sherry on the terrace. Father Hancock managed three glasses without apparent effect and talked happily to Sir George about bird-watching and to Ivo about liturgical reform on which Ivo showed himself surprisingly well informed. No one mentioned Clarissa, and it seemed to Cordelia that, for the first time since her murder, her restless, menacing spirit was subdued. For a few precious moments the weight of guilt and misery lifted from her own heart. It was possible to believe, innocently talking in the sun, that life was as well ordered, as certain, as austerely decent and reasonable as the great Anglican compromise in which they had taken part. And when they went in to their roast ribs of beef and rhubarb tart – a conventional and rather heavy Sunday luncheon provided, she suspected, primarily for the benefit of Father Hancock – it was a relief to have him there, to hear the thin but beautiful voice discussing such a harmless interest as the nesting habits of the song thrush and to watch his frank enjoyment of the food and wine. Only Simon, his face flushed, drank as steadily, downing the claret as if it were water, reaching for the decanter with a shaking hand. But Father Hancock seemed as spry as ever after a meal which would have reduced many a younger man to stupor and he took his leave of them with the same serene contentment with which he had greeted them four hours earlier.

As *Shearwater* drew away, Roma turned to Cordelia and said with gruff embarrassment:

'I'm going for a walk for half an hour. Would you care to come? I'd like to have a word with you.'

'All right. If Grogan wants us he can send for us.'

They walked together, without speaking, up the long greensward beyond the rose garden, then under the shadow of the beeches, crunching their way through the bright drifts of fallen leaves and hearing above the scuffle of their tramping feet the strengthening pulse of the sea. After five minutes they emerged from the trees and found themselves on the edge of the cliff. To their right was a concrete bunker, part of the 1939 defences of the island, its low entrance almost blocked with leaves. They moved round it and settled their backs against its rough-textured wall, looking down through a green and gold pattern of beech leaves to the narrow strip of beach and the glitter of the sea-washed shingle.

Cordelia didn't speak. The walk had been at Roma's request. It was for her to say what was on her mind. But she felt curiously peaceful and at ease with her companion, as if none of their differences could weigh against the fact of their common femininity. She watched as Roma picked up a beech twig and began methodically shredding it of leaves. Without looking at Cordelia, she said:

'You're supposed to be an expert in these things. When do you suppose we can get away? I've got a shop to look after, my partner can't manage indefinitely on his own. The police can't keep us here, surely? The investigation could take months.'

Cordelia said:

'They can't legally hold us at all unless they arrest us. Some of us will have to attend the inquest. But I should think you could leave tomorrow if you wanted to.'

'And what about George? He'll need some help. Is he going to sort out her things, jewellery, clothes, make-up, or does he expect me to?'

'Hadn't you better ask him?'

'We can't even get into her bedroom. The police still have it sealed. And she's brought drawers of stuff with her. She always did, even for a weekend. And then there'll be all the clothes in the Bayswater flat and at Brighton, suits, dresses, her furs. He can hardly dump it all on Oxfam.'

Cordelia said:

'They'd be surprised, certainly. But I expect they'd find a good use for it all. They could sell the clothes in their gift shops.' She would have found this female chat about Clarissa's wardrobe bizarre if she hadn't realized that Roma's concern about her cousin's clothes masked a deeper concern: Clarissa's money. Again there was silence. Then Roma said gruffly:

'Did you know that I'd asked Clarissa for a loan just before she was killed and that she'd turned me down?'

'Yes. I was there when she told Sir George.'

'And you haven't told the police?'

'No.'

'That was decent of you, considering that I haven't been particularly pleasant to you.'

'What has that to do with it? If they want that kind of information they can get it from the person concerned, you.'

'Well, they haven't got it so far. I lied. I'm not proud of it and I'm not even sure why. Panic, I suppose, and a feeling that it would suit them to pin the murder on me rather than on George or Ambrose. One's a baronet and war hero and the other's rich.'

'I don't think they want to pin it on anyone except the guilty person. I don't take to either of them, Grogan or Buckley. But I think they're honest.'

Roma said:

'It's odd. I've never much liked or trusted the police, but I always took it for granted that, faced with a crime as serious as murder, I'd co-operate with them up to the hilt. I want Clarissa's murderer caught, of course I do. So why do I feel so defensive? Why do I act as if Grogan and Buckley are in league against me? And it's humiliating to find oneself lying, lying and terrified, and ashamed.'

'I know. I feel the same.'

'It looks as if George hasn't told them about our quarrel either. Nor has Tolly, apparently. Clarissa sent her out while we were talking, but she must have guessed. What do you think she has in mind, blackmail?'

Cordelia said:

'I'm sure not. But I think she knows. She was in the bathroom while I was there, and she probably overheard. Clarissa was pretty vehement.'

'She was vehement with me, vehement and offensive. If I were capable of killing her, I'd have done it then.'

They were silent for a moment, then she said:

'What I can't get used to is the way we all carefully avoid discussing who it was killed her. We don't even confide what we've told Grogan. Since the murder, we've behaved to each other like strangers, telling nothing, asking nothing. Don't you find it strange?'

'Not really. We're stuck here together. Life will be intolerable if we start hurling accusations or recriminations at each other or divide into cliques.'

'I suppose so. But I don't think I can go on, not knowing, not even talking about it, pretending to make polite conversation when we're all thinking about the same thing, carefully avoiding each other's eyes, wondering, locking our doors at night. Did you lock yours?'

'Yes. I wasn't sure why. I don't think for one moment that there's a homicidal maniac on the island. Clarissa was always the intended victim. She wasn't killed by mistake. But I did lock my door.'

'Against whom? Who do you think did it?'

Cordelia said:

'One of us who slept in the castle on Friday night.'

'I know that. But which one?'

'I don't know. Do you?'

Roma's twig was a thin denuded wand. She threw it away, found another and began again the work of methodical destruction.

'I should like it to be Ambrose if anyone, but I can't believe it. Wasn't it George Orwell who wrote that murder, the unique crime, should arise only from strong emotions? Ambrose never felt a strong emotion in his life. And he hasn't the courage or the ruthlessness. He isn't capable of that much hatred. He likes to play with the toys of violence; a tag end of executioner's rope, a bloodstained nightdress, a pair of Victorian handcuffs. With Ambrose even the horror comes second-hand, disinfected by time and charm and quaintness. And it can't be Simon. He never even saw the marble limb and, anyway, he'd have confessed by now. He's a weakling like his father. He wouldn't have the psychological strength to stand up to Grogan for five minutes if the going got rough. And Ivo? Well, Ivo's dying. He's nearly served his life sentence. He may feel that he's out of the reach of the law. But where's his motive? I suppose George is the main suspect, but I don't believe that either. He's a professional soldier, a professional killer if you like. But he wouldn't do it in that way, not to a woman. It could be the Munters, singly or together, or even

Tolly, but I can't think why. That leaves you and me. And it wasn't me. And, if it's any comfort to you, I don't think it was you either.'

Cordelia said:

'Tell me about Clarissa. You spent a lot of your holidays with her as a child, didn't you?'

'Oh God, those awful Augusts! They had a house on the river at Maidenhead and spent most of the summer there. Her mother thought that Clarissa ought to have young company and my parents were glad to have me fed and boarded free. Oddly enough, we got on quite well together then, united I suppose by our fear of her father. When he came down from London she lived in terror.'

'I thought that she adored him, that he was an over-indulgent, devoted papa.'

'Is that what she told you? How typical of Clarissa! She couldn't even be honest about her own childhood. No, he was a brute. I don't mean he physically ill-treated us. In some ways that would have been more endurable than sarcasm, a cold adult anger, contempt. I didn't understand him then, of course. Now I think I do. He didn't really like women. He married to get himself a son – he had the egotism that can't imagine a world in which he hasn't at least a vicarious immortality – and he found himself with a daughter, an invalid wife who'd no intention of breeding again and a job in which divorce wasn't an option. And Clarissa wasn't even pretty when she was a child. And his coolness and her fear killed any spontaneity, any affection, even any intelligence which she might have shown. No wonder she spent the rest of her life obsessively looking for love. But then don't we all?'

Cordelia said:

'After I was told something about her, something she'd done, I thought that she was a monster. But perhaps no one is, not entirely, not when you know the truth about them.'

'She was a monster all right. But when I think of Uncle Roderick, I can understand why. Hadn't we better be getting back? Grogan will suspect us of conspiracy. We can probably scramble down to the beach from here and walk back by the sea.'

They trudged back along the edge of the surf. Roma, her

hands sunk in her jacket pockets, walked ahead, splashing through the small receding waves, seeming oblivious of the wet trouser bottoms flapping against her ankles, of her sodden shoes. The way back was longer and slower than the walk through the copse, but at last they turned the headland of a small bay and the castle was suddenly before them. They stopped and watched. A young man in bathing-trunks and carrying a rough wooden box was climbing down the fire escape from the window of Cordelia's first bedroom. He climbed carefully, hooking his arms round the rungs, being careful not to touch them with his hands. Then he glanced round, walked to the edge of the rocks and with a sudden violent gesture flung the box out to sea. Then he stood poised for a moment, arms raised, and dived. About thirty yards from the end of the terrace rocked a boat, a different boat from the police launch. A diver, sleek and glittering in his black suit, rested on the gunwale. As soon as the box hit the water he twisted his body and dropped backward out of sight. Roma said:

'So that's what the police are thinking?'

'Yes. That's what they're thinking.'

'They're after the jewel casket. And suppose they do manage to dredge it up?'

Cordelia said:

'It will be bad news for someone on this island. I think that they'll find that it still holds Clarissa's jewels.' But what else might it hold? Would the notice of Clarissa's performance in *The Deep Blue Sea* still be in the secret drawer? The police had taken very little interest in that single square of newsprint, but suddenly it seemed to Cordelia that it must have had some significance. Wasn't there just the possibility that it had a bearing on Clarissa's death? The thought at first seemed absurd, but it persisted. She knew that she wouldn't be satisfied until she had seen a duplicate. The obvious first step was to call at the newspaper office in Speymouth and examine the archives. She knew the year, Jubilee year, 1977. It shouldn't be too difficult. And at least it would give her something positive to do.

She was aware that Roma was standing absolutely still, her eyes fixed on the lone swimmer. Her face was expressionless.

Then she shook herself and said:

'We'd better go in and face another round of what, with Chief Inspector Grogan, passes for the third degree. If he were openly impertinent, or even brutal I'd find it less offensive than his veiled masculine insolence.'

But when they passed through the hall and were drawn by the sound of voices into the library they were told by Ambrose that Grogan and Buckley had left the island. They were said to be meeting Dr Ellis-Jones at the Speymouth mortuary. There would be no more questioning until Monday morning. The rest of the day was their own to get through as best they could.

CHAPTER THIRTY-FOUR

Buckley thought that Sunday afternoon was a hell of a time for an autopsy. He didn't exactly enjoy them whenever he had to attend, but Sunday, even when he was on duty, had about it a lethargic, post-prandial calm which called for a comfortable chair in the Sergeants' Mess and a desultory reading over of reports rather than an hour spent on his feet while Doc Ellis-Jones sliced, sawed, cut, weighed and demonstrated with his gloved and bloody hands. It wasn't that Buckley felt squeamish. He didn't in the least care what indignities were practised on his own body once he was dead and he couldn't see why anyone should be more perturbed by the ritual dismemberment of a corpse than he had been as a lad watching his Uncle Charlie in that exciting shed behind his butcher's shop. Come to think of it, Doc Ellis-Jones and Uncle Charlie shared the same expertise and went about their business in much the same way. This had surprised him when, as a newly appointed constable fresh out of regional training school, he had attended his first post-mortem. He had expected that it would be more scientific, less brutal, and far less messy than it had, in fact, proved to be. It had occurred to him then that the main differences between Doc Ellis-Jones and Uncle Charlie were that Uncle Charlie worried less about infection, used a smaller variety of somewhat cruder instruments and treated his meat with more respect. But that wasn't surprising when you considered what he charged for it.

He was glad to get out at last into the fresh air. It wasn't that the PM room stank. It would have been less objectionable to him if it had. Buckley strongly disliked the smell of disinfectant which overlay rather than masked the smell of putrefaction. The smell was elusive but persistent and tended to linger in his nose.

The mortuary was a modern building on upper ground to the west of the little town, and as they made their way to their Rover they could see the lights coming on like glow-worms along the curving streets and the dark form of Courcy Island lying supine as a half-submerged and sleeping animal, far out to sea. It was odd, thought Buckley, how the island seemed to draw closer or recede depending on the light and the time of day. In the mellow autumnal sunshine it had lain in a blue haze, looking so near that he could imagine it possible to swim to that multi-coloured and tranquil shore. Now it had drawn far into the Channel, remote and sinister, an island of mystery and horror. The castle was on its southern shore and no lights beckoned. He wondered what the small company of suspects was doing at this moment, how they would face the long night ahead. It was his guess that all but one of them would sleep behind locked doors.

Grogan came up to him. Nodding towards the island he said:

'So now we know what one of them knew already, how she died. Stripped of Doc Ellis-Jones's technical chat about the mechanics of force and the local absorption of kinetic energy in injuries to the head, not to mention the interesting and characteristic pattern in which the skull disintegrates under the weight of impact, what have we? Much as we expected. She died from a depressed fracture of the front of the skull made with our old friend, a blunt instrument. She was probably lying on her back at the time, much as Miss Gray found her. The bleeding was steady but almost entirely internal and the effect of the blow was intensified by the fact that the bones of the skull are thinner than normal. Unconsciousness supervened almost immediately and she died within five to fifteen minutes. The subsequent damage was done after death, how long after he can't unfortunately say. So we have a murderer who sits and waits while his victim dies and then . . . what? Decides to make sure? Decides that he didn't much like the lady and may as well make that fact plain? Decides to cover up how she died by giving her more of the same thing?

You aren't going to tell me that he waited ten minutes or so before deciding to panic?'

Buckley said:

'He could have spent the time searching for something and been enraged when he didn't find it. So he took out his frustration on the corpse.'

'But searching for what? We haven't found it either, unless it's still there in the room and we've missed its significance. And there's no sign of a search. If the room was searched it was done with care and by someone who knew what he was about. And if he was looking for something, my guess is that he found it.'

'There's still the lab report to come, sir. And they'll have the viscera within the hour.'

'I doubt whether they'll find anything. Doc Ellis-Jones saw no sign of poison. She may have been drugged – we mustn't theorize too far ahead of the facts – but my guess is that she was awake when she died and that she saw the face of her killer.'

It was extraordinary, thought Buckley, how cold the day became once the sun had gone. It was like moving from summer to winter in a couple of hours. He shivered and held open the car door for his Chief. They moved slowly out of the car park and turned towards the town. At first Grogan spoke only in laconic spurts:

'You've heard from the Coroner's Officer?'

'Yes, sir. The inquest's fixed for two o'clock on Tuesday.'

'And the London end? Burroughs is getting on with those inquiries?'

'He's going up first thing in the morning. And I've told the divers we'll be needing them for the rest of the week.'

'What about the bloody press conference?'

'Tomorrow afternoon, sir. Four thirty.'

Again there was silence. Changing gear to negotiate the steep and twisting hill which ran down to Speymouth, Grogan suddenly said:

'The name Commander Adam Dalgliesh mean anything to you, Sergeant?'

There was no need to ask of what force. Only the Met had Commanders. Buckley said:

'I've heard of him, sir.'

'Who hasn't? The Commissioner's blue-eyed boy, darling of the establishment. When the Met, or the Home Office come to that, want to show that the police know how to hold their forks and what bottle to order with the *canard à l'orange* and how to talk to a Minister on level terms with his Permanent Secretary, they wheel out Dalgliesh. If he didn't exist, the Force would have to invent him.'

The gibes might be unoriginal but there was nothing second-hand about the dislike. Buckley said:

'It's a bit old-fashioned isn't it, sir, all that stuff?'

'Don't be naïve, Sergeant. It's only unfashionable to talk like that any more, but that doesn't mean that they've changed their thinking or their actions. He could have had his own force by now – probably be chairing ACPO – if he hadn't wanted to stick to detection. That and personal conceit. The rest of you can struggle in the muck for the prizes. I'm the cat who walks alone and all places are alike to me. Kipling.'

'Yes, sir.'

Buckley paused and then asked:

'What about the Commander?'

'He knows the girl, Cordelia Gray. They tangled together in a previous case. Cambridge apparently. No details offered and none asked for. But he's given her and that Agency a clean bill. Like him or not, he's a good copper, one of the best. If he says that Gray isn't a murderess I'm prepared to take that as evidence of a sort. But he didn't say that she's incapable of lying and I wouldn't have believed him if he had.'

He drove on in a moody silence. But his mind must have been mulling over yesterday's interviews. After a space of ten minutes in which neither of them had spoken, he said:

'There's one thing which struck me as intriguing. You probably noticed it yourself. They all described the visit on Saturday morning to the Church and the crypt. They all mentioned that story about the drowned internee. But it was done a little too casually; the mere mention of an unimportant trifle; just a short excursion we happened to fancy before lunch. As soon as I invited them to dwell on the incident they reacted like a bunch of virgins who'd had an interesting experience in the Marabar caves. I suppose the allusion is wasted on you, Sergeant?'

'Yes, sir.'

'Don't worry. I'm not degenerating into one of those literary cops. I'll leave that to Dalgliesh. We did *A Passage to India* as a set book when I was at school. I used to think it overrated. But no knowledge is wasted in police work as they used to tell me at training school, not even E. M. Forster apparently. Something happened in the Devil's Kettle which none of them is prepared to talk about and I'd like to know what.'

'Miss Gray found one of the messages.'

'So she says. But I wasn't thinking of that. It's probably a long shot, but we'd better find out more about that 1940 drowning. I suppose Southern Command would be the starting point.'

Buckley's thoughts went back to that white, scientifically butchered body, to a nakedness which had been totally unerotic. And more than that. For a moment watching those gloved and probing fingers he had felt that no woman's body would ever excite him again. He said:

'There was no rape and no recent intercourse.'

'That hardly surprised us. Her husband hadn't the inclination and Ivo Whittingham hadn't the strength. And her murderer had other things on his mind. We'll call it a day, Sergeant. The Chief Constable wants a word with me first thing tomorrow. No doubt that means that Sir Charles Cottringham has been having a word or two with him. That man's a nuisance. I wish he'd stick to amateur theatricals and leave real-life drama to the experts. And then we'll get back to Courcy Island and see if a night's sleep has refreshed their memories.'

CHAPTER THIRTY-FIVE

At last the interminable hours dragged to dinner-time. Cordelia came in from a last and solitary walk with barely time to shower and change, and by the time she went down, Ambrose, Sir George and Ivo were already in the dining-room. They were all seated before Simon appeared. He was wearing a dark suit. He looked at the others, flushed and said, 'I'm sorry. I didn't realize that we were going to change. I won't be long.'

He turned to the door. Ambrose said with a touch of impatience, 'What does it matter? You can dine in your swimming-trunks if it makes you feel more comfortable. No one here cares what you wear.'

Cordelia thought that it wasn't the happiest way of putting it. The unspoken words hung on the air. Clarissa would have cared; but Clarissa wasn't there. Simon's eyes slewed to the empty chair at the top of the table. Then he sidled to a chair beside Cordelia.

Ivo said:

'Where's Roma?'

'She asked for soup and chicken sandwiches in her room. She says she has a headache.'

It seemed to Cordelia that everyone was simultaneously doubting the reality of the headache while mentally congratulating Roma on having hit on so simple an expedient for avoiding this their first formal dinner together since Clarissa's death. The table had been rearranged, perhaps in an attempt to minimize the trauma of that empty chair. The two end places hadn't been laid and Cordelia and Simon sat facing Ambrose, Ivo and Sir George, almost, it seemed, eyeball to eyeball, while an expanse of mahogany stretched gleaming on either side: Cordelia thought that the arrangement made them look like a couple of *viva-voce* candidates facing a not particularly intimidating panel of examiners, an impression which was strengthened by Simon's suit in which, paradoxically, he looked less cool and more formally overdressed than did the other three in their frills and dinner-jackets.

Neither Munter nor his wife were present. Bowls of vichyssoise were already set at each place and the second course was under covers on the sideboard hotplates. There was a faint smell of fish, an unlikely choice for a Sunday. It was obviously to be a convalescent's dinner, blandly inoffensive, unexciting to the palate or the digestion. It was, thought Cordelia, a nice point of culinary etiquette, the choice of menu for a house party of murder suspects dining together the day after the crime.

Ivo's thoughts must have been running with hers for he said:

'I wonder what Mrs Beeton would reject as the most

inappropriate meal for this kind of occasion. My choice would be bortsch followed by steak tartare. I can't decide on the pudding. Nothing too crude, but it needs to be richly indigestible.'

Cordelia said in a low voice:

'Don't you care at all?'

He paused before replying as if her question merited careful thought:

'I don't like to think that she suffered or was in terror even for a moment. But, if you mean do I care that she's no longer alive, then no, I don't really care.'

Ambrose had finished pouring the Graves. He said: 'We'll have to serve ourselves. I told Mrs Munter to take the evening off and get some rest and Munter hasn't shown himself since luncheon. If the police want to interview him again tomorrow they'll be unlucky. It happens about every four months, and invariably if I've had a house party. I'm not sure whether it's a reaction from the excitement, or just his way of discouraging me from too much entertaining. As he's usually considerate enough to wait until my guests have left I can't really complain. He has compensating qualities.'

Sir George said:

'Drunk is he? I thought he might take to the bottle.'

'I fear so. It usually lasts three days. I did wonder whether the violent death of one of my guests would break the pattern, but apparently not. I suppose it's his release from some intolerable internal boredom. The island isn't really congenial to him. He has an almost pathological dislike of water. He can't even swim.'

Ambrose, Ivo and Cordelia had moved to the sideboard. Ambrose lifted a silver lid to reveal thin fillets of sole in a creamy sauce. Ivo asked:

'Why then does he stay?'

'I've never asked him for fear that the same question might occur to him. Money, I suppose. And he likes solitude even if he would prefer it not to be guaranteed by two miles of sea. He has only me to please. An easy job on the whole.'

'And easier now that Clarissa's dead. I take it you won't be going ahead with the drama festival?'

'Not even, my dear Ivo, as a memorial to her.'

They then seemed to realize that the exchange, even though Sir George was seated too far away to overhear, was in poor taste. Both of them glanced at Cordelia. She felt a little angry with Ambrose. Helping herself to mange-tout peas she said on impulse:

'I was wondering whether he might have found a way to augment his wages, perhaps a little smuggling on the side. The Devil's Kettle would be a useful unloading point. I noticed that he keeps the trapdoor bolt well oiled and he'd hardly need to do that if you don't show the place to summer visitors. And on Friday night I saw a light flashing at sea. I thought that it might be acknowledging a signal.'

Ambrose laughed as he carried back his plate, but when he spoke the thin note of spite was unmistakable. 'Clever Cordelia! You're wasted as an amateur. Grogan would be glad to enrol you in the ranks of official snoopers. Munter may have his private arrangements but he doesn't confide in me and I certainly have no intention of inquiring. Courcy is traditionally a smuggler's haven and most sailors in these parts do a little amateur smuggling. It wouldn't amount to much, a few casks of brandy, an occasional bottle of scent. Nothing as spectacularly naughty as drugs if that's what you have in mind. Most people like a little tax-free income and a touch of risk adds to the fun. But I don't advise you to confide your suspicions to Grogan. Let him get on with the investigation he has in hand.'

Ivo said:

'What about the lights Cordelia saw?'

'Warning off his pals I expect. He'd hardly want the stuff landed with the island swarming with police.'

Ivo said evenly:

'Except that Cordelia saw the signal on Friday. How could he know that the police would be here next day?'

Ambrose shrugged, unworried.

'Then it couldn't have been the police he feared. Perhaps he knew or guessed that we were being favoured with the company of a private eye. Don't ask me how he knew. Clarissa didn't confide in me and I shouldn't have told Munter even if she had. But it's my experience that little goes on under any roof that a good servant doesn't learn first.'

They rejoined Sir George. He had already helped himself to sole and was eating with a stolid determination but with no evident enjoyment. Cordelia pondered on Munter. She thought it unlikely that he had guessed her secret or that he would have altered his plans if he had. It was more possible that with the castle full of guests he had felt the time unpropitious for the reception of his loot; too many people about, too much extra work, the possibility that he would find it difficult to slip away unnoticed. Perhaps he hadn't been able to get a message to his confederates or the message had gone astray. Or had there been an unexpected arrival on the island, someone he feared particularly, or someone who might have known of the Devil's Kettle, might even have visited it? There was only one person who fitted that bill: Sir George.

The meal seemed endless. Cordelia sensed that they all wished it over but that no one wanted to appear to hurry or to be the first to leave. Perhaps that was why they appeared to be eating with deliberate slowness. She wondered whether it was the absence of staff that made the occasion so portentous; they might be the remnants of some deserted and soon to be beleaguered garrison stoically eating their last meal with traditional ceremony, ears tuned for the first distant shouts of the barbarians. They ate and drank but were silent. The six candles in their branched entwined stems seemed to burn less brightly than on their first evening so that their features, half shadowed, were sharpened into caricatures of their daytime selves. Pale, etiolated hands reached out to the fruit bowl, to furred and flushed peaches, the curved shininess of bananas, apples burnished so that they looked as artificial as Ambrose's candle-lit skin.

The french windows had been shut against the chill of the autumn night and a thin wood fire crackled in the immense grate. But surely those fitfully leaping flames couldn't account for the oppressive heat of the room? It seemed to Cordelia that it was getting hotter by the minute, that the heat of the day had been trapped and thickened, making it difficult to breathe, intensifying the smell of the food so that she felt faintly nauseous. And in her imagination the room itself changed; the Orpens splurged and spread into amorphous colours so that the walls appeared to be hung with crude tapestries and the elegantly stuccoed roof raised smoked hammer beams to a black infinity, open to an everlastingly starless sky. She shivered despite the heat and reached for her wine glass as if the physical feel of cool glass could strengthen her hold on reality. Perhaps only now were the full horror of Clarissa's death, the strain of the police interrogation taking their physical toll.

One candle wavered as if blown by an invisible breath, flickered, and went out. Simon gave a gasp, then a long terrified moan. Hands, half-lifted to mouths, became motionless. They turned in a single movement and stared at the window. Silhouetted against the moonlight reared an immense form, its black arms flailing, hurling itself against the window. Its anger came to them faintly, something between a wail and a bellow. As they gazed in fascinated horror it suddenly ceased its frantic beating and was for a moment still, quietly looking in at their faces. The gaping mouth, raw as a wound, seemed to suck at the window. Two gigantic palms, fingers splayed, imprinted themselves on the glass. The pressed, distorted features dissolved against the window into a mess of slowly draining flesh. Then the creature gathered its strength and heaved. The doors gave, and Munter, wild-eyed, almost fell into the room. The night air rushed cool and sweet over their faces and the distant sighing of the waves became a surging tide of sound as if the swaying figure had been borne in on them by the force of a violent storm, bringing the sea with him.

No one spoke. Ambrose got to his feet and moved forward. Munter brushed him aside and shambled up to Sir George until their faces almost touched. Sir George stayed in his seat. Not a muscle moved. Then Munter spoke, throwing back his head and almost howling the words:

'Murderer! Murderer! Murderer!'

Cordelia wondered when Sir George would move, whether he would wait until Munter's fingers were actually at his throat. But Ambrose had moved behind and had seized the shuddering arms. At first the contact seemed to calm Munter. Then he gave a violent wrench. Ambrose said breathlessly:

'Could one of you help?'

Ivo had begun peeling a peach. He seemed totally unconcerned. He said:

'I'd be no use in this particular emergency, I'm afraid.'

Simon got up and grasped the man's other arm. At his touch Munter's belligerency left him. His knees buckled and Ambrose and Simon moved closer, supporting his sagging weight between them. He tried to focus his eyes on the boy, then slurred out a few words, guttural, unintelligible, sounding hardly English. But his final words were clear enough.

'Poor sod. God, but she was a bitch that one.'

No one else spoke. Together Ambrose and Simon urged him to the door. He gave no further trouble but went as obediently as a disciplined child.

After they had left, the two men and Cordelia sat in silence for a minute. Then Sir George got up and closed the french windows. The noise of the sea became muted and the wildly flickering candles steadied and burned with a clear flame. Returning to the table he selected an apple and said:

'Extraordinary fellow! I was at Sandhurst with a chap who drank like that. Sober for months at a time, then paralytic for a week. Torpedoed in the Med in the winter of '42. Foul weather. Picked up from a raft three days later. Only one of the party to survive. He said that it was because he was pickled in whisky. D'you suppose Gorringe lets Munter have the key to his cellar?'

'I shouldn't think so.' Ivo sounded amused.

Sir George said, 'Extraordinary arrangement, a butler who can't be trusted with the keys. Still, I suppose he has other uses. Devoted to Gorringe obviously.'

Ivo asked:

'What happened to him; your friend I mean?'

'Fell in his own swimming pool and drowned. The shallow end. Drunk at the time, of course.'

It seemed a long time before Ambrose and Simon reappeared. Cordelia was struck with the boy's pallor. Surely coping with a drunken man couldn't have been so horrifying an experience. Ambrose said:

'We've put him to bed. Let's hope he stays there. I must apologize for the performance. I've never known Munter to behave before in such a spectacular way. Will someone please pass the fruit bowl?'

After dinner they gathered in the drawing-room. Mrs Munter had not appeared and they poured their own coffee from the glass percolator on the sideboard. Ambrose opened the french windows and one by one, as if drawn by the sea, they walked out on the terrace. The moon was full, silvering a wide swathe to the horizon and a few high stars pin-pricked the blue-black of the night sky. The tide was running strongly. They could hear it slapping against the stones of the quay and the distant whisper of the spent waves hissing on the shingle beach. The only other sound was the muted footfalls of their walking feet. Here in this peace, thought Cordelia, it would be easy to believe that nothing mattered, not death, nor life, nor human violence, nor any pain. The mental picture of that splodge of battered flesh and congealed blood which had been Clarissa's face, scored as she thought forever on her mind, became unreal, something she had imagined in a different dimension of time. The disorientation was so strong that she had to fight against it, to tell herself why she was here and what it was she had to do. She came out of her trance to hear Ambrose's voice.

He was speaking to Simon. 'You may as well play if you want to. I don't suppose a half hour of music would offend anyone's susceptibilities. There must be something appropriate between a music-hall medley and the "Dead March" from *Saul*.'

Without replying, Simon went over to the piano. Cordelia followed him into the drawing-room and watched while he sat, head bowed, silently contemplating the keys. Then, suddenly hunching his shoulders, he brought down his hands and began playing with quiet intensity and she recognized the slow movement of Beethoven's Emperor Concerto. Ambrose called from the terrace:

'Trite but appropriate.'

He played well. The notes sang into the silent air. Cordelia thought it interesting that he should play so much better with Clarissa dead than he had when she was alive.

When he had finished the movement she asked:

'What's going to happen, about your music I mean?'

'Sir George has told me not to worry, that I can stay on at Melhurst for a final year and then go to the Royal College or the Academy if I can get in.'

'When did he tell you this?'

'When he came to my room after Clarissa was found.'

That was a remarkably quick decision, thought Cordelia, given the circumstances. She would have expected Sir George to have had other things on his mind just then than Simon's career. The boy must have guessed her thoughts.

He looked up and said quickly:

'I asked him what would happen to me now and he said that I wasn't to worry, that nothing would change, that I could go back to school and then on to the Royal College. I was frightened and shocked and I think he was trying to reassure me.'

But not so shocked that he hadn't thought first of himself. She told herself that the criticism was unworthy and tried to put it out of her mind. It had, after all, been a natural childish reaction to tragedy. What will happen to me? How will this affect my life? Wasn't that what everyone wanted to know? He had at least been honest in asking it aloud. She said:

'I'm glad, if that's what you want.'

'I want it. I don't think she did. I'm not sure I ought to do something she wouldn't have approved of.'

'You can't live your life on that basis. You have to make your own decisions. She couldn't make them for you even when she was alive. It's silly to expect her to make them now that she's dead.'

'But it's her money.'

'I suppose it will be Sir George's money now. If it doesn't worry him I don't see why it need worry you.'

Watching the avid eyes desperately gazing into hers Cordelia felt that she was failing him, that he was looking to her for sympathy, for some reassurance that he could take what he wanted from life and take it without guilt. But wasn't that what everyone craved? Part of her wanted to respond to his need; but part of her was tempted to say: You've taken so much. Why jib at taking this? She said:

'I suppose if you want to salve your conscience about the

money more than you want to be a professional pianist, then you'd better give up now.'

His voice was suddenly humble.

'I'm not all that good, you know. She knew that. She wasn't a musician, but she knew. Clarissa could smell failure.'

'Oh well, that's a different issue, whether you're good enough or not. I think you play very well, but I can't really judge. I don't suppose that Clarissa could either. But the people at the colleges of music can. If they think you're worth accepting, then they must think you have at least a chance of making a career in music. After all, they know what the competition's like.'

He looked quickly round the room and then said, his voice low:

'Do you mind if I talk to you? There are three things I must ask you.'

'We are talking.'

'But not here. Somewhere private.'

'This is private. The others don't seem likely to come in. Is it going to take long?'

'I want you to tell me what happened to her, how she looked when you found her. I didn't see her, and I keep lying awake and imagining. If I knew it wouldn't be so awful. Nothing is as awful as the things I imagine.'

'Didn't the police tell you? Or Sir George?'

'No one told me. I did ask Ambrose but he wouldn't say.'

And the police would, of course, have had their own reasons for keeping silent about the details of the murder. But they had interviewed him by now. She didn't see that it mattered any more whether he knew or not. And she could understand the horror of those nightly imaginings. But there was no way in which she could make the brutal truth sound gentle. She said:

'Her face was battered in.'

He was silent. He didn't ask how or with what. She said:

'She was lying quite peacefully on the bed, almost as if she were asleep. I'm sure she didn't suffer. If it were done by someone she knew, someone she trusted, she probably didn't even have time to feel afraid.'

'Could you recognize her face at all?'

'No.'

'The police asked me if I'd taken anything from a display cabinet, a marble hand. Does that mean they think it was the weapon?'

'Yes.'

It was too late now to wish that she'd kept quiet. She said:

'It was found by the bed. It was . . . it looked as if it had been used.'

He whispered, 'Thank you,' but so quietly that she had difficulty in hearing him. After a moment she said:

'You said there were three things.'

He looked up eagerly as if glad that his mood had been broken. 'Yes, it's Tolly. On Friday when I went swimming while the rest of you toured the castle she waited for me on the shore. She wanted to persuade me to leave Clarissa and live with her. She said that I could go straight away and that she had a room in her flat I could have until I'd found myself a job. She said that Clarissa might die.'

'Did she say how or why?'

'No. Only that Clarissa thought she was going to die and that people who thought that often did die.' He looked straight at her. 'And next day, Clarissa did die. And I don't know whether I ought to tell the police what happened, about waiting for me, what she said.'

'If Tolly were actually planning to murder Clarissa she'd hardly warn you in advance. She was probably trying to tell you that you couldn't rely on Clarissa, that she might change her mind about you, that she might not always be there.'

'I think she did know. I think she guessed. Ought I to tell the Chief Inspector? I mean, it is evidence isn't it? Suppose he found out that I'd been keeping something back?'

'Have you told anyone?'

'No. Only you.'

'You must do what you think is right.'

'But I don't know what's right! What would you do if you were in my place?'

'I wouldn't tell. But then I have a reason. If you feel that it's right to tell, then tell. If it's any comfort to you, I don't think the police will arrest Tolly on that evidence alone and they haven't any other, at least as far as I know.'

'But she'd know that I must have told them! What would she think of me? I don't think I could face her after that.'

'You might not have to. I don't suppose she'll stay on now that Clarissa's dead.'

'So you would tell if you were me?'

Cordelia's patience snapped. It had been a long day ending in the trauma of Munter's dramatic appearance and she was weary in spirit as well as body. And it was difficult to sympathize with Simon's obsessive self-concern.

'I've told you. I wouldn't tell. But I'm not you. It's your responsibility and you can't force it on anyone else. Surely there's something you're capable of deciding for yourself.'

She regretted the unkindness almost as soon as the words were out of her mouth. She turned her eyes from his scarlet face and stricken, dog-like eyes and said:

'I'm sorry. I shouldn't have said that. I suppose we're all on edge. Wasn't there a third thing you wanted to ask?'

He whispered, his mouth trembling:

'No. There's nothing else. Thank you.'

He got up and closed the piano. He added quietly and with some attempt at dignity:

'If anyone asks about me, I've gone to bed.'

Unexpectedly, Cordelia found that she, too, was close to tears. Torn between irritation and pity and despising her own weakness she decided to follow Simon's example. The day had gone on long enough. She went out on the terrace to say goodnight. The three black-clad figures were standing apart, silhouetted against the iridescence of the sea, motionless as bronze statues. At her approach they simultaneously turned and she could feel the concentrated gaze of three pairs of eyes. No one moved or spoke. The moment of moonlit silence seemed to her protracted, almost ominous, and as she said her goodnights the thought that for the past twenty-four hours she had tried to suppress surfaced in all its stark and frightening logic. 'We are here together, ten of us on this small and lonely island. And one of us is a murderer.'

CHAPTER THIRTY-SIX

Cordelia fell asleep almost as soon as she had closed her book and put out the bedside light. But her awakening was as sudden. She lay for a moment confused and then put out her hand and found the switch. Her wrist-watch, curled on the bedside table, showed her that it was just after three thirty, far too early, surely, for her to have woken naturally. She thought that her sleep had been pierced by some sound, perhaps the shriek of a night bird. The moonlight streamed through the half-drawn curtains cutting a swathe of light over the ceiling and walls. The silence was absolute except for the pulse of the plangent sea, louder now than in the stir of the daylight hours. Her mind, still drugged with sleep, took hold of the tag end of a dream. She had been back in Kingly Street and Miss Maudsley had been showing her with pride a newly rescued kitten. As is the way of dreams, she found it unsurprising that the kitten should be sleeping in a carved cradle with a red canopy and side curtains, a miniature of Clarissa's bed, or that, when she peered into the cot and pulled aside the shawl she should see, not a kitten but a baby and should know that this was Miss Maudsley's illegitimate child and that she must be very tactful and not betray that she knew. She smiled at the memory, put out the light and tried to relax into sleep.

But this time it was elusive. Once woken, she was restless. Her mind busied itself again with the mystery and horror of Clarissa's death. Image succeeded image, unsought but insistent, disconnected in time but horribly clear; Clarissa's satin-clad body gleaming pale under the crimson canopy; Clarissa gazing down into the swirl of water at the Devil's Kettle; Clarissa's slim figure passing to and fro on the terrace, pale as a ghost; Clarissa standing on the pier and stretching her arms bat-winged in welcome; Clarissa removing her make-up, turning on Cordelia one naked and diminished eye in a freakish, strange discordant gaze which seemed now to hold a look of sad reproach.

Her mind held that last picture as if unwilling to let it fade. Something about it was significant, something that she ought to have known or remembered. And then the realization came. She saw again the dressing-table, the balls of cotton wool smeared with make-up, the smaller pads shifting across the mahogany, blackened with mascara. Clarissa had used a special lotion to cleanse her eyes. But those pads hadn't been on the dressing-table when her body was discovered. Perhaps she hadn't troubled to remove her eye make-up. Was that something which the forensic pathologist would be able to detect even beneath that shattered and swollen flesh? But why should she take off her powder and foundation and leave her eyes under a weight of shadow and mascara, particularly as she proposed to rest them under the moistened pads. But wasn't there another possibility, that she had kept on all her make-up because she was expecting a visitor and that it had been the visitor who had wiped her face clean before smashing it to pulp? And that implied a man. A man was surely the most likely secret visitor. Clarissa was too obsessed with her appearance to meet even a woman with a naked face. But wouldn't a woman be more likely to realize that she must use the special pads to remove the eye make-up? Tolly would have known it certainly. But Roma? Roma's eyes were devoid of mascara and in the urgency and terror of the moment she would be unlikely to make a close inventory of the bottles on the dressing-table. A man was still the most likely to make such a mistake, except perhaps Ivo with his knowledge of theatrical make-up. But the strangest part of it all was surely Tolly's silence. The police must have questioned her about the make-up, must have asked her if everything on the dressing-table looked normal. And that meant that Tolly had held her tongue. Why and for whom?

It was impossible now to will herself to sleep. But she must have dozed at last if only fitfully for it was nearly four when she next awoke. She was too hot. The bedclothes lay heavily on her like a weight of failure and she knew that there would be no more sleep that night. The sea was louder than ever, the air itself seeming to throb. She had a vision of the tide rising inexorably over the terrace, sweeping into the dining-room, floating the heavy table and the carved chairs, rising to cover the Orpens and the stuccoed ceiling, creeping up the stairs until the whole island was covered except for the slender tower rising like a lighthouse above the waves. She lay rigidly, longing for the first flush of day.

It would be Monday, a working day in Speymouth. She would be able to get away from the island, if only for a few hours, visiting the local newspaper office, trying to trace the cutting about Clarissa's Jubilee performance. She had to do something positive however unlikely it was to prove successful and significant. It would be good to feel free, free of Ambrose's ironic, half-secret smile, Simon's misery, Ivo's gaunt fortitude; free most of all from the eyes of the police. She had no doubt that they would be back. But, short of arresting her, there was nothing they could do to prevent her spending a day on shore.

Now it seemed that the morning would never come. She gave up the attempt at sleeping and got out of bed. Pulling on her jeans and Guernsey she went to the window and drew back the curtains. Below her lay the rose garden, the last overblown heads drooping on their spiky branches, bleached pale by the moon. The water in the pond looked as solid as beaten silver and she could see clearly the smudge of lily leaves, the gleam of their blossoms. But there was something else on the surface, something black and hairy, an immense spider crawling half submerged, spreading and waving its innumerable hairy legs under the shimmering water. She gazed in fascinated disbelief. And then she knew what it was and her blood ran cold.

She wasn't aware of her flight down to the door which led from the passage to the garden. She must have banged on bedroom doors as she ran, indiscriminately, aware only that she might need help, not waiting for a response. But others must have been sleeping lightly. By the time she had reached the door into the garden and was straining upwards to shoot back the top bolt, she was aware of muffled footsteps padding down the passageway, a confused murmur of voices. And then she was standing at the edge of the pool with Simon, Sir George and Roma beside her and viewed clearly for the first time what it was she knew that she had seen: Munter's wig.

It was Simon who threw off his dressing-gown and waded into the pool. The water came up to his thrashing arms. He gulped then dived. The rest of them watched and waited. The water had scarcely steadied after the flurry of his disappearance when his head shot up, sleek as a seal's. He called:

'He's here. He's caught on some wire-netting where the lilies are rooted. Don't come in. I think I can free him.' He disappeared again. Almost at once they saw two black shapes surfacing. Munter's bald head, face upwards, looked as swollen as if it had been in the water for weeks. Simon pushed the body towards the side of the pool and Cordelia and Roma bent and tugged at the sodden sleeves. Cordelia knew that it would be easier to take his hands but the bloated fingers, yellow as udders, repelled her. She bent over his face and shifted her grasp to his shoulders. The eyes were open and glazed, the skin as smooth as latex. It was like pulling a dummy from the water, some discarded manikin with a stuffed sawdust body, waterlogged and inert in its ridiculous formal coat. The clown's mask with its sagging jaw seemed to be gazing into hers with a look of piteous inquiry. She could imagine that she smelt his breath, stinking with drink. She was suddenly ashamed of the repugnance which had rejected the sad remnant of his humanity, and in a spasm of pity she grasped his left hand. It felt like a taut bladder, fleshless, and cold. And it was in that moment of touch that she knew he was dead.

They tugged him on to the grass. Simon pulled himself out of the water. He folded his dressing-gown under Munter's head, forced back his neck and felt in the gaping mouth for dentures. There were none. Then he fastened his mouth over the thick lips and began the kiss of life. They watched silently. No one spoke even when Ambrose and Ivo came up quietly and stood among them. There was no sound but the squelch of sodden clothes as Simon bent to his task and the regular gasp of his intaken breath. Cordelia glanced at Sir George, wondering a little at his silence. He was gazing down at the bloated inverted face, at the half-shut and unseeing eyes with a look of great intensity, almost of incredulous recognition. And in that moment, Cordelia's heart jolted. Her eyes met his and she thought they flashed a warning. Neither spoke but she wondered whether he had shared her revelation. There came into her mind an old incongruous picture; the music room at the Convent, Sister Hildegarde stretching wide her mouth and eyes in an anticipatory mime, raising the white baton. 'And now my children, the Schumann. Happy, happy! Mouths wide. *Ein munteres Lied.*'

She dragged her mind back to the present. There was no time

to think about her discovery or to explore its implications. She forced herself to look again at the sodden lump of flesh on which Simon was so desperately working. He was close to exhaustion when Ambrose bent and felt for the pulse at Munter's wrist. He said:

'It's no good. He's dead. And he's icy cold. He's probably been in the water for hours.'

Simon didn't reply. He went on mechanically pumping breath into the inert body as if performing some indecent and esoteric rite. Roma said:

'Ought we to give up? I thought you were supposed to go on for hours.'

'Not when the pulse has gone and the body's cold.'

But Simon took no notice. The rhythm of his harsh, indrawn breath and the antics of his crouched body seemed to have become more frantic. It was then that they heard Mrs Munter's voice, low but harsh:

'Leave him be. He's dead. Can't you see that he's dead?'

Simon heard her. He stood up and began to shiver violently. Cordelia took his dressing-gown from under Munter's head and wrapped it round his shoulders. Ambrose turned to Mrs Munter.

'I'm so very sorry. When did it happen, do you know?'

'How can I tell?' She paused, then added, 'sir'. 'I don't sleep with him when he's drunk.'

'But you must have heard him go out. He can't have walked steadily or quietly.'

'He left his room just before three thirty.'

Ambrose said:

'I wish you had let me know.'

Cordelia thought: He sounds as peevish as if she's proposing to take a week's holiday without consulting him.

'I thought you paid us to protect you from trouble and inconvenience. He'd made enough for one night.'

There seemed to be nothing to say. Then Sir George came forward and beckoned to Simon.

'Better get him indoors.'

There was a new note in Mrs Munter's voice. She said quickly:

'Don't bring him into the servants' flat, sir.'

Ambrose said soothingly:

'Of course not, if that's how you feel.'

'That's how I feel.'

She turned and walked away. The rest of the party looked after her.

Then Cordelia ran and caught her up.

'Please let me come with you. I don't think you should be alone.'

She was surprised that the eyes lifted to hers could hold so much dislike.

'I want to be alone. There's nothing the likes of you can do. Don't worry, I'm not going to kill myself.'

She nodded towards Ambrose. 'You can tell him that.'

Cordelia returned to the group. She said:

'She doesn't want anyone with her. She says to tell you that she'll be all right.'

No one answered. They were still standing in a circle looking down on the body. Dressing-gowned as they were, their feet muffled by slippers, they loomed over the corpse like a group of oddly clad mourners: Sir George in shabby checked wool, Ivo's dark-green silk through which his shoulders stuck like wire hangers, Ambrose's sombre blue, faced with satin, Roma's padded and flowered nylon, Simon's brown bathrobe. Watching the circle of bent heads Cordelia half expected them to rise in concert and wail a threnody in the thin air. Then Sir George roused himself and turned to Simon:

'Shall we get on with it?'

Ivo had wandered a little way along the edge of the pool and was contemplating the remnants of the water lilies as if they were some rare marine vegetation in which he had a scientific interest. He looked up and said:

'But ought you to move him? Isn't it usual not to disturb the body until the police arrive?'

Roma cried:

'But that's only in a case of murder! This is an accident. He was drunk, he staggered and he fell in. Ambrose told us that Munter couldn't swim.'

'Did I? I can't remember. But it's perfectly true. He couldn't swim.'

Ivo said:

'You told us so at dinner. But Roma wasn't there.'

Roma cried:

'Someone told me, Mrs Munter perhaps. What does it matter? He was drunk, he fell in and he drowned. It's perfectly obvious what happened.'

Ivo resumed his contemplation of the water lilies. 'I don't think anything is ever perfectly obvious to the police. But I dare say you're right. There's enough mystery without making more. Are there any marks of violence on the body?'

Cordelia said:

'Not that I can see.'

Roma said obstinately:

'We can't leave him here. I think we should take him indoors.'

She looked at Cordelia as if inviting her support. Cordelia said:

'I don't think it matters if we move him. It isn't as if we found him like this.'

They all looked at Ambrose as if waiting for instructions.

He said:

'Before we move him, please come with me all of you. There's something we have to decide.'

CHAPTER THIRTY-SEVEN

They followed him towards the castle. Only Simon glanced behind him at the ungainly lump of cold flesh, still spread-eagled, which had been Munter. His glance conveyed an embarrassed regret, almost a look of apology that they should have to desert him, leave him so uncomfortably circumstanced.

Ambrose led them into the business room and switched on the desk lamp. The atmosphere was at once conspiratorial; they were like a gang of dressing-gowned schoolchildren planning a midnight prank. He said:

'We have a decision to make. Do we tell Grogan what happened at dinner? I think we ought to agree this before I telephone the police.'

Ivo said:

'If you mean, do we tell the police that Munter accused Ralston of murder, why not say so plainly?'

Simon's hair, plastered over his brow and dripping water into his eyes, looked unnaturally black. He was shivering under the dressing-gown. He looked from face to face, astounded.

'But he didn't accuse Sir George of . . . well, of any particular murder. And he was drunk! He didn't know what he was saying. You all saw him. He was drunk!' His voice was getting dangerously close to hysteria.

Ambrose spoke with a trace of impatience.

'No one here thinks it of any importance. But the police may. And anything that Munter did or said during the last hours of his life will obviously interest them. There's a lot to be said for saying nothing, for not complicating the investigation. But we have to give roughly the same account. If some tell and the others don't, those who opt for reticence will obviously be placed in an invidious position.'

Simon said:

'Do you mean that we pretend that he didn't come in through the dining-room windows, that we didn't see him?'

'Of course not. He was drunk and we all saw him in that state. We tell the police the truth. The only question is, how much of the truth?'

Cordelia said quietly:

'It isn't only Munter's shouted accusation at Sir George. After you and Simon had taken Munter out Sir George told us about an army friend of his who had drunk in just that compulsive way . . .'

Ivo finished the sentence for her:

'And had been drowned in just that way. The police will find that an interesting coincidence. So unless Sir George told you both the same story on a different occasion – which I take it he didn't – Cordelia and I are already in what you might call an invidious position.'

Ambrose took in this information in silence. It seemed to give him some satisfaction. Then he pronounced:

'In that case the choice would seem to be; do we all give a truthful account of the evening's proceedings or do we omit Munter's shout of "murder" and the story about Ralston's unfortunate friend?'

Cordelia said:

'I think we should tell the truth. Lying to the police isn't as easy as it sounds.'

Roma said:

'You speak from experience perhaps.'

Cordelia ignored the note of malice and went on:

'They'll question us closely. What did Munter say when he burst in? What did the rest of us talk about when Ambrose and Simon were helping him to bed? It isn't only a question of omitting embarrassing facts. We have to agree on the same lies. That's apart from any moral considerations.'

Ambrose said easily:

'I don't think we need complicate the decision with moral considerations. Doing evil that good may come is a perfectly valid option whatever the theologians tell you. Besides, I imagine that we all did a little judicious editing in our interviews with Grogan. I did. He seemed to feel that my staging the play for Clarissa required explaining so I told him that she gave me the idea for *Autopsy*. An ingenious but quite unnecessary lie. So our first decision is easy. We tell the truth, or we agree on a story. I suggest we take a secret ballot.'

Ivo said quietly:

'Here, or do we all repair to the crypt?'

Ambrose ignored him. He turned first to where Simon stood, his chattering mouth half open, his washed face pale under the feverish eyes, and thought better of it. He said to Cordelia with formal courtesy:

'Would you be good enough to bring me two cups from the kitchen? I think you know the way.'

The short journey, the incongruous errand, seemed to her of immense significance. She walked down the empty passages and into the kitchen and took down two breakfast cups from the dresser with grave deliberateness as if an unseen audience were watching the grace of every movement. When she got back to the business room it seemed to her that no one had moved.

Ambrose thanked her gravely and placed the cups side by side on the desk. Then he went out to the display cabinet and returned carrying the round board with its coloured marbles, Princess

Victoria's solitaire board. He said: 'We each take a marble. Then we close our eyes – no peeping I implore you – and drop them into one of the cups. We'll make it easy to remember. The left cup for the more sinister option, the right for righteousness. You'll see that I've even aligned the handles appropriately so there's no excuse for confusion. When we've heard the five marbles drop we open our eyes. It's convenient that Roma wasn't at dinner. There's no possibility of a tie.'

Sir George spoke for the first time. He said:

'You're wasting time, Gorringe. You'd better ring for the police now. Obviously we tell Grogan the truth.'

Ambrose took his marble, selecting it with some care and examining its veining as if he were a connoisseur of such trifles.

'If that's what you want, that's what you vote for.'

Ivo said:

'Do you then intend to take a second ballot to decide whether we tell the police about the first ballot?'

But he took a marble. Sir George, Simon and Cordelia followed. She closed her eyes. There was a second's silence and then she heard the first marble tinkle into the cup. The second followed almost immediately, then a third. She stretched out her hands. They were briefly brushed by ice-cold fingers. She felt for the cups and placed a hand on each so that there could be no mistake. Then she dropped the marble into the right-hand cup. A second later she heard the last marble fall. The sound was unexpectedly loud; it must have been dropped from a height. She opened her eyes. Her companions were all blinking as if the period of darkness had lasted for hours, not seconds. Together they looked into the cups. The right-hand one held three marbles.

Ambrose said:

'Well, that simplifies matters. We tell the truth, apart of course, from mentioning this little divertissement. We came together into the business room and you all sat here together appropriately subdued while I rang the police. We've only spent a few minutes so there will be no embarrassing hiatus of time to account for.'

He replaced the marbles, after carefully scrutinizing each one, handed the two cups to Cordelia, and took up the telephone receiver. As she was returning the cups to the kitchen two thoughts chiefly occupied her. Why had Sir George waited until the ballot was inevitable before announcing that he favoured the truth, and which of the other two of them had dropped their marbles into the left-hand cup? She did briefly wonder whether anyone could have transferred someone else's marble in addition to dropping his own, but decided that this would have required some sleight of hand even if done with open eyes. Her own ears were exceptionally sharp and they had detected only the four clear tinkles as the other marbles fell.

Ambrose was apparently practising a policy of togetherness. He waited until she returned before ringing the Speymouth police station. He said:

'It's Ambrose Gorringe speaking from Courcy Island. Will you tell Chief Inspector Grogan that my butler Munter is dead. He was found in the pool here, apparently drowned.'

Cordelia thought that the statement was notable for being brief, accurate and carefully non-committal. Ambrose for one was keeping an open mind on the cause of Munter's death. The rest of the conversation was monosyllabic. Ambrose eventually replaced the receiver. He said:

'That was the duty sergeant. He'll let Grogan know. He says not to move the body. The less interference the better until the police arrive.'

There was a silence in which it seemed to Cordelia that they all simultaneously recognized that they were cold, that it wasn't yet half-past six and that while it might appear unfeeling to express a wish to return to bed and hopeless to expect sleep once there, it was unreasonably early to get dressed and face the day.

Ambrose said:

'Would anyone care for tea or coffee? I don't know what's likely to happen about breakfast. You may get none unless I cook it, but I assure you I'm perfectly competent. Is anyone hungry?'

No one admitted to being hungry. Roma shivered and hunched herself deeper into her padded nylon dressing-gown. She said:

'Tea would be welcome, the stronger the better. And then I, for one, am going back to bed.'

There was a general murmur of acquiescence. Then Simon spoke.

'There's something I forgot. There's some kind of box down there. I felt it when I released the body. Ought I to bring it up?'

'The jewel casket!' Roma turned re-animated, the desire for bed apparently forgotten.

'So he had it after all!'

Simon said eagerly:

'I don't think it's the casket. It felt larger, more smooth. He must have dropped it as he fell.'

Ambrose hesitated:

'I suppose we ought to wait until the police arrive. On the other hand, I have a curiosity to see what it is, if Simon has no objection to a second immersion.'

So far from objecting, the boy, shivering as he was with cold, seemed impatient to get back to the pool. Cordelia wondered if he had temporarily forgotten that sprawled body. She had never seen him so animated, almost frantic. Perhaps it was the result of being, for once, the centre of the action.

Ivo said:

'I think I can contain my curiosity. I'm going back to bed. If anyone is making tea later I'd be grateful if you'd bring up a cup.'

He left on his own. Roma was apparently cured both of her headache and tiredness. They returned to the pool. The fading moon was tissue thin and the sky was streaked with the first light of day. The air rose in a thin mist from the water and struck them with a damp autumnal chill. Bereft of the moonlight's bleak enchantment and the sense of unreality which moonlight bestows, the body looked at once more human and more grotesque. The flesh of the left cheek, resting against the stones, was pressed upwards to distort the eye so that it seemed to be leering at them, ironic and knowing. From the drooling mouth a trickle of blood-stained saliva had hung and dried on the stubble of the chin. The sodden clothes looked as if they had already shrunk and a thin stream of water still ran from the trouser legs and dripped slowly into the pool. In the uncertain light of the first dawn it seemed to Cordelia that his life blood was seeping away, unregarded and unstaunched. She said:

'Can't we at least cover him up?'

'Of course.' Ambrose was at once solicitous.

'Could you fetch something from the house, Cordelia? A tablecloth, a sheet, a towel, or even a coat would do. I'm sure you'll find something suitable.'

Roma turned on him, her voice harsh.

'Why send Cordelia? Why should she be expected to run all the errands round here? She's not paid to take your orders. Cordelia isn't your servant. Munter was.'

Ambrose looked at her as if she were an unintelligent child who had for once succeeded in making a sensible remark.

He said calmly:

'You're perfectly right. I'll go myself.'

But Roma, in angry spate, was beyond appeasement.

'Munter was your servant and you can't even bring yourself to say you're sorry he's dead. You don't care do you? You didn't care about Clarissa and you don't care about him. Nothing touches you as long as you're comfortable and saved from boredom. You haven't said a word of regret since we found his body. And who are you, for God's sake? Your grandfather made his money out of liver pills and gripewater. You haven't even the excuse of caste for not behaving like a human being.'

For a second Ambrose's body froze and two moons of red appeared on the smooth cheeks, then as quickly faded leaving him very pale. But his voice hardly altered. 'The only human being I know how to behave like is myself. I shall grieve for Munter in my own time and place. This hardly seems an appropriate moment for a valediction. But if its absence offends you I can always emulate Prince Hal.

What! old acquaintance! could not all this flesh
Keep in a little life? Poor Jack, farewell,
I could have better spared a better man.

And if it's any comfort to you, I would rather see all of you, with one possible exception, dead at the bottom of my pool than lose Carl Munter. But you're right about Cordelia. One is too ready to take advantage of competence and kindness.'

After he had left there was an embarrassed silence. Roma, her face blotched, her chin creased with stubborn anger, stood a little apart. She had the truculent, slightly defensive air of a child who knows that she has said something indefensible but who is not altogether ungratified by the result.

Suddenly she swung round and said gruffly:

'Well, at least I managed to provoke a human reaction from our host. So now we know where we stand. I take it that Cordelia is the privileged one among us whom Ambrose would be reluctant to see dead at the bottom of his pool. Even he isn't entirely immune to a pretty face, apparently.'

Sir George stared down at the water lilies. 'He's upset. Natural, after all. Hardly the time to quarrel among ourselves.'

Cordelia felt that she ought to make some comment, but unable to think of anything appropriate, remained silent. She was puzzled by Roma's outburst which she hardly felt was the result of concern or affection for herself. It could, she supposed, have been a gesture of feminine solidarity or a blast against male arrogance. But she suspected that it was more likely a spontaneous release of pent-up terror and shock. Whatever the cause, the result had been interesting. And Ambrose had been remarkably apt with his quotation from *King Henry IV Part I.* Was that because he was a natural lover of Shakespeare, or because he had recently been spending some time looking through the Shakespearean section of *The Penguin Dictionary of Quotations*?

They heard Ambrose's returning footsteps on the stones. He was carrying a folded red-checked table-cloth. While they watched he shook it out then let it fall gently over the body. Cordelia thought that, as a temporary shroud, it was hardly the most appropriate covering he could have found. He knelt and tucked it solicitously round the body as if making it comfortable. Still no one spoke. Then Sir George turned to Simon and barked out his order. 'Right, boy. Let's get on with it.'

Simon had already judged the depth of the pool and this time he dived. His body cleft the water in a neat curve parting the water lilies. There was a flurry and a brief commotion. And then his sleek head broke the surface and he raised both his arms high. Between them he held a dark wooden box about twelve inches by nine. A few seconds later he had pushed his burden into Ambrose's waiting hands and was drawing himself up over the side of the pool. He gasped:

'It was caught under the netting. What is it?'

For reply Ambrose opened the lid. The musical-box, watertight, had emerged a little scratched but otherwise undamaged. The cylinder slowly turned and a tinkle of sweet, disjointed notes plucked out a familiar tune, one which Cordelia had last heard during the final rehearsal, 'The Bluebells of Scotland'.

They listened silently until the tune was at an end. Then there was a pause and the next tinkle began, soon to be identified as 'My Bonnie Lies over the Ocean'.

Ambrose closed the box. He said:

'The last time I saw this it was with the other musical-box on the props table. He must have been taking it back to the tower room. This would be the direct route from the theatre to the tower.'

'But why? What was the hurry?'

Roma frowned at the box as if its appearance had disappointed her expectations. Ambrose said:

'There was no hurry. But he was drunk and I suppose he was acting irrationally. Munter shared my slight obsession with order and he strongly disliked any of the things in the castle being used as theatrical props. I suppose his muddled brain thought that this was as good a time as any to start putting things to rights.'

Cordelia thought that Sir George had been remarkably silent. Now he spoke for the first time.

'What else has he moved? What about the other box?'

'That was kept in the cupboard in the business room. As far as I can remember, one box was there, the second with the clutter in the tower room.'

Sir George turned to Simon.

'Better get dressed, boy. You're shivering. There's nothing else to do here.'

It was a dismissal, almost brutal in its peremptoriness. Simon seemed to realize for the first time that he was cold. His teeth began to chatter. He hesitated, nodded, then shambled off.

Roma said:

'That boy has more talents than I gave him credit for. And how, incidentally, did he know what Clarissa's jewel box was like? I thought you only gave it to her when she arrived on Friday morning.'

Cordelia said:

'I suppose he knows in the same way as you and I know; because we've been to her room and been shown it.'

Roma turned to go.

'Oh, I realized, of course, that he must have been in her room. I was just wondering when exactly.' She added:

'And how did he know that Munter was carrying the box when he fell? It could have been lying there on the bottom for months?'

'It was a safe assumption, surely, given the position of the body and the fact that it and the box were both caught by the netting.'

Ambrose's voice held a lightness and a determined incuriosity which Cordelia sensed was a little too controlled, a little too careful. He added:

'Why not leave the questions to Grogan. One amateur detective in the house is surely enough. And accusations of murder come more appropriately from the police, don't you feel?'

Roma turned away, hunching her shoulders more deeply into the collar of her dressing-gown. 'Well, I'll get back to bed. Perhaps I could have some tea in my room too when you get around to making it. And when I've had my stint with Grogan I'll relieve you of my presence here. Either the Courcy curse is still operative or, in your paradise, death is becoming infectious.'

Ambrose watched while she stumped away and disappeared into the shadows of the arches. He said:

'That woman could be dangerous.'

Sir George was still staring after her departing back. 'Only unhappy.'

'With a woman that amounts to the same thing. And with those beefy swimmer's shoulders, she shouldn't wear a padded dressing-gown. And she shouldn't choose that shade of blue, or any blue for that matter. I suppose that we may as well see whether the second musical-box is back where it's normally kept.'

Back in the business room he knelt and opened the doors of a walnut chiffonier. Cordelia could see that it contained a number of box files, two carefully wrapped parcels which could have been ornaments as yet unpacked, and a box in dark wood similar in size to the first. He placed it on the table and raised the lid. The box plucked out the tune 'Greensleeves'. Sir George said:

'So he did return it. Odd. Probably couldn't rest until he'd started putting things to rights.'

Cordelia said:

'Except that he's changed them around. This one belonged in the tower room.'

Ambrose's voice was unexpectedly sharp.

'How can you possibly know?'

'Because I saw it there on Friday afternoon while Clarissa was rehearsing. I went to explore the tower and found the room. I couldn't be mistaken.'

'They look very alike.'

'But they play a different tune. I opened the box in the tower, this box. It played "Greensleeves". The one used at the rehearsal played the Scottish medley. You know. You were there.'

Sir George said:

'So yesterday afternoon he fetched this one from the tower and not from the business room.' He turned to Ambrose.

'Did you know that, Gorringe?'

'Naturally not. I knew that we had two boxes and that one was kept here, the other in the tower room. I didn't know which was which. They aren't a particular passion of mine. When Munter told me what he also told the police, that he hadn't left the ground-floor apartments and that he'd fetched a musical-box from the business room, I saw no reason to doubt him.'

Cordelia said:

'When Clarissa or the producer first asked for a musical-box, he acted as one would expect. He fetched the nearer and less valuable box. Why trouble to go all the way to the tower room when there was a box easily to hand here in the business room? He wouldn't have gone to the tower room if Clarissa hadn't rejected the first box.'

Ambrose said:

'The only entrance to the tower is from the gallery. Munter lied to the police. At about two o'clock yesterday he was within a few feet of Clarissa's door. That means he could have seen someone entering or leaving. The police may feel that he could have gone in to her himself, locked door or no locked door. And that's why he was so obsessive about returning the boxes, each to the room he said he'd taken it from. He needn't have troubled, of course, I don't see how anyone could have known the truth. It was pure chance that you, Cordelia, wandered into the tower and found the second box. Whether the police believe you is, of course, another matter.'

Cordelia said:

'It wasn't altogether chance. If Clarissa hadn't ordered me out of the theatre I should have watched the rehearsal to the end. And I don't see why the police shouldn't believe me. They may find it easier to believe that I was curious to explore the tower room than that you, who are so fond of your Victoriana, didn't know precisely where you kept each of your musical-boxes.'

As soon as she had spoken, she wondered whether this frankness had been wise; spoken to her host, it had hardly been courteous. But Ambrose accepted the comment without offence. He said easily:

'You're probably right. I doubt whether they'll believe either of us. After all they only have our word for it that Munter lied. And it's very convenient for us, isn't it; a dead suspect who can't now deny what any of us choose to say about him? The butler did it. Even in fiction, so I'm led to believe, that solution is regarded as unsatisfactory.'

Sir George lifted his head:

'I think the police launches are arriving.'

He must, thought Cordelia, have remarkable ears for an ageing man. Hers had caught nothing. And then she sensed rather than heard the throb of engines. They looked at each other. For the first time Cordelia saw in their eyes what she knew they must be recognizing in hers, the flicker of fear. Ambrose said:

'I'll meet them at the quay. You two had better get back to the body.'

Sir George and Cordelia were alone. If it were to be said it had to be said now, before the police questioning began. But it was hard to get out the words, and when she did they sounded harsh, accusatory.

'You recognized that drowned face, didn't you? You think he could have been Blythe's son?'

He said unsurprised:

'It did strike me, yes. Never occurred to me before.'

'You'd never seen Munter like that before, his face upturned, dead and drowned. That's how you last saw his father.'

'What made you think of it?'

'Your face when you looked down at him. The War Memorial he decorates every Armistice day. The words he shouted out at you, murderer, murderer! It was his father he meant, not Clarissa. And I think he muttered in German to Simon. Even his Christian name. Didn't Ambrose say he was Carl? And his height. His father died slowly because he was so tall. But, most of all, his name. *Munter* is German for "blithe". It's one of the few German words I know.'

She had seen that look of strained endurance on his face before, but all he said was:

'Could be. Could be.'

She asked:

'Are you going to tell Grogan?'

'No. None of his business. Not relevant.'

'Not even if they arrest you for murder?'

'They won't. I didn't kill my wife.' Suddenly he said, quickly as if the words were forced out of him:

'I don't believe I deliberately let them kill him. May have done. Difficult to understand one's motives. Used to think it was all so simple.'

Cordelia said:

'You don't have to explain to me. It's none of my business. And you were a young officer at the time. You can't have been in command here.'

'No, but I was on duty that evening. Should have discovered that something was afoot, should have stopped it. But I hated Blythe so much that I couldn't trust myself to go near him. That's one thing you never forget or forgive, cruelty when you're a child and defenceless. I shut my mind and my eyes to anything that concerned him. May have shut them deliberately. You could call it a dereliction of duty.'

'But no one did. There was no court martial, was there? No one blamed you.'

'I blame myself.'

There was a moment's silence, then he said:

'Never knew he was married. No mention of a wife at the inquest. There was talk of a girl in Speymouth but she never showed herself. No talk of a child.'

'Munter probably wasn't born. And he could have been illegitimate. I don't suppose we shall ever know. But his mother must have been bitter about what happened. He probably grew up believing that the Army had murdered his father. I wonder why he took a job on the island; curiosity, filial duty, the hope of revenge? But he couldn't have expected that you would turn up here.'

'He might have hoped for it. He took the job in the summer of 1978. I married Clarissa that year, and she has known Ambrose Gorringe nearly all her life. Munter probably kept track of me. I'm not exactly a nonentity.'

Cordelia said:

'The police have made mistakes before now. If they do arrest you I shall feel free to tell them. I shall have to tell them.'

He said quietly:

'No, Cordelia. It's my concern, my past, my life.'

Cordelia cried:

'But you must see how it will look to the police! If they believe me about the musical-box, they'll know that Munter was in the gallery a few feet from your wife's room at about the time she died. If he didn't kill her himself, he could have seen the person who did. Taken with that shout to you of "murderer" it's damning unless you tell them who Munter was.'

He didn't respond but stood rigid as a sentry, his eyes gazing into nothingness. She said:

'If they arrest the wrong person it's a double injustice. It means that the guilty one goes free. Is that what you want?'

'Would it be the wrong person? If she hadn't married me she'd be alive today.'

'You can't know that!'

'I can feel it. Who was it said we owe God a death?'

'I can't remember. Someone in Shakespeare's *Henry IV*. But what has that to do with it?'

'Nothing, I expect. It came into my mind.'

She was getting nowhere. Beneath that apparently guileless and inarticulate front of personality he harboured his private under-cover agent, a mind more complex and perhaps more ruthless than she had imagined. And he wasn't a fool, this deceptively simple soldier. He knew precisely the extent of his danger. And that could mean that he had his own suspicions; that there was someone he wanted to protect. And she didn't think that it would be either Ambrose or Ivo. She said helplessly:

'I don't know what you want of me. Am I to carry on with the case?'

'No point is there? Nothing can frighten her ever again. Better leave it to the professionals.' He added awkwardly, 'I'll pay, of course, for your time so far. I'm not ungrateful.'

Ungrateful for what? She wondered.

He turned and looked down at Munter's body. He said:

'Extraordinary business, putting that wreath on the War Memorial every year. Do you suppose Gorringe will keep up the tradition?'

'I shouldn't think so.'

'He should. I'll have a word with him. Oldfield could see to it.'

They turned to make their way across the rose garden, then stopped. Coming across the lawn towards them in the pale apricot light, their footfalls absorbed by the soft grass, were Grogan and his coterie of officers. Cordelia was caught unawares. Facing their silent, inexorable advance, their bleak, unsmiling faces, she resisted the temptation to glance at Sir George. But she wondered whether he shared her sudden and irrational vision of how the two of them must look to the police, as guilty and discomforted as a couple of poachers surprised by the gamekeepers with their dead spoils at their feet.

PART SIX

A Case Concluded

CHAPTER THIRTY-EIGHT

Munter's body was taken away with a speed and efficiency which Cordelia thought was almost unseemly. By ten o'clock the metal container with its two long side-handles had been slid from the jetty on to the deck of the police launch with as little ceremony as if it had held a dog. But what, after all, had she expected? Munter had been a man. Now he was a weight of latent putrefaction, a case to be given a file and a number, a problem to be solved. She told herself that it was unreasonable to expect that the men – police officers? mortuary attendants? undertaker's staff? – would bear him away with the solemnity appropriate to a funeral. They were doing a familiar job without emotion, and without fuss.

And with this second death the suspects were able to watch the police at work. They did it discreetly from the window of Cordelia's bedroom, watching while Grogan and Buckley walked slowly round the body like a couple of marine scientists intrigued by some bedraggled specimen which had been washed up by the tide. They watched while the photographer did his job, hardly seeming to notice or speak to the police, occupying himself with his own expertise. And this time Dr Ellis-Jones didn't appear. Cordelia wondered whether this was because the cause of death was apparent or whether he was busy elsewhere with another body. Instead, a police surgeon arrived to certify that life was extinct and to make the preliminary examination. He was a large and jovial man, dressed in sea boots and a knitted jersey patched on both elbows, who greeted the police like old drinking companions. His cheerful voice rose clearly on the quiet morning air. It was only when he knelt to rummage in his case for his thermometer that the watchers at the window silently withdrew and took refuge in the drawing-room, ashamed of what had suddenly seemed an indecent curiosity. And it was from the drawing-room windows, less than ten minutes later, that they saw Munter's body borne through the archway and across the quay to the launch. One of the bearers said something to his mate and they both laughed. He was probably complaining about the weight.

And with this second death even the police questioning didn't take long. There was, after all, not a great deal that anyone could tell, and Cordelia guessed how suspiciously unanimous that little must sound. When it was her turn she went into the business room weighed down by the conviction that nothing she said would be believed. Grogan stared at her across the desk, his pale, unfriendly eyes red-rimmed as if he had gone without sleep. The two musical-boxes were on the desk in front of him, carefully positioned side by side.

When she had finished her account of Munter's appearance at the dining-room windows, of the finding of his body and the recovery of the musical-box, there was a long silence. Then he said:

'Why exactly did you go up to the tower room on Friday afternoon?'

'Just curiosity. Miss Lisle didn't want me at the rehearsal and Mr Whittingham and I had finished our walk. He was tired and had gone to rest. I was at a loose end.'

'So you amused yourself by exploring the tower?'

'Yes.'

'And then you played with the toys?'

He made it sound as if she were a tiresome child who hadn't been able to keep her hands off someone else's kiddy car. She realized with a mixture of anger and hopelessness the impossibility of explaining, of making him understand that impulse to set the whole childish menagerie working, to drown wretchedness with a cacophony of sound. And even if she had confided the cause of her distress, Ivo telling her of the death of Tolly's child, would her story have sounded any more plausible? How did one explain to a policeman, perhaps to a judge, a jury, those small, seemingly irrational compulsions, the pathetic expedients against pain, which hardly made sense to oneself? And if it were difficult for her, so egregiously privileged, how did those others cope; the ignorant, the uneducated, the inarticulate, faced with the esoteric and uncompromising machinery of the law? She said:

'Yes, I played with the toys.'

'And you are absolutely certain that the musical-box you found in the tower room played the tune "Greensleeves"?' He smacked his great palm down on the lid of the left-hand box, then lifted the lid. The cylinder turned and the delicate teeth of the long comb once more picked out the nostalgic, plaintive tune. She said:

'I'm absolutely sure.'

'Externally, they're very alike. The same size, the same shape, the same wood, almost the same pattern on the lids.'

'I know. But they play different tunes.'

She could understand the frustration and the irritation which he was keeping so tightly under control. Had she liked him better, she might have sympathized. If she were telling the truth, then Munter had lied. He had left the ground floor of the castle some time during that critical hour and forty minutes. The only entrance to the tower was from the gallery floor. He had been within feet of Clarissa's door. And Munter was dead. Even if Grogan believed him innocent, even if some other suspect were brought to trial, her evidence about the musical-box would be a gift for the defence. He said:

'You didn't mention your visit to the tower when you were questioned yesterday.'

'You didn't ask me. You were chiefly interested in what I did and saw on Saturday. I didn't think it important.'

'There's nothing else that you didn't think important?'

'I've answered all your questions as honestly as I can.'

He said:

'Perhaps. But that isn't quite the same thing, is it, Miss Gray?'

And the small voice of her own conscience, in collusion with him, indicted her. Have you? Have you?

Suddenly he leaned across the desk and put his face close to hers. She thought she could smell his breath, sour and tainted with beer, and had to force herself not to draw back.

'What exactly happened on Saturday morning in the Devil's Kettle?'

'I've told you. Mr Gorringe told us the story of the young internee who was left to drown. And I found that quotation from the play.'

'And that's all that happened?'

'It seems to me enough.'

He sat back and she waited. He didn't speak. At last she said:

'I should like to go to Speymouth this afternoon. I want to get off the island.'

'Who doesn't, Miss Gray?'

'That's all right, is it? I don't have to ask permission? I mean, you can't stop me going where I like unless you arrest me?'

He said:

'That, no doubt, is what you'd advise your clients if you had any. And you'd be perfectly right. We can't stop you. But you must be in Speymouth tomorrow at two o'clock for the inquest. It won't take long, just a formality. We'll be asking for an adjournment. But you were the one who found the body. You were the last person to see Miss Lisle alive. The Coroner will want you there.'

She wondered whether it was intended to sound like a threat. She said:

'I'll be there.'

He looked up and said so gently that she almost believed him to be sincere:

'Enjoy yourself in Speymouth, Miss Gray. Have a good day.'

CHAPTER THIRTY-NINE

It was after twelve thirty when she was released. Strolling out to join the others who were drinking their pre-luncheon sherry on the terrace, she learned that Oldfield had already gone to the mainland to fetch the post and supplies. Ambrose was expecting a parcel of books from the London Library. Cordelia asked if *Shearwater* could be ordered for her for two o'clock and he agreed without curiosity, merely inquiring when she would like the launch to be at Speymouth quay for the return journey. Cordelia ordered it for six o'clock.

She wasn't hungry for luncheon and nor, apparently, was anyone else. Mrs Munter had provided a cold buffet in the dining-room, too much food, most of it intended for the party, set out indiscriminately in an appetite-stifling mass. The wonder was, thought Cordelia, that she had bothered at all. No one had spoken of her since the finding of her husband's body. She too had been interviewed by the police, but had spent most of the morning secluded in her flat or moving silently and unnoticed from pantry to dining-room. Cordelia doubted whether Ambrose was greatly concerned about her and there was no one else to care. She decided to see if she was all right, to ask, before setting out, whether there was anything she could do for her in Speymouth. She doubted whether her intrusion would be welcomed. What was there, after all, that she or anyone could do? But at least she could ask.

She didn't trouble to sit down but cut herself slices of cold beef and put them between bread. Then making her excuses to Ambrose, she helped herself to an apple and a banana and took her picnic on to the beach. Already her mind was moving away from this claustrophobic island towards the mainland. She felt like a refugee, waiting to be rescued from some plague-ridden and violent colony, watching with desperate eyes for the boat which would bear her away from the smell of rotting corpses, the shouting and tumult, the bodies strewn on the shore, towards the safety and normality of home. The mainland which she had seen recede with such high hopes only three days earlier now shone in the imagination with all the refulgence of a promised land. It seemed to her that two o'clock would never come.

Shortly before one thirty she made her way along the tiled passage past the business room to the baize door which she knew must lead to the servants' flat. There was no bell or knocker but while she was wondering how to attract attention, Mrs Munter came quietly up behind her carrying on her hip a basket of washing. Without speaking, she held open the door and Cordelia passed before her down a shorter passageway and into a sitting-room to her right. Like all Victorian architects, Godwin had ensured that from none of their rooms could the servants overlook their betters whether the family were disporting themselves indoors or out, and the single window gave a view only of a wide yard with, beyond it, the stable block with its charming clock tower and weather vane. Across the yard was slung a washing line from which drooped a pair of Munter's huge pyjamas. They seemed to Cordelia pathetic and embarrassing and she averted her eyes as if detected in a prurient curiosity.

The room itself was starkly furnished, not uncomfortable, but despite the artful simplicity of the art nouveau furniture almost devoid of character. There was a television set in the corner but no books or pictures and no photographs or ornaments on the dresser. It was as if the inhabitants had no past to remember, no present to celebrate. And no third person, apparently, ever sat here. There were only two easy chairs, one on each side of the elegantly carved iron grate, and only two upright chairs set opposite each other at the dining-table.

Mrs Munter didn't invite her to sit down. Cordelia said:

'I didn't mean to bother you. I just wanted to see that you are all right. And I'm going into Speymouth shortly. Is there anything I can get or do for you?'

Mrs Munter swung her basket of washing down on the table and began folding the clothes.

'There's nothing. I'll be with you on the boat likely enough. I'm leaving, Miss. I'm getting off the island.'

'I know how you must feel. But if you're frightened I could share a room with you tonight.'

'I'm not frightened. What is there to be frightened of? I'm leaving that's all. I never liked being here and now that he's gone I don't have to stay.'

'Of course not, if that's how you feel. But I'm sure Mr Gorringe wouldn't want you to do anything in a hurry. He'll want to talk to you. There are bound to be well . . . arrangements.'

'There's nothing to talk about. He's been a good enough master but it was Munter he wanted. I came with Munter. Now we're separate.'

Separate, thought Cordelia, finally and for ever. There had been no mistaking the note of satisfaction, almost of triumph. And she had come to the flat out of an embarrassed compassion, inexperienced as she might be, to try to give comfort. None, it appeared, was wanted or necessary. But surely there would be wages outstanding, offers of help to be made, funeral arrangements to be discussed? Ambrose would surely want to reassure her that she could stay on at the castle as long as it suited her. And, of course, there would be the police, Grogan and his ubiquitous experts in death, trained in suspicion and mistrust. If Munter had been deliberately pushed to his death, she could have done it. With one undetected murderer already on the island, what better time to get rid of an unwanted husband? Cordelia didn't doubt that Grogan, faced with this ungrieving widow, would place her high on his list of suspects. And the police were bound to see this hurried departure as highly suspicious. She was wondering whether she ought to say a word of warning when Mrs Munter spoke.

'I've spoken to the police. They've no call to keep me. They know where they can find me. Mr Gorringe can see to the funeral arrangements. It's no concern of mine.'

'But you were his wife!'

'I never was his wife. He wasn't the marrying kind, and nor am I. I'll be leaving in the launch as soon as Oldfield is ready.'

'Are you all right for money? I'm sure that Mr Gorringe . . .'

'I don't need his help. Munter had money. He had ways of making a bit on the side and I know where he kept it. I'll take what's due to me. And I'll be all right. Good cooks don't starve.'

Cordelia felt totally inadequate. She said:

'No indeed. But have you somewhere to go, for tonight I mean?'

'She'll be staying with me.'

Tolly came quietly into the room. She was wearing a dark-blue fitted coat with padded shoulders and a small hat pierced with one long feather. The outfit was reminiscent of the thirties and gave her a slightly raffish and outdated smartness. She was carrying a bulging suitcase bound with a strap. She moved unsmiling to Mrs Munter's side – it was impossible for Cordelia to think of her by any other name – and the two women faced her together.

Cordelia felt that she was seeing Mrs Munter clearly for the first time. Until now she had hardly noticed her. The strongest impression she had made was of an unobtrusive competence. She had been an adjunct to Munter, little more. Even her appearance was unmemorable, the coarse hair, neither fair nor dark, with its stiff, corrugated waves, the stolid body, the stumpy work-worn hands. But now the thin mouth which had given so little away was taut with an obstinate triumph. The eyes which had been so deferentially downcast stared boldly into hers with a look of challenging, almost insolent confidence. They seemed to say: 'You don't even know my name. And now you never will.' Beside her stood Tolly, unchanged in her self-contained serenity.

So they were going away together. Where, she wondered, would they live? Presumably Tolly had a house or flat somewhere in London where she had made a home for her child. Cordelia had a sudden and disconcertingly clear picture of them, not living there surrounded by memories, but installed in a neat suburban house within convenient distance of the Tube and the shopping parade, net curtains looped across the bay window, hindering inquisitive eyes, a small front garden railed against unwelcome intruders, against the past. They had thrown off their servitude. But surely that servitude must have been voluntary? Both were adult women. Surely it wasn't the fear of unemployment that had kept them from their freedom? They could have left their jobs whenever it suited them. So why hadn't they? What was the mysterious alchemy that kept people tied together against all reason, against inclination, against their own interests? Well, death had parted them now, one from Clarissa, the other from Munter; parted them very conveniently the police might think.

Cordelia thought, I'm seeing both of them clearly for the first time and still I know nothing about them. Some words of Henry James fell into her mind. 'Never believe that you know the last word about any human heart.' But did she know even the first word, she who called herself a detective? Wasn't it one of the commonest of human vanities, this preoccupation with the motives, the compulsions, the fascinating inconsistencies of another personality? Perhaps, she thought, we all enjoy acting the detective, even with those we love; with them most of all. But she had accepted it as her job; she did it for money. She had never denied its fascination, but now, for the first time, it occurred to her that it might also be presumptuous. And never before had she felt so inadequate for the task, pitting her youth, her inexperience, her meagre store of received wisdom against the immense mysteriousness of the human heart. She turned to Mrs Munter.

'I should like to have a word with Miss Tolgarth alone. May I please?'

The woman didn't reply but looked at her friend and was given a small nod. Without speaking, she left them.

Tolly waited, patient, unsmiling, her hands folded before her. There was something which Cordelia would like to have asked first, but she didn't need to. And she was less arrogant now than when she had first taken the case. She told herself that there were questions she had no right to ask, facts she had no right to be told. No human curiosity, no longing to have every piece of the jigsaw neatly fitted into place as if her own busy hands could impose order on the muddle of human lives, could justify asking what she knew in her heart was true, whether Ivo had been the father of Tolly's child. Ivo who had spoken of Viccy with knowledge and love, who had known that Tolly had refused to accept any help from the father; Ivo who had taken the trouble to get in touch with the hospital and learn the truth about that telephone call. How strange to think of them together, Ivo and Tolly. What was it, she wondered, that they had wanted of each other? Had Ivo been trying to hurt Clarissa, or assuage a deeper hurt of his own? Was Tolly one of those women, desperate for a child, who prefers not to be burdened with a husband? The birth of Viccy, if not the pregnancy, must surely have been deliberate. But none of it was her business. Of all the things that human beings did together, the sexual act was the one with the most various of reasons. Desire might be the commonest, but that didn't mean that it was the simplest. Cordelia couldn't even bring herself to mention Viccy directly. But there was something she had to ask. She said:

'You were with Clarissa when the first of the messages came, during the run of *Macbeth*. Would you tell me what they looked like?'

Tolly's eyes burned into hers with a sombre, considering stare but not, she thought, with resentment or dislike. Cordelia went on:

'You see, I think it was you who sent them and I think she might have guessed and known why. But she couldn't do without you. It was easier to pretend. And she didn't want to show the messages to anyone else. She knew what she had done to you. She knew that there were things even her friends might not forgive. And then what she hoped would happen did happen. Perhaps there had been some change in your life which had made you feel that what you were doing was wrong. So the messages stopped.

They stopped until one of the small number of people who had known about them took over. But then they were different messages. They looked different. Their purpose was different. And their end was different and terrible.'

Still there was no reply. Cordelia said gently:

'I know I've no right to ask. Don't answer me directly if you'd rather not. Just tell me what those first messages were like and I think I shall know.'

Then Tolly spoke:

'They were written by hand in capital letters on lined paper. Paper torn from a child's exercise book.'

'And the messages themselves. Were they quotations?'

'It was always the same message. A text from the Bible.'

Cordelia knew that she was lucky to have gained so much. And even this confidence wouldn't have been given if Tolly hadn't recognized some sympathy, some empathy between them. But there was one more question which she thought she might risk.

'Miss Tolgarth, have you any idea who it was who took over?'

But the eyes looking into hers were implacable. Tolly had told all she intended to tell.

'No. I concern myself with my own sins. Let others look to theirs.'

Cordelia said:

'I shall never pass on to anyone what you've just said to me.'

'If I thought that you would, I wouldn't have told you.' She paused, and then asked in the same even tone:

'What will happen to the boy?'

'To Simon? He told me that Sir George will keep him on at Melhurst for his final year and that he'll then try for a place at one of the colleges of music.'

Tolly said:

'He'll be all right now she's gone. She wasn't good for the young. And now, if you'll excuse me, Miss, I'd like to help my friend finish her packing.'

CHAPTER FORTY

There was nothing more to be said or done. Cordelia left the two women together and went to her bedroom to get ready for the afternoon's excursion. As her object was to search for the newspaper review, her full scene-of-crime kit was hardly necessary, but she slipped a hand magnifying-glass, a torch and notebook into her shoulder-bag and pulled her Guernsey over her shirt. It might be cold on the boat on the return trip. Lastly she wound the leather belt twice round her waist and buckled it tight. As always, it felt like a talisman, a girding on of resolution. As she crossed the terrace from the western front of the castle she saw that Mrs Munter and Tolly were already making their way towards the launch, both of them carrying a case in either hand. Oldfield must only recently have landed. He was still dragging his crates of wine and groceries on to the jetty, helped rather surprisingly by Simon. Cordelia thought that the boy was probably glad of something to do.

Suddenly Roma appeared from the dining-room windows and hurried down the terrace in front of her. She went up to Oldfield and spoke to him. The canvas post-bag was on top of his trolley and he unbuckled it and took out the bundle of letters. Drawing close to them Cordelia could sense Roma's impatience. It looked as if she might snatch the bundle from Oldfield's gnarled fingers. But then he found what she was wanting, and handed her a letter. She almost ran from him, then slowed to a walk and, without noticing Cordelia's approach, tore the envelope open and read the letter. For a moment she stood absolutely still. Then she gave a sob, so high that it was almost a wail, and began stumbling along the terrace, pushed past Cordelia, and disappeared down the far steps to the beach.

Cordelia paused for a moment, uncertain whether to follow. Then she called to Oldfield to wait for her, that she wouldn't be long, and ran after Roma. Whatever the news, it had devastated her. There might be something she herself could do to help. And even if not, it was impossible just to board the launch and set off as if the scene had never happened. She tried to silence the small resentful voice which protested that it couldn't have occurred at a more inconvenient time. Was she never to be allowed to get off the island? Why should she always have to be the one to act as universal social worker? But it was impossible to ignore such distress.

Roma was stumbling and reeling along the shore, her hands flung out before her, groping the air. Cordelia thought that she could hear a high continued scream of pain. But perhaps it was the cry of the gulls. She had almost caught up with the fleeing figure when Roma tripped, fell at full length on the shingle and lay there, her whole body shaking with sobs. Cordelia came up to her. To see the proud and reserved Roma in such an abandonment of grief was as physically shocking as a blow to the stomach. Cordelia felt the same rush of impotent fear, the same helplessness. All she could do was kneel in the sand and put her arms round Roma's shoulders, hoping that this human contact might at least help to calm her. She found herself softly cooing as she might to a child or an animal. After a few minutes the dreadful shaking ceased. Roma lay so still that, for a second, Cordelia feared that she had ceased to breathe. Then she heaved herself clumsily upright and threw off Cordelia's arm. Walking unsteadily into the surf she bent and began splashing her face. Then she stood upright for a moment, looking out to sea before turning to face Cordelia.

Her face was grotesque, bloated as a long-drowned visage, the eyes like gummed slits, the nose a bulbous mess. When she spoke, her voice was harsh and guttural, the sounds forcing themselves through swollen vocal cords.

'I'm sorry. That was a disgusting exhibition. I'm glad it was you, if that's any comfort.'

'I wish I could help.'

'You can't. No one can. As you've probably guessed, it's the usual commonplace sordid little tragedy. I've been chucked. He wrote on Friday night. We only saw each other on Thursday. He must have known then what he was going to do.'

She pulled the letter from her pocket and held it out.

'Go on, read it! Read it! I wonder how many drafts it took to produce this elegant, self-justifying piece of hypocrisy.'

Cordelia didn't take the letter. She said:

'If he hadn't the decency and courage to tell you to your face, he isn't worth crying over, he isn't worth loving.'

'What has worth to do with love? My God, why couldn't he have waited?'

Waited for what? thought Cordelia. For Clarissa's money? For Clarissa's death? She said:

'But if he had, could you ever have been sure?'

'Of his motive, you mean? Why should I care? I haven't that kind of pride. But it's too late now. He wrote a day too soon. Oh God, why couldn't he have waited? I told him that I'd get the money, I told him!'

A wave, larger than its fellows, broke at Cordelia's feet and rolled a woman's silver evening sandal among the brighter sea-washed stones. She found herself looking at it with an artificial intensity, making herself wonder what sort of woman had worn it, how it had come to be in the sea, from what wild party on what yacht it had been lost overboard. Or was its owner out there somewhere, a slim, half-clad body turning in the waves? Any thought, even that thought, helped to shut out the harsh unnatural voice which might any moment say those fatal words which couldn't be taken back and which neither of them would be able to forget.

'When I was a child I went to a co-educational school. All the children paired off. When the friendship cooled they used to send each other what they called a chuck note. I never had one. But then I never had a boy friend. I used to think it would be worth getting the chuck note if only I'd had the friendship first, just for one term. I wish I could feel that now. He was the only man who has ever wanted me. I think I always knew why. You can only deceive yourself so far. His wife doesn't much enjoy sex and I was a free fuck. All right, don't look like that! I don't expect you to understand. You can get love whenever you want it.'

Cordelia cried:

'That isn't true, not of me, not of anyone!'

'Isn't it? It was true of Clarissa. She only had to look at a man. One look, that's all it ever took. All my life I've watched her using those eyes. But she won't any more. Never again. Never, never, never.'

Her anguish was like an infection, strong and feverish and smelling of sweat. Cordelia could feel its contamination in her own blood. She stood on the shingle, afraid to approach Roma since she knew that physical comfort would be unwelcome, reluctant to leave her, miserably aware that Oldfield would be getting impatient. Then Roma said gruffly:

'You'd better go if you want to catch the launch.'

'What about you?'

'Don't worry. You can escape with an easy conscience, I shan't do anything stupid. That's the euphemism, isn't it? Isn't that what they always say? Don't do anything stupid. I've been taught my lesson. No more stupidity, Roma! I can tell you what will happen to me, in case you're interested. I'll take Clarissa's money and buy myself a London flat. I'll sell the shop and find myself a part-time job. From time to time I'll take a foreign holiday with a woman friend. We shan't much enjoy each other's company, but it will be better than travelling alone. We'll devise little treats for ourselves, a theatre, an art show, dinner at one of those restaurants where they don't treat solitary women as pariahs. And in the autumn I'll enrol for evening classes and pretend an interest in throwing pots, or the Georgian architecture of London or comparative religion. And every year I shall get a little more fussy about my comforts, a little more censorious of the young, a little more fretful with my friend, a little more right-wing, a little more bitter, a little more lonely, a little more dead.'

Cordelia would have liked to have said: 'But you'll have enough to eat. You'll have your own roof over your head. You won't die of cold. You'll have your strength and your intelligence. Isn't that more than three-quarters of the world enjoys? You're not a Victorian shell-gatherer, waiting for a man to give purpose and status to your life. There doesn't even have to be love.' But she knew that the words would be as futile and insulting as telling a blind man that there was always the sunset.

She turned and walked away leaving Roma still staring out to sea. She felt like a deserter. It seemed discourteous to hurry and she waited until she reached the terrace before breaking into a run.

CHAPTER FORTY-ONE

No one spoke during the passage to the mainland. Cordelia sat in the prow of the launch fixing her eyes on the gradually approaching shore. Mrs Munter and Tolly settled themselves together in the stern, their bags at their feet. When *Shearwater* finally berthed, Cordelia waited until they were ashore before herself getting up. She watched while the two women, side by side but still unspeaking, made their slow way up the hill towards the station.

The town was less crowded and less busy than on the Friday morning but it still held its slightly archaic air of cheerful sunlit domesticity. What she found extraordinary was to be so unnoticed. She had half expected that people would turn to stare at her, that she would hear the whispered word 'Courcy' at her back, that she would bear an all too visible mark of Cain. How marvellous it was to be free of Grogan and his minions, at least for a few blessed hours, no longer one of that apprehensive, self-regarding coterie of suspects, but an ordinary girl walking an ordinary street, anonymous among the early afternoon shoppers, the last holiday visitors, the office workers hurrying back to their desks after a belated lunch. She wasted a few minutes in a chemist's shop behind a charming Regency façade buying a lipstick which she didn't need, taking more than usual care over her selection. It was a small gesture of hope and confidence, a salute to normality. The only mention she saw or heard of Clarissa's death was a couple of placards advertising national dailies with the words 'ACTRESS MURDERED ON COURCY ISLAND' written, not printed, under the paper's name. She bought one at a kiosk and found a brief account on the third page. The police had given the minimum of information and Ambrose's refusal to speak to the press had obviously frustrated them in making much of a story. Cordelia wondered whether, in the end, it would prove to have been wise. She learned from the newsagent that there was now only one local paper, the *Speymouth Chronicle*, which came out twice a week on Tuesday and Friday. The office was at the northern end of the Esplanade. Cordelia found it without difficulty. It was a white converted house with two large windows, one painted with the words 'Speymouth Chronicle' and the other filled with a display of newspaper photographs. The front garden had been paved to provide a parking space for half a dozen cars and a delivery van. Inside she found a blonde girl of about her own age presiding at a reception desk and simultaneously coping with a small switchboard. At a side table an elderly man was sorting pictures.

Her luck held. She had feared that old copies of the paper might be kept elsewhere or might not be readily available to the public. But when she explained to the girl that she was researching into provincial theatre and wanted to look up the reviews of Clarissa Lisle's performance in *The Deep Blue Sea* no questions were asked and no difficulties made. The girl called out to her companion to keep an eye on the desk, ignored a light on the switchboard, and took Cordelia through a swing door and down a steep flight of ill-lit stairs to the basement. There she unlocked a small front room from which the exciting musty smell of old newsprint rose to the nostrils like a miasma. Cordelia saw that the archives were bound in springback folders filed in chronological order on steel shelves. In the middle of the room was a long trestle-table. The girl switched on the light and two fluorescent tubes glowed into harsh brightness. She said:

'They're all here, going back to 1860. You can't take anything away and you mustn't write on the papers. Don't slip off without telling me. I have to come and lock up after you've finished. OK? See you later then.'

Cordelia approached her task methodically. Speymouth was a small town and was unlikely to have a permanent theatre company. It was almost certain, therefore, that Clarissa had played with a repertory company during the summer season, most likely between May and September. She would begin her search with those five months. She found no mention of the Rattigan play in May but she did note that the summer repertory company based in the old theatre opened with each new offering on a Monday and played for two weeks. The first reviews appeared on a page devoted to the arts in each Tuesday's edition, a commendably quick response for a small provincial paper. Presumably the reviewer telephoned his copy from the theatre. The first mention of *The Deep Blue Sea* appeared in an advertisement in early June which stated that Miss Clarissa Lisle would be guest star for the two weeks beginning 18th July. Cordelia calculated that the notice would appear on the arts page, invariably page nine, on 19th July. She lugged the heavy bound volume containing the editions from

July to September on to the table and found the paper for that date. It was larger than the normal edition, consisting of eighteen pages instead of the usual sixteen. The reason was made apparent on the first page. The Queen and the Duke of Edinburgh had visited the town on the previous Saturday as part of their Jubilee Year provincial tour, and the Tuesday edition had been the first one following the visit. It had been a big day for Speymouth, the first Royal visit since 1843, and the *Chronicle* had made the most of it. The account on the first page stated that further pictures were shown on page ten. The words struck a chord of memory. Cordelia was now almost sure that the reverse side of the notice she had seen had been not newsprint but a picture.

But now that success was so close she felt a sudden loss of confidence. All she would discover would be the review by a provincial reporter of a revival which hardly anyone in Speymouth would now remember. Clarissa had said that it was important to her, important enough to keep in the secret drawer of her jewel box. But that, with Clarissa, could have meant anything. Perhaps she had liked the notice, met the reviewer, enjoyed a brief but satisfactory love affair. It could have been as sentimentally unimportant as that. And what possible relevance could it have to her death?

And then she saw that the sheet she wanted wasn't there. She checked twice. No careful turning of the newspaper disclosed pages nine and ten. She bent back the thick wedge of newsprint where it was gripped by the binder. Down the margin of page eleven she thought she could detect a thin impression as if the paper had been faintly scored with a knife or razor blade. She got out her magnifying glass and moved it slowly over the bound edges. Now she could see it clearly, the tell-tale mark, in some places actually cutting the paper, showing where the sheet had been excised. She could detect, too, minute shreds of paper where the edge of page nine was still clasped in the binder. Someone had been here before her.

The girl at the desk was busy with a customer inquiring, but without any visible signs of grief, how she went about inserting a death notice and how much extra a nice bit of verse would cost. She handed over a child's exercise book and pointed out the rounded, laboriously formed letters. Cordelia, always curious about the idiosyncrasies of her fellow humans and for a moment forgetting her own concerns, edged closer and slewed her eyes to read:

The pearly walls were shining,
St Peter whispered low,
The golden gate was opened,
And in walked Joe.

This piece of extremely dubious theology was received by the girl with a lack of interest which suggested that she had read its like before. She spent the next three minutes attempting to explain what the probable cost would be including the extras if the notice were boxed and surmounted with a wreathed cross, a consultation which was punctuated by long considering silences as they both contemplated samples of the designs on offer. But after ten minutes all was satisfactorily decided and she was then able to turn her attention to Cordelia who said:

'I've found the right edition but the sheet I think I want isn't there. Someone's cut it out.'

'They can't have. It isn't allowed. Those are the archives.'

'Well they have. Is there another copy?'

'I'll have to tell Mr Hasking. They can't go cutting the archives about. Mr Hasking will be in a rare state about that.'

'I'm sure. But I do need to see that page urgently. It's page nine of the edition of 19th July 1977. Haven't you any other back numbers I could look through?'

'Not here. The Chairman might have a set up in London. Cutting the archives! Mr Hasking sets great store by those old copies. That's history, that is, he says.'

Cordelia asked:

'Can you remember who last asked to see them?'

'There was a blonde lady from London last month. Writing a book about seaside piers she said. They blew this one up in 1939 so the Germans couldn't land, then the Council hadn't any money to build it again. That's why it's so stumpy. She said they used to have a music hall on the end when she was a girl and artistes used to come down from London in the season. She knew a lot about piers.'

Cordelia thought that a better equipped or more efficient private detective would have come with photographs of the victim and suspects for possible identification. It would have been useful to know whether the blonde woman who was so knowledgeable about piers looked like Clarissa or Roma. Tolly, unless she had disguised herself, surely an unnecessarily dramatic ploy, was obviously out. She wondered whether Bernie would have thought of photographing the house party unseen, prepared for just such an eventuality. She hadn't herself felt such a tricky procedure was possible or useful. But she did, after all, have the Polaroid in her kit on the island. Perhaps it would be worth a try. She could come back tomorrow. She said:

'And is the pier lady the only one who has recently asked to see the archives?'

'While I've been here. But then, I've only been on the desk a couple of months. Sally could have told you about anyone before that, but she's left to get married. And I'm not always on the desk. I mean someone could've come when I was in the office and Albert was on the desk.'

'Is he here?'

The girl looked at her as if astounded at such ignorance.

'Albert? Of course he isn't. Albert's never here Mondays.'

She looked at Cordelia with sudden suspicion. 'Why d'you want to know who else has been here? I thought you were just after seeing that review.'

'I am. But I was curious who could have cut out that page. As you said, these are important records. And I wouldn't like anyone to think it was I. You're quite sure there isn't a copy anywhere else in the town?'

Without looking round, the elderly man who was still arranging new photographs in the display frame with a deliberation and an eye for artistic effect which suggested that the job could well take the rest of the day, made his suggestion.

'19th July, '77 did you say? That's three days after the Queen's visit. You could try Lucy Costello. She's kept press cuttings on the Royal family for the last fifty years. Isn't likely she'd have missed the Royal visit.'

'But Lucy Costello's dead, Mr Lambert! We had an article

about her and her press cuttings the day after they buried her. Three months ago, that was.'

Mr Lambert turned round and spread out his arms in a parody of patient resignation:

'I know Lucy Costello's dead! We all know she's dead! I never said she wasn't dead. But she's got a sister, hasn't she? Miss Emmeline's still alive as far as I know. She'll have the cuttings books. Isn't likely she'd throw them out. They may have buried Miss Lucy but they haven't buried her press cuttings with her, not that I know of. I said to try her. I didn't say speak to her.'

Cordelia asked how she could find Miss Emmeline. Mr Lambert turned away again to his photographs and spoke gruffly, as if regretting his former loquacity:

'Windsor Cottage, Benison Row. Up the High Street, second left. Can't miss it.'

'Is it far? I mean, ought I to take a bus?'

'You'd be lucky. Catch yer death you would waiting for that Number 12. Ten minutes' walk at most. No trouble for a young 'un.'

He selected a picture of a portly gentleman in a mayoral chain, whose sideways glance of salacious bonhomie suggested that the official banquet had more than fulfilled expectations, and positioned it carefully beside a photograph of a well endowed and decidedly underclad bathing beauty, so that his eyes appeared to be gazing down her cleavage. Cordelia thought that here was a man who enjoyed his work. She thanked him and the girl for their help and set out to find Miss Emmeline Costello.

CHAPTER FORTY-TWO

Mr Lambert had been right about the distance. It was almost exactly ten minutes' admittedly brisk walk to Benison Row. Cordelia found herself in a narrow street of Victorian houses curving above the town. Although there was a pleasing unity in the age, architecture and height of the cottages, they were charmingly individual. Some had bow windows, others had been fitted with wooden window-boxes from which a profusion of variegated ivy, geraniums and aubrietia trailed their bright pattern against the painted stucco, while the two at the end of the row had bay trees in painted tubs set each side of the gleaming front door. Each had a narrow front garden set behind wrought-iron railings which, perhaps because of their delicate ornamentation, had escaped being sacrificed for scrap iron in the last war. Cordelia realized that she had never before seen a row of houses with their railings complete and they gave to the street, which was outwardly so English in its small-scale prettiness, a touch of charming but alien eccentricity. The little gardens rioted with colour, the warm deep reds of autumn seeming to burst against the railings. Although it was late in the season, the air was a potpourri of lavender and rosemary. There were no cars parked at the kerb, no throat-catching tang of petrol fumes. After the bustle and hot smells of the High Street, walking into Benison Row was like stepping back into the cosy simplicity of another and legendary age.

Windsor Cottage was the fourth house down on the left-hand side. Its garden was plainer than the rest, a neat square of immaculate lawn bordered with roses. The brass door-knocker in the shape of a fish gleamed bright in every scale. Cordelia rang the bell and waited. There was no sound of hurrying footsteps. Again she rang, this time a longer peal. But there was silence. She realized with a pang of disappointment that the owner was out. It had, perhaps, been stupidly sanguine to expect that Miss Costello would be waiting at home simply because she, Cordelia, wanted to see her. But the disappointment dragged at her spirit and filled her with a restless impatience. She was convinced now that the missing news cutting was vital, and only in this neat little house was there a chance of finding it. The prospect of having to return to the island with this clue unexplored, her curiosity unsatisfied, appalled her. She began pacing up and down outside the railings, wondering how long it might be worth waiting, whether Miss Costello would return, perhaps from shopping, or whether she had shut up the house and gone away for a holiday. And then she noticed that the two upper windows were open at the top, and her spirits rose. A middle-aged woman came out of the next-door house, looked up the road as if expecting someone, and was about to close the door when Cordelia ran forward:

'Excuse me, but I was hoping to see Miss Costello. Do you know if she's likely to be back this afternoon?'

The woman replied pleasantly:

'She'll be at the Washateria, I expect. She always does her washing on Monday afternoons. She shouldn't be long, unless she decides to have tea in the town.'

Cordelia thanked her. The door closed. The little street sank back into silence. She leaned against the railings and tried to wait in patience.

It wasn't long. Less than ten minutes later she saw an extraordinary figure turn the corner into Benison Row, and knew at once that this must be Miss Emmeline Costello. She was an elderly woman, trundling after her a canvas-covered shopping trolley from the top of which bulged a plastic-covered bundle. She walked slowly but upright, her thin figure obliterated by a khaki army greatcoat so long that its hem almost scraped the pavement. Her small face was as softly puckered as an old apple and further diminished by a red and white striped scarf bound round her head and tied under the chin. Over it had been pulled a knitted purple cap topped with a bobble. If such a superfluity of clothing was necessary on a warm September day, Cordelia could only wonder how she dressed in winter. As Miss Costello came up to the gate Cordelia moved to open it for her and introduced herself. She said:

'Mr Lambert of the *Speymouth Chronicle* suggested that you might be able to help me. I'm looking for a cutting from an old edition of the paper – 19th July 1977. Would it be an awful nuisance if I looked through your sister's collection? I wouldn't trouble you, but it really is important. I've tried the newspaper archives but the page I want isn't there.'

Miss Costello might present to the world an appearance of almost intimidating eccentricity, but the eyes which looked into Cordelia's were sharp, bright as beads, and accustomed to making judgements, and when she spoke it was in a clear, educated and authoritative voice, which immediately and unmistakably defined her precise place in the complicated hierarchy of the British class system.

'When you're eighty-five, my child, don't live on top of a hill. You'd better come in and have some tea.'

In just such a voice had Reverend Mother greeted her when she had first arrived, tired and frightened, at the Convent of the Holy Child.

She followed Miss Costello into the house. It was apparent that nothing would be done in a hurry and, as a supplicant, she could hardly insist that it was. She was shown into the drawing-room while her hostess went off to remove several layers of her outer clothing and to make tea. The room was charming. The antique furniture, probably brought from a larger family home, had been selected to suit the room's proportions. The walls were almost covered with small family portraits, watercolours and miniatures but the effect was of an ordered domesticity, not of clutter. A mahogany wall cupboard inlaid with a pattern of rosewood held a few choice pieces of porcelain and, on the mantelshelf, a carriage clock ticked away the moments. When Miss Costello reappeared, wheeling a trolley before her, Cordelia saw that the tea service was in green decorated Worcester and that the teapot was silver. It was an occasion, she thought, on which Miss Maudsley would have felt perfectly at home.

The tea was Earl Grey. As she sipped it from the elegant shallow cups Cordelia had a sudden and irresistible impulse to confide. She couldn't, of course, tell Miss Costello who she was or what she was really seeking. But the peace of the room seemed to enclose her with a warm security, a comforting respite from the horror of Clarissa's death, from her own fears, even from loneliness. She wanted to tell Miss Costello that she came from the island, to hear a sympathetic human voice saying how awful it must have been, a comforting elderly voice assuring her in the remembered tones of Reverend Mother that all would be well. She said:

'There's been a murder on Courcy Island. The actress Clarissa Lisle has been killed. But I expect you know. And now Mr Gorringe's manservant has been drowned.'

'I have heard about Miss Lisle. The island has a violent history. I don't suppose these will be the last deaths. But I haven't read the newspaper account, and, as you see, we don't have a television set. As my sister used to say, there's so much ugliness now, so much hatred, but at least we don't have to bring it into our sitting-room. And at eighty-five, my dear, one is entitled to reject what one finds unpleasing.'

No, there was no comfort to be had here in this seductive but spurious peace. Cordelia was ashamed of the momentary weakness that had sought it. Like Ambrose, Miss Costello had carefully constructed her private citadel, less beautiful, less remote, less extravagantly self-indulgent, but just as self-contained, just as inviolate.

Neither excitement nor impatience had impaired Cordelia's appetite. She would have been grateful for more than the two thin slices of bread and butter provided, particularly as the meagreness of the meal bore no relation to its length. It was surprising that Miss Costello could take so long drinking two cups of tea and nibbling her share of the food. But at last they had finished. Miss Costello said:

'My late sister's press cuttings are in her room upstairs. She was a dedicated monarchist' – here Cordelia thought she detected a nuance of indulgent contempt – 'and there was scarcely a royal occasion during the last fifty years which escaped her attention. But her main interest was, of course, in the House of Saxe-Coburg-Gotha. I shall leave you to search on your own if I may. I am unlikely to be able to help you. But please don't hesitate to call if you feel that I could.'

It was interesting but not altogether surprising, thought Cordelia, that Miss Costello hadn't troubled to inquire what she was seeking. Perhaps she regarded such a question as vulgar curiosity or, more likely, feared that it might only provoke one more intrusion of the disagreeable into her ordered life.

She showed Cordelia into the front bedroom. Here Miss Lucy's obsession was immediately apparent. The walls were almost covered with photographs of royalty, some of them half effaced with scribbled signatures. On a long shelf over the bed was closely ranged a collection of Coronation mugs while a glass-fronted display cabinet was filled with other memorabilia, crested and decorated teapots, cups and saucers and engraved glass. The whole of the wall facing the window was fitted with shelves holding a collection of scrapbooks. Here was the famous collection.

Each of the books was marked on the spine with the dates covered and Cordelia was able, without difficulty, to find July 1977. The local press photographers had done justice to Speymouth's big day. There was hardly an aspect of the Royal visit which had gone unrecorded. There were pictures of the Royal arrival, the Mayor in his chain, the curtseying Mayoress, the children with their miniature Union Jacks, the Queen smiling from the Royal car, hand raised in the distinctive Royal wave, the Duke at her side. But there was no cutting which precisely fitted Cordelia's memory of the shape and size of the missing piece. She sank back on her heels, the book open before her, and felt for a moment almost sick with disappointment. The microdots of grinning, anticipatory self-satisfied faces mocked her failure. The chance of success had been slight, but she was chagrined to realize how much hope she had invested in it. And then she saw that hope was not yet lost. On the bottom shelf was stacked a row of stout manilla envelopes each with the year written on it in Miss Lucy's upright hand. Opening the top one she saw that it also contained press cuttings, perhaps duplicates sent to Miss Lucy by friends anxious to help with her collection, or cuttings she had rejected as unworthy of inclusion but hadn't liked to throw away. The envelope for 1977 was plumper than its fellows as befitted Jubilee year. She tipped out the medley of cuttings, most already fading with age, and spread them around her.

And, almost immediately, she found it, the remembered oblong shape, the heading 'Clarissa Lisle triumphs in Rattigan revival', the third column cut down the middle. She turned it over. She didn't know what she had expected but her first reaction was one of disappointment. The whole of the reverse was taken up with a perfectly ordinary press photograph. It had been shot across the Esplanade and showed the opposite pavement thronged with smiling faces, a row of children squatting on the kerb their flags at the ready, their more adventurous elders perched on window ledges or clinging to lamp posts. At the back of the crowd two stout women with Union Jacks round their hats stood on the steps of a house holding up a sagging banner with the words, 'Welcome to Speymouth'. Royalty hadn't yet arrived but the picture conveyed the sense of happy expectation. Cordelia's first irrelevant thought was to wonder why Miss Costello had rejected it. But then, there had been so many pictures to choose from, many in which the Queen was actually shown. But what possible interest could this not particularly distinguished photograph, this record of local patriotism, have for Clarissa Lisle? She looked at it more closely. And then her heart leaped. To the right of the photograph was the slightly blurred figure of a man. He was just stepping out into the road, obviously intent on some private business, oblivious of all the excitement around him, his preoccupied face staring past the camera. And there could be no doubt about it. The man was Ambrose Gorringe.

Ambrose in Speymouth in July 1977. But that had been the year of his tax exile. Surely he had had to stay overseas for the whole of the financial year; she could remember reading somewhere that even to set foot in the United Kingdom would vitiate the non-resident status. But suppose he had sneaked back – and this picture proved that he must have done – wouldn't that make him liable for all the tax he had avoided, all the money he must have spent on restoring the castle, acquiring his pictures and porcelain, beautifying his private island? She would have to find an expert, discover what the legal position was. There would be firms of solicitors in Speymouth. She could consult a lawyer, put a general question on tax law; there would be no need to be specific. But she had to know and there wasn't much time. She glanced at her watch. Already it was ten minutes to five. The launch would be waiting for her at six o'clock. It was essential to get some kind of confirmation before she returned to the island.

As she gathered up the unwanted cuttings and replaced them in the envelope and went downstairs to find Miss Costello her mind was busy with this new knowledge. If Clarissa had realized the significance of that press photograph, why hadn't anyone else? But then, why should they? Ambrose hadn't lived on the island in 1977. He had probably visited it only rarely; it was unlikely that his face would be known locally. Those who knew him best lived in London and were unlikely ever to see the *Speymouth Chronicle*. And he had written his bestseller under a pseudonym. Even if someone living locally did recognize the picture, he was unlikely to realize that this was A. K. Ambrose, the author of *Autopsy*, who was supposed to be spending a year in tax exile. It was hardly the kind of thing one advertised. No, it had been his appallingly bad luck that Clarissa had been playing in Speymouth that week and had wanted to read her notice. And Clarissa had extorted her price for silence. Oh, it would have been subtly managed; there would have been nothing crude or blatant about this blackmail. Clarissa would have laid down her terms with charm, even a tinge of amused regret. But the price would have been demanded, and it had been paid. So much was clear to her now: why Ambrose had tolerated the disruption of his life by the Players, why Clarissa made use of the castle as if she were its chatelaine. Cordelia told herself that none of this proved that Ambrose was a murderer; only that he had a motive. And she held the proof of it in her hand.

Afterwards it was to strike her as strange that never for one moment did she consider taking the cutting at once to the police. First she must get confirmation; then she must confront Ambrose. It was as if this murder investigation had nothing to do with the police. It was a matter between herself and Sir George who had employed her, or perhaps, between herself and the woman she had failed to protect. And Chief Inspector Grogan's arrogant masculine voice rang in her ears:

'You may be too bright for your own good, Miss Gray. You're not here to solve this crime. That's my job.'

She found Miss Costello in her small back kitchen, folding her linen ready for ironing. She was happy for Cordelia to take away the cutting and said so without bothering to look at it or to take her attention from her pillowcases. Cordelia asked whether she could recommend a firm of local solicitors. This request did evoke a swift upward glance from the shrewd eyes; but still she asked no questions. Escorting her guest to the door she merely said:

'My own advisers are in London, but I have heard that Blake, Franton and Fairbrother are considered reliable. You will find them on the Esplanade about fifty yards east from the Victoria memorial. You would be wise to hurry. Little useful activity, professional or otherwise, goes on in Speymouth after five o'clock.'

CHAPTER FORTY-THREE

Miss Costello was right. By the time Cordelia arrived, panting, at the polished Georgian door of Messrs Blake, Franton and Fairbrother it was shut firmly against any further clients for that day. The lower rooms were in darkness, and although there was a light in the second storey, a name-plate on the side of the door showed that this part of the house was a separate flat. Even if it hadn't been, she could hardly disturb a strange solicitor in his private house for advice on what was, on the face of it, hardly an urgent matter. Perhaps there was a firm which remained open until six; but how to find it? There was always the Yellow Pages, if the Post Office provided this directory in the provinces. She was ashamed to discover that, Londoner as she was, this was a fact she didn't know. And even if she could find a directory which gave the names of local solicitors, there would be the difficulty of locating the offices without a town map. She seemed to have come on this excursion singularly ill-equipped. As she stood irresolute a young man came up bearing a carton of vegetables and pressed the bell of the flat. He said:

'Closed are they?'

'Yes, as you see. I wanted a solicitor in a hurry. It's rather urgent.'

'Yeah, that's the thing about solicitors. If you have to have 'em it's usually urgent. You could try Beswick. He's got an office in Gentleman's Walk. About thirty yards down the street and turn left. He's about half-way up on the right.'

Cordelia thanked him and ran. Gentleman's Walk was easily found, a narrow cobbled street of elegant early eighteenth-century houses. A brass name-plate, polished to the point of being almost indecipherable, identified James Beswick, Solicitor. Cordelia was relieved to see that a light still shone behind the translucent glass and the door opened to her touch.

Seated at the desk was a fat, rather untidy woman with immense scarlet-rimmed spectacles, wearing a tightly belted suit in a brightly patterned cretonne of overblown roses and intertwined vine leaves which gave her the look of a newly upholstered sofa. She said:

'Sorry, we're shut. Call or ring tomorrow, ten o'clock onwards.'

'But the door was open.'

'Literally, but not figuratively. I should have locked it five minutes ago.'

'But since I'm here . . . it's very urgent. It won't take more than a few minutes, I promise.'

A voice from an upper room called out:

'Who is it, Miss Magnus?'

'A client. A girl. She says it's very urgent.'

'Is she comely?'

Miss Magnus jerked her spectacles to the end of her nose and looked at Cordelia over the rims. Then she shouted up the stairs:

'What's that got to do with it? She's clean, she's sober and she says it's urgent. And she's here.'

'Send her up.'

The footsteps receded. Cordelia, suddenly assailed by doubts, asked:

'He is a lawyer, isn't he? A good one?'

'Oh yes, he's that all right. Nobody's ever said that he isn't a good lawyer.'

The emphasis on the last word was ominous. Miss Magnus nodded at the staircase.

'You heard him. First floor to the left. He's feeding his tropical fish.'

The man who turned to her from the window was tall and gangling with a lean, creased, humorous face and half-spectacles worn low on his long nose. He was sprinkling seed from a packet into an immense fish tank, not shaking it from the packet but pinching small quantities between his fingers and dropping the seed in a careful pattern on the surface of the water. There was a tumble of red and bright blue as the fish swirled together and snapped at the food. He pointed as one of the fish streaked to the surface in a blaze of polished bronze.

'Look at him. Isn't he a beauty? That's the dawn tetra, an expensive little fellow from British Guiana. But perhaps you prefer the glowlight tetra. There he is, lurking under the shells.'

Cordelia said:

'He's very beautiful, but I don't much enjoy tropical fish in tanks.'

'Is it the fish or the tanks or the conjunction you object to? They're perfectly happy I assure you, at least one assumes so. Their small world has been artistically and scientifically devised for their comfort, and they get their food regularly. They sow not neither do they reap. Ah, there's a beauty! Look at that flash of gold and green.'

Cordelia said:

'I wanted some urgent information. It isn't about my affairs, it's just a general inquiry. You do give that kind of advice?'

'Well, it isn't usual. I'm not sure that it's wise. Solicitors are rather like doctors. You can't really generalize or deal in hypotheses; each case is unique. You have to know all the circumstances if you're really going to help. That's an interesting analogy, come to think of it; and I'll go further. If your doctor tells you to go abroad at once you can always settle for sunny Torquay instead. If your solicitor suggests you go abroad, you'd be wise to make for Heathrow immediately. I hope you're not in that precarious situation.'

'No, but it's about going abroad that I've come to consult you. I want to know about tax avoidance.'

'Do you mean tax avoidance, which is legal, or tax evasion, which isn't?'

'The first. Suppose I came into a very large sum of money, all of it in one tax year. Could I avoid paying tax if I went abroad for twelve months?'

'That depends what you mean by "came into a large sum of money". Are you talking about an inheritance, a gift, a football pool win, a sale of property or shares or what? You're not contemplating a bank raid, are you?'

'I mean earned income. Money I received by writing a successful play or a novel, or painting a picture or acting in a film.'

'Well if you were sensible you would arrange your contracts so that the money wasn't all received during the one financial year. That would be a matter for your accountant rather than for me.'

'But suppose I didn't expect it to be so successful?'

'Then you could avoid paying tax on it by becoming non-resident for the whole of thc subsequent financial year. Money earned in that way is taxed retrospectively as you probably know.'

'Could I come home for a holiday or weekend?'

'No. Not even for a day.'

'Suppose I needed to? I might be homesick.'

'I should strongly advise you not to. Tax exiles can't afford the luxury of homesickness.'

'But if I did come back?'

He sighed.

'If you really want an authoritative answer I would have to do some delving to see if there is any case law. And as I say, it's more a question for a tax accountant than for me. My present view, for what it's worth, is that you would become liable for tax on the income received during the whole of the preceding year.'

'And if I concealed the fact of my return from the Inland Revenue?'

'Then you could be prosecuted for attempted fraud. Probably they wouldn't bother with that if the amount wasn't large, but they would see that they got the tax due. I mean, they're in the business of getting their hands on tax properly due.'

'How much would that be?'

'Well the present top rate on earned income is sixty per cent.'

'And in 1977?'

'Ah, in those unregenerate days it was rather more. Eighty per cent or more on an income of over twenty-four thousand of taxable income. Something like that.'

'So they might ruin me?'

'Bankrupt you, you mean. Indeed they might if you were so ill advised as to spend all your previous year's income in advance in the confident expectation that it wouldn't be taxable. Death and taxation catch up with us all.'

'Thank you. You've been very kind. Can I pay now? If it's more than two pounds I'm afraid I'll have to give you a cheque. I have a cheque card.'

'Well, it hasn't taken very long, has it? And I think Miss Magnus has balanced the petty cash and locked away the box. Suppose you have this consultation on me?'

'I don't think that would be right. I ought to pay for your time.'

'Then put a pound in the doggy-box and we'll call it quits. When you've written your bestseller you can come back and I'll give you some proper advice and charge you highly for it.'

The doggy-box was on his desk, the brightly painted model of a lugubrious spaniel holding between his paws a collecting-tin bearing the name of a well-known animal charity. Cordelia folded in a couple of pound notes with the mental promise that she would charge only one to Sir George's account.

And then she remembered. There probably wouldn't be any account. Perhaps she would return to the office poorer than when she had left. Sir George had reassured her that she would be paid, but how could she charge him for so tragic a failure; it would be too like blood money. And how on earth would her bill be worded? It was strange how many small complications the huge complication of murder threw up. She thought: even in the midst of death we are in life, and the petty concerns of life don't go away.

She reached the harbour with two minutes to spare. She was surprised and a little disconcerted to find that the launch wasn't waiting, but told herself that Oldfield must have been kept by some job on the island; she was, after all, a little ahead of time. She sat on the bollard to wait, glad of the chance to rest although her mind, stimulated by the excitements of the day, soon drove her to action. She got up and began restlessly pacing the harbour wall. Below her a sluggish tide sucked at the verdigrised stones and a swag of seaweed spread its gnarled and drowned hands under the darkening surface. Daylight was fading and the warmth died with the light. One by one the houses climbing the hill lit their glowing oblongs behind drawn curtains and the winding streets became festive with sparkling necklaces of light. The late shoppers and holidaymakers had gone home and she heard only the occasional echo of a solitary footfall on the harbour wall. The little town, as if regretting its hours of unseasonable frivolity, was settling into a chill autumnal calm. The smells of summer were forgotten and a rank watery smell rose from the harbour.

She looked at her watch. She saw that it was six thirty, and the time was immediately confirmed by the striking of a distant church clock. She walked to the harbour mouth and gazed towards the island. There was no sign of the launch and the sea was empty except for two or three late returning boats gliding with slackened sails towards their moorings.

Still she paced and waited. Seven o'clock. Seven-fifteen. The evening sky, layered in mauve and purple, flamed into darkness, and the moon, pale as a tissue, shed a trembling path of light over the sea. In the distance, Courcy Island crouched like an animal against the paler hue of the sky. Night had distanced it. It was hard now to believe that only two miles of water separated that black and ominous shore from the lights, the gathered domesticity of the town. Looking out at it she shivered. Ambrose's story came back into her mind with the primitive atavistic force of a childhood nightmare. She could understand why so many local fishermen down the ages had thought the island accursed. Almost she could picture that desperate sailor, fighting the onset of the Plague and the fury of the sea, wild-eyed and exultant on his way to his dreadful vengeance.

It was after seven thirty now. Whether by accident or design, Oldfield wasn't going to come. But at least she could leave the quay to ring the island and inquire without the fear of missing him. She remembered seeing two telephone boxes near the Victoria statue. Both were free, and when she had shut herself into the first she was glad to find that it hadn't been vandalized. It was irritating that she hadn't made a note of the castle number and for a moment she feared that Ambrose's obsession with privacy might have caused him to be ex-directory. But the number was listed, although under Courcy Island not his name. She dialled and could hear the ringing tone. Then the receiver was lifted, but no one replied to her voice. She thought that she could detect the sound of breathing but told herself that this must be imagination. She said again:

'It's Cordelia Gray here. I'm ringing from Speymouth. I was expecting the launch at six o'clock.' Still there was no reply. She spoke again, more loudly, but there was nothing but silence and the impression, eerie but unmistakable, that there was someone there, but someone who had lifted the receiver with no intention of speaking. She replaced the handpiece and dialled again. This time she got the engaged signal. The receiver had been taken off the rest.

She made her way back to the harbour though now with little hope that the launch would be in sight. And then she saw that there were lights and signs of activity on one of the moored vessels. Standing on the edge of the quay she looked down at a shabby but sturdy wooden boat with a crudely constructed cabin amidships, brown sails, and an outboard motor. The port and starboard lamps were lit and there was a drag-net heaped in the stern. It looked as if the sailor was preparing for a night's fishing. And he must, she thought, have a small galley. The salty, mouth-watering tang of fried bacon rose from the cabin above the fainter pervasive smell of tar and fish. As she gazed down, a stocky and bearded young man squeezed through the cabin door and looked up, first at the sky and then at her. He was wearing a patched jersey and sea boots and was biting into a thick sandwich. With his cheerful ruddy face and shock of black hair he looked like an amiable buccaneer. On impulse she called down to him.

'If you're setting out, could you land me on Courcy Island? I'm staying there and the launch hasn't come for me. It's terribly important that I get back tonight.'

He moved along the boat, still munching the wedge of greasy bread, and looked up at her with eyes which were shrewd but not unfriendly. He said:

'They say there's someone murdered there. A woman, isn't it?'

'Yes, the actress, Clarissa Lisle. I was staying there when it happened. I'm still supposed to be staying there. They should have sent the launch for me at six. I must get back tonight.'

'A murdered woman. That's nothing new for Courcy Island. I'll be fishing off the south-east point. I'll take you if you're sure you want to go.'

Neither his voice nor his face betrayed any particular curiosity. She said quickly:

'I'm quite sure. I'll pay for the petrol of course. That's only fair.'

'No need. The wind's free. There'll be enough of it out in the bay. You can crew if you like.'

'I'm not sure that I know how. But I'll pull on the right rope when you tell me.'

He transferred the sandwich to his left hand, wiped the right on his jersey and held it out to help her aboard. She said:

'How long do you think it will take us?'

'The tide's running against us. Best part of forty minutes. Maybe more.'

He disappeared into the cabin and she waited seated in the bow, willing herself to patience. A minute later he reappeared and handed her a sandwich, two rashers of bacon, greasy and strong smelling, wedged between thick slices of crusty bread. Until she bit into it, almost disconnecting her jaw in the process, Cordelia hadn't realized just how hungry she was. She thanked him. He said, with a trace of boyish satisfaction at the evident success of his catering arrangements:

'There'll be cocoa once we get under way.'

He clambered along the outside of the cabin towards the stern. A minute later the engine shuddered and the small boat began to creep from the quay.

CHAPTER FORTY-FOUR

It was almost impossible to believe that she had first seen Courcy Castle only three days earlier. In that short span of time she seemed to have lived through long, action-packed years, to have become a different person. Surely it had been some excitable expectant child who had gasped in wonder at her first sight of those sunlit walls, those patterned battlements, that high, luminous tower. But now, as the little boat turned the headland, she almost gasped again. The castle was ablaze with light. Every window shone, and from the tower, scored with pencil-slim lines of light, the high window threw a strong beam like a warning beacon over the sea. The castle seemed buoyant with light, lifted above the rocks to float in motionless serenity under an indigo sky, obliterating the nearer stars with brightness. Only the moon held her place, wan as a circle of rice paper, moving behind a thin veil of cloud.

She stood on the quay until the boat had drawn away. For a

moment she was tempted to call out to the boy to stay, at least within call. But she told herself that she was being ridiculous and fanciful. She wouldn't be alone with Ambrose. Even if Ivo were too sick to be much support, Roma, Simon and Sir George would be there. And even if they weren't, why should she be afraid? She would be facing someone with a motive. But motive alone didn't make a murderer. And she agreed in her heart with Roma: Ambrose hadn't the nerve, the ruthlessness, the capacity for hatred which drove a man to the ultimate crime.

Light lay across the terrace like a sheet of silver. She trod it as if on air, as if she, too, were buoyant, moving silently towards the open french windows of the drawing-room. And then Ambrose appeared and stood watching her approach, a dark figure silhouetted against the light. He was wearing a dinner-jacket and holding a glass of red wine in his left hand. The picture had the clarity and distinction of a painting. She found herself admiring the artist's technique; the careful positioning of the body, the artful blob of red in the glass cunningly and deftly painted in to emphasize the dark vertical lines of the figure, the splash of white at the shirt front, the dominant eyes which gave a focus and meaning to the whole composition. This was his kingdom, his castle. He was in command. He had illuminated it as if to celebrate and exult in his mastery. But when she came up to him his voice was light and casual. He might have been welcoming her home after an afternoon's shopping on the mainland. But wasn't that precisely what he thought he was doing?

'Good evening, Cordelia. Have you eaten? I didn't wait dinner, such as it is. I cooked myself some soup and a herb omelette. Would you care for one?'

Cordelia moved into the drawing-room. Here only the wall lights and one table lamp were lit, making a cosy circle of light by the fire. The corners of the room were dark and long shadows moved like fingers over the carpet and the walls. The fire must have been lit for some time. A single large log was burning steadily. She slipped off her shoulder-bag and asked:

'Where is everyone?'

'Ivo's in bed, not at all well, I'm afraid. He'll be going home tomorrow if he's fit for the journey. Roma has left. She was anxious to get back to London. Sir George had one of his mysterious calls to a meeting at Southampton and she took the launch with him. They won't be returning, although they'll both be in Speymouth tomorrow for the inquest. Simon said that he wasn't hungry. He's gone to bed.'

So they were alone after all, alone except for the sick Ivo and a boy. She asked, hoping that her voice didn't betray her dismay:

'Why wasn't the launch at Speymouth? Oldfield was supposed to meet me at six.'

'He or I must have misunderstood. He'll be back with *Shearwater*, but not until the morning. He's visiting his daughter in Bournemouth for the night.'

'I did ring, but whoever answered put down the receiver.'

'I'm afraid that's been my stock response to the telephone today. Too many calls, too many reporters.'

They stood together in front of the fire. She took the newspaper photograph from her bag and held it out to him.

'I went to Speymouth to find this.'

He didn't touch it or even glance at it.

'I did wonder. I congratulate you. I didn't think you'd succeed.'

'Because you'd already cut it out of the newspaper archives?'

He said calmly:

'Yes, I destroyed it about a year ago. It seemed a sensible precaution.'

'I found another.'

'So I see.'

Suddenly he said gently:

'You look tired, Cordelia, hadn't you better sit down? May I get you some claret or brandy?'

'I'd like a glass of claret, please.'

She had to keep her mind clear, but the thought of the wine was irresistible. Her mouth was so dry that she could hardly frame her words. He fetched a glass for her from the dining-room, poured her wine and refilled his own glass, then sat with the decanter close at hand. They settled themselves one each side of the fireplace. It seemed to Cordelia that no chair had ever been more welcoming or as comfortable, no wine had ever tasted so good. He began to speak as calmly and unemotionally as if they were sitting together after dinner discussing the ordinary events of an unremarkable day.

'I came back to visit my uncle. I was his heir and he wanted to see me. I don't think he understood that I couldn't return and still have a tax-free year. That wasn't the way his mind worked. It would never have occurred to him that a man could spend a year of his life doing what he didn't want to do, living where he didn't want to live, because of money. I wish you'd known him. You would have liked each other. It wasn't difficult getting here unnoticed. I flew from Paris to Dublin and took an Aer Lingus flight to Heathrow. Then I travelled by rail to Speymouth and rang the castle for my uncle's servant William Mogg to meet me after dark with the launch. They'd lived together here for nearly forty years. I asked Mogg not to tell anyone that he'd seen me, but it wasn't necessary. He never spoke of his master's business. Three months after my uncle died he turned his face to the wall and followed him. So you see, there wasn't really any risk. He asked me to come. I came.'

'And if you hadn't, perhaps he would have altered his will.'

'Unkind, Cordelia. You probably won't believe me, but I wasn't influenced by that disagreeable possibility. I didn't even believe that it was a possibility. I liked him. I seldom saw him – he didn't encourage visits even from his heir – but when I did pay my annual homage there was something between us which both of us recognized. Not love. I think he only loved William Mogg and I'm not sure that I know what the word means. But whatever it was I valued it. And I valued him. He had toughness, obstinacy, courage. He was his own man. He lay in that immense bedroom like some ancient chieftain gazing out over the sea and fearing nothing: nothing, nothing. And then he asked me to get for him something he fancied, a last taste of Blue Stilton. He can't have tasted it for thirty years. He and William Mogg practically lived off the island, making their own butter and cheese. God knows what put that need into his mind. He could have asked Mogg to get it for him. But he didn't, he asked me.'

'So that's why you went to Speymouth?'

'That's why. If I hadn't done that simple act of filial kindness

Clarissa wouldn't have seen that press photograph, wouldn't have forced me into staging *The Duchess of Malfi*, would still be alive. Odd, isn't it? It makes nonsense of any theory of the beneficent governance of human life. But then I learned that lesson when I was eight and my mother died because she was one minute late for the plane home and the one she caught crashed. It was a matter, you see, of whether the Paris traffic lights were red or green. We live by chance and we die by chance. With Clarissa if you look back far enough, it was a matter of eight ounces of Blue Stilton. Evil coming out of good if those two words mean something to you.'

Ivo had asked her much the same question. But this time she wasn't expected to answer.

He went on:

'A man should have the courage to live by his beliefs. If you accept, as I do absolutely, that this life is all that we have, that we die as animals, that everything about us is finally lost irrevocably, that we go into the night without hope, then that belief must influence how you live your life.'

'Millions of people live with that knowledge and still live good and kindly and useful lives.'

'Because goodness and usefulness and kindness are expedient. I have my share of them. It is necessary for comfort to be at least a little liked. And perhaps some of the virtuous unbelievers still retain a vestigial hope or fear that there could be an after-life, a measure of reward or punishment, a rebirth. There isn't, Cordelia. There isn't. There's nothing but darkness, and we go into it without hope.'

Remembering how he had sent Clarissa into her darkness, she gazed appalled at the gently smiling face with its look of spurious sorrow, as if the full knowledge of what he had done had only now come home to her.

'You smashed in her face! Not once, time and time again! You could make yourself do that!'

'It wasn't agreeable. And if it's any consolation to you, I had to close my eyes. And it seemed to go on for so long. The sensation was horribly specific, softness cushioning the brittleness of bones. And so many bones. I could feel them splintering, like smashing a tin of toffee in childhood. Our old cook used to let me make it. Smashing it when it had cooled was the best part. And when I opened my eyes and made myself gaze, Clarissa wasn't there. Of course, she hadn't been there before, but once her face was gone I couldn't even remember what she had looked like. More than anyone I know, Clarissa was her face. That demolished, I knew afresh what I'd always known, the ridiculous presumption of supposing that she had a soul.'

Cordelia told herself: I won't be sick. I won't. And I must stay calm. I mustn't panic.

His voice came to her faintly but very clear:

'When I was sixteen and first came to this island as a schoolboy I knew for the first time what I wanted of life. Not power, not success, not sex, with men or women. That has always been to me an expense of spirit in a waste of shame. It wasn't even money, except as it contributed to my passion. I wanted a place. This place. I wanted a house. This house. I wanted this view, this sea, this island. My uncle wanted to die on it. I wanted to live on it. It's the only real passion I've ever known. And I wasn't going to let a nymphomaniac second-rate actress take it from me.'

'And so you killed her?'

He refilled her glass and his own, then looked at her. She had the feeling that he was measuring something, her probable response, his need to confide, perhaps even how much time remained to them. He smiled, and the smile was one of genuine amusement which almost broke into a laugh.

'My dear Cordelia! Do you really believe that you're sitting here, sipping Château Margaux with a murderer! I congratulate you on your sang-froid. No, I didn't kill her. I thought you understood that. I haven't that brand of courage or ruthlessness. No, she was dead when I battered in her face. Someone had been there before me. She couldn't feel it, you see. Nothing matters, nothing exists as long as you can't feel it. It wasn't living flesh that I beat into a pulp. It wasn't Clarissa.'

But, of course. What had made her so blind? She had reasoned all this out before. Clarissa must have been dead when he raised the marble limb and brought it down, the limb of a dead princess who, by chance, had borne the same name as that other child who, more than a century later, had died uncomforted by her mother in a London hospital bed.

He said:

'There was no upward spurt of blood. How could there be? She was already dead. It isn't so very difficult to strike when the kill has been made. No blood, no pain, no guilt. All I did was to cover up for the murderer. Admittedly my motive was mainly self-interest. I needed to find and destroy that vital scrap of newsprint. I knew that it would be somewhere in the room. That was one of her little tricks, to keep it near her, to take it out of her handbag occasionally and pretend to read the review. But you should credit me with some disinterested concern for the killer. It pleased me to concoct for him a way of escape if he had the guts to take it. After all, I did owe him something.'

'She could have taken photocopies of the photograph.'

'Perhaps, although it wasn't likely. And what would it matter if she had? They'd be found with her effects at home, trivia to be thrown away with the detritus of her essentially trivial life, the half-used jars of face cream, the dead love-letters, the hoarded theatre programmes. And even if George Ralston had found it and realized its significance – an unlikely eventuality – he wouldn't have done anything. George wouldn't have seen it as his business to do the work of the Inland Revenue. I came back here for one day and one night to be with a dying man. Would you, or anyone you know, use that knowledge to inform on me?'

'No.'

'And will you now?'

'I must. It's different now. I have to tell, not the tax people, the police. I have to.'

'Oh, no you don't, Cordelia! No you don't! Don't try to fool yourself that you no longer have the responsibility of choice.'

She didn't answer. He leaned forward and refilled her glass.

'It wasn't the possibility of other copies that worried me. What I couldn't risk was the police finding that one copy, and in her room. And I knew that, if it were there to find, then they'd find it. They'd be looking for a motive. Everything in that room would be collected, docketed, scrutinized, examined. There was a chance, of course, that they'd take the cutting at its face value, a critic's notice kept for purely sentimental reasons. But why that particular notice, a not very important play in a provincial theatre? It's never safe to rely on the stupidity of the police.'

She said with great sadness: 'So it was Simon. Poor Simon! Where is he now?'

'In his room. Perfectly safe, I assure you. Don't you want to know what happened?'

'But he couldn't have planned it! Not Simon. He couldn't have meant it.'

'Planned it, no. Meant it? Who's to say what he meant? She's just as dead, isn't she, whatever he meant? What he told me was that she invited him to her room. He was to say that he was going for a swim, put on his swimming-trunks under his jeans and shirt, wait until thirty minutes after she'd gone to rest, then knock three times at the door. She'd let him in. She said there was something she wanted to talk to him about. There was, of course. Herself. Whatever else did Clarissa ever want to talk about? He, poor deluded fool, thought she was going to tell him that he could go to the Royal College, that she'd pay for his musical education.'

'But why send for Simon? Why him?'

'Ah, that I doubt whether we shall ever know. But I can make a guess. Clarissa liked to make love before a performance. Perhaps it gave her confidence, perhaps it was a necessary release of tension, perhaps she only knew of one way to stop herself thinking.'

'But Simon! That boy! She couldn't have wanted him!'

'Perhaps not. Perhaps, this time, she only wanted to talk, wanted companionship. And, with all respect to you, my dear Cordelia, she had never looked to a woman for that. But she may have thought that she was doing him a service in more ways than one. Clarissa is totally incapable of believing that a man exists – a normal man anyway – who wouldn't take her if he could get her. And to do her justice, my sex hasn't done much to disabuse her of the idea. And what better time for Simon to begin his privileged education than on a warm afternoon after, I pride myself, an excellent luncheon and when she needed a new sensation, a divertissement to take her mind off the performance ahead? And who else was there? George, poor chivalrous booby, would lie to the death to protect her reputation, but my guess is that he hasn't touched her since he discovered that he's a cuckold. I'm no use to her. And Whittingham? Well, Ivo has had his turn. And can you imagine her wanting him even if he had the strength? It would be like handling the dry skin of death, infecting your tongue with the taste of death, smelling corruption in your nostrils. Given dear Clarissa's peculiar needs, who was there but Simon?'

'But it's horrible!'

'Only because you're young, pretty and intolerant. It would have done no harm with a different boy and at a different time. He might even have thanked her. But Simon Lessing was looking for a different kind of education. Besides, he's a romantic. What she saw in his face wasn't desire, it was disgust. Of course, I could be wrong. She may not have thought it out very clearly. Clarissa seldom did. But she asked him to come to her. And as with me and my uncle, he came.'

She said:

'What happened? How did you find out?'

'I lied to Grogan about the time I left my room. I changed at once and quickly so that just after twenty minutes to two I was passing Clarissa's door. At that moment Simon looked out. The encounter was completely fortuitous. We stared at each other. His face was ghastly – ashen-white, the eyes glazed. I thought he was going to collapse. I pushed him back into the bedroom and locked the door. He was wearing only his swimming-trunks and I saw his shirt and jeans in a heap on the floor. And Clarissa was lying sprawled on the bed. She was dead.'

'How could you be sure? Why didn't you get help?'

'My dear Cordelia, I may have led a sheltered life but I know death when I see it. I did check. I felt for a pulse. None. I drew the corner of my handkerchief across the eyeball, a disagreeable procedure. No response. He had brought the jewel box crashing down on her head and smashed the skull. The box was actually lying there on her forehead. Oddly enough, there was very little bleeding, a small smudge on his forearm where the blood had spurted upwards, a thin trickle running from her left nostril. It had almost dried when I saw her and yet she had only been dead for ten minutes. It looked like a crooked gash, a disfigurement above the gaping mouth. That's one last humiliation which none of us can do anything about, looking ridiculous in death. How she would have hated it! But then you know. You saw her.'

Cordelia said:

'You forget. I saw her later. I saw her when you'd finished with her. She didn't look ridiculous then.'

'Poor Cordelia! I'm sorry. I would have spared you that if I could. But I thought it would look suspicious if I went up early to call her myself. That's something I've learnt from popular fiction. Never be the one to find the body.'

'But why? Did he say why?'

'Not very coherently. And I was more concerned to get him away than to discuss the psychological complications of the encounter. But neither of them had got what they wanted. She must have seen the shame and the disgust in his eyes. And he saw the loss of all his hopes in hers. She taunted him with his sexual failure. She told him that he was as useless to her as his father had been. I think it was at that moment when she lay there half-naked on the bed smiling at him, mocking him and his dead father together, destroying all his hopes, that his control snapped. He seized the jewel casket, the only weapon to hand, and brought it down.'

'And after that?'

'Can't you guess? I told him precisely what he must do. I schooled him in his story to the police. He was to say that he'd gone to swim after lunch as he told us all that he would. He'd walked along the beach until about an hour after the end of the meal and had then entered the water. He had started off back to the castle at about a quarter to three to dress for the play. I made sure that he had it by heart. I took him into Clarissa's bathroom and washed off the small spot of blood. Then I dried the basin with toilet paper and flushed it down the WC. I found the newspaper cutting. It didn't take long. Her handbag or the jewel box were the two obvious places. Then I took him next door and instructed him how to get down the fire escape from your bathroom window being careful not to touch any of the rungs with his hands. He was like a dutiful child, obedient, extraordinarily calm. I watched while he managed the fire escape, carrying the box under his arm, then as he went to the edge of the cliff and hurled it out to sea as I'd instructed him. And if the police do succeed in dredging it up, they'll find that the valuable jewels are missing. I took them out and flung them into another part of the sea. Forgive me if I don't demonstrate my confidence in you by saying precisely where. But it would never have done if all that the police found missing in the casket was one reputed sheet of newsprint. Then he dived and I watched him strike out strongly towards the west cove.'

'But someone else was watching too; Munter from the tower room window, the only window which overlooks the fire escape.'

'I know. He managed to make that plain to us in his drunken ramblings when Simon and I were helping him to his room. It wouldn't have mattered. Munter was absolutely safe. I told Simon not to let it worry him. Munter would have taken any secret of mine to the grave.'

Cordelia said:

'He took it to the grave conveniently early. And could you really trust a drunkard?'

'I could trust Munter, drunk or sober. And I didn't kill him. And nor, as far as I know, did Simon. That death, at least, was accidental.'

'What did you do next?'

'I had to work quickly. But the haste and the risk were remarkably stimulating. My plotting of this real-life mystery was almost as ingenious as it was in *Autopsy*. I cleaned the make-up from Clarissa's face so that the police wouldn't suspect that she'd invited a visitor to her room. Then I set out to destroy the evidence of how precisely she was killed and to substitute a weapon which Simon couldn't have brought with him because he didn't know it existed, a weapon which would deceive the police into thinking that the murder was connected with the threatening quotations. I didn't tell Simon what I proposed and I didn't touch the body until he'd left. His ignorance was his greatest safeguard. He never saw Clarissa's shattered face.'

'And you had the limb with you, I suppose, in the inside pocket of your cloak?'

'I had both of them ready, the marble and the note. I was

intending to put them in the casket which Clarissa would open in the second scene of Act Three. It would have had to be done under cover of the cloak and at the last minute, requiring some sleight of hand. But I think I might have managed it. And I assure you the result would have been spectacular. I doubt whether she would have got through the scene.'

'And is that why you took the job of assistant stage manager and occupied yourself with the props?'

'That's why. It was natural enough. People assumed that I wanted to keep an eye on my belongings.'

'And after you'd destroyed Clarissa's face, I suppose you took Simon's clothes to the cove, also hiding them under your cloak.'

'How well you understand duplicity, Cordelia. I should have liked to have left them further down the shore but there wasn't time. The small cove beyond the terrace was as far as I could manage. And then I entered the theatre by the arcade and checked the props with Munter. I should mention that I didn't have to worry unduly about fingerprints when I was in Clarissa's room. This is my house. The furniture and the objects, including the marble, belong to me. It was perfectly reasonable that they should bear my prints. But I did wonder about my palm print on the communicating door. That could have shown that I was the last person to touch it. That's why I took good care to open it after we found the body.'

'And the threatening quotations, you sent those too? You took over when Tolly stopped?'

'So you know about Tolly? I think I've underestimated you, Cordelia. Yes, it wasn't difficult. Poor Tolly took to religion as an opiate for grief, and I continued the good work but in a rather more artistic form. It was only then that Clarissa called the police. It wasn't a development I welcomed so I suggested a little ploy to her that effectively scotched their interest. Clarissa really was an extraordinarily stupid woman. She had instinct but absolutely no intelligence. My success depended on two things about Clarissa, her stupidity and her terror of death. So when Tolly's little notes with their remarkably apt biblical reference to millstones around necks ceased, I initiated my own brand of unpleasantness with the occasional help of Munter. The object was, of course, to destroy her as an actress and give me back my privacy, my peaceable island. It was only as an actress that Clarissa had any power over me. She would never return to Courcy if its theatre was the scene of her final humiliation. Once her confidence and her career were effectively and totally destroyed, I should be free. To do her justice she wasn't a common blackmailer. She didn't need to be. She first saw that newspaper cutting in 1977. Clarissa liked to pamper her ego with discreditable secrets about her friends and this was one she hugged to herself for three years before she needed to make use of it. It was my bad luck that the restoration of the theatre and the crisis in her career should coincide. Suddenly there was something she wanted of me. And she had the means to get it. I assure you, *that* blackmail was carried out with the greatest delicacy and discretion.'

Suddenly he leaned towards her and said:

'Look, Cordelia, it isn't going to be possible to shield him for much longer. He's beginning to drink. You must have seen it. And he's making mistakes. That gaffe which Roma noticed, for example. How could he have known what the jewel box was like if he hadn't seen or handled it? And there will be others. I like the boy and he's not without talent. I've done all I can to save him. Clarissa destroyed his father and I didn't see why she should add the son to her list of victims. But I was wrong about him. He hasn't the guts to see this through. And Grogan is no fool.'

'Where is he now?'

'I told you. In his room as far as I know.'

She looked into his face, at the smooth womanish skin burnished by the light of the fire, the eyes like black coals, the perpetually half-smiling mouth. She felt the persuasive force flowing towards her rooting her into the comfort of her chair. And then as if the claret had mysteriously cleared her mind, she knew exactly what he was doing. The careful explanations, the wine, the almost companionable chat, the seductive comfort folded like a shawl around her tiredness, what were they but a ploy to waste time, to keep her at his side? Even the place had conspired with him against her; the cheerful domesticity of the fire, the sense of unreality induced by the long restless shadows, the windows wide to the disorientating blackness of the night and the ceaseless, sleep-inducing susurration of the sea.

She snatched up her shoulder-bag and ran from the room, through the echoing hall, up the wide staircase. She flung open the door of Simon's bedroom and switched on the light. The bed was made, the room empty. She fled like a wild creature from room to empty room. Only in one did she see a human face. In the soft glow of his bedside lamp, Ivo was lying on his back staring at the ceiling. As she came up to him he must have sensed her desperation. But he smiled sadly and gave a small rueful shake of the head. There was no help here.

There was still the tower to search, that and the theatre. But perhaps he wasn't any longer in the castle. The whole island was open to him, cliffs and uplands, meadows and woodlands, the black unsearchable island holding like a shell in its dark intricacies the everlasting murmur of the sea. But there was still the business room and the kitchen quarters, unlikely as it was that he had taken refuge there. She sped down the tiled passage and flung herself at the business room door. And then she stood, arrested. The second display cabinet, the one which held the small mementoes of Victorian crime and horror had been violated. The glass had been smashed. And staring down she saw that something was missing: the handcuffs. And then she knew where she would find Simon.

CHAPTER FORTY-FIVE

She flung her shoulder-bag on the desk of the business room, taking with her only her torch. There was only one other thing she wished to have, the leather belt. But it was no longer round her waist. Somewhere and somehow during the day's activities she had lost it. She had a memory of hurriedly putting it on in the women's cloakroom of a chain store where she had stopped on her way to Benison Row. In her anxiety to find Miss Costello she must have buckled it insecurely. As she ran across the lawn and into the darkness of the wood she wished that she still felt the reassuring strength of this private talisman clasped round her waist.

The Church loomed before her, numinous and secret in the moonlight. No lights shone from the open door but the faint gleam from the east window was enough to light her to the crypt even without the aid of her torch. And that door, too, was open with the key in the lock. Ambrose must have told him where it could be found. The strong dusty smell of the crypt came up to meet her. She didn't pause to find the switch but followed the shifting pool of torchlight, past the rows of domed skulls, the grinning mouths, until it shone on the heavy iron-bound door which led to the secret passage. This too was open.

She dared not run; the passage was too twisting, the ground too uneven. She remembered that the passage lights were on a time switch and pressed each button as she passed, knowing that in a few moments the lights would go out behind her, that she was moving from brightness into the dark. The way seemed interminable. Surely that small party, only two days earlier, hadn't travelled as far as this? She had a moment of panic, fearing that she might have found and taken a hidden turning and be lost in a maze of tunnels. But then she saw the second flight of steps and there gleamed before her the low-roofed cavern above the Devil's Kettle. The single bulb suspended in its protective grille was shining steadily. The trapdoor was up, the lid resting against the wall of the cave. Cordelia knelt and gazed down into Simon's face. It strained up at her, the eyes wide and staring, the whites showing, like the eyes of a terrified dog. His left arm was stretched above his head, the wrist handcuffed to the top rail. His hand drooped from the bar of the handcuff, not the strong hand she remembered coming down on the piano keys, but tender and pale as the hand of a child. And the steadily rising water, flapping like black oil against the cave walls and glazed with light from the cavern above, was already up to his shoulders.

She climbed down beside him. The cold cut her thighs like a knife. She said:

'Where's the key?'

'I dropped it.'

'Dropped it or threw it? Simon, I have to know where.'

'I just dropped it.'

Of course. He would have no need to hurl it far. Handcuffed and helpless as he was, he couldn't retrieve it now however close it lay and however tempted or desperate he might be. She prayed that the bottom of the cave would be rock not sand. She had to find the key. There was no other way. Her mind had already done its rapid calculation. Five minutes to get back to the castle, another five to return. And where would she find a toolbox, a file sufficiently strong to cut through the metal? Even if there were someone in the castle able and willing to help her, there still wasn't time. If she left him now she would be leaving him to drown.

He whispered:

'Ambrose told me I'd be in prison for the rest of my life. That or Broadmoor.'

'He lied.'

'I couldn't stand it, Cordelia! I couldn't stand it!'

'You won't have to. Manslaughter isn't murder. You didn't mean to kill her. And you aren't mad.'

But how clearly the words of Ambrose fell into her mind. 'Who's to say what he meant? She's just as dead, isn't she, whatever he meant?'

Any additional light was welcome. She switched on her torch, resting it on the top rung. Then she gulped in a lungful of air and lowered herself carefully under the gently heaving surface. It was important not to disturb the sea bed more than she could help. The water was icy cold and so black that she could see nothing. But she felt with her hands, scraping them along the bottom, feeling the gritty sand, the spurs of sharp unyielding rock. A swathe of seaweed wound itself round her arm like a soft detaining hand. But her slowly creeping fingers found nothing that could have been the key.

She came up for air and gasped:

'Show me exactly where you dropped it.'

He whispered through his bloodless, chattering lips:

'About here. I held my right hand out like this. Then I let it fall.'

She cursed her folly. She should have taken more trouble to discover the exact place before disturbing the sand. Now she might have lost it forever. She had to move gently and slowly. She had to stay calm and take her time. But there wasn't any time. Already the water was up to their necks.

She lowered herself again trying methodically to cover the area he had indicated, letting her fingers creep like crabs over the surface of sand. Twice she had to come up for air and see briefly the horror and the despair in those staring eyes. But on the third attempt her hand found the stub of metal and she brought up the key.

Her fingers were so cold that they felt lifeless. She could hardly grasp the key and was terrified that she might drop it, that she might not be able to fit it into the lock. Watching her shaking hands he said:

'I'm not worth it. I killed Munter, too. I couldn't sleep and I was there, in the rose garden. I was there when he fell in. I could have saved him. But I ran away so that I wouldn't have to look. I pretended that I hadn't seen, that I hadn't been near.'

'Don't think about that now. We've got to get you out of here, get you warm again.'

The key was in the lock at last. She was fearful that it might not work, that it might not even be the right key. But it turned easily enough. The bar of the handcuff loosened. He was free.

And then it happened. The trapdoor crashed down in an explosion of sound physical as a blow cleaving their skulls. The noise seemed to thunder through the island, shaking the iron ladder under their rigid hands, lifting the water at their throats and bursting it against the walls of the cave in a tidal wave of concentrated fury. It seemed that the cave itself must split open to let in the roaring sea. The lighted torch, dislodged from the top rung of the ladder, curved in a shining arc before Cordelia's horrified eyes, gleamed for a second under the swirling water, then died. The darkness was absolute. And then, even before the echo of that crash had rumbled into silence, Cordelia's ears caught a different sound, the hideous rasp of metal against metal, once and then repeated, a noise so dreadful in its implication that she threw back her sea-drenched head and almost howled her protest into the blackness.

'Oh no! Please God, no!'

Someone – and she knew who it must be – had kicked down the trapdoor. Someone's hand had shot home the two bolts. The killing ground had been sealed. Above them was unyielding wood, surrounding them the rock face, at their throats the sea.

She raised herself and pressed with all her strength against the wood. She bent her head and strained against it with her shoulders. But it didn't move. She knew that it wouldn't. She was aware of Simon dragging himself up beside her, of his palms beating ineffectually against it. She couldn't see him. The darkness was thick and heavy as a blanket, an almost palpable weight against her chest. She was only aware of his terrified moans, long drawn out and tremulous as the waiting sea, of the rank smell of his fear, of the harsh indrawing of his breath, of a thudding heart which could have been his or hers. She reached out for him with her hands. They moved in what was meant to be comfort over his wet face, knowing only by the warmth which of the drops were sea water and which were tears. She felt his trembling hands on her face, her eyes, her mouth. He said:

'Is this death?'

'Perhaps. But there's still a chance. We can swim for it.'

'I'd rather stay here and have you close to me. I don't want to die alone.'

'It's better to die trying. And I won't try without you.'

He whispered:

'I'll try. When?'

'Soon. While there's still air enough. You go first. I'll be behind you.'

It was better for him that way. The first one through would have an easier passage, unhampered by the leader's thrusting feet. And if he gave up there was the hope that she might have the strength to push him through. For a second she wondered how she would cope if the passage narrowed and his inert body blocked her escape. But she put the thought away from her. He was now less strong than she; weakened by cold and terror. He must go first. The water was now so high that only a fragile ribbon of light marked the exit. Its beam lay pale as milk on the dark surface. With the next wave that, too, would go and they would be trapped in utter darkness with nothing to point the way out. She tugged off her waterlogged jersey. They let go of the ladder, joined hands, and paddled to the middle of the cave where the roof was highest, then turned on their backs and gulped in their long last lungfuls of air. The rock face almost scraped

Cordelia's forehead. Water, cool and sweet, fell on her tongue like the last taste of life. She whispered, 'Now!' and he let go of her hand without hesitation and slid under the surface. She took her final gulp of air, twisted and dived.

She knew that she was swimming for her life, and that was almost all she knew. It had been a moment for action not for thought and she was unprepared for the darkness, the icy terror, the strength of the inflowing tide. She could hear nothing but a pounding in her ears, feel nothing but the pain above her heart and the black tide against which she fought like a desperate and cornered beast. The sea was death and she struggled against it with all she could muster of life and youth and hope. Time had no reality. It could have been minutes, even hours, that passage through hell, yet it must have been counted in seconds. She wasn't aware of the thrashing body in front of her. She had forgotten Simon, forgotten Ambrose, forgotten even the fear of dying in the struggle not to die. And then, when the pain was too great, her lungs bursting, she saw the water above her lighten, become translucent, gentler, warm as blood and she thrust herself upward to the air, the open sea and the stars.

So this was what it was like to be born: the pressure, the thrusting, the wet darkness, the terror and the warm gush of blood. And then there was light. She wondered that the moon could shed so warm a light, gentle and balmy as a summer day. And the sea, too, was warm. She turned on her back and floated, arms wide spread, letting it bear her where it would. The stars were companionable. She was glad they were there. She laughed aloud at them in her joy. And it wasn't in the least surprising to see Sister Perpetua there bending over her in her white coif. She said:

'Here I am, Sister. Here I am.'

How strange that Sister should be shaking her head, gently but firmly, that the coiffed whiteness should fade and that there should be only the moon, the stars and the wide sea. And then she knew who and where she was. The struggle still wasn't over. She had to find the strength to fight this lassitude, this overwhelming happiness and peace. Death which had failed to seize her by force was creeping up on her by stealth.

And then she saw the sailing boat gliding towards her on the moonlit stream. At first she thought that it was a sea phantom born of her exhaustion and no more tangible than the white-coiffed face of Sister Perpetua. But it grew in form and solidity and, as she turned towards it, she recognized its shape and the tousled head of its owner. It was the boat which had brought her back to the island. She could hear it now, the swish of the waves under the keel, the faint creaking of wood and the hiss of the air in its sails. And now the stocky figure was standing black against the sky to fold the canvas in his arms and she heard the splutter of the engine. He was manoeuvring to draw alongside. He had to drag her aboard. The boat lurched, then steadied. She was aware of a sharp pain tugging at her arms. And then she was lying on the deck and he was kneeling beside her. He seemed unsurprised to see her. He asked no questions, only pulling off his jersey and folding it round her. When she could speak she gasped:

'Lucky for me you were still here.'

He nodded towards the mast and she saw, buckled round it like a pennant, the narrow strip of leather.

'I was coming to bring you that.'

'You were bringing me back my belt!'

She didn't know why it was so funny, why she had to fight the impulse to break into wild hysterical laughter.

He said easily:

'Oh well, I had a fancy to land on the island by moonlight and Ambrose Gorringe is none too keen on trespassers. I had it in mind to leave the belt on the quay. I reckoned you'd find it soon enough in the morning.'

The moment of incipient hysteria had passed. She struggled upright and gazed back at the island, at the dark mass of the castle, impregnable as rock, all its lights extinguished. And then the moon moved from behind a cloud and suddenly it glowed with magic, each separate brick visible yet insubstantial, the tower a silver fantasy. She gazed enchanted at its beauty. And then her numbed brain remembered. Would he be watching for her, there on his citadel, binoculars raised, eyes scanning the sea for her bobbing head? She could picture how it might have been; her exhausted body dragging itself ashore through the squelch of the shingle and the drag of the receding waves, her bleared eyes looking up only to meet his implacable eyes, his strength confronting her weakness. She wondered if he could have brought himself to kill in cold blood. She thought that it would have been difficult for him. Perhaps it would have been impossible. How much easier to kick shut the trapdoor, to shoot the bolts and leave the sea to do your work for you. She remembered Roma's words, 'Even his horror is second-hand.' But how could he have let her live, knowing what she did? She said:

'You saved my life.'

'Saved you a bit of a swim, that's all. You'd have made it. You're close enough to the shore.'

He didn't ask why, almost naked, she should be swimming at such an hour. Nothing seemed to surprise or disconcert him. And it was only then that she remembered Simon. She said urgently:

'There are two of us. There was a boy with me. We've got to find him. He'll be here somewhere. He's a very strong swimmer.'

But the sea stretched in a calm, moonlit emptiness. She made him wait and search for an hour, tacking slowly up and down the shore line with the sails furled, the engine gently purring. She lay slumped against the gunwale and stared desperately, watching for any movement on the sea's calm face. But at last she accepted what she had known from the beginning. Simon had been a strong swimmer. But weakened by cold and terror and perhaps by some despair which went beyond them, he hadn't been strong enough. She was too tired now to feel grief. She was hardly aware even of disappointment. And then she saw that they were making slowly for the quay. She said quickly:

'Not to the island, to Speymouth.'

'You'll be wanting a doctor, then?'

'Not a doctor, the police.'

Still he asked no questions, but put the boat about. After a few minutes, with warmth and energy flowing back into her limbs, she tried to get up and give him a hand with the ropes. But she seemed to have no strength in her arms. He said:

'Better go into the cabin and get some rest.'

'I'd rather stay here on deck if that's all right.'

'You'll not be in my way.'

He fetched a pillow and a heavy coat from the cabin and tucked her up beside the mast. Looking up at the pattern of unregarding stars, hearing the flap of canvas as the boom swung over and soothed by the swish of the waves under the slicing hull, Cordelia wished that the journey could go on forever, that this respite of peace and beauty between the horror passed and the trauma to come might never end.

And so in a companionable silence they sailed together towards the harbour, feeling the peace of the night flowing between them. Cordelia must have slept. She was dimly aware of the boat gently bumping the quay, of being carried ashore, of his hands under her breasts, of the strong sea-smell of his jersey, of a heart beating strongly against her own.

CHAPTER FORTY-SIX

The next twelve hours remained in Cordelia's memory only as a confused impression of time passing but disorientated, of a limbo in which individual pictures and people stood out with startling and unnatural clarity as if a clicking camera had spasmodically recorded them, fixing them instantaneously and for ever in all their capricious banality.

A huge teddy bear on the desk at the police station, humped against the wall at the end of the counter, squint-eyed, with a tag round its neck. A cup of strong sweet tea slopping into the saucer. Two sodden biscuits disintegrating into mush. Why should they produce so clear an image? Chief Inspector Grogan in a blue jersey with frayed cuffs wiping egg off his mouth, then looking down at his handkerchief as if sharing her wonder that he should be eating so late. Herself huddled in the back of a police car and feeling the rough tickle of a blanket on her face and arms. The foyer of a small hotel, smelling of lavender furniture polish with a lurid print of the death of Nelson above the desk. A cheerful-faced woman, whom the police seemed to know, half supporting her up the stairs. A small back bedroom with a brass bedstead and a picture of Mickey Mouse on the lampshade. Waking in the morning to find her jeans and shirt neatly folded on the bedside chair and turning them over in her hands as if they belonged to someone else; thinking that the police must have gone back to the island the night before and how odd they hadn't taken her with them. One old man silently sharing the breakfast room with her and two women police officers, paper napkin tucked into his collar, a vivid red birthmark covering half his face. The police launch butting its way across the bay against a freshening wind with herself, like a prisoner under escort, wedged between Sergeant Buckley and a policewoman in uniform. A seagull hovering above them with its strong curved beak, then dropping to settle on the prow like a figurehead. And then a picture which jerked all the unrealities into focus, brought back all the horror of the previous day and clamped it round her heart like a vice; the solitary figure of Ambrose waiting for them on the quay. And among all these disjointed images there was the memory of questions, endless repetitive questions, of a ring of watching faces, of mouths opening and shutting like automata. Afterwards she could recall every word of the dialogue although the place had slipped for ever from her mind, whether it had been the police station, the hotel, the launch, the island. Perhaps it had been all of these places and the questions had been asked by more than one voice. She seemed to be describing events that had happened to someone else, but to someone she knew very well. It was all clear in the mind of that other girl, although it had happened so long ago, years ago so it seemed, when Simon had been alive.

'Are you sure that when you first arrived at the trapdoor it was up?'

'Yes.'

'And the door itself resting back against the wall of the passage?'

'It must have been if the trapdoor was open.'

'If? But you said it was open. You're sure you didn't open it yourself?'

'Quite sure.'

'How long were you with Simon Lessing in the cave before you heard it crash down?'

'I can't remember. Long enough to ask about the key to the handcuffs, to dive and find it, to set him free. Less than eight minutes perhaps.'

'Are you sure that the trapdoor was bolted? Did you both try to lift it?'

'I tried at first, then he joined me. But I knew it wasn't any good. I heard the scrape of the bolts.'

'Is that why you didn't try very hard, because you knew that it wasn't any good?'

'I did try hard. I pressed my shoulders against it. I suppose it was a natural reaction, to try. But I knew it wasn't any use. I heard the bolts being shot home.'

'You heard that small sound against the rush of the incoming tide?'

'There wasn't very much noise in the cave. The tide spouted in quietly like water into a kettle. That's what was so frightening.'

'You were frightened and you were cold. Are you sure you would have had the strength to push open the door if it had fallen accidentally?'

'It didn't fall accidentally. How could it? And I heard the bolts.'

'One or two?'

'Two. The scrape of metal against metal. Twice.'

'You realize what that means? You understand the importance of what you're saying?'

'Of course.'

They made her go back with them to the Devil's Kettle. It was neither kind nor merciful; but then, they weren't in the business of being kind or merciful. There were bright lights trained on the trapdoor, a man kneeling and dusting it for prints with the careful delicate strokes of a painter. Then they raised it, not resting it against the rock face but balancing it upright on its hinges. They stood back and, after no more than a couple of seconds, it crashed down. She shivered like a puppy, remembering another such crash. They asked her to raise it. It was heavier than she had expected. And underneath was the iron ladder leading down to death, the ray of bright daylight shining from a crescent exit, the slap of dark, strong-smelling water against the rock. They even made her go down, then shut the trapdoor gently over her. As they had instructed, she pushed her shoulders against it and was able without much strength to force it open. One of the officers climbed down into the cave and they closed the trapdoor and gently shot back the bolts. She knew that they were testing how much she could have heard. Then they asked her to balance the trapdoor on its hinges and she tried but couldn't. They asked her to try again, and when she failed they said nothing. She wondered if they thought that she wasn't trying. And all the time she saw, in her mind's eye, Simon's drowned body with its gaping mouth and glazed eyes, turning and twisting, sucked to and fro like a dead fish in the ebbing tide.

And then she was sitting in a corner of the terrace, alone except for the unspeaking, unsmiling woman police officer, waiting beside the police launch which would take her away from the island for ever. Her typewriter and hand baggage were at her feet. There was still a wind but the sun had come out. She could feel its comforting warmth on her back, and was grateful. She had thought that, since yesterday, she would never be warm again.

A shadow fell across the stones. Ambrose had come up silently to stand beside her. The waiting policewoman was out of earshot but he spoke as if she were not there, as if they were totally alone. He said:

'I missed you last night. I was worried about you. The police tell me that they found a hotel for you. I hope that it was comfortable.'

'Comfortable enough. I can't remember much about it.'

'You've told them everything, of course. Well that's obvious from the mixture of coolness, speculation and slight embarrassment with which they've regarded me since they made their untimely if not unexpected visit late last night.'

'Yes, I've told them.'

'I can almost smell their exhilaration. It's understandable. If you aren't lying or mistaken or mad, then they're on to a very good thing. Promotion gleams like the holy grail. They haven't arrested me, as you see. The situation is unusual, requiring tact and care. They'll take their time. At the moment I imagine that they're still testing the trapdoor, trying to decide whether it could have crashed down accidentally, whether you really could have heard the bolts shoot home. After all, when they returned here last night, in a state I might say of some excitement, they found the trapdoor closed but not bolted. And I don't think they'll get any identifiable prints from the bolts, do you?'

Suddenly she felt an immense and overpowering anger, almost cosmic in its intensity as if one fragile female body could hold all the concentrated outrage of the world's pitiable victims robbed of their unvalued lives. She cried:

'You killed him, and you tried to kill me. Me! Not even in self-defence. Not even out of hatred. My life counted for less than your comfort, your possessions, your private world. My life!'

He said with perfect calmness:

'If that's what you believe, then a certain resentment is reasonable. But you see, Cordelia, what I'm saying to the police and to you is that it didn't happen. It isn't true. No one tried to kill you. No one shot back those bolts. When you reached the trapdoor you found it closed. You raised it just wide enough to slide through and climb down to Simon, but you didn't prop it up completely. You closed that door after you; either that or you partly raised it and it accidentally fell. You were terrified, you were cold and you were exhausted. You hadn't the strength to shift it.'

'And what about the motive, the photograph in the *Chronicle*?'

'What photograph? It was unwise of you to leave it in your shoulder-bag on the business room table. A natural oversight in your anxiety about Simon but highly convenient for me. Don't tell me that you haven't yet discovered that it's missing.'

'The police are checking with the woman who gave it to me. They'll know that I did have a press cutting. Then they'll begin searching for a duplicate.'

'Which they'll be lucky to find. And even if they do and the copy, after four years, is as clear as the one you so carelessly lost, I shall still have my defence. Obviously I have a double somewhere in England. Or he could have been a foreign visitor. Let's say that I have a double somewhere in the world. Is that so unusual? Finding any real proof that I was in the United Kingdom in 1977 will get more difficult with every month that passes. In a year or so I should have felt safe even from Clarissa. And even if they can prove I was here that doesn't make me a murderer or a murderer's accomplice. Simon Lessing's death was suicide and it was he, not I, who killed Clarissa. He confessed the truth to me before he disappeared. He fractured her skull, beat her face to pulp in his hatred and disgust, then made his escape through the bathroom window. And last night, unable any longer to face the truth of what he'd done or its consequences, he tried to kill himself. Despite your heroic attempt to save him, he succeeded. It was fortunate that he didn't take you with him. I had no hand in any of it. That, Cordelia, is my story and nothing you choose to fabricate can disprove it.'

'Why should I want to fabricate? Why should I lie?'

'That's what the police asked me. I had to reply that the imagination of young women is notoriously fertile and that you had, after all, been through an appalling experience. I added that you are the proprietress of a detective agency which – forgive me, I'm judging from externals – isn't exactly prospering. You'd have to spend a fortune to get the kind of publicity that this case will bring you if it ever comes to trial.'

'Hardly the kind of publicity anyone would want. Failure.'

'Oh, I wouldn't be too depressed about that. You showed admirable courage and intelligence. Above the call of duty is how poor George Ralston would put it. I think that George will feel that he's had value for money.'

He added:

'If you persist in going on with this it will be my word against yours. Simon's dead. Nothing can touch him further. It isn't going to be comfortable for either of us.'

Did he think that she hadn't thought of that, of the long months of waiting, the interrogations, the trauma of the trial, the speculative eyes, the verdict which could brand her as a liar, or worse, a publicity-crazed hysteric? She said:

'I know. But then I'm not much used to comfort.'

So he was going to make a fight for it. Even as he watched her rescue last night he must have been planning, scheming, perfecting his lies. He would use every ounce of his skill, his reputation, his knowledge, his intelligence. He would hold on to his private kingdom until his last breath. She glanced up at him, at the half smile, the calm, almost exultant confidence. Already he was rejoicing in the release from boredom, buoyant with the euphoria of success. He would buy the best advice, the most prestigious lawyers. But essentially it would be his fight and he wouldn't yield an inch now or later.

And if he succeeded, how would he live with the memory of what he had done? Easily enough. As easily as Clarissa had lived with the memory of Viccy's death, Sir George with his guilt over Carl Blythe. You didn't need to believe in the sacrament of penance to find expedients for coping with guilt. She had hers; he would contrive his. And was it so very remarkable, what had happened to him? Somewhere, every minute of every day, a man or woman was suddenly faced with an overwhelming temptation. It had gone ill with Ambrose Gorringe. But what had he been able to draw upon at the core of his being which could give him the strength to resist? Perhaps if you opted out long enough from human concerns, from human life with all its messiness, you opted out also from human pity.

She said:

'Please leave me. I want you to go away.'

But he didn't move. After a moment she heard him say, quietly and gently:

'I'm sorry, Cordelia. I'm sorry.'

And then, as if aware for the first time of that silent uniformed watcher he added:

'Your first visit to Courcy Island hasn't been as happy for you as I hoped. I wish it could have been otherwise. Please forgive me.'

She knew that this was the only admission that he would ever make. It had no validity in law. It would never be given in evidence. But she believed, almost despite herself, that it had been sincere.

She watched him as he walked briskly towards his castle. At the doorway Chief Inspector Grogan appeared and moved out to meet him. Without speaking they went inside together.

And still she sat and waited. A uniformed officer, painfully young and with the face of a Donatello angel, came across to her. He blushed and said:

'There's a telephone call for you, Miss Gray. In the library.'

Miss Maudsley was trying hard not to sound fussed but her voice was close to panic.

'Oh, Miss Gray, I do hope it's all right to call you. The young man who answered said that it was. He was so helpful. But I wondered when you'll be coming home. There's a new case just in. It's terribly urgent, a lost Siamese kitten, a seal point. It belongs to a child who is just out of hospital after her leukaemia treatment and she's only had it a week. It was a coming-home present. She's dreadfully distressed. Bevis is at another audition. If I go there's no one to look after the office. And Mrs Sutcliffe has just rung. Her Pekinese, Nanki-Poo, is lost again. She wants someone to go round at once.'

Cordelia said:

'Put a notice on the door to say that we'll be open at nine o'clock tomorrow. Then lock up and start looking for the kitten. Ring Mrs Sutcliffe and tell her I'll call round this evening about Nanki-Poo. I'm just on my way to the inquest, but Chief Inspector Grogan will ask for an adjournment. It shouldn't take long. And then I'll catch the mid-afternoon train.'

Putting down the receiver, she thought; and why not? The police would know where to find her. She wasn't yet free of Courcy Island. Perhaps she never would be. But she had a job waiting for her. It was a job that needed doing, one that she was good at. She knew that it couldn't satisfy her for ever but she didn't despise its simplicities, almost she welcomed them. Animals didn't torment themselves with the fear of death, or torment you with the horror of their dying. They didn't burden you with their psychological problems. They didn't surround themselves with possessions, nor live in the past. They didn't scream with pain because of the loss of love. They didn't expect you to die for them. They didn't try to murder you.

She walked through the drawing-room and out to the terrace. Grogan and Buckley were waiting for her, standing motionless, Grogan at the prow of the police launch, Buckley at the stern. In their still intensity they looked like unweaponed knights standing guardian over some fabled vessel, waiting to bear their king to Avalon. She paused and regarded them, feeling the concentrated gaze of their unwavering eyes, aware that the moment held a significance which all three recognized but which none of them would ever put into words. They were struggling with their own dilemma. How far could they rely on her sanity, her honesty, her memory, her nerve? How far dare they trust their reputations to her fortitude when the going got rough? How would she acquit herself if the case ever came to trial and she found herself standing in that loneliest of places, the witness box of the Crown Court? But she felt distanced from their preoccupations as if nothing that they could do or think or plan had any relevance to her. It would all pass as they and she would pass. Time would take their story and fold it with the half-forgotten legends of the island: Carl Blythe's lonely death, Lillie Langtry sweeping down the great staircase, the crumbling skulls of Courcy. Suddenly she felt inviolate. The police would have to make their own decisions. She had already made hers, without hesitation and without a struggle. She would tell the truth; and she would survive. Nothing could touch her. She hitched her bag more firmly on her shoulder and moved resolutely towards the launch. For one sunlit moment it was as if Courcy Island and all that had happened during that fateful weekend was as unconcerned with her life, her future, her steadily beating heart as was the blue uncaring sea.

BY THE SAME AUTHOR

The Children of Men

The year is 2021. The young are violent and the old despairing. For twenty-five years no child has been born. Nor will there by any more children, for infertility has spread like a plague and the human race faces extinction.

'As taut, terrifying and ultimately convincing as anything in the dystopian genre. It is at once a piercing satire on our cosseted, faithless and trivially self-indulgent society and a most tender love story' – *Daily Mail*

'The central images haunt the mind terrifyingly . . . It has extraordinary power and visionary passion' – *Observer*

'All the excitement of a first-class thriller' – *Daily Telegraph*

Devices and Desires

A murderer is on the loose in a remote area of the Norfolk coast . . .

'Another magnificent achievement . . . a compelling human drama that will keep your phone off the hook for days' – *Evening Standard*

'The characters are vibrant, the writing distinguished, the descriptions of mood and landscape perfect, the ironic ending nicely cynical. And over it all, a haunting Norfolk mist of dread, loneliness and ancient history' – *Sunday Express*

also published

The Black Tower
Cover Her Face
Death of an Expert Witness
A Mind to Murder
Shroud for a Nightingale
Unnatural Causes
A Taste for Death

also published

A Dalgliesh Trilogy
A Second Dalgliesh Trilogy

and with T. A. Critchley:

The Maul and the Pear Tree